MANSFIELD
PARSONAGE

KYRA C. KRAMER

Mansfield Parsonage

M
MadeGlobal Publishing

For more information on
MadeGlobal Publishing, visit our website
www.madeglobal.com

Cover image: "Lady with a Harp"
by Eliza Ridgely, 1818

This book is dedicated to my beloved husband, Casey. Thank you for demonstrating every day what true love is really like ... and for being my hero by cleaning up after the dogs when they puke.

Author's Note

Why retell *Mansfield Park*? It is Jane Austen's least-loved novel. Only confirmed Janeites or academic Austenites bother to read it, let alone reread it. Casual readers who adored *Pride and Prejudice* tend to toss *Mansfield Park* aside half-way through it, disgusted by the lack of searing wit and rapid pacing that marks Austen's other books. So why bother telling Mary Crawford's tale?

Simply put, I wanted to tell the story from Mary Crawford's point of view because she was the most amusing, most vital, and most Lizzy Bennet-like character in the book. The delight of most Austen's characters, for good or for ill, is in their flaws. Whether they are comic relief or fodder for scathing social commentary or beloved protagonists, they were imperfect. Austen's strong-willed heroines are particularly relatable for the reader *because* they are not pure paragons. Elizabeth had her prejudice, Anne was too persuadable, Marianne was too romantic, Elinor was too pragmatic, Catherine was naïve and overly imaginative, and Emma was subject to vanity. They are loved because they are inherently decent people, and lovable because they aren't revoltingly perfect models of submissive 18th century feminine ideals. Fanny Price, the heroine of *Mansfield Park*, stands alone as the main protagonist who was unable to make a mistake. Fanny Price is an apotheosis of delicacy, modesty, and tenderness. She is so meek, mild, and righteous that it is almost impossible not to hate her. Mary Crawford is the sharp one in the book. Mary Crawford is the one with uncongenial character traits to be overcome. Mary Crawford is *interesting*.

Miss Crawford is one of my favourite literary creations, and I've pondered her situation a great deal. In my opinion, the loss of Edmund Bertram – who was nearly as revoltingly faultless as Fanny Price and every bit as judgemental and prudish – *was* ultimately a stroke of luck for Mary. She loved Edmund because he was handsome and a Good Boy and if she had married him, I think she would have been bored to tears and miserable within a year. Losing Edmund to

Fanny Price was an unintended kindness to Mary by the author. Let Edmund and Fanny have each other; Mary deserved better.

Furthermore, the treatment Mary Crawford got from Fanny and Edmund appalled me and I wanted to both castigate the protagonists for their shoddy behaviour and defend the antagonist's alleged transgressions. What did Mary do that was so wicked? She was no worse than any of protagonists whom Austen rewarded with a happily ever after in other novels. She planned to marry well, and considering the fate that befell Austen's characters when they married imprudently, one wonders why the author doesn't applaud this. She wished Edmund Bertram were richer and the eldest son, but all of Austen's heroines except Catherine Moreland married the eldest son and even the "poorest" of the happy couples in Austen's novels were incredibly wealthy by Regency standards. Was Mary willing to marry without love? Yes, but Marianne Dashwood married a man she didn't love and Austen assures us she lived happily ever after with Colonel Brandon. Mary had no more vanity than Emma, no more hubris than Elizabeth Bennet, and no more practicality in matters of the heart than Elinor Dashwood. *Mansfield Park* would have been vastly improved if Mary Crawford, not the indigent epitome of womanhood Fanny Price, had been Austen's object. Since Austen chose not to, I have to made a stab at it. Considering I have the audacity to rewrite Austen, a stab is exactly what some people may wish to give me.

There are only two other things I wish to tell you, gentle reader, before you dive into the narrative. The first is that there are excerpts of the original Mansfield Park manuscript in this work, albeit those sections are also peppered with sentences of my own making. This is a technique used by other authors before me and is legal inasmuch as the copyright on the book expired long ago. I thought it would be helpful to those who had not read Mansfield (recently or at all) to follow the plot, which I was careful not to change, and to see that I did my very best not violate Mary's original characterization in my quest to make her the protagonist. It should be fairly obvious which sentences are the products of Austen's genius and which are my own scribblings; if it is not then I shall develop an unbearably swelled head from the compliment.

Secondly, I think I have an explanation for Fanny Price's weak constitution. She shows every sign of having severe anaemia. Without the appropriate amount of iron and haemoglobin in Fanny's blood, she would experience shortness of breath, become easily fatigued, suffer more from the cold, have a decreased appetite, headaches, and remain unnaturally pale. Additionally, because her heart had to labour more intensely to oxygenate her body, her heartbeat could be thrown into arrhythmia by any exertion, explaining her fluttering pulse. She probably had compromised fertility as well, although a child or two in her future is certainly possible. If Fanny was kept in a genteel environment and pampered, which she would have been as Mrs Edmund Bertram, she could easily live to an old age despite being sickly and infirm.

I sincerely hope you enjoy reading the book.

Warmest regards,

Kyra Cornelius Kramer

Chapter One

July 8, 1813

MARY CRAWFORD WAS the darling of Nature and Fortune; both had gifted her lavishly and perhaps too well.

Nature had made her hale and athletic, with more than an average share of personal beauty. Her complexion was sallow but so clear and delicate that she had no need to be fair. Her hair was very dark, with fetching auburn highlights when the sun shone upon it, and her bright eyes were the warm colour of strongly brewed tea. Her lashes were abundant and long, and they framed her eyes in such a way as to call attention to their luminosity. Although she lacked the elegance of height, Miss Crawford's figure was perfectly formed for a petite woman, which, in conjunction with her quick eyes and playful manner, gave her a sprite-like aspect that never failed to please the viewer. It was to her credit that she had very little vanity; her looks were an accident of birth and while she found them advantageous she did not pride herself on them. She was, however, proud as any peacock about her abilities on the harp. She felt entitled to that satisfaction; she had practised long hours to augment her sincere taste in music. Moreover, her fingers were slender and graceful, and being a rational creature, she was well aware of how comely they looked when she played. Miss Crawford was not a disciple of false modesty, and she knew that she had never met another amateur harpist who could match her skill, display, and feeling on the instrument.

Fortune had smiled upon her quite as much as had Nature. At twenty years of age, she was a woman of means and tolerable independence, having inherited 20,000 pounds from her parents and some further monies from her beloved aunt. This wealth, even without the addition of her beauty, would have assured her finding a husband; when coupled with her handsomeness she was secure enough of eventual matrimony to determine to be exceedingly nice in accepting an offer of marriage. Fortune had also seen to it that Mary Crawford had grown up in luxury in one of the best areas of London, been supplied with an excellent governess and superior masters for dancing and art, and had become accustomed to using only the best mantua-makers and milliners for her apparel.

Alas, neither Nature nor Fortune could grant her unmixed felicity in her friends and relations. Although luck had supplied her with an excellent brother and loving aunt, she also bore the burden of a loathsome uncle. Her father's brother and his wife had taken over the care of Mary Crawford and her elder brother, Henry, upon the death of their parents. In their uncle's house, they had found a kind home. Admiral and Mrs Crawford, though agreeing in nothing else, were united in affection for Mary and Henry, or, at least, were no farther adverse in their feelings than that each had their favourite, to whom they showed the greatest fondness of the two. The Admiral delighted in the boy, Mrs Crawford doted on the girl, and both children were given every comfort. In spite of the kindnesses that this uncle had shown Mary, she could not like him. He had made his wife miserable, and Mary had both sensibility enough to be aware of all the many slights and stings the Admiral directed at her dearest aunt and sense enough to despise him for it. His cruelty toward the woman she viewed has having a mother's place in her heart kept Mary from forming any filial attachment to her uncle. His frequently ill-bred behaviour kept her likewise from developing the respect that should have been his due. Her gratitude and fondness were all the property of her aunt.

After the death of his wife, Admiral Crawford proved himself to be a man of vicious conduct, who chose, instead of retaining his niece, to bring his mistress under his own roof. Thus, Mary found it necessary to quit her uncle's home. She had tried in vain to persuade her brother to settle with her at his own country house in Norfolk. However, to anything like a permanence of abode, or limitation of society, Henry Crawford had, unluckily, a great dislike: he could not accommodate his sister in an article of such importance.

As much as she loved her brother, Mary Crawford was well aware that although he possessed a sterling heart, he was a selfish creature underneath his casual generosity. Her brother would give those he loved anything but that which sincerely inconvenienced him. Nonetheless, his wit and gentlemen-like manner assured him the continued affections of his sister and his status as a favourite among their many acquaintances. Such was Henry's charisma that he had a reputation as an obliging fellow, regardless of how often he was actually disobliging. His innate charm had given him the happy knack of being unaccommodating in a way that left others feeling positively favoured by his refusal to be persuaded. Even better, his love of fun and society meant that he readily agreed to any interesting scheme suggested to him, which gave him a general impression of easy-going amiability.

Her love for her brother was unalloyed by her practical understanding of his egocentric habits. Having never met a man who was *not* selfish among all her friends and acquaintances, Mary had come to think of vanity and self-interest as idiosyncrasies of their sex. This philosophy didn't worry her overmuch when she thought of her future as a wife. She supposed that if someone were a true gentleman, then his conceit would prevent him from being a troublesome husband because he would be too well-bred to have disagreeable manners. Her brother had shown her that a superfluity of pride did not make men disgusting; on the contrary, it made them more likeable. Henry, for all that he was self-centred, was still liberal, kind, and cultivated. He was not vicious and objectionable, like the Admiral. As long as she chose a husband like Henry, one who was too intelligent and refined to be irksome or discourteous, then she would find matrimony tolerable enough.

When she had given up her hopes that her beloved and selfish brother would take her to Norfolk, Miss Crawford then resolved to hazard herself among her other relations, seeking refuge with a half-sister by the name of Mrs Grant. As children, Henry and Mary had been fond of their older sister, but as her own marriage had been soon followed by the death of their common parent, they had scarcely seen her since. In spite of the many years since they had been in each other's company, Mrs Grant was more than civil in her answer to Mary; she welcomed her with warm-hearted and generous eagerness and begged her to think of the Grant's as her new home.

Mrs Grant was perfectly sincere in her reply and it was a measure quite as welcome on one side as it could be expedient on the other; for Mrs Grant, having by this time run through the usual resources of ladies residing in the country without a family of children – having more than filled her favourite sitting-room with pretty furniture, and made a choice collection of plants and poultry – was very much in want of some variety at home. The arrival, therefore, of a sister whom she had always loved, and now hoped to retain with her as long as she remained single, was highly agreeable; and her chief anxiety was that a home in the country should not satisfy the habits of a young woman who had been mostly used to London.

Miss Crawford was pleased and flattered by Mrs Grant's response to her request, but not entirely free from apprehensions, though they arose principally from doubts of her sister's style of living and line of society. Mrs Grant was married to a rector, and although a clergyman was very respectable and Dr Grant's income not small, they resided in Mansfield, a small village in Northamptonshire. What did one do in the country where there were no theatres, no pleasure gardens of note, no decent shops, and an almost certain lack of good society? Mary Crawford enjoyed company to every other pursuit but music, and the idea of rustication and few acquaintance to liven her days filled her at times with something very like dread.

There were supports, however, that helped her retain mostly a sanguine attitude towards her impending provincialism. Mansfield was somewhat more than sixty miles from Town, but her brother Henry was escorting her, with the utmost kindness, into Northamptonshire and he had readily engaged himself to fetch her away again, at half an hour's notice, whenever she were weary of the place; it was not as though she were doomed to abide there if it made her unhappy. Moreover, her brother had promised to visit with her and the Grants for a few days.

Arrangements were duly made that Mary and Henry would come to Northamptonshire in early July, soon after the Henley Regatta. Mary was unhappy about leaving so much before the Season was over but an early removal could not be helped. Every day under the same roof as the Admiral's mistress, Mrs Chatsworth, was odious to her and risked exposing her to ridicule and speculation.

Henry had resolved that they would travel in his barouche instead going via post-chaise. The weather bid fair and the roads were good; the trip would take less than nine hours, even taking into account a longer stop at Luton to eat a cold luncheon while the horses were changed. An armed footman and a small trunk or two would go with them, and there was plenty of room in the barouche box for Henry's valet. Another footman and Mary's maid would go by mail coach the day before, escorting Mary's luggage. Henry was confident that if they breakfasted early and left Hill Street about an hour past sunrise, then they would be in Mansfield by four o'clock; in plenty of time to dine with the Grant's even if they kept country hours.

As was often the case, Henry was correct. The weather for the whole of their transit was sunny but not overly hot, and their passage had more the feel of a pleasure ride than serious travel. They were also running well on time. It was only half past two yet they were only an hour from Mansfield. Mary thought to herself it would be better served if they had been behindhand; as they neared their destination, she felt again some anxieties about the bucolic future awaiting her.

Mary sat pensively beside her brother, who was courteously seated in the main body of the carriage with her instead of driving the horses himself, as was his want. Even though they were travelling, Henry still managed to look as though he had just sprung to life from a fashion plate. Now wonder he was so pleased with his valet, Anderson, who sat perched on the barouche box, comfortably talking to the coachman despite the disparity in their stations; the valet had once been a footman in the Admiral's establishment and had become friendly with the coachman whilst they were both lower servants. Henry, particular in many areas, was nearly republican in his laxity toward the fraternising among the members of his staff. His lack of officious interference in the lives of the servants, a direct contrast to the intrusive and dictatorial behaviour of the Admiral to his houschold, was one of the many qualities she found endearing in her brother.

"What has you so thoughtful?" Henry asked. "You have been as silent as a stone for these last fifteen minutes at least."

Mary gave her brother a small smile. "I would have thought that a great relief to you, Henry. Don't you ever get enough of a woman trying to coax your attention with witty conversation?"

"I never get tired of talking to my sister, the only woman I have ever truly loved," Henry replied with gallantry. "She is not so silly or as artificial as other women. However, she is a slyboots for trying to misdirect the subject. Come. Tell me what it is that's bothering you."

"I am not bothered so much as I am" she paused to find the right word, "*uneasy* about the unknown. I have not been a resident of the country since my infancy; what will I find to occupy my time? I cannot play my harp forever, as appealing as I find that idea upon occasion. Reading is all well and good for rainy days, but it cannot supply *all* my felicity any more than my harp can. Even the company of sister, be she ever so congenial, cannot replace card parties every night without the risk of dullness and ennui afflicting me. Everyone lauds the fresh air of the country, but for myself there is a limit to how much I can breathe in before I long for the stinks of Mayfair."

"Not to mention," teased her affectionate brother, "you'll be without your usual crowd of lovers and beaus. Are you afraid that you'll become an old maid left to pine in the wilderness?" He grinned. "A veritable Arcadian ape-leader?"

"Bosh," Mary chided her brother. "I don't give two hoots about dandies, and you know it. Most of them are cakes or coxcombs, and I have enough brains to know that they wish to win my settlement, not my heart. (Although bear in mind that if I ever *do* marry a fortune hunter you can trust that I'll have picked the best-looking and most intelligent one of the lot!) No, Henry. Beaus are the least of my worries. I am not in Northamptonshire to look for suitors; I'd much rather be an ape-leader than marry some clod-pated bumpkin that I met out in the middle of nowhere. It is tedium, not spinsterhood, which I fear."

"It is perfectly permissible to fear both," Henry pointed out. "These are trying times."

"I'll probably be stuck playing quadrille until next spring," Mary said with exaggerated dolefulness. "When next you see me I shall be wearing glasses and calling everyone 'deary' like a proper biddy."

Henry laughed. "Oh, yes to be sure. You'll also be ready to introduce me to your betrothed. Will he be a quaint farmer, do you think? The impoverished fifth son of some local tradesman? Mayhap a vicar? Or better yet; a sweet-natured young curate."

Mary feigned a shudder. "Henry, some things are too horrible to speak of, even in jest."

"You needn't fear, Mary," Her brother still smiled but she heard the thread of seriousness in tone. "If it is all that bad, I shall simply take you with me to Bath when I leave. If need be, we can hire you a respectable widow or ageing governess as a companion and set you up in a small establishment of your own there, or even in London."

"It would be terribly gauche of me to have my own establishment when my uncle is also in Town, even with the most respectable hired companion in creation," Mary looked pensive. "It is bad enough that everyone knows why I needed to leave; that I should have to see Mrs Chatsworth at the dinner table!"

"Mrs Chatsworth is a nice old bird. She has always been kindness itself to me. You could have stayed in Town if you had really wanted to," Henry said.

"Mrs Chatsworth," Mary said severely, "is a nice old bird *of paradise* and the only thing more embarrassing than having to leave the house *because* of her would be to stay in the house *with* her."

Henry shrugged, managing to make even that uncouth movement stylish. "I cannot agree. She may be under our uncle's protection, but she is hardly a Cyprian. Before she liaised with the Admiral, she was a respectable widow. She is of low birth, but she is not so low that she was a servant. It is not as though our uncle has brought an actress or chorus girl into his home. Be rational. People are not as strict about these affairs as they have been; I cannot help but wonder if you are too fastidious about such matters."

Mary arched an eyebrow at her brother's lack of awareness. "A woman can *never* be too fastidious on such matters, Henry. You may make japes about my marrying a farmer, but it would come to that — even with my 20,000 pounds — if it was believed that association with Mrs Chatsworth had injured my character; I would be cast out of good society entirely."

"Upon my word," Henry looked genuinely concerned, "that is bleak fate you foresee. Surely it would not come to that. I would call out anyone who impugned you; I would defend your honour as my own. You know that, I hope."

"You cannot call out all the Lady Patronesses of Almack's," Mary reminded him. "They are the ones who would decide my fate."

Henry grinned, boyish dimples flashing briefly. "I could not call out Lady Lieven, that's true enough; I fear she would best me in a duel. The rest of the fair arbiters would be fair game, however."

Amused, Mary chided him, "Henry, you never treat any subject with anything but levity. You make me laugh against my will. How can I talk to you seriously, as a brother?"

"There is far too much seriousness in the world," Henry said. "I feel it my duty to prevent its encroachment, for seriousness is a fusty fellow who often brings his bosom friend tedium to tea uninvited."

"I do believe that tediousness is the one sin for which I will never be able to call you to account," Mary told him archly. "You prefer your sins more lively. Speaking of which, how is Mlle. LaVeaux?"

Henry narrowed his eyes at his sister. "I have no idea of whom you speak."

"That looked so genuine as to almost fool *me*," Mary said in admiration. "Your ability to counterfeit sincerity is astounding."

Looking resigned, Henry asked, "Was it Lady Stornoway who informed you?"

"Yes," Mary said. "How did you know?"

"She came upon me buying Mlle. LaVeaux a bottle of scent in Floris; I suspected that when she left the first thing she did was fly straight to you to gossip."

"You underestimate her. First, she found out everything she could about your opera singer, and *then* she flew to me to share the information."

Henry snorted. "I should have known. But you shouldn't know about my chere-amie, Mary; it isn't becoming in an unmarried lady."

"Well, I am not such a fool as to mention it to anyone but you," Mary assured him, "but have we not always had perfect candour between us? Besides, how could I have grown up in Admiral Crawford's household and not have learned about these matters? The house might as well have been a harbour in the isle of Cyprus, so many of those natives have docked in it. I would need to be very stupid and very dimwitted not to have noticed. As long as you are not so hulver-headed to make her, as they say, 'sprain her ankle', you need not fear reproach from me."

Henry made a sound that was very nearly a snort at the very idea of impregnating a mistress; that idiocy was for the king's sons.

"What I cannot fathom is why Lady Stornoway should bother to tell you about it," Henry was perplexed. "It is a very ill-bred thing to tell my sister."

"Do you not?" Mary replied. "Lady Stornoway is still in love with you and jealous as the devil of all your amours. You should really be more careful when you make women attached to you, Henry. It might get you into real trouble someday."

Henry, having never been in love himself, didn't really believe his sister. "Stuff and nonsense; Lady Stornoway is merely still piqued that I didn't offer for her hand. She is no more in love with me that I am in love with Mlle. LaVeaux; she probably loves me less than I love my barouche if the truth were known. Your novel reading has caused you to see romances where there are none."

"That's a bit rich, coming from you," Mary pointed out. "You read as many novels as I do and *you* are the one who must always be involved in an intrigue of some kind. How many hearts have you broken? A dozen? Two dozen?"

"It's all in good fun," Henry waved away any possibility of heartbreak. "Everyone knows I am a sad flirt and no one forms any *reasonable* expectations of me. If you could gather so much as a thimble-full of real feeling among the ladies I've paid attention to I should be surprised."

Mary was as naturally resistant to infatuations and love as her brother, but from the frank confidences of her female acquaintances she had begun to suspect that she was somewhat singular in that regard. She sometimes worried Henry was doing a great deal of damage to the women he flirted with. Then her natural scepticism of romantic love and her deep fondness for her brother would rise within her breast and she would decide that any woman silly enough to think Henry serious in his flirtations was too silly to feel sorry for. Worse, such silliness was a sign of weakness. Weakness, like hypocrisy and the wearing of pattens by a lady of rank, was something Mary despised too much have any sympathy for.

"On your own head be it," Mary said. "I am not my brother's keeper. But what shall you do for entertainment at our sister's house, with no young ladies to make fall in love with you?"

"I should hope my ego can survive a few days without such fodder," Henry smiled. "I shall content myself to win all your pin money at cards."

"You can *try*," Mary scoffed.

"Excuse me, sir," The coachman twisted in his seat to address Henry. "I believe we are coming upon Mansfield, sir."

"Thank you, Willis," Henry responded. "There, Mary. Do you see the parsonage?"

They had come out of a large wood and as the road curved the village had come into view. They ascended to the top of the arched bridge over a small tributary of the River Nene, and the rise gave them the vantage point to see almost all of the hamlet. It was a tidy place, larger than Mary had expected, with shops, snug cottages and a small number of respectable houses that were doubtlessly the property of wealthier tradesmen, many of who had risen in consequence until they were within a stone's throw of gentility. The church towered over the other dwellings, and its medieval architecture was impressive. Not far from it was a house Mary supposed was the parsonage and all its demesnes, gently rising beyond the village road. Happily, it was not some ramshackle old building with a farmyard in the front. Instead, it was a large, spacious, and modern home with a surfeit of windows that boasted that the people living there could afford King George's tax on light and air. Mary could see the edges of lace curtains moving in the breeze of the open windows, noting that it gave the parsonage the fantastical appearance that it was quivering in excitement to see them coming. The aspect was also quite good; a small gated yard filled with an abundance of flowerbeds in it fronted the home and a neat rock path paved the way to the red-painted door.

From this door burst a small, pleasingly plump woman not yet in her mid-thirties wearing a yellow voile dress over a butter-coloured petticoat. Her face was plain, but the animation of her countenance lent her a facsimile of handsomeness. A yellow bandeau restrained her upswept curls, which were identical to Mary's in colour. She hastened down the path with more joy than dignity, hallooing her greetings to her siblings.

"Mary! Henry! I am so glad you've come!" Mrs Grant embraced them both as they alighted from the barouche. "Do come in, and I'll have a dish of tea served presently. You must be so tired from the road!" She bubbled over with welcome, effusive in her warm reception. "Let me show you both to your rooms, where you can change out of your travelling clothes. My housekeeper knows you've arrived and has gone this moment to make sure hot water, soap, and towels are brought to you as quickly as possible. Oh! I am so happy you are here!"

Chapter Two

THE MEETING WAS very satisfactory on each side. Miss Crawford found a sister without preciseness or rusticity, a sister's husband who looked the gentleman, and a house commodious and well fitted up. Mrs Grant was not vulgar in any respect, and had the good sense to dress as a matron rather than, as *The Mirror of the Graces* cautioned against, grotesquely "affecting the airy garments of youth." Dr Grant was excessively civil in his address and, if not handsome, was at least devoid of clownishness and had a tolerably large income.

Dr Grant was the rector of six livings, five of which were occupied by vicars and curates who performed the offices of the church. The livings, all of which had ample land attached to them which Dr Grant could rent out, gave him nearly 1000 pounds per annum. The Grants had chosen to live at Mansfield parsonage because it was the best of the rectory houses available to them. Moreover, the glebe here was the largest. In fact, the land set aside for the use of the rector of Mansfield's church was so large that Dr Grant's household had a good kitchen garden and poultry-yard and excellent pasturage for their cattle, yet there was still plenty of acreage left over to lease to a local farmer.

Mary had not expected to be so well pleased with a parsonage. Not only was the house larger than she had hoped for, it was decorated in a modern style and unburdened with the heavy furniture of the past; clearly Mrs Grant had made good use of the catalogues! The hall was short and lacked grandeur, but it had been papered in a Chinoiserie pattern that bespoke taste; the paper's clever juxtaposition of coloured background and charcoal drawings in the foreground also provided the first impression that the hall was larger than it really was. Unlike the townhomes which situated the drawing and dining rooms on the first floor, the parsonage had its main rooms on the ground floor in the country manner. The dining room could have graced any home in Christendom, and drawing-room was particularly fine, with a floor-length window on the far wall that opened into the garden, providing a lovely view of the flowers and shrubberies.

Even better and much to Mary's pleasure, there was a very modern and very unexpected water closet. A flushable toilet with indoor plumbing had been available for thirty years, but only the well-to-do had been able to afford them. Such were the circles that Mary moved in that many homes, including those of her closest friends Lady Stornoway and Mrs Fraser, had the felicity of a toilet-room in their residences. Few people with Dr Grant's income had bothered with the expense of an indulgence of this kind, but the rector was a man devoted to his physical comforts and was willing to pay for them. The entire contraption had been enclosed in an oak commode with a decorated enamel bowl recessed into it. Mary had seldom seen more stylish facilities even in London, and would be sure to casually mention it in her letters to her friends, because it was an affirmation of the gentility and station in life of some of her nearest relations.

The stairs were too cramped for elegance, but Mary's bedroom was unexceptional and larger than she had expected. There was the blessing of a dressing-closet for her ablutions and toilette attached to her boudoir, and an additional commode in the bedroom, with a chamber pot for her use in the night. The walls of the room were covered with paper-hangings of a modern fashion that Mary particularly liked. The paper was a very modish hue of beige and patterned with floral bouquets. The blossoms in the posies were multiple shades of pink and backed with fronds of delicate greenery, all tied with light blue ribbons and surrounded by sage coloured ornamental scroll. Delicate garlands of pale orange and yellow flowers interconnected the larger bouquets, giving the paper's design a symmetry that pleased the eye. The bed's canopy, drapes and coverlet were also up-to-the-minute and stylish, made of powder blue chintz of good quality with a roller print of paired turtledoves decorating it. The same fabric was used for the window treatments, with curtains of buff coloured trolly-lolly lace hanging over the glass to obscure the view of anyone looking into the room without impeding the influx of sunshine or breezes. The bedroom also boasted a fireplace, with a slender oak mantle above it on which perched an ormolu and white marble clock, as well as a crystal vase with fresh flowers. A wooden folding screen covered by French scenic papers created a space in front of the fireplace to act as a kind of small sitting room within the larger bedroom. This bed-sit was furnished with a dainty round pedestal table and two chairs, so that she could write her letters in private or have a coze with a guest if she wished. Mary was enchanted; the room far exceeded her expectations. She felt she would be, as the saying was, as snug as a bug in a rug.

Her sister's open-hearted welcome plus the pleasing style and situation of the parsonage all combined to make Mary very happy. She may have been stuck in the country, but her relations and accommodations eased her worries of tedium and rustication considerably.

Mrs Grant was also made happy. She received in those whom she hoped to love better than ever a young man and woman of very prepossessing appearance. The manners of both were lively and pleasant, and Mrs Grant immediately gave them credit for everything else. She was delighted with each, but Mary was her dearest object; and having never been able to glory in beauty of her own, she thoroughly enjoyed the power of being proud of her sister's. Her chiefest desire was to retain the society of these beloved siblings, and the best way of securing that happiness was if either of them married into the neighbourhood.

She had not waited for Mary's arrival to look out for a suitable match for her. Mrs Grant had fixed on Tom Bertram; the eldest son of a baronet was not too good for a girl of twenty thousand pounds, with all the elegance and accomplishments which Mrs Grant foresaw in her; and being a warm-hearted, unreserved woman, Mary had not been three hours in the house before she told her what she had planned. As soon as Henry and Dr Grant had retired to the rector's library for an after-dinner sherry, Mrs Grant took advantage of her *tête-à-tête* with her sister to communicate her hopes.

"When my husband and dearest Henry join us again, we must all walk up the lane a bit so that you can see Mansfield Park, Sir Thomas Bertram's manor-house. He is a baronet, wealthy, and very much a gentleman; he is well-respected throughout the country. He has been away at his estate in Antigua for above eighteen months, and his wife, Lady Bertram, told me in April that he had written to say he should be home again at the end of summer. Lady Bertram is perfectly pleasant, but does not often take the trouble of leaving her home; I go to her at least once a week. I think it would be just the thing if their eldest son, a handsome young man who will be six and twenty this August, fell in love with you."

"My word!" Mary laughed. "Does the poor fellow get a say in it?"

"I assure you I am paying him the highest compliments! I think he will be both intelligent enough to value you exceedingly and that he is very nearly worthy of you," Mrs Grant told her sister tenderly. "His sisters are particular friends of mine, the eldest especially, and I feel I know him very well by their accounts."

"Well, then," Mary said jovially, "do tell me all there is to know of my future family. No, let me guess: they are all amiable and accomplished and respectable."

"They are all those things, so you tease me in vain. There is a Mr Edmund Bertram, just a year younger than his brother and his equal in handsomeness, if not in consequence. There are likewise two daughters, Miss Bertram and Miss Julia Bertram, both of them highly accomplished beauties. They are not as fond of quietly staying at home as their mother, and they often visit me here at the Parsonage. I find them perfectly amiable, and not at all vain in spite of their beauty. The Bertrams are also charitable to the poor of the parish, and charitable to their own relations as well. There is an indigent niece, the fruit of an improvident marriage by Lady Bertram's youngest sister, who lives with them. Her name is Miss Price and she is being raised as one of the family. She has been given the same education as her cousins, but she is aware of her place; her manners are reserved but very pleasing, and she seeks no pert distinctions for herself."

Miss Crawford was glad to find a family of such consequence so very near them, and not at all displeased either at her sister's early care, or the choice it had fallen on. Matrimony was her object, provided she could marry well: and having seen Mr Bertram in town, she knew that objection could no more be made to his person than to his situation in life. While she treated it as a joke, therefore, she did not forget to think of it seriously.

The scheme was soon repeated to Henry, as the Grants and the Crawfords strolled toward Mansfield Park in a post-dinner perambulation. The houses, though scarcely half a mile apart, were not within sight of each other; one needed to walk to the first bend in the lane past the parsonage to see the manor.

The long afternoons of the summer month gave them plenty of light, though it was nearly eight o'clock. The slanting rays of the setting sun lit the tops of the trees but left the lower branches and trunks in a pleasantly cool shadow. The air stirred easily and carried the scents

of hay and chamomile from the surrounding farmland, as well as the
woodsier smells of the copse and hawthorn hedge that bracketed the
lane. Miss Crawford found it a bit strange to hear the lowing of cows
from nearby meadows and the occasional distant baulking of chickens
in unseen farmyards rather than the rattles of carriage traffic and the
footsteps of multitudes, but after some consideration, she found that
it was a peaceful, and even welcome, change. Wild flowers rioted in
the verge and ditches, and Dr Grant pointed out and named the corn
cockles, buttercups, spearworts, water crowfoots and cornflowers
when Mary exclaimed over their prettiness.

"The cornflowers look familiar," Mary noted. She looked closer.
"Were they the flowers sprinkled on the mashed turnip dish tonight?"

Mrs Grant was pleased. "Yes, you are correct dearest. The
cornflower is an edible bloom and I think there is nothing so pretty
as a few of the bright blue petals on top of mashed yellow turnips;
the blue stands out so well against them and delights the eye in
my opinion."

"I agree with you, ma'am," Mary nodded. "The food on my
plate was as lovely as it was tasty. My congratulations on both your
menu and your cook."

"I am most fortunate in my wife's consideration to my love of
good food," Dr Grant praised her. "Although I am by no means an
Epicurean, I freely confess to being overly nice about how my food is
dressed. Between them, Mrs Grant and Cook have quite spoiled me.
I am very lucky to have a wife so dedicated to my foibles. There is no
meal so simple that she cannot offer some little delicacies to me."

Mrs Grant blushed at the praise. "It is of little consequence,
Dr Grant. It is no more than any wife should do. Pray, you'll fill me
with conceit."

Mary watched Dr Grant pat his wife's hand where it lay in the
crook of his elbow, and was somewhat amazed to see such obvious
affection between them. She had seen so few married couples in Town
who were reasonably tolerant of each other — let alone fond of one
another — that she found the marital harmony between the Grants
endearing. Nonetheless, as a natural sceptic, she could not help but
wondered if Dr Grant maintained his courtesies regularly. Her uncle
was always civil, even obliging to her aunt when they were in company
but treated his wife with indifference or contempt in the privacy
of his own household. Or perhaps, Dr Grant's attentions were the
perfunctory offerings of a husband pleased with his wife's devotions

and wanting them to continue? It had always been Mary's example that husbands were kind to their wives only when they wished to avoid a fuss or obtain a benefit.

"Who could fail to be an attentive wife when her home is a source of joy to her?" Mrs Grant asked rhetorically. "And now, I have thought of something to make it complete. I should dearly love to settle you both in this country; and therefore, Henry, you shall marry the youngest Miss Bertram, a nice, handsome, good-humoured, accomplished girl, who will make you very happy." Henry bowed and thanked her.

Mary could read Henry's expressions well, and saw the hint of a smirk in the brackets of his mouth. Her brother would not easily step into the parson's trap; he had no desire to tie himself down or truncate his pleasures even the slightest, and had given too many men horns to believe that connubial bliss and fidelity weren't as rare as an honest parliamentarian from a rotten borough. No, Henry would see thirty before he would see his wedding breakfast.

"My dear sister," said Mary, "if you can persuade him into anything of the sort, it will be a fresh matter of delight to me to find myself allied to anybody so clever, and I shall only regret that you have not half a dozen daughters to dispose of. If you can persuade Henry to marry, you must have the address of a Frenchwoman. All that English abilities can do has been tried already. I have three very particular friends who have been all dying for him in their turn; and the pains which they, their mothers (very clever women), as well as my dear aunt and myself, have taken to reason, coax, or trick him into marrying, is inconceivable! He is the most horrible flirt that can be imagined. If your Miss Bertrams do not like to have their hearts broke, let them avoid Henry."

Mary's tone was jocular, but her warnings were serious. Since her sister claimed Miss Bertrams as close acquaintance, Mary made a mental note to speak to her brother later about abusing his sister's goodwill by cutting up the peace of her friends.

"My dear brother, I will not believe this of you."

"No, I am sure you are too good. You will be kinder than Mary. You will allow for the doubts of youth and inexperience. I am of a cautious temper, and unwilling to risk my happiness in a hurry. Nobody can think more highly of the matrimonial state than myself. I consider the blessing of a wife as most justly described in those discreet lines of the poet – 'Heaven's last best gift.'"

"There, Mrs Grant, you see how he dwells on one word, and only look at his smile. I assure you he is very detestable; the Admiral's lessons have quite spoiled him."

"I pay very little regard," said Mrs Grant, "to what any young person says on the subject of marriage. If they profess a disinclination for it, I only set it down that they have not yet seen the right person."

Dr Grant laughingly congratulated Miss Crawford on feeling no disinclination to the state herself.

"Oh yes! I am not at all ashamed of it. I would have everybody marry if they can do it properly: I do not like to have people throw themselves away; but everybody should marry as soon as they can do it to advantage."

"Marrying into the Bertrams would certainly be an advantage for you both; their antecedents are beyond reproach," Mrs Grant said firmly. "They are a fine family, and as handsome as they are respected. Your connections would all be good, to be sure. The eldest daughter, Miss Bertram, is engaged to Mr James Rushworth, who has 12,000 a year; they are waiting only for Sir Thomas Bertram to return before they wed. She will remain settled in the area, for Mr Rushworth's estate of Sotherton is just ten miles from Mansfield. If Henry married Miss Julia Bertram and Mary accepted Mr Tom Bertram, think of how happy we would all be united!"

"Didn't you say there was another son?" Mary asked. "Whom shall he marry?"

"Whoever he marries, I dare say she will be a good addition to the family. Mr Edmund Bertram is a very good sort of young man; very diligent and not given to gaming or extravagance," Mrs Grant replied.

"An ideal younger son, then," Mary exclaimed playfully.

"Gibe if you must," Mrs Grant said complacently, "but he is both handsome and agreeable, and I would not be shocked if he won the hand of some fair heiress."

"And Miss Prince – a niece I believe you said — is she to marry well too? Alas, Henry can only marry one of them," Mary quizzed her elder sister.

"It is Miss *Price*," Mrs Grant corrected her. "A Miss Fanny Price. She is a poor relation, but the dearest little thing you could ever imagine. You'll never meet another young woman so meek and mild tempered. She is always ready to oblige; she is an invaluable companion. She is not so captivating as her cousins, it is true, but

I find her very amiable and she has nothing disgusting in either her looks or her manners. I am sure you will find them all very amiable. Well, almost all of them."

"What is this?" Mary cried. "Who dares to dwell in Mansfield Park without adding to its felicity?"

"She doesn't actually live at Mansfield Park; she is just a nearly constant visitor," explained Mrs Grant. "She is Mrs Norris, the widow of the former rector and Lady Bertram's sister. I am afraid that Dr Grant and Mrs Norris are not good friends; their acquaintance had begun in dilapidations, and their habits are totally dissimilar. Between us, I find her trying."

Henry's brows rose. "I fear to meet a woman who can try your gentle temper. Such a virago would unman me!"

"It's not her words you need be afraid of, "Dr Grant interjected, "she can be positively obsequious when it suits her; if Sir Thomas were home, you would wonder how the man ever dries his boots with her licking them so unreservedly. I would vow that Mrs Norris eats more toad than a heron. No, it is her manner that you must fear. She is bustling and officious; a busy-body with a long nose for sticking into other people's business. She's also scaly and cannot abide that others be liberal when she is not (excepting when they are liberal to *her*, of course). She would skin a flea for the hide and tallow, and dislikes it that every soul in the country isn't as mean as she is. She is also a dreadful bully to the lower classes. I like her not."

"I know we should try to be more charitable towards her," Mrs Grant admitted sorrowfully. "She is a widow with no children, and as such is an object of pity. How much of her behaviour is due to her disappointments in life? I try to bear that in mind when I am near her, and pour oil over troubled waters when I can. I find it easier to humour her than engage my time fussing with her. She only exposes *herself* with her behaviour, so it doesn't matter to *me* if she believes my civilities to be a petty victory over me."

"It would be a better world if we all embraced your philosophy, ma'am," Mary Crawford felt a further surge of fondness for her sister. "My temper is not as sweet as yours, I'm afraid. Yet I must confess myself eager to meet Mrs Norris, if only for the comedy of her manners. With complete candour, I admit I am eager to meet all characters whom you have sketched so fully! Who knew the countryside could provide such interesting denizens?"

Henry laughed, "And I wish to meet them as well, upon my word! What man could resist meeting the Miss Bertrams, young women are such paragons of amiability and beauty?"

Mrs Grant turned to her husband and declared with false woe, "I believe my siblings are quizzing their elder sister! What say you dear? Is such impudence possible in such affable and handsome young people?"

"More likely than not," Dr Grant replied. "The fact they are both handsome and young means people will more readily forgive them, and therefore they have learned to tease their elders to their hearts' content."

"Oh, but this is hard!" Mary exclaimed, her dimples flashing. "A docile young woman such as I would never dare tease an elder such as Mrs Grant. Why, her very augustness would render me mute should I try."

"She has a valid point, dear," Mrs Grant told her husband. "My sister is as meek as a mouse and as mild as milk, with no hint of that playful nature that would lead her to speak lightly to me. We both of us must be completely in error."

"It's true," Henry added. "Among our acquaintance in Town, my sister is well-known for her lack of opinions and her complete avoidance of bon mots and repartee. I often think that if I could just coax her into being a little less of a shy wallflower, perhaps I could find someone willing to marry her. As it is, I merely have to turn down offers for her hand on her behalf two or three times a week during the season."

"Ah, but I have told you repeatedly that I can marry no one but William Charles Macready; having seen him play Hamlet I can never love another," Mary quipped.

"Macready? Did you see him at Covenant Gardens then?" Dr Grant asked.

"Yes, sir. Henry was kind enough to escort myself and two dear friends to see *The Devil to Pay* only a fortnight ago."

"It has been almost two years since Dr Grant and I were at leisure to go to Town and enjoy the theatre there. There is no theatre within fifty miles of us," Mrs Grant lamented. "We have been to some very amusing pantos at Northampton during Christmas, though."

"I enjoy the theatre, but its loss is not such a trial to me as it would be to Henry. Poor Henry is simply mad for plays. I know him to be a great lover of opera as well." Mary gave her brother a mischievous glance, to see how he would react to the combination of "lover" and "opera" in conjunction with his name. Being Henry, he didn't turn a hair.

"It is true that the Gardens are something I frequent often, but Mary is being captious when she accuses me of being the greater lover of the theatre. It is a rare week that goes by without my sister attending a performance with some close acquaintance or another," Henry made a face of exaggerated gravity. "But what can a brother do with such a wilful sister, when she is determined to nourish her yearnings for Macready?"

Merrily disputing as to who was the most addicted to plays and operas, dramas or comedies, the Crawfords and the Grants returned to the parsonage to enjoy card games and each other's company until time for bed.

Chapter Three

A NOTE WAS delivered to Mrs Grant the next morning at a quarter past nine, not long after they had all sat down to breakfast. After a quick glance at the direction, she opened it at the table. Having read it briefly, she smiled and exclaimed, "Here's a piece of good news. Lady Bertram has already answered my request to be allowed to introduce you both at Mansfield Park. Not just a morning call, either! She has invited us all to take tea with them after dinner."

Mary handed Henry the cup of tea she had just poured for him. "Lovely! It was very good of Lady Bertram to respond to you so expeditiously and offer us such civility. A morning visit would have done; this is something above the regular. It shows a pleasing concern for your feelings which, as your sister, I must approve."

"I agree," Henry added cream to his tea. "Does she keep country hours, ma'am?

Mrs Grant shook her head. "No. Lady Bertram may not bother to keep a house in Town any longer, but she still keeps Town hours. They do not dine at the park until six o'clock, and we do likewise. Unlike the parsonage, they keep Town hours for breakfast too, so I try not to make any morning calls on them at the Park until at least midday to avoid disturbing them at the table. Which recalls it to my mind — we always have a sandwich tray or a cold luncheon put out on the sideboard from one o'clock until two, since we breakfast early and dine late. On no account would I have you go hungry in my home."

"It is all done to humour me," Dr Grant smiled, pouring himself a second cup of chocolate. "I prefer breakfast to be a family meal and of something more substantial than rolls and marmalade, and need to have it early so I can perform my ecclesiastical duties for the rest of the morning. Those to whom I must minister most often are of the class where they must rise at dawn and start their work soonest, and I must conform my hours to their needs if I am to be helpful, rather than idle. I have curates and vicars enough in my other livings; where I reside I wish to be a true shepherd to my flock."

"I honour you for it sir," Henry said sincerely. "Too often one encounters parsons who have no concern for their office, leaving the work to be done by overburdened vicars or harried curates."

Dr Grant replied, "I thank you for it, but I do not think doing one's duty should be praised over much."

"Since it is a woman's duty to make her neighbours think well of her, Mrs Grant should fear overpraise as well," Henry added gallantly.

Mrs Grant's cheeks grew faintly pink. "You flatter me, brother. Do feel free to continue."

Mary used the pause after the chuckles Mrs Grant's *bon mot* produced to redirect the topic back to the visit at Mansfield Park. "Will we be taking tea with Lady Bertram's sons and daughters, as well?"

"I am not entirely sure," Mrs Grant replied. "They may all be dining out this evening. However, it is certain that Miss Price will be there, and it is likely Mrs Norris will also join us."

"Mrs Norris never misses an opportunity to dine at Sir Thomas's expense," Dr Grant added sourly.

"True, but she is a very good card player. If we are invited to play cards (which I consider to be assured) then you will have a more enjoyable evening for having a worthy foe at the table," Mrs Grant did her best to call attention to the scant positives of having Mrs Norris in the party. "If the Miss Bertrams are there then there is a strong chance they can be prevailed upon to play and sing, which they both do remarkably well. You know how much you enjoy a good performance upon the pianoforte, my dear."

"You are right as ever, Mrs Grant," Her husband gave her a fond look. He then addresses his brother-in-law. "It is in your sister's nature to seek the greatest good in every situation, even as it is in mine to be satirical. I have seen in you, sir, a similar tendency toward sardonic observation. The greatest alloy to the avoidance of excessive cynicism is to marry a woman of a gentle, cheerful disposition and sanguine temper, as I have done."

"I honour your wisdom, sir."

"If that is the best way to find marital happiness then I shall have to give my hand only to an idealist or fanciful romantic," Mary laughed. "Provided he isn't a second son, of course."

"Now, Mary," her sister admonished, "If you should find a second son who was agreeable, of whom you became fond, I am sure you would marry him. You would not *really* choose ambition over love in such an important matter as matrimony."

"That is why I am very careful to avoid the company of second sons. One cannot be persuaded to folly where one is not tempted. No, let second sons keep to themselves."

Mary spoke lightly, but she was in earnest. She was convinced she would never risk her happiness with a second son. Marriage itself was enough of an evil; her husband would control every aspect of her life, from her residence to her pin money. Her liberties, her pursuits, even those she allowed to be her acquaintances and her time with friends would be subject to his will. She had seen very well how the Admiral had relished picking at her dear aunt, how he would solicit her opinion for the purpose of jeering at it. The only true source of felicity available to a woman was to move in good society; her aunt had received the admiration and attention she deserved from the beau monde. Mary intended to have the same happiness, and a younger son would be hard pressed to cut an important figure in society by either rank or wealth. She could think of only a handful, and since she was not vain enough to suppose she would attach such an unusual specimen, she would eschew the species altogether.

"Are you still willing to walk to the river with me today, then? There is a great risk some of the men we will see are not firstborn." Mrs Grant smiled at her sister.

"I would venture any hazard to please you, ma'am," Mary replied, "but I will own that my peril is not great. None of the men I will see would be of our class, and thus none would be able to address me and put me in danger of losing my heart to a younger son. I am resolved to avoid meeting a second son at the altar, but I harbour no such resentment toward second sons whom I shall meet on the lane. I am quite unafraid."

"I have no aversion to meeting a second son, regardless of his rank," Henry spread butter on his toast. "I am also unafraid of meeting a second son at the altar, or his sister Molly."

Dr Grant choked on a mouthful of hot chocolate. "Do you not play back gammon then?"

"Only in the parlour, with ladies present," returned Henry smoothly.

"I believe," Mary narrowed her eyes, "that they are speaking of something dreadfully rude, but I know not what."

"Neither do I, which I am grateful for," Mrs Grant avowed. "When you are through with your silliness, what is it that you will be doing Henry?"

"I shall go for a ride, ma'am. It is a fine country and I would like to see more of it. Both my hunter and I could use the exercise."

"Then I will advise you to ride toward the north. There are some fine vistas in that direction, and if you ride as far as Islip you will see the Church of St Nicholas, which is a fine old Gothic building," Mrs Grant recommended.

Her brother was startled. "How did you know that I was a lover of the Gothic? Does it appear written on my brow?"

"No, dearest. It was written in a letter from Mary."

"It is true Henry. I did indeed tell Mrs Grant that you had a fondness all things baroque and picturesque," Mary admitted, helping herself to more tea.

"You do me ill, Mary," Henry said. "You will have Dr and Mrs Grant think I am a Romantic fribble rather than an antiquarian."

"I would never say you were either a Romantic or a fribble, but I do consider you to be enamoured of medievalism and folklore. Am I wrong?" Mary asked.

"Alas, no," Henry said. "You have me in checkmate. I must concede that I thrill to all things historical and horrid."

"Then you are in good company here," Dr Grant assured him. "Both Mrs Grant and myself are excessively fond of such things. Do you read German?"

"I do indeed, sir."

"Then I must share with you my stock of Schauerroman, the German shudder-novels. As loathe as I am to admit it, there is not a single horrid novel in English that can compare to the terrors one encounters in a German shudder-novel."

"Oh! That I had asked for a German master, instead of an Italian one!" Mary lamented. "Will you read them to me, Henry? I know the agility of your mind; you can translate each line quickly enough to suit me."

"Before you agree," Dr Grant interjected, "you should be forewarned, Henry. The shudder-novel has themes and passages ill-suited to the ears of a lady. If I were you, I would save both yourself and Miss Crawford some mortifying blushes by denying her request, as much as it pains us both to deny her anything."

Henry gave a small bow to his brother-in-law. His lack of spoken agreement gave Mary the strongest suspicion that her brother would read her the books — or at least sum them up for her — clandestinely. The only thing thus far that Henry had absolutely refused to let Mary read was the Marquis de Sade, which she was determined to get a copy of as soon as she became a married woman.

"As captivating as this topic is," Mrs Grant said, "I am quite done with breakfast and must excuse myself from the table. I need to reply to Lady Bertram before I go walking with Mary, and will attend to it in the sitting room while she is finishing her tea."

"I am through with my tea just now," Mary commented. "I have promised to write Lady Stornoway; your epistolary diligence has inspired me to keep my promise. If you will allow me, I will join you."

The gentlemen stood up as the ladies rose from their seats, and Henry said "I, too, have eaten enough. I shall head to the stables directly, before the surfeit of excellent food tempts me to idle about when I should properly be active."

"Shall I give your compliments to Lady Stornoway in my letter, Henry?" Mary inquired, a twinkle in her eye.

"Of course," Henry replied without the slightest change in countenance. "And if you do not mind, tell her my particular friend from France wishes to make her acquaintance, and say that I strongly recommend it, for I know they have much in common."

Suppressing a giggle at the thought of her friend's outrage should she write such a naughty thing, Mary curtsied to her brother and trailed her sister out of the dining room.

As though the weather felt it was behaving in too Spanish a manner for an English summer, the long run of sunny days were interrupted when storm clouds blew in shortly after breakfast, preventing Mary and Mrs Grant from taking their planned walk along the river and bringing Henry's ride to an early close. However, Mary found nothing objectionable about an occasional quiet day with one's siblings, and had no complaints. Henry had been delighted to find that the Grant's library was in possession of several horrid novels which he had not yet had time to read, and had installed himself in the study with the first volume of Mrs Roche's *The Monastery of St Columb*.

Mary was in a more sociable mood and stayed with her sister in the sitting room, where they had a satisfying tête-à-tête while plying their needles. Although Mary usually netted, when she saw Mrs Grant working on a patchwork quilt, which she was told was for one of the poor families in the parish, she offered help with the project rather than continuing her reticle cover. With the basket of scraps on the sofa between them, the sisters talked with the accompaniment of the sound of gentle rain on the windows. It was deeply peaceful, and even a hardened city mouse like Mary began to see some of the allure of a country home.

As the morning passed, the conversation began to drift from the comfortable shoals of gossip and fashion into the deeper waters of more serious topics.

"You told me yesterday that Sir Thomas Bertram was on his estate of Antigua. Does he support slavery then?" Mary knew her brother-in-law was, despite his personal dislike of slavery, a staunch Tory; she and Henry had both been careful to not introduce the topic of their ardent support of abolition lest it led to a discussion of the fact Henry was a Whig and potentially cause a quarrel with their host. Mary suspected that her sister was more a friend of the Enlightenment than Dr Grant, and was determined to discover if Mrs Grant's opinions were in harmony with her own.

"Sir Thomas is not a friend to abolition, no." Mrs Grant confided. "He believes the profits on his sugar plantation were materially lessened when he was no longer able to import fresh slaves from Africa. It saddens me that it is so, because he is liberal enough with the poor of his own country."

"So it is a sugar plantation then? I thought that raising sugar was an immensely profitable enterprise?" Mary asked in faint surprise.

"It still is, in my opinion, but Sir Thomas looks more at the contraction of his wealth than its continuation. It does not help that Mr Bertram accrued gaming debts of a considerable size, which required Sir Thomas to liquidate some of assets for cash. He can no longer use his slaves for that purpose, and he feels the loss of his capital more than he feels the human sorrow of the pernicious trade. It was to satisfy Mr Bertram's debts that Sir Thomas found it necessary to sell this living."

"Is Mr Bertram an inveterate gamer, then?" Mary frowned.

"Not habitually, I am happy to report. I would not have considered him for you if he were improvident in general," Mrs Grant assured her. "He fell briefly into bad company, but has promised his father on his honour to refrain from betting anything more than his pocket money while Sir Thomas lives."

"Does Sir Thomas's wife and children also share his sentiments toward slavery?"

Mrs Grant hesitated. "Lady Bertram is of Sir Thomas's opinion, but she has such a yielding temper and such a high regard for her husband that I have never heard her to disagree with him on even the smallest matter. I cannot say for sure of what his children think; I can only give you my impression. They are all of them so very aware of the respect due to their father that they are naturally loathe to disagree with him in a frank or public manner. It is very unlike how King George and his sons got on! I believe, however, that Sir Thomas's sons are like Dr Grant; they are Tories but friends to abolition. Mr Bertram has made a few statements in private to me about his distaste for seeing slaves upon the Antigua estate, and has hinted that he would prefer his father to withdraw from sugar cultivation altogether. Mr Edmund Bertram has been more cautious in his opinions, but his silence on the matter speaks of a lack of agreement between himself and his father on this point. In confidence, Miss Bertram and Miss Julia Bertram have confessed themselves to be the admirers of the writings of Mr Clarkson, and I cannot fathom how anyone can have read his works and remained supporters of slavery."

Mary nodded, and then quietly continued to feather-stitch her section of the quilt, clearly lost in thought. Finally she spoke, "I find it curious how some men — or *people* I should say, since women are as prone to it as men — wish to alleviate the wants of those in need nearby yet have no compassion for those who suffer abroad, while others wish to right the wrongs of distant strangers but cannot see the suffering of the poor when it is under their noses. It has been very seldom in my experience that anyone wishes to do both. Sir Thomas has no feeling for his slaves, but you say he acts to reduce the pains of poverty here. My brother has great feeling for the abolition of slavery, but I am sorry to tell you that he neglects the poor of his Norfolk estate. They are both gentlemen, but their concerns are so disparate; I wonder what makes mankind so divergent in principles? Do you think it is a result of their natures, or as a result of what one is instructed to use as a guide for one's morals?"

"My dear!" Mrs Grant laughed. "These are deep questions! Are these reflections from philosophy? No one would believe such a pretty girl to have such information."

Mary looked slightly rueful. "I confess to reading philosophy. Henry loves debate on such topics, and it intrigues me. I am careful, though, not to read or learn overmuch. Doctors say being *too* studious will make a woman begin to harden and lose her bloom. Some may call it vanity to worry too much about one's appearance, but until men chose wives for their erudition rather than beauty I believe my concerns to be prudence, rather than vanity.

Mrs Grant nodded. "That's true, dearest. You are wise to be cautious. They say that if a woman overindulges in scholarly pursuits, it can prevent her from having a family later in life. It can warp the more delicate feminine organs."

"I fear it has already cost me some femininity," Mary said. "I have read too much; I am a rationalist. It is indelicate for a woman to be as impervious to feeling as I am. I flatter myself that I am *sensible* rather than sardonic, but I am lacking in that *sensibility* that is so valued in our sex. I am not romantic. I find nothing to admire in a consumptive poet or bloodthirsty revolutionary. My pragmatism would always triumph over idealism."

"But I know you enjoy horrid novels and Cowper's poetry; is that not a sign of sensibility? A desire to experience a depth of feeling?"

"I will not, cannot, deny my enjoyment of horrid novels, or novels in general for that matter. I also cannot deny that I relish the poetry of Cowper and Pope and suchlike. To read work that quakes the nerves, that breeds fancies in the mind; who could not be fond of such titillation? It is simply that romance belongs in print or in art and should not intrude into one's reality. I can admire Byron's poems without wishing to die for love."

"No one would be that silly!" Mrs Grant was appalled at the idea.

"I assure you," Mary was wry, "that such silliness flourishes among the young ladies of the Ton. To perish for love is all the thing. Thinking on it, perishing from love is all the crack among the gentlemen of the beau monde as well. Occasionally some would-be swain will imply he shall die of love for me. I always tell them that, 'men have died and worms have eaten them, but not for love'. One can always be as rude as one likes provided one is quoting Shakespeare, you know. The only penalty I have suffered is that someone has published some truly execrable poetry to 'a Lady named Rosalind from her Orlando' that is reputed to refer to *me*. I wouldn't mind being the subject of such absurdity if only the fellow could produce an acceptable couplet."

Mrs Grant was amused. "Still, I am surprised that you disavow sensibility. You seem to be too lively, too sociable, to be a pragmatist."

"Why should you be surprised?" Mary shook her head. "My rationality does not make me sober. Can one not be both lively and a realist? Henry is far more unsentimental than I am — he is constantly on his guard lest he becomes a true cynic — but he has a cheerful disposition and loves company. Rationalism does not make one dull or stupid. Its dangers are those of apprehension; it makes one more scornful of the dullness and stupidity of others and more sceptical of human nature."

Mrs Grant pondered over her sewing. "I am sentimental myself. I hope, however, that my sensibility does not make me seem foolish to you."

"Of course not!" Mary exclaimed. "I find your cordiality and sweetness of temper to be a great boon. You are all that delights me as a sister. It is only that I appreciate your nature *rationally;* I value your benevolence and solicitude with my *understanding,* as well as from my heart. A person of sense would always look for such characteristics in a friend."

"You are all kindness," Mrs Grant looked at Mary fondly. "I cannot believe you are so much a disciple of enlightenment; your impulses are too good."

"I must dissuade you from your opinion," Mary laughed. "I am enlightened to the point that I could deter shipwrecks; I could serve as a lighthouse beacon."

"Come! Be serious!"

"Can a woman be serious? Do you allow it to be possible for our sex?"

"You know well that they can, Mary. Cannot sensibility be coupled to seriousness?"

"In truth, I am of your opinion about it," Mary admitted with an engaging grin. "Have you read the novel *Sense and Sensibility?*"

Mrs Grant said that she had not, nor had she seen it in Mansfield's circulating library.

"It was published only last year, so perhaps it has not come to the countryside yet," Mary surmised. "It has been very popular in Town though. Princess Charlotte has great admiration for it."

Mrs Grant was intrigued. "Who is the author? Is it a work of Mrs Edgeworth or Mrs Burney?"

"No one knows the exact author, ma'am, except the publisher. It was written by 'a Lady'. It is quite as good as a novel written by either Mrs Edgeworth or Mrs Burney, though; perhaps even better. The superior style of the writing makes me suspect it might have been written by one of the ton, except for the fact it has real taste and feeling in it unlike any I've encountered among them," Mary said with derision.

"Mary! You make me laugh but you cannot think that way about all your friends and acquaintance. You know you cannot," Mrs Grant protested.

"It is not quite that bad," Mary said with a smile, "but there is a sad want of real taste and feeling among the beau monde as a general thing. The characters in the novel, Elinor and Marianne Dashwood, have such *heart* between them that they do not strike me as having been written by any member of London's glittering throng."

"Are they allegories of sense and sensibility then?" Mrs Grant asked.

"Not really. Each of them have too much of one, and must learn to balance it with more of the other. Elinor is *too* sensible, and Marianne has *too* much sensibility. Elinor must learn to give more importance to her feelings, and Marianne must learn to be rational. Like you have just argued, Marianne has great sensibility, but is serious rather than lively. I believe you would like it. It is excellently done, with a strong romantic theme. I have seldom liked a novel that *wasn't* horrid better."

"Then I shall read it," Mrs Grant promised. "I do like novels wherein the characters learn something about *themselves.* I just hope their introspection does not make them unfeminine; I do not like novels where the heroines are almost made masculine by their exertions or education."

Mary paused thoughtfully. "Have you read Wollstonecraft?"

Mrs Grant started. "Of course not!"

"Well, I have," Mary stated with a hint of defiance. "Whatever the unorthodoxy of the author's personal life, her philosophy on the rights of women does not offer any impropriety. If you were to read her work you would see that it merely calls for women to be treated as rational beings and educated. There is nothing to unsex them; an education befitting their station in life would make them better wives, in that they could be true helpmates to their husbands, and better mothers, since it is women who first educate the young."

"I cannot agree with you, Mary," Mrs Grant was hesitant. "Such a life as she led, with a love child and to marry an anarchist! No, as much as I wish us to be always in agreement I cannot join you in admiration of Wollstonecraft."

"Then let us speak no more of her, Mrs Grant. I would be a very unfeeling friend indeed to wish to distress a sister who has been kindness itself to me," Mary's expressive eyes were filled with contrition. "Let us speak of more pleasant topics, such as music and whether Liverpool can convince the Prince of Wales to stop living with Mrs Fitzherbert and return to his wife."

Mrs Grant laughed. "May the Lord have mercy on Princess Caroline, if he should do so. Poor woman, I shall support her as long as I can, because she *is* a woman and because I hate her husband."

Merrily, the sisters wiled away the morning in the discussion of the Regent's foibles, and finished nearly half the quilt.

Chapter Four

"SHALL I TAKE a shawl, do you think?" Mary asked her sister as they sat in the parlour and waited for the carriage to be brought round. The earlier rain had made the short walk to Mansfield Park inadvisable, even though there were several hours of daylight remaining. It would not do to appear before Lady Bertram with their slippers and petticoats coated in dirt.

"I think a shawl would be wise, dearest. The evening air is often chill after a day of rain, and the drawing-room at the Park is large enough that its fireplace cannot keep every nook comfortable should the day lose too much of its warmth."

"Thank you," Mary turned to instruct her maid to bring down the golden Kashmir shawl, which Beatty did with admirable speed. "May I ask your opinion on this shawl, ma'am? Is it too ornate for half-dress?"

Mrs Grant shook her head. "Even in half-dress I hold it that a shawl cannot be too fine. What is the purpose of having a Kashmir, if one cannot make full use of it? And I think that such a dark shade of gold looks very well on you, Mary. I think I may tell you that you are lovely without causing undue vanity, and it would be a shame not to show yourself to advantage."

Mary smiled her thanks to her sister and reached out to press Mrs Grant's hand with affection. She had dressed with care for an evening at Mansfield Park, bearing in mind that she was not opposed to Tom Bertram falling in love with her, and was glad her sister had noticed.

Her dress had a squared neck with the smallest of sleeves, and was gathered just under her small bosom. It was made of a beige Madras muslin, which she believed suited her much better than the white usually worn by young women, and was cunningly decorated with tiny golden beads scattered over the fabric. If their visit extended past sunset, then the candlelight would spark on the beads, giving an effect was reminiscent of random flashes of sunshine on rippling water. Under the see-through muslin, she wore two chemises. The one closest to her skin was a sleeveless shift of serviceable white cotton that came only to her knees. The other was an under-dress of amber coloured crepe de chine that was nearly as transparent as the muslin gown which covered it.

The extra layers of fabric and the style of the garment gave the impression that she was more rounded below the waist than was actually the case. Her sylph-like figure was both a blessing and a curse; a blessing because it was light and pleasing, but a curse because she was bereft of the voluptuous hindquarters that were considered a mark of true beauty. She had been in high luck when she found a modiste who could conjure the illusion of fleshiness that she lacked in truth.

As much as she would have liked a little more backside, it was her hair that was her least fashionable characteristic; it steadfastly resisted curl. Not for her were the irregular ringlets of Romanesque elegance. Most of her locks were confined to a braided chignon, and only the shorter hair around her face could be subdued into twists by Beatty's valiant assaults with curling tongs. In addition to her crimped fringe, she had a few small fresh flowers laced into her tiny decorative braids.

Mary had fretted over her jewellery for a good quarter of an hour. To wear no jewellery at all was impossible, but to wear too much or the wrong kind of jewellery would be in bad taste. As far as Mary was concerned, bad taste was a sin equivalent to any of those listed in the Ten Commandments. It was possibly even worse since God would forgive the sincerely penitent for breaking any of the Ten Commandments, whereas the Ton would neither forgive nor forget bad taste. A thin gold chain with a topaz cross would usually do very well for evening half-dress, but would it be enough for a making Lady Bertram's acquaintance? Should she wear pearls? Her smallest strand of pearls and most discrete pearl earrings were silvery white, and would look ill with her gown, so she would have to wear a longer necklace with pearls of a very dark cream; was it too long? Finally, Mary decided to split the difference and wear her most ornate gold chain, without any pendant, and simple gold earrings.

When Henry entered the drawing-room to inform his sisters that the carriage was at the door, he was generous in his compliments to both of them. Then, as he was helping Mary on with her cloak in the hall, he murmured to her, "Poor Mr Tom Bertram, I fear he is in great danger."

"You are a rattle, Henry. His heart maybe as well-guarded as yours, and thus an unbreachable fortress." Mary was flattered by Henry's assurance of her powers over his sex, but she did not take them seriously; he was far from impartial in his estimation of her virtues.

"Then let us once more into the breach," Henry offered her his arm, "and see if he falls."

"

Shortly after their introduction to Mansfield Park, the Crawfords were disposed to find the Bertrams as amiable as the Grants had claimed them to be. Lady Bertram was, to be sure, neither witty nor vivacious, but she was as affable and elegant a gentlewoman as they had ever met. Her sons were both handsome and men of information, and although the younger brother did not have the easy charm of Mr Bertram, his calm good manners were pleasing. Lady Bertram's daughters, who were both of them uncommonly pretty and gracious, as well as accomplished, were ideal additions to the Crawford's society. In them, Mary found ladies to equal her in their taste for music and their conversational abilities.

Maria and Julia Bertram were a source of particular felicity for Henry Crawford. He could never see a beauty without wishing to beguile her, and he had been introduced to them less than a quarter of an hour before he resolved to make Miss Bertram, rather than Miss Julia Bertram, his object. He would have to restrain his attentions to Julia, since they might give rise to expectations that would touch upon his honour, but Maria was engaged; he was safe to flirt as much as he chose. Henry felt sure he would choose to flirt with her a great deal. Seldom had he seen, even in London, a woman of such good looks. She was tall and golden-haired, and had the most perfect figure imaginable. Her eyes, though blue, were not soft; they had a depth of colour and expression that rendered them captivatingly bright. In short, she was the quintessential English Rose and Henry's vanity would not be appeased until he won her admiration.

He gave no thought to Miss Price, although she was also introduced. Her shyness and uninteresting looks did not inspire him in any way. Her spiritless demeanour bordered on the insipid.

"What a lovely tea caddy, Lady Bertram," Mary remarked civilly, when the trolley was brought out. "I have never seen shell-work like it, or with such vivid colours."

"Thank you", Lady Bertram replied complacently. "It is West Indian shell-work, with coral beads. My husband, Sir Thomas, sent it to me recently. He had been on his estate in Antigua for more than a year, and has made us all several presents during his absence. He is a most attentive husband and father."

"I honour him," Henry said. "My uncle, who has been generosity itself to me in almost all respects, seldom thinks to bring home curios or send interesting gifts from his travels. The Admiral has sailed many times to West Africa, but any ivory I possess has been obtained at Gray's, in Sackville Street."

Henry politely left out the fact his uncle was part of the West African Squadron, the Naval force employed to crush the Atlantic slave-trade. Even if Lady Bertram did not make the connection between the Squadron and her husband's estate, her children would doubtlessly have felt some awkwardness.

"I daily feel my good fortune," Lady Bertram assured her visitors while she blended the tea and added it to the pot. Although her love for her husband was not ardent or something that occupied much of her thoughts, it was sincere.

"We all feel our good fortune in my brother, Mr Crawford," Lady Betram's sister Mrs Norris interjected. "He is everything estimable in a man of his position."

Mrs Norris was the most unexpected member of the Park's family in the opinion of the Crawfords. With such descriptions of her vinegary disposition, Mary and Henry had both expected her to be an old sourpuss and thin as a rake. Instead, Mrs Norris was nearly as pretty as her sister, lacking only a modicum of plumpness to equal her sister in looks. In her face and in her demeanour to Lady Bertram's guests, there was nothing to mark a choleric temper.

Lady Bertram poured the tea into the cups, and both her daughters rose to pass it around to their guests. It was customary for the lady of the house to serve the tea to her guests, but since Maria and Julia had come out it had been given to them to do the honours. This not only allowed their mother to remain seated, as was her preference, it allowed the sisters an opportunity to show off both their abilities as hostesses and their stately figures.

"This blend is excellent, Lady Bertram," Mary took another sip of tea. "My sister told me that you blended a very good tea, and — as it ever is — her judgement on this matter was correct."

"My mother," Tom said, "has quite spoiled me for tea. When I am away I always miss her blend. Other women can, and do, blend excellent teas, but my mother's is always the superior to my taste."

Conversation, as is usual for such first meetings between new acquaintance, moved from tea to the weather, and from the weather to music. Both Maria and Julia were prevailed upon to play the pianoforte, and after a few well-done pieces, the Crawfords and Tom Bertram were invited to join them in a glee. Mary, with a good ear for music, was impressed with Tom's singing voice, which was nearly as good as Henry's. It was another point in the gentleman's favour.

Edmund did not join in the singing, but his attention and requests for more showed him to be a man of musical taste. Even the timid Miss Price crept nearer to the pianoforte, to hear the music better. Mary saw that Edmund, alone of his siblings, noticed and coaxed Miss Price to come closer and join the group.

Poor little Miss Price was unable to enjoy the company of other young people or music long. She was summoned away, in no gentle manner, by Mrs Norris for the purpose of making up a table for loo. The Grants, Lady Bertram, and her sister had decided upon playing loo and they needed a fifth player to assure a tolerable game. It occurred to none of them that Miss Price should be asked her preference, but even if they had asked her it was almost certain that she would have declared herself to be instantly at their disposal.

Mary observed a slight tightening in Edmund's countenance, and she believed he was vexed on his cousin's behalf but hiding it well, as a true gentleman. "Miss Price is most obliging. Even upon such short acquaintance, I perceive her to have a very sweet temper." It was in Mary's nature, as much as Mrs Grants, to try to smooth over little social troubles when there was no active ill-will to counter.

Edmund's face relaxed and he smiled. "You are not deceived, Miss Crawford. I can say that I know no one who is more obliging or fearful of giving offence than my cousin. She has, though, a good deal of sense; I suspect her patience must be tried upon occasion by the expectations of her compliance, but she never gives any hint of resentment."

"Perhaps she feels none," Mary offered. "If her temper is naturally sweet and her character formed to give comfort to others, then she would feel more honoured than put upon when her services were called for."

"I had not thought of that. You have a quick insight," Edmund gave her a slight bow. "Do you see all our characters with such perspicacity?"

"By no means," Mary declared. "One does not need deep insight to see that Miss Price is sweet tempered; it is plain. I would not venture to sketch the character of anyone else upon such short acquaintance. It is natural for those who have been in the world to have some artifice; it keeps their feelings properly restrained. Your cousin is singular in that her lack of artifice reveals no impropriety. One does not often encounter such in Town."

"I can say, with sincerity, that I have never met anyone as naturally modest and fearful of giving offence as my cousin," Edmund paused. "I do not mean false-modesty; that is common enough. It is that most women, being rational creatures, are aware of their charms and their virtues. This does not always equal a lack of modesty or indicate vanity. We are all of us capable of making some judgements as to our weaknesses and our strengths. Nevertheless, my cousin seems to be unaware of any good parts she processes."

Mary was pleased. "Not everyone gives women the credit of being rational creatures, but I agree with you Mr Bertram. Both sexes recognise their best features and attempt to cultivate and display them, as well as hide and attempt to ameliorate their worst ones."

"I find it hard to believe that you have faults; I must take your word upon the matter." Edmund rejoined. He was not unaware of her beauty, and he found the mixture of liveliness and archness in her manner enchanting.

He was rewarded with the sight of her dimples. "If I have them, you may sure I shall not own them."

Tom, who had finished speaking to Henry about horses a short time before, turned to Miss Crawford and his brother. "Pardon me, but I could not help but overhear your conversation. I must say that I agree with my brother, and believe that if you do not own your faults it is because it is unlikely that you have them."

Mary swept her gaze down in imitation of modesty, and then tilted her head and looked up at Tom through her thick lashes. "You flatter me, sir."

Tom protested that he did not, for there could be no flattery in the truth. "I feel myself something of an expert in the matters of faults and false modesty, since my encounter with Miss Hawkins in Bath last year. Do you remember me telling you of it Edmund?"

"If it is the same Miss Hawkins who was giving herself air due to an elder sister's advantageous marriage, then indeed I do."

"That is the one I am speaking of. She was the most disgusting case of false modesty I have ever come across. Everything she said to flatter herself was couched as a phrase from her friends," Tom put on a simpering face and raised his voice to a falsetto. "I do not claim to be a virtuoso on the pianoforte, but my friends say I am not devoid of talent. I am no expert, but my friends say I am not without taste. My travels are not broad, but my friends tell me that my brother — Mr Suckling — has a home that would be not out of place in France." He resumed his normal tone. "She fished me for compliments as if I were a trout stream."

"Her error was clearly in the bait. One does not use a fat worm to angle for trout; one uses a delicate fly or one is lost," Mary remarked.

Tom and Edmund both looked surprised and delighted. "Are you an angler then, Miss Crawford?" Tom asked.

"I am, I must confess it." Mary put on a simpering falsetto in mimic of Tom's and continued, "My friends say I am not entirely devoid of skill."

The Bertram brothers laughed. "How came you to be an angler, Miss Crawford? Tom queried. "It is a somewhat unusual pursuit for your sex."

"My father would take me trout fishing along with Henry, when I was a young girl," Mary explained. "There was no sport he loved better than fishing and there was nothing Henry and I loved so much as being with him, so it was natural that I develop a liking for the activity. When my parents passed away so suddenly, I was, as you could expect, plunged into deepest melancholy. Henry, though two years my elder, was hardly less distraught. My dear aunt was desperate to make us feel some form of enjoyment, and knew we loved fishing, but the Admiral did not fish. She did, however, have a dear friend whose husband was an angler of repute and who had a fine trout stream on their estate. My aunt appealed to her friend, who very kindly invited us all to Derbyshire." Noticing a lull in Henry's conversation, she raised her voice slightly as asked, "Henry, do you remember the summer we went fishing in Derbyshire?"

"Vividly; it is one of my happiest memories. The pains our uncle took to learn to fish with us! If he had not come to love the sport as well, I think the poor man would have suffered greatly. He's never been overly fond of the countryside."

"And our aunt, dutifully trailing behind us ankle deep in mud and having her gowns splashed with fishy water!"

"Yes!" Henry laughed. "They were both so kind. We can neither of us ever give them too much credit for their care."

"Certainly they were both unexceptional caregivers when we were youngsters." Mary, having grown into a deep dislike for the Admiral because of his cruelties to her aunt, hedged her agreement without resorting to falsehood. "Do you recall when I fell into the stream?"

"How could I ever forget it?" Henry cried.

"I hope you were unhurt, Miss Crawford!" Julia said with some real concern. It was not uncommon for children to drown, and living near the River Nene had meant she and Maria had been constantly cautioned to avoid going too close to the water when they were young.

"I was unharmed, but I did a great deal of damage to my aunt's nerves, I believe," Mary replied.

"Not just out aunt's nerves, Mary," Henry exclaimed. "You did not see the Admiral and the footman and the groom and the gamekeeper all leap into the water to retrieve you. Our uncle was shaking for some time after, and white as a new sheet."

"True," Mary agreed. "I was much more aware of my aunt's scream of horror and her tears as she and nanny rushed me to the house."

"Did the scare curtail your fishing afterwards?" Tom asked.

"Surprisingly, no," Mary told him. "But you may be certain I was never allowed to get too close to the bank of the stream ever again."

"The Admiral also taught us both to swim," Henry reminded her.

"Ah! I haven't swum since I became old enough to need a governess. I had nearly forgotten."

"Is it only trout you enjoy fishing for?" Edmund inquired.

"By no means," Mary replied. "I enjoy any sport fishing. In truth, I am better at hook fishing than I am with flies. I will even stoop to coarse fishing if I have to."

"It is to my chagrin that I have to admit I am the one who has convinced Mary to join me in coarse fishing," Henry admitted. "Her friend Lady Stornoway invited us to her estate and she had the most large and delightful pond not half a mile from the house. I do not enjoy solitary fishing as much as I enjoy it with company, so Mary would join me almost every day."

"Then let us scheme to go fishing!" Tom exclaimed. "Edmund and I often take a small boat out on the Nene to fish. It would be of little consequence to obtain one large enough for all our party."

Henry, noticing some disgruntlement at being excluded on the faces of the Bertram daughters, requested that they go as well. "Even if you choose not to fish, your company would make the day a pleasant one."

"You should be aware that the best fishing is to be had in the early morning, before breakfast," Edmund warned his sisters, aware of how little they liked rising before nine o'clock.

Maria and Julia both made haste to assure him they would not mind rising at dawn, and they were eager to learn to fish.

"I have a splendid idea," Tom said. "Let us go on an early fishing expedition, and then perhaps Mr and Miss Crawford would consent to join us for breakfast?"

Consent was readily obtained, with the codicil that it not be an inconvenience to the Grants, and it was decided that if the day after next were fair, they would meet at seven o'clock to go fishing.

The day of the fishing expedition was breezy, and the early morning air was cool enough that Mary had worn a lightweight sarsnet pelisse over her walking dress. The fishing party, which included gamekeepers to bait the hooks and to unhook the fish, was large enough that two boats had been employed. On one, Henry endeavoured to teach Maria and Julia the rudiments of fishing, assisted by two gamekeepers. On the other, Mary and the Bertram brothers fished with the minimal help of the remaining servant.

Although the second boat has a good deal of conversation, everyone aboard was dedicated enough to fishing to speak softly, lest they scare away their finned prey. The first boat, being noisy and gay, returned to the dock that day without having caught so much as a solitary perch. In contrast, Tom and Edmund were able to catch both tench and bream that were worthy of keeping, while Mary not only caught as many fish as they did, she secured the largest prize: a carp weighing twenty pounds that had caused the men in her boat to gape at in amazement when a woman as small as herself was able to land it.

In honour of Mary's achievement, the Bertrams' unanimously decided that the whole catch should be dispatched to the vicarage. Leaving the gamekeepers to put away the gear and transport the fish, the Bertrams and Crawfords returned to the Park. Considering the heat which was already rising, they walked a more circuitous path that remained almost entirely in the shade. Between the shade and the brisk wind they were all comfortable enough, albeit several times the warmth of the day was remarked upon, and they all speculated as to how long the heat would last.

Mary was glad she had worn her pelisse, in spite of the warmth. The thinness of a summer walking dress and a single petticoat meant that even a mild wind could blow the garment against the wearer and reveal her body in such a way that left almost nothing to the imagination. Julia Bertram had also worn a pelisse, but her sister had not. Maria had chosen a cotton spencer, which encased her arms and shoulders in thin material but stopped at the top of her high waisted gown — only an inch below her full bosom. As a result the wind was moulding Maria's diaphanous walking dress to her in a way that not only revealed the curves of her thighs, but pushed the dress between them to outline the triangle of her temple of Venus. Since, by the rules of etiquette, such a revelation could not be directly looked at, mentioned, or used even in private to censure the lady, it was a very effective way to show off a good figure with impunity. Mary suspected Maria was well aware of how much of her limbs were being displayed, but was honest enough with herself to suspect that if *her* lower limbs were as wonderfully rounded then she would be as tempted to exhibit them.

As they were all breakfasting, recounting the morning's fun to an attentive Miss Price and languid Lady Bertram, a note arrived from the parsonage. In it, Mrs Grant most civilly thanked the Betrams for the fish, and asked if they would all dine at the parsonage the next day to help the Grants and Crawfords eat such an abundant catch. Lady Bertram, who was inclined to always stay at home if possible, was urged to accept the invitation by her eldest son. It was soon settled that she would write to Mrs Grant directly after breakfast, and allow Mary and Henry to deliver the note as they went.

Chapter Five

THE CRAWFORDS AND the Grants remained a small family party that evening, and spent their time after dinner in whist and conversation. All four were superlative whist players, and a cosy card game with real hazards and triumphs was no small source of felicity for any of them.

"Mrs Grant, you have undone me!" Henry cried jovially. "I had suspected that Dr Grant would be quite the card sharp, but I was deceived by your sweetness to think you were not ruthless enough to truly excel at a game like whist. How wrong I was!"

Dr Grant smiled at his wife and addressed Henry. "I have never found any partner equal to my wife for whist, sir. I believe I fell in love with her when she first trounced me while partnering with Mrs Arkwright."

"Is how your romance began?" Mary delighted in such stories. "I was too young to be much aware of the particulars."

"I cannot speak for Mrs Grant, as for when she decided she would accept my suit, but for myself I can say it was during a dinner with my friend Dr Arkwright that I first laid eyes upon her and by the end of the evening I had determined she should be my wife will all the speed delicacy would allow."

"That's my eye, Beatty Martin!" Mrs Grant laughed. "You are speaking a humbug sir, to quiz me. You know that you did not think of me so soon. Your attentions that evening were all for Miss Dwerryhouse."

"Miss Dwerryhouse was a very amiable, pretty girl, but she could only command my civilities. It was your bright eyes that attached my notice. I can prove it. I asked for your hand before Mr Holmwood asked Miss Dwerryhouse to take his name, and we had both known her for at least a six month before I met you."

"And how do I know you did not suspect Miss Dwerryhouse of partiality to Mr Holmwood, and turn your thoughts to me?" Mrs Grant needled her husband lightheartedly.

"Because the former Miss Dwerryhouse could not beat me at whist. Who could think of Miss Dwerryhouse when there was a Miss Owston at the table? That a woman could be so soft of temper and sharp of mind had not occurred to me. I was helplessly bewitched."

Mrs Grant laughed with elation, although she did not believe her husband to be fully serious or entirely candid. The simple idea that he would trouble to flatter her with nonsense after more than a dozen years of marriage was delightful enough to raise her spirits.

"There, Henry!" Mary exclaimed. "That is your warning. You must avoid the card table if you do not want Miss Julia Bertram to steal your heart. Her brother Mr Bertram told me that Julia was the best whist player among them, and her reputation at loo is fearsome. Beware your danger."

Henry bowed, but did not reply. Mr Crawford did not mean to be in any danger! the Miss Bertrams were worth pleasing, and were ready to be pleased; and he began with no object but of making them like him. He did not want them to die of love; but with sense and temper which ought to have made him judge and feel better, he allowed himself great latitude on such points.

The Bertrams came to dinner the next day, and it all went very well; Henry flirted with the daughters of the house, Mary charmed Mr Bertram, Dr Grant talked politics with Edmund, and Mrs Grant played cribbage with Lady Bertram.

"I like your Miss Bertrams exceedingly, sister," said he, as he returned from attending them to their carriage after the said dinner; "they are very elegant, agreeable girls."

"So they are indeed, and I am delighted to hear you say it. But you like Julia best."

"Oh yes! I like Julia best."

"But do you really? for Miss Bertram is in general thought the handsomest."

"So I should suppose. She has the advantage in every feature, and I prefer her countenance; but I like Julia best; Miss Bertram is certainly the handsomest, and I have found her the most agreeable, but I shall always like Julia best, because you order me."

"I shall not talk to you, Henry, but I know you *will* like her best at last."

"Do not I tell you that I like her best *at first*?"

"And besides, Miss Bertram is engaged. Remember that, my dear brother. Her choice is made."

"Yes, and I like her the better for it. An engaged woman is always more agreeable than a disengaged. She is satisfied with herself. Her cares are over, and she feels that she may exert all her powers of pleasing without suspicion. All is safe with a lady engaged: no harm can be done."

"Why, as to that, Mr. Rushworth is a very good sort of young man, and it is a great match for her."

"But Miss Bertram does not care three straws for him; *that* is your opinion of your intimate friend. *I* do not subscribe to it. I am sure Miss Bertram is very much attached to Mr. Rushworth. I could see it in her eyes, when he was mentioned. I think too well of Miss Bertram to suppose she would ever give her hand without her heart."

"Mary, how shall we manage him?"

"We must leave him to himself, I believe. Talking does no good. He will be taken in at last."

"But I would not have him *taken in*; I would not have him duped; I would have it all fair and honourable."

"Oh dear! let him stand his chance and be taken in. It will do just as well. Everybody is taken in at some period or other."

"Not always in marriage, dear Mary."

"In marriage especially. With all due respect to such of the present company as chance to be married, my dear Mrs. Grant, there is not one in a hundred of either sex who is not taken in when they marry. Look where I will, I see that it *is* so; and I feel that it *must* be so, when I consider that it is, of all transactions, the one in which people expect most from others, and are least honest themselves."

"Ah! You have been in a bad school for matrimony, in Hill Street."

"My poor aunt had certainly little cause to love the state; but, however, speaking from my own observation, it is a manoeuvring business. I know so many who have married in the full expectation and confidence of some one particular advantage in the connexion, or accomplishment, or good quality in the person, who have found themselves entirely deceived, and been obliged to put up with exactly the reverse. What is this but a take in?"

"My dear child, there must be a little imagination here. I beg your pardon, but I cannot quite believe you. Depend upon it, you see but half. You see the evil, but you do not see the consolation. There will be little rubs and disappointments everywhere, and we are all apt to expect too much; but then, if one scheme of happiness fails, human nature turns to another; if the first calculation is wrong, we make a second better: we find comfort somewhere – and those evil-minded observers, dearest Mary, who make much of a little, are more taken in and deceived than the parties themselves."

"Well done, sister! I honour your *esprit du corps*. When I am a wife, I mean to be just as staunch myself; and I wish my friends in general would be so too. It would save me many a heartache."

"You are as bad as your brother, Mary; but we will cure you both. Mansfield shall cure you both, and without any taking in. Stay with us, and we will cure you."

The Crawfords, without wanting to be cured, were very willing to stay. Mary was satisfied with the Parsonage as a present home, and Henry equally ready to lengthen his visit. He had come, intending to spend only a few days with them; but Mansfield promised well, and there was nothing to call him elsewhere. It delighted Mrs. Grant to keep them both with her, and Dr. Grant was exceedingly well contented to have it so: a talking pretty young woman like Miss Crawford is always pleasant society to an indolent, stay-at-home man; and Mr. Crawford's being his guest was an excuse for drinking claret every day.

II

It had been exactly one week since the Crawfords had come to Mansfield, when Mary took it upon herself to speak to her brother about his intentions toward Maria and Julia Bertram. It was late in the morning, and she and Henry were, excepting the servants, alone in the house; Dr Grant had been summoned to a sick parishioner's bedside and his excellent wife had gone with him in order to give comfort and succour to the patient's distraught wife and children. Henry had returned from a long ride and had changed early into his dinner clothes, and now sat upon the drawing-room sofa reading a novel entitled *Zastrozzi: A Romance*, a book which was giving some reviewers fits because of its monstrous antihero. Obliging as ever, Henry promised Mary she could have the first volume as soon as he had finished it.

"Henry, I would speak with you."

Mary's brother, truly a gentleman in almost every particular, closed his book and straightened his posture to give her his full attention. "Of course. What is it, dearest? Are you troubled?"

"I am fine, I thank you," Mary assured him. "No, I want you to give me your honest opinion of the Bertrams."

"Of course, but what makes you ask me with so solemn a countenance?"

Mary hesitated. "In truth, it is the fact that our sister has such hopes for you and Julia Bertram. Mrs. Grant is not like us Henry; she is all warmth with no cynicism to chill it. We know too much of the world to enjoy any naivety but Mrs Grant doesn't have enough of the commonplace mind to see things as we do. She is as free of guile as a tib! I mean to try to discourage her hopes for you and Miss Julia Bertram, unless you tell me there is no occasion for it."

Henry replied with unaccustomed gravity, "Miss Julia Bertram is a very pretty and accomplished young lady, but she does not tempt *me*; she is as silly and vain as any other."

Mary ignored this slight to her sex. She was well aware that Henry considered her superior in all ways to the average chit of the beau monde. When he spoke derisively of women, it was understood between them that Mary was not included in his scorn.

"And what of Miss Maria Bertram? She was more attentive to you last night that was entirely proper for a woman in her situation; you did not seem insensible to it."

Her brother smirked. "I will freely admit she is lovely in both face and figure, with no small talent for music and has what appears to be a brain in her head. However, even with all that she is no match for her good opinion of *herself*. Her manners seem easy, but I see the vanity behind them. It will do her good to be a little trifled with; Mr Rushworth will thank me when she comes to the marriage with less conceit than she came to the engagement. He may have little enough to be thankful for. I would be much surprised if Miss Maria Bertram has a petticoat that will never stain."

"You would be the expert on lady-birds among the ladies of the Ton," Mary rebuked him. "As many men as you've fitted for horns you should know of which you speak, though it is no flattery to the future Mrs Rushworth. Yet I would not have her gulled, Henry. Vain she may be but she is also country-bred and green as grass; flirt but do not pluck roses you have no wish to keep. Promise me."

"I promise, Mary. You know I never besmirch the women you befriend — regardless of how much they want me to."

"Henry!" Mary laughed. "You shock me!"

"Nothing shocks you, sister of mine. You have more *savoir faire* than anyone else I have ever met. You did not turn a hair when we walked in on the Admiral and Mrs Chatsworth!"

"Please don't remind me of that," Mary shuddered. "I only regret that it did not blind me on the spot."

"Don't be missish."

"It is not missish to be repulsed by that sort of behaviour Henry, and you know it. Even the notorious Lady Jersey would have blushed at such a sight."

Henry picked his book up again. "Be that as it may, you have no need to fear for the supposed virtue of your friend, or that I should make an offer for her sister. Do all you can to dissuade Mrs Grant from such hopes, but she may not thank you for it. It is more pleasant to daydream than it is to be wise." A sudden thought struck Henry, and he refrained from opening his retrieved volume. "I say, Mary. Are you forming a tendre for Mr Bertram?"

"Don't be a goose Henry. My blood is too cold for that. As Beatrice said in *Much Ado About Nothing*, 'I would rather hear a dog bark at a crow than a man swear he loves me'. No, I may think about whether or not I should accept Mr Bertram should he ask for me, but I am not one to sigh over any man born. Remember, 'my hate is general, I detest all men; some because they are wicked and do evil, others because they tolerate the wicked, refusing them the active vigorous scorn which vice should stimulate in virtuous minds.' I like no one well enough to love them, save for you, and I know that even you are a terrible rogue."

He shook his head. "It is unnatural that you should quote so much of Moliere. You should be noting that "many a flower is born to blush unseen" or "soul meets soul on lovers' lips" or how a beetle feels as much pang as a giant if we should step on it; not singeing the air with French cynicism. Besides, you always start quoting when you are avoiding a topic, or wish to divert attention. I have known you for your whole life, so use no cunning with me. "

Mary shrugged. "In truth Henry, my heart is untouched but my mind is aware of possibilities. Mr Bertram may do, or he may not. I have not decided and he has certainly given no indication of asking. Even if all else recommends him, I would be cautious; 'they dream in courtship, but in wedlock wake'. I will not risk my happiness for romantic folderol."

Henry arched a brow and opened his book. "If you say so then I believe you, but I wonder if you are as impervious to cupid as all that. 'Methinks the lady doth protest too much'. Is it that your heart is more tender than you would have it be?"

"You leave me no choice but to play my trump and quote Socrates: 'be as you wish to seem'. An ancient Greek philosopher has precedence over even Shakespeare. You must admit your defeat." Mary then swept from the room to go change for dinner, the sound of her brother's mirth following her up the stairs.

ǁ

Mary had no intention of falling prey to cupid, but she was giving more serious deliberation to the idea of marrying Tom Bertram that she had ever had anyone else before him. Marriage was necessitous, but dangerous, and was not something she would enter into for so ephemeral a boon as love; she was too shrewd. However, Mr Bertram was, when looked at rationally, a good choice. Not only was he handsome and the eldest son, he was also gallant, lively, and appeared to prefer society and Town to provincial life. He had undeniable potential.

Tom Bertram's situation and eligibility was much on her mind, but Mary was not one to sit idly and dwell on a topic, or mope about. Since it was Mrs Grant's habit to make daily excursions, weather permitting, to check in on parishioners and to see if anyone was ill or starving, it quickly became Mary's custom to join her sister on these goodwill missions, both for information about the Mansfield area and for the exercise. Having no duties as a rector's wife, Mary was careful to hang back whenever Mrs Grant approached the more humble abodes. It would have been rude and prying for Mary to listen in to the woes and worries of the labouring class, especially since the disparity of rank meant that Mrs Grant could not introduce Mary to anyone. If Mrs Grant's visits were to the prosperous farmers and merchants of the parish, then Mary could at least be introduced, although she could never allow them to be more than a nodding acquaintance. She and Mrs Grant would sometimes be offered refreshments at the home of one of the more well-off yeomen or tradesmen, which they could accept, but it was understood that there could never be a return invitation to the parsonage. The class system was ingrained to the bone, and Mary no more wondered why an educated and genteel farmer could not join them at the rectory for tea than she wondered why she could not marry one of King George's many sons. There were some things so unthinkable that very few people ever thought of them.

As they were leaving the home of Mr and Mrs Triggs, a large and thriving family with a good income who leased some of the parsonage's glebe, Mrs Grant, who took every occasion to encourage thoughts of matrimony in her sister, saw an opportunity to point out the felicities of a good match.

"I suspect Mrs Triggs is increasing; this will be her fifth."

"She is fortunate then," Mary replied civilly, but without much interest.

"They are a fortunate couple. Mrs Triggs was once thought barren. She was a widow who had been married five years without fruit when she married Mr Triggs. It was a love match, and considered imprudent on Mrs Triggs's part when it was announced. She had been left a small fortune by her first husband and Mr Triggs was greatly in debt. There was some fear that if they wed she would have to supply his creditors with her marriage portion. She wished to keep her money and the interest on it separate, but since her possessions would become her husband's by law, there was some concern that even articles giving her dower rights over her goods would be insufficient."

"I can hardly fault her for wanting to keep her fortune from going to her new husband's creditors, but I am amazed that she knowingly married someone with such a burden. Did he have some peculiar advantage of family or situation?" Mary asked.

"No, he was quite alone in the world by then, not that his family had been advantageous when they were alive," Mrs Grant informed her. "He used a small inheritance to become a chandler, and had just begun to turn a small profit when his shop was consumed in a conflagration. He had borrowed against his store to purchase stock, which is some sort of common thing for tradesmen, and when he lost everything he was plunged into terrible debt without a farthing to bless himself with. He had, just before his losses, asked Mrs Triggs (who was at the time Mrs Odell) for the honour of her hand. She had asked for three days to consider the matter, and it was at that time that the poor man suffered his reversal of fortune. He expected Mrs Odell to refuse his suit, of course. Nevertheless, to his surprise — and I must say the amazement of the county — she accepted him. If Mrs Odell's fortune could be used to set them back upon their feet, then all would be well; if the creditors took it then Mr Triggs might never recover his advantages. Dr Grant and I had not been in Mansfield a month when this happened, and I was quite engrossed in the saga. I did not know what was to be done for them. I didn't know *then* what a shift marriage was."

"A shift marriage? You have the advantage of me ma'am, for I have never heard of such a thing. I am all eagerness to hear of it." Mary was highly diverted by her sister's tale.

"It is a local custom, my dear. If a woman should marry in her shift, then her debts are not transferred to her new husband, nor his to her."

"But isn't the woman excessively mortified to appear before the parson with only a shift to clothe her?" Mary was more amused than scandalised by the thought.

"When it came time to wed Mrs Odell and Mr Triggs, it was Dr Grant who was excessively mortified I think." Mrs Grant giggled. "When he returned home from performing the ceremony that morning he was as flustered as I have ever seen a man."

"Oh! Do tell!"

"Perhaps I shouldn't," Mrs Grant teased. "You are an unmarried lady after all."

"Don't be cruel; tell me or I shall never cease to wonder."

"Alright then, but remember that this is in strictest confidence and prepare yourself to be astounded. When Dr Grant arrived at the rectory, he found Mr Triggs awaiting him and Mrs Odell retired to the necessary room. Not long thereafter, Mrs Odell emerged, enswathed in a cloak from head to foot. Dr Grant, of course, assumed it was because she was in her shift and wanted to be covered as much as possible for as long as possible. However, my dearest husband had underestimated her determination that her husband's debts would not be the cause of their ruination. As soon as Dr Grant assumed his position at the altar, and the wedding service was to begin, Mrs Odell threw off her cloak and proceeded to say her vows in the exact same state in which she was born!"

"No!" Mary gasped, truly shocked yet simultaneously profoundly entertained. "Without one stitch upon her?"

"It was if she were Eve in Paradise, and knew not her nakedness. Even her hair was unbound. Dr Grant said that he blushed and knew not where to look, and Mr Triggs stammered like a schoolboy, but that Mrs Odell became Mrs Triggs with as much *sang-froid* as if she had been draped with a nun's habit."

Mary started laughing. "Oh, how did Dr. Grant endure it when he next saw her in Sunday service? How does he look her in the eye even now?"

"To tell the truth, my husband could not converse with Mrs Triggs for more than a twelvemonth without becoming discomfited and inarticulate. He grew more composed with time, but still to this day every time he must speak of original sin and Eve's temptation his eye seeks her out among the congregation, no matter how sternly he tells himself not to."

Any hope Mary had of moderating her levity evaporated with this intelligence, and she was so convulsed with guffaws that she had to cease walking. When she could get breath enough to speak, she exclaimed, "How I am to keep my countenance when I next see Mrs. Triggs I don't know."

Mrs Grant patted her arm. "You shall conduct yourself in a ladylike manner, as always. I have absolute faith in it. But do you know why I revealed such a marvellous occurrence?"

"To see if I would fall down from hilarity?"

"No, goose. I set the Triggs as a good example of a woman's decision to risk matrimony, even to a man in impecunious circumstances, if his character is known to be good and she has true affection for him and the conviction of his constant regard. Her belief in Mr Triggs's principles was justified; he paid back his creditors from the sweat of his own brow and he keeps Mrs Triggs in a comfortable home, treating her with all the sincere appreciation that a husband should. She risked her happiness on his honour, and she was satisfied. Although I would never advise you to look for an imprudent match, let the man's character and feelings, rather than his circumstances, be your guide in accepting any proposal."

"Your advice is, as ever, both sound and appreciated, ma'am. However, I shall be careful to marry a man with no debt. If I should come to the ceremony as Mrs Triggs did I do not think Dr Grant could survive it, and if his life did not extinguish from mortification on the spot then I know mine *would*."

ıı

Mary heeded her sister's prescription, but only in part. While she *did* contemplate Tom Bertram's character, she still weighted it *less* than the other, more tangible, advantages to the match. Mr Bertram was the sort of young man to be generally liked, his agreeableness was of the kind to be oftener found agreeable than some endowments of a higher stamp, for he had easy manners, excellent spirits, a large acquaintance, and a great deal to say; and the reversion of Mansfield Park, and a baronetcy, did no harm to all this. Miss Crawford soon felt that he and his situation might do. She looked about her with due consideration, and found almost everything in his favour: a park, a real park, five miles round, a spacious modern-built house, so well placed and well screened as to deserve to be in any collection of engravings of gentlemen's seats in the kingdom, and wanting only to be completely new furnished – pleasant sisters, a quiet mother, and an agreeable man himself – with the advantage of being tied up from much gaming at present by a promise to his father, and of being Sir Thomas hereafter.

Although she was an ardent abolitionist, the fact that a large percentage of the Bertram fortune was provided by the slavery taking place on their Antigua estates wasn't something she thought of as an impediment to enjoying that wealth. Like many abolitionists of her class, the evils of slavery were not conflated with the money it generated. Neither did she find it strange that a man could own slaves, which she thought immoral, and still be a fine and moral gentleman in society. For Mary, and indeed almost every single soul among her contemporaries, social ranking and breeding trumped any other consideration.

Thus, after much deliberation, she decided that Tom Bertram might do very well; she believed she should accept him; and she began accordingly to interest herself a little about the horse which he had to run at the Burnleyraces.

These races were to call him away not long after their acquaintance began; and as it appeared that the family did not, from his usual goings on, expect him back again for many weeks, it would bring his passion to an early proof. Much was said on his side to induce her to attend the races, and schemes were made for a large party to them, with all the eagerness of inclination, but it would only do to be talked of.

Chapter Six

MR BERTRAM SET off for Lancashire, and Miss Crawford was prepared to find a great chasm in their society, and to miss him decidedly in the meetings which were now becoming almost daily between the families; and on their all dining together at the Park soon after his going, she retook her chosen place near the bottom of the table, fully expecting to feel a most melancholy difference in the change of masters. It would be a very flat business, she was sure. In comparison with his brother, Edmund would have nothing to say. The soup would be sent round in a most spiritless manner, wine drank without any smiles or agreeable trifling, and the venison cut up without supplying one pleasant anecdote of any former haunch, or a single entertaining story, about "my friend such a one."

Notwithstanding her expectations of tedium, Mary was not one to surrender herself to dullness without an effort. She must try to find amusement in what was passing at the upper end of the table, and in observing Mr Rushworth, who was now making his appearance at Mansfield for the first time since the Crawfords' arrival.

Dispassionately studying Rushworth, Mary thought her friend Maria could have had a much larger cross to bear to get 12,000 pounds a year. If Rushworth were stupid and not a man of information, he was at least well-looking and convivial in his imbecility. She could detect no harm in him, and he was amazingly lacking in conceit for a man of such wealth. His pride seemed in good order, which was more than she could say for Maria Bertram.

Mr Rushworth had been visiting a friend in the neighbouring county, and that friend having recently had his grounds laid out by an improver, Mr Rushworth was returned with his head full of the subject, and very eager to be improving his own place in the same way; and though not saying much to the purpose, could talk of nothing else. The subject had been already handled in the drawing-room; it was revived in the dining-parlour. Miss Bertram's attention and opinion was evidently his chief aim; and though her deportment showed rather conscious superiority than any solicitude to oblige him, the mention of Sotherton Court, and the ideas attached to it, gave her a feeling of complacency, which prevented her from being very ungracious.

"I wish you could see Compton," said he; "it is the most complete thing! I never saw a place so altered in my life. I told Smith I did not know where I was. The approach *now*, is one of the finest things in the country: you see the house in the most surprising manner. I declare, when I got back to Sotherton yesterday, it looked like a prison – quite a dismal old prison."

"Oh, for shame!" cried Mrs Norris. "A prison indeed? Sotherton Court is the noblest old place in the world."

"It wants improvement, ma'am, beyond anything. I never saw a place that wanted so much improvement in my life; and it is so forlorn that I do not know what can be done with it."

"No wonder that Mr Rushworth should think so at present," said Mrs Grant to Mrs Norris, with a smile; "but depend upon it, Sotherton will have *every* improvement in time which his heart can desire."

"I must try to do something with it," said Mr Rushworth, "but I do not know what. I hope I shall have some good friend to help me."

"Your best friend upon such an occasion," said Miss Bertram calmly, "would be Mr Repton, I imagine."

"That is what I was thinking of. As he has done so well by Smith, I think I had better have him at once. His terms are five guineas a day."

"Well, and if they were *ten*," cried Mrs Norris, "I am sure *you* need not regard it. The expense need not be any impediment. If I were you, I should not think of the expense. I would have everything done in the best style, and made as nice as possible. Such a place as Sotherton Court deserves everything that taste and money can do. You have space to work upon there, and grounds that will well reward you. For my own part, if I had anything within the fiftieth part of the size of Sotherton, I should be always planting and improving, for naturally I am excessively fond of it. It would be too ridiculous for me to attempt anything where I am now, with my little half acre. It would be quite a burlesque. But if I had more room, I should take a prodigious delight in improving and planting. We did a vast deal in that way at the Parsonage: we made it quite a different place from what it was when we first had it. You young ones do not remember much about it, perhaps; but if dear Sir Thomas were here, he could tell you what improvements we made: and a great deal more would have been done, but for poor Mr Norris's sad state of health. He could hardly ever get out, poor man, to enjoy anything, and *that* disheartened me from doing several things that Sir Thomas and I used to talk of. If it had not been for *that*, we should have carried on the garden wall, and made the plantation to shut out the churchyard, just as Dr Grant has done. We were always doing something as it was. It was only the spring twelvemonth before Mr Norris's death that we put in the apricot against the stable wall, which is now grown such a noble tree, and getting to such perfection, sir," addressing herself then to Dr Grant.

"The tree thrives well, beyond a doubt, madam," replied Dr Grant. "The soil is good; and I never pass it without regretting that the fruit should be so little worth the trouble of gathering."

"Sir, it is a Moor Park, we bought it as a Moor Park, and it cost us – that is, it was a present from Sir Thomas, but I saw the bill – and I know it cost seven shillings, and was charged as a Moor Park."

"You were imposed on, ma'am," replied Dr Grant: "these potatoes have as much the flavour of a Moor Park apricot as the fruit from that tree. It is an insipid fruit at the best; but a good apricot is edible, which none from my garden are."

Mary hid a smile behind her napkin. She could see Mrs Norris swelling up like a pricked finger at the aspersions cast upon her alleged Moor Park apricots. Why the old biddy should care about such a trivial matter or take it personally was a mystery to Mary, but it was clear Mrs Norris was deeply offended by Dr Grant's refusal to pretend the apricot tree at the parsonage produced anything but inferior fruit.

"The truth is, ma'am," said Mrs Grant, pretending to whisper across the table to Mrs Norris, "that Dr Grant hardly knows what the natural taste of our apricot is: he is scarcely ever indulged with one, for it is so valuable a fruit; with a little assistance, and ours is such a remarkably large, fair sort, that what with early tarts and preserves, my cook contrives to get them all."

Mrs Norris, who had begun to redden, was appeased; and, for a little while, other subjects took place of the improvements of Sotherton.

Mary looked fondly at her sister. She would have not troubled herself to be kind to Mrs. Norris; she saved her good deeds for good people. Mrs Grant was kind to all without prejudice. Mary knew that she was the handsomer sister on the exterior, but Mrs Grant was the superior beauty in character.

Mr Rushworth began again. "Smith's place is the admiration of all the country; and it was a mere nothing before Repton took it in hand. I think I shall have Repton."

"Mr Rushworth," said Lady Bertram, "if I were you, I would have a very pretty shrubbery. One likes to get out into a shrubbery in fine weather."

Mr Rushworth was eager to assure her ladyship of his acquiescence, and tried to make out something complimentary; but, between his submission to *her* taste, and his having always intended the same himself, with the superadded objects of professing attention to the comfort of ladies in general, and of insinuating that there was one only whom he was anxious to please, he grew puzzled, and Edmund was glad to put an end to his speech by a proposal of wine. Mr Rushworth, however, though not usually a great talker, had still more to say on the subject next his heart. "Smith has not much above a hundred acres altogether in his grounds, which is little enough, and makes it more surprising that the place can have been so improved. Now, at Sotherton we have a good seven hundred, without reckoning the water meadows; so that I think, if so much could be done at Compton, we need not despair. There have been two or three fine old trees cut down, that grew too near the house, and it opens the prospect amazingly, which makes me think that Repton, or anybody of that sort, would certainly have the avenue at Sotherton down: the avenue that leads from the west front to the top of the hill, you know," turning to Miss Bertram particularly as he spoke. But Miss Bertram thought it most becoming to reply—

"The avenue! Oh! I do not recollect it. I really know very little of Sotherton."

Mary overheard Miss Price, who was sitting exactly opposite of her, say to Edmund in a low voice. "Cut down an avenue! What a pity! Does it not make you think of Cowper? 'Ye fallen avenues, once more I mourn your fate unmerited.' "

He smiled as he answered, "I am afraid the avenue stands a bad chance, Fanny."

"I should like to see Sotherton before it is cut down, to see the place as it is now, in its old state; but I do not suppose I shall."

"Have you never been there? No, you never can; and, unluckily, it is out of distance for a ride. I wish we could contrive it."

"Oh! it does not signify. Whenever I do see it, you will tell me how it has been altered."

"I collect," said Miss Crawford, "that Sotherton is an old place, and a place of some grandeur. In any particular style of building?"

"The house was built in Elizabeth's time, and is a large, regular, brick building; heavy, but respectable looking, and has many good rooms. It is ill placed. It stands in one of the lowest spots of the park; in that respect, unfavourable for improvement. But the woods are fine, and there is a stream, which, I dare say, might be made a good deal of. Mr Rushworth is quite right, I think, in meaning to give it a modern dress, and I have no doubt that it will be all done extremely well."

Miss Crawford listened with submission, and said to herself, "He is a well-bred man; he makes the best of it." Mary admired good breeding more than anything else. Even vast wealth and social position could not equal the worth of a truly well-bred man of moderate means in her estimation. She looked at Edmund Bertram carefully. He lacked elan, but his extreme handsomeness and gentlemanlike behaviour made him quite a prize for some country maiden. She good-naturedly hoped the deserving younger son would find an heiress.

"I do not wish to influence Mr Rushworth," Edmund continued, after a little more thought; "but, had I a place to new fashion, I should not put myself into the hands of an improver. I would rather have an inferior degree of beauty, of my own choice, and acquired progressively. I would rather abide by my own blunders than by his."

"*You* would know what you were about, of course; but that would not suit *me*," Mary replied. "I have no eye or ingenuity for such matters, but as they are before me; and had I a place of my own in the country, I should be most thankful to any Mr Repton who would undertake it, and give me as much beauty as he could for my money; and I should never look at it till it was complete."

All things false were Mary's abhorrence; false-friends, false-praise, and false-pride were the things that gave her unalloyed revulsion. She would not pretend to be adept at improving or an admirer of the picturesque, regardless of how fashionable such things were, because that sort of sham approbation without genuine feeling disgusted her. She would rather be thought tasteless, or even of having the dreadful affliction of bad taste, than to expose herself as a humbug.

"It would be delightful to *me* to see the progress of it all," said Fanny.

Mary nodded in agreement. "Ay, you have been brought up to it. It was no part of my education; and the only dose I ever had, being administered by not the first favourite in the world, has made me consider improvements *in hand* as the greatest of nuisances. Three years ago the Admiral, my honoured uncle, bought a cottage at Twickenham for us all to spend our summers in; and my aunt and I went down to it quite in raptures; but it being excessively pretty, it was soon found necessary to be improved, and for three months we were all dirt and confusion, without a gravel walk to step on, or a bench fit for use. I would have everything as complete as possible in the country, shrubberies and flower-gardens, and rustic seats innumerable: but it must all be done without my care. Henry is different; he loves to be doing."

What Mary did not tell was that the injury of the improvement had been given excessive insult when the Admiral gave the cottage over to his paramour the following summer. Mary and her aunt had been forced to seek relief from the London heat elsewhere, because the lovely little home in Twickenham was being enjoyed by a Parisian strumpet in their stead.

Edmund was sorry to hear Miss Crawford, whom he was much disposed to admire, speak so freely of her uncle. It did not suit his sense of propriety, and he was silenced, till induced by further smiles and liveliness to put the matter by for the present.

"Mr Bertram," said she, "I have tidings of my harp at last. I am assured that it is safe at Northampton; and there it has probably been these ten days, in spite of the solemn assurances we have so often received to the contrary," Edmund expressed his pleasure and surprise. "The truth is, that our inquiries were too direct; we sent a servant, we went ourselves: this will not do seventy miles from London; but this morning we heard of it in the right way. It was seen by some farmer, and he told the miller, and the miller told the butcher, and the butcher's son-in-law left word at the shop."

"I am very glad that you have heard of it, by whatever means, and hope there will be no further delay."

"I am to have it to-morrow; but how do you think it is to be conveyed? Not by a wagon or cart: oh no! nothing of that kind could be hired in the village. I might as well have asked for porters and a handbarrow."

"You would find it difficult, I dare say, just now, in the middle of a very late hay harvest, to hire a horse and cart?"

"I was astonished to find what a piece of work was made of it! To want a horse and cart in the country seemed impossible, so I told my maid to speak for one directly; and as I cannot look out of my dressing-closet without seeing one farmyard, nor walk in the shrubbery without passing another, I thought it would be only ask and have, and was rather grieved that I could not give the advantage to all. Guess my surprise, when I found that I had been asking the most unreasonable, most impossible thing in the world; had offended all the farmers, all the labourers, all the hay in the parish! As for Dr Grant's bailiff, I believe I had better keep out of *his* way; and my brother-in-law himself, who is all kindness in general, looked rather black upon me when he found what I had been at."

"You could not be expected to have thought on the subject before; but when you *do* think of it, you must see the importance of getting in the grass. The hire of a cart at any time might not be so easy as you suppose: our farmers are not in the habit of letting them out; but, in harvest, it must be quite out of their power to spare a horse."

"I shall understand all your ways in time; but, coming down with the true London maxim, that everything is to be got with money, I was a little embarrassed at first by the sturdy independence of your country customs. However, I am to have my harp fetched to-morrow. Henry, who is good-nature itself, has offered to fetch it in his barouche. Will it not be honourably conveyed?"

Miss Crawford's dark eyes sparkled with even greater effect when she talked of such beloved subjects as her brother and her harp. Her audience was not insensible to her beauty. Both Miss Price and her fair cousin were rendered nearly breathless by Mary's charms; Fanny from aesthetic admiration and Edmund from admiration of a more corporeal kind.

Edmund spoke of the harp as his favourite instrument, and hoped to be soon allowed to hear her. Fanny had never heard the harp at all, and wished for it very much.

"I shall be most happy to play to you both," said Miss Crawford; "at least as long as you can like to listen: probably much longer, for I dearly love music myself, and where the natural taste is equal the player must always be best off, for she is gratified in more ways than one. Now, Mr Bertram, if you write to your brother, I entreat you to tell him that my harp is come: he heard so much of my misery about it. And you may say, if you please, that I shall prepare my most plaintive airs against his return, in compassion to his feelings, as I know his horse will lose."

"If I write, I will say whatever you wish me; but I do not, at present, foresee any occasion for writing." Edmund did not wish to talk of his brother; he preferred Tom to stay far away from the alluring Miss Crawford and leave the field clear for himself.

"No, I dare say, nor if he were to be gone a twelvemonth, would you ever write to him, nor he to you, if it could be helped. The occasion would never be foreseen. What strange creatures brothers are! You would not write to each other but upon the most urgent necessity in the world; and when obliged to take up the pen to say that such a horse is ill, or such a relation dead, it is done in the fewest possible words. You have but one style among you. I know it perfectly. Henry, who is in every other respect exactly what a brother should be, who loves me, consults me, confides in me, and will talk to me by the hour together, has never yet turned the page in a letter; and very often it is nothing more than – 'Dear Mary, I am just arrived. Bath seems full, and everything as usual. Yours sincerely.' That is the true manly style; that is a complete brother's letter."

"When they are at a distance from all their family," said Fanny, blushing for her brother William's sake, "they can write long letters."

"Miss Price has a brother at sea," said Edmund, "whose excellence as a correspondent makes her think you too severe upon us."

"At sea, has she? In the king's service, of course?"

Fanny would rather have had Edmund tell the story, but his determined silence obliged her to relate her brother's situation: her voice was animated in speaking of his profession, and the foreign stations he had been on; but she could not mention the number of years that he had been absent without tears in her eyes. Miss Crawford civilly wished him an early promotion.

Mary looked at Fanny with more interest and empathy from that moment on. She also knew what it was to dearly love a brother. Perhaps she had more in common with the timid girl than she had thought. Miss Price might be an acceptable companion once the child came out.

"Do you know anything of my cousin's captain?" said Edmund; "Captain Marshall? You have a large acquaintance in the navy, I conclude?"

"Among admirals, large enough; but," with an air of grandeur, "we know very little of the inferior ranks. Post-captains may be very good sort of men, but they do not belong to *us*. Of various admirals I could tell you a great deal: of them and their flags, and the gradation of their pay, and their bickerings and jealousies. But, in general, I can assure you that they are all passed over, and all very ill used. Certainly, my home at my uncle's brought me acquainted with a circle of admirals. Of *Rears* and *Vices* I saw enough. Now do not be suspecting me of a pun, I entreat."

Mary, used to the wit and bon mots of London society, was completely oblivious to the fact her drollery was unappreciated. Burlesque caprice in particular fell upon stony ground when sown on the humourless fields of Edmund and Fanny.

Edmund again felt grave, and only replied, "It is a noble profession."

"Yes, the profession is well enough under two circumstances: if it make the fortune, and there be discretion in spending it; but, in short, it is not a favourite profession of mine. It has never worn an amiable form to me."

Edmund reverted to the harp, and was again very happy in the prospect of hearing her play.

The subject of improving grounds, meanwhile, was still under consideration among the others; and Mrs Grant could not help addressing her brother, though it was calling his attention from Miss Julia Bertram.

"My dear Henry, have *you* nothing to say? You have been an improver yourself, and from what I hear of Everingham, it may vie with any place in England. Its natural beauties, I am sure, are great. Everingham, as it *used* to be, was perfect in my estimation: such a happy fall of ground, and such timber! What would I not give to see it again?"

"Nothing could be so gratifying to me as to hear your opinion of it," was his answer; "but I fear there would be some disappointment: you would not find it equal to your present ideas. In extent, it is a mere nothing; you would be surprised at its insignificance; and, as for improvement, there was very little for me to do – too little: I should like to have been busy much longer."

"You are fond of the sort of thing?" said Julia.

"Excessively; but what with the natural advantages of the ground, which pointed out, even to a very young eye, what little remained to be done, and my own consequent resolutions, I had not been of age three months before Everingham was all that it is now. My plan was laid at Westminster, a little altered, perhaps, at Cambridge, and at one-and-twenty executed. I am inclined to envy Mr Rushworth for having so much happiness yet before him. I have been a devourer of my own."

"Those who see quickly, will resolve quickly, and act quickly," said Julia. "*You* can never want employment. Instead of envying Mr Rushworth, you should assist him with your opinion."

Mrs Grant, hearing the latter part of this speech, enforced it warmly, persuaded that no judgement could be equal to her brother's; and as Miss Bertram caught at the idea likewise, and gave it her full support, declaring that, in her opinion, it was infinitely better to consult with friends and disinterested advisers, than immediately to throw the business into the hands of a professional man, Mr Rushworth was very ready to request the favour of Mr Crawford's assistance; and Mr Crawford, after properly depreciating his own abilities, was quite at his service in any way that could be useful. Mr Rushworth then began to propose Mr Crawford's doing him the honour of coming over to Sotherton, and taking a bed there; when Mrs Norris, as if reading in her two nieces' minds their little approbation of a plan which was to take Mr Crawford away, interposed with an amendment.

"There can be no doubt of Mr Crawford's willingness; but why should not more of us go? Why should not we make a little party? Here are many that would be interested in your improvements, my dear Mr Rushworth, and that would like to hear Mr Crawford's opinion on the spot, and that might be of some small use to you with *their* opinions; and, for my own part, I have been long wishing to wait upon your good mother again; nothing but having no horses of my own could have made me so remiss; but now I could go and sit a few hours with Mrs Rushworth, while the rest of you walked about and settled things, and then we could all return to a late dinner here, or dine at Sotherton, just as might be most agreeable to your mother, and have a pleasant drive home by moonlight. I dare say Mr Crawford would take my two nieces and me in his barouche, and Edmund can go on horseback, you know, sister, and Fanny will stay at home with you."

Lady Bertram made no objection; and everyone concerned in the going was forward in expressing their ready concurrence, excepting Edmund, who heard it all and said nothing.

‖

"How kind and charitable of you to assist Miss Bertram's fiancé with his improvements, Henry. I dare say you would take many tasks off the poor fellow's hands if you could." Mary could not resist teasing her brother the following morning during breakfast.

"I strive to do my best for any fellow man," Henry complacently assured his sister. "Especially one so dimwitted as Mr Rushworth."

"He *is* a bit of a simpleton," Mrs Grant reluctantly agreed, "but he is also obliging and amiable. Those are qualities that might make Miss Bertram more fortunate in her choice of a husband than a woman who accepted a man of information but of an ill-temper."

"He is rich, too. What he lacks in information he makes up for in gelt," Henry pointed out.

"But I do not think Miss Bertram would marry him solely for such mercenary gains," Mrs Grant was a little distressed at the implication.

Henry, perceiving her dismay, qualified, "Of course not, ma'am. But she would be a foolish woman to not have thought it in the gentleman's favour, just as I am equally sure that Mr Rushworth does not marry Miss Bertram only because she is a beauty, but that her beauty does her no disservice in his eyes." He saw Mary raise her cup of tea to hide her smile, and knew that she thought the match was as avaricious and shallow as he conjectured it to be.

Mrs Grant, having a less suspicious outlook on the subject of engagements, was mollified by Henry's explanation, and began to talk cheerfully of how kind Henry was to take such an interest in the improvements of Sotherton.

Chapter Seven

EDMUND BERTRAM WAS early invited to come hear Mary play the harp, and he found it added to her beauty, wit, and good-humour; for she played with the greatest obligingness, with an expression and taste which were peculiarly becoming, and there was something clever to be said at the close of every air. Edmund was at the Parsonage every day, to be indulged with his favourite instrument: one morning secured an invitation for the next; for the lady could not be unwilling to have a listener, and every thing was soon in a fair train.

A young woman, pretty, lively, with a harp as elegant as herself, and both placed near a window, cut down to the ground, and opening on a little lawn, surrounded by shrubs in the rich foliage of summer, was enough to catch any man's heart. The season, the scene, the air, were all favourable to tenderness and sentiment. Mrs Grant and her tambour frame were not without their use: it was all in harmony; and as everything will turn to account when love is once set going, even the sandwich tray, and Dr Grant doing the honours of it, were worth looking at. Without studying the business, however, or knowing what he was about, Edmund was beginning, at the end of a week of such intercourse, to be a good deal in love; and to the credit of the lady it may be added that, without his being a man of the world or an elder brother, without any of the arts of flattery or the gaieties of small talk, he began to be agreeable to her. She felt it to be so, though she had not foreseen, and could hardly understand it; for he was not pleasant by any common rule: he talked no nonsense; he paid no compliments; his opinions were unbending, his attentions tranquil and simple. There was a charm, perhaps, in his sincerity, his steadiness, his integrity, which Miss Crawford might be equal to feel, though not equal to discuss with herself. She did not think very much about it, however: he pleased her for the present; she liked to have him near her; it was enough.

‖

"I have recently purchased a new mare," Edmund said one day, during his visit to the parsonage.

"Have you? Is it a purchase of the moment, having seen a beautiful stepper, or the work of some thought?" Mary inquired.

"It was a matter of deliberation. My cousin, Miss Price, was without a mount; the pony she had been accustomed to riding died nearly a fortnight ago. Miss Price is not strong; she is easily knocked up; the best means of exercise for her is to ride. If she is left without a horse, she is either kept with my mother, who finds exercise of all kinds odious and never thinks that it's good for others, or she is kept busy by my Aunt Norris, who has such prodigious strength she cannot fully comprehend the limits of Fanny's endurance. Fanny must have a horse. Nevertheless, my good mother reminded me I had no such authorization for such expenditure in my father's absence; a fact I must pay heed to. I had, however, in my possession two fine hunters and a very useful road-horse; they were entirely at my own disposal. I resolved to exchange my road-horse for one Fanny could ride. My friend, Mr Owen, had just such a mare as would suit Fanny like no other. Owen is an obliging and agreeable fellow, and was willing to swap my horse for the mare. Fanny likes the new mare well; it suits her."

"How thoughtful of you Mr Bertram!" Miss Crawford praised him as much with her eyes as with her words. "Miss Price is lucky to have such a good cousin; you have the tenderness of a brother. I honour you."

"Indeed, Mr Bertram," Mrs Grant added, "It is like the kindness that Henry so often shows Mary. I need not praise you too highly, however, because if anyone has the sensibility to be grateful for your considerate behaviour it is Miss Price; anything I can say has surely been said better, and with more feeling, by Miss Price."

Edmund blushed. "I would not like you to think that I told you of this to earn your praise. I was only talking about what I had done of late. A kindness done for the praise of others is no kindness at all."

"We suspect no such puppyism from you; upon my word," Mrs Grant assured him, "but it is beyond a woman's ability not to express pleasure when she hears of such deeds."

"Indeed, Edmund," Mary said, "if we had supposed that you had told us to earn blandishments you would have gotten no such compliments from us; I would have quizzed you instead. I abhor the hypocrisy of those who do good for show, without genuine feeling behind it. If I praise you, it is because I see your sincerity."

Seeing Edmund's cheeks gain further colour, Mary tactfully changed the subject.

"I have been meaning to ask your advice about a matter of great similarity. I have never learned to ride; in Town one has a carriage or a curricle. Now that I am in the country, I should like to learn the sport. Would you be so kind as to advise me in the purchase of a good horse? One gentle enough to allow me forbearance in my novice attempts? It is too much to hope that Mr Owen has two such mares, but have you any other information of a soft-mouthed horse?"

"I regret that I do not know of another such horse, but I believe I can still be of service. I am sure that my cousin Fanny would be agreeable to the loan of her horse for a half hour or so in the mornings before her ride. You can learn upon Fanny's horse whilst your friends and I look for a suitable horse for a young lady without much experience in the saddle."

Mary looked at his face quickly, seeing if he had indulged in a *double entendre* about riding. She saw there, however, no knowing look or flirtatious glance. He really was the top of the trees; a man of sincere delicacy. If she were not careful, she would end up with a lifetime lease on a second son. Could there be something as ridiculous as a woman trapped in the country with a second son? How her friends would stare! To be the butt of snide gossip or false-pity was a fate worse than death to Mary Crawford; she resolved to guard her heart from such foolish weakness more carefully.

II

Miss Price was, to no one's surprise, agreeable and willing to allow Miss Crawford's use of the mare. Fanny, on its being first proposed, so far from feeling slighted, was almost over-powered with gratitude that he should be asking her leave for it.

Miss Crawford, as it turned out, was a natural equestrian. Active and fearless, and though rather small, strongly made, she seemed formed for a horsewoman; her progress on the first day was speedy, and praised by everyone. Everyone found enjoyment in it, excepting Miss Price. Fanny, unsuspected by everyone but servants, was hopelessly in love with her cousin Edmund. His delight in Miss Crawford's riding could bring no happiness to *her*; Fanny could only suffer in silence.

Fanny's growing misery was as unknown to Mary as it was to Edmund. All that they were aware of was their own pleasure in the activity. Who could think of Fanny when Edmund was touching Mary's delicate ankle – albeit through the thickness of her riding boot – to make sure her foot was placed correctly in the stirrup? Mary Crawford was brilliant sunshine compared to Fanny's wan moonlight, and the sight of her neat figure on a horse burned away the pale wisp of his cousin from Edmund's mind. As for Mary, she never thought of Miss Price unless the girl was directly before her. Everything about Fanny's shrinking demeanour begged not to be noticed, so Mary did her the unthinking kindness of not noticing her.

The second day's riding lesson brought further joy to Mary Crawford. Her enjoyment of riding was such that she did not know how to leave off; and to the pure genuine pleasure of the exercise, something was probably added in Edmund's attendance and instructions, and something more in the conviction of very much surpassing her sex in general by her early progress, to make her unwilling to dismount.

The morning grew late, and still Edmund stayed to instruct Miss Crawford. They practised in the parsonage's meadow attended by the Grants and Henry. Mary had risen to a trot, and now was riding demurely at a walking pace with the stalwart Edmund by her side on his own mount.

"You are doing very well, Miss Crawford." Edmund's compliment was evidently sincere. "I have never seen such a prodigious rider."

Mary rewarded him with another of her dimpled smiles. "I thank you, Mr Bertram! I confess I did not expect such unalloyed enjoyment from the exercise, and now repine that I have never before attempted to become a horsewoman. Perhaps there is something in the excellence of the teaching?"

Edmund's colour rose. Mary had discovered no better proof of her power over a suitor than her ability to bring a blush to his cheeks, and was satisfied that at least one of the Bertram brothers had been captivated by her.

"I assure you your merit is all your own," Edmund avowed with a very endearing earnestness.

"Then shall we test it?" A fresh breeze grabbed for Mrs Grant's borrowed flat-crowned Shako riding hat, but it was secured to Mary's head too well for Zephyr to steal. Tossing her head to allow the wind to blow the plume of ostrich feathers away from her eyes, Mary demanded, "Cannot I not yet canter?"

Edmund looked briefly worried, but then smiled at her. "Yes; if you can trot so easily you can probably canter. But you must remember to pull back on the reins if you feel your seat is anything other than completely secure. Do not allow the mare to run away with you."

"You won't run away with me, you pretty girl, will you?" Mary addressed the horse playfully.

"Come then," Edward said and instructed her how to induce her horse to canter.

They made a full circuit of Dr Grant's meadow, and Mary was exhilarated by the speed of the horse and the thrill of novelty. Her countenance seemed lit from within as they pulled to a halt, and Edmund Bertram – already half in love with her – fell head over heels when she laughed and looked at him with sparkling eyes.

To cover his confusion, Edmund tried to explain to Miss Crawford how to better hold the reins for a canter, but he made the fatal mistake of touching her hand to do it. Even through the leather of her riding gloves, she scorched him. He was holding her hand. He held it too long, unspeaking, and Miss Crawford looked at him quizzically. He dropped the hand as if it were a purloined jewel he was trying to steal, and Miss Crawford's quizzical look became complacently knowing. She was no less aware of her power over him than he was.

Henry hid his smile and took pity on his sister's swain by stepping forward and suggesting that Mary had enough of lessons for the day. When she began to protest, he admonished her that she would be too sore from the unaccustomed exercise to ride the following morning if she did not use moderation. Edmund, recalling that Fanny was awaiting the horse, agreed with Henry, but added that Miss Crawford could ride the mare to Mansfield Park and he would escort her there on foot, with her family's leave.

The Grants and Henry acquiesced easily, and waved the pair on their way.

Mary was speaking to Edmund of her great love of riding when they passed through a gate into the lane, and so into the park. Edmund, looking toward the manor, saw his cousin Fanny and made towards the spot where she stood. Fanny, with every appearance of polite accommodativeness, walked toward them in a friendly – albeit diffident – manner.

"My dear Miss Price," said Miss Crawford, as soon as she was at all within hearing, "I am come to make my own apologies for keeping you waiting; but I have nothing in the world to say for myself – I knew it was very late, and that I was behaving extremely ill; and therefore, if you please, you must forgive me. Selfishness must always be forgiven, you know, because there is no hope of a cure."

Fanny's answer was extremely civil, and Edmund added his conviction that she could be in no hurry. "For there is more than time enough for my cousin to ride twice as far as she ever goes," said he, "and you have been promoting her comfort by preventing her from setting off half an hour sooner: clouds are now coming up, and she will not suffer from the heat as she would have done then. I wish *you* may not be fatigued by so much exercise. I wish you had saved yourself this walk home."

"No part of it fatigues me but getting off this horse, I assure you," said she, as she sprang down with his help; "I am very strong. Nothing ever fatigues me but doing what I do not like. Miss Price, I give way to you with a very bad grace; but I sincerely hope you will have a pleasant ride, and that I may have nothing but good to hear of this dear, delightful, beautiful animal."

At last Fanny was mounted upon her mare, but it was a pleasure much alloyed; as she rode away her last glimpse of Edmund was her cousin walking Miss Crawford back to the parsonage, and laughing at some witticism.

ıı

"You cousin is very generous and tolerant of discourtesy; I am thoroughly ashamed of myself for monopolising her horse," Mary said, as she and Edmund walked through the Park toward the Grant's home.

"If there is any creature alive who could be less offended than my cousin, I would be surprised; I am sure Miss Price does not begrudge you a loan of the mare," Edmund assured her.

"Nevertheless, her difficulty to offend does not give *me* license for offence. I must be more careful to end my lesson with alacrity. It does not do to become habituated to getting one's own way simply because someone else is too sweet natured to think ill of you for it. That is how one becomes Russian."

Edmund laughed. "Is my cousin Poland, then?"

"I hope not. To be a battleground between Napoleon and Czar Alexander is no place for a nice young lady like Miss Price."

"Miss Price is stronger than she appears, and more resolute than one would suspect with such a yielding temper. If she is to be Poland then she would be Poniatowski; earning admiration and respect regardless of her subjugation to France," Edmund argued.

"That is easy for the French to say," Miss Crawford gave Edmund a pointed look.

Edmund was quiet for a long moment, leading Mary to worry she had offended him, then said, "You think we are all of us tyrannical to Fanny?"

He seemed genuinely worried, and Mary responded with sincerity and warmth, "No, I see no tyrants at Mansfield Park. That is, no one who lives within seems to be despotic toward Miss Price. It is just that Miss Price's acquiesce is assumed, because it is always so readily given. Your mother, I am convinced, loves her niece, and your brother and sisters seem to be aware of her virtues; but I cannot help but be of the opinion that you alone think about what *Miss Price* would like or choose to have. Forgive me if I am mistaken, or too forward in my observations. If I am wrong, I am happy to be corrected."

"No," Edmund said soberly, "you are not wrong. Fanny is not always given the attention she deserves, even though she herself never fails to give everyone around her their due attention. She has such a gentle spirit than even I can forget she may have wants that she is suppressing for our convenience."

Mary shook her head. "This will not do. I have introduced a solemn topic where it was not needed. It is the fancy of my own guilt, and I beg that we speak of lighter things."

"Of course. I am at your service. We have lately defeated the Americans at a place called Beaver Dam, and captured two sloops; we can share information of those victories," Edmund suggested with humour.

"War is beyond contestation a light topic, but I wish to go lighter still," Mary replied with a smile.

"We could discuss the ramifications of the end of the East India Company's monopoly on tea," he sallied again.

"I cannot but agree that the subject of trade monopolies is both light and very diverting, yet I must ask that we go lighter still."

"Shall we discuss the Doctrine of the Trinity Act and whether toleration of Unitarian worship is a good thing for Great Britain?"

"We shan't; try again."

Edmund appeared to be thinking hard. "There has been lately printed a treatise called *The Necessity of Atheism* written by the poet Percy Shelley and barrister of the surname Hogg when they were university students; we could discuss rebellion against the Almighty."

"We could not. At any rate, I have read Milton's "Paradise Lost" and feel there could be nothing new to add."

"Then I have no choice. Did you hear of the fracas between Beau Brummell and the Prince Regent?"

Mary was delighted. "That is the very thing! I have heard there was an absolute rupture between them, but I know none of the details yet; papers are so slow to arrive here and my friends are very lackadaisical correspondents. If you know the particulars of what occurred, then I beg you to share it with me!"

"I cannot swear that the particulars I know are Gospel, but I think they give a fair account. I received a letter from Tom yesterday, and the event had been recounted to him by a friend who was in Watier's at the time. Brummell, Avanley, Mildmay and Pierrepoint were all hosting a masquerade ball at the club …. I trust you know who those gentlemen are?"

"Certainly. Is there anyone in Town who does not know the names of the foremost gentleman of "the Dandy Club"? Henry is a member at Watier's, but he has never introduced me any of them."

"Then your brother is wise; I would not have a sister of mine in such company. As I was saying, the Prince Regent was, naturally, invited to the event. When his highness came up to greet his hosts, he spoke only to Alvanley and Pierrepoint; he gave Brummell and Mildmay the cut direct."

"Good God!" Mary's hand flew up to cover her mouth. "He gave a cut to his hosts at their own ball? Could even Prinny be so rude, so uncouth?"

"Can there be any doubt? Has he not proven himself repeatedly to be of a very low character, regardless of how high his birth? Nevertheless, it is not the cut itself that has caused the breach. Brummell, whose audacity is astonishing, addressed Alvanley and asked him, "Who is your fat friend?" before the Prince Regent had even turned away."

Mary's dark eyes were shining. "He didn't!"

"He did."

"What did the Prince Regent do? What did he say?"

"According to Tom's report, his highness said nothing. However, those in attendance say the Prince Regent went very white, then very red, and appeared to be deeply mortified. This is likely to be the end of Brummell's place in society."

"Do you know," Mary mused, "I am not entirely sure of that. Were the Prince Regent despised *less*, or Brummell *less* popular, your prognostication would be accurate, without question. Nevertheless, Prinny is so very despised and Brummell is so very admired that I believe Brummell may well continue in good society."

"It is possible," Edmund conceded, "but royalty, regardless of their transgressions, are still the leaders of society and fashion. I believe his remarks will catch up with Brummell, and he shall suffer for his impudence, no matter how witty or deserved the comment."

"Perhaps," Mary was not invested enough in the subject to pursue it and risk disagreement, so she changed the topic. "This talk of the Dandy club puts Lord Byron in my mind, which reminds me of his poetry, and which leads me to remember that it is rumoured that should Sir Walter Scott refuse the honour, Robert Southey will be named the Poet Laureate. Do you like poetry Mr Bertram?"

Edmund smiled at her. "That is a circuitous route of thought, and reminds *me* that a lively mind is an altogether good thing. To answer your question, yes, I read poetry, and in anticipation of your next question, yes, I like the work of Southey."

"Reading poetry is, for me, a favourite pastime. In truth, it is second only to music in my pursuits. I must confess that, in spite of my lively mind," she gave Edmund a flirtatious look to acknowledge his compliment, "I enjoy most the poems that are clearly the work of blue devils; the more wracked with sorrow the poet and the more sorrowful the subject, the more I enjoy it. It is some perversity in my makeup that I should be blessed with a naturally sanguinary temper, but revel in the melancholy and horrid. Odd, I know, but since it *is* so, I am not an avid reader of Southey."

"You do not find the subject of Joan of Arc sorrowful enough?"

Mary shook her head. "Not the way the Southey writes it, no. There is an element of hope that threads his work, a belief that change can be effected, that does not allude to true despondency in my opinion. However, I will concede that he is a very good wordsmith and that I did read "After Blenheim" with great satisfaction."

"You prefer the romantic poets, then?"

"Oh yes. I have often thought," Mary continued, "that my lukewarm feelings for Southey are the children of my zealous admiration for Byron."

"Because the style between the two is so dissimilar?"

"Sadly, no," Mary replied. "That would at least be rational. I believe it stems more from Byron's distaste for Southey's work. My enthusiasm for Byron allows his taste to influence mine. Because Byron mocks Southey as a ballad-monger, I am prejudiced when I read his works. It makes me feel as though my opinion is a very malleable, will o' the wisp thing. Yet if I try to convince myself to like Southey's poems before I read them, that is just as much a reaction to Byron's sentiments, although in the opposite direction, and does not lessen Byron's influence over me a jot less."

"Does Byron have so strong an opinion on Southey, then?" Edmund asked in surprise. "I did not know."

"Byron wrote an anonymous satirical poem about Southey in '09, which was found to be his work within weeks. My governess shewed it to me; it had been reprinted in several newspapers. My fervour for poetry was still fresh and had the sharp edge of a schoolgirl's fancy, and because I enjoyed Byron's *Hours of Idleness* his estimations were given the most serious attentions by me. I read it so often that I believe I can still recite the last quarter or so of the poem." Actually, she knew she could. She had often done so to amuse friends in the drawing-room once Byron had published *Childe Harold's Pilgrimage* and become monstrously famous almost overnight. Nonetheless, she had been repeatedly warned by her aunt that it was not advisable to display her erudition too flagrantly to an admirer and did not want to reveal her prodigious memory to Edmund so openly.

"Can you then? Would you be willing to do so for me?"

"I am willing, but I must beg your indulgence for any mistakes." Mary gave a small cough to clear her throat and began, "Oh! Southey! Southey! cease they varied song! A bard may chant too often and too long; As thou art strong in verse, in mercy spare! A fourth, alas! were more than we could bear. But if, in spite of all the world can say, Thou still wilt verseward plod thy weary way; If still in Berkley ballads most uncivil, Thou wilt devote old women to the devil, The babe unborn thy dread intent may rue: 'God help thee,' Southey, and thy readers too."

Edmund laughed. "That is satirical condemnation indeed. It is not surprising that such words influenced you. But does not our education mark us all?"

Mary was thoughtful. "I believe it is one thing for my respect for my aunt or the words of some sage author of antiquity to mark my opinions, but I feel it is overly-compliant to be so influenced by satire or comedy. It bespeaks a weakness of character that I should not like to admit to in myself."

"I cannot concur," Edmund said. "Comedy or satire *can* contain as much wisdom as the writings of St Augustus or Plato. The truth coated in a jest is still the truth. In my opinion, a farcical tale can prove as educational as a tomb of philosophy. Look at Aesop's fables; they contain morals that are of great service in dealing with the world. Or think upon Swift's novel *Gulliver's Travels*; its mockery of pretension and vanity is highly instructive."

Mary's dimples winked once more into captivating existence. "I have no choice but to be persuaded by you, Mr Bertram. Firstly, your examples are incontrovertible. Secondly, your opinion flatters *me*, and therefore *must* be true."

Chapter Eight

MISS CRAWFORD'S DELIGHT in riding and her early excellence in it was greatly admired by Edmund and his sisters. Mary soon began to express a great desire to get as far as Mansfield common, since Mrs. Grant had been telling her of its fine views, and Edward had no doubt of her being perfectly equal to the trip. With the lady's felicity in mind, Edward asked Fanny if she were willing to lend Miss Crawford her mare for the entire morning so that they could form a riding party for that purpose. Fanny, ever obliging, consented to the scheme.

The ride to Mansfield common took place the next morning. All the young went except for Fanny, and not even Edmund gave her a second thought as they rode away from the Park. All of his attention was for Mary, who looked exceptionally pretty in her newly made olive-coloured riding habit.

"What a fine thing this is! Why did I never learn to ride sooner?" Mary was in high spirits.

"I cannot answer that," Maria responded, "but I can tell you that I am glad you can do so now."

"As am I," said Henry. "There is a great satisfaction in riding on a sunny morning, with company as beautiful as the day itself."

"You are my brother; you are obligated to think me beautiful," Mary shooed away his compliment.

"Believe me when I say I am sincere in my opinion as to the beauty of the company." Henry's reply was to his sister, but his heavy-lidded gaze was directed toward Maria Bertram. He caught her eye, had the satisfaction of her flush, and then turned to smile at Julia and flatter her more directly, but with perfectly gentlemanly decorum.

"If you will not accept a brother's praise, may I give you mine?" Edmund asked.

"Are you being a gallant?" Mary quizzed him.

"That is no risk. I am woefully without banter or gallantry." Edmund assured her.

"I can attest to that, Miss Crawford," Maria said. "Did I tell you of Edward's compliments to me upon the occasion of my first ball?"

"No, and I beg you to hear it," Mary grinned.

"And I beg you to remain silent," Edward only half-pretended to plead.

Ignoring her brother, Maria continued. "I was as nervous as any other débutante and just before we entered Mr and Mrs Pickering's ballroom, I turned to my brother for comfort. I asked him if he thought I looked well, hoping he would pour some soothing flattery on my irritated feelings, and he, cold-hearted sibling that he is, looked me over and said, 'well enough' in a very tepid way. If I had been vain, that would have put an end to on the spot."

Mary laughed. "Oh! Mr Bertram, how could you be so abominable to your dear sister?"

Edmund smiled. "Maria has a mirror; she has no need of compliments from *me*."

"That is where you are wrong, sir. A woman's security is as fragile as Venetian glass and must be supported at all times," Mary explained.

"I wonder if that applies to all women?" Julia remarked. "Mama had a letter from a friend today with the information that Princess Charlotte's flirtation with Captain George Fitzclarence is at an end, and that Lieutenant Charles Hesse, who is thought to be her cousin through the Duke of York, has taken the captain's place in her affections. She can have no say in who she weds, so does she welcome the attentions of suitors to raise her vanity, or simply to raise her spirits?"

"Considering that her father keeps her locked away like anchoress nun, I cannot find it in my heart to fault her for either impulse," Mary replied spiritedly. "Why should she not flirt, when all other manner of normal intercourse is denied her?"

"I think it very hard that the Princess should have no say in the matter of who she weds," Maria said. "This is not the medieval period; there is no reason why she shouldn't have some choice, provided the suitor be a proper match. *She* is the one most qualified to know in what manner she is to be happy."

"Alas, many ladies do not marry to be happy," Henry said. "They marry where the feel duty calls them, rather than Cupid." His voice was wistful, as if he were sad because he knew one particular lady who was wedding where her heart was not, and was satisfied to see a look of consciousness on Maria's face. "I would wish all ladies would follow their heart."

"I cannot completely agree with your there," Edmund frowned. "While I would certainly advise against marrying for esurience, neither can I say the fairer sex should unreservedly go wherever their heart should lead. An imprudent marriage that would disoblige her family could never bring true happiness, not even if her affection for her misalliance remains undimmed by time. I am thinking, of course, of my mother's sister, Mrs Price. She married a lieutenant of the marines without education or connections or any ability to make his fortune, and although there still seems to be harmony enough between them, the inconveniences and trials of such meagre income and so many children materially lesson her comforts and injure her tranquillity."

"You are right, of course," Henry affably agreed, "but I would still say that w*here circumstances are nearest to equal*, the heart can often make a better choice than the head."

Edmund and his sisters concurred, but Mary did not.

"The heart," she said, "is a very poor compass in many respects. It frequently leads one astray where the head would not. Think of the trouble the heart has caused the Earl of Uxbridge and his second wife. Or the trouble her heart has caused Lady Caroline Lamb."

"But there it is not the heart that causes the trouble; the ill lies in the lack of principles and moral fortitude by the parties," Edmund argued.

"Yes, but it was the heart that led them astray in the first place. Had Uxbridge or Lady Wellesley considered the shame, the turmoil, and the irreversible stains on their character that would occur if they abandoned their spouses and eloped with one another, they would have immediately eschewed one another's company the moment they felt the danger of attachment. If Lady Lamb had used even an ounce of sense, she would have never hazarded her reputation or happiness on Lord Byron. If she had schooled her heart properly, she would not have let her sensibility run wild and make her the laughingstock and mockery of society," Mary was unswayed. She knew foolishness was the root of the problem. Intelligent persons would have kept their affairs discrete and not opened themselves to censure, even if there were speculation.

Edmund's handsome face was set into serious lines. "I do not wish to cavil, but would not firmness of principle and the urge to do right not have prevented them from such behaviour, without having to *think* upon it? Sound morals would have safeguarded their hearts from such exigence of emotion."

"Are not principles birthed from the mind?" Mary rejoined.

"You are right," Edmund's face relaxed. "I believe we are arguing from the same perspective. You are calling egg-shaped what I name as oval." He had convinced himself that Mary, with her feminine illogic and misunderstanding, had confused firmness of principle with mental acuity and good judgement. His appreciation for her beauty did not blind him to *all* her faults, but it certainly encouraged him to perform mental gymnastics to reconcile her worldly opinions to his theological ones.

"It is my opinion that the heart is not as easily ruled for everyone," Henry proffered. "Great sensibility, high spirits, and strong emotions are harder to manage. It is the difference between controlling my hunter and my sister's control over her docile mare."

"If one cannot keep a firm hand on the reigns, one ought not try to ride a hunter," Edmund replied.

"It is much easier to risk riding a hunter if you know you will be unharmed if you are thrown," Mary said archly. "If a man should lose control he can always count on a patch of moss to break his fall, whereas a woman can be assured of landing on sharp rocks … in a waterfall … off a high cliff."

"Better to stay on the mare, then," Julia commented cheerfully.

"Yes, and merely *read* about the hunter. That is what Sir Walter Scott is *for*," Mary quipped. "If *Marmion* cannot convince you that it is a far better thing to live a life of honest purity than to succumb to your passions, then you are beyond hope or amendment."

"Passions, properly schooled, are assets," Henry contended. "The passion for learning and for discovery is transforming our world. Think of all that our short lifetimes have seen: the voltaic pile bottles of miniature lighting, the thermolampe and other gas lights that can give steady illumination in ways myriad candles cannot, the cotton gin and weaving factories that make cloth readily available, and steamboats are rendering canal travel faster by the day. A man named Robert Bell is even saying he will have a steam-powered passenger service along the River Clyde in Scotland soon! All these things are accomplished by passion, even *obsession*, on the part of their creators."

"Then passion is elemental," Maria observed. "Other elements, such as water or fire, are good when harnessed and detrimental when unchained. A waterwheel will grind corn, but a deluge will drown the crop. It is the direction and control of passion that makes it useful."

"But it is its unbridled form that makes it useful in art," Julia was enthusiastic. "It is wild, natural passions — whether of sadness or joy, pain or pleasure — that makes a piece of music or a painting touch the viewer. For the artist, passions must be unrestrained or the art suffers."

"I would say, rather, that the artist suffers." Edmund had none of his sister's wild admiration for Romanticism or Rococo. He preferred pleasant landscapes and the well-done portraits done by Blake and Runge to the idylls of Canaletto and the pink-tinged orgies of Boucher. "As a general rule, those with artistic temperaments and those who allow their passions a free reign are likely to achieve great fame and wealth, squander it, and then die in a spunging house."

"You were never a friend to naturalism, Edmund," Julia sighed at her brother's lack of whimsy and feeling.

"No," her brother smiled, "but, like Diederot, I am a friend to art that is moral and reasonable."

Henry could not resist; the opportunity for a pun was too good. "For myself, I prefer the *Baroque* to the whole."

His companions groaned, and his sister implored him, that as he loved her, to say no more puns. She reminded him that Shakespeare had called the pun the lowest form of wit. In turn, Henry claimed he must stoop to conquer. In this lively way, the party spent the morning in merriment and sightseeing.

The day's ride was much enjoyed at the time, and doubly enjoyed again in the evening discussion. A successful scheme of this sort generally brings on another; and the having been to Mansfield common disposed them all for going somewhere else the day after. There were many other views to be shewn, and though the weather was hot, there were shady lanes wherever they wanted to go. A young party is always provided with a shady lane. Four fine mornings successively were spent in this manner, in shewing the Crawfords the country, and doing the honours of its finest spots. Every thing answered; it was all gaiety and good-humour, the heat only supplying inconvenience enough to be talked of with pleasure—till the fourth day, when the happiness of one of the party was exceedingly clouded. Miss Bertram was the one. Edmund and Julia were invited to dine at the parsonage, and *she* was excluded. It was meant and done by Mrs Grant, with perfect good humour, on Mr Rushworth's account, who was partly expected at the park that day; but it was felt as a very grievous injury, and her good manners were severely taxed to conceal her vexation and anger, till she reached home.

"

After dinner and port Edmund, Julia, the Crawfords, and the Grants played loo at the round table in the drawing-room. It was not an overly large table, so Julia was obliged to sit close to, almost in contact with! her neighbour Henry, and Edmund to Mary, which was a hardship for neither Bertram sibling. In the course of the game, the subject of luck came to the fore, and soon after, the subject of superstitions in general.

"You would be astounded to know even a small part of the many superstitious that thrive among the vulgar here in the country," Dr Grant told Mary and Henry. "And worst of all is their fear of spirits, haunts, ghouls, ghosts, and other spectres."

"Oh tell!" Mary enthused. "I love a good ghost story. But do not, I entreat, explain it away rationally at the end as Mrs Radcliffe does in her books. I wish to remain thrilled and horrified, my chills unalloyed by reason."

Edmund smiled at her. "Are you sure Miss Crawford? Will it not disturb your rest tonight, when your candle is blown out, and you lay in your bed?"

"Of course not," Mary assured him. "I will shudder twice then fall into a deep and dreamless slumber. It is my way; I am impervious to the after-effects of spooky tales."

"I, however, am *not*," Henry made a distressed face. "I shall quake in my bed and call for someone to bring me light."

The table laughed, and there was raillery amongst them over who was to be the most afraid for the longest time.

"Please, Dr Grant, I implore you to share with us the fearful and dread yarns of Mansfield," Mary entreated her brother-in-law.

"Very well," Dr Grant answered her, pleased to have his anecdotes made much of by his wife's lively sister. "Shall I tell you of the black dog that is said to haunt the Rice's mill? Or the weeping woman whom some have seen walking along the River Nene, who disappears if one approaches too closely? Or shall I tell you of the one time I was genuinely and sincerely made astonished and afraid by something in my parish?"

There was an immediate outcry that he should tell them all of the events that so cowed him, and so Dr Grant began the story.

ıı

"It was late one evening, nearing bedtime, in the first year I was rector here, when there came a pounding at my door that startled me. I was so concerned by the ruckus that I did not wait for Jensen to bring me word of the visitor, but went to the door in time to see him open it. Upon my stoop were Mrs Bell, a very respectable widow who runs a girl's school in Mansfield, and a strange man whom I had never met before. Both Mrs Bell and the stranger were very white and greatly agitated."

"I, of course, urged them to enter and offered both of them wine. Mrs Bell was crying so abjectly that the stranger had to beg my pardon and tell me his name himself, which he did in as gentlemanly a manner as possible under the circumstances. He was, he told me, Colonel Brandon of Devonshire. He was travelling to visit a friend of his in Brixworth when his carriage lurched and threw off a wheel about a mile from Mansfield. Fortunately, neither he nor his servants were injured, but it was coming on very dark. The Colonel, as a soldier, was unafraid to approach Mansfield on his own, so leaving his coach and his possessions under the care and guard of his servants, he decided to walk to Mansfield to seek lodging and procure help to mend his coach in the morning, when there would be light to affect repairs."

"There was only a crescent moon, but the Colonel felt equal to the task and believed he should not go astray from such a broad road. As he approached the bridge leading into Mansfield from the south, he saw a soldier, a lieutenant by his insignia, with a bandage around his head. The bandage was very white and plainly seen, but the man's face was in shadow. The Colonel was afraid the man had either been beset by bandits, or *was* one, but the stranger addressed him civilly and begged his assistance as one soldier to another. The lieutenant claimed to be unable to carry his rucksack any further, but was loathe to leave it. The Colonel saw that the man had a crutch as well as a bandage about his head, and therefore he kindly offered to carry it for the injured soldier. The Colonel was surprised, he told me, by the small weight of the sack."

"The lieutenant was effusive in his thanks, and told the Colonel that his home was not far from the bridge, and that his wife took in lodgers. The Colonel believed this to be a marked piece of serendipity, since he needed lodging for the night. The lieutenant spoke of his great longing to see his wife at least once more, before he departed from this earth. Surmising that the man's wounds must be more severe than he reckoned, the Colonel thought that the soldier had been allowed to return home to die in comfort, and told me he felt exceedingly sorry for the fellow."

"The man led the Colonel to Mrs Bell's house, and saying how he was near the end of his strength, petitioned the Colonel to rap upon the door and summon his wife. The Colonel used the knocker, and it was Mrs Bell herself who answered the door, her manservant being engaged in some work elsewhere."

"When the light from Mrs Bell's candles fell upon the Colonel and his companion, she made a choked noise and fainted dead away. If the Colonel had not been quick, the dropped candle would have set her dress alight. In the confusion, he hallooed for help, and Mrs Bell's servants hurried to the door with more lights to assist their mistress."

"By the time the Colonel had finished his part of the tale, Mrs Bell had consumed the better part of her glass of Madeira and was coherent, if not composed. She then told me that the man standing behind Colonel Brandon was none other than her own dear husband, whom she had received news of regarding his death in France not three days before. She saw his face clearly before he disappeared into the ether, for which cause she fainted."

"The sack that the Colonel had carried, when opened, was revealed to contain only a winding shroud. He and Mrs Bell had come to me in haste for my advice, and to ask me to return with them to see the evidence. I did, and found three terrified servants and a handful of lodgers milling about all in confusion. There was, indeed, a winding shroud in a soldier's kit bag, lying on the stoop. Mrs Bell was in agony lest her husband's spirit be lost and doomed to wander, and was greatly anxious that I should give the winding shroud a Christian burial in proxy of her husband's body, which had been interred in France."

"Mrs Bell had never, as long as I had known her, been a hysterical woman, nor one prone to fancy, and the Colonel had the look and address of a sensible man. I felt I had no choice but to believe them and bury the shroud, especially since the servants were working themselves into a froth for fear that Lieutenant Bell's ghost might return to the house. Colonel Brandon came with me to the graveyard, where he attended the brief service during which I interred the shroud."

"Mrs Bell had a headstone placed to mark the grave (such as it was), and attends it. No one has ever reported seeing Lieutenant Bell's shade from that day to this. I know not what to think, other than that Lieutenant Bell's spirit was so determined to take his leave of his wife and have a marker in England that he would not rest or go to his reward until he could accomplish those tasks."

II

His audience had listened to Dr Grant's recitation in a hush, and when he finished speaking there were a great many sighs and exclamations. Nothing would do but that they all make a short progress to the graveyard, to see the tombstone and the dates engraved on it. Agreeably frightened, they returned to the parsonage to drink tea or claret.

II

"Upon my word!" Henry declared. "My story is very small beer compared to that one."

"Is it the time you saw the spectral woman standing in your path?" Mary asked him knowingly.

"Ah yes, it is indeed." He addressed the others, "My sister knows this tale well, but I am willing to share it with fresh ears if you will hear it."

He was, of course, encouraged to continue.

"My tale is a simple one. I was a boy at the time, no more than nine years old, and still living in Norfolk at Everingham. My father's steward had two sons, one a year older than I and one a year younger, and they were my constant playfellows. One day, late in the fall, we were so consumed with our games and frolics that none of us realised how late it was getting. Finally, when it started to get too dark to see the ball we were kicking, it dawned on us that perhaps the lack of light indicated that the day was done and we should away to home. We were to go in opposite directions; me to Everingham and them to their father's house in the village. To get to Everingham, I must needs go through a wood that was reported to be haunted by the spirit of an old woman. To go around the wood would add a mile to my walk, and I was already afraid of being scolded for my lateness as it was."

Henry took a sip of his claret, enjoying the eager attention and the heightened anticipation such a small delay could incur. He had always had a natural actor's ability to play an audience. "I resolved to go through the wood, ghost or nor ghost, but I will admit I went through it as quickly as possible. Yet, in spite of my speed, the wood grew darker still while I was in it until the whole was in a thick gloom. It was then that I espied a bent old woman standing next to the path some yards ahead of me. She was clearly visible, because she was all silvery when the whole wood around her was dark. She waited, still as death, for me to pass her."

"Oh my goodness! What did you do?" Mrs Grant could not help but ejaculate.

"I was rooted to the spot by fear. How could I force myself to go past this apparition? What would happen to me if I did? Would she reach out a cold spectral hand to accost me? Or worse, a clammy dead hand? I could feel my heart beating as if it would fly from my breast. Little by little, I became ashamed of my fear, which to my young mind smacked of cowardice instead of prudent apprehension of the uncanny. With trembling hands, I picked up a stout branch and screwing my courage to the sticking point I ran toward the ghost with a terrible shout … and struck at her!"

Even Mary, who had heard him recount the story multiple times before, gasped as he demonstrated the sudden forward movement of his body. Henry always moved when his listeners least expected it.

"What then, Mr Crawford? What then?" Julia cried out.

Henry lowered her voice to almost a whisper. "I felt a terrible pain throughout my young arms, as though I had been struck by lightning." He then sat back and raised his voice to a normal, jovial tone. "I had struck an old silver birch stump as hard as I could and the reverberations of the stick had nearly torn my limbs off!"

His small audience pealed with laughter, all envisioning the young Henry assaulting a stump with his weapon.

||

Edmund and Julia stayed some few hours longer, enjoying games and lively conversation, and did not leave until after ten o'clock.

Chapter Nine

SUNDAY BROUGHT A serious Edmund to visit the parsonage. His pensiveness was obvious, and as soon as he was seated, Mary Crawford asked him, "Is there something the matter, Mr Bertram? You seem out of sorts."

"I regret to say there is," Edmund replied. "I am extremely reluctant to abridge any pleasure of yours, but I must withdraw the use of my mare."

Exclamations of concern for the health of the mare were made by the party, which Edmund was quick to assure them of.

"It is, however, something in regards to health which has forbidden me from providing you with the mare. My cousin is sorely in decline from the want of proper exercise. I must make sure she has her mare at her disposal."

"Then we are all of us brutes," Mary declared decisively. "None of us considered Miss Price as we ought. I, for one, am thoroughly ashamed."

Edmund rushed to absolve Miss Crawford of any guilt, but her brother shook his head.

"I am afraid I cannot agree with you Edmund; my sister is right; we are all brutes and should all be ashamed. *I* should be more ashamed than anyone. My groom has found a horse that would do for Mary but I have been too busy enjoying my time with the intimates of Mansfield than taking care of business; I could have gone to purchase the gelding two days ago.

Edmund looked rueful, "We have made a sad business of doing our duties, Crawford; but only I can be accused of neglecting my cousin. She is not dependent on your kindness."

"But his neglect is worse," Mrs Grant chimed in. "*You* may have been neglecting a cousin; *he* has been neglecting a sister."

Henry laughed, "My word! This is hard coming from you, Mrs Grant. Have I neglected my sisters so much then?"

"Oh yes," his elder sister rejoined. "I have been simply desperate for someone to help me sort my thread this whole morning; yet you read. What could be more cruel?"

Edmund shook his head. "Miss Price is as dear to me as a sister, and thus my neglect is commensurate to Crawford's. Worse, in fact. For *his* sister's health was not endangered by his thoughtlessness."

Edmund continued at the parsonage for another quarter of an hour before making his adieus. When invited to dine there later, he was forced to decline; his sister's fiancé and Mrs Rushworth would be coming to Mansfield Park for dinner and he must return hither. He very civilly invited the Grants and Crawfords to visit Mansfield the next day to meet the Rushworths, and regretfully left them for the less congenial company of his own home.

II

Mrs Grant and Miss Crawford walked up to Mansfield Park on Monday, as they had promised Edmund they would, and when they entered the drawing-room, they were introduced to Mrs Rushworth and told that they had lately missed Mr Rushworth, who had left to call on Mr Crawford at the parsonage. Comfortable hopes, however, were given that he would find Mr Crawford at home. A scheme that all the young people should go to Sotherton on Wednesday morning to discuss how to improve it was forthwith mentioned. It was hardly possible, indeed, that anything else should be talked of with Mrs Rushworth present.

Mrs Rushworth, under the conviction that everybody must be wanting to see Sotherton, proceeded to include Miss Crawford in the invitation; and though Mrs Grant, who had not been at the trouble of visiting Mrs Rushworth, on her coming into the neighbourhood, civilly declined it on her own account, she was glad to secure any pleasure for her sister; and Mary, properly pressed and persuaded, was not long in accepting her share of the civility. Mr Rushworth came back from the Parsonage successful; Edmund made his appearance just in time to learn what had been settled for Wednesday, and to attend Mrs Rushworth to her carriage.

"It is very good of you to invite us all, Mrs Rushworth," Edmund addressed his future brother's mother respectfully. "Am I assuming too much in thinking Miss Price is included in your hospitality?"

"I have, of course, invited Miss Price; she is a very pleasant gel," Mrs Rushworth replied, "but I have been told she will be needed to stay home with Lady Bertram. Are you sure Lady Bertram would not like to come?"

"I thank you, but my mother would find such a trip fatiguing; however, perhaps I can arrange it so that Miss Price should have the felicity of visiting Sotherton. I know she particularly wishes to see it."

"I am sure she does," Mrs Rushworth said in a self-satisfied way, "and she is very welcome to come."

After carefully assisting Mrs Rushworth into her carriage and giving his most polite farewells to her and her son, Edmund escorted Mrs Grant and Mary Crawford halfway across the Park.

"What do you know of Sotherton?" Miss Crawford asked him. She was still determined to never marry a second son, but she unquestionably wanted Edmund to admire her. She had dressed with care, wearing a walking gown patterned with Bengal stripes in pale shades of Devonshire brown and a peach shawl with ecru and gold embroidery; she thought she saw appreciation in his eyes.

"It was built during Elizabeth's time, I believe," Edmund informed her. "It is a fine old place of that style. It is well lit in the interior, or should be, being like Hardwick Hall "more glass than wall"; but it has several trees that encroach too near and block the light. Mr Rushworth is right in improving it."

"I am undecided about the Elizabethan style," Mary said. "I cannot make up my mind if I find it oppressive or picturesque. I cannot help but thrill at heavy stone-work, but is it taste or sentiment that I feel?"

"I comprehend you perfectly. The houses of that era are impressive, but can be repressively cold and seem more suited to gloomy tales and doomed loves than contented living. Happily for my sister Sotherton is, like Longleat House, very symmetrical and elegant of design and conducive for familial enjoyment."

"Men may not know it," Mrs Grant said, "but a need for improvements is a source of cheer for a bride. To refurnish and fit up a residence all to one's own taste brings a young woman many a happy hour, so long as her husband can afford to indulge her."

"My sister may look forward to many days of pleasure then; not only is Sotherton large but there is also a house in Mayfair that she will no doubt want to newly furnish."

"In truth, to feather her nest was one of the few sources of happiness my aunt had," Mary said without thinking. Her sister reached out to press her hand in comfort, and Mary altered her tone to one lighter and more jocular. "She changed the paper and furniture so often that the Admiral was often thrown into confusion trying to find the correct parlour after supper. My aunt assigned a footman to direct him whenever she had instituted a new colour scheme."

Lightness restored, Mrs Grant and Mary bid Edmund adieu and continued to the parsonage.

ɪɪ

The next meeting of the two Mansfield families produced another alteration in the plan, and one that was admitted with general approbation. Mrs Grant offered herself as companion for the day to Lady Bertram in lieu of her son, and Dr Grant was to join them at dinner. Lady Bertram was very well pleased to have it so, and the young ladies were in spirits again. Even Edmund was very thankful for an arrangement which restored him to his share of the party; and Mrs Norris thought it an excellent plan, and had it at her tongue's end, and was on the point of proposing it, when Mrs Grant spoke.

ɪɪ

Wednesday was a fine, and soon after breakfast the barouche arrived, Mr Crawford driving his sisters; and as everybody was ready, there was nothing to be done but for Mrs Grant to alight and the others to take their places. The place of all places, the envied seat, the post of honour, was unappropriated. To whose happy lot was it to fall? While each of the Miss Bertrams were meditating how best, and with the most appearance of obliging the others, to secure it, the matter was settled by Mrs Grant's saying, as she stepped from the carriage, "As there are five of you, it will be better that one should sit with Henry; and as you were saying lately that you wished you could drive, Julia, I think this will be a good opportunity for you to take a lesson."

Mary bit her lip to keep from smiling, not at Mrs Grant's unsubtle attempts to push Julia and Henry together, but at the frozen look on Maria's face that was clearly hiding vexation. The immobility of her countenance was a good as a scowl to indicate her unhappiness. In contrast, Julia was beaming at the chance to sit by Henry, obviously thrilled. Such adulation could not be good for Henry's already full-bodied estimation of his own charms, in Mary's opinion. Would that the Bertram daughters have a little more discretion in their preference for her brother! Mary felt almost as much embarrassment *for* them as she felt amusement *at* them.

Happy Julia! Unhappy Maria! The former was on the barouche-box in a moment, the latter took her seat within, in gloom and mortification; and the carriage drove off amid the good wishes of the two remaining ladies, and the barking of Pug in his mistress's arms.

Their road was through a pleasant country; and Fanny, whose rides had never been extensive, was soon beyond her knowledge, and was very happy in observing all that was new, and admiring all that was pretty. Miss Crawford was very unlike her. She had none of Fanny's delicacy of taste, of mind, of feeling; she saw Nature, inanimate Nature, with little observation; her attention was all for men and women, her talents for the light and lively. In looking back after Edmund, however, when there was any stretch of road behind them, or when he gained on them in ascending a considerable hill, they were united, and a "there he is" broke at the same moment from them both, more than once.

Julia was enjoying the trip more than anyone else in the party. When Julia looked back from the top of the barouche box, it was with a countenance of delight, and whenever she spoke to them, it was in the highest spirits: "her view of the country was charming, she wished they could all see it," etc.; but her only offer of exchange was addressed to Miss Crawford, as they gained the summit of a long hill, and was not more inviting than this: "Here is a fine burst of country. I wish you had my seat, but I dare say you will not take it, let me press you ever so much;" and Miss Crawford could hardly answer before they were moving again at a good pace.

When they came within the influence of Sotherton associations, it was better for Miss Bertram, who might be said to have two strings to her bow. She had Rushworth feelings, and Crawford feelings, and in the vicinity of Sotherton the former had considerable effect. Mr Rushworth's consequence was hers. She could not tell Miss Crawford that "those woods belonged to Sotherton," she could not carelessly observe that "she believed that it was now all Mr Rushworth's property on each side of the road," without elation of heart; and it was a pleasure to increase with their approach to the capital freehold mansion, and ancient manorial residence of the family, with all its rights of court-leet and court-baron.

"Now we shall have no more rough road, Miss Crawford; our difficulties are over. The rest of the way is such as it ought to be. Mr

Rushworth has made it since he succeeded to the estate. Here begins the village. Those cottages are really a disgrace. The church spire is reckoned remarkably handsome. I am glad the church is not so close to the great house as often happens in old places. The annoyance of the bells must be terrible. There is the parsonage: a tidy-looking house, and I understand the clergyman and his wife are very decent people. Those are almshouses, built by some of the family. To the right is the steward's house; he is a very respectable man. Now we are coming to the lodge-gates; but we have nearly a mile through the park still. It is not ugly, you see, at this end; there is some fine timber, but the situation of the house is dreadful. We go down hill to it for half a mile, and it is a pity, for it would not be an ill-looking place if it had a better approach."

Miss Crawford was not slow to admire; she pretty well guessed Miss Bertram's feelings, and made it a point of honour to promote her enjoyment to the utmost. Mary often felt sorry for those who fell in love with Henry, and did her best to lessen their wounds and pangs. While she loved her brother too much to ever attempt to strenuously check his flirtations or call him to task for anything but the most extreme actions, she was kind-hearted enough to wish to comfort those who fell prey to his charms, even as she harboured contempt for their foolishness in taking a rattle like Henry at all seriously. The general ease with which Henry captivated women made her feel that she was unusual in more than just her resistance to blandishments and falling in love; she could not help feel she was wiser than the average lady. Could they not see that Henry was a sad flirt? Could anything but their own stupidity and vanity account for their blindness?

Mrs Norris was all delight and volubility; and even Fanny had something to say in admiration, and might be heard with complacency. Her eye was eagerly taking in everything within her reach; and after being at some pains to get a view of the house, and observing that "it was a sort of building which she could not look at but with respect," Fanny added, "Now, where is the avenue? The house fronts the east, I perceive. The avenue, therefore, must be at the back of it. Mr Rushworth talked of the west front."

"Yes, it is exactly behind the house; begins at a little distance, and ascends for half a mile to the extremity of the grounds. You may see something of it here – something of the more distant trees. It is oak entirely."

Miss Bertram could now speak with decided information of what she had known nothing about when Mr Rushworth had asked her opinion; and her spirits were in as happy a flutter as vanity and pride could furnish, when they drove up to the spacious stone steps before the principal entrance.

Mary was very impressed with the Rushworth abode. The aspect and approach to the house may have wanted improvement, but the house itself was imposing and majestic. It was two storeys tall, formed in the symmetrical 'E' shape so common of Elizabethan country homes and manors, and built of the pale, orangey-brown sandstone quarried in Northamptonshire. The many gables of the Rushworth residence were done in the Dutch 'crow-stepped' style and the Italianate façade was adorned with pillars, carvings, and a strapwork frieze that would have looked fussy on a smaller building but just gave an air of grandeur to Sotherton. Even the clusters of rectangular chimneys were grand and stately, being tall and thin and made to resemble Tuscan columns.

Sotherton was also a monument to the glazier's art, and its many windows announced the family's past and present wealth. Most noticeable was the immense bay window jutting out from on the left wing of the house, where the family living area would be. Mary assumed it was attached to the drawing-room or receiving room. Such light it would bestow upon a drawing-room! It was a delight to think of. A magnificent curved and panelled stain-glass lunette window topped the round-head arch of the entrance.

The front gardens were immaculate to the point of dullness; a triumph of boxwood, gravel, and closely-shorn grass. Several peacocks roamed the front garden, fanning their tails and strutting for the unimpressed hens, several of which were followed by half-grown, drab offspring just beginning to show iridescence in the feathers on their necks. One large peacock sat on the decorative stone pillar on the right side of the entrance steps, his aureate train sweeping down almost five feet. His crest bobbed as he turned his head this way and that to watch the visitors alight from the barouche. Mary thought his appearance a fitting welcome for Maria's arrival at her soon-to-be marital home. No other bird in creation could be as aware of the beauty of its plumage as Maria was of hers.

Chapter Ten

MR RUSHWORTH WAS at the door to receive his fair lady; and the whole party were welcomed by him with due attention. In the drawing-room they were met with equal cordiality by the mother, and Miss Bertram had all the distinction with each that she could wish. After the business of arriving was over, it was first necessary to eat, and the doors were thrown open to admit them through one or two intermediate rooms into the appointed dining-parlour, where a collation was prepared with abundance and elegance. Much was said, and much was ate, and all went well. The particular object of the day was then considered. How would Mr Crawford like, in what manner would he chuse, to take a survey of the grounds? Mr Rushworth mentioned his curricle. Mr Crawford suggested the greater desirableness of some carriage which might convey more than two. "To be depriving themselves of the advantage of other eyes and other judgements, might be an evil even beyond the loss of present pleasure."

Mrs Rushworth proposed that the chaise should be taken also; but this was scarcely received as an amendment: the young ladies neither smiled nor spoke. Her next proposition, of shewing the house to such of them as had not been there before, was more acceptable, for Miss Bertram was pleased to have its size displayed, and all were glad to be doing something.

The whole party rose accordingly, and under Mrs Rushworth's guidance were shewn through a number of rooms, all lofty, and many large, and amply furnished in the taste of fifty years back, with shining floors, solid mahogany, rich damask, marble, gilding, and carving, each handsome in its way. Of pictures there were abundance, and some few good, but the larger part were family portraits, no longer anything to anybody but Mrs Rushworth, who had been at great pains to learn all that the housekeeper could teach, and was now almost equally well qualified to shew the house. On the present occasion she addressed herself chiefly to Miss Crawford and Fanny, but there was no comparison in the willingness of their attention; for Miss Crawford, who had seen scores of great houses, and cared for none of them, had only the appearance of civilly listening, while Fanny, to whom everything was almost as interesting as it was new, attended with unaffected earnestness to all that Mrs Rushworth could relate of the family in former times, its rise and grandeur, regal visits and loyal efforts, delighted to connect anything with history already known, or warm her imagination with scenes of the past.

The situation of the house excluded the possibility of much prospect from any of the rooms; and while Fanny and some of the others were attending Mrs Rushworth, Henry Crawford was looking grave and shaking his head at the windows. Every room on the west front looked across a lawn to the beginning of the avenue immediately beyond tall iron palisades and gates.

Mary, having no small talent for pricing objects at a glance, saw enough of glass-drop chandeliers, mirrors in gilded frames, silver candlestick holders, Indian fancies, oriental carpets, ormolu clocks, Serves porcelains, and *objets d'art* that even she, who was used to London opulence and conspicuous consumption, was impressed. Maria Bertram was marrying a very stupid man, but he was a very rich one who had been brought up be accustomed to the finest luxury goods possible. Maria would be surrounded by tell-tale signs of wealth, wear the best clothes in the latest fashions, have jewels worthy of a Harem favourite, and be denied nothing she wanted. Looking around, Mary believed that if Mr Rushworth had offered for her, *she* would have been tempted to accept him, regardless of how dull his company would be. He was a tedious man, truly, but also an easily led one; it would be nothing for a wife to convince him to live a life of gaiety in Town during the season and to host large house parties the rest of the year. A plethora of interesting guests would make up for the lack of an interesting husband. And although Mary herself had no plans to besmirch her *own* vows, she saw how easy it would be to conduct an *affaire de cœur* under Rushworth's unperceptive nose if his wife should wish to take a lover to alleviate her boredom. A woman married to a man as brainless as Rushworth need not suffer for it, had she so much as a teaspoon of brains in *her* head. It became Mary's decided opinion that if Maria was willing to give all this up for Henry (and she believed that Maria would jilt Rushworth in an instant, should Henry ask for her hand instead) then Maria was a simpleton. Perhaps it would have been different if Henry – wonderful, witty, and urbane Henry – had actually loved Maria, but as they were all circumstanced, Mary believed Maria Bertram to be as foolish as she was vain.

Having visited many more rooms than could be supposed to be of any other use than to contribute to the window-tax, and find employment for housemaids, "Now," said Mrs Rushworth, "we are coming to the chapel, which properly we ought to enter from above, and look down upon; but as we are quite among friends, I will take you in this way, if you will excuse me."

Mary stifled a sigh. She had seen nothing in the house – magnificent though it was – that she had not seen equalled or surpassed in other estates. Now she would be forced to pretend to admire the chapel. She deplored sameness, and of all the rooms in country houses, the chapel was the one most like all the others. Perhaps, if the family were Papists some grandeur of the former times remained, but the reign of Cromwell and his Puritans had turned all Anglican chapels into beastly dull images of themselves with whitewash. As one *had* to believe in God, let there at least let there be grandeur and beauty to acknowledge the Almighty. If there was anything worse than seeing an abode of worship turned into a plain workaday place of penitence and prayer, Mary did not know what it was.

In this regard for solemn chapels, she and Fanny Price finally had tastes that converged. Fanny's imagination had prepared her for something grander than a mere spacious, oblong room, fitted up for the purpose of devotion: with nothing more striking or more solemn than the profusion of mahogany, and the crimson velvet cushions appearing over the ledge of the family gallery above. "I am disappointed," said she, in a low voice, to Edmund. "This is not my idea of a chapel. There is nothing awful here, nothing melancholy, nothing grand. Here are no aisles, no arches, no inscriptions, no banners. No banners, cousin, to be 'blown by the night wind of heaven.' No signs that a 'Scottish monarch sleeps below.'"

"You forget, Fanny, how lately all this has been built, and for how confined a purpose, compared with the old chapels of castles and monasteries. It was only for the private use of the family. They have been buried, I suppose, in the parish church. *There* you must look for the banners and the achievements."

"It was foolish of me not to think of all that; but I am disappointed."

Mrs Rushworth began her relation. "This chapel was fitted up as you see it, in James the Second's time. Before that period, as I understand, the pews were only wainscot; and there is some reason to think that the linings and cushions of the pulpit and family seat were only purple cloth; but this is not quite certain. It is a handsome chapel, and was formerly in constant use both morning and evening. Prayers were always read in it by the domestic chaplain, within the memory of many; but the late Mr Rushworth left it off."

"Every generation has its improvements," said Miss Crawford, with a smile, to Edmund. It did not occur to her that Edmund and his cousin did not share the general aversion to lingering and multitudinous church services.

Mrs Rushworth was gone to repeat her lesson to Mr Crawford; and Edmund, Fanny, and Miss Crawford remained in a cluster together.

"It is a pity," cried Fanny, "that the custom should have been discontinued. It was a valuable part of former times. There is something in a chapel and chaplain so much in character with a great house, with one's ideas of what such a household should be! A whole family assembling regularly for the purpose of prayer is fine!"

"Very fine indeed," said Miss Crawford, laughing. "It must do the heads of the family a great deal of good to force all the poor housemaids and footmen to leave business and pleasure, and say their prayers here twice a day, while they are inventing excuses themselves for staying away."

"*That* is hardly Fanny's idea of a family assembling," said Edmund. "If the master and mistress do *not* attend themselves, there must be more harm than good in the custom."

"At any rate, it is safer to leave people to their own devices on such subjects. Everybody likes to go their own way – to chuse their own time and manner of devotion. The obligation of attendance, the formality, the restraint, the length of time – altogether it is a formidable thing, and what nobody likes; and if the good people who used to kneel and gape in that gallery could have foreseen that the time would ever come when men and women might lie another ten minutes in bed, when they woke with a headache, without danger of reprobation, because chapel was missed, they would have jumped with joy and envy. Cannot you imagine with what unwilling feelings the former belles of the house of Rushworth did many a time repair to this chapel? The young Mrs Eleanors and Mrs Bridgets –

starched up into seeming piety, but with heads full of something very different – especially if the poor chaplain were not worth looking at – and, in those days, I fancy parsons were very inferior even to what they are now."

Mary gave little attention to what she said; it was a commonplace form of pleasantry among her set in London to jeer the buffoonery of churchmen and the unwillingness to suffer through a tedious church service. To respect the Church as a profession in anyone who had any *choice* in the matter was an alien concept to her. A man who was to be a parson was either bred to it or forced to it. To *enjoy* church services were beyond comprehension; they were to be endured.

For a few moments she was unanswered. Fanny coloured and looked at Edmund, but felt too angry for speech; and he needed a little recollection before he could say, "Your lively mind can hardly be serious even on serious subjects. You have given us an amusing sketch, and human nature cannot say it was not so. We must all feel *at times* the difficulty of fixing our thoughts as we could wish; but if you are supposing it a frequent thing, that is to say, a weakness grown into a habit from neglect, what could be expected from the *private* devotions of such persons? Do you think the minds which are suffered, which are indulged in wanderings in a chapel, would be more collected in a closet?"

"Yes, very likely. They would have two chances at least in their favour. There would be less to distract the attention from without, and it would not be tried so long."

"The mind which does not struggle against itself under *one* circumstance, would find objects to distract it in the *other*, I believe; and the influence of the place and of example may often rouse better feelings than are begun with. The greater length of the service, however, I admit to be sometimes too hard a stretch upon the mind. One wishes it were not so; but I have not yet left Oxford long enough to forget what chapel prayers are."

While this was passing, the rest of the party being scattered about the chapel, Julia called Mr Crawford's attention to her sister, by saying, "Do look at Mr Rushworth and Maria, standing side by side, exactly as if the ceremony were going to be performed. Have not they completely the air of it?"

Mr Crawford smiled his acquiescence, and stepping forward to Maria, said, in a voice which she only could hear, "I do not like to see Miss Bertram so near the altar."

Starting, the lady instinctively moved a step or two, but recovering herself in a moment, affected to laugh, and asked him, in a tone not much louder, "If he would give her away?"

"I am afraid I should do it very awkwardly," was his reply, with a look of meaning.

Mary was diverted by Maria's reaction to Julia's comment and she wondered how no one else could see how reluctant the bride was to tie the knot with Mr Rushworth. She worried Henry's flirtatious expression was too obvious, but no – she was surrounded by the wilfully blind.

Julia, joining Henry and Maria at the moment, carried on the joke.

"Upon my word, it is really a pity that it should not take place directly, if we had but a proper licence, for here we are altogether, and nothing in the world could be more snug and pleasant." And she talked and laughed about it with so little caution as to catch the comprehension of Mr Rushworth and his mother, and expose her sister to the whispered gallantries of her lover, while Mrs Rushworth spoke with proper smiles and dignity of its being a most happy event to her whenever it took place.

Mary was hard-pressed to hide a smile as she watched Maria struggle to look something other than repulsed by her intended husband.

"If Edmund were but in orders!" cried Julia, and running to where he stood with Miss Crawford and Fanny: "My dear Edmund, if you were but in orders now, you might perform the ceremony directly. How unlucky that you are not ordained; Mr Rushworth and Maria are quite ready."

Miss Crawford's countenance, as Julia spoke, might have amused a disinterested observer. For once, her ironbound sangfroid had deserted her. She looked almost aghast under the new idea she was receiving. Fanny pitied her. "How distressed she will be at what she said just now," passed across her mind.

"Ordained!" said Miss Crawford; "what, are you to be a clergyman?" Had Edmund been declared to be destined as a human sacrifice she could not have been more appalled.

"Yes; I shall take orders soon after my father's return – probably at Christmas."

Miss Crawford, rallying her spirits, and recovering her complexion, replied only, "If I had known this before, I would have spoken of the cloth with more respect," and turned the subject.

The chapel was soon afterwards left to the silence and stillness which reigned in it, with few interruptions, throughout the year. Miss Bertram, displeased with her sister, led the way, and all seemed to feel that they had been there long enough.

II

"This is insufferably hot," said Miss Crawford, when the party had gone out onto the lawn. She, Edmund Bertram, and Miss Price were walking together, as they had for most of the tour of Sotherton. "Shall any of us object to being comfortable? Here is a nice little wood, if one can but get into it. What happiness if the door should not be locked! of course it is; for in these great places the gardeners are the only people who can go where they like." Mary, still discomfited by her gaffe in the chapel regarding clergymen, did not expect anything to be as she liked it.

The door, however, proved not to be locked, and they were all agreed in turning joyfully through it, and leaving the unmitigated glare of day behind. A considerable flight of steps landed them in the wilderness, which was a planted wood of about two acres, and though chiefly of larch and laurel, and beech cut down, and though laid out with too much regularity, was darkness and shade, and natural beauty, compared with the bowling-green and the terrace. They all felt the refreshment of it, and for some time could only walk and admire.

Mary was recovering her spirits. Mr Bertram was not lost at present. There was still time to save him from his fate. Surely *she* could make him see the folly of his choice. At length, after a short pause, Miss Crawford began with, "So you are to be a clergyman, Mr Bertram. This is rather a surprise to me."

"Why should it surprise you? You must suppose me designed for some profession, and might perceive that I am neither a lawyer, nor a soldier, nor a sailor."

"Very true; but, in short, it had not occurred to me. And you know there is generally an uncle or a grandfather to leave a fortune to the second son."

"A very praiseworthy practice," said Edmund, "but not quite universal. I am one of the exceptions, and *being* one, must do something for myself."

"'But why are you to be a clergyman? I thought *that* was always the lot of the youngest, where there were many to chuse before him."
Do you think the church itself never chosen, then?"
"*Never* is a black word. But yes, in the *never* of conversation, which means *not very often*, I do think it. For what is to be done in the church? Men love to distinguish themselves, and in either of the other lines distinction may be gained, but not in the church. A clergyman is nothing," Mary spoke decisively. To her knowledge, no one had ever given a contradictory opinion to this assertion.

"The *nothing* of conversation has its gradations, I hope, as well as the *never*. A clergyman cannot be high in state or fashion. He must not head mobs, or set the ton in dress. But I cannot call that situation nothing which has the charge of all that is of the first importance to mankind, individually or collectively considered, temporally and eternally, which has the guardianship of religion and morals, and consequently of the manners which result from their influence. No one here can call the *office* nothing. If the man who holds it is so, it is by the neglect of his duty, by foregoing its just importance, and stepping out of his place to appear what he ought not to appear."

Mary refrained from rolling her eyes at such idealistic monkeyshine. She had never known a clergyman to set a good example in her life. Even her brother, Dr Grant, who obeyed more of the Ten Commandments than most parsons, could be faulted for gluttony and idleness. Who, outside of Edmund's ecclesiastical Shangri-La, looked to the clergy for guidance?

"*You* assign greater consequence to the clergyman than one has been used to hear given, or than I can quite comprehend. One does not see much of this influence and importance in society, and how can it be acquired where they are so seldom seen themselves? How can two sermons a week, even supposing them worth hearing, supposing the preacher to have the sense to prefer Blair's to his own, do all that you speak of? govern the conduct and fashion the manners of a large congregation for the rest of the week? One scarcely sees a clergyman out of his pulpit."

"*You* are speaking of London, *I* am speaking of the nation at large."

"The metropolis, I imagine, is a pretty fair sample of the rest."
Mary, a Town lass to the hilt, could think of no other *worthy* measure of England but London.

"Not, I should hope, of the proportion of virtue to vice throughout the kingdom. We do not look in great cities for our best morality. It is not there that respectable people of any denomination can do most good; and it certainly is not there that the influence of the clergy can be most felt. A fine preacher is followed and admired; but it is not in fine preaching only that a good clergyman will be useful in his parish and his neighbourhood, where the parish and neighbourhood are of a size capable of knowing his private character, and observing his general conduct, which in London can rarely be the case. The clergy are lost there in the crowds of their parishioners. They are known to the largest part only as preachers. And with regard to their influencing public manners, Miss Crawford must not misunderstand me, or suppose I mean to call them the arbiters of good-breeding, the regulators of refinement and courtesy, the masters of the ceremonies of life. The *manners* I speak of might rather be called *conduct*, perhaps, the result of good principles; the effect, in short, of those doctrines which it is their duty to teach and recommend; and it will, I believe, be everywhere found, that as the clergy are, or are not what they ought to be, so are the rest of the nation."

"Certainly," said Fanny, with gentle earnestness.

"There," cried Miss Crawford, "you have quite convinced Miss Price already." Mary was amused by the girl's warmhearted agreement with her cousin's viewpoint.

"I wish I could convince Miss Crawford too."

"I do not think you ever will," said she, with an arch smile; "I am just as much surprised now as I was at first that you should intend to take orders. You really are fit for something better. Come, do change your mind. It is not too late. Go into the law."

"Go into the law! With as much ease as I was told to go into this wilderness."

"Now you are going to say something about law being the worst wilderness of the two, but I forestall you; remember, I have forestalled you."

"You need not hurry when the object is only to prevent my saying a *bon mot*, for there is not the least wit in my nature. I am a very matter-of-fact, plain-spoken being, and may blunder on the borders of a repartee for half an hour together without striking it out."

A general silence succeeded. Each was thoughtful. Mary was confused by how unhappy Edmund's declaration he would be a clergyman made her. Why should she care what a second son was to do with his life? What could it be to *her*? She had not realised she had been forming designs on the handsome younger brother until he had said something which shattered any hope that he would be a possible husband. Wed a parson? Faugh! Yet ...

Fanny made the first interruption by saying, "I wonder that I should be tired with only walking in this sweet wood; but the next time we come to a seat, if it is not disagreeable to you, I should be glad to sit down for a little while."

"My dear Fanny," cried Edmund, immediately drawing her arm within his, "how thoughtless I have been! I hope you are not very tired. Perhaps," turning to Miss Crawford, "my other companion may do me the honour of taking an arm."

"Thank you, but I am not at all tired." She took it, however, as she spoke, and the gratification of having her do so, of feeling such a connexion for the first time, made him a little forgetful of Fanny. "You scarcely touch me," said he. "You do not make me of any use. What a difference in the weight of a woman's arm from that of a man! At Oxford I have been a good deal used to have a man lean on me for the length of a street, and you are only a fly in the comparison."

"I am really not tired, which I almost wonder at; for we must have walked at least a mile in this wood. Do not you think we have?"

"Not half a mile," was his sturdy answer; for he was not yet so much in love as to measure distance, or reckon time, with feminine lawlessness.

"Oh! do not consider how much we have wound about. We have taken such a very serpentine course, and the wood itself must be half a mile long in a straight line, for we have never seen the end of it yet since we left the first great path."

"But if you remember, before we left that first great path, we saw directly to the end of it. We looked down the whole vista, and saw it closed by iron gates, and it could not have been more than a furlong in length."

"Oh! I know nothing of your furlongs, but I am sure it is a very long wood, and that we have been winding in and out ever since we came into it; and therefore, when I say that we have walked a mile in it, I must speak within compass."

"We have been exactly a quarter of an hour here," said Edmund, taking out his watch, oblivious to Mary's slight emphasis on the words 'long' and 'wood'. He was impervious to double entendre. "Do you think we are walking four miles an hour?"

Mary smiled up at him with a saucy look, oddly pleased he was unable to ascertain any hint of the risqué in their conversation. "Oh! do not attack me with your watch. A watch is always too fast or too slow. I cannot be dictated to by a watch."

A few steps farther brought them out at the bottom of the very walk they had been talking of; and standing back, well shaded and sheltered, and looking over a ha-ha into the park, was a comfortable-sized bench, on which they all sat down.

"I am afraid you are very tired, Fanny," said Edmund, observing her; "why would not you speak sooner? This will be a bad day's amusement for you if you are to be knocked up. Every sort of exercise fatigues her so soon, Miss Crawford, except riding."

"How abominable in you, then, to let me engross her horse as I did all last week! I am ashamed of you and of myself, but it shall never happen again." Mary did not speak entirely in jest. It *was* terribly rude of her to monopolise the mare and she was truly repentant for her selfishness. She disliked selfishness in others too much to forgive it easily in herself.

"*Your* attentiveness and consideration makes me more sensible of my own neglect. Fanny's interest seems in safer hands with you than with me."

"That she should be tired now, however, gives me no surprise; for there is nothing in the course of one's duties so fatiguing as what we have been doing this morning: seeing a great house, dawdling from one room to another, straining one's eyes and one's attention, hearing what one does not understand, admiring what one does not care for. It is generally allowed to be the greatest bore in the world, and Miss Price has found it so, though she did not know it."

"I shall soon be rested," said Fanny; "to sit in the shade on a fine day, and look upon verdure, is the most perfect refreshment."

Fanny may have found it to be the perfect refreshment, but Mary was bored to tears simply sitting and gawking at the same trees. After sitting a little while Miss Crawford was up again. "I must move," said she; "resting fatigues me. I have looked across the ha-ha till I am weary. I must go and look through that iron gate at the same view, without being able to see it so well."

Edmund left the seat likewise. "Now, Miss Crawford, if you will look up the walk, you will convince yourself that it cannot be half a mile long, or half half a mile."

"It is an immense distance," said she; "I see *that* with a glance."

He still reasoned with her, but in vain. She would not calculate, she would not compare. She would only smile and assert. The greatest degree of rational consistency could not have been more engaging, and they talked with mutual satisfaction. At last it was agreed that they should endeavour to determine the dimensions of the wood by walking a little more about it. They would go to one end of it, in the line they were then in – for there was a straight green walk along the bottom by the side of the ha-ha – and perhaps turn a little way in some other direction, if it seemed likely to assist them, and be back in a few minutes. Fanny said she was rested, and would have moved too, but this was not suffered. Edmund urged her remaining where she was with an earnestness which she could not resist, and she was left on the bench to think with pleasure of her cousin's care, but with great regret that she was not stronger. She watched them till they had turned the corner, and listened till all sound of them had ceased.

Chapter Eleven

THEY HAD NOT walked far from Fanny when they were tempted into the Park by and unfastened side gate, and they soon came upon the very avenue which Fanny had been hoping the whole morning to reach at last, and had sat down under one of the trees. Mary was perched most becomingly on an oak tree's thick root, and Edmund reclined back onto one elbow near her feet. Her suitor had plucked a daisy for her, and she twirled the stem in her long, elegant fingers, well aware of the delightful picture she made. She had even, oh so artlessly, exposed a bit of ankle as if unawares, and was enjoying the sight of Edmund *not* looking at it with such ardent determination more than she had many gentlemen looking at it with admiration.

"I wish Fanny could see these oaks," Edmund said, without taking into account that he was the one who had abandoned her to walk on with Miss Crawford. "She loves an avenue, and an avenue of oaks is always very fine. She particularly wished to see this one."

"I wish Miss Price were not always so knocked up, so that she *could* be with us to see the oaks," Mary replied. "Has she always had such frail health?" Being of robust health herself, Mary thought that to be so feeble would be a terrible thing to endure, and pitied Fanny greatly.

"Ever since I have known her, and she came to the Park when she was only ten years old. We learned quickly that she was very tender and easily fatigued. She has always wanted appetite, and been extraordinary pale. If she does too much walking she will get dreadful headaches, and becomes dizzy if she stands too quickly. Occasionally she has alarmed us all with chest pains, and an erratic pulse brought on by too much exertion. Even during last week's heat, her hands were cold to the touch; I have never known her hands to *not* be cold. If she is not kept well bundled up during bitter weather, her lips and her fingernails will take on the most frightening blue tinge," Edmund sighed. "She is a very delicate creature, both in body and in mind."

"My nurse used to say people who suffered from blue nails and were easily knocked up had weak blood, and that beef broth and coddled eggs would feed their blood and make them stronger," Mary offered. "Perhaps such dishes would help Miss Price?"

"I'll mention it to my mother," Edmund smiled at Mary's concern, "and recommend that those dishes be put more frequently on the menu. We can but hope that Fanny will eat them, though."

"If you would encourage her, I am sure she would. She looks upon you as her guide to everything. No father nor elder brother could have a more devoted kinswoman than you have in your cousin."

"You are very devoted to your brother as well; do you look to Henry for guidance?" Edmund was a little flustered by the praise, but very flattered.

"Goodness, no!" Mary laughed. She dared not tell Edmund that if she took Henry as her guide she'd have multiple lovers and intrigues with half of London; she knew Edmund would be quite shocked by her knowledge of the less seemly side of life. "Henry has abhorrence for serious concerns and wishes to be no one's model. I had my aunt as my archetype, and now I have my sister. I am well enough."

"And your aunt? What manner of woman was she?" Edmund was entranced by Miss Crawford's enthusiasm, which made her countenance even more alluring.

"My aunt was the best of women," she declared. "She was a woman of learning and information, charitable to the poor, eager to assist her friends, and loved by all who knew her," Mary's face darkened briefly, "save one." Then her dimples made their reappearance. "Did I ever tell you of my friend Mrs Fraser's passion for taking likenesses?"

"You have not."

"This relates to my aunt, and will help you understand that I loved her as much for her wit as I did for her more admirable characteristics. Perhaps that is to my shame, but I must own it to be so. My friend Mrs Fraser, who was still Miss Janet Ross at the time, was all in a tither for about half a year with the desire to take likenesses, but she, poor dear, did them very ill and none of us had the heart to tell her. She once did a likeness of Henry that resembled a chicken very much, but still we praised it and Henry had it placed in a frame rather than burned as he ought. She would take likenesses of anyone she could convince to sit for her, and my aunt, being a very obliging woman, agreed when the future Mrs Fraser asked her to pose as an allegory of spring. For three days my dearest aunt sat every morning for my friend, as patient as an oyster, while Mrs Fraser flurried with her crayons. Finally, it was finished and it was, not to put too fine a point on it, the most ghastly likeness I have ever seen. Nonetheless, my aunt praised it and furthermore promised to have it mounted and hung in the receiving room. As soon as Mrs Fraser absented herself on an errand, I asked my aunt what she was about to have such a dreadful likeness of herself hung where it could not help but be seen by visitors. My aunt, with perfect composure, told me that she had no fear that anyone would recognise it as her and that is was not everyone who could boast of a picture of a codfish wearing a wreath of flowers and a pink silk gown."

Edmund laughed. "She sounds like a woman of good humour. She must have been an ideal aunt for a lively young girl." His dark blue eyes were very warm as he looked at Mary.

Basking in his approbation, Mary joked, "Is not your Aunt Norris equally ideal?"

"Alas, I cannot say that she is. She feels a good deal of attachment to us (Maria especially), but her temper is too variable to be as attaching in return." Edmund was thoughtful. "In truth, her treatment of Fanny is too unkind to make her partiality to me or my siblings seem like a sign of true feeling. It is impossible to feel gratitude toward her for so uneven a preferment."

"I can understand that," Mary sympathised. "There was some little preferment in my home, in that my aunt doted on me a bit more and the Admiral gloried in Henry, but it was not *in extremis*. My aunt was plainly attached to Henry, and there was no cause for resentment over so moderate a favouritism."

"You speak of your aunt; was your uncle's favouritism resented?" Edmund wondered if that was the root of Mary's dislike for her uncle.

Mary's voice was chilly. "You must *want* someone's approval or attention in order to resent its absence. I care nothing for the admiral's preferences." She recollected herself, and regained her congenial tone and expression. "But that is no fit topic for such a sunny day, and such a delightful environment. Let us speak of more pleasant things. Tell me of your interests, Mr Bertram. You know all about my tastes, but I know little of yours."

Edmund, made unhappy by Miss Crawford's lack of respect for her uncle, was more than willing to allow a change of subject.

"Perhaps my tastes are all bad?" He said depreciatingly.

"I doubt that, but if they are then I will help you amend them."

"Perhaps you will find my pursuits tedious?" Edmund persisted.

"Then I will help enliven them."

He smiled at Miss Crawford, but was clearly sceptical of her assurances. "And if I told you I like botany?"

"Then I would tell you I have talked with Sir Joesph Banks many times."

Edmund was impressed. Sir Joseph Banks was one of the most reknown botanists in London, and was famous for his travels with Captain James Cook and his studies of native plant life in Australia, New Zealand, North and South America, and several South Seas Islands. As head of the Royal Society, the foremost academy of science in England, he also had also advised King George III on the development of the Royal Botanic Gardens at Kew.

"Upon your word, have you really?"

Mary had never seen Edmund so animated. "Yes, I have *really*. He is an acquaintance of my uncle, formed when Sir Joseph was arranging a science expedition with the Royal Navy. Nonetheless, I am fudging a bit. I have seldom asked him about plants; we have always spoken entirely upon the topic of China. Sir Joseph was with the Macartney Embassy to China, and he told me that he had carefully collected a veritable *forest* of tea plants in the hope of growing them here at home. Alas that he should have been as unable to produce a tea crop outside of China as everyone else has been! How pleasant it would be to grow one's own tea!"

The Macartney Embassy, led by Lord George Macartney and George Staunton, had traversed to China in 1793 in the hopes of convincing the Quianlong Emperor of China to establish better trade relations between the two nations and to allow the British to establish a permanent embassy in Beijing, and Mary was not the only person to have been fascinated by the reports of that embassy. The British public had been captivated by the exotic orient and the details of the Chinese way of life had continued to fuel the ongoing rage for 'Oriental' or 'Chinoiserie' decorations throughout Europe.

"Are you an amateur sinologist, then?" Edmund asked with an inward chuckle at the idea of a woman being skilled in the natural sciences.

"I am an amateur in name only," Mary told him archly. "I have been fascinated by the Far East ever since I read the accounts of the Macartney Embassy as a schoolgirl, and although it is considered only dabbling, I dabble *ferociously*. Have you read Percy's translation of the Chinese novel *Hau Kiou Choann?*"

Edmund shook his head. "I haven't. I have read Macartney's account, of course, but I have not been more interested than that. I am more fond of botany than the Orient."

"I think you would like this book, regardless of your *inexplicably* tepid feelings toward China." Mary half-jested, her dark eyes sparkled with her keenness on the topic. "Too many people believe the Chinese to be a mysterious race, unfathomable to us. *Hau Kiou Choann* demonstrates that the gulf between the Oriental and ourselves is not large; while the *manners* are different, the underlying *ideals* are the same."

Edmund looked unconvinced, so Mary pressed on.

"Take, as an example, the topics of romantic love and virtue. In many European novels of sensibility, only a strong adherence to principles and morals assures the protagonists of their mutual reward in marriage. In the estimable Mrs Radcliffe's novel, *The Mysteries of Udolpho*, it is only Emily St Aubert's unswerving devotion to her principles that allows her resist all attempts at seduction and provides her eventual happy resolution with her true love, Valancourt. Likewise, in *Hau Kio Choann* a virtuous beauty and a virtuous scholar adhere so firmly to their principles that their enemies are defeated and the couple are eventually allowed to wed. Their virtues of chastity and incorruptibility are not different from our ideals of virtuous behaviour. The Chinese are neither licentious nor immoral, even if they *are* heathen."

Edmund gave her a condescending smile. "I am afraid, Miss Crawford, that you are confusing *worldly* virtues with the *true* virtues of Christianity. The Chinese cannot be both moral and heathens; it is impossible."

"How so?" Mary, looking at Edward's handsome face, hid her annoyance at his words.

"Without faith in Christ, and the spiritual reliance on the Almighty, all principles are inherently shallow." Edmund was almost painfully earnest, hoping to correct Miss Crawford's mistaken belief that there could be morality outside of European religion. "It is not virtue; it is merely the *mimicry* of virtue."

Mary looked thoughtful. Edmund was not the first person in Mary's acquaintance to have this opinion, by far; it was much more commonly held than her own. Nonetheless, it was an opinion which she believed to be pure twaddle. Her urge to contradict Edmund was strong, but by custom and habit she could not tell a gentleman that he was full of malarkey. She must frame her opposition delicately, or not at all.

"So chastity cannot be true chastity and constancy cannot be true constancy in heathens?" Posing questions as a method of disagreeing with a man was a skill women of the gentry learned early and learned well.

"That is correct." Edmund seemed relieved that she was grasping the concept.

"But by that rationale, a Christian who commits the sins of licentious and adultery – but who then repents and is forgiven, wiping away the sin – is more virtuous than a heathen who remains unstained by corruption. I do not see how that is possible." Mary assumed her best 'adorably confused' façade.

"Because faith is the only indicator of the virtue of a person's soul," Edmund explained portentously. "Only our faith is 'the Way, the Truth, and the Life'. We are all of us born into evil, and it is only through our religion that any evil can be removed from us. Anything else is mere window-dressing. While there are some sects of Christianity, like the Catholics, who believe that *works* are as important as *faith*, the Church of England is wiser than that. Just look at the degradation in the rookeries of the Irish in London; all of them idolaters and drunkards because of the false theology of Papists. Or the way Catholic countries such as Italy are so full of corruption and vice. It is one of the many reasons I am so stridently against Catholic Emancipation, which the Whigs perniciously support."

Edmund's gem-like eyes were radiant with his sincerely held bigotry.

Mary had heard or read the same sentiments dozens of times before, almost in those same words, and considered it more of the same common balderdash as the prevailing opinion no morals could be found outside Anglican England. It was as if those espousing those opinions forgot that any corruption and vice existed among the English or the English Church, even if they had been railing about how the country was going to the mischief only a moment before. Their deep and abiding belief that all that was familiar to them — in manner and religion and habit — was inherently superior to the rest of the world amused her even as she scoffed at it. It sounded as if they were children claiming that *their* papa was the tallest, regardless of how tall any other man in the kingdom was, simply because he the tallest in their hearts.

Nonetheless, she could not spurn Edmund as readily as she did the others who irked her with the same nonsense. He was, in her experience, unique; the oddity that he actually *followed* the dictates he expressed regarding his own faith fascinated her. It was delightfully singular. It prevented her from dismissing him as a hypocrite unworthy of her further regard or acquaintance, and made her want to coax him away from his mean opinions.

"Then you do not support the argument, espoused by many learned scholars, that the Chinese belief in a Divine Providence, which they term as 'Heaven', is commensurate with the belief in God? I have read the works of some of the first missionaries to China, including the dissertation *The True Meaning of the Lord of Heaven* by a Jesuit priest named Matteo Ricci, wherein he goes into great detail about the similarities of Confucianism and Christianity. Although you believe the Catholic faith to be misguided in some of their dogma, you would not say that they are not Christians — and therefore unknowledgeable about Christian tenets – would you?"

"I have no doubt," Edmund spoke gravely, "that there is a similarity between Christianity *as it is practised by Papists* and Confucianism. Their customs of worship, of exalting certain persons, of superstition and idolatry, are alike. However, this does not mean that there is any deeper connection between the heathen belief of the Orient and the Gospel. It merely demonstrates the degradation of Popery, rather than raises the value of the Chinese cult."

She was infatuated with Edmund enough that she thought she could soften his prejudices and persuade him to her viewpoint, but Mary was unwilling to bother with further argument at the present. She did not like discourse on profundities when the discussion might degenerate into a quarrel, and thus far the only person she trusted to debate with equanimity was her brother Henry. She had no desire to risk even a mild breech with Edmund Bertram when she still wished to see the grounds of Sotherton in his attentive company. "Well, on this we do not agree, and I am more than willing to discuss all the ins and outs of the topic some evening by the fireplace, when the weather is inclement. Today, however, is a day of pleasure; it is designed for exercise and felicity, not existentialism and philosophy. Shall we walk further along the avenue before returning to Miss Price?"

Edmund agreed, and leapt to his feet to help Mary rise. For a brief moment they were, upon her standing up, less than a hand's breadth apart. Edmund retained her hand in his and became so tense she wondered if he were about to kiss her. She had no objection to Edmund being her first kiss, and therefore did not pull away. Rather to her chagrin Edmund seemed to regain command of himself again and stepped back, a conscious blush overspreading his cheeks. Mary mercifully called his attention to hawk circling the park, and looked at it while he cobbled his composure back together. Then, taking his arm again, they meandered further away from Fanny, and deeper into the shade of the avenue.

ii

Edmund and Mary found Fanny up and looking for them when they returned to the wilderness, and explained to them how Miss Bertram and Mr Crawford had walked on together across the ha-ha, with Miss Julia Bertram and Mr Rushworth in pursuit. In turn, Edmund and Miss Crawford told her they ha seen the avenue, and had very much wished she had been with them, which was very little comfort to Fanny. Afraid of his cousin becoming knocked up even more than she had already endured that day, Edmund convinced Fanny to return with Miss Crawford and himself to the comfort of Rushworth's abode.

Upon the trio reaching the bottom of the steps to the terrace, Mrs Rushworth and Mrs Norris presented themselves at the top, just ready for the wilderness, at the end of an hour and a half from their leaving the house. On this *rencontre* they all returned to the house together, there to lounge away the time as they could with sofas, and chit-chat, and the Tory newspaper Quarterly Reviews, till the return of the others, and the arrival of dinner. It was late before the Miss Bertrams and the two gentlemen came in, and their ramble did not appear to have been more than partially agreeable, or at all productive of anything useful with regard to the object of the day. By their own accounts they had been all walking after each other, and the junction which had taken place at last seemed, to Fanny's observation, to have been as much too late for re-establishing harmony, as it confessedly had been for determining on any alteration. She felt, as she looked at Julia and Mr Rushworth, that hers was not the only dissatisfied bosom amongst them: there was gloom on the face of each. Mr Crawford and Miss Bertram were much more gay, and she thought that he was taking particular pains, during dinner, to do away any little resentment of the other two, and restore general good-humour.

The slight dishevelment of Miss Bertram's hair, and her general air of being mussed, along with her solo walk with Henry, made Mary somewhat suspicious. Her brother, she was aware, was not adverse to his lovemaking passing beyond the verbal, even with unmarried maidens. Mary was well aware that one of Henry's amours, a Miss Talbot, had born her little boy so few months after she had become Mrs Aker as to indicate the child was not a post-marital conception, and that the boy was widely suspected to be Henry's love child.

Mary cornered Henry under the pretence of showing him a porcelain rhinoceros figurine near an alcove and hissed, "Tell me you did not deflower Miss Bertram under a bush in the park! The Grants have to *live* in Mansfield and they don't need to see Robert Aker's half-brother every time they visit the Rushworths."

Henry smiled devilishly. "Do not fret. I would never risk exposure by *visiting Mrs Quimbly* in the open air on her betrothed's estate." Mary's relief was short-lived when Henry winked and continued, "We were in the gazebo."

Mary cut him a sharp glance, which only made him grin more mischievously before he returned his attentions to Julia Bertram, leaving his sister to stew over whether or not he had dallied too intimently with Maria Bertram. Comforting herself with the thought that Henry was surely not so much of an imbecile as to have dishonoured a baronet's daughter outdoors in broad daylight, Mary returned to sit by Fanny Price and Edmund.

Dinner was soon followed by tea and coffee, a ten miles' drive home allowed no waste of hours; and from the time of their sitting down to table, it was a quick succession of busy nothings till the carriage came to the door, and Mrs Norris, having fidgeted about, and obtained a few pheasants' eggs and a cream cheese from the housekeeper, and made abundance of civil speeches to Mrs Rushworth, was ready to lead the way. Mary was very pleased to see her brother approach Julia Bertram and say, "I hope I am not to lose my companion, unless she is afraid of the evening air in so exposed a seat." The request was very graciously received, and Julia's day was likely to end almost as well as it began.

Mary covertly watched Miss Bertram's reaction very carefully, and was relieved to see Maria receive Mr Rushworth's parting attentions as she ought. Mary thought Mr Rushworth was certainly better pleased to hand his fiancée into the barouche than to assist her in ascending the box, and his complacency seemed confirmed by the arrangement.

It was a beautiful evening, mild and still, and the drive was as pleasant as the serenity of Nature could make it; but when Mrs Norris ceased speaking, it was altogether a silent drive to those within. Their spirits were in general exhausted; and to determine whether the day had afforded most pleasure or pain, might occupy the meditations of almost all.

Chapter Twelve

"MR EDMUND BERTRAM seems to be in your thrall, sister dearest. As you pipe, he must dance. What do you mean to do about it?" Henry asked, as he and Mary walked along the banks of the River Nene.

Mary, who never had to hide her pragmatism from her brother, did not bother to pretend she didn't know what Henry was talking about. "Frankly, I don't know. It is strange, because my path should be clear. He is a younger son and is to be *japanned* (of all things!) so I should not even be considering anything except how to avoid a proposal or to decline him with the most civility if I cannot. Yet, I am unsure. I waver. He is so congenial, so handsome, so upright and principled, and so much the gentleman in all his dealings. I had not thought such men existed outside the covers of books."

"Oh, thank you *very* much, Mary!" Henry huffed.

"Don't 'oh Mary' me, you great goat. You are a gentleman to the core and there is no one with more pleasing manners, but your principles are havy-cavy and we both know it. You would never cheat at cards but you would never be constant to a wife. Those are your traits, just as they are for most of the beau monde. Do you say I lie?"

"But your beau would be a Greek at cards and tie himself to your petticoats like Jerry Sneak, would he?" Henry asked snidely. He was in a bit of a pet to be placed lower than Edmund Bertram in his sister's estimation.

Mary gave him an exasperated side-eye. "Don't be absurd. Edmund Bertram would never cheat at cards, and neither would he be henpecked. I am saying that he, unlike almost every other man who exists on this earth, would not take a mistress or ever be less than attentive to his wife."

Henry had his faults, but he was not one to deny the truth. With some reluctance, he admitted he agreed with his sister. "I was speaking to Tom Bertram, before he went away, and he told me his brother had *never* had a mistress, or even an affair, that he knew of. It exceeds even the morality of their father, who has never had a lady of comfort in Town but has at least a mulatto common-law wife on his estate. Although it has to be said that Sir Thomas is apparently even faithful to *her* when he is in Antigua. Edmund Bertram is cut from the same cloth."

"If only he weren't going to be a *man* of the cloth," Mary fretted. "For *me*, to rusticate as a parson's wife in the country! I would be a laughingstock." Her place in society was everything to her. The idea of becoming an object of ridicule, to lose her place as a leader of fashion and conversation among her set, filled her stomach with a cold ball of dread to contemplate.

"Not necessarily," her brother comforted her. "Let Mr Bertram be seen amongst our acquaintance, parade him and let him be seen his handsomeness, his manners, his genteel behaviour, and let be known his Puritan morals; then you'll be acknowledged to have been lucky in a love match and it will be *romantic* rather than *ridiculous*." They walked on a bit further. "Besides, it is not as if you shall be poor or can never enter London in a new gown again. Between your dowry and his tithes you shall easily be able to keep a carriage, and even if you cannot afford a house in Town you both can stay with me during the season."

"You live with the Admiral when you are in Town, and I do not think Mr Bertram could sit down at the table with Mrs Chatsworth and keep his countenance. Even if the Admiral were to make an honest woman of her, it would be too much to ask of a man of Mr Bertram's stamp that he should keep company with her. It would even be too much to ask of *me*, though I am no moralist. A white gown is easily smudged if next to a dirty one; *my* reputation would suffer if I did anything other than spurn her presence like a pestilence."

Henry shrugged. "So you assure me. I cannot keep up with the niceties of it all, particularly when so many married women of the ton have lovers as well. How are they different than Mrs Chatsworth?"

"You would know more than I about married women taking lovers, from all your horn-work," Mary said dryly. "Nonetheless, I can tell you why a discret affair won't ruin a lady's reputation but association with a woman like Mrs Chatsworth would. The difference is, my dear brother, that no decent woman would be taken into a man's protection. It would take a ring, rather than a *carte blanche*, to place her under the same roof as her amour. Moreover, a lady only risks becoming a woman of ill-repute if she takes a lover *before* she has first produced a heir and a spare for her husband and *if* she still shares connubial relations with her lord and master while involved with a lover. Of course, if she is indiscreet enough to get caught and cause a scandal her reputation is tarnished beyond repair even if she had lived as a saint until the day she was found out. As for myself, I intend to follow my aunt's example and never make my husband Acteon."

"Considering that I would shoot the fellow that is for the best."

"That is a bit rich, coming from you."

"You are my sister," Henry explained patiently, "not some piece of muslin to be winked at about in the ton. What is sauce for the gander is *not* sauce for the goose. I will not have you talked of among men as I have heard other ladies talked of."

"Or as you have talked of them?" Mary was arch.

"Or as I have talked of them," Henry agreed, ignoring her archness as adroitly as ever.

Mary took her brother's arm, more pleased than not by his protectiveness, and they walked quietly for a few minutes. A family of swans paddled by, a trail of cygnets stretched between the hen and her cob.

"So many offspring," Mary murmured.

"I beg your pardon, I didn't quite catch that."

"It does not really signify," Mary told him. "It was mostly to myself. I was just looking at the dozen cygnets and wondering what it would be like to have so many."

"Do you *want* so many?" Henry was aghast at the thought of so numerous a family.

Mary gave a very unladylike snort. "Yes, Henry. I *want* to emulate our queen and bear my husband fifteen stalwart babes, including a half dozen of the most useless sons to ever embarrass father. It is to be entirely my *choice* in the matter."

Henry was silent. Although he was always frank with his sister, she was unmarried and not yet aware of the particulars of what occurred between the sexes, or how pregnancy truly came about. Her comment indicating that she thought she was helpless to stop an onslaught of a child every year made him determined to have a courtesan write instructions for preventatives that he could leave anonymously in her room shortly after her wedding. If she married someone like Edmund Bertram, he would probably not use a 'French letter', because condoms were so associated with vice and venereal disease, or because he would feel it was sinful to prevent conception, so Henry could not rely on a future brother-in-law having the sense not to risk Mary's life in childbirth a dozen times. Mary could also not use one that would be noticeable from the odour, like a vinegar and tansy-oil sponge, lest her husband become angry at her desire to prevent conception. He would have Harriet Wilson, who was as good-tempered as she was bold, write the directions for the preventative she used, which he believed to be simply a sponge soaked in olive oil, because it was odourless and the most effective.

Mary broke into Henry's contraceptive reverie, saying, "When I am a mother, I shall take our aunt's friend Mrs Tench as my model. She is an ideal mother, and her advice on children is thought to be of the utmost soundness. Many women in society are encouraging her to write a book about parenting, for the general edification of all."

"Mrs Melesina Trench?" Henry asked. When his sister answered in the affirmative, he mentioned that even he had heard of her and the great regard for her expertise in mothering.

"Yes, she lives at Bursledon in Hampshire, for the most part, but she has many correspondents in society and her letters are often shared among women. She has made me quite determined to suckle my own children, and to spend a prodigious amount of time with them in the nursery. It is then, she says, that the firm bonds are created between a mother and her offspring which will solidify her influence over them for the good. It is important to procure the best, most moral nursemaids, of course, but of the *most* importance is the mother's attendance."

"Are you going to give up society, as other women give up music when they marry?" Henry was sceptical.

"Don't speak nonsense, love. It becomes you ill. No, I shall have time for society in the evenings and for a few hours during the morning. Children need to go to bed very early, you know. It is just that instead of frivolling away my time doing nothing much but looking ornamental, I shall spend a good deal of it with my darlings in the nursery."

"You shall perish from boredom in a fortnight."

"I shan't," Mary was resolute. Her memories of her own dear mama and aunt were too sentimental for her to think of motherhood as anything other than a near-vocation.

"Well, that will please Mr Edmund Bertram, I am sure," Henry couldn't resist saying. "Motherly devotion is an altogether excellent thing for morality and sobriety."

"*If* I were intending to marry Mr Edmund Bertram, then that knowledge would be conducive to my happiness," Mary said with some asperity. "However, since I do *not* intend to marry Mr Edmund Bertram, his opinions on motherhood are moot."

"I thought you were not entirely decided against Mr Bertram," her brother reminded her.

Mary bit her lip. "I do not see how I could accept him. While I approve of Mr Bertram's morality in *general*, in particulars it can be problematic. I have to guard against almost every topic of conversation for worry that I shall shock or disgust him. I broached the topic of the Duke of Cumberland, but had to hastily make reference to his malice against his siblings, because Mr Bertram was clearly about to have an apoplexy over fear I would mention the Sellis murder. Is there to be no scandal I can speak of for the rest of my life? Should I put on blinkers, like carriage horse? How tedious that would be!"

King George's fifth son, the inaptly named Earnest, Duke of Cumberland, was believed by some to have seduced and murdered his valet, Joseph Sellis, while others postulated that Sellis had interrupted Cumberland having sex with his valet Neale, and then Cumberland murdered Sellis to prevent him from revealing the homosexual activity. As motives for murder went, either was suitable because sodomy was punishable by death — not to mention the scandal that would occur if found out for certain — and Cumberland would have been desperate to keep Sellis from talking. Almost no one believed the 'official' version, which was that Sellis attacked Cumberland in a fit of madness and then killed himself by slitting his own throat. If nothing else, it was rendered unbelievable by the fact that the physician who examined Sellis's body said that a left-handed man could *not* have made the cut across his throat, yet Sellis was left-handed. The whole of England speculated upon the Sellis affair ... with the exception of Edmund Bertram and his cousin Fanny Price; one of whom pretended the issue did not exist and the other who was the only creature in the kingdom left unaware of it.

Henry raised an eyebrow. "Bertram attended Oxford; surely he knows about ... that sort of love? It is too common a vice to be missish about. There are Molly-walks and Molly-houses in London that are known to everyone; he cannot be ignorant of it. Why should the Sellis murder cause him such a flutter?"

"Because a delicate young lady should *not* know about that sort of love, is why," Mary made a grimace. "He is nearly delusional about that sort of thing. He would probably have to lie down three days together if he knew that his own sisters had heard so many details of the Sellis murder from their aunt Norris that they could almost instruct *me* about it."

Henry was puzzled. "I do not know why Edmund is so unaccountably tender in such matters. His brother and sisters are normal enough, and as quick with a *double entendre* as any other member of the ton."

"Is constancy and blamelessness in a husband worth losing so much worldly enjoyments?" Mary wondered. "Would it not be as though I had become a Methodist, determined to have no fun at all in case it be sinful?"

"Perhaps he would bend with time?"

"Him? I doubt it. I have never met a more unbendable spirit than Mr Edmund Bertram."

"You are yourself a do-gooder; could you not find a common ground for his high-mindedness there?"

Mary gave her head a shake. "No, he is more determined to live a life of scrupulous respectability than any other concern; that is his religion. Not that he is without heart, mind you; he is liberal enough with those whom he knows the particulars of their situation and deems them worthy of his help. It is just that he fears helping the poor *as a general thing* will simply coddle them and make them lazy, without considering the immorality of allowing a small child working from dawn to dusk in a manufactory in Leeds. I cannot even talk politics; almost all the Whiggish reforms I support would be anathema to him. What common ground do we have? How can we have marital felicity? No," Mary shook her head again, with more determination. "I should better not accept him and I need to stop cavilling about the matter."

"With so much against him, why *do* you cavil?"

"He is just so amiable and handsome!" Mary was almost despairing. "I like him against my reason, and against my will."

"Well, his brother will return in a few weeks. He is an amiable and handsome fellow, too. Perhaps he will cure you," Henry comforted. "It is not as though you will be an old maid, dearest. You are too pretty and have too much of a dowry for that to be a risk. You need only worry about whom you shall choose."

"Would you recommend one of your intimate friends, then?" Mary looked over the river to hide her smile.

"Gracious God, no! None of them are worthy to be your shoe-leather," Henry was severe.

Mary laughed. "Then my choices are a bit more restricted than you realised, aren't they?"

The siblings walked on companionably, one another's best friend and confidant. London had taught them early that they could truly trust no one but each other, and it had cemented the closeness that had formed in their infancy.

"It *is* pretty to walk in the countryside," Mary said after a while, "and I like very much being free of stench, but I think I still like Town best."

"There is certainly more to entertain one there," Henry concurred. "Do you know what I miss the most about London?" When Mary gave him an inquiring look, he continued. "The gaslights at dusk. I love the look of the bright dots along the streets. It looks as though we have captured stars to do our service."

"There are real stars to be seen here," Mary pointed out. "Oodles of them."

Henry nodded. "True, but I cannot command them. They will not do a human's bidding and light my way to the theatre at ten o'clock."

"Edmund Bertram can name almost every star, and all the constellations I would warrant." She frowned. "Blast. Why does he intrude on my thoughts so? I cannot possibly be so foolish, such a sapscull, as to cut up my peace over a gluepot! To wear the willow over a cushion thumper! It cannot be; I shan't allow it."

"If he weren't to be a Jack-in-a-Pinch, would you accept him then?" Henry wanted to know.

"How could I, after all the differences in opinion and character that I have enumerated? No, I need to put him out of my mind, and reminding myself that he is to be a clergyman is the most economical way of doing it."

A large fish jumped in the river, snatching an insect snack and flopping back into the water with a plunk and a splash.

"We should have our tackle," Henry comment. "That was a monster."

"There must be a great many of his brethren down there, yet it looks so still on the surface," Mary mused. "Do you ever feel that Mansfield village is the same? That there is a great deal going on that we aren't privy to?"

"Perhaps, but it probably signifies as much to us as do the concerns of the fish. Less, in fact, because at least the fish we would wish to catch and eat for dinner. What is it to us who marries who, and who among the riff-raff is the least vulgar?"

"I don't know, Henry. I am in a thoughtful, odd mood today. It is not quite a brown study, but I am not myself. I cannot help but feel something of import is coming; something that I cannot quite make out."

"Been to a gypsy fortune-teller then? Did she lay out your cards and warn you that unless you buried gold under a certain tree you would have ill-luck?" Henry quizzed with a grin.

"Pish-tosh," Mary replied with an answering smile. "It is nothing so silly. It is merely a queer feeling, as they say, in my waters."

"It is probably no more than an oncoming thunderstorm," Henry soothed. "It will bring nothing worse than a break from this wretched heat."

"You are right, I am sure."

The walked on companionably, until Henry thought of something to cheer his sister. "I say, Mary, did I tell you I got a letter from my friend Mr Honeycutt today?"

"No, you didn't. Was there anything of interest in it?"

"It depends," Henry said with a sly smile. "Are you at all interested in Lord Byron's affair with Lady Caroline Lamb?"

The effect on his sister was as Henry had hoped; electrifying.

"Oh, tell me! Do not tease! Have they eloped? Is there are terrible scandal?"

"Peace! Peace, and I'll tell you," Henry was laughing at his sister's animation. "I swear Mary, I have seen hounds less aquiver during a hunt."

"Leaving aside that you just compared me to hound, if you do not tell me your news I shall push you in the river and see what *that* does to your boots!" Mary was trying to look fierce, but spoiled the effect by giggling.

"Spare my boots, if you please," Henry begged. "What should have happened but that Byron and Lady Lamb have had a rupture? A complete breach."

Mary was flabbergasted. "How can this be? Their affair — it was so immoderate! so hot! How can it be over so soon? Can Mr Honeycutt not be mistaken?"

"That is unlikely, since Honeycutt got it from Hobhouse himself," Henry replied.

Considering the John Hobhouse was Byron's dearest friend and confident, Mary was forced to admit that the information was probably accurate.

"But how did it all come about? Was Byron driven to yet another jealous rage by her affection for her husband? Did he become someone else's lover? Did it end with a sigh or a cry?"

"Your avidity amuses me, sister. I wish I had half your energy! But have done with your entreaties; I'll tell you all I know. According to Honeycutt, on the last Wednesday of July Hobhouse and Byron were to leave London for Harrow to the express purpose of escaping Lady Lamb, who had grown too persistent and open in her affections for Byron's comfort. However, before they could affect their hegira, Lady Lamb showed up at No. 8 St James Street, without an escort or even her maid, and demanded an entrance."

"No!" Mary was actually shocked. To do such a thing was an unforgivable action in a well-born lady. She could not imagine love for anyone driving her to such a rash and foolish act as visiting a man's home unattended.

"Yes. Moreover, she was 'disguised' as a *page*."

"She never!"

"She did, indeed. Upon my honour, that's what Honeycutt wrote to me that she did. Breeches, jacket, boots, and all. You could, Hobhouse told Honeycutt, clearly see every inch of her lower limbs and the cleft of her buttocks." Henry felt free to tell his sister this detail, and bravely mention anatomy, because they were still fortunately decades away from the Victorian uber-modesty which would deny that women, chairs, and pianos possessed legs. "Even with her hair cut into such a close crop, there was no mistaking her as anything but a woman."

Mary was enthralled by the scandal. "Good God," she gasped, "what did Byron *do*?"

"Well, he couldn't just throw her out into the street, now could he? She was a *lady*, even if she was dressed as a boy. Honeycutt is given to understand a *crowd* was gathering. Moreover, Hobhouse was petrified that Lady Lamb would demand an elopement, and then what could Byron do but comply? When the poor devil tried to tell her that an elopement was infeasible, she grabbed a knife and threatened to commit self-murder. Byron – if Honeycutt can be believed, which I think he might inasmuch as he is an honest fellow – had to restrain Lady Lamb as if she were a madwoman."

Mary nearly shrieked. What horrid novel could have such a dramatic turn of events? She had seen Lady Lamb at Almack's, and could easily envision that slender, pale figure clasping a knife and threatening to end it all for love. In her mind's eye she saw Byron, dashing and somehow windswept even in a windless room, rush to his lover and prevent her from making the fatal wound. Oh! What she would have given to be a fly on the wall!

Henry was enjoying revealing the scandal as much as Mary was enjoying hearing it. "Finally, after a dint of persuasion from both Byron and Hobhouse — all that they could do in fact — Lady Lamb was willing to don a servant's dress and bonnet and let Hobhouse take her to a third party's home. Byron had to promise to come to her again rather than leave London, though, for her to agree to leave. It was in every way a fracas."

"How could you have waited all morning to tell me of this?" Mary demanded.

Henry shrugged. "I was going to tell you immediately, but you were out with Mrs Grant and by the time you returned to the parsonage my mind was filled with other thoughts. You know my brain cannot rest; it must be doing something. But I have not yet told you all my news, Mary."

"There's *more*?" Her voice was nearly ecstatic.

"What I have to tell you is so scandalous that I am not sure I should even breathe a word of it."

"I will beat you to death with my reticule if you do *not*."

"Under such a threat I have no choice but to comply," Henry sighed dramatically. "Lady Lamb sent Byron a letter."

"That's it? A letter?"

"Not quite. Within the letter was a lover's token," Henry paused.

"Well, go on!"

"It was a lock of hair."

"A lock of hair? That's all? Why should that be so scandalous that I couldn't hear it?" Mary was perplexed.

"It was a lock of hair of a most … *personal* … nature, dear sister. A very *private* lock of hair, if you will," Henry smirked.

Mary was rendered absolutely speechless, and gaped at her brother like a very pretty fish. Finally, she spoke, "Can this be true?"

"I've always found Honeycutt a reliable source," Henry said.

"Is that all?"

"Isn't that *enough?*"

Mary made an exasperated sound. "You know well what I meant."

"One final bit of news then. Lady Lamb has gone to Ireland with her husband. It is said that Byron himself ordered her to go. They are over forever," Henry ended his tale with a flourish.

His sister's bright eyes gleamed. "What a delightful débâcle. The Ton will feast on this for *months.*"

"Just don't tell Mr Bertram," Henry reminded her. "He'd faint if he knew half of the tale, and develop a brain-fever if he thought you knew a tenth of it."

Chapter Thirteen

A FEW DAYS after the fraught trip to Sotherton, Miss Crawford, on walking up with her brother to spend the evening at Mansfield Park, heard the good news that Sir Thomas was to return from Antigua in a few months; and though seeming to have no concern in the affair beyond politeness, and to have vented all her feelings in a quiet congratulation, heard it with an attention not so easily satisfied. Mrs Norris gave the particulars of the letters, and the subject was dropt; but after tea, as Miss Crawford was standing at an open window with Edmund and Fanny looking out on a twilight scene, while the Miss Bertrams, Mr Rushworth, and Henry Crawford were all busy with candles at the pianoforte, she suddenly revived it by turning round towards the group, and saying, "How happy Mr Rushworth looks! He is thinking of November."

Edmund looked round at Mr Rushworth too, but had nothing to say.

Mary could not help but notice his silence, and commented, "Your father's return will be a very interesting event."

"It will, indeed, after such an absence; an absence not only long, but including so many dangers."

"It will be the forerunner also of other interesting events: your sister's marriage, and your taking orders."

"Yes."

"Don't be affronted," said she, laughing, "but it does put me in mind of some of the old heathen heroes, who, after performing great exploits in a foreign land, offered sacrifices to the gods on their safe return."

"There is no sacrifice in the case," replied Edmund, with a serious smile, and glancing at the pianoforte again; "it is entirely her own doing."

Mary gave a careless wave. "Oh yes I know it is. I was merely joking. She has done no more than what every young woman would do; and I have no doubt of her being extremely happy. My other sacrifice, of course, you do not understand."

"My taking orders, I assure you, is quite as voluntary as Maria's marrying."

And as self-destructively certain to make you unhappy, was Mary's private thought. Aloud, she said, "It is fortunate that your inclination and your father's convenience should accord so well. There is a very good living kept for you, I understand, hereabouts."

"Which you suppose has biased me?"

"But *that* I am sure it has not," cried Fanny.

Mary and Edmund smiled indulgently at Fanny's quick defence of her cousin.

"Thank you for your good word, Fanny, but it is more than I would affirm myself. On the contrary, the knowing that there was such a provision for me probably did bias me. Nor can I think it wrong that it should. There was no natural disinclination to be overcome, and I see no reason why a man should make a worse clergyman for knowing that he will have a competence early in life. I was in safe hands. I hope I should not have been influenced myself in a wrong way, and I am sure my father was too conscientious to have allowed it. I have no doubt that I was biased, but I think it was blamelessly."

"It is the same sort of thing," said Fanny, after a short pause, "as for the son of an admiral to go into the navy, or the son of a general to be in the army, and nobody sees anything wrong in that. Nobody wonders that they should prefer the line where their friends can serve them best, or suspects them to be less in earnest in it than they appear."

"No, my dear Miss Price, and for reasons good. The profession, either navy or army, is its own justification. It has everything in its favour: heroism, danger, bustle, fashion. Soldiers and sailors are always acceptable in society. Nobody can wonder that men are soldiers and sailors."

"But the motives of a man who takes orders with the certainty of preferment may be fairly suspected, you think?" said Edmund. "To be justified in your eyes, he must do it in the most complete uncertainty of any provision."

Mary made a playfully aghast face, but it reflected the truth as much as it concealed her seriousness. "What! take orders without a living! No; that is madness indeed; absolute madness."

"Shall I ask you how the church is to be filled, if a man is neither to take orders with a living nor without? No; for you certainly would not know what to say. But I must beg some advantage to the clergyman from your own argument. As he cannot be influenced by those feelings which you rank highly as temptation and reward to the soldier and sailor in their choice of a profession, as heroism, and noise, and fashion, are all against him, he ought to be less liable to the suspicion of wanting sincerity or good intentions in the choice of his."

"Oh! no doubt he is very sincere in preferring an income ready made, to the trouble of working for one; and has the best intentions of doing nothing all the rest of his days but eat, drink, and grow fat." Mary did an admirable job of keeping her voice light enough to obscure the true disdain in her words. "It is indolence, Mr Bertram, indeed. Indolence and love of ease; a want of all laudable ambition, of taste for good company, or of inclination to take the trouble of being agreeable, which make men clergymen. A clergyman has nothing to do but be slovenly and selfish – read the newspaper, watch the weather, and quarrel with his wife. His curate does all the work, and the business of his own life is to dine."

"There are such clergymen, no doubt, but I think they are not so common as to justify Miss Crawford in esteeming it their general character. I suspect that in this comprehensive and (may I say) commonplace censure, you are not judging from yourself, but from prejudiced persons, whose opinions you have been in the habit of hearing. It is impossible that your own observation can have given you much knowledge of the clergy. You can have been personally acquainted with very few of a set of men you condemn so conclusively. You are speaking what you have been told at your uncle's table."

Edmund's pompous assumptions that he knew what influenced her thoughts more accurately than she did herself began to grate on Mary's nerves. "I speak what appears to me the general opinion; and where an opinion is general, it is usually correct. Though *I* have not seen much of the domestic lives of clergymen, it is seen by too many to leave any deficiency of information."

"Where any one body of educated men, of whatever denomination, are condemned indiscriminately, there must be a deficiency of information, or (smiling) of something else. Your uncle, and his brother admirals, perhaps knew little of clergymen beyond the chaplains whom, good or bad, they were always wishing away."

"Poor William! He has met with great kindness from the chaplain of the Antwerp," was a tender apostrophe of Fanny's, very much to the purpose of her own feelings if not of the conversation. However, she might as well have held her tongue for all the attention Edmund and Miss Crawford gave her.

"I have been so little addicted to take my opinions from my uncle," said Miss Crawford, "that I can hardly suppose – and since you push me so hard, I must observe, that I am not entirely without the means of seeing what clergymen are, being at this present time the guest of my own brother, Dr Grant. And though Dr Grant is most kind and obliging to me, and though he is really a gentleman, and, I dare say, a good scholar and clever, and often preaches good sermons, and is very respectable, *I* see him to be an indolent, selfish *bon vivant,* who must have his palate consulted in everything; who will not stir a finger for the convenience of any one; and who, moreover, if the cook makes a blunder, is out of humour with his excellent wife. To own the truth, Henry and I were partly driven out this very evening by a disappointment about a green goose, which he could not get the better of. My poor sister was forced to stay and bear it."

Mary was displeased with both Edmund and herself; at him for baiting her and at herself for being baited into revealing more of the Grants' dirty laundry than she customarily aired in public.

She was mollified a little when Edmund exclaimed, "I do not wonder at your disapprobation, upon my word. It is a great defect of temper, made worse by a very faulty habit of self-indulgence; and to see your sister suffering from it must be exceedingly painful to such feelings as yours. Fanny, it goes against us. We cannot attempt to defend Dr Grant."

"No," replied Fanny, "but we need not give up his profession for all that; because, whatever profession Dr Grant had chosen, he would have taken a – not a good temper into it; and as he must, either in the navy or army, have had a great many more people under his command than he has now, I think more would have been made unhappy by him as a sailor or soldier than as a clergyman. Besides, I cannot but suppose that whatever there may be to wish otherwise in Dr Grant would have been in a greater danger of becoming worse in a more active and worldly profession, where he would have had less time and obligation – where he might have escaped that knowledge of himself, the *frequency*, at least, of that knowledge which it is impossible he should escape as he is now. A man – a sensible man like Dr Grant, cannot be in the habit of teaching others their duty every week, cannot go to church twice every Sunday, and preach such very good sermons in so good a manner as he does, without being the better for it himself. It must make him think; and I have no doubt that he oftener endeavours to restrain himself than he would if he had been anything but a clergyman."

Mary smiled at Miss Price's sweetly naive perspective. "We cannot prove to the contrary, to be sure; but I wish you a better fate, Miss Price, than to be the wife of a man whose amiableness depends upon his own sermons; for though he may preach himself into a good-humour every Sunday, it will be bad enough to have him quarrelling about green geese from Monday morning till Saturday night."

"I think the man who could often quarrel with Fanny," said Edmund affectionately, "must be beyond the reach of any sermons."

Fanny turned farther into the window; and Miss Crawford had only time to say, in a pleasant manner, "I fancy Miss Price has been more used to deserve praise than to hear it"; when, being earnestly invited by the Miss Bertrams to join in a glee, she tripped off to the instrument, leaving Edmund looking after her in an ecstasy of admiration of all her many virtues, from her obliging manners down to her light and graceful tread.

Mary had the satisfaction of watching Edmund inch ever nearer to her during the glee, almost as if he were unable to help himself, and to be urgently entreated by him to sing again.

ǁ

"Did you suffer overmuch from our absence?" Mary asked her sister the next morning after breakfast, as they walked together toward town to visit the circulating library.

"No, not at all, for once you and Henry were gone, Dr Grant could tell me what was really bothering him so much. It is his way to seem discontent over a small thing, like a green goose, when a larger problem is on his mind. Once I have coaxed him to tell me the true topic of his perturbation, his mood improves vastly. If anything, he was more pleasant to me last evening than usual as an apology for his shortness of temper beforehand."

Mary was surprised and confessed herself to be so. "I believed Dr Grant's vexation to be entire because of the goose; I have wronged him. Why would he not say what was truly upsetting him? Why would he suffer us to think he was piqued enough to grumble in the gizzard over such a trivial matter?"

Mrs Grant shrugged. "Who knows? I suspect it is because he tries to hide his feelings from himself, and that curdles his temper, but I cannot swear to it. I doubt if Dr Grant himself knows. We all have a strange kidney and quirk about us, when it comes to it."

"What, if I may ask, was provoking my good brother's spleen?"

Mrs Grant hesitated. "I am not sure if I should tell you. It is a shocking thing, and unfit for delicate ears."

"Come now," Mary said, "am I not a woman of sense? I am not such a squeamish tib of the buttery that I must hear nothing but bluebirds singing. If I faint, I have my vinegar in my reticule; feel free to use it to revive me."

"All right then," her sister agreed, amused by Mary's bravura, "but if your ears are singed you must not complain. Yesterday Dr Grant was called upon to perform a forced marriage and it was very disagreeable to him. The bride was Nan Horne, the daughter of a local alewife. The girl is very young, not quite fourteen years of age, but needed to be wed because she was with child and very near to her confinement, and the child must not be left to burden on the parish. The father of the babe had been taken into custody the day prior, and was behaving very unbecoming about his obligations to her. Mrs Horne was in floods of tears, as was poor little Nan, and upon talking to them in private, Dr Grant discovered that the seduction had been forced upon Nan and she was loathe to marry the man. What was he to do? The babe must have upkeep, but to wed such a villain to Nan Horne seemed like a blasphemy. Dr Grant demanded that they hold the man, a local tanner by the name of George Wragge, in custody one more night so that he could see what could be done in consultation with the magistrate. The magistrate saw no reason why Nan Horne should not be wed, forced seduction or not. That is why Dr Grant was in such ill temper last night."

"That would be irksome indeed, and try the temper of a saint. I pity Dr Grant! Did he have to marry them this morning, then?" Mary thought of poor little Nan Horne being forced to be the wife of a tanner brute and shuddered.

"I am thankful to report that he did *not*. He went very early this morning to see Mr Edmund Bertram and explain the situation to him. Mr Bertram, whose influence is not small, persuaded the magistrate that George Wragge should be forced to pay upkeep for

Nan's babe, but not be required to marry her. Furthermore, Wragge has been warned that if he should go near her again, or attempt to claim the infant as his own, then he will be publicly whipped and put in the stocks."

"Oh what good news! How glad I am that Dr Grant and Mr Bertram found a solution," Mary exclaimed.

"Yes, it could only be done with Mr Bertram's help," Mrs Grant gave her sister a knowing look. "One must think of Mr Edmund Bertram with admiration, do you not agree?"

"Of course Mr Bertram is admirable; I greatly esteem him," She spoke firmly. "I cannot say enough good things of his character, but that does *not* make me his admirer."

Mrs Grant was placid. "I am sure."

"I am sincere, ma'am."

"I did not say you were not, dear."

"I hear doubt in your tone, sister."

"How so? How can you hear doubt where there is none?"

They walked together quietly for a few paces, and then Mary said, "He *is* something of a Galahad, isn't he?"

"If Mr Bertram were to be compared to any knight errant, that is the very one I would settle on," Mrs Grant agreed.

The sisters walked on quietly for a few more steps, before Mary burst out, "This is *most* irksome!"

"What is dear?" Her elder sister asked as if she did not already know.

"Mr Edmund Bertram is too often in my head. I feel myself to be in some danger. Yet he is not at all suitable to me! His opinions are far different from my own, his pursuits, his habits, his pleasures — all the opposite of mine! He is the Country Mouse, and I am the City Mouse. While such dispairity might be put in abayence for a short while, I do not see how such mismatched mice can *live* together. It is folly to contemplate. Even if he is a Galahad, I am not the Holy Grail; it would be better if he does not quest for *me*."

Mary knew that her sister would phoo-phoo away any concerns about his status as a younger brother, and she could not mention her abhorrence for marrying a clergyman without offending Mrs Grant (who had chosen to do so); therefore she restricted her concerns about Edmund to the not inconsiderable differences in their tempers and preferred mode of living. Even if Edmund had been Sir Thomas's eldest son, the dissimularity between them would have given her pause to accept his suit.

"My dear sister, you worry unnecessarily," Mrs Grant looped her arm through Mary's. "You do not take into account that Mr Bertram is a *gentleman*. You have not seen his father's conduct toward Lady Bertram, which must be Mr Bertram's model of marital behavoir. Lady Bertram does not need to ever raise her voice; her words are attended to, her needs are considered. If you should desire to spend even so much as half the year in London, I am sure a truly amiable husband would not prevent it. He might not be able to stay in Town so long himself, but there is no reason why he would forbid you to visit your friends and relations. Although, to be sure, you may find yourself not wishing to be apart from him. London, with all its pleasures, may not atone for the pains of separation. You may find yourself more content to be a Country Mouse than you would think."

Mary shuddered with half-serious fear. "What? I should think the high point of my day should be how many eggs my hens have laid, or how yellow is my butter? No, I think one must be bred and reared as a Country Mouse before those pleasures are more estimable than outings to Covent Garden or Vauxhall. I am too much of the cosmopolitan to change."

"When one is happily married," Mrs Grant suggested, "eggs and butter gain more pleasure than one can think of when one is still a City Mouse with no husband to bring her joy."

"Oh, dear Mrs Grant. It is much more than just my city habits. I am so unlike you. Your sweetness of temper is matched with a calmness that is *formed* for happiness in domestic tranquillity. *You* do not long to hear political chatter chitter. You are the ideal parson's wife. Your concerns are all for those around you, and you do not shirk the poorest or the most vulgar cottager. I look at them with disgust, and wish only to avoid their presence. How, then, could I be a fitting wife for a clergyman?"

Mrs Grant was shocked. "Mary! How can you say such things about yourself! I know of your great liberality to charitable institutions. I am aware of how many pounds you outlay for the provision of the destitute. You speak nonsense."

"I regret to inform you that I am speaking the truth." Mary was many things, but delusional about her own character she was not. "I like my charity distant. I do not wish to go among the ignorant and unwashed, seeing to their needs and delivering them from their wants. No, for me to organise a charity social, or art exhibit, or ball, or musical concert is all I wish to do. I do it *well*. I often raise large sums for the aid of the indigent. I and three particular friends hosted a ball that raised nearly five hundred pounds for the Foundling Hospital. Yet I do not *myself* perform acts of charity. I funnel the monies into worthy hands, like yours; people who are willing to come face to face with the lowest orders. I would very much like to see all the poor relieved, but have no wish to actually *see* them at any time."

"Then why do you walk with me so often?" Her sister was confused.

"For three reasons. First, I find such pleasure in your company that any activity with you is congenial. Secondly, the poverty here is not dire. Here are not the backstreets of London filled with hungry, dirty, hollow-eyed children and their beggared parents. Here are not the tiny children working in the factories, half-starved and full-wearied. If I should see them Oh! how they tear at my heart! But I do not wish to run to them and give them succour. They make me want to rush to give someone *else* direction and funds to alleviate them, and then rush to find entertainment that will purge their images from my mind. I would feed them all if I could, just do not make me *look* upon them until they are well-fleshed. And for the third, you shield me from it so that I am always a degree separated. I need but stand in the lane and wait while you comfort and supply eatables to those who have neither friends nor food. There is no hardship *there*. It pains me to make you see me as I am, but I cannot pretend to have that likeness to an angel which romantic heroines possess. It is not only my feet that are made of clay; I fear that I am earthenware to my *neck*."

Mrs Grant stopped and embraced her sister. "Dearest Mary, do you think I was always so sanguine when I was first a parson's wife? Do you think I had not the same fears or worries? No one who is capable of sensibility can look upon want unmoved, but many who are moved by it wish to be removed from it by the farthest degree possible. You are not alone. And I would wager that you would find, as I did, that the act of comforting begins to make your feelings less *intense* because they can be relieved by *action*."

Mary's face was full of doubt, but she didn't want to contradict her sister. Let Mrs Grant think her better than she was; it flattered even if it did not reassure.

"You do not believe me?" Mrs Grant began to walk again, and Mary fell in alongside her.

"You have never told me a falsehood," Mary hedged.

"I could set you up a fine example in Miss Price. The sweet little thing is a watering pot, and her heart is softer than a rabbit's fur, yet she ministers to the poor as Lady Bertram's deputy. If someone as extremely tender as Fanny Price can manage, how can you fail?"

"Miss Price cannot be *my* model," Mary protested. "You might as well compare a sparrow to a hawk, or milk to brandy."

"Then put yourself to the proof, dearest. Tomorrow, I shall be going to the most meagre cottages in the village and instead of waiting in the lane, you can come in with me. You can hand out a bundle or two, and a few groats. You can see and feel the good it does, so that you can know your own capabilities better." Mrs Grant could not believe her sister was unable to dispense charity as well as pay for it.

"I would much better like to give a musicale for the cause," Mary could not resist a little jest. Her lively nature could not be confined to seriousness for very long.

"That can be done later," Mrs Grant smiled at her.

Mary sighed. "Even if you cure me of my revulsion for going among the poor, how will you bring me into harmony with Mr Bertram in politics?" She became playful. "No, if I am to learn to overcome my bad habits and frailties, he can too. He shall just have to become a Whig."

Mrs Grant chuckled at the idea. "Mr Bertram? Dearest, he is a Tory to the soles of his boots."

"Then he can take them off and find himself a new cobbler," Mary quipped. "I think it can be done. Mr Bertram is truly affable and truly interested in helping the poor. How can I not introduce him to Lord Byron's first parliamentary speech without stirring his conscience? Byron's speech on the Luddites and the wretched poor was sublime! I cut a copy of it from a paper and pasted it in my album, so that I can read it whenever I wish and have leisure. Who can forget his rebuke against the hard-hearted villainy of the Lords who would condemn them! Who can forget his defence of the oppressed! 'These men were willing to dig, but the spade was in other hands; they were not ashamed to beg, but there was none to relieve them. Their own means of subsistence were cut off; all other employments pre-occupied; and their excesses, however to be deplored and condemned, can hardly be the subject of surprise.' I cannot praise Lord Byron's good feelings enough."

"Yes, and after Mr Bertram becomes a Whig, I shall have my flying pig wing a pamphlet with an ode to him and Byron all over the county," Mrs Grant snorted.

Mary dimpled at her sister. "The same pig can deliver the invitations to the wedding breakfast."

Chapter Fourteen

THE APPROACH OF September brought tidings of Mr Bertram, first in a letter to the gamekeeper and then in a letter to Edmund; and by the end of August he arrived himself, to be gay, agreeable, and gallant again as occasion served, or Miss Crawford demanded; to tell of races and Weymouth, and parties and friends, to which she might have listened six weeks before with some interest, and altogether to give her the fullest conviction, by the power of actual comparison, of her preferring his younger brother.

It was very vexatious, and she was heartily sorry for it; but so it was; and so far from now meaning to marry the elder, she did not even want to attract him beyond what the simplest claims of conscious beauty required: his lengthened absence from Mansfield, without anything but pleasure in view, and his own will to consult, made it perfectly clear that he did not care about her; and his indifference was so much more than equalled by her own, that were he now to step forth the owner of Mansfield Park, the Sir Thomas complete, which he was to be in time, she did not believe she could accept him.

Although she could not accept Mr Bertram while preferring his brother, she had no intention of changing her name to Bertram for Edmund's sake either. Yes, Edmund was handsome and she had a pash for him – but that was a far cry from considering matrimony. She saw her potential danger, but was as sure as her brother that she could not *really* come to harm because of a flirtation. She was unwilling to give up the enjoyment of being wooed by a handsome man just yet. She would remove herself from Edmund Bertram's sphere later, when she tired of his attentions.

The knowledge that her intention to risk her happiness in order that she could continue to enjoy the addresses of an agreeable man was not so very different (barring only an intended husband) than the practices of Maria Bertram, whose behaviour she most heartily jeered at in the privacy of her own thoughts, eluded Mary. Although Mary was good about eschewing hypocrisy whenever she detected it in herself, she was as blind to her own follies as anyone else could be when folly was also a pleasure. Just as Maria's vanity was so deeply embedded in her makeup that she could not recognize it in herself, Mary's self-centeredness was so much a part of her habits that she could not recognize it as a species of selfishness akin to her brother's.

As for Mary's brother, the season and duties which brought Mr Bertram back to Mansfield took Mr Crawford into Norfolk. Everingham could not do without him in the beginning of September. He went for a fortnight – a fortnight of such dullness to the Miss Bertrams as ought to have put them both on their guard, and made even Julia admit, in her jealousy of her sister, the absolute necessity of distrusting his attentions, and wishing him not to return; and a fortnight of sufficient leisure, in the intervals of shooting and sleeping, to have convinced the gentleman that he ought to keep longer away, had he been more in the habit of examining his own motives, and of reflecting to what the indulgence of his idle vanity was tending; but, thoughtless and selfish from prosperity and bad example, he would not look beyond the present moment. The sisters, handsome, clever, and encouraging, were an amusement to his sated mind; and finding nothing in Norfolk to equal the social pleasures of Mansfield, he gladly returned to it at the time appointed, and was welcomed thither quite as gladly by those whom he came to trifle with further. Every thing returned into the same channel as before his absence; his manners being to each so animated and agreeable, as to lose no ground with either, and just stopping short of the consistence, the steadiness, the solicitude, and the warmth which might excite general notice.

It was not only the Bertram sisters who were glad to see Henry return on the 10th, as he had promised; Tom and Edmund were equally happy to welcome him. Henry was a gentleman of wit, and a genial companion. Furthermore, he was a good shot, and a pleasure to hunt with. Partridge season had opened on the first day of the month, and the gentlemen were all very keen for the sport. The Bertram brothers had always enjoyed fowling with each other, and enjoyed it still, but they found that the pithy comments and bon mots of Henry Crawford made a morning's hunt more amusing by far.

The second week of September brought another visitor to Mansfield park; a new intimate friend of Tom Bertram's, the Honourable John Yates. This new friend had not much to recommend him beyond habits of fashion and expense, and being the younger son of a lord with a tolerable independence. Mr Bertram's acquaintance with him had begun at Weymouth, where they had spent ten days together in the same society, and the friendship, if friendship it might be called, had been proved and perfected by Mr Yates's being invited to take Mansfield in his way, whenever he could, and by his promising to come; and he did come rather earlier than had been expected, in consequence of the sudden breaking-up of a large party assembled for gaiety at the house of another friend, which he had left Weymouth to join.

Tom Bertram was happy to have him at the Park, since the addition of young people helped relieve the tedium of spending quiet evenings in the country. Maria and Julia had no misgivings about his arrival either, since he made it very clear he admired them both exceedingly. He was not Henry Crawford, with that beau's abilities to charm and beguile, but he had enough rank and personal attractions to make his addresses flattering to them. Yates was also a good excuse for an impromptu dance. It had been thought of only that afternoon, built on the late acquisition of a violin player in the servants' hall, and the possibility of raising five couple with the help of Mrs Grant.

Mary and Henry Crawford, were very glad of it, for it offered each of them an opportunity to flirt with their object; Mary with the object of her growing affection, and Henry with the objects of his growing vanity.

Edmund, aware that it was Fanny's first chance to dance in any kind of public setting, very properly stood up with her for the first two dances. A significant look in Henry's direction by Mary also secured Miss Price a partner for the third and fourth dance, when Miss Crawford became Edmund's partner. Mary did not think often of Fanny Price, but when she was reminded of her, the girl's situation always inspired some such kindness on Mary's part.

"Your sister seems out of spirits this evening, Mr Bertram," Mary commented, looking at Maria, who was dancing with Mr Tom Oliver from Stoke with a decided want of sparkle.

"Yes, but not so much as you might suppose. Maria has never been lively *in general*. She is not possessed of strong feelings or a desire to stand out in company."

Mary, disagreeing with Edmund in every particular about his sister, changed the subject. "Did you hear that your favourite poet, Southey, has been working on a biography of Lord Nelson, which he hopes to have in print by next summer?"

"I think it goes too far to call him my *favourite* poet, though I do enjoy reading him, but I had not heard of his writing about Lord Nelson. I look forward to reading it, when it is published. Will your disdain for Southey's poetry extend to his prose?" Edmund took her hand as part of the dance, and he trembled a little at the contact.

"I will admit freely that I plan to read his biography of Nelson as soon as I can get a copy." Mary turned gracefully, as sprightly in dance as she was on horseback. "I expect all of England will feel the same, and have resigned myself to a disappointingly long wait before I have it. When a book is popular, it can be monstrously difficult to come by. When Mrs Edgeworth's novel *The Absentee* came out I could not get my hands on the first volume for almost three months. There is a book of German ghost stories entitled *Fantasmagoriana* that I am wild to read, but I have had to send to London for a copy of it because the circulating library here will not have it until after Christmas, perhaps not even until Candlemas."

Edmund smiled, charmed by her enthusiasm even as he inwardly derided her choice of reading material. "It is only biography that appeals to you, or do you like reading history as a general thing?"

"I do not read history in the common way," Mary looked up at him through her thick lashes, "but I shall make an exception for Nelson. Who does not want to know more about the Hero of Trafalgar?"

"You were but a child when Trafalgar was fought. Did it leave an impression on you then, or only later when you could think upon it with a more developed mind?"

"When *I* was but a child?" Mary was amused at his wording. "And were you a man grown, a veritable elder, in '05?"

Edmund smiled. "I was not full-grown, but neither was I a child. I had just gone down to Oxford, and remember well the stir the victory and Nelson's death caused. *You*, however, would have been a child under the care of your governess. Had you gone to London yet?"

"I had moved there to live with my aunt just a fortnight before Trafalgar. My uncle became an Admiral as a result of his action in that battle and was still at sea, so we were solely the property of my aunt then. To be frank, I was caught up too much in the drama of my own loss to notice a national one. When everyone in Town seemed to be mourning, I childishly though they were also grieving my parents."

"It must have been a grievous loss for you."

"Yes, but it is an old one, and we should not let it dampen our pleasure in the dance. Do you like to read history in particular?" Mary's hand looked very small in Edmund's large one, and she realised anew how tall he was. She wished he was not so strikingly handsome. If he were plain, or even *less* handsome, then perhaps she would not have developed such an aggravating preference for him.

"I do. There is something about history that fascinates me, and soothes my mind when I read it. It is even more delightful to me when it is about a figure I can so fully admire, such as Lord Nelson," Edmund paused a moment, then said, "Nelson was the son of a parson, yet he rose to distinction."

"He rose to distinction because he joined His Majesty's navy, rather than taking orders like his father," Mary rejoined.

"Is there nothing good about being a parson, then?" Edmund asked, still hoping to win her approval for his career choice.

"Nothing at all, except good Christmas dinners," Mary was unaware of how determined Edmund was to take orders. She hoped to tease him toward another path. Although she was not yet ready to believe would accept any proposal from him, she could not help but think that if she *was* able to turn him away from the cloth, it would be a good thing. If she changed her mind and accepted him, dissuading him from becoming a parson would not only give her the benefit of *not* marrying an Autem jet, it would be proof of her power over him and prognosticate a union more congenial to her than the one her aunt suffered with the unyielding, uncaring Admiral.

"My aunt's cook is already thinking of Christmas dinner and winter dining," Miss Crawford continued, when Edmund was silent. "She is contriving to put up an immense amount of jams and preservatives, especially of the wild berries that grow here so profusely in the Midlands, that she can turn into sauces and add to pies or puddings. As a child in Everingham, we called the berries on the gorse bushes bilberries or whortleberries, but the children hereabout and Cook call them huckleberries or blackberries. Did you eat them as a boy?"

"I still do," Edmund smiled at her again, her beauty and lively manners overcoming once again any resentment he might have as to her opinion of the clergy. "Our old nurse will still warn me not to eat them uncooked, for fear I will fall dead on the spot from a gripe."

"Your nurse is still near?"

"I think you have met her, or at least she knows of you. She is Granny Flowers, and lives in Bluebell cottage with her eldest son and his wife."

"Ah, yes! I know them. Or, that is, I know *of* them. Mrs Grant and I were walking toward the Sudley farm when we heard a terrible racket and the outcries of several children. We dropped our baskets and ran toward the commotion, fearing (from the noise) that bears had returned to Northampton and one was eating a village youngster. It was fortunately not so. However, a child by the name of Perkin Hibbert had fallen from a tree and split the skin on his forehead, as well as obtaining many other scrapes and bruises. The other children surrounding him, his siblings and cousins all, had been convinced by his copious bleeding that their playmate was soon to cease his time on this earth. To tell you the truth, I was positive myself that the child would exsanguinate! Mrs Grant assured the children (and *me* although she did not know it) that a wound to the head normally bleeds so freely and the boy was in no danger. My sister ordered some of the children to fetch Mrs Hibbert and some of the children to fetch Granny Flowers and bid her come to the Hibbert's lodge. Soon Mrs Hibbert arrived and scooped up her offspring and bore him away. Mrs Grant told her we would come as soon as we had retrieved our goods."

Here there was a pause as Edmund and Mary began a very energetic part of the dance.

"Since I have not heard of the Hibbert's suffering a great loss, may I assume the child survived?" Edmund asked, when they were less strenuously engaged.

"Yes, with thanks to Granny Flowers. She came and bandaged the boy, and gave him physic and his mother instructions, and when she told the company that the child would be well, we all were relieved and believed her immediately. I find those old, wise women to be of more comfort than the most educated doctor, I must own it."

"I trust Granny Flowers implicitly, but it is the habit of youth rather than any well thought out design. Too often have her hands comforted me and soothed my hurts for me to regard them as scarcely less than magical." Edmund was a little rueful as he confessed his faith in his old nurse.

"Since we are exchanging confidences, I will tell you that if I am afflicted with a cold or ague, I long for my aunt to nurse me; it was such bliss to feel so loved and petted. I am sure, though, that if I should become feverish or develop a sore throat, Mrs Grant will tend me with every care. She is a most loving sister."

Mary and Edmund were mutually sorry to see their dances end, but managed to sit together during tea to their conjoint satisfaction.

II

While her attention was principally preoccupied by Edmund, Mary could not help but notice Henry's interactions with the Bertram sisters at the sofa across from hers. While Mr Rushworth was looking on, Henry was paying the chief of his attention to Julia. Nevertheless, at Henry's slightest notice Maria would forsake her intended, even in the middle of his sentence, to smile and flirt with Mr Crawford in the manner opposite of her cold treatment of Mr Rushworth. Mary was worried; Maria was within an inch of exposing herself and causing everyone in the company acute embarrassment. Fortunately, Henry was as savvy to these social niceties as Mary, and he requested that Julia comes to play for him on the pianoforte, and honour him with a duet, thus leaving Maria in complete procession of Mr Rushworth. Maria may have glanced after her sister and Henry, but she had the self-command to not get up and follow Mr Crawford like a pet spaniel.

It was nearing eleven o'clock when Mary and Henry finally said their adieus and set out arm in arm across the Park for the rectory. Dr and Mrs Grant had left more than two hours before, after earnestly assuring the Crawfords that they should stay for as long as they and the Bertrams wished, so the siblings had the privacy needed to discuss Maria's clear tendre for Henry.

"Henry, I beg of you to be more careful. You have done nothing that would open you to the criticism of having raised Maria Bertram's expectations, but she is not bothering to conceal her preference for you. Why Mr Rushworth tolerates it, I do not know."

"Because Mr Rushworth is too stupid to see more than a half of it and too much of a dolt to know what to think of the half he perceives," Henry was cavalier. "Her brothers are perspicacious men; I am more amazed that they do not see it."

"None are as blind as those who will not see." The night air was cool, and Mary was glad she had thought to have her pelisse fetched from the parsonage. "Tom Bertram does not care enough to notice, and Edmund Bertram cares too much to *believe* what he notices. He thinks his sister's treatment of Mr Rushworth is the natural result of her lack of strong feelings."

Henry could not help but laugh. "*Her* feelings lack strength? That is claiming that there are too many raisins in a plum pudding! I fear to be alone with her for dread she will ravish *me*."

Mary would have liked to have defended Maria from the charge, but could not. "It is this rustication, Henry. If she had been properly put on the marriage mart and had become accustomed to Town manners, she would not act so rashly in the presence of the first flirt she has ever met. It is like watching an infant grab at a candle flame."

"My God, when she does get to London ..." Henry was thoughtful. "Mr Rushworth will be lucky if his heir is his own get."

"Surely she won't go that far!" Mary protested.

Her brother shrugged. "I have met many like her, Mary. They are so vain they must have admiration, and they will allow their lovers liberties, either from inclination or in an attempt to solidify their hold on their cicisbeo. With Maria Bertram, I believe it will be from inclination. Her blood runs so hot I would swear she were Spanish. She will always be too elegant to be a wagtail, but she will be as short heeled as any in the demimonde. Mark my words."

"I cannot think so ill of her," Mary enjoyed Maria's company too much to allow such a bleak future for her friend. "You are too callous, Henry. You do not make allowances for the wisdom of maturity or her pride. She would rather die than be thought *squirrelly*. She is a woman of education and information. When she sees how the Ton treats women of ill repute, she will be cautious. She will learn from the examples of Lady Jersey and Dora Jordan."

"Or she will set her course by the newest Countess of Jersey and learn to be discrete," Henry was unmoved.

"I hope, for Edmund Bertram's sake, that you are wrong. His shame and pain if his sister conducted herself in such a way would be violent."

"Well, if Edmund Bertram is out here in the country seeing to his parish and spending his worries on the acreage afforded his cows, he'll not know."

"I have hopes," Mary confided, "that I'll coax him to become a Black Fly rather than a Black Box."

"You wish him to be a lawyer?" Henry thought about it. "He does have an excellent speaking voice and the solemn demeanour of a judge. Yes, I think he would make a very good lawyer."

Mary was pleased. "We think alike then. Even though I do not see him being happy in Town, as a lawyer he would be someone of importance in the country. It would be a shame to see him reduced to a parson when he could be more." She also thought that she could stand to live in the country most of the year if she were the wife of a judge; *that* would not be such a hardship.

As though he had read her thoughts, Henry said with an unusually staid candour, "It is a sign of good taste in him that he sets his sights on you. He could not do better. And, if I may say it, a mark of good taste in you as well, that you would accept him. He is a thoroughly decent fellow."

She was made happy by her brother's comment. Henry was sage in his dealings with people, and his good opinion was difficult to earn. If Henry liked Edmund well enough to think of him as a worthy spouse for his sister, then Edmund was as meritorious as Mary believed him to be. She liked to think that only a sterling example of a second son could tempt her, rather than she had in any way lowered her standards of what was due to her position and wealth.

"What about you Henry? Do you think to form an attachment? If you asked for Miss Julia Bertram's hand, she would make you a good wife. She is not so proud or strong tempered as her sister."

"No, she is pretty enough and hasn't her sister's high spirits, but I do not love her. Marriage is a wretched enough business; I intend to be in love to soften the blow when my own time comes."

"I don't see why you think marriage is a hazard," Mary told him. "Your sex risks very little when you wed."

"Ah, but look at the misery a bad marriage can cause, even when the man is free in all but name. Think of Prinny and Caroline of Brunswick."

"What you fail to take into account, brother," Mary informed him, "is that *you* would never behave so abominably and drive a wife to such vicissitude. Moreover, Prinny's suffering is nothing compared to what his wife must endure. Princess Caroline is the much harder done by in that union, and you know it."

"Yes, but *her* misery does not make *him* any the happier."

"Are you sure? He seems to positively wallow in his wife's unhappiness. I think the entire Delicate Investigation into her activities in Montagu House were more because Prinny feared she was enjoying herself than for any of her possible indiscretions," Mary made a dismissive noise. "You shall never convince me a man's lot in an uncongenial marriage can ever go as badly as a woman's, Henry.

Your wife can never shut you up in the country or forbid you to see your children."

Henry's only response was a sigh, and the siblings continued along the moonlit path without talking for a few minutes, before Henry spoke again.

"You do not account for the shame of an inconstant wife, Mary. If a man should have a mistress, no blame or pity or mockery is directed toward his wife, but if a man is cuckolded then his mortification is beyond expression. To be crowned in horns is grievous and unmans him."

"Bosh. Many, many men of the Ton ignore that their wives have lovers," Mary retorted.

"While you are right about older men, or couples who have long since gone their separate ways, I am speaking of young men and new wives. For a wife to take a lover before a husband has tacitly given her leave to live her life without his care; *that* is humiliating beyond expression."

"Then why have you done it?" Mary asked.

"I have not!" Henry was indignant. "All my amours have been with women who are not living with their husbands most of the year, or still bearing him heirs. I do not seek to humble my brethren. I am a not a cad."

Mary squeezed her brother's arm. "Of course you aren't dearest. I am sorry for saying so." She waited a moment, then challenged him, "But what of unmarried women, Henry? Can you say you have been a moralist among them?"

"When I was first of age, I did not give it serious enough thought," he admitted with a voice laced with chagrin, "but now that I am older I know it to be very wrong. Dangerous as well! I have been very careful to not dabble where I may be forced to wed against my inclination. And, to tell you the truth, I worry that I would have a natural child I could not acknowledge. I know Mrs Aker's son is rumoured to be mine, but I cannot be sure of that; she and Mr Aker had been *precipitous* in their vows. There is every chance the child is his. In fact, it is more likely, considering whom she saw the most frequently."

"So both Maria and Julia are safe?"

"Safer from me that Edmund Betram is from *you*."

"Then they are safe enough, for Mr Bertram is quite safe from me … as long as he stays on his present course."

Chapter Fifteen

MR YATES HAD come to Mansfield Park on the wings of disappointment, and with his head full of acting, for it had been a theatrical party; and the play in which he had borne a part was within two days of representation, when the sudden death of one of the nearest connexions of the family had destroyed the scheme and dispersed the performers. To be so near happiness, so near fame, so near the long paragraph in praise of the private theatricals at Ecclesford, the seat of the Right Hon. Lord Ravenshaw, in Cornwall, which would of course have immortalised the whole party for at least a twelvemonth! and being so near, to lose it all, was an injury to be keenly felt, and Mr Yates could talk of nothing else. Ecclesford and its theatre, with its arrangements and dresses, rehearsals and jokes, was his never-failing subject, and to boast of the past his only consolation.

Happily for him, a love of the theatre is so general, an itch for acting so strong among young people, that he could hardly out-talk the interest of his hearers. From the first casting of the parts to the epilogue it was all bewitching, and there were few who did not wish to have been a party concerned, or would have hesitated to try their skill. The play had been Lovers' Vows, and Mr Yates was to have been Count Cassel. Mr Yates had been well-nigh crushed with disappointment when it all came to naught.

"It was a hard case, upon my word"; and, "I do think you were very much to be pitied," were the kind responses of listening sympathy. Tom Bertram even went so far as to say, "Yates, I think we must raise a little theatre at Mansfield, and ask you to be our manager."

This, though the thought of the moment, did not end with the moment; for the inclination to act was awakened, and in no one more strongly than in him who was now master of the house; and who, having so much leisure as to make almost any novelty a certain good, had likewise such a degree of lively talents and comic taste, as were exactly adapted to the novelty of acting. The thought returned again and again. "Oh for the Ecclesford theatre and scenery to try something with." Each sister could echo the wish; and Henry Crawford, to whom, in all the riot of his gratifications it was yet an untasted pleasure, was quite alive at the idea. "I really believe," said he, "I could be fool enough at this moment to undertake any character that ever was written, from Shylock or Richard III down to the singing hero of a farce in his scarlet coat and cocked hat. I feel as if I could be anything or everything; as if I could rant and storm, or sigh or cut capers, in any tragedy or comedy in the English language. Let us be doing something. Be it only half a play, an act, a scene; what should prevent us? Not these countenances, I am sure," looking towards the Miss Bertrams; "and for a theatre, what signifies a theatre? We shall be only amusing ourselves. Any room in this house might suffice."

Such was Henry's enthusiasm that when he returned the parsonage he was very sorry to hear that Mary had already gone to bed, and he would be forced to wait until the morning to tell her of the acting scheme. He resolved to tell his sisters and Dr Grant the interesting tidings at breakfast, and to relieve his temptation to communicate it early to half the party, he retired to bed as well.

II

"I have the most marvellous news to relate," Henry began, as soon as they had all sat down at the table. "The Bertrams and their friend Yates mean to be acting, and have invited me to join in the exercise, and Mary too if she would like it."

"I should like that excessively!" Mary enthused. "I've never acted before, and I think I will be wonderfully diverted by it. What are we to be acting?"

"It hasn't been decided yet," Henry informed her and helped himself to a slice of ham.

Dr Grant frowned. "I do not wish to be a killjoy, but I am unsure the Bertrams should be acting. Private theatricals, although they chafe the Methodist, are all well and good if done with propriety, but as the Bertrams are circumstanced it is indelicate. Their father is not home. He is on a fever-ridden island and about to take a perilous sea-crossing. Their determination on something as gay as a private theatrical shows a want of concern for their father, a want of gratitude and sensibility. It's not tying one's garter in public, but it is indecorous."

Mrs Grant was reluctant to amend any of her siblings' pleasures, and tried to persuade her husband that nothing unbecoming would occur. "It is only intimate friends, dear. It is but for intimate friends. The Bertram's surely would not do anything improper. They have no plans to invite half the gentry from three counties to see it, do they, Henry?"

"Not to the best of my knowledge, ma'am," Henry replied. "If they should show any signs of such a thing, I will do my best to caution them against it."

"Do you really think it would be disreputable, sir?" Mary asked her brother-in-law.

"More that it seems uncouth," the parson replied. "It is a bit coarse. I am surprised the Miss Bertrams are willing, especially since the eldest in engaged."

"I am sure Mr Rushworth will be participating," Henry soothed. "If a woman can be callow for spending time with her intended, who can escape censure? It is but small enjoyment for, as Mrs Grant pointed out, *intimate* friends. No one will be exposing themselves."

Dr Grant's brow was still furrowed. "I cannot think it a good idea, but I am willing to consider that I am being overly nice."

"It is only because you must think of everyone's good, dearest," Mrs Grant flattered him.

He smiled at his wife. "I must think of that, but neither can I expect young people to be as hidebound and fusty as myself. I promise to keep any misgivings silent."

"I shall endeavour to give you no misgivings," Henry promised.

"Oh, I am not worried about you and Mary," Dr Grant assured him. "There is no reason for you not to do as *you* wish. There are no circumstances that would make a private theatrical improper for either of *you*. It is only the Bertrams who surprise me."

||

After breakfast, Henry told Mary that he was returning to the Park to confer with their fellow would-be thespians, and asked if she wanted to go with him. She declined, having already made plans to accompany Mrs Grant on her errands, but told him to report to her what play was chosen as soon as he possibly could and assure the company that she was happy to accept any trifling part.

She had expected them soon to have settled on a play, but she found out that was not to be. Daily she asked Henry if they had chosen, and daily Henry told her that no consensus had been reached.

"

"Have you all decided on a play yet?" Mary asked her brother on the fourth day, before she stooped to bowl her wood toward the smaller jack. Henry would be going to the Park again that morning, but he had promised to play a game of bowls on the lawn with her first.

"I am in despair that we ever shall," Henry watched Mary's ball curve gracefully toward the jack. "Good roll, that one." He and his sister had avoided the topic of acting during breakfast, in deference to Dr Grant's continuing concerns.

"Whatever is the difficulty?" The sun was out and the Michaelmas daisies were still in bloom, with the year's last stalwart butterflies flitting among them. The air was just cool enough that Mary needed a pelisse. With the ends of the pelisse and her skirts swishing and her bonnet's ribbons floating and swooping with every tug of the breeze, she looked not unlike a butterfly herself.

"Pure, unadulterated, unalloyed selfishness," Henry said scornfully. "You have never seen such squabbling pretending to be polite obligingness in your life." He was ready to act and wanted to get one with it; this seemingly unnecessary delay in his gratification was irritating.

"And you are not as determined to get your way as anyone else?" Mary asked with amused disbelief.

"Compared to the others, I am flexibility incarnate," Henry claimed. "I wish it to be a tragic piece, a dramatic piece, rather than comedic one, but if all the others would decide on a comedy, I would not demure. The trouble is that the Miss Bertrams and Mr Yates are determined on tragedy but Tom Bertram is *more* determined on comedy. Do you remember in the Odyssey how Zeus claimed to be able to win a tug-of-war against all the other gods combined? Such is Tom Bertram's strength of opinion."

"It was the Iliad," Mary reminded him. "Book eight if I am not mistaken."

Henry gave her a look of mock outrage. "*Must* you correct me? Must you have such a prodigious memory? It is unseemly in a woman."

Mary laughed. "Be comforted brother; I cannot read it in *Greek*. I, lowly woman that I am, never learned that scholarly language and have to trust the translations of others."

"As long as you acknowledge my superiority," he joked, "I will concede that the tug of war between Zeus and the gods occurred in the Iliad."

"Would you forgive me further if I could provide you comfort from the same source?"

"Of course," Henry lacked Mary's dimples, but his smile was charming nonetheless.

"Then let me point out that in the thirteenth book of the Iliad Zeus gets into a tug-of-war with merely *one* god, Poseidon, and can do no better than a draw. Poseidon says that Zeus is greater, and Zeus brags of his superior strength, but when the contest comes it is equal. Moreover, Hera disarms Zeus when he storms angrily into Olympus. Mr Bertram may yet be swayed to tragedy."

"When I consider that, with Zeus's backing, the Greeks prevailed against Troy, I feel my hopes are dimmed." Henry watched his wood come close to the jack. "That's a point for me."

"Zeus initially forbade the gods to interfere, and helped the Greeks only when cajoled into it or from his spite for a god that favoured the Trojans. I still say there is hope you will do a tragedy yet."

"The tragedy is already upon me; my younger sister schools me on the Iliad."

"That is because I was fated to be your sister, and the fates rule even the gods."

"Would you care to wager on the fate of this game?"

"If *you* would care to wager on the category of play that will be chosen."

"That would assume a play will *ever* be chosen. I doubt it will ever be resolved. I will be an octogenarian, and be forced to return to Mansfield Park to finally assume my role," Henry complained.

"Then I will give you some news to cheer you. I have received a letter from Mrs Fraser, with some choice information in it," Mary told him.

Henry perked up. "Do tell."

Mary walked over to stand closer to her brother, glancing around to make sure there wasn't an undergardener nearby, and lower her voice. "Mrs Fraser has told me that the *on dit* in Town is that Byron is now keeping company with Lady Oxford."

"Lady Oxford!" Henry was surprised. "Blast! I wagered with Honeycutt that Byron's next paramour would be Mrs Wilson."

"Silly Henry!" His sister chided him. "Byron does not need the *demimonde*. He is so beautiful that Harriette Wilson would give *him* diamonds in exchange for his company. Byron need only beckon, and ladies will come to him."

Her brother gave her a severe look. "*You* shall never meet him then."

"No, I have no desire to meet him. I am content to hear of him and see him from a distance and read his work. One sits near a fireplace but does not climb into the flames because one knows that burning is painful." Mary was too familiar with men who trifled with women to ever be willing to be trifled with herself.

Henry looked sceptical, but refrained from commenting on her assertion. "How does Mrs Fraser know that Byron is Lady Oxford's lover?"

"Mrs Savage told her. Mrs Fraser encountered Mrs Savage in Vauxhall a few days ago, and Mrs Savage's is a good friend of one of Oxford's cousins."

"Will Byron contribute to the Harleian Miscellany do you think?" Henry snickered. The earl of Oxford's surname was Harley, and the first two earls of Oxford had given their collection of books and other literary materials to posterity, which was famously known as the Harleian Miscellany. Since it was rumoured that none of Lady Oxford's children were sired by Lord Oxford — or indeed the same father — her offspring were also referred to as a Harleian Miscellany.

Mary giggled. "It will be easy to tell if he does. The newest Harley would be a *handsome*."

"Yes, and when he came of age he could come to Mansfield to watch the production; we *might* be ready to perform in twenty-one years time" Henry said in a somewhat sour tone, and bowled a perfect pitch within inches of the jack.

"You are all impatience, Henry. It will not hurt you to have something a little out of your reach. It will do you good to wait," Mary reproved him.

"I could wait more patiently if they were not all so stupid in how they are going about choosing, or if their arguments were a little more rational. Everyone is petulant. Everyone claims to not care *which* play we do but whatever play that is suggested there is at least someone who moans about it, claiming we could not do worse,"

Henry gave a small huff. "It is bad enough in the Bertram women, but in Bertram and Yates it is maddening."

"Which play would you do, if the choice were yours?" Mary was curious.

Henry's answer was instantaneous. "I would not make it a single play. There are too many different tastes to account for, too many strong roles called for. I would do an evening ensemble, where an act from several familiar plays are performed. That way everyone could have it their own way. Bertram could have his comedy and we could be his foils, and then Yates can be the Baron in *Lover's Vows* with some of us supporting, and Miss Bertram could do a scene from whatever tragedy she thought would make her most like Sarah Siddons, and so forth."

"Perhaps she could take on a breeches role, like Siddons, and dress as a man?" Mary said to rib her brother.

"Perhaps she would. From Edmund Bertram's disapproving looks, *he* could not think it worse than theatricals in general. He is making very heavy weather of us doing anything at all," Henry watched Mary take her turn to bowl. "You were right about him being a very stiff-necked creature. He is a good fellow, but he could teach Cromwell how to be a Puritan."

"His head isn't round enough," Mary quipped. "You would need to affix a billiard ball atop his neck."

"Ah, but then he'd be vulnerable to being in a play," Henry looked very serious.

"How so?"

"He would have to learn to take a *cue*."

Mary stood as one stunned. "That may be the worst pun I have ever encountered in my entire life."

Her brother grinned, proud of himself.

ll

It was a full week before the Mansfield amateur thespians could decide on a play. It was to be *Lover's Vows*, the very play Mr Yates would have originally performed in. Mary Crawford would have won her wager, for it was a drama, but neither was Tom Bertram overset; he was to play the Butler, a very comedic part. There were two principle female parts in the play, Amelia and Agatha. Neither lady was modest, delicate, or proper. Amelia, the baron's daughter, was in love with a parson and she defies social convention by expressing her love to him in the hopes he feels the same. The role of Agatha was less delicate still, since she was the abandoned mistress of Amelia's father, and had given birth the baron's son more than twenty years previously. That son, Frederick, was to be played by Mr Crawford, while Mr Yates performed as the baron. Amelia's swain, the pious and respectable Anhalt, should have been played by Edmund Bertram, but Edmund was absolutely refusing to do it. Julia Bertram, having lost the part of Agatha to her sister, had also refused to participate in the play, leaving the part of Amelia for Mary Crawford.

Maria Bertram, perhaps eager to escape the recriminating eye of her bitterly disappointed sister, resolved to go down to the Parsonage herself with the offer of Amelia to Miss Crawford. Maria was in a triumphant mood as she tramped toward the Parsonage. She was certain of Henry Crawford's preference for herself, and was nearly trembling from the thought of the intimate scenes the two would be engaged in. He would be playing her son, but the role would call for her to lean on him, caress him, embrace him, and breathlessly explain how she had been seduced; intoxicated "by the fervent caresses of a young, inexperienced, capricious man." It was titillating to think upon.

Mary was playing her harp, and Mrs Grant was embroidering with the help of her tambour, when Miss Bertram arrived. Both women received her very cordially, and suspended their pursuits to converse with their visitor. Mary thought she had never seen Maria in better looks. She was practically glowing, her face was so flushed from walking across the park. The wind had also served her as a lady's maid, tousling her hair most becomingly and putting animation and sparkle into her blue eyes.

"I am come, Miss Crawford, to tell you we have chosen a play, and beg you to take one of the parts. It is *Lover's Vows*, and we need an Amelia."

"Of course I shall be Amelia!" Mary Crawford assured her guest. "I would be delighted to be of service. Happily, I have seen the play more than once, and although I am sure I shall do the part badly, I at least know how it *should* be. Have you seen the play, Miss Bertram?"

Mary was very interested to know if Maria knew what she was letting herself in for. Such a part for an engaged woman of quality! Was Maria blundering into it, or did she trip in with her eyes wide open?

"I have not *seen* the play, but I have read it more than once," Maria replied.

Mary was very glad that Mrs Grant began to speak of the
play to Maria, because she needed a moment's struggle to keep her
countenance before she spoke again. To accept Agatha, circumstanced
as Maria was! Mary, who knew herself to be bold and liberal in
her concept of propriety, believed *she* would have rejected the part
of Agatha. From her point of view, Amelia almost as bad, and if it
were not going to be a very private group of genteel people she didn't
think she could have agreed to do it. Maria Bertram as Agatha! If
Miss Bertram was Mrs Rushworth, it would be tolerable. But for an
unmarried woman, in an engagement that had not yet had the articles
signed, with a father away from home ... it was indelicate in the
extreme. When Dr Grant found out, his opinion would be decidedly
against it.

Regardless of her semi-scandalised thoughts on Maria's actions,
Mary had no intention of missing out on the play. She loved bustle
and schemes. She loved to be watching people for intrigues and
follies. All her nerves and pulses were alive with the desire to see how
the performers would act and what they would do when not acting.
Dr Grant would disapprove, but he was not her father; it did not
signify. She would laugh at Maria and be shocked, but it would be
between Henry and herself. To Maria she would be all courtesy and
unsuspected mockery.

"So you are to be Agatha. How will you appear aged? Your
untouched youth will make the sight of your mothering a grown man
appear comic in the midst of drama, if you are not aged." Mary asked.

"Oh, I think something like a mobcap and powder in my hair
will do," Maria told her blithely. There was no mention of drawing
fine wrinkles on her face with the help of a little lamp-black and a
fine brush.

"And who is to be Frederick?" Mary asked, already certain it
would be Henry.

"Mr Crawford is to be Frederick," Maria confirmed.

"My brother is to play your son? How droll!" Mrs Grant
laughed. "It must be, as the Orientals believe, a case of reincarnation.
You became his mother in a past life, died, and are now younger than
he is but you still recognise him. That would make an interesting
edition to the play."

Maria smiled politely, but it did not reach her eyes. "It is certain
I will need all my acting ability to convince the audience that Mr
Crawford is my son, but what is life without a challenge?"

"It will certainly be a challenge to Henry to envision you as his mother," Mary told her.

"I'm sure he's up to the task," Maria's smile warmed a bit. "We shall just have to audition until our performance is sufficient."

I am positive that you will, Mary thought to herself. I suspect that the first act will be rehearsed more often than it would be by professional actors.

"Tell us more, please. What roles do your brothers and sister take?" Mrs Grant asked.

"Tom will be Verdun, the butler, but Edmund and Julia do not intend to act," Maria's face was composed.

Mrs Grant was taken aback. "Mary has told me that Edmund and Miss Price have no wish to be acting, but I am surprised Miss Julia Bertram does not mean to act. When I spoke to her last, she was ebullient on the subject."

"Julia did not think any of the available parts would amuse her, so she has chosen to merely watch." There was enough chill in Maria's voice to warn Mrs Grant away from the topic.

"Is Mr Rushworth to be Anhalt?" Mary asked. When Maria said she did not know Mr Rushworth's part yet, Mary continued. "I suppose he *will* be Anhalt. I wonder how I will keep my countenance when I must make love to your betrothed. You must promise not to laugh at me Miss Bertram. It will be the end of any acting on my part if you let me see your humour in watching me give Mr Rushworth some of Amelia's addresses."

Maria promised she wouldn't laugh, and Mary suspected that Miss Bertram wouldn't be *jealous* either. No one who cared as much as a fig for their intended would countenance a role that would bring the gentleman into such intimate contact with another lady. To have her beg him to teach her love and have him declare he loves her more than life! Even Lady Stornoway would have gone yellow from jealousy — a jealousy based on ownership if nothing else – and she had not loved her husband one jot either before or after their wedding.

"I am very much looking forward to seeing the play. I am sure it will be capital," Mrs Grant beamed approvingly. No thought of propriety or impropriety alienated Mrs Grant's enthusiasm for the play. Her siblings were both happy; that was enough to secure her blessing. "When do you think it shall be performed?"

"I should think around mid-October. Six weeks will be enough time to do the thing properly." Miss Bertram did not wish it to take longer. All evidence of the play would need to be removed before her father returned in November. If things went as she hoped, her engagement would be equally removed, and Henry Crawford would step into Mr Rushworth's former place.

The visit was short. Maria stayed no longer than a quarter of an hour before she rushed back to Mansfield Park and Mr Crawford, leaving Mary and Mrs Grant to discuss the play and await Henry to return to the parsonage for fresher information.

Chapter Sixteen

THE PLAY WAS the thing. That evening Tom, Maria, and Mr Yates, soon after their being reassembled in the drawing-room, seated themselves in committee at a separate table, with the play open before them, and were just getting deep in the subject when a most welcome interruption was given by the entrance of Mr and Miss Crawford, who, late and dark and dirty as it was, could not help coming, and were received with the most grateful joy.

"Well, how do you go on?" and "What have you settled?" and "Oh! we can do nothing without you," followed the first salutations; and Henry Crawford was soon seated with the other three at the table, while his sister made her way to Lady Bertram, and with pleasant attention was complimenting *her*. "I must really congratulate your ladyship," said she, "on the play being chosen; for though you have borne it with exemplary patience, I am sure you must be sick of all our noise and difficulties. The actors may be glad, but the bystanders must be infinitely more thankful for a decision; and I do sincerely give you joy, madam, as well as Mrs Norris, and everybody else who is in the same predicament," glancing half fearfully, half slyly, beyond Fanny to Edmund.

Mary was deeply curious as to whether or not Edmund would continue to make such a fuss when he had the opportunity to act with her. Would he show himself persuadable, or would he be no different than the Admiral in his selfish determination to have his own way?

She was very civilly answered by Lady Bertram, but Edmund said nothing. His being only a bystander was not disclaimed. After continuing in chat with the party round the fire a few minutes, Miss Crawford returned to the party round the table; and standing by them, seemed to interest herself in their arrangements till, as if struck by a sudden recollection, she exclaimed, "My good friends, you are most composedly at work upon these cottages and alehouses, inside and out; but pray let me know my fate in the meanwhile. Who is to be Anhalt? What gentleman among you am I to have the pleasure of making love to?"

For a moment no one spoke; and then many spoke together to tell the same melancholy truth, that they had not yet got any Anhalt.

"Mr Rushworth was to be Count Cassel, but no one had yet undertaken Anhalt." Tom Bertram informed her with real regret, knowing he was putting the pretty Miss Crawford in an awkward position. He was a spoilt young man, but was not a deliberate cad.

"I had my choice of the parts," said Mr Rushworth; "but I thought I should like the Count best, though I do not much relish the finery I am to have."

"You chose very wisely, I am sure," replied Miss Crawford, with a brightened look; "Anhalt is a heavy part."

"*The Count* has two-and-forty speeches," returned Mr Rushworth, "which is no trifle."

There were some polite noises of assent from the group, but every person was internally sneering at Mr Rushworth. He was not only a dullard; his obliviousness to his own lack of brains made him clownish. What could be more absurd?

"I am not at all surprised," said Miss Crawford, after a short pause, "at this want of an Anhalt. Amelia deserves no better. Such a forward young lady may well frighten the men."

"I should be but too happy in taking the part, if it were possible," cried Tom; "but, unluckily, the Butler and Anhalt are in together. I will not entirely give it up, however; I will try what can be done – I will look it over again."

"Your *brother* should take the part," said Mr Yates, in a low voice. "Do not you think he would?"

"*I* shall not ask him," replied Tom, in a cold, determined manner.

Miss Crawford talked of something else, and soon afterwards rejoined the party at the fire. She liked light-hearted teasing and raillery, but this want of harmony made her uncomfortable. This was more than ruffled feathers; this was seething resentment. She wished to soothe everyone's feelings by coaxing Edmund into being a part of the players.

"They do not want me at all," said she, seating herself. "I only puzzle them, and oblige them to make civil speeches. Mr Edmund Bertram, as you do not act yourself, you will be a disinterested adviser; and, therefore, I apply to *you*. What shall we do for an Anhalt? Is it practicable for any of the others to double it? What is your advice?"

"My advice," said he calmly, "is that you change the play."

"*I* should have no objection," she replied; "for though I should not particularly dislike the part of Amelia if well supported, that is, if everything went well, I shall be sorry to be an inconvenience; but as they do not chuse to hear your advice at *that* table" (looking round), "it certainly will not be taken."

Edmund said no more. Mary was taken aback by his uncivil lack of response, but endeavoured not to show it.

"If any part could tempt *you* to act, I suppose it would be Anhalt," observed the lady archly, after a short pause; "for he is a clergyman, you know."

"*That* circumstance would by no means tempt me," he replied, "for I should be sorry to make the character ridiculous by bad acting. It must be very difficult to keep Anhalt from appearing a formal, solemn lecturer; and the man who chuses the profession itself is, perhaps, one of the last who would wish to represent it on the stage."

Miss Crawford was silenced, and with some feelings of resentment and mortification, moved her chair considerably nearer the tea-table, and gave all her attention to Mrs Norris, who was presiding there. She was out of charity with Edmund. Let him wallow in his priggishness alone.

"Fanny," cried Tom Bertram, from the other table, where the conference was eagerly carrying on, and the conversation incessant, "we want your services"

Fanny was up in a moment, expecting some errand; for the habit of employing her in that way was not yet overcome, in spite of all that Edmund could do.

"Oh! we do not want to disturb you from your seat. We do not want your *present* services. We shall only want you in our play. You must be Cottager's wife."

"Me!" cried Fanny, sitting down again with a most frightened look. "Indeed you must excuse me. I could not act anything if you were to give me the world. No, indeed, I cannot act."

Mary Crawford, soft-hearted for all her cynicism, hurt to hear the genuine fright in Miss Price's voice. If the poor girl had been a horse, she would have been trembling and showing the whites of her eyes.

"Indeed, but you must, for we cannot excuse you. It need not frighten you: it is a nothing of a part, a mere nothing, not above half a dozen speeches altogether, and it will not much signify if nobody hears a word you say; so you may be as creep-mouse as you like, but we must have you to look at."

"If you are afraid of half a dozen speeches," cried Mr Rushworth, "what would you do with such a part as mine? I have forty-two to learn."

Mary carefully did not look at Mr Rushworth for fear she would be unable to disguise her contempt.

"It is not that I am afraid of learning by heart," said Fanny, shocked to find herself at that moment the only speaker in the room, and to feel that almost every eye was upon her; "but I really cannot act."

"Yes, yes, you can act well enough for *us*. Learn your part, and we will teach you all the rest. You have only two scenes, and as I shall be Cottager, I'll put you in and push you about, and you will do it very well, I'll answer for it."

How ill-bred of Tom Bertram to push his cousin in so heartless manner! Mary was grateful she had not enticed him and accepted him before he revealed this streak of wilful disobligingness. She could forgive him being a slave owner but not for the sin of behaving in an ill-bred manner.

"No, indeed, Mr Bertram, you must excuse me. You cannot have an idea. It would be absolutely impossible for me. If I were to undertake it, I should only disappoint you."

Mary's heart hurt to hear Miss Price plead so desperately. Why would Bertram not give over? Why didn't Edmund or his sisters help their cousin?

"Phoo! Phoo! Do not be so shamefaced. You'll do it very well. Every allowance will be made for you. We do not expect perfection. You must get a brown gown, and a white apron, and a mob cap, and we must make you a few wrinkles, and a little of the crowsfoot at the corner of your eyes, and you will be a very proper, little old woman."

"You must excuse me, indeed you must excuse me," cried Fanny, growing more and more red from excessive agitation, and looking distressfully at Edmund, who was kindly observing her; but unwilling to exasperate his brother by interference, gave her only an encouraging smile. Her entreaty had no effect on Tom: he only said again what he had said before; and it was not merely Tom, for the requisition was now backed by Maria, and Mr Crawford, and Mr Yates, with an urgency which differed from his but in being more gentle or more ceremonious, and which altogether was quite overpowering to Fanny;

and before she could breathe after it, Mrs Norris completed the whole by thus addressing her in a whisper at once angry and audible – "What a piece of work here is about nothing: I am quite ashamed of you, Fanny, to make such a difficulty of obliging your cousins in a trifle of this sort – so kind as they are to you! Take the part with a good grace, and let us hear no more of the matter, I entreat."

Mary almost forgot herself and spoke up at this harangue from Mrs Norris. She had to collect herself and remind herself forcefully that it was not her place to intervene. Mrs Norris's ill-breeding and the careless treatment of Miss Price by the Bertrams did not give her room to be ill-bred in turn.

"Do not urge her, madam," said Edmund. "It is not fair to urge her in this manner. You see she does not like to act. Let her chuse for herself, as well as the rest of us. Her judgement may be quite as safely trusted. Do not urge her anymore."

"I am not going to urge her," replied Mrs Norris sharply; "but I shall think her a very obstinate, ungrateful girl, if she does not do what her aunt and cousins wish her – very ungrateful, indeed, considering who and what she is."

Edmund was too angry to speak; but Miss Crawford, looking for a moment with astonished eyes at Mrs Norris, and then at Fanny, whose tears were beginning to shew themselves, immediately said, with some keenness, "I do not like my situation: this *place* is too hot for me," and moved away her chair to the opposite side of the table, close to Fanny, saying to her, in a kind, low whisper, as she placed herself, "Never mind, my dear Miss Price, this is a cross evening: everybody is cross and teasing, but do not let us mind them"; and with pointed attention continued to talk to her and endeavour to raise her spirits, in spite of being out of spirits herself. By a look at her brother she prevented any farther entreaty from the theatrical board, and the really good feelings by which she was almost purely governed were rapidly restoring her to all the little she had lost in Edmund's favour.

Mary was not so forgiving of Edmund as he was of her. Why had he not defended Fanny more ably? How could he remain silent when Miss Price was being torn apart by wolves in front of his eyes? Never had Mary more wished to be back in Town; she wished she had never been introduced to any of the Bertrams.

Fanny did not love Miss Crawford; but she felt very much obliged to her for her present kindness; and when, from taking notice of her work, and wishing *she* could work as well, and begging for the pattern, and supposing Fanny was now preparing for her *appearance*, as of course she would come out when her cousin was married, Miss Crawford proceeded to inquire if she had heard lately from her brother at sea, and said that she had quite a curiosity to see him, and imagined him a very fine young man, and advised Fanny to get his picture drawn before he went to sea again – she could not help admitting it to be very agreeable flattery, or help listening, and answering with more animation than she had intended.

Miss Crawford was utterly bamboozled by Fanny's show of gratitude, and had no suspicions of Fanny's resentful and jealous heart. Her kind feelings for Miss Price were unreciprocated even after becoming the young woman's only champion in her travail. Fanny wanted Edmund for her own and wished Miss Crawford at the Devil.

The consultation upon the play still went on, and Miss Crawford's attention was first called from Fanny by Tom Bertram's telling her, with infinite regret, that he found it absolutely impossible for him to undertake the part of Anhalt in addition to the Butler: he had been most anxiously trying to make it out to be feasible, but it would not do; he must give it up. "But there will not be the smallest difficulty in filling it," he added. "We have but to speak the word; we may pick and chuse. I could name, at this moment, at least six young men within six miles of us, who are wild to be admitted into our company, and there are one or two that would not disgrace us: I should not be afraid to trust either of the Olivers or Charles Maddox. Tom Oliver is a very clever fellow, and Charles Maddox is as gentlemanlike a man as you will see anywhere, so I will take my horse early to-morrow morning and ride over to Stoke, and settle with one of them."

While he spoke, Maria was looking apprehensively round at Edmund in full expectation that he must oppose such an enlargement of the plan as this: so contrary to all their first protestations; but Edmund said nothing.

Mary was deeply chagrined at the thought of having a near-stranger brought into such an intimate activity. After a moment's thought, she calmly replied, "As far as I am concerned, I can have no objection to anything that you all think eligible. Have I ever seen either of the gentlemen? Yes, Mr Charles Maddox dined at my sister's one day, did not he, Henry? A quiet-looking young man. I remember him. Let *him* be applied to, if you please, for it will be less unpleasant to me than to have a perfect stranger." A deaf man could have heard the reluctance in her tone, and a blind man could have seen the chill on her countenance. Tom Bertram chose to ignore both her tone and her expression in favour of having his play.

Charles Maddox was to be the man. Tom repeated his resolution of going to him early on the morrow; and though Julia, who had scarcely opened her lips before, observed, in a sarcastic manner, and with a glance first at Maria and then at Edmund, that "the Mansfield theatricals would enliven the whole neighbourhood exceedingly," Edmund still held his peace, and shewed his feelings only by a determined gravity.

"I am not very sanguine as to our play," said Miss Crawford, in an undervoice to Fanny, after some consideration; "and I can tell Mr Maddox that I shall shorten some of *his* speeches, and a great many of *my own*, before we rehearse together. It will be very disagreeable, and by no means what I expected."

"

"What a sad business this is!" Mary began when she and her brother were safely out of earshot and walking back to the parsonage. "To be acting Amelia with a man I barely know is very disagreeable to me."

"I am heartily sorry for it," Henry patted her hand where it lay on his forearm. "I have no idea of how to remedy the situation. If only Edmund Bertram would bend! But there is no use hoping for that."

"None at all," Mary frowned, remembering his uncivil rejection of her hint he should play Anhalt. He had wounded her pride and hurt her feelings, and had lost a great deal of ground in her estimation of him. When he was addressing her so coldly, she could not even think him very handsome.

"At least Charles Maddox is a very gentlemanlike man. Maddox is a barrister, and he is a man of property and education, even if his father *is* a farmer," Henry consoled her.

"That is easy for *you* to think," Mary said sharply. "*You* are not the one who will be making love to him repeatedly, and for the entertainment of others. Furthermore, he may be a gentleman but he is also a dead bore. I thought I should die of tedium when he was at dinner. Worst yet, his eyes are too small and too close together; he looks like a fish. I will feel as though I am making love to a mackerel."

Henry chuckled. "It could be worse yet; it could be Rushworth. Tell me the truth, which would you rather have to make love to? Maddox or Rushworth?"

"My God!" Mary feigned horror. "I would have to choose between making love to a mackerel and making love to a codfish. The heart revolts!"

"Take the mackerel, dearest. It is better to deal with the fish-faced than the fish-brained." Henry advised her.

"Rushworth *is* buffle-headed, ain't he?" Mary agreed. "Can he not see you making love to his fiancée before his face? And what will he do if he *does* notice."

Henry shrugged. "That is Miss Bertram's lookout, not mine."

"It would be your lookout if he challenged you, you know."

"He's too much of a buffoon to challenge anyone, Mary", Henry was blasé about the whole matter. Trifling with Maria was not something that worried him, even on the rare occasions when he thought about it.

"Don't underestimate him, Henry," Mary's voice was grave, and it caught her brother's fullest attention. "Mr Rushworth has two-and-forty speeches you know."

"Two-and-forty speeches!" Henry guffawed. "How proud he was of his two-and-forty speeches. What a nincompoop. If you hesitate to pretend to make love to him, how does Miss Bertram endure him making love to *her*?"

"Well, she certainly does not bother to pretend she is making love to *him*," Mary was scornful. "I have never in my life seen a woman treat her future husband with such cavalier dismissal. Even he must know she doesn't care for him."

"She is careless, ain't she?" Henry agreed. "For all her elegance she sorely wants delicacy. Still, Rushworth is easy to dupe. He is the embodiment of that old saw, 'as the bell clinks, so the fool thinks'. He wants to believe she loves him, so he will not see what is in front of his eyes."

"Is she is so lacking in elegance or care, why do you flirt with her so?" Mary asked mockingly, well aware it was Maria's physical charms alone that tempted Henry.

"What else is there to do? I cannot flirt too noticeably with Julia, lest she form expectations, and there is nothing much else to do in the country after one is done with the morning's hunting."

"Yes, but it is not like you to go after such low-hanging fruit. You are someone who prefers pursuit, although you seldom meet a fox that bothers to run even a meagre course," Mary faked a large sigh. "Alas, my brother is growing too old to do anything but let the fox run to *him*."

Henry was amused. "I confess I am afraid she will declare herself to me. I have no idea what to do if she *does*."

"Blush and faint?" Mary suggested.

"It may be my only hope of escape," Henry said ruefully.

"Your mention of escape reminds me," Mary's agile mind jumped to a new topic, "can there be any escape for Miss Price from that dreadful aunt of hers?"

"Mrs Norris is a brute," Henry agreed. "I heartily wish I had not also entreated Miss Price to be the Cottager's Wife; upon reflection it made me feel as brutish as that Norris woman. To remind Miss Price that she is a dependent relation! It not only lacked proper delicacy, it was repulsively unkind. I did not like Mrs Norris before, but now I am of Dr Grant's opinion and despise her as a villain."

"Poor little Miss Price," Mary was indignant on the girl's behalf, "she had tears standing in her eyes and if I had not intervened I believe she would have mortified herself by crying in public. How could Mrs Norris be so savage to such a dear girl? I have never met anyone as modest and shy as Miss Price, or anyone so deserving of kindness."

"That was a jolly good thing you did when you went to Miss Price, Mary. I was proud of you, because I could see you were having to labour hard to bring her any tolerable peace of mind."

Mary made a shooing gesture with her free hand. "It was not such a labour for me. Miss Price was already struggling to be composed before I sat next to her. All I did was give her something happy to think upon; her brother William Price. I am convinced she loves her brother as much as I love you, Henry. Perhaps her love is even more than my own. I love you with a rational mind. I can see you have faults. To Miss Price, her brother is faultless and she loves him perfectly."

"You think I have faults? That is cruel Mary, because I consider you as faultless as an angel."

"Balderdash," Mary laughed softly. "You are too intelligent to see me other than how I am."

"Miss Price is intelligent, but you just declared that she sees her brother as faultless. Why can I not be intelligent and discern your perfections as well?"

"Alright then, I shall say that you are too *knowledgeable* to see me as faultless. You are a man of the world and you know something of folly and vices. Therefore, it comes as no shock to you when others are imperfect. That is what lets you identify my flaws. Miss Price is as innocent as a babe. She cannot think of her brother as less than perfect because she cannot conceive of any evils that normal men may do. She thinks William Price to be as much of a paragon as Edmund Bertram. It would never occur to her that her brother may have a mistress, or may be a tartar to his subordinates, or may swear like the sailor he is. Because she cannot fathom that he may have these vices, she cannot see that he would have faults."

"I will still argue that you are faultless, Mary," Henry smiled affectionately at his sister. "I know you have some little imperfections, but they only serve to endear you to me."

Mary was touched. "Dearest Henry, you are the best brother in the world. I would not trade you for a gross of William Prices, even if he should be all that his sister believes him to be."

"I should hope not. For one thing, William Price is always at sea, and would not be here to keep you diverted."

"Nor could he read to me so well, I am certain. No one reads as well as you do, Henry. Tomorrow, let us stay home, and you can read to me and Mrs Grant while we work. It has rained so much that the lanes are all very dirty, and a morning spent cosy in the drawing-room would be pleasant. All this bustle about the play is *usually* agreeable, but the Mackerel and Mrs Norris have put me out of spirits. I feel disposed to an avoidance of it, at least for *one* evening."

Henry agreed instantly, solicitous for his sister and not averse to avoiding the attentions of Maria and the sulks of Julia for a little while. "What shall I read to you? Will it be one of your favourite horrid novels? Or one of your favourite poets? Do I read *Childe Harold* again for the one-hundredth time?"

"For a change, I am not quite in the humour for a horrid novel or poetry." She ignored his dramatic pretence of shock. "I would like to hear *Belinda*. But I want you to read the first printing, before the publishers replaced Juba with James Jackson or made Belinda become so unaccountably cool to Mr Vincent. I detest that sort of abominable tampering with a narrative; it always renders a book milquetoast."

"Does our sister have such a copy?"

"Yes, I saw it in the library the other day, and that's what has brought it into my mind."

"Did you check to see if Dr Grant had avoided Bowdler's *The Family Shakespeare* as well?"

"Thank God, I could not find that blasphemous thing among his books," Mary was facetious only in part; had Dr Grant owned the expunged and 'sanitised' version of Shakespeare's works she would have thought less of him. "I still cannot conceive of the audacity in tampering with the Bard's writings. Mr Bowdler must think very well of himself."

"Taking your strong feelings on the matter into consideration, I have dire news to impart," Henry said playfully. "The Bertram's have Bowdler's version."

Mary stopped dead. "No!" Her horrified revulsion was only partly exaggerated.

"This, I am afraid, will scuttle any of Edmund Bertram's chances to woo and win your heart," Henry mocked his sister without spite.

"If his priggish and cold behaviour tonight had not been enough to sink him in my estimation, then the idea that he approved of such a watered-down and sad-sack edition of Shakespeare is surely the final blow. I can like a man who is a strait-laced prude, but I cannot like one that would countenance defiling Shakespeare. Some things are beyond the pale, Henry."

"Is a greater sin than being a second son?"

"It is close *enough*."

"And if I told you there was also a copy of Wilkes and Potter's poems, "An Essay on Woman"? What would you say then?"

For once Mary was sincerely shocked. The collection of poems was beyond scandalous. Even Lady Stornoway and Mrs Fraser, who as married women could now read it, would not let Mary see their copy until she was married as well. They did, however, let her know that it contained, among other odes, an erotic parody not only of Pope's poem "An Essay on Man", but also a parody of Pope's "A Dying Christian to his Soul" called "A Dying Lover to his Prick." The thought of the upright and starched-rumped Edmund Bertram reading such a thing boggled her mind.

"Gracious God. That cannot be possible!" Mary exclaimed.

"Of course it is not," Henry said calmly. "I am pulling your leg."

It was ominously quiet for almost a minute before Mary told her brother, "When you least expect it, I shall push you down a flight of stairs."

"You would never hurt me; I am your favourite brother," Henry said with a smugness calculated to tease his sister further.

"I will shoot you and make it look like a hunting accident."

"Stuff and nonsense."

"I will bury you alive in a Gothic mausoleum."

"Mausoleums are *above* ground, ninny. You mean tomb."

"I will stab you with an assassin's dagger."

"That you obtained where? Cloudberry's dry-goods shop?"

"I will spill wine on your new silk waistcoat."

"Now, I say! That goes too far!" Henry cried in an aggrieved manner, which caused Mary to burst into giggles.

"See, now you laugh again, Edmund Bertram's coldness and the misfortunes of the Mackerel alleviated by mirth," Henry said, as they approached the parsonage.

"Ah, Henry. I really would have no other brother but you," Mary patted his cheek and preceded him through the door.

Chapter Seventeen

EARLY THE NEXT morning, Mary sought out her sister and asked her to take a turn in the shrubbery before breakfast. Mrs Grant, as eager to please as always, agreed immediately.

"That is a very pretty bonnet, ma'am," Mary complimented her sister as soon as possible. While she did think that the new straw bonnet, with its pomona green silk lining and a cluster of strawberries nestled in the bows of multi-hued green ribbons that wound around the crown and extended as ties, was pretty, she had other motives for the compliment. She wished to butter Mrs Grant up, because she had a favour to ask. Although she was almost certain that her good-natured and obliging sister would agree, she thought a little weight on the side of agreeableness wouldn't go amiss.

"Thank you, Mary," Mrs Grant preened a little. "It is just my old bonnet, trimmed afresh."

"Yes, but you have given it more elegance than is usually found in a morning walking bonnet. I have seldom seen better, even in Town," Mary laid it on thickly.

Mrs Grant smiled. "You are a dear sister; you flatter me."

"No, I merely observe," Mary assured her.

The ladies walked on among the flowerbeds in the garden, prompting Mrs Grant to lament she had not brought her basket with her, because the yarrow was blooming beautifully and she should cut some to display indoors.

"The nice thing about yarrow is that it also dries so well. I must always dry a good supply for Cook's use, because Dr Grant is partial to the flavour of dried yarrow in his pork ragouts. They call yarrow old man's mustard or old man's pepper in this part of the county, which is odd because it tastes like neither," Mrs Grant mused aloud.

"Considering that Cook's ragouts would not embarrass a table in France, I must say that she — and Dr Grant — know what they are about," Mary waited a moment to make sure her sister had nothing further to say about yarrow or any other pernicious blooming weed that Mary cared less than three straws about, before continuing. "I do not like to bring this up in front of Dr Grant, who I know has reservation about the Mansfield theatrics, but we are having some little difficulties with the play already. Mr Edmund Bertram is steadfast in his refusal to act, meaning that Mr Charles Maddox will be solicited to play the part of Anhalt."

"Oh dear! That must be disagreeable to you. You hardly know Mr Maddox," Mrs Grant was instantly sympathetic.

Mary nodded. "It is, ma'am, I must confess it. But unless I want to be so uncivil as to leave the play *now*, I must make the best of it. There is also trouble with the role of Cottager's Wife."

"How so?"

"Poor Miss Price finds acting abhorrent (I believe she quite dreads the thought!) and does not want the part, yet Mr Tom Bertram, with a decided lack of delicacy, is badgering her to be useful in that manner. Worse still, the hateful Mrs Norris is trying to bully Miss Price into the role with intimations of what she owes her cousins, considering her dependence."

Mrs Grant's face showed her revulsion. "That is appalling! Poor Miss Price. I thought little of Mrs Norris before, but I think less of her now. I am sure they will pressure Miss Price into the role eventually. As obliging and meek as she is, she cannot withstand them long."

"Well," Mary began, "if you would consent to be our Cottager's Wife, then no one would try to chivvy Miss Price into the part. She would be safe. Nonetheless, if the idea of acting is uncongenial to you, I would not have you do it for the world." Mary wanted to spare Miss Price pain, because she felt pity for her, but would not save her at a sibling's expense.

"Me?" Mrs Grant thought for a moment, then smiled broadly. "I should like that I believe. It is a small role?"

"Very small, but very important," Mary informed her.

"I must, of course, ask Dr Grant's opinion on it, but if he makes no difficulties I don't see why I should not take the part," Mrs Grant said.

"Dear Mrs Grant, that is so very obliging of you! I am certain Miss Price will feel it as she aught."

"I am certain she will as well. If there is any creature in the wide world who is less capable of ingratitude than Miss Price, I should like to see it. No little favour may be done without incurring her thanks. She is a very sweet girl," Mrs Grant said.

Mary had a mischievous idea. "There is perhaps something you could do to alleviate my situation with Mr Maddox," Mary kept her countenance sober.

"If there is any good I might do you, just tell me," Mrs Grant was all consideration.

"You could take the role of Anhalt, as well as that of the Cottager's Wife."

Mrs Grant looked flabbergasted. "Me? As Anhalt?"

"Oh yes," Mary said cheerfully. "Some of the finest female performers excel at a breeches role, you know. Why, didn't Dora Jordan take Drury Lane by storm in such roles? My only concern is that the Duke of York should hear of it, and demand an invitation to the play. Now that he and Mrs Jordan have parted company, his heart would be yours for the taking."

Mrs Grant burst into a booming laugh. "Mary, you had me convinced you were serious for half a moment! Me, in a breeches role; the absurdity of it diverts me excessively."

"But I am very serious," Mary claimed, but gave away her jocosity by her own uncontrollable smile. "I am sure Dr Grant could have no objection to his wife prancing on the Park's little stage in breeches. The wife of a respectable rector would face no opprobrium from her husband, nor censure from his parishioners, simply for donning inexpressibles and a short coat."

"No, not a bit I'm sure," Mrs Grant replied in the same vein. "Would the breeches be buckskins then?"

"I think they should be satin, sewed as tightly as possible. Perhaps in a modest colour like coquelicot?" The poppy-red of coquelicot was the most noticeable colour in Christendom, and to wear too much of it was to court scandal even if the dress was in all other ways decorous.

"And what shall I wear to pair with it?" Mrs Grant's tongue was firmly in her cheek. "A spencer? Or perhaps just a shirt and waistcoat?"

"I think it advisable that you wear Tahitian garb, ma'am, such as Capitan Cook described," Mary recommended.

"Tahitian garb?" Mrs Grant was momentarily perplexed. "I am unfamiliar with Tahitian garb."

"That is because they wear *none*, ma'am."

Mrs Grant went into a positive fit of hilarity. "Lord!" she said when she got her breath back, "That would make me a popular actress, indeed. I'll be sure to mention it to Dr Grant tonight, and discover his opinion on it."

Tittering at their own naughtiness, the sisters made no less than three turns around the shrubbery before they felt themselves composed enough to return inside the parsonage.

ıı

Mary had just changed into her new mustard-coloured wool riding habit when a maid came to tell her that Mr Edmund Bertram had arrived. She was glad she wearing clothes that clearly indicated that she was about to be active; it was a good excuse for leaving Mr Bertram's company in as short a time as possible. She was in no mood to give him consequence after his negligent attention to her the night before.

"Mr Bertram," Mary swept into the drawing-room with her brightest smile. She wanted him to feel the full force of her beauty, so that he might regret his haughtiness sufficiently. She had even applied the faintest hint of Pear's Liquid Blooms of Roses on her cheeks and an alkanet-hued lip salve, to gild the lily. "How good of you to visit. Please have a seat. I'm afraid I cannot offer to play the harp for you, though. As you see, I was about to go for a ride. My brother has already gone to the stables to await me."

Edmund bowed and then sat. He looked uncomfortable, and seemed hesitant. Mary waited patiently for him to speak. "I have come with some information I hope will be pleasing to you," he finally said.

"Really?" Mary was civil, but her air was distant and uninterested.

Edmund shifted in his seat and cleared his throat. "I have agreed to play the role of Anhalt, if that is agreeable to you."

Instantly Mary became all lively warmth. She poured out her delight upon Edmund. "How happy I am to get this news, Mr Bertram! I was very discomposed by the idea of someone not familiar to me — someone not an intimate friend — in that role. But with *you* I am sure I shall be easy. With *you*, there is nothing to concern me."

This was not spoken to an insensible audience. Edmund felt the compliment as deeply as Mary could have wished. His face coloured, and he did his best to brush away any untoward praise. He was merely doing what he ought in consideration of Miss Crawford. Her feelings should be respected.

"In turn, I have some happy news for you, Mr Bertram." Mary's dimples were once again his to command. "Or at least it is happy news for Miss Price, and as you are a very good friend to her, I think it reasonable to suppose it be happy news for you as well."

"Anything you could have to tell me is pleasant, I am sure." Edmund wasn't a gallant man, but he *was* a smitten one, and that sometimes caused a sort of inadvertent gallantry.

"Mrs Grant has been so obliging as to accept the part of the Cottager's Wife. Miss Price is safe from any further importune requests that she fill the role."

"I am very glad to hear it," Edmund was so happy he looked almost lively. "This is your doing, Miss Crawford. This is your amiable consideration at work. I honour you for it."

Mary, to her own surprise, blushed. "It was but the work of a moment, Mr Bertram. The chiefest merit goes to my sister, for her good nature and obligingness."

"I know it is unchivalrous to contradict a lady, but I must dispute that, Miss Crawford." Edmund was earnest. "It was *your* thoughtfulness that made you seek to find some way of relieving Fanny. It was *your* thoughtfulness that prompted your petition to Mrs Grant. It displays an affability and delicacy that cannot be valued highly enough."

"You give me too much credit, Mr Bertram." If Mary had been a cat, she would have purred under his heated onslaught of praise.

While Edmund was protesting that there could never be too much credit to Miss Crawford's merits, Henry entered the room looking for his sister. Hasty explanations and apologies were made by Mary and Edmund; she for having kept her brother waiting and he for detaining her. Henry waved them away as a matter of little concern, and instead made merry with the fact that Edmund was to be Anhalt.

"That is splendid of you, Bertram," Henry was so moved he shook Edmund's hand. "You have come to my sister's rescue. You have brought peace and happiness with you. I cannot thank you enough, sir."

Again, Edmund's cheeks took on a crimson shade. "Please, speak of it no more, I beg you. It is a small matter. It is nothing of true importance."

"Since you will not accept my effusions, will you accept my invitation?" Henry asked. "Would you like to join us for a ride?"

Regretfully, Edmund explained that he could not. "I have promised to return as expediently as possible to the park. I trust I will see you both there later in the morning? And perhaps you and the Grants will dine with us tomorrow?"

Henry and Mary assured him that he would see them at the Park shortly after noon, and that they would be happy to dine with them, and that they were positive the Grants would be happy to as well, if they were not engaged elsewhere. Then, in a stately flurry of thanks and counter-thanks, Edmund was gone, leaving Henry and Mary to make their way to the stables and ride out in a superlative mood.

॥

"Well, Mary," Henry asked when they were mounted and striking across the meadow for the trail alongside the River Nene, "how do you feel about Mr Edmund Bertram *now?*"

Mary gave him an impish smile. "He was in better looks this morning. He was nearly handsome again."

Henry snorted. "Yes, I am sure as soon you felt your power over the poor chap has been proved, he was handsome again. Women do like to see a man at their beck and call. They soon form as much affection for him as they do for their lapdogs."

"You are a nigmenog," Mary rolled her eyes. "Edmund Bertram is no lapdog. Edmund Bertram is perhaps a mastiff, but he's no little spaniel for me to carry about in my arms and shed fur everywhere. No, it is not my *power* over him that makes me happy; it is that he showed such consideration of my feelings, and put my needs ahead of his own determination. *That*, brother, is sweet indeed."

"This is different from power over him, then? I think you are splitting the hair very fine."

"It *is* different," Mary insisted. "Power over a man, as it is expressed in conversation, means very little. All coxcombs and puppies swear some woman has power over them, but all that means is that they wish her to flirt with *them*, not some other fellow. Or they want to make her believe she has power over *them*, so they may gain power over *her*. I do not wish for power over a man. I wish for a man to treat me as though *my* happiness is more important to him than what *he* wants. Besides, the very term 'power over a man' is detestable. It is something Maria Bertram would say about Rushworth – and she would likely be right. Power over a man indicates he is lacking strength. No, for me let his subjugation be voluntary. Only then will I know that it is *for* me and not because of me."

"You seem to have given this a great deal of thought," Henry's voice was surprised. "I had no idea you felt so strongly about the proper way for a man to prove his courtship."

"If you, Henry, were a woman who had seen how our aunt was so disdainfully treated by the Admiral, then you would be leery as well. He married her for her wealth, and his superciliousness began almost as soon as the wedding cake was eaten. Our aunt always made it clear to me that the safest path to matrimony was to marry a very wealthy man, who wanted *you* rather than your blunt, or to marry a man who put his lover ahead of himself. Since I have never met the later, I am determined on the former," Mary was firm.

"Bertram seems to have put you first; is he not exactly what you suspect doesn't exist?" Her brother asked, leaving aside his disagreement regarding their uncle's treatment of their aunt.

Henry did not consider the subject of selfishness as a measure of love to encompass him, but it did. Mary was aware that she was the only woman in the world he had ever really loved, and that he had never felt the slightest urge to put her needs first in anything other than the most trivial concerns. He would buy her presents and travel with her, but he would not bestir himself enough to establish a house when she had to flee the Admiral's residence. However, the small efforts he made were leviathan concessions compared to the relentless insolence and contempt the Admiral showed his wife. Mary had chalked the whole business up to the idea that Henry was a gentleman of wealth and ease, but the Admiral was *not*. Only men of wealth and ease could be trusted to provide a tolerable marriage. Mere love would not do. Even Dr Grant, for all that he loved his wife, expected her to give way to his every whim and quibble. Mary was determined that a man should prove himself *extremely* obliging before she could hazard herself in wedlock.

Mary put on a sportive air to reply to Henry. "Perhaps he is a paragon, but his being a second son is too great a flaw. If he were the second son and in the army … that might be bearable. But a clergyman? I would wind up deranged, and be found wandering the moors reciting Burn's "Holy Willie's Prayer" while I wept and beat my breast."

"There are very few moors in Northamptonshire," Henry pointed out reasonably.

"If I married a parson, some would spring up, like Athena from her father's brow, just so I could wander them."

"It's almost a shame. I think Bertram would treat you well. Would that not make a rusticated life bearable?"

Mary looked at him askance. "And when are *you* proposing to leave Town behind and embrace the idylls of nature and the quaint yeomanry that infests it? For myself, I agree with Crabbe:

'Go! if the peaceful cot your praises share,
Go, look within, and ask if peace be there:
If peace be his—that drooping weary sire,
Or theirs, that offspring round their feeble fire,
Or hers, that matron pale, whose trembling hand
Turns on the wretched hearth th' expiring brand.

"One day I shall catch you out with no ready borrowed wit or verse to refute me or mock me, and then you shall have to admit my superior wisdom," Henry jested in false woe.

"You shan't," Mary laughed, but she was certain.

They were forced to let their horses go single file for a small stretch of narrowed path, and then Henry came alongside Mary once more.

"Do you know what this talk of power and puppies and poems has made me think of?" Mary asked.

"I am afraid," was his reply.

"It's recalled Colonel Tilney to my mind."

"Colonel Tilney! I haven't thought of him in an age," Henry searched his memory. "He was a particularly pernicious suitor when you first came out, back in '08, wasn't he? Brother of the Viscountess Painswick? Handsome, but the most affected puppy to have ever barked in a ballroom?"

Mary nodded. "That is the self-same Colonel Tilney of whom I speak. If he wasn't Eleanor's brother I would not have given him the civility that *he* felt to be encouragement."

"The Viscountess Painswick is one of the most gentle ladies I have ever met; that Colonel Tilney is her brother never ceases to astound me," Henry said. "Didn't he make the most confounded nuisance of himself all that season?"

"It wasn't until the end of the Season in '09 — that was the August I went to Twickenham with the Aylmers; do you recall? – that

I was finally able to escape him. How grateful I was to hear he was gone to Portugal again!"

Henry smiled. "It was not altogether disagreeable to have such an ardent swain, though was it? His ardour increased your popularity."

"True, but at what a sacrifice? He was so *tedious* and his flirtation has all the subtlety of a bellowing bull. 'Oh Miss Crawford! Your beauty torments me! You have such power over me!' What a bag of moonshine he tried to get me to buy from him."

"Yes, but I think your tricks on him brought you more amusement than his courtship cost you."

Mary snickered. "I will always remember when I made up that poem to gull Colonel Tilney, that is true. I have never been more diverted in my life! He was always and forever more misquoting poets around me, unaware that I could see through his sham erudition to the ignorance underneath, until I could bear it no longer and *had* to tease him for his foolishness. Lord! How amused I was when I pretended to read him a romantic poem from an anthology that I wished his opinion on, since I trusted his *judgement* in such matters, when it was only the most dreadful mish-mash of oft-quoted couplets I could devise. Anyone who had actually *read* poetry would have heard immediately what I had done, but someone like Tilney – some coxcomb who had just learned to *use* snips of poetry in conversation to feign an appreciation of it – would be properly caught out. And how I did catch him out! Did you know I even included the words 'fee, fie, fum' somewhere in it! I bamboozled him completely. He gave me the most *solemn*, the most *earnest* opinion of the tommyrot I had just read. I had to pretend to be overcome by emotion, as an excuse to hold my handkerchief to my face in order to hide my mirth."

Her brother laughed heartily at the idea of Colonel Tilney trying to convince Mary that her fiddle-faddle had deep meaning. "What a buffoon! I pity the Viscountess Painswick her brother."

"Happily, Eleanor has another brother for whom she need not blush. She says he is witty and kind, and that his wife is as much her sister in truth as she is by law. I cannot give you a first-hand account of him, though; he's not been to London since '07. He's a rector content to stay in Gloucestershire with his wife and their ever-growing brood of children," Mary made a noise that would have been called a snort if she weren't so ladylike in manner. "Isn't that what all rectors do if they can?"

"But wouldn't that give you all the time you need to spend in the nursery with your children, as you have told me you wish to do?"

"That would give me *more* than enough time. I wish to be with my children often but I don't intend to eat dinner at three o'clock and go to bed an hour later. I wish for some amusement *other* than watching trees grow, no matter *how* much nature is eulogised in verse." Mary hesitated, then honestly compelled her to say, "Not that our time here has been unhappy."

"It has been more pleasurable than expected, hasn't it?" Henry's horse shied when a hare broke from the tall grass, but he reined the roan in expertly. "It's not been so different than a house-party. It is having society worth mingling with that has made it so much more congenial than we were expecting."

"True," Mary agreed. "I was afraid that it would be all half-gentlemen and underbred squires in the neighbourhood; I had not foreseen Mansfield Park. The society of people who have gentility and manner enlivens existence as much in Northamptonshire as in Town. If I would have had to have endured the nothing but the Olivers or Mr Maddox as the pinnacle of company I would have been here less than a fortnight before I wrote to you for a rescue. I am very glad we made the acquaintance of the Bertrams."

"The Bertrams have been very agreeable," Henry mouth curled upwards, "especially the Park's fair ladies."

Mary said slyly, "I do not think the Park's fair ladies will be as glad to have met *us* as we have been to meet *them* once you leave, Henry. I think they shall both have their hearts broke."

"Their vanity will be the only thing injured, I assure you." Henry remained nonchalant about the feelings of Maria and Julia, even though Julia's recent snit and present coldness should have enlightened him as to how much the sisters were dependent on his attentions. It would have been inconvenient for him to see their passions; it would have lessened his pleasure. Thus, he did not see it.

"Perhaps, but Maria Bertram's vanity is not a trivial concern. She is good company, but her conceit is a colossus that could bestride the earth. You may regret having called the giant's notice to you, Henry."

Her brother did not heed her warnings. How could a flirtation with Maria Bertram harm *him*? There was, in Henry's opinion, no reason to curtail his enjoyment over the unreasoning fear that his trifling with Maria Bertram could ever cut up *his* peace and happiness.

Chapter Eighteen

ALTHOUGH EDMUND HAD given Mary assurances that Fanny would be grateful to Mary for her thoughtfully soliciting Mrs Grant to play the role of Cottager's wife, he was sorely mistaken. If either Mary or Edmund could have read Fanny Price's thoughts, they would have seen that she was in no wise as fond *of* or as thankful *to* Miss Crawford as her cousin assumed her to be. Fanny was in love with Edmund, and she was sullenly resentful that she was beholden to Miss Crawford's kindness. There was no appreciation in her heart; no gratitude. She was full of jealousy and agitation.

Fanny was deep into her bitter spirits when practice for the play began. Miss Crawford came with looks of gaiety which seemed an insult, with friendly expressions towards herself which she could hardly answer calmly. Every body around her was gay and busy, prosperous and important; each had their object of interest, their part, their dress, their favourite scene, their friends and confederates, all were finding employment in consultations and comparisons, or diversion in the playful conceits they suggested. She alone was sad and insignificant; she had no share in any thing; she might go or stay; she might be in the midst of their noise, or retreat from it to the solitude of the East room, without being seen or missed. She could almost think any thing would have been preferable to this. Mrs Grant was of consequence; *her* good nature had honourable mention—her taste and her time were considered—her presence was wanted—she was sought for and attended, and praised; and Fanny was at first in some danger of envying her the character she had accepted. But reflection brought better feelings, and shewed her that Mrs Grant was entitled to respect, which could never have belonged to *her*, and that had she received even the greatest, she could never have been easy in joining a scheme which, considering only her uncle, she must condemn altogether.

Mary and Edmund, completely oblivious to Fanny's jealous petulance, saw only what was endearing in her actions and looks. She was retiring. She was humble. She was, as her cousin Tom called her, "creepmouse", but it was the gentle and easily domesticated dormouse that she reminded them of. They could have both put her in their pockets if they could have. They were, both of them, fooled by Fanny's docile manner into thinking she was a friend to Miss Crawford. Neither of them knew that Mary's every action was ascribed the worst motivations by Fanny, or that Mary's every kindness was being repaid by malicious dislike, or that the seemingly-delicate Fanny harboured such stern acrimoniousness toward Miss Crawford in her breast.

With a great goodwill, Mary continued to treat Fanny with unceasing consideration and cordiality as the rehearsals carried on, unknowing that if Miss Price had been initiated into the secrets of Voodoo then there would be a small effigy of Miss Crawford bristling with pins hidden away in Fanny's trunks. Fanny's blushes and stammers when Mary addressed her were misinterpreted as pleasure and shyness by Miss Crawford rather than as proofs of Fanny's implacable enmity. Mary, foolishly, made *more* efforts to distinguish Miss Price, seeing how forlorn she was amidst the bustle and enjoyment of the players, much to Fanny's chagrin and displeasure.

Mary also honoured Fanny for her attempts to help and coach Mr Rushworth to learn his part. Rushworth was as thick as a yard of lard, and no one but Fanny had the patience to go over his lines with him. For herself, Mary would have gladly stuffed his gob with his copy of the script every time he yammered or nattered about his pink satin cloak or two-and-forty speeches. Watching Miss Price calmly and with unvaried forbearance try to teach Rushworth his lines came very near to convincing Mary that Fanny was a saint.

Sainthood was very far from Maria Bertram, however. Mary saw how contemptuously Maria treated Rushworth, and how coquettishly she behaved with Henry, and came close to blushing for Maria, such was Miss Bertram's exposure of herself.

Maria's insolence toward Rushworth and unctuousness toward himself did nothing to endear her in Henry's eyes. She lowered herself daily. He saw her as nothing but a very pretty would-be jilt and hanger-on. Henry had been the recipient of too many honeyed words and manners for them to inspire his gratitude to the woman who bestowed those blandishments. Maria was not a prize. She was his for the taking. Thus, he was uninterested in her beyond the immediate amusement she could afford him.

Tom and Edward, much to the Crawfords' amazement, remained blind to the antics of their oldest sister. Mary believed that Tom simply did not care enough about his siblings to pay close attention, and that Edmund was too pure of heart to realise *what* he was seeing. Henry agreed with Mary about the cause of Edmund's lack of discernment, but he believed Tom's denseness regarding his sister's folly to be the result of the stupidity that attends self-absorption, rather than carelessness. The inattention of the Bertram brothers meant that Henry felt completely free to bask in Maria's flummery without the least obligation to return her regard.

Julia was clearly in a pet, and if she were behaving with more dignity then Mary might have even felt pity for her. As it was, Julia's obvious and unchecked discontent as a result of her jealousy of Maria engendered more disparagement than compassion in Mary's breast. It was so lacking in self-command! Julia's brothers were equally unsympathetic to her plight, considering her to be behaving with petty childishness about the role of Agatha, rather than believing her to be heart-burningly envious of Mr Crawford's addresses to Maria. Only Mr Yates was concerned and solicitous of Julia. Mary was suspicious that Yates was falling under Julia's spell, and she was likewise suspicious that Julia did not care about Yates except to use his attentions in a futile attempt to make Henry jealous.

Henry was not jealous in the least, of course. He had some initial qualms about Julia's pique, and wished to lessen her umbrage so that he could enjoy peace and harmony when he was at the Park. For a day or two after the affront was given, Henry Crawford had endeavoured to do it away by the usual attack of gallantry and compliment, but he had not cared enough about it to persevere against a few repulses; and becoming soon too busy with his play to have time for more than one flirtation, he grew indifferent to the quarrel, or rather thought it a lucky occurrence, as quietly putting an end to what might ere long have raised expectations in more than Mrs Grant.

Mrs Grant was not pleased to see Julia excluded from the play, and sitting by disregarded; but as it was not a matter which really involved her happiness, as Henry must be the best judge of his own, and as he did assure her, with a most persuasive smile, that neither he nor Julia had ever had a serious thought of each other, she could only renew her former caution as to the elder sister, entreat him not to risk his tranquillity by too much admiration there, and then gladly take her share in anything that brought cheerfulness to the young people in general, and that did so particularly promote the pleasure of the two so dear to her.

Nonetheless, Mrs Grant was too good-natured to forget Julia entirely, or to be apathetic to Julia's interest of Henry. It worried her.

"I rather wonder Julia is not in love with Henry," was her observation to Mary.

"I dare say she is," replied Mary coldly. "I imagine both sisters are." Why should she bother to deny it when the Bertram sisters did so little to hide it?

"Both! no, no, that must not be. Do not give him a hint of it. Think of Mr Rushworth!"

"You had better tell Miss Bertram to think of Mr Rushworth. It may do *her* some good. I often think of Mr Rushworth's property and independence, and wish them in other hands; but I never think of him. A man might represent the county with such an estate; a man might escape a profession and represent the county."

"I dare say he *will* be in parliament soon. When Sir Thomas comes, I dare say he will be in for some borough, but there has been nobody to put him in the way of doing anything yet."

Splendid. Another imbecilic know-nothing in parliament. Mary felt herself becoming cross at the thought, and it added to her general reluctance to see Sir Thomas return from his travels.

"Sir Thomas is to achieve many mighty things when he comes home," said Mary, after a pause. "Do you remember Hawkins Browne's 'Address to Tobacco,' in imitation of Pope? –

Blest leaf! whose aromatic gales dispense; To Templars modesty, to Parsons sense.

I will parody them –

Blest Knight! whose dictatorial looks dispense; To Children affluence, to Rushworth sense.

Will not that do, Mrs Grant? Everything seems to depend upon Sir Thomas's return."

"You will find his consequence very just and reasonable when you see him in his family, I assure you. I do not think we do so well without him. He has a fine dignified manner, which suits the head of such a house, and keeps everybody in their place. Lady Bertram seems more of a cipher now than when he is at home; and nobody else can keep Mrs Norris in order. But, Mary, do not fancy that Maria Bertram cares for Henry. I am sure *Julia* does not, or she would not have flirted as she did last night with Mr Yates; and though he and Maria are very good friends, I think she likes Sotherton too well to be inconstant."

Mary carefully prevented a smirk from keeping house on her countenance. "I would not give much for Mr Rushworth's chance if Henry stept in before the articles were signed."

"If you have such a suspicion, something must be done; and as soon as the play is all over, we will talk to him seriously and make him know his own mind; and if he means nothing, we will send him off, though he is Henry, for a time."

"I am sure he will heed your advice, ma'am," Mary lied without guilt, then changed the topic to her more immediate concern. "But I cannot occupy my mind with Henry. I am too anxious about this evening. After dinner, I am to be rehearsing the third act with Mr Edmund Bertram. It will be just us in the little theatre unless we can get Miss Price to come be our audience. I am quite discomposed when I think of the things I must say to him! To all but declare my love, and offer to teach him to love me, or that he should teach *me* that art!"

"It *is* a very forward topic, I'll own," Mrs Grant attempted to comfort her sister. "But think of how much of a gentleman Mr Edmund Bertram is. He would never press such an advantage, or make more of it than he should. If there is any man in England to whom it is safe to say those lines, it is Edmund Bertram."

Mary smiled at her sister, but was not reassured. *Edmund* might not be moved by Amelia's declarations, but what of *her*? To look at that handsome face — to gaze into those dark blue eyes — and say she loved him; how would she not feel it? He was already too much in her heart. He must be rooted out, but this act would nourish her disturbing preference for Edmund. It was not what she wanted; and yet it *was*. She wanted to be in the play. She wanted him to be Anhalt. She wanted him to admire her. What she did *not* want was her own weakness to his strange allure.

Yet why *should* she like him? He was not charming. He gave no gallant compliments. She did not agree with him on many topics, and absolutely disagreed with him on many topics she felt were of utmost importance. He should have no hope of winning her. She should be indifferent to him, or even dismissive of him. Nonetheless, this plain-spoken, church-bound second son had come near to captivating her. It was beyond her understanding of herself.

"I have an idea!" Mary brightened as a sudden inspiration came to her. "I shall go ask Miss Price to rehearse with me, and help me grow comfortable. Will that not suit, Mrs Grant?"

Mrs Grant approved of Mary's idea with all the support Mary could have hoped for. "What a perfect plan! No one could happier to be of service than Miss Price, and no one could be a safer foil for your rehearsal. She is so delicate, so unmanly in characteristics, you could recite the balcony scene in Romeo and Juliet to her without a blush."

"Dear Miss Price," Mary mused. "I only wish I could do more to give her that respect and attention which her cousins — excepting Edmund Bertram — are appallingly remiss in giving her."

"I saw the great pains you took to require her help when Mrs Norris came looking for Fanny to press her into more needlework," Mrs Grant looked at her sister fondly. "If you had not said you had already claimed Fanny's help in prompting you in the second act, the poor girl would have been trapped sewing seams for hours while Mrs Norris harangued her. I am sure she would have patiently stitched until her fingers bled and her eyes gave out without complaint, but listening to the constant attacks of her odious aunt would have fatigued her beyond endurance."

Some little domestic matter called Mrs Grant from the room, leaving Mary in the drawing-room with tatting. Mary didn't like thread-craft without conversation to accompany it, and was debating between reading or playing her harp when Mrs Grant returned, making such a change in occupation unneeded.

"Do you know what Mrs Norris reminds me of?" Mrs Grant asked, when she had resettled herself with her tambour frame.

"We are too close to a farmyard for my guess not to be indelicate."

Mrs Grant laughed. "You are closer than you know, but it is a farm *animal* that she reminds me of. Mrs Norris reminds me of one of my hens; the first one who will try to peck another chicken to death the minute she spots a weakness in the bird."

"Do chickens *do* that?" Mary's experience with chickens involved her dinner plate.

"Oh yes," her sister told her, "it is distressingly common in chickens. If one of the hens is ill or injured, and I do not find it out and separate the bird from the rest of the flock, the other fowl will peck the poor thing to death. It is very gruesome. Sometimes the hen will still be alive in the morning, but with her feathers mostly gone and her eyes pecked out. I have to have Jackie the farm-lad come and wring its neck to put it out of its misery."

Mary was appalled. "My God! I thought chickens were timid and cowardly birds. I had no idea the bloodthirsty horrors that their coups hide."

Her sister shrugged. "It is nature my dear; it is the way God made them and it is not worth worrying about. I only mention it because Mrs Norris reminds me of one particular hen who always looks for a weaker bird to peck, even if the other fowl is hale and whole. Jackie the farm-lad says that it that hen that always leads the first attack on an injured chicken. Mrs Norris pecks at Fanny because she sees Fanny is shy and timid; she believes these qualities to be a weakness, and so she attacks."

"I beg you to show me this dastardly hen tomorrow," Mary falsely pleaded with a grin. "I shall christen her Mrs Norris and know to watch for her from the corner of my eye."

"You are so silly. Do you think the hen will stalk you, as if it were some Indian tiger?"

"I've read somewhere that the native Indians wear masks on the back of their heads, because the tiger will only pounce when no one is watching. The mask fools the beast into thinking it is seen, so it does not attack. Perhaps I should get a mask in case Mrs Norris the hen creeps up behind me in the shrubbery?"

Mrs Grant began to giggle. "Is that common in your Gothic novels? Do innocent maidens flee through the shrubbery, chased by a demonic chicken? Are the damsels kept imprisoned in a mouldering abbey, unable to leave lest the dread hen attack?"

"What a fine book that would make," Mary laughed as well. "I can see it now. *The Cursed Chicken of Castle Cully: A Tale of Murder Most Fowl* by Mrs Ima Simkin-Sapscull."

"You are a sauce box, Mary!"

"You only say that because you would be the villainess of the piece; the cruel half-sister determined to have me killed because you will either inherit my fortune or plan to console my true-love until he loves you in return. Change the parsonage into a decrepit castle atop an Italian cliff and me into an ethereally lovely ingénue and our situation is straight from between the covers of a horrid novel."

"Mrs Grant is much too commonplace a name for such a villainess as I will be. I need a title and an ominous surname."

Mary thought for a minute. "I think you should be Baroness Brunhilda De Praved."

"And you?"

"Miss Dotty Von Noddy would do, I should think."

"And the hero?"

"Mr Jacob Broadshoulder, future Lord of Feeble, from Mediocre-upon-Insipid, of course."

"If there were such a book in the circulating library, I vow that I would be on its doorstep tomorrow morning as soon as it should open in the hopes of obtaining a copy," Mrs Grant was very entertained by her lively sister's flights of fancy.

"Woe it is then," Mary moaned as she raised one hand dramatically to her brow, leading with the wrist, "that I should have no talent for writing," She lowered her hand and spoke naturally again. "Although it must be said that many authors I have encountered have as little talent for writing as I do."

"You are uncharitable, dear," Mrs Grant reprimanded her gently. "Not everyone can be Mrs Radcliffe or Mrs Edgeworth."

"Then not everyone should pick up their pen and make their scritch-scratch public," Mary remained unrepentantly tart-tongued. As far as Mary was concerned, the world was full of folly that deserved unceasing raillery. "It invites comment."

"If I were you Mary, I should be careful what I said aloud about authors."

"Whyever for?"

"They might be tempted to set a chicken loose upon you in the shrubberies of their imaginations."

When the Henry and Dr Grant entered the room a few minutes later, they were baffled as to why Dr, Grant's comment that the chicken had been a little tough at dinner inspired such unchecked hilarity in Mary and Mrs Grant.

An explanation followed, which led to the moniker of The Old Chook being ascribed to Mrs Norris for perpetuity.

ǁ

Fanny worked and meditated in the East room, undisturbed, for a quarter of an hour, when a gentle tap at the door was followed by the entrance of Miss Crawford.

"Am I right? Yes; this is the East room. My dear Miss Price, I beg your pardon, but I have made my way to you on purpose to entreat your help." Mary smiled warmly at Fanny Price, whom she sincerely thought of as dear girl.

Fanny, quite surprised, endeavoured to shew herself mistress of the room by her civilities, and looked at the bright bars of her empty grate with concern.

"Thank you; I am quite warm, very warm. Allow me to stay here a little while, and do have the goodness to hear me my third act. I have brought my book, and if you would but rehearse it with me, I should be *so* obliged! I came here to-day intending to rehearse it with Edmund – by ourselves – against the evening, but he is not in the way; and if he *were*, I do not think I could go through it with *him*, till I have hardened myself a little; for really there is a speech or two. You will be so good, won't you?"

Fanny was most civil in her assurances, though she could not give them in a very steady voice. Mary assumed the trembling was the result of Miss Price's excessive diffidence.

"Have you ever happened to look at the part I mean?" continued Miss Crawford, opening her book. "Here it is. I did not think much of it at first – but, upon my word. There, look at *that* speech, and *that*, and *that*. How am I ever to look him in the face and say such things? Could you do it? But then he is your cousin, which makes all the difference. You must rehearse it with me, that I may fancy *you* him, and get on by degrees. You *have* a look of *his* sometimes."

"Have I? I will do my best with the greatest readiness; but I must *read* the part, for I can say very little of it."

Miss Crawford gave the girl an encouraging smile. "*None* of it, I suppose. You are to have the book, of course. Now for it. We must have two chairs at hand for you to bring forward to the front of the stage. There – very good school-room chairs, not made for a theatre, I dare say; much more fitted for little girls to sit and kick their feet against when they are learning a lesson. What would your governess and your uncle say to see them used for such a purpose? Could Sir Thomas look in upon us just now, he would bless himself, for we are rehearsing all over the house. Yates is storming away in the dining-room. I heard him as I came upstairs, and the theatre is engaged of course by those indefatigable rehearsers, Agatha and Frederick. If *they* are not perfect, I *shall* be surprised. By the bye, I looked in upon them five minutes ago, and it happened to be exactly at one of the times when they were trying *not* to embrace, and Mr Rushworth was with me. I thought he began to look a little queer, so I turned it off as well as I could, by whispering to him, 'We shall have an excellent Agatha; there is something so *maternal* in her manner, so completely *maternal* in her voice and countenance.' Was not that well done of me? He brightened up directly. Now for my soliloquy."

She began, and with such an Anhalt Miss Crawford had courage enough. It was hard to imagine Miss Price as a lover, and there was no consciousness to stay Mary's voice. They had got through half the scene, when a tap at the door brought a pause, and the entrance of Edmund, the next moment, suspended it all.

Surprise, consciousness, and pleasure appeared in each of the three on this unexpected meeting; and as Edmund was come on the very same business that had brought Miss Crawford, consciousness and pleasure were likely to be more than momentary in *them*. He too had his book, and was seeking Fanny, to ask her to rehearse with him, and help him to prepare for the evening, without knowing Miss Crawford to be in the house; and great was the joy and animation of being thus thrown together, of comparing schemes, and sympathising in praise of Fanny's kind offices. Mary and Edmund were delighted to have shown such shared delicacy of feeling. The admiration they each gave the other was a reflection of the pride they each felt for their own refinement of taste.

They must now rehearse together. Edmund proposed, urged, entreated it, till the lady, not very unwilling at first, could refuse no longer, and Fanny was wanted only to prompt and observe them. Bitterly unwilling but placid in appearance, Miss Price did as she was bid. In watching them she forgot herself; and, agitated by the increasing spirit of Edmund's manner, had once closed the page and turned away exactly as he wanted help. It was imputed to very reasonable weariness, and she was thanked and pitied; but she deserved their pity more than she hoped they would ever surmise. At last the scene was over, and Fanny forced herself to add her praise to the compliments each was giving the other. Neither Edmund nor Mary was mistrustful of Fanny's kindness, since neither knew what a worm-eaten heart was buried in the affectionate sentimentality. Both were credulous regarding Fanny Price's avowed regard for Mary Crawford.

Chapter Nineteen

THE FIRST REGULAR rehearsal of the three first acts was certainly to take place in the evening of October 10th: Mrs Grant and the Crawfords were engaged to return for that purpose as soon as they could after dinner; and every one concerned was looking forward with eagerness. There seemed a general diffusion of cheerfulness on the occasion. Tom was enjoying such an advance towards the end; Edmund was in spirits from the morning's rehearsal, and little vexations seemed everywhere smoothed away.

They did not wait long for the Crawfords, but there was no Mrs Grant. She could not come. Dr Grant, professing an indisposition, for which he had little credit with his fair sister-in-law, could not spare his wife.

"Dr Grant is ill," said Miss Crawford, with mock solemnity. "He has been ill ever since he did not eat any of the pheasant today. He fancied it tough, sent away his plate, and has been suffering ever since." The fact that he was discommoding the Crawfords and the Bertrams as well as his spouse had not deterred Dr Grant's insistence on being coddled by his wife.

Here was disappointment! Mrs Grant's non-attendance was sad indeed. Her pleasant manners and cheerful conformity made her always valuable amongst them; but *now* she was absolutely necessary. They could not act, they could not rehearse with any satisfaction without her. The comfort of the whole evening was destroyed. What was to be done? Tom, as Cottager, was in despair. After a pause of perplexity, some eyes began to be turned towards Fanny, and a voice or two to say, "If Miss Price would be so good as to *read* the part." She was immediately surrounded by supplications; everybody asked it; even Edmund said, "Do, Fanny, if it is not *very* disagreeable to you."

But Fanny still hung back. She could not endure the idea of it. Miss Crawford and Edmund each felt a stir of guilt in asking Miss Price to do something she disliked so excessively, but their desire to act the scene together once more squashed their normal considerations.

"You have only to *read* the part," said Henry Crawford, with renewed entreaty.

"And I do believe she can say every word of it," added Maria, "for she could put Mrs Grant right the other day in twenty places. Fanny, I am sure you know the part."

Fanny could not say she did *not*; and as they all persevered, as Edmund repeated his wish, and with a look of even fond dependence on her good-nature, she must yield. She would do her best.

They *did* begin; and being too much engaged in their own noise to be struck by an unusual noise in the other part of the house, had proceeded some way when the door of the room was thrown open, and Julia, appearing at it, with a face all aghast, exclaimed, "My father is come! He is in the hall at this moment."

Mary's sharp eye saw that Julia's three siblings were equally alarmed, although they all quickly schooled their countenances. After a brief consultation with one another, they walked off, utterly heedless of Mr Rushworth's repeated question of, "Shall I go too? Had not I better go too? Will not it be right for me to go too?" but they were no sooner through the door than Henry Crawford undertook to answer the anxious inquiry, and, encouraging him by all means to pay his respects to Sir Thomas without delay, sent him after the others with delighted haste.

As soon as he had gone, the other three, no longer under any restraint, were giving vent to their feelings of vexation, lamenting over such an unlooked-for premature arrival as a most untoward event, and without mercy wishing poor Sir Thomas had been twice as long on his passage, or were still in Antigua. Mary Crawford amused Yates and Henry by wondering aloud why they had not beseeched Poseidon to send an errant current or two to delay the ship; did they not have plenty of doves that they could have sacrificed?

The Crawfords were more warm on the subject than Mr Yates, from better understanding the family, and judging more clearly of the mischief that must ensue. The ruin of the play was to them a certainty: they felt the total destruction of the scheme to be inevitably at hand; while Mr Yates considered it only as a temporary interruption, a disaster for the evening, and could even suggest the possibility of the rehearsal being renewed after tea, when the bustle of receiving Sir Thomas were over, and he might be at leisure to be amused by it. The Crawfords laughed at the idea; and having soon agreed on the propriety of their walking quietly home and leaving the family to themselves, proposed Mr Yates's accompanying them and spending the evening at the Parsonage. But Mr Yates, having never been with those who thought much of parental claims, or family confidence, could not perceive that anything of the kind was necessary; and therefore, thanking them, said, "he preferred remaining where he was, that he might pay his respects to the old gentleman handsomely since he *was* come; and besides, he did not think it would be fair by the others to have everybody run away."

Mary and Henry could do nothing else but wish Mr Yates a good evening, and leave him to his folly.

॥

Dr and Mrs Grant were startled and concerned when Mary and Henry returned to the parsonage so soon after they had left it. Once the initial fears of injury or illness were soothed away, Mary and Henry could inform their sister and her husband of Sir Thomas Bertram's return to Mansfield Park.

"Did he look well?" Mrs Grant inquired. "Was he much fagged by such a trip?"

"I regret I cannot answer your question, ma'am," Henry explained. "We were not near the front of the house when he returned, and we thought it prudent not to force an introduction on him tonight, when he was so newly returned."

"You did absolutely right," Dr Grant approved. "I mean to pay my respects to Sir Thomas as soon as possible, which to my mind will be the day after tomorrow."

"We tried to get Mr Yates to come away with us," Mary said, "but it was like talking to a block of wood. He saw no need to allow the family some privacy to rejoice in the modern Odysseus's homecoming."

Dr Grant smiled at Mary's comparison of the staid English baronet to a Greek hero-king gone from home for twenty years. "At least Sir Thomas does not find Mr Yates to be a suitor for his wife."

"If anyone could out wait a dozen ardent suitors, it is Lady Bertram," Henry couldn't help but point out. "She would just *defer* them to their deaths." Henry, a naturally active man, was both fascinated and repulsed by Lady Bertram's seemingly unshakable inertness. He had occasionally considered setting her dress alight, just to see if she *could* be roused to quick movement or agitation.

"Since we speak of suitors, how did Mr Rushworth react to the arrival of Maria's father?" Mrs Grant was very curious to find out what Sir Thomas thought to his future son.

"As Mr Rushworth usually reacts: stupidly." In the privacy of the parsonage, Mary had no mercy on Maria's very wealthy dunce of a lover. "Henry and I had to advise him for a solid five minutes that he should join the family party before he finally went. If I had known the method of semaphoric communication I would have tried *that* to impart my message, since words were not penetrating Mr Rushworth's fog of dullness."

"I am sure he will improve under Sir Thomas's guidance," Mrs Grant's optimism was shared by no one else in their small group.

"I have a great admiration for the character and abilities of Sir Thomas, but I do not believe him capable of miracles," said a sardonic Dr Grant.

Mrs Grant frowned, and looked unusually serious, so much so that Dr Grant asked if he had offended her with his less than charitable assessment of Mr Rushworth's capabilities for improvement.

"No, dear. I know he is a *stolid* young man," which was as close as Mrs Grant ever came to calling someone bacon brained. "I am worried about something else, and unsure how to best approach the topic," She cut a look towards her brother. "It is to do with Maria Bertram and Henry, and I do not wish to be officious or meddlesome."

Henry immediately attempted to reassure her. "My dear madam, do not make yourself uneasy. Anything you wish to say to me is welcome, and I will take it as proof of your regard that you are concerned."

Mrs Grant still looked a little worried. "It is just that — I mean to say — are you perhaps too fond of Maria Bertram for your own happiness?"

A smile spread across Henry's face. "Mrs Grant, you have made yourself disquieted without cause. I can assure you, from the bottom of my heart, that I am not in love with Maria Bertram. She is a beauty, and elegant, and because she was engaged I could be gallant without raising expectations in her. I am sadly addicted to being gallant, you know. I must have an object to admire. Miss Bertram is too intelligent to have suspected anything else, or to take my civilities seriously. She knows what she is about. She does not love Mr Rushworth but she is fond enough of Sotherton to marry him without repining. Do not worry for either me or your friend."

Henry's explanations — which sounded sincere because he wished it to be true, and thus have his conscience remain untroubled — satisfied Mrs Grant. The idea that Henry was a cad, a cold-hearted flirt who did not care about the hearts he might break, was too abhorrent to his sister for her to entertain any suspicions of him. Dr Grant thought that perhaps Henry was a little *too* sure of Maria Bertram's knowing he was not serious, but Dr Grant liked Henry too well to be much concerned about any proclivities his brother-in-law might have toward making conceited young women fall in love with him. Mary could only turn her head so that Mrs Grant could not see her amusement at Henry's self-deluding platitudes.

Mary knew that Henry was capable of genuine feeling. He had grieved as deeply as she had where their parents had died within a year of one another, and he was sincerely attached to herself, Mrs Grant, and the Admiral. Henry had even become very fond of Dr Grant, in spite of his being an occasional valetudinarian. There were even members of his acquaintance that he cared for, and did everything in his power to facilitate their happiness. Nevertheless, Henry was, in the common way, a misanthrope. He regarded most people as heartless and self-serving and shallow as puddles. She could not even say he was wrong. It was only with people whom Henry considered *worthy* of his attachment and effort that he became attached. Of the Bertram siblings, Mary knew that he thought Edward to be the only one who was deserving of true friendship.

Although she wished Tom and his sisters no *harm*, and thought them very pleasant company, Mary agreed with her brother as to their merits as *friends*. Tom would be just another handsome young man she would flirt with, and enjoy dancing with, but she could not esteem him. Maria and Julia would always be welcome in her circle, and she could chat with either with great enjoyment for hours altogether, but they would never be boon companions. Even her boon companions, Lady Stornoway and Mrs Fraser, were not as dear to her as she was to them. Her closeness with them had been from habit more than feeling for many years. She had liked them well enough at the London seminary they had attended as girls, but their continued friendship owed more to the fact she found no reason to *not* continue friendship. She liked the Viscountess of Painswick much more, and thought she could come to love her, but she saw Eleanor too seldom to have invested much of her heart. As it was, the only two people still in existence that she truly loved were her brother and Mrs Grant. This did not bother her. Like Shakespeare's heroine in *Much Ado About Nothing*, she thanked God for her cold blood.

"Mr Yates," Mary said in manner meant to lessen the soberness of the subject at hand, "is the only one at Mansfield Park who risks a broken heart at present. When he discovers that, once again, the play has been quitted before he could perform, I sure he will wail and gnash his teeth and perhaps rub ashes on his head. If he didn't value his tailor so much, he would probably rend his garments."

Henry interjected, "In truth, I am fond of Yates's tailor. At least when he was talking about clothes he was not practising one of his dreadful rants. It was more bearable to hear him natter on like he was the second coming of Beau Brummel than to listen to him storm and bloviate as the Baron."

Mrs Grant, in spite of her kindly disposition, could not help but giggle and add, "You *could* hear him hallooing his lines from every corner of the house, couldn't you? Mr Yates will be cruelly disappointed by Sir Thomas's return, I'm afraid."

"Not as disappointed as Sir Thomas himself," Dr Grant sighed. "I believe he will be very unhappy to discover what has been afoot in his absence. A play would, in itself, be a mark that his children were unfeeling about his dangers and toils, but a play such as *Lover's Vows* would compound the error greatly. To know his children, particularly his daughters, would consent to act in that play would be hard enough. To know that they would do while he was not there would be mortifying."

"Mr Tom Bertram will jolly him out of his ill humour soon enough," Mary remarked, without caring much about whether Tom would succeed or not. She bore a grudge against Sir Thomas, erroneously seeing him as the malevolent force driving Edmund into taking orders.

Henry echoed this sentiment. "I do not believe he will harbour any ill-will that his daughters cannot cajole away. From what The Old Chook says, Sir Thomas favours his daughters considerably."

"The Old Chook may have a harder time of soothing Sir Thomas than anyone," Dr Grant speculated. "She was left to guard the welfare of his children, and she has done an abominable job of it."

"Do you speak of her encouraging the play, or her encouragement of Maria's engagement to Mr Rushworth?" Mary asked with sweet acidity. "For myself, I know which one I should find the greater evil if I were Sir Thomas."

Mrs Grant was again moved to defend Mr Rushworth, who in his bumbling and stupidity had won her sympathy. "Mr Rushworth is not such terrible choice for a daughter. He is not witty, but he is not viscous or unprincipled. He will be kind to Maria."

"I can think of twelve-thousand reasons a year why Sir Thomas will consider the connection worth preserving," Henry said sardonically.

"Oh pooh! Sir Thomas would not promote his daughter making a match only for ambition," Mrs Grant insisted.

"Perhaps not, but I am sure it factors into the gentleman's favour," Henry pointed out, and Mrs Grant could not refute it. Seeing that he had caused her mild distress, Henry qualified, "As does the fact that as Mrs Rushworth his daughter will be within an easy ten miles distance from her family. Sir Thomas will doubtlessly prefer her to settle nearby."

"If Maria, as Mrs Rushworth, has a house in Town for the Season, I wonder if Lady Bertram will begin to join her husband in London when the Parliament is in session again?" Mary wondered.

"I sincerely doubt it," Mrs Grant replied. "Lady Bertram would not think it worth the trouble and effort."

"Lady Bertram is a good woman," Dr Grant opined, "and through Miss Price she does considerable good for the poor of the parish, but she does not stir herself for anything other than to call for her pug."

"Considering the dog's devotion to her mistress, Lady Bertram need not stir herself much there either," Henry said.

"I should not mind a lapdog," Mrs Grant said wistfully, surprising them all.

A chorus of various ways of saying "would you really?" broke out, and when it subsided, Mrs Grant spoke again.

"Yes. Mother, that is *your* mother, Henry and Mary, but she is the only mother I can recall so I think of her as *my* mother as well, had a squirrel spaniel and I loved the tiny thing fiercely. It died when you were both still in the nursery – although Henry was close to being breeched, now that I think on it – so I don't think either of you will remember it."

Both Henry and Mary admitted they did not, but Mary continued, "I do have friends with squirrel spaniels, and I can see why you would want one. Their frolics and antics are very amusing. Although I must say, Mrs Hornsby was not amused when her dog brought a pair of her husband's smalls up the stairs from the wash room and dragged them like a dead rat throughout the company in her drawing-room while a three desperate footmen and the butler chased the poor little thing to try and reclaim them."

General laughter rose from this picture, and entreaties were made that Mary tell them how the débâcle was resolved.

"I, and nearly a score of other guests, did our best to pretend we did not see the dog as it ran by, even as it scampered over our slippers, dodged between the gentleman's boots, darted under the furniture we were sitting on, and knocked over the fire irons … all while Mr Hornsby's smalls fluttered in its jaws. Seldom has the weather and chance of rain in the morning been so *fervently* discussed by people who were unable to so much as glance at the floor. Finally the dog bolted from the room, footmen and butler still pursuing it like hounds after a fox. Mrs Hornsby stood, and said with an unshakable calm, "I believe I need something stronger than tea; would anyone care to join me in a glass of wine or spirits?" Needless to say, we all needed, at the very least, a glass of wine, while several of the gentleman required something stronger."

When the mirth had abated to a reasonable level, the Grants and Crawfords agreed that wine or 'something stronger' were ideal to drink on such a night as this, either as a restorative for the disappointment of the play or as a celebratory glass to welcome Sir Thomas home.

"I don't particular want a squirrel *spaniel*, but I would like to have a *squirrel*." At the flash of his sister's dimples, Henry clarified. "The *tree dwelling animals* make superlative pets." Prostitutes where sometimes called squirrels in modern cant, and Mary's quick smirk had nearly made Henry blush, and required him to take a fortifying sip of his peach brandy. Thankfully, the Grants only thought of squirrels as the red arboreal rodents in the woods that were not infrequently kept as pets by the wealthy since medieval times.

Mary, her countenance under control after a sip of her Madeira, asked her brother to elaborate on his love of squirrels. "You mean the fancy squirrels, with the diamond collars, I assume?"

"My goodness!" Mrs Grant exclaimed. "Do some people actually put diamond collars on their pet squirrels?"

"They do indeed, ma'am. However, the kind of people who put diamonds on squirrels are not likely to be close friends of mine, so I will have no compunction about giving my pet squirrel something much less impressive as its collar," Henry replied.

"What makes you want a squirrel?" Dr Grant asked.

Henry was beginning to regret having mentioned his interest in such a pet, because his younger sister was disconcerting him by turning bright red and coughing delicately into a handkerchief. "It is the animal's intelligence, sir. It is a marvel to see the kind of tricks a squirrel can learn to perform."

Mary, who had just taken another drink of wine, choked and sputtered, and became the object of concern to the Grants. Henry, took the opportunity of the Grant's turned backs to shoot Mary a *serves you right* look.

When the small flurry of assiduity revolving around Mary's accidental inhalation of wine was over, and the family had resettled, Dr Grant brought pets up again, but fortunately had no yen for squirrels.

"My dear," he told his wife, "if I had known you wanted a dog in the house I would have let old Rufus in months ago." Rufus was the unfortunate by-product of Sir Thomas's pure-bred bloodhound bitch's liaison with a mutt of undetermined origin, and one of his many litter-mates now lolloped beside genteel non-hunters and half-gentleman in Mansfield and Stoke. He was a friendly, slobbering beast with a penchant for rolling in dung wherever he found it. He accompanied Dr Grant on his walks, both pastoral and recreational in nature, and guarded the chicken coop from foxes and weasels. Dr Grant was very fond of Rufus, but the dog slept in the stables where his fleas and stench would not unduly upset Mrs Grant.

"If you are willing to let Rufus sit under *your* chair during meals, then I have no objection." Mrs Grant called his bluff.

"Then again, Rufus is a bit large for a lapdog," Dr Grant conceded.

"I have no desire for a lapdog," Mary re-entered the conversation. "When I have my own establishment I shall get a parrot."

"Yes, but what kind?" Henry quizzed her. "The type of bird you wish to have, changes nearly every fortnight."

"I am quite determined on an African parrot," Mary told him with spirit.

"Are those the brightly coloured ones with the purple heads and green breasts?" Mrs Grant asked.

"I believe you are speaking of the cardinal parrot, ma'am," Mary explained. "The African parrot is all-over grey, excepting vermilion tail feathers. They can mimic speech very well, so much so that it is sometimes hard to distinguish between their words and the original speaker. My friend the Viscountess of Painswick has one named Echo, and I quite adore it, but she warns me that you must be careful what you say in front of it. Her father, General Tilney, discovered this fact the hard way. If it sees the General, it immediately cries out, "Quiet you bloody bird!" in his voice."

Henry looked mischievous. "I cannot *wait* to instruct your bird, Mary. The first thing I shall teach it to say is 'who's a good squirrel then' whenever a lady enters your drawing-room."

Chapter Twenty

THE DAY AFTER Sir Thomas's homecoming dawn clear and mild, an ideal situation for a long walk, of which Mary and Henry took advantage. Soon after breakfast the siblings departed on their ramble, this time heading away from the River Nene and into the meadows and woods to the northwest.

"I have some bad news, I'm afraid," Henry said, helping his sister over a stile.

"Is it to do with Russia?" Mary asked. Ever since Napoleon's sack of Moscow and the conflagration that rendered it a veritable pile of ash roughly a month before, the British had been waiting for the news that Czar Alexander had surrendered and sued for peace.

"No, it has nothing to do with Russia — although that does remind me to tell you that it appears that the Russians set fire to the city during their flight, rather than acts of arson by the French. Rather it has to do with someone we both like; Lady Hamilton."

Mary's brows contracted in concern. "Is she ill?"

"Worse," Henry's was not speaking in his usual jocose manner.

"She has died?" Mary was saddened, but not surprised. Lady Hamilton had grown older than her true age since Nelson died at Trafalgar, and had driven herself into debt trying to keep her home in Merton Place a veritable monument to her deceased lover. The government and the crown had broken their promise to Nelson to provide for Lady Hamilton and their daughter Honoria Thompson, and the ladies resources were rapidly depleting. Their relative poverty and their status as the beloved mistress and daughter of the heroic Lord Nelson had made them figures of sympathy among the populace and beau monde.

"Worse," Henry's face was grim.

Mary could only look her question at him.

"She had been thrown into debtor's prison," His sister gave a soft cry of dismay, and he continued. "Miss Thompson has gone with her."

"Is there no one who will give Miss Thompson shelter? Does the entire Admiralty forget what is owed to Nelson, and how much he loved his daughter and Lady Hamilton? Would not our uncle give her succour?" Mary was dismayed. She could think of nothing worse than to be scourged from society as a pauper. She, like Henry, thought of being cast out of the ton as a fate worse than death.

"Our uncle wrote to tell me of it, and he did offer to take Miss Thompson and a suitable companion for her into his home. He even made it clear that he would set up Mrs Chatsworth in her own house so that Miss Thompson's delicacy would not be wounded."

Mary could not help the reflexive and corrosive bitterness that information caused her. She did not begrudge Miss Thompson the civility, but she was deeply offended that the admiral had not shown a similar concern for *her*.

"Miss Thompson," Henry went on, "is so young that it has been decided she will stay by her mother's side. They have been given rooms by the jailer in his own house, so they are not being left to rot with the rabble in common cells or a hulk in the harbour, at least. Our uncle and several of the other men who served under Nelson in the Mediterranean are paying the jailer to keep Lady Hamilton and Miss Thompson in comfort."

"Is there nothing to be done? Will not Nelson's sisters and their husbands come forward to help?" Mary wondered.

"There is little they *can* do," Henry said regretfully, "Lady Hamilton's debts are too massive to be fully addressed by anyone but the royal family, and you can imagine how likely *that* is. The Admiral tells me that he, and some of Lady Hamilton's other friends, hope to free her and her daughter by stealth and get them to Calais, where they can be kept up in freedom with very little expense."

"What an ignoble end for one of the most glittering jewels in the ton," Mary said mournfully. "A woman is never truly safe unless she has led a blameless life. If she had been merely Lord Hamilton's widow, and not Nelson's famous paramour, she would have found more friends willing to help her."

"That is not always true," her brother disagreed. "Prinny's inamoratas have all done rather well."

"Not because of *his* efforts, though," Mary was sharp. "If Mary Robinson had not been the English Sappho and so celebrated for her writing, she would have died in penury, so little did he care about his promise of an annuity. Most of his other mistresses were too highly born to suffer much."

"Dearest Mary, you are overly nice about such things. This is the nineteenth century England, not fourteenth century Spain; there is much more liberality in matters of love nowadays than formerly. When Mrs Armistead, one of London's brilliant courtesans, married the Honourable Charles Fox, that was the death knell of such Gothic obsessions with absolute virtue. Lady Hamilton is in her current predicament because of her gambling debts; no other reason."

Mary couldn't help it. She rolled her eyes at her brother. "One of the many qualities I love about you is that you are a *fantasist*. What fairy story will spin for me next? That you narrowly escaped Raw-Head and Bloody-Bones when you were a tot?"

Henry, rather offended by Mary's cynical dismissal of his brave new world, was silent. The siblings walked on, traversing a beech copse and entering a meadow, until the progression of time restored equilibrium and harmony between them. This took a little more than a quarter of an hour.

The hard reality of it was that Henry was wrong. The death rattle of liberalism and tolerance could be heard in England, the last shaky gasps of aristocratic license. Moral panic was on the ascendant, spurred by the fears of the upper-classed that an English revolution to match the one in France would occur, and by the growing intolerance of the lower-classes for the socio-economic inequality that keep millions starving while the wealthy elites gorged. Pretentious pseudomorality and national pride in military conquest would be used as a band-aid to cover up Britain's gaping social wounds, a stop-gap measure that at least partially hid the rot of festering disparity. In the not too distant future, the hidebound prudery of the middle classes would compel those both higher and lower on the social scale to at least *pretend* they were conforming to austere respectability, especially in regards to anything sexual. This rigorous obsession with purity would become so scrupulous that it would become more lewd than any open display of wantonness. The natural and inescapable side effect of being constantly told "don't think about sex" would be that sex was never very far from anyone's mind. Queen Victoria's coming reign would spawn the golden-age of written pornography and the beginning of psychoanalysis, but bequeath few positive influences to its cultural descendants.

Mary was the first to extend an olive branch. "I am disappointed that the play is at an end, but for your sake more than mine. You were far and away the best actor in the company. I know you were keen to have a bigger audience."

"Thank you," Henry was mollified. "I thought you did well, also. For myself, I have never enjoyed a pursuit more. It is a shame a gentleman must be satisfied with private theatricals, and not pursue a career on stage."

"It is a shame, at that. I could easily see you commanding an audience at Drury Lane or Covenant Garden. In my opinion, your natural talent is such that you could have played Macbeth with Sarah Siddons."

"Your sisterly affection has addled your brains, Mary. *No one* is truly worthy of performing Macbeth with Mrs Siddons."

"Do you really think she had retired for good?" So many actors and actresses had said 'farewell' and then come out of retirement a year or two later that she had hopes Mrs Siddons would do the same.

Henry and Mary were one of the lucky Londoners who had gotten to see Sarah Siddon's final performance of Lady Macbeth, less than a fortnight before they left Town for Mansfield. Her sleepwalking scene was so powerful, so evocative, that the audience had cheered so loudly and so long that the play had been forced to end. Mary had clapped fiercely enough that her hands were swollen the next day. Even Henry had wept during Mrs Siddons final address to her well-wishers and admirers.

"I don't know. All I know is we will never see her equal."

A pheasant exploded out of the long grass almost under their feet, causing Mary to shriek and jerk backwards, and only Henry's quick reflexes in steadying her kept her from falling on her backside. It flew away, joined by several other panicked fowl, all of them calling kok-kok-kok as they fled.

Mary flattened her hand against her chest, and felt the rapid beating of her heart. "I think that bird nearly scared me to death!"

"If I had brought my fowling piece, I would exact revenge on him for you. Sadly, my gun is at home," Henry shaded his eyes and tracked the pheasants' flight toward some thick brush at the edge of the meadow where it became woodland again.

Mary recited:

"The whirring Pheasant springs,
And mounts, exulting on triumphant wings:
Ah! What avails his glossy, varying dyes,
His purple crest, and scarlet-circled eyes,
The vivid green his shining plumes unfold,
His painted wings, and breast that flames with gold.

"Is that Pope?" Henry asked.

"Yes, from *Windsor Forest*," Mary replied. "It seemed to be the most appropriate for the moment, but I also thought of Clare's "blund'ring pheasant, that from covert springs; his short sleep broke by early trampling feet; makes one to startle with his rustling wings; as through the boughs he seeks more safe retreat."

"Your ability to remember poetry is a marvel," Henry admired his sister's gift. "Do you know every poem about pheasants, then?"

"I know that *you* are a *goose*," Mary laughed. "But I must confess, I remember one more bit of verse regarding that noble bird; Cowper's couplet about how "the pheasant's plumes, which round enfold; his mantling neck with downy gold." Now, isn't that well-done of me?"

"I also remember a verse regarding pheasants," Henry informed her loftily.

"Really?" Mary was sceptical, because her brother was not a great reader of poetry.

"Yes."

"Well, come then, and let me hear it."

With an affectedly poetic voice, booming and full of feigned emotion, Henry cried, "Up gets a guinea, bang goes a penny-halfpenny, and down comes half a crown!"

Mary fell into a fit of giggling. "I don't think doggerel about pheasant hunting that is sung out by urchins in the streets is *poetry* about pheasants."

"It is all I can do; you don't let me quote prose," Henry complained.

"No, and I don't let you quote those infernal papers by Thomas Young and Benjamin Thompson, either."

"Ha!" Henry scoffed. "You let me read them to you, though. Don't pretend you don't like the science of physics."

"Not well enough to let you *quote* it at me."

"One of these days," Henry said, "I shall introduce you to Conversation Sharp, for I believe you could give him a run for his money in wit."

"I *have* met Mr Sharp," Mary told him.

Henry was taken aback. "Have you? When? Where the deuce was I?"

"It was last February, the day after Candlemas. I went with Lady Stornoway to a meeting on the effectuation of the abolition of slavery at Mrs Dormer's house. (The Dormer's live on Harley Street and are great friends with the Sharrows; you met them at the Botweight's ball last April, remember? You danced with Mrs Dormer's step-daughter, who had just come out.) Mr Sharp was one of the guests and I was introduced. I cannot say I talked *with* him, though. I mostly listened, as did everyone around me. Such wit! Such affability! As to where you were, I believe you were in *supposed* to be in Bath but had instead gone to Lyme Regis to visit the beautiful widow Mrs Crewe, who went there to take in some sea bathing."

"How do you find out so many particulars about my life?" Henry frowned. "Is there no privacy in this world?"

"Not if you are connected to the ton, dearest. You *know* that." What her brother did not know, and what she would never tell him, is that his valet Anderson was her housekeeper's son by her first marriage, and that her liberality and kindness to Mrs Brown, and Mrs Brown's closeness to her son, meant that anything Anderson heard or saw soon became Mary's property without the valet ever realising he was Mary's chiefest spy.

"I suspect you spy on me with a crystal ball, having been taught those black arts by an old gypsy woman," Henry groused.

"Stuff. If I could do that I'd spy on Princess Caroline. *That* would be entertainment indeed!"

"The crystal would smoke and then immolate itself, possibly with the explosive force of one of those bombs thrown by grenadiers." In Henry's voice was a kind of admiration for Caroline of Brunswick's exploits. She was not only a valuable ally for the Whigs, who were currently taking a vicious electoral drubbing at the hands of Liverpool and his Tories, she was a consistently riveting object of gossip.

"I think that would only result if I were foolish enough to spy on Prinny and Lady Hertford," Mary rejoined, causing Henry to shudder.

The siblings were united in their hatred of Lady Hertford, a plump and matronly woman in her fifties who was suspected of being the Regent's mistress. This doubtful speculation had become a sacred truth among the Whigs when it became evident that she was using her friendship with Prince George to induce him to betray his Whiggish allies and bring him round to the Tory faction. Lady Hertford's supposed affair with Prinny was also fodder for mockery and censure by the Londoners who weren't fond of the Regent, of whom there were legion.

The Prince Regent didn't help himself any by arriving nearly daily at the Hertfords' home in a virulently yellow carriage that announced his visitations to even the most casual and disinterested observer. Lord Hertford's presence at Manchester House did nothing to quell the rumours about Lady Hertford and her royal beau. It was assumed he just looked the other way in exchange for the political and monetary favours Prinny lavished him with.

Like many in their social set, Mary and Henry had been vitriolic against the Hertfords earlier in the year when Lord Hertford was appointed Lord Chamberlain of the Regent's household, and their son, Lord Yarmouth, was given the position of Vice-Chamberlain. This vitriol, as is too often the case, would often express itself as derision against Lady Hertford and Prinny for their age and weight. Cartoons lampooning the supposed lovers as bloated, elderly perverts were prevalent in London papers, and print shops sold copies of well done and especially vicious caricatures.

After a several minutes entertaining raillery and insult of both Lady Hertford and the Regent, the siblings came to a deep stream that obliged them to walk along it for nearly a quarter of mile before they found a bridge to cross it. The view from the middle of the bridge was such that Mary was forced to stop and wait while her brother waxed eloquent about its beauty.

It was still early enough in October that as many trees were still green as those that had donned a flashier raiment, but several scarlet and gold leaves had already fallen to confetti the grass along the bank or to make colourful fairy-boats as they floated along on the stream's placid current. The floating leaves were thrown into sharp relief by the sun's rays, which slanted in brightly from the east through the gaps in the tree canopy over the water. The sunshine sparkled on the water, creating frisking motes to surround the harlequined leaves as they sailed serenely along.

"It *is* very pretty," Mary agreed.

"Pretty?" Henry was flabbergasted anew by his sister's lukewarm praise of the beauties of nature. "How can you read poetry lauding the glorious verdure and picturesque views of England without actually appreciating those views for yourself?"

Mary's mouth quirked at her brother's astonishment. "I *do* think it is pretty, Henry, but I cannot pretend to have raptures over it. That is why I *read* poetry but do not *write* it. It brings me great pleasure to hear a poet's ecstasy over nature, but I do not experience euphoria at a lovely view, the way you do. Besides, the poetry I like best, and which I read most often, is more likely to describe the emotional agonies autumn reflects than the beauties of the season."

Henry smiled ruefully as they resumed their walk. "I am not feeling 'emotional agonies', but I will own that I am feeling somewhat brown."

"Why?" Mary was concerned. It was unlike Henry to be less than cheerful, let alone experience the ennui-like condition of feeling brown. "What is bothering you?"

"I believe it is only disappointment that the play has been sunk," Henry confessed. "It is such a little thing, yet I was looking forward to it with so much pleasure! I am like a child who has been told they can have no pudding after all."

"What a great pity it is that we are not in Town. You could go to Astley's, or your club, or find some other form of amusement," Mary said.

"I thought about going down to London, but I don't feel as though it would suit me at the present," Henry shrugged. "Perhaps I shall go to Brighton, or Bath. Yes, I think I shall go to Bath. *There* I can find fresh amusement. The society there changes so often that I am sure to find some novelty. Within a week, I shall be merry as a cricket again."

"Will you be going to meet the Admiral?" Mary did not quite succeed in keeping her voice neutral, but Henry let it pass unmentioned.

"He'll probably be there in a week or two, I suppose. He's usually there the first week of November at the latest."

Mary tried not to be disappointed. "I shall miss you, of course. Will you come back, or do you stay there through Christmas?"

"I am not certain when I can return to Mansfield, but I know I cannot join you at Christmas. I'll be in London then. I have promised a friend that I will spend a week at Christmas time in her company."

"Mlle. LaVeaux or Mrs Crewe?" Mary teased.

"Mrs Van Neck," Henry gibed in return.

"Oh, Lord! What an impudent whelp you are!" Mary crowed.

"Mrs Van Neck, indeed!" Mrs Van Neck denoted not a person, but rather any woman with a very large bosom. Although the ideals of the day dictated that an overly-endowed woman was not a fashionable beauty, many men retained an admiration for a bursting bodice, including Henry Crawford.

When her laughter had died down, she said more soberly, "I *will* miss you. You make me laugh more than any other creature. No one else would dare to tell me such outré poppycock."

"Would I be a better brother if I talked of Peacock instead of poppycock? As in, the poet Mr Thomas Love Peacock?" Henry asked with a grin.

"What have you to tell me of the author of *Palmyra*?"

"That Davencourt has written me to say that Mr Peacock has just had a new poem published, called *Philosophy of Melancholy: etcetera etcetera*, and that he has purchased a copy for me as a token of his friendship and is sending it to me here at the parsonage as a gift." Waiting until Mary had finished squealing and clapping her hands with joy, Henry continued. "He also sends his compliments to you."

"May I open it when it arrives?" Henry's assent brought forth more squealing and clapping. "I cannot wait to read it! But why does Captain Davencourt send *you* a book of poetry? Surely he knows you well enough to know you are not an avid reader of verse."

"Because, my woolly-headed sister, he is courting *you*."

Mary was disconcerted for a moment then rallied. "If true, then he is canny and sly and I shall be very wary of him," she jested.

A suitor could not give a lady anything more expensive than flowers or food. Captain Davencourt, in an effort to make himself stand out, needed to give Mary something she would truly appreciate, and thus think kindly of the man who gave it to her. Poetry was the obvious answer, but buying her something as extravagant as a book was just not acceptable. Thus, Davencourt had clearly figured away around the problem by sending the book to *Henry* as a gift. His plan was a good one, because he was suddenly raised several notches in Mary's estimation. He was an eldest son and not unhandsome, but he was not particularly wealthy or connected either; she had not thought of him seriously before. His perspicacity had made him more interesting to her. Not enough to banish the handsome Edmund Bertram from her mind, but enough to render him an object of interest.

"Captain Davencourt's principle residence is in Wales, is it not?" Mary inquired.

"You are correct. He lives near Cardiff; a small village called Penarth or Pentarth I believe. He bought a house there after his father died. His father was a rector, and his mother was left without an establishment upon the elder Davencourt's passing. Good fellow that he is, Davenport got a home so she could keep house for him."

"Why did he choose a small village in Wales?"

"His mother's family is from that area. He still has cousins there. Also, it is only five miles from Cardiff, so he is not completely starved of good society."

Mary was thoughtful. "How often does Capitan Davencourt come to Town?"

"I believe it depends on the year. If he is on leave during the season, he brings his mother and sisters to London to see the sights. I tell a lie; it is only one sister now. The other three are all married."

"I remember you introducing the captain at a ball — or was it Almack's? — the Elwyn's ball then — and I recall dancing with him, but I don't think I ever asked how *you* knew him so well."

Henry hesitated. "I met him through our uncle. The Admiral considers Captain Davencourt to be one of his finest officers."

"Oh. How charming," Mary replied. Henry could see poor Davenport sinking again in his sister's esteem.

"Now, Mary," Henry coaxed her, "don't be prejudiced against him just because our uncle admires him. All that the Admiral's approval of Davencourt means is that he is a good captain. It is not fair to suppose that our uncle and Davencourt are in sympathy with one another."

Mary made a non-committal noise of not-quite-agreement.

Henry, more in favour of his sister forming an alliance with Edmund Bertram than anyone else, left off. Captain Davenport must shift for himself.

Their wanderings had taken them in a wide arc so that they had turned in the direction of the parsonage during the course of the walk. Mary could see the distant spire of the church, and the slight haze smoke from the village of Mansfield's chimneys. She could not see the Bertram's manor house because of some low hills with beech hangers atop them, but she knew it was there.

"You must make your introductions to Sir Thomas before you go to Bath," Mary observed, "and it would be terribly bad manners not to make your farewells to the family."

"I shall be going with Dr Grant in the morning to pay my respects to the returned *pater familias*, and I can take my leave of them all then," Henry said absently. He was speculating that he could still make it to Banbury the next day, even if he left so late after breakfast.

What neither he nor Mary were thinking about was Maria Bertram's hopes. Unbeknownst to them, Maria Bertram would wait all day, with her heart in her throat, in the hopes that Henry Crawford would come and declare his love, allowing her to break off her engagement to Mr Rushworth and marry the man she *actually* loved. In her vanity, she had taken Henry's flirtation to be serious, and Henry's adieus the next morning would grievously injure her pride, and though the Crawfords would not credit it, her heart.

Chapter Twenty-One

HENRY'S DEPARTURE, AND Sir Thomas's abhorrence of social intercourse with anyone but the Rushworths threatened to make the last weeks of October very dull for Mary. Only Edmund prevented such a wretched occurrence. On any day that rain had not made it too wet or too dirty to venture out, Edmund walked to the parsonage. Mary noticed with contentment that there was seldom a day so wet or so dirty that Edmund considered it impossible to make the journey. It flattered her. It made her feel complacent in *his* affections, even though she was still uncertain as to her own. Or rather, she knew she had a strong partiality for Edmund, but she didn't know if her partiality was so strong that she was willing to give up all her hopes of a more equal alliance.

||

"How do the inhabitants of the Park get on?" Mary asked one morning as she handed Edmund a cup of tea, creamed to perfection. "Have plans for Maria's wedding driven everyone batty as a belfry?" Mrs Grant had excused herself to answer a note, but since she was nearby and the drawing-room door was open, not even Edmund worried that his tête-à-tête with Miss Crawford was improper.

"Not very much, I am glad to tell you. Maria will be waiting for next spring to make any decisions regarding a new carriage or furniture for Sotherton, and she wishes to eschew a wedding breakfast. She is merely waiting for her trousseau to be finished, and then she and Mr Rushworth shall be married. I expect my father to send Dr Grant a letter fixing the happy day soon," Edmund replied.

"And between us, will the day be happy?" Mary asked without her customary liveliness. She would not have asked if Mrs Grant had been with them, but hoped the privacy would allow Edmund to be candid.

Edmund looked even more serious than usual. "May I speak in confidence?"

"Of course," Mary promised.

"It troubles me. I can see that Maria is indifferent to Mr Rushworth, as can my father. As a parent, he was concerned enough about the engagement to offer to break it off for her, regardless of the embarrassment that a rupture would bring, if she were repenting of having accepted Mr Rushworth. Yet Maria says she is content. She points to Rushworth's good nature and placid temper, and says she is secure in her belief that he will make her happy. Personally, I fear that it is Sotherton and twelve thousand pounds a year that make her so secure of her happiness, as much as it pains me to say that about my own sister. Whatever her reasons, she is determined to have Rushworth. My father puts the best face on it, speaking of how Rushworth's youth allows him plenty of time for improvement, and the likelihood that Maria's tepid feelings for her husband will mean she will be often at the Park after she weds. I, however, do not share his hopes. I am afraid she will be unhappy, and repent the marriage."

Mary gave Edmund a look that expressed her agreement, but tried to comfort him. "There is a great deal still to hope for, though. Mr Rushworth is a gentleman, and unlikely to prevent Maria from pursuing her interests and seeking enjoyment. He will probably encourage her in anything that would make her merry. He is kindly disposed toward all the world, and is not in the least vicious. I believe she *does* have a good chance of happiness with such a man."

"I hope you are right," Edmund smiled at her.

"And where do they go for the honeymoon?" Mary inquired. She had bet Mrs Grant that they would head straight for London, but Mrs Grant was risking her shilling on the guess that they would head for Weymouth or Bath first before they plunged into Town.

"They go to Brighton for a month or so, and Julia goes with them."

Since their rivalry over Henry Crawford had ended, the Bertram sisters had been gradually recovering much of their former good understanding; and were at least sufficiently friends to make each of them exceedingly glad to be with the other at such a time. Some other companion than Mr Rushworth was of the first consequence to his lady, and Julia was quite as eager for novelty and pleasure as Maria, though she might not have struggled through so much to obtain them, and could better bear a subordinate situation.

Mary made a mental note to give her sister half a shilling. While the newlyweds weren't going to Weymouth or Bath, they *were* heading to a similar kind of watering place, and that should be good for at least a portion of the bet.

"Mansfield Park's comforts will be sadly contracted with the absence of both daughters at once. It is a fortunate thing for your parents that they have Miss Price with them," Mary noted.

"I agree, and know that both my parents feel their good fortune in having Fanny there. She had been a rich reward for a small kindness. My mother could not do without her," Edmund was pleased to have Mary praise his cousin.

Mary *did* feel affection for Fanny, and *did* like her a great deal, but she was also aware of how happy it made Edmund to hear Miss Price talked of with kindness, so she had a twofold motive in her compliments. She dismissed her niggling fears of being a toad-eater-by-proxy by reminding herself that she was speaking nothing but the truth. Mary often went out of her way to please people by flattering them where they were most proud or had the deepest concern, and she didn't mind lying when she was buttering up someone she didn't much care for, but she liked Edmund too well to give *him* Spanish coin.

"It was hard to make Miss Price out at first; I could not get her character easily. Usually such reserve is disgusting, but she is so obviously unpretentious and meek that her shyness cannot offend. I do not believe I have ever met anyone that was more humble, *sincerely* humble, than Miss Price. She seems almost as fearful of notice and praise as other women are of neglect."

Edmund's face radiated his happy agreement. "You are absolutely right. Fanny is more than merely shy; she is positively timid. She would be as invisible as a housemaid if we let her. She needs coaxing to talk of herself or her concerns. I will never forget with what goodhearted alacrity you acted to help her the night Mrs Norris mortified her by mentioning her … situation. I honoured you for it."

"It was no effort on my part," Mary said modestly, and not quite truthfully. It spite of her former assurances to Henry as to the ease of the task, and her assurances to Edmund at present, distracting and consoling Miss Price had been a Herculean chore, made harder by Fanny's reluctance to supply her side of the conversation. "Who would not wish to protect Miss Price from (if I may boldly name it for what it was) *cruelty*? To see someone be sharp or unkind to your cousin is akin to setting mastiffs on a kitten — an act too brutal to watch with indifference. I could not help but be moved to aid her in some way."

"Let us be honest enough to admit that not everyone would have acted to alleviate her mortification," Edmund said. "As much as it saddens me to comment on it, both my sisters were within the room and neither of them were spurred to comfort Fanny. *You*, however, were quick to act, to console. Before I could even find my voice, *you* had already moved your chair close to Fanny's, and were making every effort to divert her. Please, you must allow me to honour you for it."

Blushing from the sincerity of his praise, Mary made light of it. "I must, if you *insist*. I would be a fool not to let a man think so well of me. Go on then, make a squeeze wax of yourself regarding my charity; I shan't say any differently."

"Your lively mind will make jokes, but I *will* honour you. I wish Fanny had some of your liveliness. If I could gift her with more animation and less fear I would (provided it did not alter her sweet nature, of course), but she is dear to me as she is. She is sound in morals, principles, and mind, which is worth a great deal more than to be generally pleasing, in my opinion," Edmund mused.

Mary could not resist the temptation to tease him. She made her face as sober as a judge's and asked, "Are pleasing manners a sign that someone's morals, principles, and mind are *not* sound?"

Edmund looked dismayed, and began to stammer at an answer, but Mary laughed and raised her hand to forestall him. "Peace! I am only bedevilling you! I am sorry, but my lively mind is a very mischievous one I am afraid. I cannot resist a chance to prank. Will you forgive me?"

"Of course," Edmund smiled at her again. "How could I bear a grudge against such pleasant company?"

"How, indeed?" Mary replied flippantly. "Especially when I am complimenting your cousin."

"It is a regrettable fact that she does not often get the compliments she deserves, except from you and Mrs Grant."

"Your mother praises her."

"But she does not remember to do so *often*."

"Then I will make up for the lack," Mary sipped her own tea. "I will tell you what I like *best* about Miss Price. It is her *fortitude*. She is tender and easily knocked up, but she never makes a fuss about it. She is the opposite of a "poor honey"; she makes *less* of her ailments and tries to keep them from inconveniencing others. You never hear *her* complaining about her nerves, or flutters, or palpitations, or headaches. I find it in every way admirable."

"Fanny's frail health worries me, but you are right; she never makes much of it. It is not in her nature to complain," Edmund's brow creased. "Because she does not complain, she is often overlooked. I wish everyone were as kind to Fanny as you are, Miss Crawford."

"I believe I could look the world over, from China to Peru, and not find a better soul than Miss Price." Mary said benignly. "I suspect she has sensibility enough, but she never uses it as an excuse for dramatics or hysterics. I have never met anyone who does *less* to anxiously parade her feelings."

"You are not one to anxiously parade your feelings, either," Edmund commented.

"Perhaps, as lively as I am, I have little feeling?" Mary quipped.

No one with *little* feeling would act with such alacrity to give succour to those in distress."

"True, true. Then I must have *too* many feelings to anxiously parade them all. It is too crowded to have them all marching as one. It would cause an intolerable crush."

"You speak playfully, but there is truth in it, I believe."

"I am glad you believe me to be feeling, because if you are to be a man of the cloth then it is important for you to have strong *beliefs*. But how far will those beliefs take you? Shall you become an Evangelical? Will you teach your parishioners Wesley's mantra of Bible, cross, conversion and activism to perfect the Christian society?" Mary asked archly.

In spite of her disdainful tone of voice, Mary was actually more tolerant of evangelicalism than were many other high-church Anglicans. Being active in the abolitionist movement, she met and mingled with the Clapham Sect of intellectual evangelicals and low-church adherents, and agreed with them in regards to many social issues, especially the alleviation of poverty. She, therefore, knew many evangelicals that she liked as *individuals*. What she could not abide was the Evangelical movement as a *whole*. Their incessant moralising and the desire to reform all the fun out of life reminded her too much of what she had learned about the Puritans. Moreover, she had read some Evangelical materials, and was appalled by the general conflation of any enjoyment with sin, and the idea that humans were so inherently bad that they deserved severe affliction at every turn.

"Me? Evangelical?" Edmund looked grave. "No, I would never do that. I dislike evangelicalism excessively. Not only do they threaten the unity of the Church of England — they threaten the very fabric of our society."

Mary was surprised by his vehemence. "I can understand why you would worry that protestant groups splintering away from the Anglican Church will weaken it by their absence, but why do you think that the evangelicals are a danger to the very fabric of our society?"

"They have no respect for proper authority, and do not know how to keep their place." Edmund's well-shaped lips thinned with irritation at the thought. "They think Jack is as good as his master and that a 'call' to preach is as good as an education. It is no wonder that the Luddites sprang from them."

"You have no sympathy for the Luddites, then?"

"Sympathy for the Luddites?" Edmund was astonished she would ask. "Why would any right thinking individual have sympathy for the Luddites? They are hooligans who destroy private property from their fear of modern machinery!"

"I cannot agree with you," Mary said mildly. Her attraction to Edmund was the only thing stopping her from calling him an imbecile to his face. "The Luddites do not fear either modernisation or machinery; they fear the loss of their jobs. They only want an opportunity to provide for themselves and their families. Is it so wrong that a man should wish to work and feed his wife and children?"

"I am sure I cannot fault their desire to work," Edmund's voice was cold, "but that does not justify — does not excuse — their ruffianism. The mill owner has a right to conduct his business as he sees fit, and not to have his income disrupted by Luddite riots and disorder."

"How can the textile workers have their claims addressed in any other fashion?" Mary queried. "It is not as if they can vote, or move to another county to seek work, or easily find another profession."

"You approve of machine breaking and attacks on magistrates and grocers then?"

"I said no such thing, Mr Bertram, and you know it," Mary was firm. "And that question does not answer *my* question regarding the ways in which textile workers can seek address."

"But how can Luddites be discussed without taking into account their assaults on their betters and their destruction of property?"

"How can Luddites be discussed without defining the underlying causes of their unrest?" Mary rejoined.

"I would say that it doesn't matter the *reasons* for their actions. The actions of the Luddites are outrageous and offensive regardless of their cause." Edmund was convinced he had the moral high ground.

"Forgive me for saying so, but that is balderdash. If you left a candle burning and it caught your bedclothes on fire, you cannot blame the candle; it was your action in falling asleep without extinguishing it that caused the tragedy."

"The candle is inanimate. *It* cannot reason or know right from wrong. Luddites, as men, have reason and are thus always to blame for their own actions," Edmund argued. "Your defence is the same sophistry used by those defending poachers or thieves. It appeals to the emotions to say 'the man poached or committed thievery because his children were starving', but the actions of poaching and thievery are inherently, absolutely wrong regardless of the motivation of the miscreant."

Mary's eyebrows rose in mocking surprise. "But I know from Dr Grant that you recently released a poacher. You gave the fellow a stern warning but did not remand him to authorities because you knew his family was in need. You even gave him some money and wrote a letter recommending him for a job as game-keeper to your friend Lynwood, so that he would no longer be tempted to poach. Dr Grant was quite in raptures about it, as a model of Christian charity. What is that but mercy for a crime committed from desperation?"

Edmund looked uncomfortable, and his cheeks took on a faint colour. "That is different; I am not the law. I can look at extenuations, but the law cannot."

"Reasons for a crime are only applicable when a private citizen deals with them, rather than the law? Then, I ask you, how can a soldier commit murder in battle without being a murderer? His actions are not judged by an individual; they are subject to military law. Isn't the soldier's crime expunged because he was acting on orders, and because his motivation for killing was to serve his nation?" Mary's questions were barbed.

Henry had once told Mary that the rhetorical devise of asking questions in order to force someone to reveal their flawed logic was called Socratic irony, a fact she found amusing considering how she and every woman she knew had used it from infancy to successfully argue with men without gaining reputations as harridans. Thankfully, men never recognised Socratic irony when it was employed by a woman; what would a woman know of logic, rhetoric, the philosophy of Socrates?

"That is not the same thing at all." Edmund frowned. "A soldier is not breaking the law."

"Are all laws just?" Mary asked. "If a law regarding the enclosure of land is the reason a man is starving, does it not bear some responsibility when he is driven by extremity to steal so he and his family might eat?"

"Simply by becoming a law, the law is just; it stands for justice. Whether one thinks the law is *fair* or not is of no import. The law is the law and it cannot be waived when convenient." English law had not yet embraced the concept of extenuating circumstances for a confessed crime. Every punishment was preset, and had to be applied without alterations.

"When crimes are committed by soldiers, the military takes circumstance into account," Mary reminded him.

"Martial law and civil law are different," Edmund neatly avoided the point.

"Then there is to be no temperance or mercy for any crime? Desperation, want, hunger, maltreatment — none of these are legitimate grievances?"

"It does not matter whether they are legitimate grievances or not," Edmund insisted. "The law is clear cut and final. If a crime is committed, then punishment will occur. The Luddites cannot claim they were unaware of the severity of their crimes. They knew the penalties for such wanton destruction of property."

Mary cocked her head. "Parliament has passed a law wherein machine breaking is now a capital crime; do you think that a fair punishment for men desperate to have their livelihood back?"

"In truth, I do not. I think transportation or imprisonment would be sufficient," Edmund sighed. "It does not matter, though, what I think or my personal opinion on the punishment. That is the law of the land. The law must be obeyed, or we will have nothing but anarchy."

"Then it appears to me that the law is very different from *justice*, because there can be no justice where there is no merciful judgement based on circumstance."

Edmund smiled condescendingly. "It is your warm and generous heart that tells you this, Miss Crawford. You can think of no one suffering without wishing to assuage their difficulty. It is a womanly heart, but it is why women cannot go into the law. The legal system needs hardened resolve if it is to be effective. It must be done rationally, rather than with feeling."

While he continued to believe Miss Crawford was completely wrong to have sympathy for the Luddites, Edmund was in love with her and therefore made excuses for her erroneous thinking. Her misunderstandings of right and her inability to comprehend the superiority of English law were doubtlessly the effects of being improperly instructed by her aunt and uncle. She had not been taught that there should be no mercy regarding violence or rebellion in the lower classes. However, Edmund gave Mary credit for having a fine mind, and was sanguine that he could teach her how to think correctly; that over time and with patience all her thoughts and opinions would begin to align with his own.

For her part, Mary was determined to try to persuade Edmund that mercy toward the poor and unjustly treated should be taken into account, even by the law. She had seen his kindnesses, and Mrs Grant had told her of his compassionate aid for those in poverty within the parish, so she did not despair of changing his opinions if given enough time. She still felt more fondly toward him than any other man. She was actually giving some thought to accepting him, if he would show himself willing to compromise on her behalf. He must show himself to be unlike the Admiral; he must think of her needs and wishes as having equal importance with his own. Let him give up the idea of being a parson — let him choose another profession — and he could have her hand, a relatively impecunious second son or not.

"Perhaps you should rethink your refusal to go into the law. You seem to have a great respect and affection for it," Mary said glibly. "Surely to become a parson you would need to have more to do with *feeling* and *mercy*? Would not the law suit you best?"

Edmund shook his head. "No, I feel that the best profession for myself is the church. It suits me best, in habit and in preference."

Mary was stymied, but undaunted. "Then you should take up service to the crown. Your father has many acquaintances and connections in Parliament and the government; you could easily obtain a post in the diplomatic corp. Perhaps not as an ambassador, but as envoy or attaché. Consider the benefits! You could see so much of the world. You could be asked to go somewhere truly interesting, such as Japan or India."

To travel the world, to see the exotic locals she had heretofore only read about, would be a dream come true for Mary. She couldn't begin to understand how reluctant Edmund was to leave the county of Northampton, let alone England. A dislike of travel and adventure was so alien to her makeup that she didn't understand they *could* be present in the characters of others. She could not see it, but Edmund's homebody ways were diametrically opposed to Mary's free spirited approach, and her yen to travel. What Edmund loved most of all was the familiar, the tame, and the sedate.

Edmund looked almost aghast at the thought of such unwelcome adventuring. "That would not suit me at all."

It took all of Mary's self-command not to recoil in consternation. It would not suit him to travel, and to be seen in the best society? He would prefer the banality of the clergy to the excitement and prestige of diplomacy? Was he a man, or a timid little tit?

She recovered herself, and spoke as if it were a matter of no great importance. "Well, then. You shall be a parish bull in prunella and I shall be a *femme heureuse citadin* in poplin; to everyone their own I suppose. Fortunately, I will be able to visit you whenever I am with my sister and Dr Grant, and I am sure I will call upon the future Mrs Rushworth."

Mary smiled at Edmund, satisfied that her airy tone of voice hid most her antipathy while letting him know that *she* would not be stuck in the country as a parson's wife. If he wanted to rot in the sticks, so be it. He would have to give up his hope of *her*. It was just as well, since he clearly never thought of her *seriously*, or he would have given up his plans to be a provincial devil catcher. If he could be satisfied without *her*, she would certainly be satisfied without *him*.

Edmund looked flustered. "Indeed, Miss Crawford, I would hope to see you often in the future ..."

She took advantage of his minute pause to exclaim, "Of course you will! You'll see Henry quite often as well, I would imagine; he is as much of a sportsman as you or your brother. We expect him back after Christmas, and I am sure he will be eager to fox hunt. He particularly admires your chestnut gelding, and has told me he wants to see it being put through its paces. It is an Irish hunter, I believe?"

"Yes, it is."

"When will you and Mr Bertram hunt next?"

"We hope to go tomorrow, if the weather is fine."

"Does Sir Thomas go as well?"

"No, my father gave up field hunting almost five years ago. It aggravates his rheumatism too much." Edmund looked as though he were unsure how he had wound up discussing fox hunting and his father's aching joints with the woman he was seeking to woo.

"Perhaps the day after next we, that is you and your sisters and brother and I, can go for a ride? The Welsh Cob my brother bought me is the most delightful animal imaginable, and I would rather exercise her than have a groom do it. Did I tell you I have finally settled on a name for her?"

"No, you haven't. Which did you choose?"

"None of the ones we previously discussed! I have named her Dilly, short for Daffodil. I thought that a suitable nod to her country of origin, and her gait is so smooth it reminds me of a field of daffodils bobbing in a soft wind. Have you read Wordsworth poem about daffodils? You haven't? Dr Grant has the volume in his library — would you like me to read it to you? Oh, I would so much like to hear you read it to *me*. You have a wonderful reading voice. Henry's reading is excellent, so I am exceedingly nice about those I wish to hear read."

With friendly chatter and several requested poems, Mary kept Edmund distracted for the rest of his visit. He was completely unaware she was internally livid at the insult of of his preferring to take orders rather than wining her hand in marriage.

Chapter Twenty-Two

NOVEMBER 9TH WAS set as the day of Maria Bertram's marriage to Mr Rushworth, and Mary was one of the handful of people invited to attend. Weddings were very quiet affairs, on the whole, and Maria had not wanted a breakfast afterwards, preferring to eat quietly at home first and then go straight to Sotherton after the ceremony rather than to have to pretend to be happy for guests over her egg and toast.

It was a very proper wedding. The bride was elegantly dressed—the two bridesmaids were duly inferior—her father gave her away—her mother stood with salts in her hand, expecting to be agitated—her aunt tried to cry—and the service was impressively read by Dr Grant. Nothing could be objected to when it came under the discussion of the neighbourhood, except that the carriage which conveyed the bride and bridegroom and Julia from the church door to Sotherton, was the same chaise which Mr Rushworth had used for a twelvemonth before. In every thing else the etiquette of the day might stand the strictest investigation.

Mary watched Maria promise to love, honour, and obey Mr Rushworth with a jaded eye. She knew Maria didn't mean a word of it, although Mr Rushworth seemed to believe it well enough. What would their life together be like? Would the groom ever come to understand that his lovely bride despised him? Would the new Mrs Rushworth be satisfied with the 12,000 pounds per annum she was receiving for her body and, to some extent, her soul? Would fripperies, flirtations, and frolics make up for a disagreeable marriage to a stupid husband? Would Mr Rushworth feel he had gotten a bad bargain, or would he never see past Maria's beautiful façade?

It was times like these that Mary wished she had the courage to remain a spinster. Would freedom and independence perhaps be *worth* the jeers she would have to endure as an old maid? And jeer people would. It was not some Cock Lane ghost to provide false fright. Her fears were based on reality. She would, if unwed, become an object of pity and sport. It wouldn't be as bad as it would be if she were poor, but knowing that 'I wonder why Miss Crawford never married?' would be said snidely in almost every drawing-room was too humiliating a thought to be born. No, she thought, better to marry and risk unhappiness than to remain single and guarantee ridicule and shame.

Mrs Grant, ever the optimist who thought well of everybody, saw none of the worm-eaten wood beneath Maria's veneer of satisfaction. She spoke contentedly of her friend's certain conjugal felicity as she and Mary sat in the parlour with their needlework.

"Maria's 20,000 pounds is secured to her for her younger sons in the marriage articles, and Mr Rushworth is to give her 1000 pounds a year in pin money," Mrs Grant informed Mary. There was no such thing as privacy regarding money, and Maria's access to wealth was considered a very important — perhaps the *most* important — aspect of her marital happiness. "They will have a house in Town, and she will almost certainly have a curricle to drive in Hyde Park. Oh! How stylish she will be. She will be one of the leading lights in London. Her marriage is a blessing indeed."

Blessed by the Old Lady of Threadneedle Street, Mary thought cynically. Mr Rushworth's wealth in the Bank of England was the only source of felicity that Mary could see in the marriage. However, she had no desire to damped Mrs Grant's sanguine hopes, so she said only, "Well, until she gets to Town she will have fun enough in Brighton. Mrs Rushworth and Julia will be shown a gay time there."

"You went in the autumn of '11, didn't you Mary?"

Mary bit off a piece of thread and responded. "Yes, my aunt and I went to Brighton while the Admiral and Henry went to Bath. We were lucky enough to have been invited to stay with Lady Clinkson in her house along the Steyne. She was just two houses down from Mrs Fitzherbert."

"Mrs Fitzherbert!" Mrs Grant was delightfully scandalised. "Did you meet the Regent's mistress face to face?"

"We saw her walking and sometimes at the balls, and once in the grand saloon, but we were never introduced. She was a very handsome woman, and seemed very respectable and elegant. She is well known for her taste there, as well. Her demeanour made me convinced that Prinny *did* secretly marry her in '85; she looked too much like a wife not to consider herself one."

"She can *think* herself married, but a *Catholic* service without the king's permission was no wedding at all," Mrs Grant sniffed. "She is no more married to the Prince Regent than I am."

"I suppose she thinks a service before the Lord God trumps a king, but you know how the Catholics are." Mary was droll, but she couldn't resist being scornful of anti-Catholic sentiment, even when it came from a dearly beloved sister. She couldn't really fathom all the hatred and blather about religion. It seemed to require such pettiness from God, and a pettiness she did not see in her sister under any other circumstance. And the Catholics were fellow Christians; what would her sister say of her Jewish or Mohometan acquaintance? Mary was fairly sure that if her sister knew of her warm acquaintanceship with Miss Rosenburg, Mrs Grant would faint.

Mrs Grant, detecting the faint censure in her sister's jape, sought to change the subject. "Tell me all about Brighton, dear. I know little about it from first-hand information."

"What do you want to know?" Mary asked with a smile, tickled by her sister's unsubtle divergence from the subject of Catholicism.

"Everything!"

Mary's smile widened at her sister's enthusiasm. "My word! I don't know if I can tell you *everything* about Brighton. Will you be satisfied just to know what my aunt and I did there?"

After Mrs Grant swore she would be satisfied with only such paltry information as *that*, Mary did her best to recall the most pleasurable parts of the sea resort.

"Let me think. The first thing my aunt and I did was to go sea bathing. My aunt's doctor had recommended it or she wouldn't have gone Brighton — she always felt as though sea breezes were the absolute *ruin* of beauty and health — but she trusted Dr Godmersham and was willing to try. We were dipped by Martha Gunn herself, who is considered the best of the sea dippers. I found out the locals call her the Venerable Priestess of the Bath, and I cannot say they were wrong. She was a woman of very sturdy proportions — fat and tall and strong as an ox! – and I felt very safe as she dipped me, even though the waves were a little rough that day. You need only to relax as Mrs Gunn keeps you afloat and pulls you gently through the waters. We were dipped twice a week for the six weeks we were there, although we were only able to secure Martha Gunn's services for about half of those times. The other dippers did their jobs well, but I never felt as safe or content with them as I did when Martha Gunn dipped me. I recommended her strongly to Maria."

"Did the sea bathing help your aunt?"

"It *did* help, and the air at Brighton was so good that she hardly felt any ill effects from its breezes, for a mercy. She felt much better after the visit there, and we were to go again the next autumn, but she felt too ill to make the trip." Mary's jaw briefly clenched as she remembered her aunt's slow, wasting death over the course of year. It wasn't until the very last that the Admiral would admit his wife was truly ailing.

"I should like to go sea bathing at Brighton," Mrs Grant said wistfully. "However, Dr Grant prefers Bath so it is there that we go every spring for his gout."

To Mary, this was yet further proof that even a husband like Dr Grant, one who was amiable and loved his wife, would only put *his* concerns first. Mary wondered if Maria was perhaps *lucky* to have married Rushworth. The man was a Tom Noddy but he would give way to any of her suggestions or preferences, having few fixed ideas of his own.

"Perhaps Dr Grant can be persuaded to go to Brighton next autumn," Mary said consolingly, "and I shall go with you."

"Perhaps," Mrs Grant agreed without much conviction. "But until then I wish to at least *hear* more about it."

"It is a very social place, ma'am, with many opportunities to make new acquaintance. There are two sets of Assembly Rooms; one set at the Old Ship Inn and the other set at the Castle Inn. The Castle Inn is considered the most elegant, but in my opinion the Old Ship Inn had the best food and drink. Both establishments made sure to keep their schedules in harmony, so that visitors to Brighton could have as much enjoyment as possible. The Castle Inn has a ball on Mondays and a card party on Wednesdays, while the Old Ship Inn has a ball on Thursdays and a card party on Fridays. Then, of course, they both have a public tea on Sundays."

"My word! That is a whirl of gaiety!" Mrs Grant exclaimed. "Did you ever have an unengaged day?"

"Seldom, if I tell the truth. There was often someone having a private ball during the week as well, so I could go to as many as six balls in a fortnight."

"Did that not satisfy even *your* insatiable appetite for balls?" Mrs Grant chuckled.

"You would *think* so, but no — I was foot-sore but determined to dance at them all! The tradesmen and laundresses of the town had good reason to thank me, I believe. I must have worn through a score of slippers and dozens of shoe roses, and I had to buy more gloves several times, not to mention needing new underthings to wear while all my others were being washed. There were so many dinners and balls that my aunt and I even bought three new evening dresses apiece from the mantua maker."

"Three?" Mrs Grant was somewhat amazed by the exorbitance.

"Yes, but think of how unfit a gown is to be worn after a ball until it has been properly cleaned and aired. Since we are alone, I will say it frankly: I sweat like a horse while dancing at a large ball. There is so little air, and the great number of people and candles make it so warm, that it is like a miniature August in one room. After a public ball, or even a large private one, I find that perspiration has usually *soaked* my stays and shift, and that necessitates a wash for the petticoat and gown as well, even assuming no one has splashed negus or punch on me in the crush. Sometimes only the sleeves of a gown need to be removed and washed, but it takes time for Beatty and I to sew them back on. Besides, it isn't as if I wouldn't need them in London as well. It is only here in the country that having seven evening dresses is seen as exorbitance, my dear Mrs Grant."

"You are right, of course. I had not thought of that. Are the stores in Brighton as good as the ones in Bath?" Mrs Grant asked.

"I would say better. Bond Street in London offers nothing better than what can be purchased on St James's Street in Brighton. I was as able to buy the most perfect muslin for dresses and the best poplin and silk for petticoats there as I am able to in Town. Everything there, every furbelow and bonnet, was the latest crack of fashion, and excellent half-boots could be bought for rather less money than one must pay for them at home – that is, in London. You could buy any household goods you wished, as well. The breakfast china I sent you for New Year's was purchased in Brighton."

"That reminds me, I must complain about the china you gave me."

Mary was nearly dumbstruck. For Mrs Grant to be so rude as complain about a *gift*, especially a gift Mary saw on the table daily? It was some of Spode's finest bone china! It was a pattern of red flowers and gilding on white, which was the most modern fashion available. It was the same pattern of breakfast dishes used by Lady Castlereagh!

When Mary was able to find her voice again, she asked, "What about it offends you ma'am?"

"It put my dinner china to shame and I was forced to buy new," Mrs Grant fell into giggles. "The look on your face!"

"What abominable lessons in teasing you have learned from my brother!" Mary cried in mock dismay, before joining Mrs Grant in giggling.

"Yes, I have become quite arch in my old age," Mrs Grant pretended to brag.

"You had better keep a civil tongue inside your head, madam, or I'll not say another word about Brighton."

"Woe is me! Alas! Alack!" Mrs Grant's facial expressions during her feigned distress were so comical that Mary's giggles burst into a full-throated laugh.

"You are a goosecap," Mary playfully scolded her sister.

"Better than a gooseberry, I suppose," Mrs Grant retorted saucily. "Or gooseberry-eyed."

"There is little worse than gooseberry-eyed, it's true," Mary agreed. "I had a would-be beau in Brighton named Mr Frye that had the worst eyes I have ever seen. Not only were they the dull grey colour of boiled gooseberries, but one eye was always wandering away to look at something else when we spoke. It was very disconcerting."

"Oh, that poor man!"

"It was a pity, because he would have been handsome otherwise. Not that it signifies, because Mr Frye was the son of a rich tradesman and should have little trouble getting a wife in his own set, or even to marry above himself. He was receiving encouragement from Miss Dierdre Dalrymple when I left. She is the youngest daughter of a baron, but the family doesn't have a brass farthing to bless themselves with. Her elder two sisters were obliged to go abroad, one to India and the other to the West Indies, to marry men of newly made fortunes there. One of the sisters, the eldest I think, is doing well in India, but I heard that the other is *very* unhappy with her husband in the islands, and he will not let her return to England to visit her family lest she refuse to return to him. I think the last Miss Dalrymple and her parents didn't want to risk that kind of misfortune falling upon *her*. She would be wise to marry Mr Frye."

"I would hate to think of a genteel woman marrying for such a mercenary reason," Mrs Grant said.

Mary shrugged. "Is it mercenary or prudent? Mr Frye would make good connections and his fortune would aid Dalrymples; as long as the couple does not loathe one another, I cannot see the harm in it."

"I suppose you are right," Mrs Grant admitted. "Not everyone can marry for love."

"There is no reason to suppose they will be entirely devoid of affection," Mary tried to cheer her sister. "Perhaps they will come to love each other. He was a well-spoken man of information, and not *ugly* in spite of his unfortunate eyes, and she is all together well-looking in spite of being nearly thirty and penniless. Their mutual *gratitude* toward one another may make them mutually fond. Stranger things happen every day."

"That's true," Mrs Grant conceded, "and Brighton must be quite the place for romance."

"For me, it was quite the place for *books*," Mary said. "There is a circulating library there called Donaldson's and it is a delight. It had a wonderful selection of novels and music. I copied at least three pieces from there into my music-book."

Mary was not jesting about her preference for libraries and her indifference to romance at Brighton. She turned twenty-one at the seaside resort, and she had believed that she had plenty of time to choose a husband; maybe even as long as four or five years. It was not until her aunt's death and the Admiral's choice to move his paramour into his home that Mary began to feel a pressing need to marry. It was only when it became clear that she needed the security of a home of her own that she began to *seriously* consider her marriage prospects. Although she had considered accepting Tom Bertram's theoretical proposal just a few months before, he would have been scarcely regarded a year prior. Sometimes she wondered if her attraction to Edmund was also bolstered by her need to marry. Was she merely infatuated with Edmund because he was clearly interested in her, and thus the most likely candidate for marriage here and now?

"What else was delightful at Brighton?"

"Haven't I told you of felicitousness enough?" Mary joshed.

"*Is* there any end to felicitousness in Brighton?" Mrs Grant joked in return.

"There must be, but I confess *I* didn't find it. There seemed to be always something to be doing there. One morning my aunt and I hired a pony-cart and driver and were taken to the village of

Rottingdean, which is very picturesque. It has a stone church (called St Margaret's if my memory hasn't failed me), which has exceptionally beautiful stain glass windows and what we were told was a Saxon tower; it was quite Gothic looking. We were also told we must see the windmill in there, which was thought to be a marvel when it was built in '02, but we did not find it special. It is just a black wooden smock mill, and for the life of me I do not know why it causes such a stir. But I will tell you what *did* cause a stir."

"What?" Mrs Grant leaned forward, her white-on-white work forgotten in her hands.

"On our fourth day at Brighton, and I remember it *quite* clearly, it was our privilege to see what I can only assume to be a foreign gentleman strip entirely naked on the beach to go bathing."

"Gracious God! Really?"

"Oh, yes. He was obviously a man of some means, and was wearing some of Beau Brummel's style of trousers so he was clearly up to date on the latest fashions in Town. He and what I can only *assume* was his wife were sitting on a beach-rug and they appeared so unexceptional I didn't give them the slightest notice at first. However, when he began to strip off his clothes to go sea bathing he caught my attention, as well as the observance of everyone for a mile in either direction. At first, I thought he would at least retain his smalls, scant modesty though *they* would provide when wet, but no — he was as Adam in paradise when he approached the water."

Mrs Grant could not help her amusement. "I should be reprimanding you for looking but I confess I would have been unable to ignore such a spectacle either!"

"I found it mighty *educational*," Mary said dryly, "but I will never be able to look upon a cooked goose's neck the same way again."

She had to wait some time for Mrs Grant to stop fizzing and spluttering with mirth before she could continue.

"When the good fellow emerged from the water, his lady helped him dry himself with towels, and he redressed with the nonchalance of an emperor. My aunt and I waited at our posts for more than half an hour to see if the wife would do the same, but I am sad to report that the couple was done providing entertainment for the day."

"Now I am *determined* to go to Brighton one day," Mrs Grant said. "I have never seen *that* sort of thing in Bath."

"In truth, I cannot say it was an everyday occurrence at Brighton, either."

"What about more sedate amusements. Did you go on any sailing parties?" Mrs Grant had never had a chance to be on a sailing party, but hoped to do so one day.

"Just one, ma'am. I enjoyed it, but it made my poor aunt so ill she nearly turned green. Henry has promised to escort me on more sailing parties when I next come to Bath, but I don't know if I shall go. I don't think the sea air at Bath is as mild as the sea air in Brighton; a Bath sailing party might not suit me as much."

"I wish Mansfield had more amusements, dearest. I am afraid you will feel the loss of Mrs Rushworth and Julia as the winter sets in," Mrs Grant fretted a little, fearful of her sister's being made unhappy by the lack of company.

"Mrs Rushworth and Miss Bertram have been here so infrequently in the last four weeks that I do not think I shall miss them as much as I did when Sir Thomas first arrived home," Mary said. "As long as I have *you* for company I shall be content. We can always send one of the footmen to the circulating library if the lane becomes too dirty to for us to walk on, and I can ride Dilly as easily across muddy ground on cold days as I can dry ground on warm ones. It is not as if she need to worry about ruining *her* shoes. We have cards, and needlework, and I have my music. I am sure there will be some times of tedium, but tedium can strike even in London. If you don't believe me, you need only watch a friend's children put on one of Monsieur Berquin's plays from *L'Ami des Infants* to discover the terrible truth. I know M. Berquin's skits are an excellent way for children to learn good morals while also learning French elocution, but they are the most dreadful pabulum to endure watching."

"I shall endeavour to help you avoid tedium," Mrs Grant promised.

"If it comes near, we shall set the dog on it," Mary agreed, "and as long as I eschew reading French philosophy then tedium's friend ennui should avoid the house as well."

"I think the parsonage will have *some* visitors who will bring amusements," Mrs Grant said with jovial slyness. "Mr Edmund Bertram will come, I am sure."

Mary, much to her chagrin, felt her cheeks heat. To cover her blush, she carelessly replied, "Oh, I am sure he will want to visit Dr Grant often to discuss his future as a parson."

"Yes, that is sure to be the *only* reason for his calls," Mrs Grant was gamesome.

"Miss Price may come as well," Mary attempted to channel the conversation into a new area. "She will be coming out soon, I suppose, and will need to go about more in society."

Mrs Grant made a small grimace. "I fear you will have to go to *her*, dearest. Lady Bertram will be reluctant to allow Fanny to leave unless Mrs Norris is there to keep her sister company."

"Considering how often Mrs Norris goes to the Park, there will be many mornings when Miss Price will have the freedom and leisure to visit us here," Mary pointed out. "Let Mrs Norris do something to earn her keep; she dines at the Park more often than she does at her own home."

"True. Mrs Norris should do *something* good for Fanny Price for a change, even if it is simply allowing her the freedom to visit us."

"I am hopeful it will be so, and for that reason I shall look forward to becoming more intimately acquainted with Miss Price," Mary said optimistically, totally unaware of how much Fanny hated and despised her.

Chapter Twenty-Three

AS FORTUNE WOULD have it, it was not very long after Maria Bertram became Mrs Rushworth that something occurred to allow Miss Price to be established as a regular visitor at the parsonage. Fanny, having been sent into the village on some errand by her aunt Norris, was overtaken by a heavy shower close to the Parsonage, and being descried from one of the windows endeavouring to find shelter under the branches and lingering leaves of an oak just beyond their premises, was forced, though not without some modest reluctance on her part, to come in. A civil servant she had withstood; but when Dr Grant himself went out with an umbrella, there was nothing to be done but to be very much ashamed and to get into the house as fast as possible; and to poor Miss Crawford, who had just been contemplating the dismal rain in a very desponding state of mind, sighing over the ruin of all her plan of exercise for that morning, and of every chance of seeing a single creature beyond themselves for the next twenty-four hours; the sound of a little bustle at the front door, and the sight of Miss Price dripping with wet in the vestibule, was delightful. The value of an event on a wet day in the country, was most forcibly brought before her. She was all alive again directly, and among the most active in being useful to Fanny, in detecting her to be wetter than she would at first allow, and providing her with dry clothes; and Fanny, after being obliged to submit to all this attention, and to being assisted and waited on by mistresses and maids, being also obliged on returning down stairs, to be fixed in their drawing-room for an hour while the rain continued, the blessing of something fresh to see and think of was thus extended to Miss Crawford, and might carry on her spirits to the period of dressing and dinner.

The two sisters were so kind to her and so pleasant, that Fanny might have enjoyed her visit could she have believed herself not in the way. The dual assurances of Miss Crawford and Mrs Grant that she was very welcome could not convince her that she was anything other than an intruder to the family's private time. Fanny was so often obliging when she did not truly wish to be that she could not believe the occupants of the Parsonage were not also bearing her presence with the same false complacency.

It was beginning to look brighter, when Fanny, observing a harp in the room, asked some questions about it, which soon led to an acknowledgement of her wishing very much to hear it, and a confession, which could hardly be believed, of her having never yet heard it since its being in Mansfield. To Fanny herself it appeared a very simple and natural circumstance. She had scarcely ever been at the Parsonage since the instrument's arrival, there had been no reason that she should; but Miss Crawford, calling to mind an early-expressed wish on the subject, was concerned at her own neglect;— and "shall I play to you now?"—and "what will you have?" were questions immediately following with the readiest good humour. She wished to make amends for being remiss in inviting Fanny to hear the harp sooner.

She played accordingly; happy to have a new listener, and a listener who seemed so much obliged, so full of wonder at the performance, and who shewed herself not wanting in taste. She played till Fanny's eyes, straying to the window on the weather's being evidently fair, spoke what she felt must be done.

"Another quarter of an hour," said Miss Crawford, "and we shall see how it will be. Do not run away the first moment of its holding up. Those clouds look alarming." Fanny was delightful, and Mary was reluctant to release her.

"But they are passed over," said Fanny.—"I have been watching them.—This weather is all from the south."

"South or north, I know a black cloud when I see it; and you must not set forward while it is so threatening. And besides, I want to play something more to you—a very pretty piece—and your cousin Edmund's prime favourite. You must stay and hear your cousin's favourite."

Fanny felt that she must; and after Mary had played Edmund's piece and reluctantly agreed that the sky was clear, Fanny was so kindly asked to call again, to take them in her walk whenever she could, to come and hear more of the harp, that she felt it necessary to be done, if no objection arose at home. Her manner in nowise let her audience into the secret of her aversion to visiting the Parsonage, and both Mary and Mrs Grant assumed the dear girl was made happy by their attentions and invitations. The ladies of the Parsonage were pleased with themselves for prevailing on Miss Price to return in spite of her shyness and unwillingness to give trouble.

‖

Fanny left nothing but goodwill behind her. Mrs Grant was grateful to her for providing some source of enjoyment for Mary, and Mary herself found Miss Price an object of great interest. Fanny was her cousin Edmund's favourite, which predisposed Mary to like her as well, and Fanny was such a demure, trembling, baby-rabbit of a girl that Mary's generous heart could not help but warm to her. Her budding friendship with Miss Price had the beneficial felicity of feeling philanthropic on Mary's part; she felt like a better person for wanting to befriend such a timorous young woman as Miss Price because she felt she could do her some good. She hoped to coax the girl into talking more, and gaining some measure of ease in company, before Fanny came out. Perhaps the bashful girl would even inspire a romance, and thus be freed of the eternal drudgery of being an indigent niece to an indolent Lady Bertram. Mary was not too hopeful of this satisfaction, though. Miss Price was pretty in a soft way and a more good-tempered young lady would never be found, but she was without a bean. It was rare to find a man of their class who could, or would, marry a moneyless dependent relation whose father's family was of low birth. Miss Price would have to be very lucky indeed to ever receive an offer for her hand.

‖

Such was the origin of the sort of intimacy which took place between them within the first fortnight after the Miss Bertrams' going away, an intimacy resulting principally from Miss Crawford's desire of something new, and which had little reality in Fanny's feelings. Fanny went to her every two or three days; it seemed a kind of fascination; she could not be easy without going, and yet it was without loving her, without ever thinking like her, without any sense of obligation for being sought after now when nobody else was to be had; and deriving no higher pleasure from her conversation than occasional amusement, and *that* often at the expense of her judgement, when it was raised by pleasantry on people or subjects which she wished to be respected. She went however, and they sauntered about together many an half hour in Mrs Grant's shrubbery, the weather being unusually mild for the time of year; with Mary being without the slightest inkling of the animosity toward her festering in her seemingly pleasant companion.

"This is pretty—very pretty," said Fanny, looking around her as they were thus sitting together one day, and launched into soliloquy regarding the majesty of ever-changing nature worthy of the raptures Henry Crawford often broke out in when regarding landscapes. Miss Crawford, long used to her brother's eloquence on the topic, remained untouched and inattentive, and had nothing to say; and Fanny, perceiving it, brought back her own mind to what she thought must interest.

"It may seem impertinent in *me* to praise, but I must admire the taste Mrs Grant has shewn in all this. There is such a quiet simplicity in the plan of the walk!—not too much attempted!"

"Yes," replied Miss Crawford carelessly, "it does very well for a place of this sort. One does not think of extent *here*—and between ourselves, till I came to Mansfield, I had not imagined a country parson ever aspired to a shrubbery or any thing of the kind." For Mary, there was nothing in the country that she could not enjoy just as well in a London park.

"I am so glad to see the evergreens thrive!" said Fanny in reply. "My uncle's gardener always says the soil here is better than his own, and so it appears from the growth of the laurels and evergreens in general.—The evergreen!—How beautiful, how welcome, how wonderful the evergreen!—When one thinks of it, how astonishing a variety of nature!—In some countries we know the tree that sheds its leaf is the variety, but that does not make it less amazing, that the same soil and the same sun should nurture plants differing in the first rule and law of their existence. You will think me rhapsodising; but when I am out of doors, especially when I am sitting out of doors, I am very apt to get into this sort of wondering strain. One cannot fix one's eyes on the commonest natural production without finding food for a rambling fancy."

"To say the truth," replied Miss Crawford, amused at Fanny's enthusiasms but unwilling to court hearing more of them, "I am something like the famous Doge at the court of Lewis XIV; and may declare that I see no wonder in this shrubbery equal to seeing myself in it. If had told me a year ago that this place would be my home, that I should be spending month after month here, as I have done, I certainly should not have believed them!—I have now been here nearly five months! and, moreover, the quietest five months I ever passed."

"*Too* quiet for you I believe."

"I should have thought so *theoretically* myself, but"—and her eyes brightened as she spoke—"take it all and all, I never spent so happy a summer.—But then"—with a more thoughtful air and lowered voice—"there is no saying what it may lead to." Mary recalled herself and with renewed animation, soon went on:

"I am conscious of being far better reconciled to a country residence than I had ever expected to be. I can even suppose it pleasant to spend *half* the year in the country, under certain circumstances—very pleasant. An elegant, moderate-sized house in the centre of family connections—continual engagements among them—commanding the first society in the neighbourhood—looked-up to perhaps as leading it even more than those of larger fortune, and turning from the cheerful round of such amusements to nothing worse than a tête-à-tête with the person one feels most agreeable in the world. There is nothing frightful in such a picture, is there, Miss Price? One need not envy the new Mrs Rushworth with such a home as *that*."

"Envy Mrs Rushworth!" was all that Fanny attempted to say. Mary wondered that her meaning wasn't plain. While no one would envy Mrs Rushworth her *Mr* Rushworth, everyone should envy her Sotherton and a fat bank balance. One must be a fool not to, and Miss Price wasn't a simpleton.

"Come, come, it would be very unhandsome in us to be severe on Mrs Rushworth, for I look forward to our owing her a great many gay, brilliant, happy hours. I expect we shall be all very much at Sotherton another year. Such a match as Miss Bertram has made is a public blessing, for the first pleasures of Mr Rushworth's wife must be to fill her house, and give the best balls in the country."

Fanny was silent—and Miss Crawford relapsed into thoughtfulness, till suddenly looking up at the end of a few minutes, she exclaimed, "Ah! here he is." It was not Mr Rushworth, however, but Edmund, who then appeared walking towards them with Mrs Grant. "My sister and Mr Bertram—I am so glad your eldest cousin is gone, that he *may* be Mr Bertram again. There is something in the sound of Mr *Edmund* Bertram so formal, so pitiful, so younger-brother-like, that I detest it." The warmer Mary's feelings grew for Edmund, the colder she became toward the things that marked him out as a second son.

"How differently we feel!" cried Fanny. "To me, the sound of *Mr* Bertram is so cold and nothing-meaning—so entirely without warmth or character!—It just stands for a gentleman, and that's all.

But there is nobleness in the name of Edmund. It is a name of heroism and renown—of kings, princes, and knights; and seems to breathe the spirit of chivalry and warm affections."

"I grant you the name is good in itself, and *Lord* Edmund or *Sir* Edmund sound delightfully; but sink it under the chill, the annihilation of a Mr—and Mr Edmund is no more than Mr John or Mr Thomas." Mary shook off the thought as a vexation without remedy. "Well, shall we join and disappoint them of half their lecture upon sitting down out of doors at this time of year, by being up before they can begin?"

Edmund met them with particular pleasure. It was the first time of his seeing them together since the beginning of that better acquaintance which he had been hearing of with great satisfaction. A friendship between two so very dear to him was exactly what he could have wished; and to the credit of the lover's understanding be it stated, that he did not by any means consider Fanny as the only, or even as the greater gainer by such a friendship.

"Well," said Miss Crawford, "and do you not scold us for our imprudence? What do you think we have been sitting down for but to be talked to about it, and entreated and supplicated never to do so again?" The nippy air had brought a fine rosy colour to Mary Crawford's face, and her eyes were even brighter than usual. Edmund was struck anew by her beauty.

"Perhaps I might have scolded," said Edmund, "if either of you had been sitting down alone; but while you do wrong together I can overlook a great deal."

"They cannot have been sitting long," cried Mrs Grant, "for when I went up for my shawl I saw them from the staircase window, and then they were walking."

"And really," added Edmund, "the day is so mild, that your sitting down for a few minutes can be hardly thought imprudent. Our weather must not always be judged by the Calendar. We may sometimes take greater liberties in November than in May."

"Upon my word," cried Miss Crawford, her mock dismay spoiled by laughter, "you are two of the most disappointing and unfeeling kind friends I ever met with! There is no giving you a moment's uneasiness. You do not know how much we have been suffering, nor what chills we have felt! But I have long thought Mr Bertram one of the worst subjects to work on, in any little manoeuvre against common sense, that a woman could be plagued with. I had very little hope of *him* from the first; but you, Mrs Grant, my sister, my own sister, I think I had a right to alarm you a little."

"Do not flatter yourself, my dearest Mary. You have not the smallest chance of moving me. I have my alarms, but they are quite in a different quarter: and if I could have altered the weather, you would have had a good sharp east wind blowing on you the whole time—for here are some of my plants which Robert *will* leave out because the nights are so mild, and I know the end of it will be that we shall have a sudden change of weather, a hard frost setting in all at once, taking every body (at least Robert) by surprise, and I shall lose every one; and what is worse, cook has just been telling me that the turkey, which I particularly wished not to be dressed till Sunday, because I know how much more Dr Grant would enjoy it on Sunday after the fatigues of the day, will not keep beyond to-morrow. These are something like grievances, and make me think the weather most unseasonably close."

"The sweets of housekeeping in a country village!" said Miss Crawford archly. "Commend me to the nurseryman and the poulterer." She was not entirely in jest; she had no desire to care as much about plants and fowl as her sister. Not while there were books to read and people to talk to and music to play.

"My dear child, commend Dr Grant to the deanery of Westminster or St Paul's, and I should be as glad of your nurseryman and poulterer as you could be. But we have no such people in Mansfield. What would you have me do?"

"Oh! you can do nothing but what you do already; be plagued very often and never lose your temper." Mary was really very fond of her sister, and she marvelled at Mrs Grant's patience with the vagaries of a country life and the difficulties of a gourmand husband.

"Thank you—but there is no escaping these little vexations, Mary, live where we may; and when you are settled in town and I come to see you, I dare say I shall find you with yours, in spite of the nurseryman and the poulterer—perhaps on their very account. Their remoteness and unpunctuality, or their exorbitant charges and frauds will be drawing forth bitter lamentations."

"I mean to be too rich to lament or to feel any thing of the sort. A large income is the best recipe for happiness I ever heard of. It certainly may secure all the myrtle and turkey part of it."

"You intend to be very rich?" said Edmund, with a look which, to Fanny's eye, had a great deal of serious meaning.

"To be sure. Do not you?—Do not we all?" Mary was surprised by the seriousness of his reply and the question of it. Who did not *mean* to be rich?

"I cannot intend any thing which it must be so completely beyond my power to command. Miss Crawford may choose her degree of wealth. She has only to fix on her number of thousands a year, and there can be no doubt of their coming. My intentions are only not to be poor."

"By moderation and economy, and bringing down your wants to your income, and all that. I understand you—and a very proper plan it is for a person at your time of life, with such limited means and indifferent connections.—What can *you* want but a decent maintenance?" She tutted in overwrought sympathy. "You have not much time before you; and your relations are in no situation to do any thing for you, or to mortify you by the contrast of their own wealth and consequence. Be honest and poor, by all means—but I shall not envy you; I do not much think I shall even respect you. I have a much greater respect for those that are honest and rich."

"Your degree of respect for honesty, rich or poor, is precisely what I have no manner of concern with. I do not mean to be poor. Poverty is exactly what I have determined against. Honesty, in the something between, in the middle state of worldly circumstances, is all that I am anxious for your not looking down on."

"But I do look down upon it, if it might have been higher. I must look down upon any thing contented with obscurity when it might rise to distinction." Mary was in earnest. She did not approve of a lack of ambition. She loved her brother despite his idleness and could see why a gentleman of wealth would lack an occupation, but she could not look at complacency with anything but disdain. If *she* were a man, she would be active and determined to rise in a respectable profession. She could not respect a man who was motivated to better his circumstances.

"But how may it rise?—How may my honesty at least rise to any distinction?"

This was not so very easy a question to answer, considering Edmund's resistance to any previous suggestion Mary had made, and occasioned an "Oh!" of some length from the fair lady before she could add "You ought to be in parliament, or you should have gone into the army ten years ago."

"*That* is not much to the purpose now; and as to my being in parliament, I believe I must wait till there is an especial assembly for the representation of younger sons who have little to live on. No, Miss Crawford," he added, in a more serious tone, "there *are* distinctions which I should be miserable if I thought myself without any chance— absolutely without chance or possibility of obtaining—but they are of a different character."

There was a look of consciousness as he spoke, and what seemed a consciousness of manner on Miss Crawford's side as she made some laughing answer about a determination to wed one of the King's unmarried sons, that revealed the underlying seriousness of the conversation. Edmund was still determined to be a country parson; could Mary be content with a moderate income in the country rather than wealth in the city?

The sound of the great clock at Mansfield Park, striking three, alerted Miss Price to the late hour and she directly began her adieus; and Edmund began at the same time to recollect, that his mother had been inquiring for her, and that he had walked down to the Parsonage on purpose to bring her back.

Fanny's hurry increased; and without in the least expecting Edmund's attendance, but she found from Edmund's manner that he *did* mean to go with her.—He too was taking leave.— In the moment of parting, Edmund and Fanny were invited to dinner at the Parsonage the next day. Fanny was unsure she would be permitted, but Edmund answered that he was tolerably certain they could both accept the invitation.

The two cousins walked home together; and except in the immediate discussion of this engagement, which Edmund spoke of with the warmest satisfaction, as so particularly desirable for her in the intimacy which he saw with so much pleasure established, it was a silent walk—for having finished that subject, he grew thoughtful and indisposed for any other.

Chapter Twenty-Four

SHORTLY BEFORE FOUR o'clock, as Mary was putting the finishing touches on her toilet in her dressing closet, she heard a sound of a carriage pulling up to the entrance of the parsonage. Surprised to hear Edmund and Fanny arriving so soon, she looked out of the window, and saw with great pleasure that it was Henry's barouche. She practically flew from her boudoir and down the stairs to throw herself into her brother's arms with delight.

"Hey now!" Henry laughed. "My greatcoat is wet, and will spot your dress! Hold off while I shuck it."

"I care not a whit for spots on my dress," Mary cried. "I am too happy to have you come."

Henry looked at her askance. "*You* don't care about spots on your dress? *You?* Have you suffered a blow to the head?"

"You are such a Sammy!" Mary laughed.

The butler, having already taken Henry's hat and gloves, now helped extricate Mary's brother from his greatcoat. Once freed, Henry gave Mary a fierce hug and a resounding smack of a kiss on the forehead.

"How was Bath?" Mary asked, as she took Henry's arm and they walked toward the drawing-room.

"About the usual," Henry said, with maddening ambiguity.

"And how was Mlle. LaVeaux?"

Henry looked naughty. "About the usual."

Mary was still laughing when Mrs Grant entered the drawing-room and gave an effusive greeting to her brother. Henry told her that she was more beautiful than daylight in French, and kissed her on both cheeks in a continental manner, making his older sister giggle at his silliness. Dr Grant made his appearance close on the heels of his wife, and was given a hearty handshake and a manly slap on the shoulder by his affectionate brother-in-law.

"We are so happy you have come, Henry! We did not expect you until after Christmas." Mrs Grant eyes sparkled with gladness to see her brother.

"I have commitments to be in London by Christmas Day," Henry explained, "but I missed my sisters and brother so much that I decided to leave Bath early and come back here for a day or two, supposing I am welcome. The Admiral was surrounded by his old friends and cronies, and I felt that I could leave to please myself without discommoding him. I would rather be in Northamptonshire and spending time with my family than lounging about Bath."

The Grants were immensely flattered, but Mary suspected that there was another motive for Henry's arrival. She knew he loved her, and the Grants, but she also knew that for him to forsake a mistress in Bath while having no object of flirtation in Mansfield to be properly distracting was very odd behaviour on his part. When she got him alone, she would ceaselessly quiz him until he told her what had happened.

"You are always welcome, Henry, as well you know. You have picked an excellent day to arrive. Mrs Edmund Bertram and Miss Price are coming to dine with us, so I there is a feast to celebrate your arrival. Cook has dressed a turkey, and there will be baked apples in pastry for pudding. I know that is your prime favourite, and cook has used honey to sweeten it so that you and Mary will eat it. With Mary in the house we have saved a fortune on sugar!" Mrs Grant burbled.

Mary and Henry, like many abolitionists, avoided sugar since it was almost entirely produced by the efforts of slaves.

"You have no need of sugar, ma'am; you are sweet enough," Henry said gallantly, inspiring a blush and a depreciating moue from his elder sister.

"There is also orange crème, and it has sugar aplenty in it," Dr Grant warned. "You and Mary can avoid it, but we needed *something* of sugar on the table. It would not be seemly to provide a sugarless table to Mr Bertram."

"I cannot but agree with you, sir," Henry sketched a bow. "But if I am to join you for dinner I must go dress for it. My valet will have enough unpacked by now, surely."

"You had better make haste, dearest," Mrs Grant urged. "We expect them in less than half an hour."

"I shall be as fleet as Mercury, my dear sister. You need only listen to the flutter of wings on my heels," Henry excused himself and they heard his footsteps leaping the stairs two at a time as he went to his room.

ɪɪ

Henry, in spite of his dedication to sartorial splendour, was indeed ready by the time Edmund and Fanny arrived, entering the drawing-room a full five minutes before the guests from the Park. When Edmund and Fanny were ushered in by the butler, they saw Henry in the centre of attention, as was often the case. The smiles and pleased looks of the three others standing round him, shewed how welcome was his sudden resolution of coming to them for a few days on leaving Bath. A very cordial meeting passed between him and Edmund; and with the exception of Fanny, the pleasure was general; and even to *her*, there might be some advantage in his presence, since every addition to the party must rather forward her favourite indulgence of being suffered to sit silent and unattended to. Fortunately for the shy young woman, this indulgence was granted. Although Fanny, as the principle female guest, was forced to endure the particular attentions of the Grants and Crawfords, the conversation flowed around her in such a lively manner that she was seldom called on to talk, even in response.

"I thought of you whilst in Bath, Mary," Henry said.

"I should hope so!" Mary quipped. "It is my belief I should be in the forefront of everyone's mind. I am a gilflurt, and it pleases my vanity."

"I mean, I thought of you on a *particular* occasion, rather than just my general and constant preoccupation with your absence."

"Well, then. That will do."

"I thank you," Henry simpered like a complete puppy, to the amusement of his fellow diners, before returning to a normal tone of voice. "It was in Molland's pastry shop that you sprang to my mind. They have a new flavour of iced cream, and I know how fond you are of ices."

"They have nearly every fruit under the sun to flavour the ices; what can they have done new?" Mary asked. She and Henry both had a weakness for cream ices, the one exception they made to their avoidance of sugar. They consoled themselves that their guilty pleasure was very rarely done, but felt positively sinful as they devoured the sweet, cold, and creamy treat.

"Parmesan cheese ice," Henry told her.

"Pull the other one; it's got bells on," Dr Grant interjected.

"No, I assure you, sir," Henry smiled. "It is an ice flavoured with Parmesan cheese."

"How did it taste?" Mrs Grant's nose wrinkled, unable to conceive how ice cream that tasted like cheese could be anything but vile.

"It had a pleasing taste, which I must confess surprised me. However, not everyone likes it. The Admiral was disgusted with it, claiming that it tasted of a cross between a mouldy stocking and sweet milk."

"Has the Admiral been eating many mouldy stockings in sweet milk as of late?" Mary asked.

"Well ..." Henry drew the word out. "His new cook *is* from Calcutta."

Amid the laughter, Mary cried out, "Unfair! *Now* he gets an Indian cook. I love Indian cuisine and cannot have it here, and the Admiral gets curry every night."

"If you gave us a recipe, I am sure Cook could make some Indian dish," Mrs Grant said with a tinge of worry as if she had failed Mary by not suspecting a secret longing for channa masala.

"My dear Mrs Grant, I don't believe Cook could get the ingredients for an Indian dish nearer to here than London," Mary lovingly consoled her sister. "Moreover, Indian dishes are made with such complexity that I am afraid Cook would either poison *me* or *herself* to avoid having to make them."

"I've never had Indian cuisine," Edmund admitted, "yet I have long wanted to try it."

"Then visit my uncle and me when you next come to London, sir," Henry offered amiably. "The Admiral loves Indian cuisine and you will enjoy all the Indian dishes you could ever want. You must be warned, though, that some of them are spicy enough to have your tongue off."

"How did the Admiral come to like Indian dishes. Did he serve in India?" Edmund asked.

"No, he has not had that pleasure. His taste for Indian dishes is second-hand; several of his good friends *did* serve in India and it was on their tables that he first sampled it. One of my uncle's officers, Captain George Elliot, even has an Indian cook aboard his ship, but considering that Caption Elliot's father is Governor-General of India, his love of Indian cookery is very natural. My uncle's enjoyment of the flavours of Indian cuisine was so great he became determined to get an Indian cook, but such cooks are hard to come by, even in London. It took him nearly three years before he could hire his present cook. The fellow had jumped ship at Cardiff, and had made his way to Bath, where he was promptly snatched up by the Admiral."

"I am not surprised Captain Elliot likes Indian food if his father is Baron Minto," Dr Grant harrumphed in disapproval. "I suspect Minto has gone native, what with the treat of Amritsar in '09."

"What do you find so distasteful about the treaty, sir?" Henry asked politely.

"It gives that Ranjit Singh man complete control north of the Sutlej river! We had the forces there in Malwa. We should have crossed the bloody river and put an end to this so-called Sikh empire," Dr Grant was incensed that an Indian could get away with thumbing his nose at the British.

"I do not think we *gave* power over the north to Ranjat Singh, so much as he *took* it." Henry rejoined in a non-confrontational tone. "India is vast, and there are only so many troops on the ground, especially with so much of our military might needed to fight Napoleon. In my opinion, Minto was wise to use diplomacy. He has kept the peace in India admirably, and he *did* capture Java."

"Bah," Dr Grant waved away Java's significance. "Minto is just another Whig who has climbed to power in India on the back of General Hastings and Impey. Minto was in the thick of it, helping Burke and Fox and Sheridan tear down Hastings and Impey. The whole nonsense of impeachment was just to create a power vacuum in India so that the Whig friends of both Fox and Burke could be rewarded with plum positions there."

"I agree with you, sir," Edmund chimed in. "My father has always said Burke was appallingly anti-British, what with his support for the colonial revolt in America and his Irish-Catholic sympathies, and resented General Hastings's work to secure British interests. Minto is too lenient, as a general rule."

"Meaning no disrespect to you gentleman, I must disagree," Henry said. "Having been only five years of age when Hastings was acquitted, I have little first-hand knowledge of the trial, but I *can* read and I *can* do sums and it appears that General Hastings feathered his own nest more than Britain's during his tenure in India."

"And why shouldn't he have a good income for his hard work?" Edmund demanded. "He was risking all manner of tropical diseases and discomforts to stay in India. Furthermore, he was respected and admired by the natives. My esteemed father told me that Hastings received a very complimentary letter from the ruler of Oudh."

Henry sipped his wine. "I do not begrudge the General remuneration, nor do I think him a bad man or one unduly unkind to the natives. What I am saying is that his gains were such that they call his tenure into question and that *if* the Whigs are *now* seen as bestowing Indian sugar-plums to themselves, Hastings long rule of India *then* must likewise be seen as a plum from the Tories, who were great friends with the East India Company."

"*All* politicians are great friends with the East India Company," Mary was driven by fairness to say.

"This is true," Henry bowed to her.

"I for one am grateful to the East India Company," Mrs Grant commented. "I cannot lie; I enjoy having cotton, silk, and tea."

"The lotophagi are very grateful to them as well." Mary said cynically.

"*You* should be grateful for *that*, Mary," Henry said.

"Why? *I* am not an opium-eater."

"Yes, but so many of your beloved poets *are*," Henry smirked.

"Touché!" Mary threw up her hands in surrender. "I cannot deny I have enjoyed *The Rhyme of the Ancient Mariner*."

"Hunting has been so poor of late that I have been nearly driven to eating opium myself," Edmund was wry. "I've been out after fox three times since the season began and have yet to actually achieve the goal."

"Is Monsieur Reynard outwitting your hounds?" Mary asked with a grin.

"And the hounds' master, I am afraid," Edmund replied with a depreciating movement of his shoulders. "I am beginning to think I have been chasing a witch's familiar."

"I think Mary has hit upon the problem. Monsieur Reynard is French, and thus dashed hard to catch," Henry said.

"Not as hard to catch as a Russian fox would be," Dr Grant contradicted. "Napoleon took Moscow only to find there was not a Russian soul in it."

"Yes, but the fox did not burn down its own den, so it cannot be Russian," Edmund joked. "Napoleon was not expecting the Russians to burn their own crops and cities. There are reports that the Little General is having a miserable time of it, and will have to retreat rather than stay in Moscow and starve. I think it has been a very Pyrrhic victory for the French."

"But with fewer elephants," Mary quipped.

"Alas for Napoleon, there is no longer an Egyptian Pharaoh to lend him any, the way Ptolemy II did for Pyrrhus," Henry pretended to lament.

"If there *were* still an Egyptian Pharaoh, I am sure he would have been hauled back to the British Museum, elephants and all, along with the Rosetta Stone, and Dr Thomas Young would be studying him," Edmund smiled.

"Do you think linguists will ever be able to translate the ancient Egyptian on the stone, sir?" Mary asked him.

Edmund nodded. "I believe so, yes. However, I cannot begin to speculate how long it will take them. They have known for more than a decade now that the stone has three versions of the same text, and that the foreign names upon it are spelled phonetically, yet scholars are not materially closer to being able to read it."

"For me, the stone's greatest value is what it represents to *us* — the capitulation of the French in Egypt," Dr Grant smiled in a very satisfied way.

Henry and Mary glanced at one another and then hid their grins. Let Dr Grant be happy that the French had been vanquished. Neither of them would point out that the British had been subsequently forced out of Egypt in short order by the Ottoman forces, and the country was now ruled by an Albanian named Muhammad Ali. If that was something Dr Grant chose to ignore, then they would not drag it into the light.

"While it is always pleasant to contemplate a British victory, I am not so satisfied with the French being driven out of Egypt as I am of our recent triumphs in Spain," Edmund said.

Dr Grant's brow creased. "I cannot entirely support that notion as yet, I fear. It remains to be seen how Wellington's siege of Burgos will do, besides which I am unsure that the Spaniards deserve our aid, even against Napoleon. Have you seen that travesty that they are calling a *constitution*? I've never seen such poppycock."

Edmund responded gravely. "The constitution is, I grant you, fearsomely and radically humanistic, but Napoleon is such a danger that anything that stops his subjugation of the continent is worth doing."

Mary bit her tongue and resisted the urge to defend the Spanish constitution. For a lady to jump into political waters in this kind of company and at this time would be *coarse*. Thankful, Henry was there and she need only *look* her agreement to him.

"I think the Spanish constitution a splendid document," Henry said, causing Dr Grant to nearly drop his fork. "It entails universal male suffrage and a free press, which are, to my mind, the cornerstones of a civilised government."

"Are you saying that *our* government is uncivilised?" Edmund was made uneasy by Henry's dangerous liberalism.

"Can you look at the Prince Regent and say that it *is* civilised?" Henry asked in return.

"Ha!" Dr Grant scoffed. "I have your number, Henry. You just want the rabble and the vulgar to have a vote because of the drubbing the Whigs just took in the general election."

Henry, always easygoing, replied with a smile. "I cannot be other than disappointed by the Tory landslide, sir, and I will hold my peace about rotten boroughs and suchlike, yet it is true that I think universal suffrage would bring the Whigs once more into power. However, I will add not all Whigs are those whose politics I support. For example, I did not weep to see General Tarleton of Liverpool defeated by a Tory."

Whig or not, Banastre Tarleton was one of the most pro-slavery politicians in the country; Mary and Henry were united with the Admiral in detesting him.

Dr Grant sighed, "You are just like your uncle the Admiral in your politics. I can only hope to teach you wisdom as you grow older."

"Supposing I live long enough to doddering, I'm sure you are right," Henry rejoined, causing Mary to put down her wine glass suddenly lest she choke on more than suppressed laughter.

"I am surprised your uncle is a Whig," Edmund said. "Aren't most military men more sympathetic to the positions of the Tories?"

"I cannot speak for the Army, sir, but I can tell you that in my experience the Navy has nearly as many Whigs as it does Tories," Henry elucidated.

Henry was determined to avoid the topic of why his uncle had become a Whig if at all possible, for fear of insulting Edmund's father. It was the Admiral's experience in raiding slave ships, and seeing the execrable conditions and degradations that African captives were subjected to, that had driven him to become a resolute and ardent abolitionist. As an abolitionist, he had become a de facto Whig, and the more the Admiral was exposed to the Whig arguments in favour of religious freedom, parliamentary reform, prison reform, and education reform, the more he found that he agreed with them. Henry knew that there was no way to explain this all to Edmund, a Tory with a slave-owning father, without casting aspersions on his friend's family. If Edmund ever wanted to debate the topic, then Henry was game for it, but he would not spring it upon Edmund at the dinner table.

"Well, I am glad the Tories won, and I wish Lord Liverpool the best of luck," Mrs Grant said with pluck.

"I wish him luck as well, ma'am," Henry told her. "He is very progressive for a Tory, and no more hidebound than some of the old Friends of Mr Pitt. Besides, the former Foxite Whigs have been abandoned entirely by the Prince Regent, who turned his coat to such an extent I expected him to kiss Earl Grey on the cheek and receive thirty pieces of silver from his mother the queen."

"I cannot say I have any faith in the Prince Regent's support, either," Edmund made a gesture that was almost but not quite a shrug. "His opinions are so unfixed and mercurial, yet so correspondingly stubborn for their short course, that he is ludicrously unpredictable. It is no more safe to turn your back on him than on a bull. There is a reason we are cautioned to put not our faith in princes."

"My dislike of him is less political than it is from his appalling treatment of his daughter," Mary said. "It is hideous to think of how he keeps Princess Charlotte under lock and key at Windsor. He doesn't even let her stay long enough at the opera to see the end, before he entombs her away again with her maiden aunts and Lady de Clifford. It is positively medieval, or like one of those fictional fathers in a horrid novel, except that even fictional villains give their daughters a sufficient clothing allowance."

"Perhaps he is punishing her for blowing kisses to Earl Grey at the opera last year," Edmund suggested.

"Do you justify his conduct, sir?" Mary raised an eyebrow.

"By no means," Edmund assured her. "I am merely speculating on his highness's motivation for his shabby treatment of the princess."

"We could invite the regent to hunt your Franco-Russian fox, Mr Bertram," Mrs Grant smiled broadly. "The frustration generated by the animal's constant escape would be suitable punishment for all his crimes."

"Perhaps the skulking and elusive Monsieur Reynard would drive the regent into eating opium, as it has threatened to drive Mr Bertram," Mary said mockingly. "I believe opium-eating is the one vice Prinny does not indulge in … *yet*."

"Henry, *you* should come and hunt with Mr Bertram," Dr, Grant recommended.

"I know you disagree with my politics sir, but do you really wish to drive me to eating opium?" Henry looked aghast in a very affected and artful manner, which made even Fanny Price smile.

"No, you wiseacre," Dr Grant laughed. "I thought you might enjoy the sport. Send for your hunters from Norfolk, and stay for a while here with us."

"Yes, please do," Edmund encouraged Henry. "Tom has left to visit with friends, and I would very much like the company."

"In fox hunting, or consolatory opium eating?" Henry jested.

"In fox hunting, alone. I give you my word." Even the naturally serious Edmund enjoyed Henry's wit.

Mrs Grant also urged her brother to stay with the warmest language she could.

"Oh, *please* do, Henry," Mary begged. "Do it for Miss Price's sake."

"How would my staying be of any good to Miss Price? Does she need a coxcomb to laugh at?" Henry smiled at Fanny, but she was looking away and blushing.

"There is no doubt you *are* a coxcomb," Mary gibed with her brother, "but I was thinking that Miss Price would be relieved of the burden of having to walk with me and listen to my prattle so many days of the week if she had someone to share the chore with her."

"That would be a boon for any young lady, indeed," Henry tried to engage Fanny in conversation again. "What is your opinion, Miss Price? Do you think the open weather will continue? Or will we shiver in a freezing downpour as we hunt Monsieur Reynard?"

Fanny's answers were as short and indifferent as civility allowed. She could not wish him to stay, and would much rather not have him speak to her.

This was a new experience for Henry Crawford. Women never snubbed his conversation or attention; they courted it assiduously. Maidens, matrons, or madwomen, all ladies wanted Henry's company and gallantries. What was the meaning of Miss Price's indifference? Was she miffed because she felt slighted during his flirtation with her cousins? If so, Henry had no doubts that he could soon charm any little ill-will away. Henry could not bear to have one of her sex *not* enthralled with him. All women must love Henry for him to be happy, and Henry was usually happy for a reason.

"You seem indifferent to the plight of the poor hunter Miss Price; perhaps your sympathy is with Monsieur Reynard?" Henry tried again to get her notice, and again was given a very polite but very flat answer.

"If anyone could feel pity for a fox it is Fanny," Edmund patted his cousin's hand.

"Provided she has never seen a chicken coup after a fox has been in it," Mrs Grant specified. "Even Miss Price's soft heart could not feel pity for a fox after *that*."

"It is possible that Miss Price does not love chickens the way you do, Mrs Grant, and thus would be indifferent to their slaughter," Mary teased. "Not everyone bears your affection for poultry."

"*That* is because she hasn't got to know my hens," Mrs Grant replied serenely, to the general merriment of the table.

Chapter Twenty-Five

HENRY, IN HIS plans to coax Miss Price into finding him an agreeable fellow, was unaware of how angry she was at him for her cousins' sake. The idea that she could hold a grudge for a light flirtation on their behalf was not something he ever considered. That sort of loyalty to cousins who treated her slightingly was too alien to the manners and customs of his friends and acquaintances. Loyalty could and did exist among the ton, but it required a measure of reciprocity that Maria and Julia never showed Fanny.

They were all re-assembled in the drawing-room, when Edmund, being engaged apart in some matter of business with Dr Grant, which seemed entirely to engross them, and Mrs Grant occupied at the tea-table, when Henry brought up the subject of Mrs Rushworth and Miss Bertram. With a significant smile, which made Fanny quite hate him, he said to Mary, "So! Rushworth and his fair bride are at Brighton, I understand—Happy man!"

"Yes, they have been there—about a fortnight, Miss Price, have they not?—And Julia is with them," Mary smiled as significantly as her brother. She did not think having her pride hurt had done Mrs Rushworth any harm. Vanity such as Maria's was always better off deflated.

"And Mr Yates, I presume, is not far off."

"Mr Yates!—Oh! we hear nothing of Mr Yates. I do not imagine he figures much in the letters to Mansfield Park; do you, Miss Price?—I think my friend Julia knows better than to entertain her father with Mr Yates." Mary had too much respect for Julia's intelligence and too much understanding of Julia's enjoyments in London to think the young lady would risk Sir Thomas calling her home for any reason ... let alone a dalliance with a crowing puppy like Yates.

"Poor Rushworth and his two-and-forty speeches!" continued Crawford. "Nobody can ever forget them. Poor fellow!—I see him now;—his toil and his despair. Well, I am much mistaken if his lovely

Maria will ever want him to make two-and-forty speeches to her"—
adding, with a momentary seriousness, "She is too good for him—
much too good." And then changing his tone again to one of gentle
gallantry, and addressing Fanny, he said, "You were Mr Rushworth's
best friend. Your kindness and patience can never be forgotten, your
indefatigable patience in trying to make it possible for him to learn his
part—in trying to give him a brain which nature had denied—to mix
up an understanding for him out of the superfluity of your own! *He*
might not have sense enough himself to estimate your kindness, but I
may venture to say that it had honour from all the rest of the party."

Fanny coloured, and said nothing. Mary and Henry jointly
mistook Fanny's reddened cheeks for a blush of pleasure at the
compliments.

"It is as a dream, a pleasant dream!" he exclaimed, breaking
forth again after a few minutes musing. "I shall always look back on
our theatricals with exquisite pleasure. There was such an interest,
such an animation, such a spirit diffused! Everybody felt it. We were
all alive. There was employment, hope, solicitude, bustle, for every
hour of the day. Always some little objection, some little doubt, some
little anxiety to be got over. I never was happier."

Mary gave Henry a look indicating she knew better than
anyone why he was happy, but she refrained from commenting.

"We were unlucky, Miss Price," he continued in a lower tone, to
avoid the possibility of being heard by Edmund, and not at all aware
of her feelings, "we certainly were very unlucky. Another week, only
one other week, would have been enough for us. I think if we had had
the disposal of events—if Mansfield Park had had the government of
the winds just for a week or two about the equinox, there would have
been a difference. Not that we would have endangered his safety by
any tremendous weather—but only by a steady contrary wind, or a
calm. I think, Miss Price, we would have indulged ourselves with a
week's calm in the Atlantic at that season."

He seemed determined to be answered; and Fanny, averting her
face, said with a firmer tone than usual, "As far as *I* am concerned, sir,
I would not have delayed his return for a day. My uncle disapproved it
all so entirely when he did arrive, that in my opinion, every thing had
gone quite far enough."

Mary was surprised by Fanny's contradiction. Miss Price was
trembling and blushing, but she had been brave enough to disagree
with Henry. Mr Crawford seemed taken aback, but after a few

moments silent consideration of her, replied in a calmer, graver tone, and as if the candid result of conviction, "I believe you are right. It was more pleasant than prudent. We were getting too noisy."

Miss Crawford, who had been repeatedly eyeing Dr Grant and Edmund, now observed, "Those gentlemen must have some very interesting point to discuss."

"The most interesting in the world," replied her brother—"how to make money—how to turn a good income into a better. Dr Grant is giving Bertram instructions about the living he is to step into so soon. I find he takes orders in a few weeks. They were at it in the dining-parlour. I am glad to hear Bertram will be so well off. He will have a very pretty income to make ducks and drakes with, and earned without much trouble. I apprehend he will not have less than seven hundred a year. Seven hundred a year is a fine thing for a younger brother; and as of course he will still live at home, it will be all for his *menus plaisirs*; and a sermon at Christmas and Easter, I suppose, will be the sum total of sacrifice."

His sister tried to laugh off her feelings by saying, "Nothing amuses me more than the easy manner with which every body settles the abundance of those who have a great deal less than themselves. You would look rather blank, Henry, if your *menus plaisirs* were to be limited to seven hundred a year."

Mary, with her 20,000 pounds would receive 1,000 pounds a year in interest; 300 pounds more than Edmund would make as income. Although a family making 300 pounds a year was respectably middle class in London, to be a proper member of the gentry as Mary had always expected – to have a house in Town and keep a carriage and have an opera box – would require at least 2,000 pounds a year. If she married Edmund, they would fall short off the mark, and some uncomfortable economy would have to be practised. Henry, who made well over twice what was required to be wealthy even by the standards of the ton, would suffer no such inconvenience or lessening in *his* station if he married someone with a relative lack of funds. Mary thought to herself that Henry could stuff his complacent platitudes about Edmund's *menus plaisirs* in an inconvenient bodily cavity.

"Perhaps I might; but all *that* you know is entirely comparative. Birthright and habit must settle the business. Bertram is certainly well off for a cadet of even a baronet's family. By the time he is four or five and twenty he will have seven hundred a year, and nothing to do for it."

Miss Crawford *could* have said that there would be a something to do and to suffer for it, which she could not think lightly of; but she checked herself and let it pass; and tried to look calm and unconcerned when the two gentlemen shortly afterwards joined them. Inwardly, she was deeply agitated by the reality of Edmund's fortune ... or lack thereof.

Miss Crawford was too much vexed by what had passed to be in a humour for any thing but music. With that, she soothed herself and amused her friend while the Grants, Henry, and Edmund conversed over cards.

The assurance of Edmund's being so soon to take orders, coming upon her like a blow that had been suspended, and still hoped uncertain and at a distance, was felt with resentment and mortification. She was very angry with him. She had thought her influence more. She *had* begun to think of him—she felt that she had—with great regard, with almost decided intentions; but she would now meet him with his own cool feelings. It was plain that he could have no serious views, no true attachment, by fixing himself in a situation which he must know she would never stoop to. She would learn to match him in his indifference. She would henceforth admit his attentions without any idea beyond immediate amusement. If *he* could so command his affections, *hers* should do her no harm.

II

That evening, after the Bertram's carriage had spirited away Edmund and Fanny, and Dr Grant and his wife had retired to bed, Mary and Henry sat together talking while they drank a final glass of wine.

"At last we having a *tête-à-tête* and you can tell me the real reason you left Bath." Mary demanded of her brother.

"I told you the truth. I missed you all," Henry protested.

"That is, I believe, at least *half* the truth. What I want you to tell me is the *other* half."

"You are relentless; have I ever told you that?"

"Yes, now sing out."

"Fine. You have badgered me into submission. I left Bath in part to escape Mlle. LaVeaux."

"Escape her? Why?" Mary was flabbergasted.

"She was, as Henry V put it, hanging about my neck like a new-married wife. She was decidedly *clingy*. I know now how a tree feels when ivy sets upon it. Worse, she found out about my little peccadillo with the lovely widow in Lyme and was bawling like a calf," Henry was disgusted.

"I *told* you that making women fall in love with you was a dangerous game."

"Stuff and nonsense. She doesn't *love* me. She was, however, greatly enamoured of my pocketbook. I gave her a hundred quid to go with her *conge* and sent her back to London to find a new protector. She'll be tickety-boo in no time," Henry was unbothered.

"Until then you shall hide out here in Northamptonshire for a fortnight?"

"I don't know if I am going to stay that long yet or not," Henry was, as usual, non-committal under pressure.

"You must stay until my birthday at least. It is but the day after tomorrow, and how often does a sister turn twenty two?"

"I see through your supposed affection," Henry joked with his sister, "you just want your birthday present. Perhaps I haven't gotten you one?"

"Perhaps you didn't come so far out of your way just to make sure I received it from your hand? And perhaps I'll find pixies in stockings in the morning," Mary razzed him.

"Did I not just recently get you a horse?" Henry protested.

"What has *that* to do with my birthday?" Mary giggled.

Henry huffed with feigned resignation. "Oh well, if I must." He reached into a waistcoat pocket and pulled out a small box. "Here you are; you may have it a day early."

Determined not to squeal and disturb the house, Mary trembled in silent glee as Henry handed her the gift. Her resolve was almost broken when she opened it.

"Good God!" She gasped. "It is the most beautiful thing I have ever seen!"

Henry had gotten her an ivory cameo showing the bust of a classical goddess, encircled with pearls embedded in gold filigree and sporting a loop that would allow her to wear it on a chain as well as pin it to her dress. The goddess looked familiar, and Mary examined it more closely. When she looked again at her brother, tears were welling in her eyes.

"It is our aunt, isn't it?" She whispered, her throat tight with emotion.

"I had a jeweller do it from her miniature." Henry cleared his own throat. "I could think of nothing that would make you happier."

Mary wiped the tears from her cheeks. "You are a marvel, Henry. Only tell me you will stay for a fortnight and my birthday will be complete."

Henry smiled at his sister. "I am not sure I can; I did half-promise the Admiral to attend him in Town soon."

"It is easy enough to send the Admiral a letter. If he wants you to come, he'll not hesitate to tell you. The man is able to positively *bellow* even on paper," Mary said dismissively.

"I wish you liked the Admiral more," Henry sighed.

"I wish you liked him *less*," Mary bantered.

Henry became unusually serious. "Speaking of liking someone less … Bertram is determined to be japanned. Does this injure your peace at all?"

Mary waved the idea away with a false laugh. "Of course not!"

"That is much less than half the truth, I think," Henry looked at her kindly.

She closed the gift box gently. "You might be right, but what good would it do to speak of it? He appears to woo me, knowing I will never marry a parson, but yet he is determined to become one. What am I to think? *My* happiness is clearly no concern of his. He must have no serious intention toward me. I will not droop about like a … a … well, something *droopy*. I will be fine. If his heart is safe, then so is *mine*."

Henry gave her one of his penetrating looks, so at odds with his guise as a careless gad-about. "If you love him, Mary, I will do all in my power to support you. There are other livings he could be given."

"And should he have *five*, what good will they do? Even if we had the income to live in London as I should like, would we? Or would my wishes be worth as much as my aunt's were to *her* husband? That is galling me more than the money, which is worry enough. If he makes but seven hundred a year (and there is no telling when he will get another living), I would have to put in my one thousand per annum for us to have a tolerable income. I would not be able to set my twenty thousand aside for one of my younger sons or for a daughter, as I had thought to do, and there is no telling *how* many of those there will be. Shall I be a stay-at-home, never seeing London unless my brother has the mercy to invite me? Or live hand to mouth on a small income with a dozen children? Because *that* is what happens when you believe that love-in-a-cottage folderol. How long before I would become Xantippe from the misery of it, and nag like a fishwife? *That* is what Mr Bertram is asking me to hazard upon. No, he cannot love me if *that* is what he could want for me."

"I would not want that for you," Henry said sorrowfully.

Mary straightened her back and stood, almost visibly shaking off her melancholy. "Why are we talking on such rubbish as might-be? I have become maudlin from wine, and need to go to bed before I infect you with my false-anguish. Pray, do not worry for me. I am fine."

Henry stood and embraced his sister. "I don't worry about you at all, dearest. I worry for the poor earl or viscount who marries you."

Mary laughed in truth, and kissed her brother's cheek before turning and walking up the stairs into the dark, clutching her precious cameo.

II

Henry Crawford had quite made up his mind by the next morning to give another fortnight to Mansfield, and having sent for his hunters and written a few lines of explanation to the Admiral, he looked round at his sister as he sealed and threw the letter from him, and seeing the coast clear of the rest of the family, said, with a smile, "And how do you think I mean to amuse myself, Mary, on the days that I do not hunt? I am grown too old to go out more than three times a week; but I have a plan for the intermediate days, and what do you think it is?"

"To walk and ride with me, to be sure." Mary, engrossed in a book, was not giving Henry her full attention.

"Not exactly, though I shall be happy to do both, but *that* would be exercise only to my body, and I must take care of my mind. Besides, *that* would be all recreation and indulgence, without the wholesome alloy of labour, and I do not like to eat the bread of idleness. No, my plan is to make Fanny Price in love with me."

This startled Mary enough to close her book with a snap. "Fanny Price! Nonsense! No, no. You ought to be satisfied with her two cousins."

"But I cannot be satisfied without Fanny Price, without making a small hole in Fanny Price's heart. You do not seem properly aware of her claims to notice. When we talked of her last night, you none of you seemed sensible of the wonderful improvement that has taken place in her looks within the last six weeks. You see her every day, and therefore do not notice it, but I assure you, she is quite a different creature from what she was in the autumn. She was then merely a quiet, modest, not plain looking girl, but she is now absolutely pretty. I used to think she had neither complexion nor countenance; but in that soft skin of hers, so frequently tinged with a blush as it was yesterday, there is decided beauty; and from what I observed of her eyes and mouth, I do not despair of their being capable of expression enough when she has any thing to express. And then—her air, her manner, her *tout ensemble* is so indescribably improved! She must be grown two inches, at least, since October."

Mary rolled her eyes at her brother. "Phoo! phoo! This is only because there were no tall women to compare her with, and because she has got a new gown, and you never saw her so well dressed before. She is just what she was in October, believe me. The truth is, that she was the only girl in company for you to notice, and you must have a somebody. I have always thought her pretty—not strikingly pretty—but 'pretty enough,' as people say; a sort of beauty that grows on one. Her eyes should be darker, but she has a sweet smile; but as for this wonderful degree of improvement, I am sure it may all be resolved into a better style of dress and your having nobody else to look at; and therefore, if you do set about a flirtation with her, you never will persuade me that it is in compliment to her beauty, or that it proceeds from any thing but your own idleness and folly."

Her brother gave only a smile to this accusation, and soon afterwards said, "I do not quite know what to make of Miss Fanny. I do not understand her. I could not tell what she would be at yesterday. What is her character?—Is she solemn?—Is she queer? Is she prudish? Why did she draw back and look so grave at me? I could hardly get her to speak. I never was so long in company with a girl in my life— trying to entertain her—and succeed so ill! Never met with a girl who looked so grave on me! I must try to get the better of this. Her looks say, 'I will not like you, I am determined not to like you,' and I say, she shall."

"Foolish fellow!" Mary was both exasperated and amused by Henry's inability to leave a feminine puzzle well enough alone. "And so this is her attraction after all! This it is—her not caring about you—which gives her such a soft skin and makes her so much taller, and produces all these charms and graces! I do desire that you will not be making her really unhappy; a *little* love perhaps may animate and do her good, but I will not have you plunge her deep, for she is as good a little creature as ever lived, and has a great deal of feeling."

"It can be but for a fortnight," said Henry; "and if a fortnight can kill her, she must have a constitution which nothing could save. No, I will not do her any harm, dear little soul! I only want her to look kindly on me, to give me smiles as well as blushes, to keep a chair for me by herself wherever we are, and be all animation when I take it and talk to her; to think as I think, be interested in all my possessions and pleasures, try to keep me longer at Mansfield, and feel when I go away that she shall be never happy again. I want nothing more."

"Moderation itself!" said Mary. "I can have no scruples now. Well, you will have opportunities enough of endeavouring to recommend yourself, for we are a great deal together."

And without attempting any farther remonstrance, she left Fanny to her fate.

II

Mary would have used stronger remonstrates on Henry, if he had not been so obviously taking the whole thing as a lark. It was Henry's way to make strong, jesting statements about anything which he did not take seriously. If he had meekly promised to make Miss Price like him just a *little*, Mary would have been alarmed and feared seduction. His threats to make Fanny sigh after him were comforting piffles to his sister's mind. She also thought Fanny's lack of attractions would keep her safe. While the girl was pretty, in a delicately consumptive way, her charms were not those that had ever appealed to Henry. Her brother had always admired tall, voluptuous woman with the rosy glow of health upon their cheeks. Fanny was rather short, slimly made, and pallid. No, she felt sure there would be no temptation there strong enough to make Henry woo Fanny with enough verve to cut up the girl's peace.

What Mary did not understand was that it was a fate which, had not Fanny's heart been guarded in a way unsuspected by Miss Crawford, might have been a little harder than she deserved; for although there doubtless are such unconquerable young ladies of eighteen (or one should not read about them) as are never to be persuaded into love against their judgement by all that talent, manner, attention, and flattery can do, I have no inclination to believe Fanny one of them, or to think that with so much tenderness of disposition, and so much taste as belonged to her, she could have escaped heart-whole from the courtship (though the courtship only of a fortnight) of such a man as Crawford, in spite of there being some previous ill-opinion of him to be overcome, had not her affection been engaged elsewhere. With all the security which love of another and disesteem of him could give to the peace of mind he was attacking, his continued attentions—continued, but not obtrusive, and adapting themselves more and more to the gentleness and delicacy of her character,—obliged her very soon to dislike him less than formerly. She had by no means forgotten the past, and she thought as ill of him as ever; but she felt his powers; he was entertaining; and his manners were so improved, so polite, so seriously and blamelessly polite, that it was impossible not to be civil to him in return.

Henry was an intelligent man, and one who knew how to be pleasing. He soon learned that Fanny had an older brother by the name of William, who was a midshipman on the *Antwerp*, and that this brother was the dearest object of Fanny's heart. Crawford therefore made himself thoroughly master of the subject, and was determined on his return to town to apply for information as to the probable period of the *Antwerp's* return from the Mediterranean, &c.; and the good luck which attended his early examination of ship news, the next morning, seemed the reward of his ingenuity in finding out such a method of pleasing her, as well as of his dutiful attention to the Admiral, in having for many years taken in the paper esteemed to have the earliest naval intelligence. The *Antwerp* would be docking in Portsmouth that very day, and William Price would almost certainly have leave. Henry went hastily to Mansfield Park, hoping to be the first to deliver this good news to her, and planned to offer to go and get her brother himself if need be. He proved, however, to be too late. All those fine first feelings, of which he had hoped to be the excitor, were already given. But his intention, the kindness of his intention, was thankfully acknowledged—quite thankfully and warmly, for she was elevated beyond the common timidity of her mind by the flow of her love for William.

Chapter Twenty-Six

WILLIAM PRICE WAS among them by the 7ᵗʰ of December, and the joy shining from Fanny's eyes every time she beheld him aroused tenderness in everyone but Mrs Norris. William returned Fanny's love and devotion with interest, and the mutual friendship and fondness between the brother and sister was obvious to all that saw them together. An affection so amiable was advancing each in the opinion of all who had hearts to value any thing good. Henry Crawford was as much struck with it as any. It was a picture which Henry Crawford had moral taste enough to value. Fanny's attractions increased—increased two-fold—for the sensibility which beautified her complexion and illumined her countenance, was an attraction in itself. He was no longer in doubt of the capabilities of her heart. She had feeling, genuine feeling. It would be something to be loved by such a girl, to excite the first ardours of her young, unsophisticated mind! She interested him more than he had foreseen. A fortnight was not enough. His stay became indefinite.

Mary was also enchanted by Fanny and William's great rapport with one another. She seldom encountered another pair of siblings as devoted to one another as were she and Henry. She even spared a moment to think what a great pity it was that William Price, who was active and sensible, should have been born to the Price family; he would have made such an admirable young squire in the gentry. Much better than that gadabout Tom Bertram. Mary was still determined to harden her heart to Edmund Bertram if he should persist in his folly of taking orders, but she could not help but think of how different things would have been had *he* been the eldest born. Not only would she have doubtlessly accepted him, and even now might have been ordering her trousseau, but Mansfield Park would have materially benefited from such an alteration in fate. Oh! it was very hard to believe in a Providence who ordered society so ill. One was tempted to embrace the Greek pantheon, who were no better than they should be and made it clear someone who counted on any of their lot for omnipotent competency was doomed to disappointment.

Both Mary and Henry were disposed to be helpful to young Price, and when William expressed an inclination to hunt Crawford offered to mount him without the slightest inconvenience to himself, and with only some scruples to obviate in Sir Thomas, who knew better than his nephew the value of such a loan, and some alarms to reason away in Fanny. William Price rode so well, and was such pleasant company that the animal was one minute tendered to his use again; and the next, with the greatest cordiality, and in a manner not to be resisted, made over to his use entirely so long as he remained in Northamptonshire. Henry could be as thoughtless and selfish as any young man with his wealth and station, but he did *try* to be obliging to those he found worthy of his efforts.

ii

Mary was walking in the shrubbery when she heard the noise of her brother's hunter trotting toward the stable, and Henry's voice halloo for the groom. He sounded cheerful, so she assumed some poor fox hand been run to earth and torn to pieces by the hounds. She knew, having been told all her life that it was true, that foxes were vermin and she should no more pity them than she should a rat, but still — she did not like to think of successful fox hunts. Nonetheless, she had a duty as a sister to listen to her brother's enthusiastic recounting of the chase, and as she was also growing too cold in the December winds, she headed toward the parsonage so Henry could regale her with his retelling of his morning's hunt.

She met her brother in the vestibule, where the butler was relieving him of his muddy hunting coat, gloves, and hat.

"Mary!" Henry cried out when spying her, "what a run I have had! Hugo Meynell and all the Quorn Hunt never had better quarry! We rode for hours and we never did catch that little red rum beggar."

"Monsieur Reynard has eluded you again, I take it?" Mary grinned at her brother's jubilation in defeat.

"I think Bertram may have the right of it and Monsieur Reynard may turn back into a witch when it pleases him. Come to think on it, I did see a wizen old woman tottering down one of the lanes. It was probably him," Henry's face was glowing from his exertions. "Let me change into my dinner clothes and I'll come tell you all about it."

"Fine, fine," Mary agreed. "I'll be in the drawing-room so mind you don't dawdle too long with your cravat. There is only so much human ingenuity and starch can do."

Henry stuck out his tongue like he had done as a small boy, causing Mary to give an involuntary blast of laughter and then clap her hand to her mouth in embarrassment. Then he winked, and bounded up the stairs two at a time, as was his habit.

The butler moved to assist Mary with shedding her outerwear. "Dawson, have Beatty fetch me down my puce merino shawl, house shoes, and my warmest mitts," she instructed him, "and tell her to bring them to me in the drawing-room."

Beatty, as ever, was quick in her work and Mary was snugly established on the sofa, wrapped in a brownish-purple wool shawl with her embroidery on her lap and her feet perched on a small footstool, by the time her brother entered the drawing-room.

"You look a picture," Henry said as he kissed her cheek and sat down in the chair nearest the sofa. "With that frilly mob cap on you have a proper wifely appearance."

"Laugh if you will, but this cap keeps my head warm; in weather such as this, these caps are a good reason for sticking my head in the parson's noose. Besides, should visitors be announced it is easy to remove it and hide it in my sewing box."

After weeks of warmer than normal weather, the north wind had come whistling down from Scotland with a vengeance. While Mary was walking, her redingote and the exercise kept her warm, but once she was sitting still, even in a room with a good fire and bundled in a shawl over her sturdy chemisette and long-sleeved camblet gown, she could soon be reduced to a shivering pile of gooseflesh. When the day was particularly bitter, she considered emigrating to Morocco.

"It actually looks well on you. You have no need to fear that either matrimony or spinsterhood will injure your appearance," Henry assured her.

"Thank you. Your opinion on such matter carries great weight with me," Mary informed him was sweet sarcasm.

"It should, for I am always in the first stare of fashion," Henry smiled. "I believe I shall begin to tell Anderson to black my boots with champagne, like Beau Brummell does."

"You will be the most elegantly dressed dandy in Northampton," Mary said wryly. "The local milkmaids and scrubbers will swoon when they see you."

"They do *that* now, dearest; no need for champagne on my boots just for *them*."

"Well, *Miss Price* won't think it manly and appealing; I can tell you that for nothing."

Henry smiled complacently. "I am making some headway on Miss Price; I detect a spring thawing in her heart. I am sure she will love me soon."

"If by *love you* you mean *detest you less*, then I agree."

"No, no. I detect symptoms of softened feeling toward me."

"*That* is but her love for her brother making her feel in charity towards everyone. You are a drawcansir if you think her heart is softening towards you in *particular*," Mary teased.

"What you do not take into account, Mary, is my formidable charm. As my sister, *you* cannot see it. Miss Price, however, cannot fail to be moved by it."

"If you are *half* so charming as you *think* you are then she will be moved indeed."

Henry laughed. "I am sure Miss Price would never speak to *her* brother this way."

"That is because William Price is not the cockalorum you are."

"Are you really calling *me*, your beloved *brother*, a self-important little man?" Henry gave Mary his fiercest glare.

"Yes."

"Fair enough," he shrugged, "but I am a *charming* self-important little man."

Mary's smile lit her face. "I cannot deny it, when it comes down to it. You are in truth a charming rogue. Miss Price must prepare herself to meet her fate; she will love you just as all other women do."

"To be honest, I was afraid for a moment today she would *not*. Sugarfoot stumbled on some hidden obstacle and William Price was thrown arse over elbow into a pile of muck," Henry said in a dolorous manner.

"Oh! May I assume Mr Price is well, since you are in such high spirits?"

"The fellow was right as rain. Leapt to his feet, not a scratch on him. I believe that Bertram and I had a much worse fright when he landed than *he* did."

"That's because you and Mr Bertram would have both committed self-murder before choosing to be the one to tell Miss Price of her brother's extinction," Mary noted.

"It would seem the better option than watching her shatter like a dropped Dresden shepherdess, yes," Henry said.

Mary frowned. "We jest, at least in part, but as a sister I can tell you I could never forgive anyone who brought me the news of your demise. I believe I would rather lose my own life than lose yours."

Henry was touched, and tried to make light of it. "Of course you would. You are too good to deprive the world of its brightest jewel."

"Blatherskite," Mary said mildly.

"I can tell you about a throw from a horse that will cheer you excessively," Henry declared.

"I prepare myself for excessive amusement then."

"One fine day William Chute — you know him; he's that Tory dunderhead who speaks up only for the sugar planters' interests — was out on a hunt and he was badly thrown. Worse for him, his horse stepped on his upper leg. His friends rushed to his aid, and one of them said, "Good God, sir! I thought we were going to lose our member!" Mr Chute replied, "Well, considering where my horse stepped on me, I can tell you I thought *I* was going to lose *mine*."

Mary shook with silent mirth before gasping out, "Henry! You shouldn't tell me such anecdotes! You'll corrupt my delicacy!"

"If you had any delicacy left to corrupt, I would be concerned," Henry retorted.

"My lack of delicacy is a great secret. Do not breathe a word of it!" Mary giggled.

"A woman can have delicacy *or* she can have brains," Henry said. "If you had less sense you could be delicate enough."

"That is no *quite* true, dearest," Mary argued. "Mrs Grant and Fanny Price have brains and good sense, so far as I can tell, and neither or *them* lack delicacy."

Henry thought for a moment. "True, true. Yet, I would argue that Mrs Grant and Miss Price lack knowledge of the world. You cannot be a realist, or embrace rationality to its full effect, without sacrificing delicacy. I should have rather said that a woman can be worldly-wise or she can be delicate, she cannot be both."

Mary nodded. "I can see that viewpoint. I believe you are correct. Nonetheless, I would add that there is a peculiar goodness in our sister and Miss Price that allows them to see all manner of sin (and believe me you *cannot* do charity in the village without seeing all manner of sin) without those sins ever touching them or spoiling their innocence. I admire it, and honour it."

"It is honourable, but I do not think it is *safe* for any woman who would move in society," Henry looked thoughtful. "Our sister, and your friend, would be in mortal danger in the ton. They would not know how to gird their loins to face their enemies with a smile, to harden their hearts to flattery, to form armour against amour. You must be sensible and *suspicious* of everyone to survive unscathed among the glittering throng. Mrs Grant is safe here as a country parson's wife. Miss Price should avoid the beau monde as well."

"I am not certain it is a compliment to *me*, that you feel I am safe among ton," Mary said ruefully.

"I mean it only as a compliment, dearest. *You* are too much a queen to ever be trumped by a fool or knave. *Yours* will always be a winning hand."

Mary was thoughtful. "I wonder how Mrs Rushworth will do in London? She has Town manners but I think she has country *substance*. I think she felt more for you than any woman of sense or experience in the ton would have. You might have done her harm."

Henry's lips curled into something close to a sneer. "You give her too much credit, Mary. I am sure I harmed her *vanity*, but that is all. She was a self-satisfied, conceited beauty prepared to be inconstant and too inclined to see every flirtation as love. If she would have given her honour where she gave her hand, I could not have gotten close enough to wound her. She'll be wiser now. Rushworth will wait longer to wear his horns than if I had not trifled with her. The man owes me a note of thanks."

Mary was too honest to defend her friend. Maria *had* flirted with Henry while carelessly plotting to jilt Rushworth; she *was* self-important, vain, and conceited. Nevertheless, Mary felt sorry for her. Could injured vanity cause as much suffering as a broken heart?

Henry continued, "If Mrs Rushworth, while still Maria Bertram, had acted more like her cousin Miss Price – if she had shown more resistance to blandishments, and had given her fiancé the consideration Miss Price always gave the poor man, and had, in short, acted with more real *feeling* — I would not have toyed with her to such an extent. *Her* impropriety fed *my* mischievousness."

"Then I assume that Miss Price, having more decorum and more feeling, is safe from your *mischievousness*, as you call it. Honestly, Henry! It was the kind of *mischievousness* a cat shows to a wounded mouse. You might as well name it cruelty, because that is what it was. Tell the truth and shame the devil, as they say."

"My sex cannot be cruel. It is a well-known fact that only women can be cruel in love." Henry was not in the least convinced that he had done anything worse than be slightly ungallant to Maria Bertram.

"You are safe enough, then, by flirting with Miss Price. She hasn't a cruel bone in her body."

"She is altogether sweet," Henry smiled, thinking of her blushes and shyness. "I will be chivalry itself to her, have no fears."

"Men always promise chivalry, and they sometimes *are* chivalrous … until they become bored with it," Mary felt free to be as sardonic as she wanted with Henry.

"I would like to defend my sex with due indignation, but I received news while I was in Bath that makes me hesitate to do so," Henry admitted.

"News, or gossip?" Mary asked.

"Gossip, then, to give it a true name."

"Well, do not hesitate a moment longer! Tell me."

"Berekley Pagent has abandoned his wife and children."

"What?" Mary was dumbfounded. She lowered her voice, "For whom?"

"Amy Wilson."

Mary was stupefied. Her mouth hung open while she struggled to form words. Finally she managed, "The *courtesan* Amy Wilson?"

"Indeed."

"Did he not understand," Mary recovered her equilibrium and humour, "that the whole *point* of a courtesan is that you do not have to leave your wife for her? You simply send round the money."

"This nuance seems to have escaped him," Henry said flatly.

Mary cocked her head. "Does he think he can follow his elder brother's example, do you think?"

"He's a fool if he *does* think so," Henry said bluntly. "Anglesey's situation was altogether different. First, Anglesey will be the Earl of Uxbridge as soon as his father pops off; what a peer can do is not what a mere 'honourable' younger son can do. Even then, when Anglesey divorced his wife to marry Lady Wellesley he was damn near ruined in society. If Lady Anglesey had not been having an affair with the duke of Argyll and married him immediately after her divorce from Anglesey, then Anglesey and his new lady would have had the devil of a time of it. As it is, the whole lot of them are lucky to be received anywhere, and that's only because Prinny is kiss-kiss with the Tories right now. Berekley Paget is a nonce if he thinks that leaving his wife for a bit o'muslin is the same thing as eloping with Lady Wellsley."

"I confess that what is most occupying my mind right now is trying to remember which one of the 'three Graces' is Amy Wilson. Is she the tall one with auburn curls and alabaster complexion, or the fair one?" Mary had seen the trio of courtesans known as the three graces often in opera boxes or in the park. Like everyone else in London, Mary looked at famous courtesans as exemplars of fashion; what the modern hetaerae were wearing, soon everyone was wearing.

"Amy Wilson isn't one of the three Graces," Henry explained. That's Harriette and Fanny Wilson and their friend Julia Johnson. Amy Wilson is, for whatever reason, not part of their little trio. Harriette calls ... that is, I have *heard* that Harriette Wilson calls her sister Amy one of the Furies. You have seen Amy Wilson about Town and at the theatre, though. She always has the opera box next to the three graces. She is the one with the coal-black hair; it is curly and she always wears it without any adornment or ornament. There is so much of it that one could say it wears *her*."

"I know the one, I think," Mary was always quick on the uptake, but refrained from teasing Henry about his supposedly second-hand information about what Harriette Wilson said about her sister. "She favours yellow; I have seen that she wears primrose frequently. Didn't she used to be the watercolour wife of Captain Benjamin Sydenham, who went to be minister at Lisbon a few years ago?"

"That's the very one," Henry confirmed.

"And what does Lady Paget think of all this?" Mary wanted to know. "Isn't she the granddaughter of the second Viscount Grimston, and cousin of the current Viscount Grimston?"

"Quite right," Henry smiled, seeing where his sister was going.

"Viscount Grimston, the MP who is married to the *sister* of our current Tory prime minister, the Earl of Liverpool?"

"Amen, dearest sister, you are singing truth like a Whitfielite Methodist."

"So, Berkeley Paget is a Tory MP who has left the cousin of Liverpool's wife, and has now surely offended the leader of his party and through Liverpool the entire government?"

"Got it with the first arrow."

Mary was quiet for a moment. "What a cretin," she finally said.

"What's more, the fine and upstanding moralist the Duke of York refuses to receive Paget at Oatlands because of Paget's debauchery," Henry jeered.

"The Duke of York? The same Prince Frederick who does not live with his wife, is said to have fathered one of Lady Melbourne's sons, and who resigned as Commander-in-Chief of the army because his mistress Mary Ann Clarke was selling commissions through him? *That* Duke of York?" Mary laughed at the absurdity of Prince Fredrick judging any man's morals. "What's next? Prinny will scold Paget for eating too much?"

"Most of Paget's friends have cut him as well," Henry shrugged. "It is amazing how quickly the beau monde will turn on a man."

"But with such a fine and moral example of a royal family, what else can the beau monde *do* but cut Paget for doing openly what they are all doing themselves?" Mary said with a perfect imitation of servile innocence.

Henry, himself a master of saying something venomous in a sugared tone, felt that he was second best in that game to Mary. Regardless of how rancorous her words, the meanings were often hidden beneath honeyed civility. It was astonishing how many people were tricked by her tone of voice into thinking the words only the superciliousness or liveliness of a japester.

"I agree with you completely, dear sister. Ever since the Duke of Clarence left Dora Jordan and their ten natural children last year, the family has been the very *embodiment* of morality," Henry said fawningly.

"The duke's *slight* indiscretion can hardly be counted against him," Mary tittered like a simpleton, "after all, he was only with her for twenty years. That is merely *two* decades. No time at all, *really*."

Henry grinned. "By Jove, you are a convincing ingénue, Mary. Butter wouldn't melt in your mouth."

Her dimples made an appearance. "Butter wouldn't melt ... but cheese *would*. And now I must go dress for dinner."

Chapter Twenty-Seven

MRS GRANT AND her husband wished to invite the inhabitants of the Park to dinner, but it was a subject that required many debates and many doubts as to whether it were worth while, "because Sir Thomas seemed so ill inclined! and Lady Bertram was so indolent!"— but their worries were in vain; Sir Thomas readily accepted the invitation with the good-will and good breeding that made up the most of his character.

The meeting was generally felt to be a pleasant one, being composed in a good proportion of those who would talk and those who would listen; and the dinner itself was elegant and plentiful, according to the usual style of the Grants. In the evening it was found, according to the predetermination of Mrs Grant and her sister, that after making up the Whist table there would remain sufficient for a round game, and every body being as perfectly complying, and without a choice as on such occasions they always are. Speculation was decided on, and any hesitation on account of Lady Bertram and Fanny Price being unfamiliar to the game was smoothed away by Henry Crawford's stepping forward with a most earnest request to be allowed to sit between her ladyship and Miss Price, and teach them both, it was so settled; and Sir Thomas, Mrs Norris, and Dr and Mrs Grant being seated at the table of prime intellectual state and dignity, the remaining six, under Miss Crawford's direction, were arranged round the other. It was a fine arrangement for Henry Crawford, who was close to Fanny, and with his hands full of business, having two persons' cards to manage as well as his own—for though it was impossible for Fanny not to feel herself mistress of the rules of the game in three minutes, he had yet to inspirit her play, sharpen her avarice, and harden her heart, which, especially in any competition with William, was a work of some difficulty; and as for Lady Bertram, he must continue in charge of all her fame and fortune through the whole evening; and if quick enough to keep her from looking at her cards when the deal began, must direct her in whatever was to be done with them to the end of it.

Mary watched her brother coach Fanny and direct Lady Bertram, all while doing well with his own hand of cards, with an indulgent inward smile. How happy Henry was when he must exert himself to use even a small portion of his brains! She wished, with all his charm and intelligence, that he would go into politics. He would make an excellent MP, and *she* would not be shocked should he rise to Prime Minister.

Henry himself was in high spirits, doing every thing with happy ease, and pre-eminent in all the lively turns, quick resources, and playful impudence that could do honour to the game; and the round table was altogether a very comfortable contrast to the steady sobriety and orderly silence of the other.

"Bertram," said Crawford, taking the opportunity of a little languor in the game, "I have never told you what happened to me yesterday in my ride home." They had been hunting together, and were in the midst of a good run, and at some distance from Mansfield, when his horse being found to have flung a shoe, Henry Crawford had been obliged to give up, and make the best of his way back. "I told you I lost my way after passing that old farmhouse, with the yew trees, because I can never bear to ask; but I have not told you that with my usual luck—for I never do wrong without gaining by it—I found myself in due time in the very place which I had a curiosity to see. I was suddenly, upon turning the corner of a steepish downy field, in the midst of a retired little village between gently rising hills; a small stream before me to be forded, a church standing on a sort of knoll to my right—which church was strikingly large and handsome for the place, and not a gentleman or half a gentleman's house to be seen excepting one—to be presumed the Parsonage, within a stone's throw of the said knoll and church. I found myself, in short, in Thornton Lacey."

Mary's countenance did not change from a polite notice of Henry's words, but her entire being was alerted, and she listened with acute attention. She did not hesitate, however, to bid for William Price's knave at her turn. *She* would not give Edmund the compliment of her obvious regard in the matter of Thornton Lacey.

"It sounds like it," said Edmund; "but which way did you turn after passing Sewell's farm?"

"I answer no such irrelevant and insidious questions; though were I to answer all that you could put in the course of an hour, you would never be able to prove that it was *not* Thornton Lacey—for such it certainly was."

"You inquired, then?"

"No, I never inquire. But I *told* a man mending a hedge that it was Thornton Lacey, and he agreed to it."

"You have a good memory. I had forgotten having ever told you half so much of the place."

Miss Crawford's interest in a negotiation for William Price's knave increased. She looked as if there could be no matter of greater importance to her than the acquisition of the elusive knave.

"Well," continued Edmund, "and how did you like what you saw?"

"Very much indeed. You are a lucky fellow. There will be work for five summers at least before the place is live-able."

Miss Crawford did not wince.

"No, no, not so bad as that. The farm-yard must be moved, I grant you; but I am not aware of any thing else. The house is by no means bad, and when the yard is removed, there may be a very tolerable approach to it." Edmund glanced at Miss Crawford to see if she was listening to his defence of his living, but she was engrossed in the game and seemed heedless to his conversation with her brother.

"The farm-yard must be cleared away entirely, and planted up to shut out the blacksmith's shop. The house must be turned to front the east instead of the north—the entrance and principal rooms, I mean, must be on that side, where the view is really very pretty; I am sure it may be done." Henry's easy assumption that the expense would be no object was irksome to Mary, but she laughed at a jest William Price made and smiled at him to sweeten her attempt to inveigle away his knave.

"And *there* must be your approach," said Crawford, "through what is at present the garden. You must make a new garden at what is now the back of the house; which will be giving it the best aspect in the world—sloping to the south-east. The ground seems precisely formed for it. I rode fifty yards up the lane between the church and the house in order to look about me; and saw how it might all be. Nothing can be easier." Henry beamed, and Mary inwardly swore. "The meadows beyond what *will be* the garden, as well as what now *is*, sweeping round from the lane I stood in to the north-east, that is, to the principal road through the village, must be all laid together of course; very pretty meadows they are, finely sprinkled with timber. They belong to the living, I suppose; if not, you must purchase them. Then the stream—something must be done with the stream; but I could not quite determine what. I had two or three ideas."

Mary could envision Henry's description of what had *not* been done more than she could his improvements. A country house, just good enough to declare the owner a gentleman, but with enough of chickens and goats and a blacksmith's shop in the yard to make it look the residence of a gentleman *farmer*. Mary had the greatest respect for the yeomanry, but she had no desire to descend into being one of their class. Thornton Lacey sounded appalling to her,

"And I have two or three ideas also," said Edmund, "and one of them is that very little of your plan for Thornton Lacey will ever be put in practice. I must be satisfied with rather less ornament and beauty. I think the house and premises may be made comfortable, and given the air of a gentleman's residence without any very heavy expense, and that must suffice me; and I hope may suffice all who care about me."

Miss Crawford, a little suspicious and resentful of a certain tone of voice and a certain half-look attending the last expression of his hope, made a hasty finish of her dealings with William Price, and securing his knave at an exorbitant rate, exclaimed, "There, I will stake my last like a woman of spirit. No cold prudence for me. I am not born to sit still and do nothing. If I lose the game, it shall not be from not striving for it."

The game was her's, and only did not pay her for what she had given to secure it. Another deal proceeded, and Crawford began again about Thornton Lacey.

"My plan may not be the best possible; I had not many minutes to form it in: but you must do a good deal. The place deserves it, and you will find yourself not satisfied with much less than it is capable of." Here, Henry broke off to instruct lady Bertram in her play, before resuming his speech. "The place deserves it, Bertram. You talk of giving it the air of a gentleman's residence. *That* will be done by the removal of the farm-yard, for independent of that terrible nuisance, I never saw a house of the kind which had in itself so much the air of a gentleman's residence, so much the look of a something above a mere Parsonage House, above the expenditure of a few hundreds a year. It is not a scrambling collection of low single rooms, with as many roofs as windows—it is not cramped into the vulgar compactness of a square farm-house—it is a solid walled, roomy, mansion-like looking house, such as one might suppose a respectable old country family had lived in from generation to generation, through two centuries at least, and were now spending from two to three thousand a year in."

Miss Crawford listened, and Edmund agreed to this. The image in Mary's mind of a farmer's humble cottage gave way to the picture of a more suitable squire's abode. Perhaps Thornton Lacey was not so very bad?

"The air of a gentleman's residence, therefore, you cannot but give it, if you do any thing," continued Henry merrily. "But it is capable of much more. By some such improvements as I have suggested, (I do not really require you to proceed upon my plan, though by the bye I doubt any body's striking out a better)—you may give it a higher character. You may raise it into a *place*. From being the mere gentleman's residence, it becomes, by judicious improvement, the residence of a man of education, taste, modern manners, good connections. All this may be stamped on it; and that house receive such an air as to make its owner be set down as the great land-holder of the parish, by every creature travelling the road; especially as there is no real squire's house to dispute the point; a circumstance between ourselves to enhance the value of such a situation in point of privilege and independence beyond all calculation.

Mary was feeling a bit more hopeful as to the tone of the place, when her brother turned to Fanny Price and said in a gentle voice, "*You* think with me, I hope – Have you ever seen the place?"

"Mr Bertram," said Miss Crawford, a few minutes afterwards, "Mr Bertram, you know Henry to be such a capital improver, that you cannot possibly engage in any thing of the sort at Thornton Lacey, without accepting his help. Only think how useful he was at Sotherton! Only think what grand things were produced there by our all going with him one hot day in August to drive about the grounds, and see his genius take fire. There we went, and there we came home again; and what was done there is not to be told!" Mary was unhappy with her brother for introducing the topic and for showing more concern for Fanny's opinion of Thornton Lacey than her own, despite his knowing of Mary's quandary regarding Edmund Bertram, and felt it behoved Henry to be reminded that his career as an improver was perhaps not uncheckered.

Fanny's eyes were turned on Crawford for a moment with an expression more than grave, even reproachful; but on catching his were instantly withdrawn. With something of consciousness he shook his head at his sister, and laughingly replied, "I cannot say there was much done at Sotherton; but it was a hot day, and we were all walking after each other and bewildered." As soon as a general buz gave him shelter, he added, in a low voice directed solely at Fanny, "I should be sorry to have my powers of *planning* judged of by the day at Sotherton. I see things very differently now. Do not think of me as I appeared then."

Mary felt a moment's remorse seeing Henry appear genuinely sorrowed to have Sotherton brought up, but forgave herself instantly when her brother sent her a look of apology. He knew very well why she had introduced the topic of improvements, and was sorry that he had not thought of her feelings on the subject. Mary gave him a small smile and the hint of a nod. The siblings were in harmony again.

As yet Sir Thomas had seen nothing to remark in Mr Crawford's behaviour toward Fanny Price; but when the Whist table broke up at the end of the second rubber, and leaving Dr Grant and Mrs Norris to dispute over their last play, he became a looker-on at the other, he found his niece the object of attentions, or rather of professions of a somewhat pointed character.

Henry Crawford was detailing to his fair neighbour, with a look of considerable earnestness, his scheme to rent the house himself the following winter, that he might have a home of his own in that neighbourhood; and it was not merely for the use of it in the hunting season, (as he was then telling her), though *that* consideration had certainly some weight, feeling as he did, that in spite of all Dr Grant's very great kindness, it was impossible for him and his horses to be accommodated where they now were without material inconvenience; but his attachment to that neighbourhood did not depend upon one amusement or one season of the year: he had set his heart upon having a something there that he could come to at any time, a little homestall at his command where all the holidays of his year might be spent, and he might find himself continuing, improving, and *perfecting* that friendship and intimacy with the Mansfield Park family which was increasing in value to him every day.

Mary was well pleased by the idea, but the object of Henry's attention received the information very mildly. Sir Thomas, however, seemed as interested in Henry's plans as Miss Crawford.

Finding by whom he was observed, Henry Crawford addressed himself on the same subject to Sir Thomas, in a more every day tone, but still with feeling.

"I want to be your neighbour, Sir Thomas, as you have perhaps heard me telling Miss Price. May I hope for your acquiescence, and for your not influencing your son against such a tenant?"

Sir Thomas, politely bowing, replied—"It is the only way, sir, in which I could *not* wish you established as a permanent neighbour; but I hope, and believe, that Edmund will occupy his own house at Thornton Lacey. Edmund, am I saying too much?"

Edmund, on this appeal, had first to hear what was going on, but, on understanding the question, was at no loss for an answer.

"Certainly, sir, I have no idea but of residence. But, Crawford, though I refuse you as a tenant, come to me as a friend. Consider the house as half your own every winter, and we will add to the stables on your own improved plan, and with all the improvements of your improved plan that may occur to you this spring."

Mary looked down and busied herself with her cards. She had been suddenly and unexpectedly moved almost to tears by the idea of her brother being the guest of Thornton Lacey. She had seen, unbidden, a tableau wherein she and Edmund welcomed their now-mutual brother. The idea attracted her more than she believed to be prudent, and certainly more than she felt to be comfortable.

Sir Thomas made a very civil speech regarding how welcome Mr Crawford would be to live among them, but also stressed the importance of Edmund's abiding in his living and being an active for his parishioners before reiterated "that Thornton Lacey is the only house in the neighbourhood in which I should *not* be happy to wait on Mr Crawford as occupier."

Mr Crawford bowed his thanks.

"Sir Thomas," said Edmund, "undoubtedly understands the duty of a parish priest.—We must hope his son may prove that *he* knows it too."

Whatever effect Sir Thomas's little harangue might really produce on Mr Crawford, it raised some awkward sensations in Mary, who, startled from the agreeable fancies she had been previously indulging on the strength of her brother's description, no longer able, in the picture she had been forming of a future Thornton, to shut out the church, sink the clergyman, and see only the respectable, elegant, modernized, and occasional residence of a man of independent fortune—was considering Sir Thomas, with decided ill-will, as the destroyer of all this, and suffering the more from that involuntary forbearance which his character and manner commanded, and from not daring to relieve herself by a single attempt at throwing ridicule on his cause.

All the agreeable of *her* speculation was over for that hour. It was time to have done with cards if sermons prevailed, and she was glad to find it necessary to come to a conclusion and be able to refresh her spirits by a change of place and neighbour. Mrs Norris was not a pleasant person, but her blend of obsequious flattery and gossip was almost always diverting to listen to.

The chief of the party were now collected irregularly round the fire, and waiting the final break-up. William and Fanny were the most detached. They remained together at the otherwise deserted card-table, talking very comfortably and not thinking of the rest, till some of the rest began to think of them. Henry Crawford's chair was the first to be given a direction towards them, and he sat silently observing them for a few minutes; himself in the meanwhile observed by Sir Thomas, who was standing in chat with Dr Grant.

After some discussion of his hopes for a promotion, William asked his sister, "Are you fond of dancing, Fanny?"

"Yes, very;—only I am soon tired."

"I should like to go to a ball with you and see you dance. Have you never any balls at Northampton?—I should like to see you dance, and I'd dance with you if you *would*, for nobody would know who I was here, and I should like to be your partner once more. We used to jump about together many a time, did not we? when the hand-organ was in the street? I am a pretty good dancer in my way, but I dare say you are a better."—And turning to his uncle, who was now close to them—"Is not Fanny a very good dancer, sir?"

"I am sorry to say that I am unable to answer your question," Sir Thomas replied in his usual grave manner. "I have never seen Fanny dance since she was a little girl; but I trust we shall both think she acquits herself like a gentlewoman when we do see her, which perhaps we may have an opportunity of doing ere long."

"I have had the pleasure of seeing your sister dance, Mr Price," said Henry Crawford, leaning forward, "and will engage to answer every inquiry which you can make on the subject, to your entire satisfaction. But I believe (seeing Fanny looked distressed) it must be

at some other time. There is *one* person in company who does not like
to have Miss Price spoken of."

True enough, he had once seen Fanny dance; and it was equally
true that he would now have answered for her gliding about with
quiet, light elegance, and in admirable time, but in fact he could not
for the life of him recall what her dancing had been, and rather took
it for granted that she had been present than remembered any thing
about her.

He passed, however, for an admirer of her dancing; and
Sir Thomas, who was by no means displeased with Mr Crawford's
attentions toward Fanny, made a mental note to give the young man
an opportunity to see her dance again at the earliest possible time.

Chapter Twenty-Eight

THE NEXT WEEK brought multiple but mixed sources of delight to Mary Crawford. First, a letter arrived from Mrs Fraser, which claimed a long visit from her in London. Henry kindly offered to remain where he was till January, that he might convey her thither.

On the first day of its being settled, within the first hour of the burst of such enjoyment, when nothing but the friends she was to visit, was before her, Mary's feelings were entirely of happiness. She spoke of the forthcoming journey with animation and pleasure. She considered all that was to be done in London in January. She thought of the playhouses, such as the Sans Pareil across from the Adelphi Buildings in Winchester and the theatres on Drury lane and at Haymarket, and of the opera house in Covent Gardens, and of seeing the circus performances at Astley's. She thought of dancing in Almack's, and of getting a new gown made for the occasion. To go to Grafton House or Layton and Shear's! She thought of the shops of Cheapside and Fleet Street and Cavendish Square. Oh, to go shopping on Bond Street or to go to Tunbridge Wells! She longed to see Pall Mall lit up with its coal gas street lights. How fun it would be to go to Ackerman's again and see the prints, or to the Royal Academy's exhibition of real art! She thought of the multitude of circulating libraries and booksellers. She thought of fine days when she could ride through Hyde Park in Mrs Fraser's curricle, and of the guilty pleasure of ices at Gunter's confectionery on Berkeley square. She imagined the private balls, dinners, card parties, and musicals she would attend. It was as a beautiful dream!

But even with all these inducements she soon experienced other feelings—more chequered feelings. She told Mrs Grant that she should leave her with regret; that she began to believe neither the friends nor the pleasures she was going to were worth those she left behind; and that though she felt she must go, and knew she should enjoy herself when once away, she was already looking forward to being at Mansfield again. There was such comfort at Mansfield! Mrs

Grant was a trusted confidant in a way Mary could not rely on her friends Lady Stornoway and Mrs Fraser. Only with Henry could she lay open her heart as much as she could with Mrs Grant. She would be leaving the quiet, sweet-tempered Miss Price, and would no longer be able to provide Fanny with the amusement conversation that she knew the young woman lacked at her home. She would be leaving the avuncular kindnesses of Dr Grant, who treated her with all the care and attention of an indulgent father. And most of all, she would be leaving Edmund.

Edmund! It seemed that no sooner did she make up her mind to harden her heart against him, because he was so determined to become a clergyman and live at Thornton Lacey and undertake all the same labours that Dr Grant was forevermore doing for Mansfield, then Edmund would say or do something to soften it. His attentions were so much more constant, serious, and real-seeming than the feelings of the gentlemen of the ton that she could not help but find them agreeable. He asked her questions regarding her opinion, and seemed pleased to find she could be a woman of thought and information as well as liveliness. He was, it appeared to her, the only person other than her siblings who was interested in who she truly was, as opposed to her lovely, jocund façade. She believed he might actually love *her*, rather than a pretty face with twenty thousand pounds.

If only he would give up his asinine desire to be a man of the cloth, she would accept him without condition or reservation. She could even withstand being buried in the country for more months of the year than not, if only she weren't expected to be a parson's wife on top of it. Although she loved and respected her sister, there was no getting around the fact that there was no *style* in being the wife a country rector. Mrs Grant could never be a leader in society and fashion, as Mary's aunt had been, and as Mary aspired to be. If Edmund would go into the law, there was at least a chance. He could become a judge, and someone of importance. If *he* would but become a barrister, then *she* would give up her dreams of travel and excitement. Why could he not budge an inch, but she must give a mile? It was in every way vexing to think upon.

While she was still in this agitation of spirits, pinging back and forth between her eagerness to go to London and her desire to stay in Mansfield as if she were a shuttlecock in a game of battledore, she and Henry and the Grants received an invitation for a ball at Mansfield Park on the 22nd. *This* event she could look forward to with less alloyed happiness. To be at a ball again would be the utmost felicity. Mary loved to dance, and did it extraordinarily well. She would finally be able to wear her best evening dress again, which had lain folded in a nest of tissue-paper in her armoire for the better half of a year. Surely, *surely*, when he saw her in such a gown Edmund would be so dazzled by her that he would renounce taking vows and promise to take up another profession. She was sure that Fanny Price, who would be coming out at the ball, would be treated as the queen of the evening, but it would be Mary herself who would rule the dance as the loveliest woman there.

Mary was not the only one thinking of Miss Price. Henry brought her up as soon as he and Mary had a moment to themselves.

"I have been thinking," Henry began, only to be interrupted by Mary's exclaiming on the novelty of such an event. Giving her the look of exasperated that every elder brother has used on a younger sister. Henry continued, "*As I was saying*, I was thinking that Miss Price will wish to wear the amber cross William Price bought her in Sicily, but I do not think she has a chain for it. That is, I have never seen her wear any adornment but a ribbon around her neck. I don't believe she has any proper necklace at all."

Mary thought it over. "I believe you are right, Henry. I cannot recall Miss Price ever wearing a necklace, and I know she was ecstatic over the gift of the amber cross. It *was* a very pretty cross, but I think he could have handed her sheep's doings in a locket and she would have trembled just as much, because it was from *him*."

"She certainly seems to appreciate a gift from her brother more than *you* do," Henry teased.

"Become poor and respectable and I am sure your gifts will make me tremble too," Mary told him flippantly. "Until then, you must bear up under my yawns and my disdainful sneers when you give me a present."

"I wish that *I* could make a present of a gold chain to her, for her brother's cross," Henry sighed.

Mary's eyebrows rose almost to her hairline. "Give Miss Price a gift like that and, even as shy and mild as *she* is, she will slap your face hard enough to send your nose round the back. Not to mention that Edmund Bertram will call you out and you have yourself told me what an excellent shot he is."

To give Fanny a gift of jewellery would be tantamount to offering her a cart-blanche and an establishment under his protection in London. It would be highly offensive to a lady, implying that she was a woman whose favours could be bought. Fanny was so innocent that Mary wasn't even sure if the gel knew *why* the offer of jewellery was to be treated as a great affront. It was a common thing for men and women to make such contracts, in a general way, but where Fanny would have heard of it, Mary couldn't think. Mary herself had known about those sorts of shenanigans since she had come out and had learned what the other young women had heard while eavesdropping on the gossiping matrons.

Last summer Mary had discovered, while snooping through the Admiral's personal papers, that the offer of protection could be an *actual* contract, and could be quite lucrative for the woman involved. The Admiral had promised Mrs Chatsworth 500 pounds per annum, plus a liberal dress allowance and pin money, during the time they were together, and should he make her a grass widow, she would be given a further 500 pounds upon separation. She had subsequently questioned Henry and had discovered that the offer of a contract was more common than not amongst older men, although the young bloods such as himself were less likely to want matters formalised.

Mary herself would never accept any man's contract, not even one from a duke or royalty, because it would mean the end of all good society for her. Even if she were a peer who would still be accepted everywhere, like Lady Villiars or Lady Jersey, it would not be worth enduring the behind-the-hand talk that would plague her. Fanny Price would doubtlessly refuse upon more moral grounds. Mary did not believe that a girl like Fanny, who had rock-like principles that even Oliver Cromwell would admire, would accept such terms even if she were given three of Henry's four thousand pounds a year and a castle in the Kingdom of Bavaria to top it off.

"Of course I wouldn't offer her a necklace!" Henry protested in disgruntlement. "I'm not a complete fool. I was merely saying I *wished* I could."

Mary smiled at her brother's peeved expression. "Do not despair, Henry. I can give her one of mine; I have an abundance. I only wish that *I* had thought of it."

Henry looked speculative. "Perhaps we can both give her a necklace."

"I assume you mean something *other* than disguising yourself as me with a wig and dress, and giving her the chain in that way?" Mary jested.

Henry ignored her comment. "There is a decent jeweller in Northampton. I can go this afternoon and purchase a chain, and then you may give it to her tomorrow with friendly spontaneity."

"Why do you want to go to all that bother?" Mary was mystified. "I can just give her one I already have. I can even give her one *you've* gotten me. Why must you purchase it?"

"I am not sure, myself," Henry laughed a little self-consciously. "All I know is that I wish, very much, to be the one to buy her such a gift."

"If I didn't know better, I would think you were turning into a romantic."

"Nonsense." Henry stood up. "Is there anything you need or wish for from Northampton while I am there?"

"No, thank you. I can get shoe-roses and anything else I might need easily enough in Mansfield," Mary grinned. "Except a new necklace of course. Unlike Miss Price, I shall make do with one my brother bought last year."

ıı

The following morning Miss Crawford was just setting out to call on Miss Price when she ran into that very same young lady within a few yards of the Parsonage. Mary immediately turned to walk back to the parsonage with Fanny, but could not quite keep her disappointment completely off her face. She had been very much looking forward to offering Fanny the gold chain which Henry had bought the day before, and was reluctant to lose the opportunity. She could only offer Fanny the chain in private, since an open acknowledgement of her lack might mortify her.

Fanny explained her business at once, saying that she had come to ask Mary's advice about how to dress for the ball tomorrow evening, and observed that if Miss Crawford would be so kind as to give her opinion, it might be all talked over as well without doors as within. Mary was gratified by the application, and after a moment's thought, urged Fanny's returning with her in a much more cordial manner than before, and proposed their going up into her room, where they might have a comfortable coze, without disturbing Dr and Mrs Grant, who were together in the drawing-room. It was just the plan to suit Fanny; and with a great deal of gratitude on her side for such ready and kind attention, they proceeded in doors, and upstairs, and were soon deep in the interesting subject. Miss Crawford, pleased with the appeal, gave her all her best judgement and taste, made every thing easy by her suggestions, and tried to make every thing agreeable by her encouragement.

The dress being settled in all its grander parts,—"But what shall you have by way of necklace?" said Miss Crawford. "Shall not you wear your brother's cross?" And as she spoke she was undoing a small parcel, which Fanny had observed in her hand when they met. Fanny acknowledged her wishes and doubts on this point; she did not know how either to wear the cross, or to refrain from wearing it. She was answered by having a small trinket-box placed before her, and being requested to chuse from among several gold chains and necklaces.

Mary almost laughed when Fanny's modest scruples caused the girl to start back at first with a look of horror at the proposal of accepting such an expensive gift.

"You see what a collection I have," said she, "more by half than I ever use or think of. I do not offer them as new. I offer nothing but an old necklace. You must forgive the liberty and oblige me." Fanny's reluctance was so endearing that Mary wished more than ever to give her a chain for her amber cross.

Fanny still resisted, and from her heart. The gift was too valuable. But Miss Crawford persevered, and argued the case with so much affectionate earnestness through all the heads of William and the cross, and the ball, and herself, as to be finally successful. Fanny found herself obliged to yield that she might not be accused of pride or indifference, or some other littleness; and having with modest reluctance given her consent, proceeded to make the selection. She looked and looked, longing to know which might be least valuable; and was determined in her choice at last, by fancying there was one necklace more frequently placed before her eyes than the rest.

Mary did her part by putting Henry's chain down before Fanny the most frequently, so that the girl would believe she was choosing what Miss Crawford least wished to keep. Miss Crawford smiled her perfect approbation; her efforts were rewarded and her brother's happiness made complete. She hastened to complete the gift by putting the necklace round Fanny's slender white throat and making her see how well it looked.

Fanny had not a word to say against its becomingness, and excepting what remained of her scruples, was exceedingly pleased with an acquisition so very apropos. She would rather perhaps have been obliged to some other person. But this was an unworthy feeling. Miss

Crawford had anticipated her wants with a kindness which proved her a real friend. "When I wear this necklace I shall always think of you," said she, "and feel how very kind you were." "You must think of somebody else too, when you wear that necklace," replied Miss Crawford. "You must think of Henry, for it was his choice in the first place. He gave it to me, and with the necklace I make over to you all the duty of remembering the original giver. It is to be a family remembrance. The sister is not to be in your mind without bringing the brother too." Henry, she thought, owed her a favour for her good work on his behalf.

Fanny, in great astonishment and confusion, would have returned the present instantly. To take what had been the gift of another person—of a brother too—impossible!—it must not be!— and with an eagerness and embarrassment quite diverting to her companion, she laid down the necklace again on its cotton, and seemed resolved either to take another or none at all.

Miss Crawford thought she had never seen a prettier consciousness. "My dear child," said she laughing, "what are you afraid of? Do you think Henry will claim the necklace as mine, and fancy you did not come honestly by it?—or are you imagining he would be too much flattered by seeing round your lovely throat an ornament which his money purchased three years ago, before he knew there was such a throat in the world?—or perhaps—looking archly— you suspect a confederacy between us, and that what I am now doing is with his knowledge and at his desire?"

With the deepest blushes Fanny protested against such a thought. Mary had no doubt Miss Price had not considered it before, but she would serve at Queen Dick's court if the girl did not think it likely now that she had been given so broad a hint.

"Well then," replied Miss Crawford more seriously but without at all believing her, "to convince me that you suspect no trick, and are as unsuspicious of compliment as I have always found you, take the necklace, and say no more about it. Its being a gift of my brother's need not make the smallest difference in your accepting it, as I assure you it makes none in my willingness to part with it. He is always giving me something or other. I have such innumerable presents from him that it is quite impossible for me to value, or for him to remember half. And as for this necklace, I do not suppose I have worn it six times; it is very pretty—but I never think of it; and though you would be most heartily welcome to any other in my trinket-box, you have happened to fix on the very one which, if I have a choice, I would rather part with and see in your possession than any other. Say no more against it, I entreat you. Such a trifle is not worth half so many words." Mary was a very good liar for a good cause.

Fanny dared not make any farther opposition; and with renewed but less happy thanks accepted the necklace again.

ıı

"Well, Henry, it is done and, as they say, done well," Mary said to her brother, upon the first instance she had him alone following Fanny's departure. "I have given your necklace to Miss Price. From her stammers and blushes, I believe she may *suspect* that the gift is indirectly from you, but she could not refuse it without *certainty*. She has a very pretty chain, and she will be unable to avoid thinking of you while she wears it."

Henry looked all satisfaction. "I am glad she has a chain for her brother's cross, will she think of me or no."

"Oh yes, all modesty and altruism from *you*," Mary scoffed.

"Mock if you will, but I am glad Miss Price has the necklace. Thank you."

Mary smiled. "Of course. I am glad she has it as well. No one in the ballroom wearing diamonds will consider themselves so richly adorned as Miss Price will believe herself to be while wearing her brother's amber cross. Her heart is a simple one, but it is very deep."

"Your heart is not so simple, but I believe it is as deep as Miss Price's could ever hope to be," Henry gave Mary's hand an affectionate squeeze. "Now, ask me why I went to Northampton again today."

"To exercise your horse and allow the country lasses to blush and smile at you, I suppose."

"Not quite, although to be sure both those things happened. I had a package I had to pick up. It was not ready yesterday."

"Oh? And what sort of package was it? Do you have a new waistcoat or coat for the ball?"

"No, it is not for me at all." Henry rang for a footman, and when the servant came he instructed the man to fetch his valet. "When Anderson comes, you shall be enlightened."

Henry would not give Mary a single clue as to what the package was, inveigle and pester as she might. She had to wait until Anderson entered the drawing-room, bearing a cedar box in his arms. The box was large enough to hold a coat or a brocade gown, and Mary arose from the sofa and began to jiggle about like a small child at the sight of cake.

"Is it for me? Dear Henry, is it for me?" She asked, with breathless excitement.

"It *is* for you, silly girl. Sit back down and be calm and you shall have it." Once she was seated, Henry handed the box to her with a flourish.

Mary lifted the lid, placed it beside her on the couch, and attacked the tissue-paper covering the garment within. She very quickly revealed a luxurious pile of dark brown fustian and fur, which she withdrew from the box with a gasp.

"It is a witzchoura! Oh, Henry! It is gorgeous!" She was overwhelmed by the generosity of the gift, even from Henry, who was usually lavish in his presents to his sister.

The witzchoura was a fur trimmed mantle with wide, open sleeves, and was the first stare of fashion; it was an expensive indicator of wealth and good taste. Mary immediately tried it on. The mantle was long enough to fall to her mid-calf, and most of the outer fabric was a fustian fabric called moleskin, a nearly-waterproof, soft material made from closely woven wool. The trimming around the hood, sleeves, and hem was a band of Croatian marten fur that was as wide as her hand, and the entire inner lining of the mantle was the same silky fur. It was considered entirely too showy to display oneself in a full cape or cloak of fur, but by using the fur as lining and trim, you could announce to the world that you had the *ability* to buy a full marten coat but were simply to *tasteful* to do so. The milk chocolate colour of the moleskin and the amber of the marten fur both set off Mary's clear olive complexion and dark eyes wonderfully.

Mary clutched a double handful the witzchoura and rubbed the creamy, feathery fur against her cheeks. "It is in every way delightful, but what is the occasion? You have already given me my birthday gift!"

Henry embraced her. "It is because I was reminded of what a good sister you are. I have never had a wish you have not done your best to facilitate, and never had a problem that you have not attempted to resolve. I put in the order for the witzchoura some weeks ago in Northampton, thinking I could have it delivered to you for Christmas, but yesterday I stopped by to check on its progress, and when I saw that it was nearly finished I told them I would return for it today. I thought it would make you happy to have it for the ball tomorrow."

Although she was no means a weepy woman, tears of emotion were standing in Mary's eyes. "You are such an excellent brother, to think of me."

It was then that Mrs Grant entered the drawing-room and nearly squawked when she saw what Mary was wearing. Nothing would do but that witzchoura should be modelled by Mary, with Henry and Mrs Grant complimenting both the mantle and her ability to wear it as she walked up and down the room. Even Dr Grant was moved to admire the garment when he returned to the parsonage. Mary claimed she felt as though she were the Empress of Russia in such a magnificent covering.

When it was time to enter the dining room, it was with the greatest reluctance that Mary gave the witzchoura to Beatty so that the maid could hang the extravagant mantel in the wardrobe, and when Mary went to bed that night she took the opportunity to stroke her new apparel once more. No child receiving a doll on Christmas morning could be as happy as Mary was with her new witzchoura.

Chapter Twenty-Nine

THE DAY OF the ball was an eventful one at the parsonage, as well as at the Park. Early that morning Henry wrote a very friendly note to William Price stating, that as he found himself obliged to go to London on the morrow for a few days, he could not help trying to procure a companion; and therefore hoped that if William could make up his mind to leave Mansfield half a day earlier than had been proposed, he would accept a place in his carriage. Henry explained that he meant to be in town by his uncle's accustomary late dinner-hour, and William was invited to dine with him at the Admiral's.

In response to the note, Henry quickly received a visit from William himself to convey his acceptance and gratitude. The young Mr Price expressed himself well, declaring that the idea of travelling post with four horses and such a good-humoured agreeable friend was the best of all possible ways of going to London. William's original plan was that he should go up by the mail from Northampton the following night, which would not have allowed him an hour's rest before he must have got into a Portsmouth coach, so his thanks to Mr Crawford was as sincere as it was exuberant.

Their discussion moved, as discussions will, from the details of their travel, to the weather, horses, to sport, and finally to politics. So pleasant did the young men find talking to one another that it was nearly an hour before either gentleman could suffer that William return to the Park. They found themselves in agreement about so much of what they exchanged opinions on that they were both well content with the idea of several hours' worth of confabulation during the trip to Town.

As soon as William left, Mary came downstairs to talk to her brother. Like any woman with good sense, she was spending much of the morning before a ball resting, preferably napping, in her dressing room and bedroom. However, craving for human contact drove the gregarious Mary downstairs by noon, in the hopes of chatting with Henry. She was in her oldest morning gown, and in a valiant effort to make her coiffure the fashionable clusters of ringlets that she craved, her hair was still in its curl papers, covered by a very plain mob cap. She was not fit to be seen by anyone not family, but if any more visitors should be announced, which did occasionally happen even on days when Mary and Mrs Grant were not officially 'at home', she could nip through the dining room and up the servants stairs to her bedroom.

"May I help you madam?" Henry pretended not to recognise her when she came into the drawing-room. "Are you here to apply for the position of charwoman?"

"Oaf," Mary laughed. "Even in curl papers, I am *clearly* worthy of being a parlour maid."

Her brother did an exaggerated double-take and squinted his eyes to peer at her. "Mary? Mary, is that you?"

Mary looked around quickly to make sure they were alone, then made a very rude sign with her fingers.

"Where on *earth* did you learn *that*?" Henry cried, inspiring Mary to make another hand gesture to indicate he should lower his voice.

"Not so loud, if you please! Your voice is like the blast of Roland's horn; I think the birds on the wallpapering perished. As for where I learned that particular gesture — I've seen you and your friends do it, when you are in your cups and think, for some reason, that your open opera box has suddenly become opaque."

"Do you have any idea what that means?" He asked her sternly.

"Not really, but I could hazard a guess."

"No, no," Henry hurried to forestall her, "I don't want to hear a guess. What are you doing downstairs in such dishabille?"

"I was bored out of my mind," Mary told him. "Napping and books are all well and good, but *some* conversation *must* be had or I go mad. Too much quiet puts maggots in the brain. I take it that Mr Price will be going with you to London?"

"He will indeed."

"And you still will not give me a single hint as to why you go?"

"I shan't."

"Cruel. How ever shall I bear it," She gave a theatrical yawn.

"Would it help you bear up under the agony of suspension if I told you what news I had from Lambton today?" Henry grinned.

"Lambton! I am always eager to hear about our friend Radical Jack. How does he? Are Mrs Lambton and baby Charlotte still well?"

"Yes, Mrs Lambton and the baby are both thriving, according to Lambton, but there is more happy news; Lambton has received the confirmation that he was elected to Parliament in the general election. He'll represent County Durham, to his credit I am sure."

"Bravo!" Mary's did a small caper of joy, much to Henry's amusement. "That should roast the Earl of Cholmondeley's goat."

George Cholmondeley was a powerful Tory who had been recently made the Lord Steward of the Household, a royal posting that was the political equivalent of a cabinet position. John Lambton, whom Henry had befriended at Eton, was the very rich son of a radical reformer, and an unabashed reformer in his own right. Mary and Henry were already disposed to dislike Cholmondeley because of his politics, but when he decided his natural daughter, Harriet, was too good for Lambton and forbade the couple to marry last Christmas, the Crawford siblings were incensed on behalf of their friend. The Crawfords, always ones for intrigue, aided Harriet and John in their elopement to Gretna Green, and once the elopement had occurred, Cholmondeley had no choice but to allow the couple to be *officially* wed on his estate in Malpas a fortnight later.

"Yes, and Grey has another ally in parliament. I would offer to toast the good news with champagne, but I am not drinking a French vintage with a ragged-robin in curl papers and a Kersey frock; it would be a disgrace to good bubbly."

"Mutton-head. Did Lambton have any other news?"

"Yes he did, but I shan't tell you because you've called me mutton-head."

"If you *don't* tell me, I shall call you *worse*."

"It puts my mind under a strain, it truly does."

"It's a word I learned from your friend Mr LeFroy."

"In *that* case, I shall tell you my news, and sharpish. The verdict of the Hunts' trial was announced on the 20th."

"And will Mr Leigh Hunt and his brother be consigned to prison for telling the truth about Prinny?" Mary made a face eloquently indicating her disdain for the prince regent.

Leigh Hunt had gone on trial for slander earlier in the month for an opinion he had printed in his newspaper, The Examiner, calling the Prince Regent, among other things, "a violator of his word, a libertine over head and ears in debt and disgrace, a despiser of domestic ties, the companion of demi-reps, a man who has just closed half a century without a single claim on the gratitude of his country or the respect of posterity." This was, of course, nothing but the gospel truth, and its substantial truth meant that it was indubitably not slander. However, it had hurt Prinny's feelings to see the majority of the country's opinion of him in black and white, so he had demanded that Leigh Hunt, as well as his brother John Hunt, be prosecuted for their so-called slanderous denouncements.

"I wish I could tell you no; that English jurisprudence triumphed. Alas, I must instead tell you that both the Hunts have been found guilty, and are sentenced to serve two years in gaol as well as being forced to pay a 1000 pound fine between." Henry mouth twisted into a cynical smile.

He spoke lightly on the matter, but the idea that the Leigh Hunt had been punished for publishing the truth vexed him severely. He'd move to America, where there was a free press, if he could stomach the lack of refinement in Colonial manners.

Mary was likewise upset, but covered it in her usually lively veneer. "Perhaps the judge didn't like his poetry. The law can have a shocking aversion to the romantic and fanciful. I am sure it is *nothing* to do with Hunt's radical reformist writing."

"I am sure Hunt's radical reformism wasn't even a topic to be discussed."

"And we know how *readily*, how *easily*, a poet and newspaperman can get his hands on 500 pounds in ready cash," Mary cooed. "I am likewise sure his time in gaol will be a delightful one."

Henry, attuned as he was to the nuances of his sister's inflections, heard the bitterness and disquiet in her voice. He had forgotten that Hunt was more of a poet than a journalist. Of course Mary would be disturbed by the news of Hunt's impending imprisonment.

"It may be, at that," Henry sought to reassure her. "Hunt is not without friends with influence. There are gaols, and then there are *gaols*. Much can be done before his sentence begins in February."

Mary smiled at her brother. "Will you be one of those friends?"

"Certainly," Henry smile became a naughty boy's grin. "I will make sure he is thrown into the dankest, most rancid, and vile prison possible so it might inspire him to write better verses for my sister's enjoyment."

"You can *do* that?" Mary pretended to be agog. "Then *why* haven't you thrown Byron in the clink? Can you imagine how sublime his poetry would be after a bit of racking?"

Dawson appeared in the south door of the drawing-room. "There is a Mr Edmund Bertram here to see you, ma'am. Shall I tell him you are at home?"

Mary's eyes widened with horror. "Good God! I will wager anything he has come to ask me for the first two dances." She had expected him to ask her when she came to the ball that evening, but she had obviously underestimated her suitor. She turned to her brother and begged Henry to say they were at home and to keep Edmund entertained for a short while, and then nearly bolted out of the eastern door of the drawing-room, scurrying through the kitchen and running up the servant's staircase as fast as she could.

Henry, chatting amiably with Edmund in the drawing-room, was surprised when his sister reappeared a quarter of an hour later. She was dressed as though she were going for a walk, with her redingote and bonnet on, and sturdy half-boots. Henry turned away on a pretext, in order to hide his smile; Mary had obviously put the bonnet on over her curl papered hair and used the redingote, which was as long as her dress, to disguise the drab woollen morning dress she was wearing.

"Mr Bertram," she said pleasantly, giving him her hand to shake. "What an unexpected pleasure. I was just going for a walk among the shrubbery, being much in want of fresh air. Would you join me, sir?"

Edmund, as was to be expected, expressed his delight in accompanying Miss Crawford in her perambulations. Henry bowed them out, admiring his sister's quick thinking and ingenuity. To take Edmund out of doors not only gave her an excuse for her bonnet and coat to cover her dishabille, but it also gave them some privacy so that her beau could solicit her hand for the first two dances.

ᴵᴵ

The day was sunny, which raised the spirits, but the light was too pale and weak to give any warmth. The wind was frigid and occasionally gusty, and when it blew it nipped Mary's nose something terrible. She would have vastly preferred to be back by the fire in her own sitting room, boredom or not, just for the warmth. Nonetheless, she affected complete unconcern about the weather and happiness to be walking, as if life held no greater felicity than an icy stroll in the shrubberies on an algid morning.

"I am amazed at how tenaciously the leaves have clung to their branches this winter," Edmund said. "One would think that the wind or rain would have dislodged them."

"It is probably because the rains, while frequent, have all been soft," Mary responded. "I am sure the next hard downpour or even suitably blustery day will denude the limbs."

She saw Edmund's faint blush after she had mentioned nudity and limbs, and was well pleased with herself. Mr Bertram may seem a Banbury-man with his almost Puritanical propriety of address, but he *was* affected by her. Mary wasn't stupid. Too many men had attempted to steal a kiss, and her married friends had been too frank, for her to be ignorant of male desire. Edmund Bertram wanted her, but if he meant to have her then Mary was determined that he must show he was willing to take her wishes for the future into consideration.

"You are undoubtedly right," He was flustered.

"Although I shall miss the leaves, there is much to say of the denuded limb, don't you think? The bare limbs have a certain kind of essential elegance." Her expression and inflections were as innocent as a newborn lamb's. "They look very pleasing when they stand out against the winter's sky, whether the sky be cerulean or grey. Sometimes the juncture where the limb attaches to the trunk is particularly interesting, because it reveals some bend or crevasse that one does not get to see when the limb and trunk are hidden from view under a profusion of leaves."

"You have a keen eye for nature, ma'am," Edmund sounded as if his cravat was tied as little too tightly.

Mary decided to be merciful, and stop mentioning limbs. "Of course, once the leaves are gone, one cannot practice botanomancy."

Edmund's eyebrows rose. "You practice the art of divination from leaves?"

"No, no. I am merely interested in how such a thing was done by the ancients," She paused. "I use chicken entrails and human sacrifice like everyone else when I want to know the future."

Edmund, for all his formality and sober mien, had a joyous laugh. She always felt triumphant when she could get him to at least chuckle, because he so rarely did more to indicate amusement than give a courteous smile. She wanted to swagger like a coxcomb when he burst into laughter, but resisted the urge.

"You are, beyond contestation, one of the most amusing and witty people I have ever known," Edmund praised her.

"You flatter me, sir," Mary looked demure. "I can only assume your society has been limited if *I* am one of the wittiest among them."

"To the contrary. My society includes my brother Tom and your brother Mr Crawford, both of whom are quick witted. My sisters are not without conversational abilities, either. You, however, shine even among luminaries of the *bon mot.*"

Mary's dimpled at him, and warned him in a lively manner, "You will make me vain. Soon I shall be quoting Pope's translations of Ovid, claiming that 'To me what Nature has in charms denied; is well by Wit's more lasting flames supplied/ Tho' short my stature, yet my name extends; to Heav'n itself, and earth's remotest ends.' When I am puffed up with pride, you shall be sorry you spoke such palaver."

"I think you are too lively to be either flattered or humbled by anything I say; you will make a jest of it," Edmund assured her.

"Is that my future, as you foretell? Are you skilled in botanomancy, then?"

"Sadly, I have no skills in prognostication. I must rely on discernment, extrapolation and reason."

"Reason often goes astray," Miss Crawford said playfully. "For myself, I will take up xylomancy; it is advised one do so in the Bible you know, so it must be an accurate science."

"Where is xylomancy advised in the Bible?" Edmund demanded in good humour. "I assure you that I have seen no such text that recommends predication based on branches of wood."

"Doesn't the Bible say that 'as the twig is bent, the tree's inclined?' What is that but the suggestion that studying tree limbs will tell you the future?"

Edmund gave her a look. "I am sure you know very well that is a quote from Alexander Pope, not a reference from the Bible."

"Are you *sure*?" Mary ribbed him. "Isn't in the same chapter as "to thine own self be true" and "neither a borrower nor a lender be"? I am *positive* I have heard people citing those things as Biblical text."

"*Those* sayings are advice from Polonius to his son Laertes in *Hamlet.*"

Mary made a thoughtful sound. "I suppose you may be right. Nonetheless, I still say xylomancy is at least *somewhat* Biblical. The phrase 'as the twig is bent the tree's inclined' is from Pope's *Epistles to Several Persons.* I am absolutely *certain* there are epistles in the Bible."

"Is there no subject your lively mind cannot find humour in?" Edmund asked.

"Is there anything so serious that it should not be lightened?" Mary rejoined.

"Many things," Edmund assured her pedantically, "and I would count holy writ as the foremost among those things that should not be laughed about."

Mary was slightly peeved at Edmund's fustiness. "Really? But the Bible often mentions laughter, and the laughter of the righteous. It says there is a time to laugh and dance, just as there is a time to weep and mourn; Sarah claimed that God made laughter for her, and Isaac is named for his mother's laughter, and I have sung psalms in service that mention a mouth filled with laughter and joy because the Lord does great things, and the Lord Himself laughs at the wicked."

Like the majority of the English of her time, Mary attended church weekly, and sometimes more than weekly. The Anglican liturgy was beautiful, but it was also, by necessity and design, repetitious. Although she sometimes found fault in the way sermons were read or presented, Mary was enough of a logophile that she read and listened to the cadence and poetry of the liturgy, and thus — while not particularly religious — had absorbed a great deal of Biblical verses and teachings.

Edmund was silenced for a moment, clearly pondering something that was giving him difficulty. Finally and unexpectedly, he smiled. "Your mind is too animated, and you are too good-tempered, to dwell upon what is sombre, even when the subject you think on is a serious one. You are blithesome. Your light heart cannot be sunk deep."

Her swain's obvious, albeit delusional, infatuation mollified Mary, and furthermore prevented her from becoming irked by his assumptions that she could not think profoundly when she needed too. Edmund was too handsome, and his assiduous courtship was too flattering, for her to hold any grudges.

"Does this mean I can practice xylomancy in peace?"

"I would by no means impose upon you; you must do what makes you happy."

With her irritation at him completely soothed, Mary made a slight allusion to her ankles being fatigued, so that Edmund immediately offered her his arm. She found it very pleasant to walk with her arm tucked into Edmund's, and enjoyed the tall strength of his body being just a few inches away from her own slight frame.

"There is something of the future that I wish a xylomancer would tell *me*," Edmund said. "I would like to reserve your first two dances at the ball tonight. Can you foresee whether that will happen or not?"

Mary looked at him coyly through her thick eyelashes. "How can I practice xylomancy when so many leaves stubbornly stay on the branches? I must consult other oracles."

"And which oracles will you consult?"

"My favourite one, of course; my own inclinations. They say your quest for two dances shall not be in vain. However, like all oracles they must give you a caution as well as an answer. It is to be the last time that I ever will dance with you. I never have danced with a clergyman and I never *will*. When you go to take your orders over Christmastide, make sure you are resolved to never dance with me again."

"I hope you are speaking playfully," Edmund looked grave.

"Are you so certain that I am speaking playfully that you would hazard everything upon it?" Mary asked him, smiling archly. "Remember, the oracle at Delphi told Croesus that if he crossed the river, a great empire would be destroyed, without bothering to mention that it was *his* empire that would perish, not the Persian Empire he attacked. You really must be careful with oracles."

Edmund tried to smile back. "Are you Pythia then?"

"I can assure you, unequivocally, that I have no desire to sniff at a decomposing snake in order to hear Apollo. I am given to understand that sufficient laudanum will perform the same office."

They walked on, unspeaking, only the crunch of desiccated leaves underfoot breaking the silence.

"Thinking on predictions, what do you think of Mrs Barbauld's augury for Great Britain in her poem *Eighteen Hundred and Elven*? I am assuming, of course, that you have read it," Edmund sought a diversion.

"I have indeed read it. In point of fact, I had bespoke a copy while the poem was still at the publishers. I am a great admirer of Mrs Barbauld's writing. But you must clarify for me; do you mean her outrageous prediction that Britain will fall because it has squandered its wealth and men in the unending wars with Napoleon? Or that the United State of America will rise as an empire as Britain falls?" Mary asked.

"Either and both."

"Considering that the poem is *clearly* Juvenalian satire, I was surprised how poorly the reviewers received it. You would think that Mrs Barbauld had called for immediate surrender to Napoleon, and that all British subjects begin speaking French. The irony of it all is that many of the people castigating her for verses warning of the dangers of prolonged military engagement are the same ones who groan about the taxes to pay for it. And is she wrong? Are we entirely safe? She asks if we think always "To sport in wars, while danger keeps aloof; Thy grassy turf unbruised by hostile hoof?" If we continue to meddle in Continental affairs, is there not a risk of Continental affairs meddling with *us*? Mrs Barbauld's only sin is to have dared to suggest that Britain may not win the war, and even if it *does* we have lost more than we can ever gain. As for her declaration that America will one day be richer and greater than Britain; what *can* that be but hyperbolic satire? Surely she does not *really* think that America will rise to greatness after the United Kingdom has overstretched its limits in war. That is clearly preposterous. I find the attacks on Mrs Barbauld nonsensical and hypocritical. What do you think?"

Edmund considered the matter. "It is always risky to criticise one's country when we are at war, but I, too, feel the reaction to her work has been disproportionately against her. It certainly does not reflect the *skill* of the poem, its artistry. Nonetheless, I *do* believe that Mrs Barbauld went too far into the darkness of despair for the poem to be liked as a general thing; she took no account of her audience."

It was Mary's turn to be thoughtful. "I understand what you are saying, but I cannot wholly agree. Art is art; it must come forth from the artist regardless of whether or not the audience approves it. Otherwise, art is just rhymes and pretty pictures."

"But the artist cannot live on vapour and romance. If the audience does not like the art, and therefore does not purchase it, then the artist is no more."

"True. Yet I would also argue that the function of art is to make the audience *feel* something. Mrs Barbauld certainly commanded an emotional reaction."

"Then shall we agree that Mrs Barbauld is indeed an artist, but one who was unwise?"

Mary smiled. "That sounds like a perfect compromise, Mr Bertram."

Chapter Thirty

MARY CRAWFORD TOOK particular care when getting ready for the ball. She hoped that if she looked well enough, it would nudge Edmund Bertram into deciding to give up his plans to become a clergyman so that he could have her as his wife. She knew he wanted her, but did he love her enough to make her wishes and hopes in life a priority? Mary, like many women, was under the delusion that if she were just attractive *enough*, she would be wholly and unselfishly loved.

Only her very best dress would do. It was gold muslin, a cotton so fine as to be diaphanous, shot through with gilt threads. The gown had been liberally covered with golden spangles, making the entire dress shimmer and reflect the light with each movement. Daringly, Mary had chosen a completely sleeveless gown, electing to go to the ball with her "arms bare as Juno's." Her bodice, in contrast, was higher than average for an evening dress, which served to both make her appear more modestly dressed than she really was and allow for discrete padding over her rather meagre bosom. She had learned early that cotton batting and the right sort of half-stays could do much to disguise the fact she was chicken breasted. Her sleeveless petticoat was made of a warm-beige satin that nearly matched Mary's skin tone and made her seem, at first glance, to be naked under her muslin. Even her slippers were made of finest kid nearly the same shade as her skin, and she would have been thought barefoot if not for the shoe-roses of stiffened gold tissue and past diamonds that winked at the viewer from under the hem of her gown.

Beatty's efforts with the curl papers and pomade had worked; Mary's hair was in ringlets. Beatty had swept the hair up into a seemingly loose bunch of curls on the crown of Mary's head, and had anchored a tiara comb in front of it. The comb had been one which Mary's aunt had worn often, and it had been left to Mary in her aunt's will. It was a magnificent piece of rococo jewellery, consisting of gold filigree, 'brilliant' cut diamonds, and creamy seed pearls.

With so much sparkle on her dress and tiara comb, Mary wisely chose more simple jewellery for the rest of her ornaments. Her necklace and earrings were small and made of unadorned gold that glinted dully in the candlelight. However, she could not resist adding a thin, triple-spiraled gold cuff to her right upper arm; it looked too well on her to leave off.

Finally content with her appearance, being both expensively and nakedly dressed, she nearly floated into the drawing-room, where she received compliments and praise for her looks from everyone.

Mary, in turn, complimented her brother and the Grants. Her sister was wearing a very becoming maroon gown of lutestring silk with a hand's breadth of embroidery and beading at the hem, and matching trim along the bodice and cuff of the sleeves. Dr Grant, as always, looked the gentleman, but Henry was a fashion plate. His hose, breeches, and waistcoat were as white as an Easter lily's petals, and looked nearly as soft. His cravat, starched to perfection and the colour of snow, was tied in the latest style and the creases looked crisp enough to cut one's finger. His coat was a very dark navy blue, with the 'shawl' collar of the latest French fashion and de rigueur gold buttons. No one would look better than Henry in the ball room. Certainly, Edmund Bertram was more handsome, but he would never be able to achieve her brother's natural elan and charisma that made everyone notice him and admire what they saw.

Henry helped his sister on with her new witzchoura, and took the opportunity to tell her, "Mr Bertram will be lucky if he does not faint when he sees you," making Mary flush happily as her brother handed her into the carriage.

॥

Upon arrival, the guests from the parsonage saw that there was a lack of circulation and cheer among the crowd. Sir Thomas, as polite as he was, nevertheless weighted down the room with his formally. Edmund Bertram, while cordial in every civility, had no ease of address that would facilitate jocundity, and Lady Bertram could not be bothered to try. Mrs Norris, although capable of pleasing dullards with her blandishments, could not enliven a ballroom. Thus, the entrance of the Grants and Crawfords was a favourable epoch. The stiffness of the meeting soon gave way before their popular manners and more diffused intimacies:—little groups were formed and every body grew comfortable.

When the company were moving into the ball-room Mary looked around to see the belle of the ball, Miss Price, was near to her. Mary lost no time in complementing her friend's appearance, looking pointedly at the necklace she and Henry had conspired to put around Fanny's neck. She was not sure why the ornate chain was accompanied by a plain one bearing the amber cross, but the extra gold was modest enough it did no harm to Miss Price's unpretentious prettiness. Fanny, anxious to get the story over, hastened to give the explanation of the second necklace—the real chain. Edmund had supplied the second chain, and the amber cross would not fit upon the one Miss Crawford was so good to bestow on her.

Mary listened; and all her intended compliments and insinuations to Fanny were forgotten; she felt only one thing; and her eyes, bright as they had been before, shewing they could yet be brighter, she exclaimed with eager pleasure, "Did he? Did Edmund? That was like himself. No other man would have thought of it. I honour him beyond expression." And she looked around as if longing to tell him so. He was not near, he was attending a party of ladies out of the room; and Mrs Grant coming up to the two girls and taking an arm of each, they followed with the rest.

The ball began. It was known that the dance was in Fanny Price's honour, and henceforth the girl would officially be out. The lady of the hour was retiring and shy, but inasmuch as Miss Price was young, pretty, and gentle, however, she had no awkwardnesses that were not as good as graces, and there were few persons present that were not disposed to praise her. She was attractive, she was modest, she was Sir Thomas's niece, and she was soon said to be admired by Mr Crawford. It was enough to give her general favour. Sir Thomas himself was watching her progress down the dance with much complacency; he was proud of his niece, and without attributing all her personal beauty, as Mrs Norris seemed to do, to her transplantation to Mansfield, he was pleased with himself for having supplied every thing else;—education and manners she owed to him.

Miss Crawford saw much of Sir Thomas's thoughts as he stood, and having, in spite of all his wrongs towards her in his insistence that his son Edmund be such a detestable figure as a county parson of small income, a general prevailing desire of recommending herself to him, took an opportunity of stepping aside to say something agreeable of Fanny. Her praise was warm, and he received it as she could wish, joining in it as far as discretion, and politeness, and slowness of speech would allow, and certainly appearing to greater advantage on the subject, than his lady did, soon afterwards, when Mary, perceiving her on a sofa very near, turned round before she began to dance, to compliment her on Miss Price's looks.

"Yes, she does look very well," was Lady Bertram's placid reply. "Chapman helped her to dress. I sent Chapman to her." Not but that she was really pleased to have Fanny admired; but she was so much more struck with her own kindness in sending Chapman to her, that she could not get it out of her head. Mary knew that she could expect no better from the indolent but good-natured Lady Bertram.

Miss Crawford knew Mrs Norris too well to think of gratifying *her* by commendation of Fanny; to her it was, as the occasion offered,—"Ah! ma'am, how much we want dear Mrs Rushworth and Julia to-night!" and Mrs Norris paid her with as many smiles and courteous words as she had time for, amid so much occupation as she found for herself, in making up card-tables, giving hints to Sir Thomas, and trying to move all the chaperons to a better part of the room.

Miss Crawford blundered most towards Fanny herself, in her intentions to please. She meant to be giving her little heart a happy flutter, and filling her with sensations of delightful self-consequence; and misinterpreting Fanny's blushes, still thought she must be doing so—when she went to her after the two first dances and said, with a significant look, "perhaps *you* can tell me why my brother goes to town to-morrow. He says, he has business there, but will not tell me what. The first time he ever denied me his confidence! But this is what we all come to. All are supplanted sooner or later. Now, I must apply to you for information. Pray what is Henry going for?"

Fanny protested her ignorance as steadily as her embarrassment allowed.

"Well, then," replied Miss Crawford laughing, "I must suppose it to be purely for the pleasure of conveying your brother and of talking of you by the way."

Fanny was confused, but it was the confusion of discontent; while Miss Crawford wondered she did not smile, and thought her over-anxious, or thought her odd, or thought her any thing rather than insensible of pleasure in Henry's attentions.

Mary, in spite of her willingness to be pleased, found little pleasure at the ball. The stone in her shoe was none other than Edmund Bertram, whose attentions should have elevated her feelings.

Miss Crawford had been in gay spirits when they first danced together, but Edmund's stubborn determination to enter orders quickly ruined Mary's gaiety. He showed himself to be impervious to her hopes. He did not love her enough to oblige her in so material a concern. Angered and unwilling to reveal her hurt, Mary became flippant on the subject of the cloth, and she had absolutely pained him by her manner of speaking of the profession to which he was now on the point of belonging. They had talked—and they had been silent—he had reasoned—she had ridiculed—and they had parted at last with mutual vexation.

Fanny, not able to refrain entirely from observing them, had seen enough to be tolerably satisfied. It was barbarous to be happy when Edmund was suffering. Yet some happiness must and would arise, from the very conviction that he did suffer. Mary and Edmund, blissfully unaware that Fanny's sentimentality covered a sly and covetous heart, did not suspect that Miss Price's soft blue eyes studied them with the guileful gaze of a Greek goddess watching for hubris.

II

When Mary entered the carriage at half-past four in the morning, she was, like Fanny Price had been several hours earlier, overly full of negus, footsore, tired, and wound up from the night's hurly-burly. However, unlike Fanny, Mary had no delightful memories of the ball to make it seem wonderful in spite of everything. On the contrary, Mary was vexed almost to the point of tears. She felt as though she never wanted to see Edmund Bertram again in this life. Hateful man!

All her hopes had come to naught. Edmund, while seeming as enchanted with her appearance as even she could wish, did not speak of — did not hint at — any idea of refusing to take his orders in the coming week. Rather, he had tried to bamboozle *her* into thinking it to be a good idea. His repeated attempts to argue that going into the church was not only rational, but *appealing*, quickly ignited her choler. He *knew* she loathed the idea of it. He *knew* she would never consent to be a clergyman's wife. Yet he *insisted* on doing it. He would not be swayed. He would not be flexible in any particular. He clearly did not love Mary enough to consider her feelings. He was as arrogant and uncaring as the Admiral. She would have *nothing* more to do with him.

The worst thing for Mary, the absolute nadir of the evening, was the fact Edmund looked so unerringly handsome while he was trying to coax her into giving her approval of his wretched yen to become a cushion-thumping parson. There was no denying the manly comeliness of his face, or the graceful athleticism of his body. Muscles honed from hours on horseback were outlined more than obscured by his breeches and hose. His shoulders were alluringly broad under his severely cut black coat. She could not escape the recollection of dancing with him, of placing her gloved hand in his and being led to the floor, of seeing how much larger he was than any other man in the room.

Such was her unhappiness that Mary even found her brother's jaunty good spirits irksome. She would have much preferred a silent carriage ride, and Henry's jolly recollections of the ball, his comments on the graces of Miss Price, and his hopes for the morning breakfast with her before escorting William Price to London, were annoying in the extreme. Mary could not recall when she had ever been in a fouler mood, and it was all Edmund's fault. How dare he court her with such selfish views in mind! How dare he make her believe that he cared for her! All he wanted was her capitulation to *his* plans. What sacrifice was *he* willing to make for her, in exchange for *her* sacrifices of situation and income? Edmund was arrogant and – as only Shakespeare could insult – as loathsome as a toad. She would think of him no longer.

Mary was still fuming that she would never think of him again as she fell asleep in her own bed, curtains drawn tightly against the lightening eastern sky, with Edmund Bertram very much on her mind.

⁞

The following week was a miserable one for Mary. Edmund's absence, his removal to his friend Mr Owen's house for the purpose of taking orders, was simultaneously maddening and disheartening. To Mary it was every way painful. She felt the want of his society every day, almost every hour; and was too much in want of it to derive any thing but irritation from considering the object for which he went. He could not have devised any thing more likely to raise his consequence than this week's absence, occurring as it did at the very time of her brother's going away, of William Price's going too, and completing the sort of general break-up of a party which had been so animated. She felt it keenly. They were now a miserable trio, confined within doors by a series of rain and snow, with nothing to do and no variety to hope for. Angry as she was with Edmund for adhering to his own notions and acting on them in defiance of her, (and she had been so angry that they had hardly parted friends at the ball,) she could not help thinking of him continually when absent, dwelling on his merit and affection, and longing again for the almost daily meetings they lately had. His absence was unnecessarily long. He should not have planned such an absence—he should not have left home for a week, when her own departure from Mansfield was so near.

The more Mary missed Edmund, the more she began to reflect on whether or not she could really do without him. Was she being unreasonable? Was it too much to ask of a man that he make a significant sacrifice for his future bride? She thought over the angry way they had parted. Then she began to blame herself. She wished she had not spoken so warmly in their last conversation. She was afraid she had used some strong—some contemptuous expressions in speaking of the clergy, and *that* should not have been. It was ill-bred—it was wrong. She wished such words unsaid with all her heart.

The limited company was doing nothing to lessen Mary's yearning for Edward. She had always been happiest in a crowd, moving among friends, and meeting many acquaintances. The isolation of the parsonage was wearying to her spirits. She had little to distract her from her own thoughts. It only made her more dejected.

She tried, repeatedly, to master herself. She was not without reserves. She played her harp frequently, but would find her fingers plucking out Edmund's favourite pieces without thinking of it. Needlework made her want to scream. She read, but nothing could hold her attention long. Poetry had always agitated her feelings, but now those agitations stayed with her after she closed the book. Horrid novels failed to thrill her. She could not concentrate on any serious volume of prose. She couldn't even read a prime favourite, *Sense and Sensibility*, without being made unhappy by her realisation that she now understood Marianne's passions and Elinor's sorrows.

Mrs Grant made every effort to help her sister's evident doldrums. She talked at length, brought out playing cards, her ludo board and dice, and even tried charades. Still, nothing helped for long. Mary continued to mope around the house looking like a dying duck in a thunderstorm.

The only thing that Mary could do very well for very long was *fret*. She fretted almost constantly. She fretted that she, like Moloch, was sacrificing what she held most dear. Was her determination to reject Edmund unless he relinquished his plans to be a man of the cloth a conceit or fancy in her addled brain? She wanted him to prove he was unlike the Admiral, but didn't his principled and constant attentions already prove that? Had he not already shown, repeatedly, that he was nothing like her uncle?

She thought of Edmund almost without ceasing. She tried to think of the things that she didn't like about him, but his kindnesses kept creeping into her mind. His stated political opinions were so harsh, so controversial to her own, that she thought that could be a reason to abhor him, but his *actions* were so much of everything she approved of that she could not hold his words against him. It was Edmund who had intervened to prevent a young girl from being compelled to marry her forcible seducer. It was Edmund who had shown mercy repeatedly to poachers. Even Sir Thomas, stuffed-shirt that he was, forbade mantraps from being laid down in the park, and no one in the village could remember him ever sending a poacher to be transported or hung; Edmund was obviously as hidebound but kind as his father. It was Edmund whom Mrs Grant informed of pecuniary or physical distress among the poor and vulgar, and it was Edmund who saw that his mother's charity was directed properly, or made sure aid was given. And when she thought of how blamelessly, how generously, how benevolently Edmund treated Miss Price! None of the Bertrams were *cruel* to the girl, but only Edmund seemed to know how to be *kind* to her and to value her as a cousin as well as a companion. If the Admiral had treated his wife with *half* the graciousness that Edmund showed Fanny, then Mary would not be so leery of marriage.

Why did she resent his becoming a clergyman so much? Was not her longing to shine brightly in society merely a manifestation of her design to have *some* happiness in life? She had never expected happiness in marriage. At best, she had hoped for enough politeness and courtesy from her husband that she would not be *miserable*. But what if marriage to Edmund *could* make her happy? Would she need society so much then?

As for her fears of rustication — saving this week alone she had never been more content. As long as she had been able to have *some* social intercourse with Edmund, she had been satisfied. What was there to fear about the country, if it meant nearly daily visits with those she loved and friendly acquaintance, with nothing worse than *only* seeing Edmund when the weather made her housebound? It probably wouldn't even be only Edmund! Her brother could come to stay, and Fanny could be invited to live with them, and Mrs Rushworth would surely be glad to escape her moronic husband for a few days visit. She had many friends who could be invited to take in the country during hunting season, if Thornton Lacey could be turned into a suitable squire's residence.

If she married Edmund, it wasn't as though she would never see London again. She and Edmund could visit Mrs Rushworth, or her own brother when he eventually married. Sir Thomas was in Parliament. If she and Edmund said they would go with him, would he not get another house in Town for the season?

She had been a fool. She would accept him, despite his being a clergyman.

Mary went to bed Thursday night with the hopes that the next day could bring Edmund back to Mansfield; he was expected to return on Friday. If he failed to come to the parsonage, she was resolved to visit the Park and bewitch him anew. When people were determined to succeed they would often say, "over Edom I will cast my shoe"; Mary paraphrased it to herself, thinking "over Edmund I will cast my shoe," and fell into a hopeful slumber.

Chapter Thirty-One

SADLY FOR MARY, her vexation did not end with the week. Friday came round again and brought no Edmund—when Saturday came and still no Edmund—and when, through the slight communication with the other family which Sunday produced, she learned that he had actually written home to defer his return, having promised to remain some days longer with his friend!

If she had felt impatience and regret before—if she had been sorry for what she said, and feared its too strong effect on him, she now felt and feared it all tenfold more. She had, moreover, to contend with one disagreeable emotion entirely new to her—jealousy. His friend Mr Owen had sisters—he might find them attractive. But at any rate his staying away at a time, when, according to all preceding plans, she was to remove to London, meant something that she could not bear. Had Henry returned, as he talked of doing, at the end of three or four days, she should now have been leaving Mansfield. It became absolutely necessary for her to get to Fanny and try to learn something more. She could not live any longer in such solitary wretchedness; and she made her way to the Park, through difficulties of walking which she had deemed unconquerable a week before, for the chance of hearing a little in addition, for the sake of at least hearing his name.

The lane was, sadly, as dirty as Mary feared. She was above her ankles in mud most of the walk and the hems of her petticoats would probably need to be replaced entirely; Northampton mire being of a persistently staining kind. She was grateful she was alone and could hitch her dress and redingote high enough to reveal calf. When she had finally slogged her way to Mansfield she retired to the necessary room immediately, where a maid helped her remove her filthy boots and Mary replaced her footwear with the slippers her maid had carried for her. With her boots and redingote whisked away to be sponged as free as possible from smutty terra firma, and her dressed dropped down to hide the offensive state of her petticoats, Mary felt nearly presentable for the drawing-room.

The first half hour was lost, for Fanny and Lady Bertram were together, and unless she had Fanny to herself she could hope for nothing. But at last Lady Bertram left the room—and then almost immediately Miss Crawford thus began, with a voice as well-regulated as she could—"And how do *you* like your cousin Edmund's staying away so long?—Being the only young person at home, I consider *you* as the greatest sufferer.—You must miss him. Does his staying longer surprise you?"

"I do not know," said Fanny hesitatingly.—"Yes—I had not particularly expected it."

"Perhaps he will always stay longer than he talks of. It is the general way; all young men do." Mary gave a light laugh to indicate her lack of concern.

"He did not, the only time he went to see Mr Owen before."

"He finds the house more agreeable *now*.—He is a very—a very pleasing young man himself, and I cannot help being rather concerned at not seeing him again before I go to London, as will now undoubtedly be the case.—I am looking for Henry every day, and as soon as he comes there will be nothing to detain me at Mansfield. I should like to have seen him once more, I confess. But you must give my compliments to him. Yes—I think it must be compliments. Is not there a something wanted, Miss Price, in our language—a something between compliments and—and love—to suit the sort of friendly acquaintance we have had together?"

Mary nearly blushed from fear she was revealing too much, and lightened her tone, although she could not help but seek out more information. "So many months acquaintance!—But compliments may be sufficient here.—Was his letter a long one?—Does he give you much account of what he is doing?—Is it Christmas gaieties that he is staying for?"

"I only heard a part of the letter; it was to my uncle—but I believe it was very short; indeed I am sure it was but a few lines. All that I heard was that his friend had pressed him to stay longer, and that he had agreed to do so. A *few* days longer, or *some* days longer; I am not quite sure which."

Mary tried not to become irritated with Fanny for her quavering half-answers.

"Oh! if he wrote to his father—But I thought it might have been to Lady Bertram or you. But if he wrote to his father, no wonder he was concise. Who could write chat to Sir Thomas? If he had written to you, there would have been more particulars. You would have heard of balls and parties.—He would have sent you a description of every thing and every body. How many Miss Owens are there?"

"Three grown up."

"Are they musical?" Mary heard herself ask.

"I do not at all know. I never heard."

"That is the first question, you know," said Miss Crawford, trying to appear gay and unconcerned, "which every woman who plays herself is sure to ask about another. But it is very foolish to ask questions about any young ladies—about any three sisters just grown up; for one knows, without being told, exactly what they are—all very accomplished and pleasing, and *one* very pretty. There is a beauty in every family.—It is a regular thing. Two play on the piano-forte, and one on the harp—and all sing—or would sing if they were taught—or sing all the better for not being taught—or something like it."

"I know nothing of the Miss Owens," said Fanny calmly.

Mary smiled, and did not let her desire to pinch Miss Price for her tepid answers show. "You know nothing and you care less, as people say. Never did tone express indifference plainer. Indeed how can one care for those one has never seen?—Well, when your cousin comes back, he will find Mansfield very quiet;—all the noisy ones gone, your brother and mine and myself. I do not like the idea of leaving Mrs Grant now the time draws near. She does not like my going."

Fanny felt obliged to speak. "'You cannot doubt your being missed by many," said she. "You will be very much missed."

Miss Crawford turned her eye on her, as if wanting to hear or see more, and then laughingly said, "Oh! yes, missed as every noisy evil is missed when it is taken away; that is, there is a great difference felt. But I am not fishing; don't compliment me. If I *am* missed, it will appear. I may be discovered by those who want to see me. I shall not be in any doubtful, or distant, or unapproachable region."

Now Fanny could not bring herself to speak, and Miss Crawford was disappointed; for she had hoped to hear some pleasant assurance of her power, from one who she thought must know; and her spirits were clouded again. Was Fanny trying to spare her feelings by hiding how vexed Edmund was with her? Had he made it known to his cousin that he was resolved against any further courtship of Miss Crawford?

"The Miss Owens," said she, soon afterwards—"Suppose you were to have one of the Miss Owens settled at Thornton Lacey; how should you like it? Stranger things have happened. I dare say they are trying for it. And they are quite in the right, for it would be a very pretty establishment for them. I do not at all wonder or blame them.—It is every body's duty to do as well for themselves as they can. Sir Thomas Bertram's son is somebody; and now, he is in their own line. Their father is a clergyman, and their brother is a clergyman, and they are all clergymen together. He is their lawful property, he fairly belongs to them. You don't speak, Fanny—Miss Price—you don't speak.—But honestly now, do not you rather expect it than otherwise?"

"No," said Fanny stoutly, "I do not expect it at all."

"Not at all!"—cried Miss Crawford with alacrity. "I wonder at that. But I dare say you know exactly—I always imagine you are—perhaps you do not think him likely to marry at all—or not at present." Mary was not proud of how clumsily she hinted.

"No, I do not," said Fanny softly—hoping she did not err either in the belief or the acknowledgement of it.

Her companion looked at her keenly; and gathering greater spirit from the blush soon produced from such a look, only said, "He is best off as he is," and turned the subject. It was enough for her to know Edmund had not turned from her to the Miss Owens.

ıı

Miss Crawford's uneasiness was much lightened by this conversation, and she walked home again in spirits which might have defied almost another week of the same small party in the same bad weather, had they been put to the proof; but as that very evening brought her brother down from London again in quite, or more than quite, his usual cheerfulness, she had nothing further to try her own. His still refusing to tell her what he had gone for, was but the promotion of gaiety; a day before it might have irritated, but now it was a pleasant joke—suspected only of concealing something planned as a pleasant surprise to herself. And the next day *did* bring a surprise to her. Henry had said he should just go and ask the Bertrams how they did, and be back in ten minutes—but he was gone above an hour; and when his sister, who had been waiting for him to walk with her in the garden, met him at last most impatiently in the sweep, and cried out, "My dear Henry, where can you have been all this time?" he had only to say that he had been sitting with Lady Bertram and Fanny. "Sitting with them an hour and a half!" exclaimed Mary. What could henry have found in that company to divert his attention that long? Was he so very determined to get Miss Price to fall in love with him that he was willing to endure the tedium of Lady Bertram's listless small talk? Then he was much more determined that Mary had suspected!

But this was only the beginning of her surprise.

"Yes, Mary," said he, drawing her arm within his, and walking along the sweep as if not knowing where he was—"I could not get away sooner—Fanny looked so lovely!—I am quite determined, Mary. My mind is entirely made up. Will it astonish you? No—You must be aware that I am quite determined to marry Fanny Price."

The surprise was now complete; for in spite of whatever his consciousness might suggest, a suspicion of his having any such views had never entered his sister's imagination; and she looked so truly the astonishment she felt, that he was obliged to repeat what he had said, and more fully and more solemnly. The conviction of his determination once admitted, it was not unwelcome. There was even pleasure with the surprise. Mary was in a state of mind to rejoice in a connection with the Bertram family, and to be not displeased with her brother's marrying a little beneath him. She was speechless with delight, but her happiness for him was written clearly upon her countenance.

"Yes, Mary," was Henry's concluding assurance, "I am fairly caught. You know with what idle designs I began—but this is the end of them. I have (I flatter myself) made no inconsiderable progress in her affections; but my own are entirely fixed."

"Lucky, lucky girl!" cried Mary as soon as she could speak— "what a match for her! My dearest Henry, this must be my *first* feeling; but my *second*, which you shall have as sincerely, is that I approve your choice from my soul, and foresee your happiness as heartily as I wish and desire it. You will have a sweet little wife; all gratitude and devotion. Exactly what you deserve. What an amazing match for her!

Mary laughed as a thought struck her. "Mrs Norris often talks of her luck; what will she say now? The delight of all the family indeed! And she has some *true* friends in it. How *they* will rejoice!" Edmund, she knew, would be as happy with the match as she was herself.

"But tell me all about it. Talk to me for ever. When did you begin to think seriously about her?" Mary urged her brother, wanting to hear of it as much as she was sure he wished to speak of it.

Nothing could be more impossible than to answer such a question, though nothing could be more agreeable than to have it asked. "How the pleasing plague had stolen on him" he could not say, and before he had expressed the same sentiment with a little variation of words three times over, his sister eagerly interrupted him with, "Ah! my dear Henry, and this is what took you to London! This was your business! You chose to consult the Admiral, before you made up your mind."

But this he stoutly denied. He knew his uncle too well to consult him on any matrimonial scheme. The Admiral hated marriage, and thought it never pardonable in a young man of independent fortune. Mary could only agree with this; she could not contradict it.

"When Fanny is known to him," continued Henry, "he will doat on her. She is exactly the woman to do away every prejudice of such a man as the Admiral, for she is exactly such a woman as he thinks does not exist in the world. She is the very impossibility he would describe—if indeed he has now delicacy of language enough to embody his own ideas. But till it is absolutely settled—settled beyond all interference, he shall know nothing of the matter. No, Mary, you are quite mistaken. You have not discovered my business yet!"

Mary doubted the Admiral would be happy that Henry was marrying a dowerless girl regardless of how sweet her temper, but she let the matter lie. It was a matter for the future and Henry's burden to bear. "Well, well, I am satisfied. I know now to whom it must relate, and am in no hurry for the rest. Fanny Price—Wonderful—quite wonderful!—That Mansfield should have done so much for—that *you* should have found your fate in Mansfield! But you are quite right, you could not have chosen better. There is not a better girl in the world, and you do not want for fortune; and as to her connections, they are more than good. The Bertrams are undoubtedly some of the first people in this country. She is niece to Sir Thomas Bertram; that will be enough for the world. But go on, go on. Tell me more. What are your plans? Does she know her own happiness?"

"No."

"What are you waiting for?" Mary was surprised. Patience was one of the many virtues her brother eschewed.

"For—for very little more than opportunity. Mary, she is not like her cousins; but I think I shall not ask in vain." This was not ego; this was a rational supposition. He had wealth and station and she had nothing. Therefore, she would surely accept him.

"Oh! no, you cannot. Were you even less pleasing—supposing her not to love you already (of which however I can have little doubt,) you would be safe. The gentleness and gratitude of her disposition would secure her all your own immediately. From my soul I do not think she would marry you *without* love; that is, if there is a girl in the world capable of being uninfluenced by ambition, I can suppose it her; but ask her to love you, and she will never have the heart to refuse."

As soon as her eagerness could rest in silence, he was as happy to tell as she could be to listen, and a conversation followed almost as deeply interesting to her as to himself, though he had in fact nothing to relate but his own sensations, nothing to dwell on but Fanny's charms.—Fanny's beauty of face and figure, Fanny's graces of manner and goodness of heart were the exhaustless theme, albeit Henry did his best to exhaust it.

The gentleness, modesty, and sweetness of Fanny Price's character were warmly expatiated on, that sweetness which makes so essential a part of every woman's worth in the judgement of man, that though he sometimes loves where it is not, he can never believe it absent. Her temper he had good reason to depend on and to praise. He had often seen it tried. Was there one of the family, excepting Edmund, who had not in some way or other continually exercised her patience and forbearance? Her affections were evidently strong. To see her with her brother! What could more delightfully prove that the warmth of her heart was equal to its gentleness?—What could be more encouraging to a man who had her love in view? Then, her understanding was beyond every suspicion, quick and clear; and her manners were the mirror of her own modest and elegant mind. Fanny Price was, in short, a paragon in his opinion – an opinion which his sister fully shared.

Nor was this all. Henry Crawford had too much sense not to feel the worth of good principles in a wife, though he was too little accustomed to serious reflection to know them by their proper name; but when he talked of her having such a steadiness and regularity of conduct, such a high notion of honour, and such an observance of decorum as might warrant any man in the fullest dependence on her faith and integrity, he expressed what was inspired by the knowledge of her being well principled and religious. For her part, Mary agreed with the notion of Fanny's constancy. She was certain that Henry would be one of the few men in the Beau Monde who would never where horns.

"I could so wholly and absolutely confide in her," said he; "and *that* is what I want."

Well might his sister, believing as she really did that his opinion of Fanny Price was scarcely beyond her merits, rejoice in her prospects. Her dearest Henry, to be so happy! Sweet little Fanny, to be so rewarded! It was everything pleasing.

"The more I think of it," she cried, "the more am I convinced that you are doing quite right, and though I should never have selected Fanny Price as the girl most likely to attach you, I am now persuaded she is the very one to make you happy. Your wicked project upon her peace turns out a clever thought indeed. You will both find your good in it."

"It was bad, very bad in me against such a creature! but I did not know her then. And she shall have no reason to lament the hour that first put it into my head."

Mary squeezed his arm, and looked her approval at his self-awareness and resolve to make Miss Price happy.

Henry was determined. "I will make her very happy, Mary, happier than she has ever yet been herself, or ever seen any body else. I will not take her from Northamptonshire. I shall let Everingham, and rent a place in this neighbourhood—perhaps Stanwix Lodge. I shall let a seven years' lease of Everingham. I am sure of an excellent tenant at half a word. I could name three people now, who would give me my own terms and thank me."

"Ha!" cried Mary; "settle in Northamptonshire! That is pleasant! Then we shall be all together."

When she had spoken it, she recollected herself, and wished it unsaid; but there was no need of confusion, for her brother saw her only as the supposed inmate of Mansfield Parsonage, and replied but to invite her in the kindest manner to his own house, and to claim the best right in her.

"You must give us more than half your time," said he; "I cannot admit Mrs Grant to have an equal claim with Fanny and myself, for we shall both have a right in you. Fanny will be so truly your sister!"

Henry was silenced as he pondered the happy spectacle of his wife and sister living together in blessed accord.

Mary had only to be grateful and give general assurances; but she was now very fully purposed to be the guest of neither brother nor sister many months longer.

"You will divide your year between London and Northamptonshire?"

"Yes."

"That's right; and in London, of course, a house of your own; no longer with the Admiral," Mary sighed with heartfelt relief. "My dearest Henry, the advantage to you of getting away from the Admiral before your manners are hurt by the contagion of his, before you have contracted any of his foolish opinions, or learned to sit over your dinner, as if it were the best blessing of life!—*You* are not sensible of the gain, for your regard for him has blinded you; but, in my estimation, your marrying early may be the saving of you. To have seen you grow like the Admiral in word or deed, look or gesture, would have broken my heart."

"Well, well, we do not think quite alike here. The Admiral has his faults, but he is a very good man, and has been more than a father to me. Few fathers would have let me have my own way half so much. You must not prejudice Fanny against him. I must have them love one another." Henry could not understand why Mary had such resolve against the Admiral. So the old sailor was a bit bluff and had not coddled their aunt; was that such a sin?

Mary refrained from saying what she felt, that there could not be two persons in existence, whose characters and manners were less accordant; time would discover it to him; but she could not help *this* reflection on the Admiral. "Henry, I think so highly of Fanny Price, that if I could suppose the next Mrs Crawford would have half the reason which my poor ill used aunt had to abhor the very name, I would prevent the marriage, if possible; but I know you, I know that a wife you *loved* would be the happiest of women, and that even when you ceased to love, she would yet find in you the liberality and good-breeding of a gentleman."

The impossibility of not doing every thing in the world to make Fanny Price happy, or of ceasing to love Fanny Price, was of course the ground-work of his eloquent answer. Mary listened with amusement as her previously impervious brother waxed on and on about the splendours of falling victim to Cupid's arrow.

"Had you seen her this morning, Mary," he continued, "attending with such ineffable sweetness and patience, to all the demands of her aunt's stupidity, working with her, and for her, her colour beautifully heightened as she leant over the work, then returning to her seat to finish a note which she was previously engaged in writing for that stupid woman's service, and all this with such unpretending gentleness, so much as if it were a matter of course that she was not to have a moment at her own command, her hair arranged as neatly as it always is, and one little curl falling forward as she wrote, which she now and then shook back, and in the midst of all this, still speaking at intervals to *me*, or listening, and as if she liked to listen to what I said. Had you seen her so, Mary, you would not have implied the possibility of her power over my heart ever ceasing."

"My dearest Henry," cried Mary, stopping short, and smiling in his face, "how glad I am to see you so much in love! It quite delights me."

Mary had a sudden thought; a small grey cloud in the blue skies of Henry's good news. "But what will Mrs Rushworth and Julia say?" Mrs Rushworth as both a cousin and a jilted lover was a fearsome prospect.

"I care neither what they say, nor what they feel," Henry was adamant. "They will now see what sort of woman it is that can attach me, that can attach a man of sense. I wish the discovery may do them any good. And they will now see their cousin treated as she ought to be, and I wish they may be heartily ashamed of their own abominable neglect and unkindness."

Mary doubted that Mrs Rushworth would be anything other than peeved. That she should repent of her treatment of Fanny or learn any lesson from Henry's preference was improbable. Maria was would be more likely to spit and shriek in a conniption fit than to reflect on her own deeds, in Mary's considered opinion.

"They will be angry," he added, after a moment's silence, and in a cooler tone, "Mrs Rushworth will be very angry. It will be a bitter pill to her; that is, like other bitter pills, it will have two moments ill-flavour, and then be swallowed and forgotten; for I am not such a coxcomb as to suppose her feelings more lasting than other women's, though *I* was the object of them. Yes, Mary, my Fanny will feel a difference indeed, a daily, hourly difference, in the behaviour of every being who approaches her; and it will be the completion of my happiness to know that I am the doer of it, that I am the person to give the consequence so justly her due. Now she is dependent, helpless, friendless, neglected, forgotten."

Mary jumped to her lover's defence. "Nay, Henry, not by all, not forgotten by all, not friendless or forgotten. Her cousin Edmund never forgets her."

"Edmund—True, I believe he is (generally speaking) kind to her; and so is Sir Thomas in his way, but it is the way of a rich, superior, long-worded, arbitrary uncle. What can Sir Thomas and Edmund together do, what *do* they do for her happiness, comfort, honour, and dignity in the world to what I *shall* do?"

Mary could not deny this. As much as Edmund loved his cousin, he could not elevate her *situation*, her standing in the neighbourhood. She was but poor little Miss Price, indigent and dependent niece of Sir Thomas, useful and modest, liked because she was humble enough even for her circumstances. There was nothing about Fanny that could give disgust, but neither was their anything that could give respect and attention, beyond what was due to a niece of Sir Thomas's. Oh! But how different that would be when Miss Price became Mrs Crawford!

To become the wife of a rich, respectable man was the highest rank a woman could fairly achieve. Her status and respectability could only be a reflection of his. It was why a man could stoop to marry beneath him for money, but a woman seldom dared to do the same. A woman of low birth would rise when she married, but even a duchess would sink if she married a tradesman, be he as rich as King Midas.

There were even greater felicities possible for Fanny. Henry, active in politics, connected with all the right people, was in a fair way of become a peer — a baronet or perhaps even a baron – when the Whigs returned to power. A high appointment and his service to the government; that is all it would take to secure it. It was possible that one day Mrs Rushworth and Mrs Whomever Julia Married would have to give precedence to Lady Crawford. Surely even Fanny, as modest as she was, could not fail to exult in the change. To be first when she was least! Mary did not even mind that Fanny would go before her, so happy would she be to see her brother and his wife among the foremost in the country.

Mary was soon lost in a pleasant reverie wherein Edmund, properly coaxed over to the Whigs by herself and Henry, also became more active in politics. Perhaps he would even stand for MP one day. Mary was born to be an MP's wife. She would glitter among society, invitations to her salons and parties as envied in the future as invitations to Holland House were today. She would never *rank* as high as Lady Holland, but neither would she have scandal or impropriety in her background. With wit and merit she might rise to levels other women would need a title to achieve.

It was surprising that wreaths of pink birds and red hearts weren't visibly floating around Henry and Mary's heads, so happy were their contemplations of future connubial bliss.

Chapter Thirty-Two

MARY HAD OBTAINED Henry's promise that they would not leave for London until she had seen and made peace with Edmund, a promise easily given because it meant Henry would get to spend more time with Fanny Price, and she was feeling infinitely more sanguine about her future prospects. Even better, Henry's conversation and company had enlivened her spirits to such an extent that she could once again play her harp, read, or do needlework and chat with her sister with reasonable enjoyment and attention.

Immediately after breakfast the next morning, Henry found a moment alone with Mary, and asked her to wish him luck; he was going to Mansfield Park to try to get Fanny Price alone long enough to propose.

Mary was all good wishes and happiness. "I have no doubts of your success, so I need not wish you *luck*. However, with all my heart I wish you *joy*."

"I never gamble without an ace, though. An ace if often good luck," Henry was more nervous than he thought he should be. "I have badgered the Admiral until he has secured William Price's promotion to second lieutenant aboard the HMS *Thrush*."

Unable to shout out her gladness lest she have to explain it to all the household, Mary spontaneously embraced her brother. "I am delighted beyond words, both for Lieutenant Price and you! Never has the Admiral bestowed his good offices on a more worthy candidate and for a better cause. My word! Fanny will be so happy she will likely faint. You'd better bring my smelling salts with you."

"If she faints, I shall bring her round with a kiss, like the prince did for Sleeping Beauty," Henry grinned roguishly.

"Kiss her before the wedding and her cousin and Sir Thomas might bring you round with a second and duelling pistols," Mary cautioned in jest. "Better to bring my smelling salts."

"I am so happy thinking about her answer, imagining the blush of gratitude on her tender cheeks and those soft eyes filled with emotion, that I might need the smelling salts for myself," Henry laughed at his own romanticism.

Mary shook her head. "Not manly enough. Someone will have to wave a burnt feather under your nose."

"Should I bring the feather?"

"A peacock like yourself? Don't you already have feathers on you?"

"As if I would waste one of *my* feathers!" Henry swelled in mock indignation. "I'd as soon pebble my fountain with diamonds."

"Well, don't let Prinny know, because he'll soon follow suit and none of us can afford more taxes."

"Provided he does not tax love, I am safe enough."

"Good God, Henry! When did you become such a gushing romantic? Did Byron shake your hand while you were in London and pass the contagion onto you?"

"I fear Fanny Price is infectious; I am laid low by her charms."

"Well, to paraphrase Beatrice, it will cost you a thousand pound ere you be cured."

"A hundred thousand pounds would not be enough, Mary. The sweet poison has seeped into my bones."

"And if you don't stop blathering such romantic claptrap, my vomit will seep into your boots."

"I cannot have that! These are my best boots. I cannot ask for a lady's hand while wearing my second best boots. I must away."

"It is still their breakfast hour, dearest. You might catch them all at the table," Mary warned him.

"True." Henry considered the matter. "I shall walk the long way around, through the copse."

"It's shockingly dirty I fear. Your boots will suffer for it."

"Then what do you suggest?"

"That you wait a quarter hour. Come, I'll let you read me some of *The Swiss Family Robinson*. We can laugh about the veritable Ark of animals Mr Wyss's island boasts. If a polar bear turns up, I shall not be shocked."

"We cannot read that one; I have engaged to read it to you and Mrs Grant together." Henry thought for a moment. "I'll read you one or two of the *Rejected Addresses* instead."

"Will you read "Fire and Ale" and do the hissing sound when the Fire King is baptised?"

"Of course," Henry promised, and went to Dr Grant's library to get the book.

‖

Mary and Mrs Grant were sitting on the drawing-room sofa contentedly sewing, wrapped in shawls and benefiting from a hearty fire, when Henry returned from his early morning trip to Mansfield Park.

"Well, I have asked Fanny price for her hand in marriage," He stated boldly, causing Mrs Grant, who had no suspicions in that direction whatsoever, to goggle at him.

"Oh! Let me be the first to wish you joy!" Mary nearly squealed and leapt up to embrace her brother.

"My dearest Henry! What a surprise! I am so happy for you!" Mrs Grant also rose and gave her brother a hug. "Tell us everything, spare no details," she begged.

"First I must tell you that you are premature in wishing me joy; she has refused me." Henry said it so mildly, and with such a look of good-humoured calm, that it took some time to convince Mary and Mrs Grant that he was serious.

"What?" Mary cried. "How is this possible? Has she had her brains knocked out in an accident?"

Mary was incensed. How *dare* Fanny Price reject Henry Crawford! Was the girl a fool? Did she not see that he was a gentleman of fortune, property, and importance? Henry was one of the most sought after men in London! There was *no* chance that Fanny would ever get an offer that was half so good! Mary wanted to grab the girl by the shoulders and shake her until some sense was released in her skull.

"She does not believe me to be serious," Henry admitted ruefully. "She thinks I am merely trying to flirt with her. She mistakes my proffering of my heart as the same ... *civilities* I gave her cousins. I am but a coxcomb and would-be Lothario to Miss Price. *She* is not likely to fall in love with such a fellow."

Mrs Grant pressed her fist against her lower mouth, as if she were suppressing a cough, to hide her smile, but Mary grinned openly.

"Oh ho!" His younger sister crowed. "You are hoist on your own petard, you flirt you! How will you ever convince Fanny Price to take you seriously? What Herculean task must you perform as a lover to assure her of your pure intentions?"

"I have no doubt that if I were able to bring her three captured stars in a locket she would *still* scorn me. Here is a heart worth having Mary! There will be no hornswoggling *her* with sweet words. She demands only the true worth of the thing."

"And your much-valued ace? Was it merely a pam after all?"

Henry looked chagrined. "It was more the knave of *hearts* than the knave of clubs, but yes, it was trumped by the lady's good judgement. She thinks me an absolute puppy; I can tell."

"That cannot possibly be true!" Mrs Grant interjected with feeling. "There is not the slightest whiff of puppyism about you!"

"Perhaps not in the *common* way," Henry agreed, "but in matters of lovemaking Miss Price sees me as quizzing rapscallion. Her delicacy is so refined that my rattle toward the Miss Bertrams must have made me seem quite the scoundrel."

"Yet you are not despondent," Mary gave him a knowing look. "What is the trick you have up your sleeve?"

"I shall have you write her a note."

"*Me?*" Mary was nonplussed. "You want *me* to make love to Fanny Price *for* you? Why, for Heaven's sake?"

Henry pinched the bridge of his nose, a sure sign that he wanted to roll his eyes at her. "No, I want you to write her a note vouching for my *sincerity*. It seems the most expedient way to let her know I am truly offering her my hand as well as my heart. I can give it to her today, since I am invited to dine at the Park."

Mary bit her lips, trying not to laugh at the spectacle of the great lover Henry Crawford reduced to getting a note from his sister. Her brother narrowed his eyes at her, well aware she was amused at his expense.

"Very well," she said. "Let me fetch paper and pen, but I will not have it dictated to me. You'll take what I write and be grateful."

"And if I don't like it?" Henry demanded.

"Then you can lump it."

She got her materials from her sister's writing desk and sat at the breakfast table to write:

> "My dear Fanny, for so I may now always call you, to the infinite relief of a tongue that has been stumbling at *Miss Price* for at least the last six weeks—I cannot let my brother go without sending you a few lines of general congratulation, and giving my

most joyful consent and approval.—Go on, my dear Fanny, and without fear; there can be no difficulties worth naming. I chuse to suppose that the assurance of *my* consent will be something; so you may smile upon him with your sweetest smiles this afternoon, and send him back to me even happier than he goes. Yours   affectionately, M. C."

Henry was not entirely satisfied with Mary's note. He felt it lacked gravitas. Mary told him he could add his own verbal furbelows later, when his lady had consented to marry him. *She* wasn't doing it for him. Disgruntled, Henry announced that he was going for a long ride, and bowed himself from the room.

‖

"Was that kind, Mary?" Mrs Grant scolded her gently.

"Oh, yes." Mary assured her, "Henry's pride can well withstand such a puny blow, and a slight deflation of his opinion of himself will make him a better lover."

"I wonder that he can ride," Mrs Grant mused. "The wind is bitter today."

"He's encased in woollens from head to toe and will have a Kersey greatcoat over top of it all. He'll be warm as toast. If I could dress as warmly I would go for a ride. As it is, I would freeze stiff."

Mrs Grant was instantly concerned. "Why can't you dress as warmly? Do you lack something? I have an Irish cloth chemise we can alter to fit you."

Mary smiled at her sister's eager solicitude. "My dear Mrs Grant, you are too kind. I am well equipped in the *general* way. My riding habit is spanolet of a good thickness and my cloak is a very sturdy superfine. My cloak is, perhaps, not as warm as my witzchoura, but it is every bit as warm as my redingote. No, the problem lies in the *Netherlands*. When the wind is as blustery as it is today, it becomes very *inquisitive* when I ride and soon nips more than the cheeks on my *face*. Thick wool stockings are all well and good, but they can only go so far."

"Have you tried drawers?" Mrs Grant asked. "I have a pair, and I find they help keep the Netherlands from experiencing hard frosts."

Drawers of this time were usually rudimentary and seldom worn. They were basically two tubes of cloth serving as legs attached to a waist. Although lady's drawers closer to the 'gent's knee-length step-ins' of a later date had started to appear, they were still lesser known items of clothing. There was no reason for Mrs Grant to assume Mary already wore them.

"I had a very bad experience with a pair of drawers last winter, and I am in no humour to repeat the mortification," Mary explained.

"My goodness! What happened?"

"It was the first time I had ever worn them. At the outset, I thought they might be a good idea. They certainly helped keep my upper legs warmer. However, I soon found them to be an instrument of Satan. I was walking along with my friend, Lady Stornoway, down a very busy thoroughfare, when suddenly one leg of the drawers detached itself from the waist-tape of the garment and slid down to my ankle."

Mrs Grant shook with silent laughter. When she won back her breath she asked, "Whatever did you *do*?"

"The only thing I *could* do," Mary shrugged. "I walked out of the blessed thing and left it lying in the street. My only hope is that in the crowd people might think it belonged to Lady Stornoway. I like awake at night shuddering and wondering what I would have done if it had caught around my foot and I had dragged it with me as I walked. I can only assume I would have had no choice but to have hanged myself … provided I had not expired from mortification on the spot. I would have made a very sad ghost; the Lady of the Leg, doomed to roam for an eternity while dragging half of her drawers."

"Stop! Stop, or I shall die from laughing," Mrs Grant pleaded, hiccuping.

Mary waited patiently for her sister's laughter to wind down to a kind of quiet chuckle and occasional soft hoot.

"My dear sister," Mrs Grant said, "There are now drawers that attached together at the legs, not unlike men's smalls. You would not need to fear losing a leg ever again. I am wearing a flannel pair right now and they are as comfortable and warm as you could ever wish for."

Mary looked sceptical. "How do they fasten? It would do me no good if the *whole* thing fell down while I was walking. The only thing worse than dragging one leg along the street would be to totter along like a hobbled horse, bound at the ankles by what looked to be a pair of men's smalls." She then had to wait for Mrs Grant to finish another paroxysm of laughter.

Her sister finally stopped chortling and told her that the drawers fastened with drawstrings or laces and they were very, very unlikely to lose their moorings. Mary agreed, albeit somewhat reluctantly, to try a pair, and Beatty was duly dispatched to town to purchase the requisite flannel. Mary made a point of warning her sister that should *these* drawers fall down and mortify her to death, then she would be haunting Mrs Grant for the rest of eternity.

"

Henry returned from the Park that evening much earlier than anyone at the parsonage had expected him to, coming in shortly after nine o'clock. Dr and Mrs Grant were enjoying a game of nine men's morris on the drawing-room table, and Mary was playing her harp. They were all three surprised when Henry walked into the drawing-room.

"Henry! Why are you home so early?" Mary cried. "I thought you would be billing and cooing like a lovebird with Fanny until eleven o'clock at the least."

"I would be doomed to bill and coo alone," Henry said ruefully, collapsing onto the sofa. "She still does not believe in the sincerity of my attentions. Here, look at this note she wrote you; excuse me, but it was unsealed so I took the liberty of reading it."

Mary took the note and read:

"I am very much obliged to you, my dear Miss Crawford, for your kind congratulations, as far as they relate to my dearest William. The rest of your note I know means nothing; but I am so unequal to any thing of the sort, that I hope you will excuse my begging you to take no further notice. I have seen too much of Mr Crawford not to understand his manners; if he understood me as well, he would, I dare say, behave differently. I do not know what I write, but it would be a great favour of you never to mention the subject again. With thanks for the honour of your note,

I remain, dear Miss Crawford,

&c. &c."

"What on *earth* is the matter with her?" Mary asked, passing the note to Mrs Grant. "Does she think a man must take coals to Newcastle in the form of getting his sister to aid him in a light flirtation? Does she think that every man declares his love so openly when he is but *flirting*? I may have to revise everything I have said of her good sense."

"I fear the poor girl has no experience at all with this sort of thing," Mrs Grant answered. "If I had to guess, I would have to say that Fanny Price's natural and profound modesty cannot let her believe that *she* has secured Henry's affections when all that Julia Bertram could do failed. It is impossible that any man should prefer her to one of her cousins, and dowerless as she is she cannot have thought matrimony a likely thing. She is bewildered by you both; she cannot make it out."

Mary was nearly stupefied. "That is the *oddest* thing I have ever heard. I can barely wrap my mind around the thought of a woman so modest she does not believe she could be loved. That is unnatural. Henry, I forbid the marriage; Fanny Price is insane."

Henry, knowing she wasn't serious, ignored her and addressed Mrs Grant. "What can I do then, to convince her of my sincerity? What do you recommend me to do, ma'am?"

Mrs Grant told him, "My advice would be to go straight to Sir Thomas tomorrow, and apply for his permission to ask for Fanny's hand in marriage. He is acting as her father, and so he must have a father's place in the proceeding. I know one usually solicits the lady *before* her father, but I do not think that is practicable in this case. Only Sir Thomas could make Fanny understand that this *is* a proposal."

"I confess I find it singular," Dr Grant frowned. "Are you sure she is the right woman for you, Henry? You are worldly wise, and she is innocent as a nun in a cloister. Can she make you happy?"

Henry smiled. "Yes, a thousand times yes! What it would be to win such a heart! Principled, modest, innocent women are not two-a-penny in Town. That which is rare, has more value; I will treasure her more for her uniqueness. No knight errant can be as devoted to keeping his lady safe from worldly things as I will be."

Dr Grant did not look convinced. Alone of those in the parsonage he regretted Henry's falling in love with Fanny Price. He had heard of Henry's plans too late to offer advice or to caution his brother-in-law, but he felt it was his duty to remind Henry that physical love and heirs, not only exalted emotions, were the function of marriage. Even when the wife was healthy and conjugal love was frequent (or, at least it had been frequent before he had become middle aged, alas) there may be no offspring. Why would a reasonable man stack the deck against having children by marrying a wan and weak woman like Miss Price? Should Henry manage to get the chit pregnant, as frail as she was it would be a miracle if she survived the birth. That is assuming that there was even a chance for children to be conceived in the first place. He could not image Fanny Price ever doing more than *submitting* to marital love, and that sort of thing could crush a man's soul. He knew Henry would doubtlessly find comfort elsewhere, but to lay with your wife, the woman you loved, was such a boon that he would not have Henry cast it aside lightly. Worse, everyone knew a woman's pleasure was needed for conception; a cold woman like Miss Price, even if she were in the bloom of health, all but doomed her marriage to childlessness. Before Henry talked to Sir Thomas in the morning, Dr Grant was determined to have a serious word with the young cub.

"Well, you are certainly going to have to have as many obstacles to overcome and dragons to slay as any knight of the Round Table," Mary joked. Her brother's continued resolve to marry Fanny Price forced Mary to try to cover her annoyance with his intended by making light of it all. "Avoid the Green Knight, if you can, and best you call on St George for help."

"It's cupid, not St George, I shall rely on to help me," Henry grinned. Fanny's resistance was, for him, a mere delay. He was certain he would win her as soon as she realised he was truly offering her his heart. When had he ever failed, regardless of how little he cared? How could he fail now, when he cared a great deal?

Henry's feelings for Fanny were intensified by the novelty of them. He had never fallen into calf's love as a boy, or been rejected by a woman; nothing regarding matters of the heart had either touched him or hurt him. He was in the throws of first love as intense as any experienced by a school boy, and he had the school boy's inability to understand that love must have sturdy fuel as well as a blazing tinder if it was to burn for long. Worse, Henry did not know he should be cautious in opening himself up and becoming vulnerable to the woman he loved, lest her feelings for him not be reciprocated. He did not fear a broken heart because he was unaware of how much pain it caused. He was as open, artless, and eager as toddler reaching for a shiny knife, oblivious to the fact it could cut him deeply.

Mary was as incognisant of what heartbreak entailed as Henry was, but she was nonetheless uneasy for him. Fanny's behaviour was unappreciative; Fanny was showing herself ungrateful and aloof. Before this, Mary would have wagered one hundred pounds on Fanny's sweetness and gratitude, but now she was suspicious that she did not know Fanny as well as she thought she had done. There was a certain coldness in her reply to Mary, a certain judgemental carelessness. Fanny did not think Henry capable of being sincere. She said that she had seen too much of Henry's manners not to understand them, but Fanny had shown that her understanding was hollow.

Mary was also profoundly insulted by Fanny's claiming that her note 'means nothing' in regards to Henry's suit. Who was Fanny Price to write such a thing to Miss Crawford? She had, in essence, accused Mary of trying to trick her into accepting Henry's false addresses. Mary was not accustomed to accusations of mendacity. If anything, she was always *too* truthful in such matters. Her blunt speech had gotten her into trouble a time or two, requiring all of her charm to soothe away hurt feelings. Yet Fanny Price was implying — no, stating — that Mary was lying for Henry's convenience. Mary had believed Fanny to be her friend; Fanny's misjudgement of her stung.

Mary read the note again in her dressing room that night while Beatty braided her hair for bed. There was no getting around the lines, "The rest of your note I know means nothing; but I am so unequal to any thing of the sort, that I hope you will excuse my begging you to take no further notice. I have seen too much of Mr Crawford not to understand his manners." It was insulting. Those lines were saying that Mary was a liar and her brother a cad. Mary was profoundly angry with Fanny Price, and if Fanny had been before her then the silly girl might have gotten her nose pinched.

Fanny Price was, in Mary's opinion, making a tempest in a teapot about Henry's flirtation with Maria and Julia Bertram. Her brother had made no promises and had not paid overly particular attentions to an unattached woman. He had not deflowered, ruined, or cast off either Bertram sister. If Maria had been more principled and more disinterested in her choice of a fiancé, or if either sister had been less vain, then Henry could not have affected them any more than a summer zephyr can blow down a house. It was ridiculous and unfair for Fanny Price to place all the blame of that romancing on Henry.

By the time Mary fell asleep, she had delivered several blistering internal lectures to Fanny Price on the topic of intrigue, lovers, romance, and gratitude on Henry's behalf.

Chapter Thirty-Three

MARY AWOKE MUCH less angry with Fanny Price than she had been the night before. She was, she believed, ready to be rational about Fanny's near-hysterical response to Henry's proposal. Perhaps Fanny's fears and veiled accusations would be insulting if written by a member of the beau monde, but could they be considered insulting when written by a countrified lamb like Fanny Price? Was there not panic and confusion in her words? The handwriting was so poor in the final sentences that it was plain the girl's hand was shaking.

She now saw Fanny's inability to comprehend the sincerity in Henry's addresses in a more merciful light. It was probably not a reflection on Henry or herself; it was rather the manifestation of Fanny's own negligible self-pride. Mrs Grant's supposition was doubtlessly correct. How could Fanny, who was constantly treated as the least important member of the household by everyone but Edmund, think she could have inspired the love of a man like Henry? The poor girl must have thought that Mary and Henry were being japesters at her expense. While it was not *flattering* to be seen as so overly fond of heartless jollity, it was not as offensive as being thought cruel and careless. She reminded herself that she was a friend of Fanny Price, and as a friend she should give the poor girl the benefit of the doubt.

Mary had no doubts that Fanny *was* her good friend in return. It did not occur to her that someone so avowedly moral and principled would counterfeit something as important as regard and affection. That Fanny was capable of spurious friendliness was something Mary did not think possible. She had an honest and very misplaced faith in Fanny's fraudulent attachment to her.

At breakfast, Henry talked eagerly of his plans to see Sir Thomas as soon as possible that morning. He would have left instantly after he ate if Dr Grant had not requested his presence in the library for a short time. As it was, Henry was closeted with their brother-in-law for almost three-quarters of an hour before he could leave. Mary was exceedingly curious about what the men had talked about, but she assumed Henry would tell her later. It was probably just advice on the best way to approach Sir Thomas; nothing of excessive interest.

The Grants had no expectations of seeing Henry again until evening, for surely he would be invited to dine at the Park after he and Fanny became engaged, but Mary thought that Henry might come home briefly to sing the praises of his fiancée and reap the congratulations of his family. She believed he would at least send a note as soon as Fanny accepted him, and suspected that they would all be invited to dine with the Bertrams in celebration. What neither Mary nor the Grants were expecting was that Henry would be home shortly after noon.

Dr Grant was out, and Mrs Grant was sitting on the sofa, sewing a new pair of flannel drawers for her sister, while Mary read Bage's *Hermsprong: or, Man as he is not* aloud, which Mrs Grant had assiduously avoided for the nearly twenty years it had been published. The book, full of themes of pride and prejudice, was a radically progressive narrative couched as a romantic novel. Mary was enjoying reading it again, and was especially pleased that her sister was enthralled by the narrative as she was shocked by ideology of it. The hero, Mr Charles Hermsprong, had been raised by 'noble savages' in America and was thus able to penetrate and decry the hypocrisy of so-called civilised society, as well as act as a champion of the oppressed workers of Britain. Moreover, both Hermsprong and his love interest, Maria Fluart, propounded the ideology that women were just as capable of rational discourse and excellence in education as men, and should be given equal rights under the law. It was Mary Wollstonecraft's *A Vindication of the Rights of Women* wrapped up in a story palatable to the English public.

So engrossed were they in the tale that they did not hear the small bustle in the vestibule, and they were completely surprised when Henry entered the drawing-room.

"Henry!" Mary cried out. "Have you come to tell us the happy news, and let us wish you joy?" She put her book down and rose to embrace her brother.

Mrs Grant leapt to her feet with equal alacrity, and begged Henry to tell them everything. Neither sister had the slightest doubt that Henry had been successful.

"Regrettably, I must ask that you refrain from wishing me joy, *as yet*. Fanny's uncle has given his joyous consent, but Fanny has *not*." Henry did not look dejected in the least by this turn of events.

Love such as his, in a man like himself, must with perseverance secure a return, and at no great distance; and he had so much delight in the idea of obliging her to love him in a very short time, that her not loving him now was scarcely regretted. A little difficulty to be overcome, was no evil to Henry Crawford. He rather derived spirits from it. He had been apt to gain hearts too easily. His situation was new and animating.

Mary, however, was greatly offended on his behalf. "*What?* You have shown her that you are sincere by every possible manner and she *still* does not accept you? How can this be? What sort of ninnyhammer *is* she? The most shatterbrained pigwidgeon in the kingdom would have the good sense to accept you! She need never fear drowning, for her head is made entirely of cork!"

"Now, now, Mary," Her brother sought to soothe her. "Don't get yourself into a great tweague; there is no need to be so upset. Fanny is only proving herself *disinterested* in marital affairs. It is beyond her to marry for reasons of wealth or with an eye towards a comfortable establishment. I am happy to know that she will never marry me for my money; I must woo her and win her heart before she can consent with a clear conscience. Truthfully, I fear for the poor girl. Her uncle looked very down in the mouth when he told me of her answer. If it were up to him, I would be procuring a special license without delay. Fanny, for all her meekness, shows a strong character in refusing me. She cannot be pressured into doing what she feels to be wrong. I honour her for it!"

"*You* can honour her then," Mary said sourly. "As for myself, *I* cannot honour such a feather-headed lack of sense. Any rational woman would accept you for your wit and gentlemanlike manner, even if you didn't have a farthing. She is a right twit, she is."

"My dear, you are only angry with Fanny Price because the fellow she refused to marry is our Henry," Mrs Grant tried to dulcify Mary's ire. "If she were to come to you and say she could not marry a man she did not love, even though he were rich, you would be more likely to praise her than to think her a fool."

The firm set of Mary's jaw indicated otherwise, but she did not openly contradict her sister.

Henry could tell Mary was stewing, and made every attempt to tranquillise her feelings. "I am grateful that you, as always, are biased in my favour, but in this instance you need not be. My spirits are not lowered by her refusal. I am content to know she will only marry me for the most sincere love. I have been too hasty, too precipitate in asking for her hand. I must give her time to learn to love me. I must learn from the tortoise and the hare; slow and steady will win this race."

Mary breathed heavily through her nose, but said no more against Fanny. She knew there was little point in criticising a lover's inamorata to him; he would always find excuses for her. She was far from satisfied with Fanny's behaviour, but Henry was not someone in whom she could confide her scruples.

"Well, then," Mary said calmly, "what did Fanny say when she refused you? Was she civil and full of gratitude at least?"

Henry looked slightly uncomfortable. What he was to reveal was no credit to Fanny.

"I did not see Fanny herself," he said slowly. "Her discombobulation at the thought of rejecting my suit in person was too much for her. Sir Thomas explained that she was very distraught at the idea of seeing me this morning, so I ceased to ask it of her, of course. She will see me later this evening, in private, when she is more collected."

Mary's silence spoke volumes.

Mrs Grant excused Fanny as best she could be remarking, "Everyone knows she is exceedingly timid and shy. I am sure it was hard enough to tell you no when she had no idea you were serious; to have to decline an offer approved by her uncle would have her positively faint."

"I hope Sir Thomas was not too severe upon her," Henry worried. "He is not used to Fanny going against his wishes. *He* made it very plain he was delighted with the match. He was very sombre when he returned to me. Even his being disappointed would be frightening to Fanny; what if he were angry at her? I would not wish her to be hectored into a wedding."

And well she would deserve it if Sir Thomas lambasted her hide, Mary thought. *Silly, ungrateful, foolish girl.*

"Sir Thomas is too polite, too blamelessly and consistently well-mannered, to harangue his niece," Mrs Grant protested. "Only a brute would treat Fanny so ill, and Sir Thomas is the farthest thing from a brute imaginable. One need only look at how courteously he treats his wife, and how kindly he treats those dependent on him, to understand he has no cruelty in his nature, despite his sobriety of manner."

"You are right," Henry smiled at his elder sister. "I am seeing bugaboos where there are none. I need not worry that Sir Thomas will be harsh with Fanny."

Mary was moved to add, "*He* might not, but I pity Fanny when Mrs Norris finds out. It is only a matter of guessing whether the Chook will try to peck her to death for refusing Henry, or for the audacity of being preferred to Julia Bertram."

"When she is my wife, Fanny need never fear the ill nature of Mrs Norris again," Henry said firmly. "I shall put the Chook in her place if she dares squawk at *Mrs Crawford*. It's scandalous how she is allowed to treat Fanny."

"Since we are speaking of scandalous behaviour, I will ring for scandal *broth*," Mrs Grant offered laughingly. "Dr Grant will be home soon, and he will want luncheon. Some cold meat and hot tea will do us all good, and when Dr Grant is with us then Henry can tell us all the whole of what Sir Thomas said."

॥

After dinner, Henry once again walked to the Park, this time for a private moment with Fanny. Mary took the opportunity of his absence to vent her feelings to the Grants.

"I would have never thought Fanny would show such *unfeeling* and *selfish* behaviour," Mary fumed. "It makes me wonder if she is too perverse and wilful to make Henry a good wife."

"Mary, you are only angry for Henry's sake. You know Fanny Price is not wilful; she is as free from impertinent independence as any creature in the country. She can only be so firm because she believes herself to be morally just in her refusals. If she does not love Henry, she knows it would be very wrong to marry him," Mrs Grant reasoned.

"Well, I still think her *selfish*," Mary was adamant. "Think of how much good for her whole family that she is throwing away for her own sake. Henry is the favourite of the Admiral, and has already secured William Price's promotion. There is much more the Admiral could do for her brother in the future. Moreover, Fanny has *another* brother going to sea this year, and the Admiral could assist him as well. She supposedly loves her brother William with all her heart, yet she does not think of what would best for *him*. And what of those other siblings, who need help and preferment? Why should Sir Thomas bear the whole of the labour when Henry could help his new brothers and sisters so ably? What pleasure and happy relief her secure establishment would give Edmund and Sir Thomas! Does she not owe *them* something for all the care she has been given? And what is her sacrifice for the happiness of so many of those she claims to love? That she has to marry a rich, agreeable gentleman! Woe unto *her*. Is her heart so hard that she doesn't think she could *learn* to love Henry, if nothing else from the *gratitude* she should feel for his kindness to her and those she *professedly* holds so dear? Hers is a strange, selfish, *conceited* sort of love if she puts her own wishes above the welfare of her family, her friends, and all her relations."

Mrs Grant looked pained. "I will admit that when you lay it out in such a way, it does seem self-indulgent. But we must also understand that to marry Henry for those reasons would be, especially in the mind of a girl as principled as Fanny Price, mercenary and avaricious. There is *nothing*, so far as her principles are concerned, that could justify her wedding Henry without true affection. Would you really want Henry to marry a woman who would wed him simply for gain?"

"Of course I wouldn't!" Mary cried. "Yet I think that Fanny is being obstinate and foolish, because it would be so *easy* for her to come to love Henry. Is he not everything agreeable and charming? Would he not make her life, and the life of her siblings, so much better? I know I would be a good wife to a man who excited so much gratitude in *me*. I would love him *rationally*, which is better than romantic love because romantic love is ephemeral while rational love – a real rational love based on the content of a lover's character – is *enduring*."

"My dear, I must say that I agree with your sister," Dr Grant said to his wife. His sonorous voice lent an air of wisdom to his manner that Mary well liked when he concurred with her. "Miss Price shows herself to be uncongenial and thoughtless by her intransigent refusals. Morality and principle should not be used as a cudgel to beat Lady Fortune about the head. It would be one thing if the gel were planning on *not* being a good wife, but as long as she knows she will devote herself to Henry then she should think of her duty to *others* as well as her duty to her conscience."

Mrs Grant, soft-hearted as she was, continued to plead Fanny's case. "I cannot think *she* would see marrying without affection as a duty to others. I think she looks upon it as the most despicable acquisitiveness possible. To marry Henry without a material change of feelings would be, to her and in the opinions of many people, sordid and unscrupulous."

Mary shook her head. "I cannot agree, ma'am. It would only be sordid if she married Henry solely for her *own* pecuniary gains, or married him knowing that he was a vicious, ill-tempered fellow whom she could *never* love. This is not the case. She would be making an advantageous marriage for herself and all her dearest connections, and she would be marrying a man of good character."

"I am not saying that Fanny Price is *correct* in her assessment of the marriage's unethical nature," Mrs Grant explained. "I am just giving you my reasoned guess as to Fanny's feelings, and how *she* would feel about marrying Henry without love."

Dr Grant sighed. "I cannot say I would whole-heartedly rejoice in Henry's marriage to Miss Price, even if she loved him more than Juliet had ever loved Romeo."

Mary had not expected this. "Why not? She is clearly a sweet little thing, apart from her current stubborn self-indulgence. I know of no ill about her excepting her refusal of Henry."

"First, she is constitutionally weak," Dr Grant counted the reasons off on his fingers. "Henry is so hale himself that I am afraid he would find such a sickly wife irksome after a short time. Secondly, she speaks like a mouse in a cheese. She would do Henry no good among his friends in the ton. She could never be more than a *civil* hostess at best. Her excessive timidity would turn out to be an albatross around his neck. Thirdly, she is watery-headed. Henry is so sanguine and cheerful that her excessive weeping and trembling sorrows at *any* adversity, regardless of how small, would wear upon his nerves. He would be forevermore trying to cheer his cowering wife. Fourthly, she would be such a Mrs Princum Prancum that he could not be himself in his own home. He is a man of gamesome, Rabelaisian humour. He likes to frolic, and jest, and make puns at every turn. What could Fanny Price do for him, but teach him to be dour against his inclination? And to clinch it all, they have so few opinions and tastes in common that there would be no harmony. Oil and vinegar are good together on a sallet, but marriage must be a more substantial dish. For that you want cream, which must have undisturbed peace before it will rise."

"I now find myself wanting to defend his choice of Fanny, even though I am extremely vexed at her," Mary laughed at herself for her own contrariness. "I think that she would be such an adoring and humble little wife, so used to giving way on everything, that Henry would have nothing *but* peace. He might grow bored with her, but she would be in no way be a check upon his manner of living."

Dr Grant smiled at his sister-in-law. "I know I seem to be a croaker, foretelling doom at every turn, but my age and position as a parson has given me some understanding of the variety and vagaries of married life. Not everyone is as fortunate as I am in their choice of a wife, and the excessive misery of two people ill-united can hardly be overstated. However, if anyone could shake off such a mistake it would be Henry. His is an active mind, and he would be more likely to solve a problem than knuckle under to it."

"I would think that Henry would raise Fanny's spirits, and animate her," Mrs Grant postulated consolingly.

"Whether he would or not, it is pointless to talk sense to a young man in love. He'd only resent me for interfering. I shall keep my opinions among the three of us," Dr Grant shrugged.

"Well, I know some way to get relief from all this seriousness and lugubriosity," Mrs Grant announced. "My dear Dr Grant, will you read us something comic until our Henry returns home? It would cheer us all up immensely I believe."

"What would you have me read?" Dr Grant asked affably.

"If I may suggest something," Mary interjected, "I would recommend the book I received lately from London. It is a new comedic poem entitled *Tour of Dr Syntax in Search of the Picturesque* and I have found it amazingly humorous. It is a wonderful burlesque of the obsession some niminy-piminy people have for the picturesque."

Mary was convinced that for every one person, like Henry, who truly rhapsodised over the beauties of nature, there were a dozen who affected to adore any given panorama but were utterly devoid of taste or actual appreciation. *She* would not fly such false flags and pretend to love where she did not, and she despised people who did.

"That sounds perfect to *me*," Mrs Grant said. "Would it please you my dear?"

"If Mary will be so good as to fetch the book, I would be most happy to read it," Dr Grant declared.

Dr Grant was as good as his word, and all three inhabitants of
the parsonage found relief from any lingering gloom in the uninhibited
laughter elicited when the poem's hero was nagged by his vulgar wife,
fell into a lake trying to find the best angle to draw a ruined castle,
attempted to chivvy a herd of cows into charming groups of threes,
and angered a bull that chased him hither and yon, all in his pursuit
of the fabled picturesque. Thus, Henry returned home to hear the
sound of merriment pouring forth from the drawing-room.

"What's all this, then?" Henry asked with a smile. "I beg that
you share the amusement."

"First, you must share *your* news!" Mary cried. "I will extinguish
on the spot if you do not tell all."

Henry sat, and explained the reasons Fanny Price gave him for
refusing his suit. She had told him, that she did not love him, could
not love him, was sure she never should love him; that such a change
was quite impossible, that the subject was most painful to her, that
she must entreat him never to mention it again, to allow her to leave
him at once, and let it be considered as concluded for ever. And when
farther pressed, she had added, that in her opinion their dispositions
were so totally dissimilar, as to make mutual affection incompatible;
and that they were unfitted for each other by nature, education,
and habit.

While Fanny's reasoning raised her in Dr Grant's opinion, it
did nothing to discourage Henry in the slightest. He was in love, very
much in love; and it was a love which, operating on an active, sanguine
spirit, of more warmth than delicacy, made her affection appear of
greater consequence, because it was withheld, and determined him to
have the glory, as well as the felicity, of forcing her to love him.

He would not despair: he would not desist. He had every well-
grounded reason for solid attachment; he knew her to have all the
worth that could justify the warmest hopes of lasting happiness with
her; her conduct at this very time, by speaking the disinterestedness
and delicacy of her character (qualities which he believed most rare
indeed), was of a sort to heighten all his wishes, and confirm all his
resolutions. He knew not that he had a pre-engaged heart to attack.
Of *that* he had no suspicion. He considered her rather as one who
had never thought on the subject enough to be in danger; who had
been guarded by youth, a youth of mind as lovely as of person; whose
modesty had prevented her from understanding his attentions, and
who was still overpowered by the suddenness of addresses so wholly

unexpected, and the novelty of a situation which her fancy had never taken into account.

Must it not follow of course, that when he was understood, he should succeed?—he believed it fully and he assured the others that it was so.

Mary heard her brother with mixed feelings. She could admit that Fanny's reasons were rational and just; Henry *was* very different from Fanny in education, temper, and habit and Fanny was not ill-judging to think such difference might be too great to allow for marital happiness. Hadn't Mary thought something the same of herself and Edmund? Did it not take many weeks for her to resolve to take him even if he *were* a clergyman? What if Edmund had asked her for her hand in September? Would she have been able to say yes? Yet Mary could not see any *sufficient* reasons for Fanny's refusals. There were not obstacles of fortune or precedence, as Mary had faced with Edmund. For Fanny, all would be ease and advancement. Mary had to be in love with Edmund, because she was *lowering* herself in her choice of husband, and only love would make that justifiable or tolerable. Fanny would rise like a French hot air balloon if she married Henry. It was, In Mary's mind, as if Mary had decided to turn down a handsome, wealthy, agreeable duke for the trivial reasons that he preferred the country to London and she was not in love with him. To become a rich duchess Mary would *learn* to love both the countryside and her husband, and thought any other choice in the matter to be nonsensical, perhaps even imbecilic.

No, unlike Henry, Mary was still angry at Fanny Price and considered her friend pig-headed and overly nice at the expense of rational behaviour.

Chapter Thirty-Four

MARY AND HENRY were walking in Mansfield together, taking advantage of the newly dry weather to wander about the village a bit and go shopping. They first went to the principle, in fact the *only*, linen and woollen draper in order to make a purchase of more flannel. Mary had discovered the joy and wonder of connected flannel drawers and had resolved to never spend another cold day without them. Henry was in need, or at least felt himself in need, of new stockings, so they were on their way to the haberdasher's when, to their surprise and Mary's elation, they saw Edmund Bertram riding in the main street.

Edmund saw them almost at the same instance, and looked flustered. However, when Henry called to him and Mary curtsied, he dismounted and led his horse over to them. Henry shook hands with him in a hearty manner and told him it was very good to see him again.

"How glad I am to see you returned, Mr Bertram!" Mary gave him her hand to shake as well. "I was afraid that I would go to London without being able to bid you farewell. I shan't be returning to Mansfield for at least three or four months, and wanted to say my adieus to all my *particular* friends before I left."

Edmund blushed with delight when Mary called him her particular friend with such emphasis. "I am very glad to see you as well, Miss Crawford. You look very well, as ever." He hesitated for a moment and then plunged on. "I elected to stay with my friend Mr Owen and his family for a few days after being ordained, since Mr Owen's father is a rector as well, and I wished to ask his advice on a few matters."

Rather than appearing cold or vexed, Mary's dimples only deepened. "Well, don't tell Dr Grant; I am sure he prefers to be your source of advice. He considers all young clergymen twenty miles round to be his property, I do believe."

It was a weak jest at best, but Edmund laughed at it. "I shall never let him know I was inconstant in my advice seeking."

"All shall be well, then. Do you go to the Park sir?"

"Yes, yes I do. I have not yet been home. I must apologise for my travel-stained appearance," Edmund was acutely conscious of the mud that his horse's hooves had thrown upwards to spatter on his buckskins and boots.

"No need for that," Henry assured him. "You look like you've stepped from a catalogue. So dirty as these roads are, I would look much worse."

Edmund bowed his thanks.

"We must not keep you from Sir Thomas and Lady Bertram," Mary declared. "I know that they and Miss Price have missed you very much. Fanny and I talked of it."

Flushing again at the thought of Miss Crawford and Fanny discussing how much they (for the "they" was very much implied) missed him, Edmund replied, "I have missed everyone at Mansfield as well. It is good to be home."

"Then next time you must shorten your visit to Mr Owens, to ensure that so much missing you won't occur," Mary was as lively as ever. "Mansfield cannot seem to do without you."

Edmund blushed harder, bowed again, shook hands with both Crawfords once more, and took his leave of them.

"Mary," her brother said sternly, once Edmund was out of earshot, "you've laid a spell on that poor fellow. He looked absolutely betwattled when he saw you. I demand that you surrender your potion-making ingredients immediately."

"Are you saying I cannot captivate a man without black magic?" Mary quizzed him in return.

"To make such a dignified gentleman as Edmund Bertram act like a great booby just because you smiled at him requires, at minimum, a sacrificial goat."

"Nonsense. A black cockerel and a toad will suffice."

"Aha! *That's* where out sister's prize cockerel went! Blaming a fox was merely a cover for your dark arts."

"That cockerel was a plain brown one; I had no need of him. My grimoire is *very* specific about needing a black cockerel for the sacrifice, if you want to turn dignified parsons into cupid-struck boobies."

"Infamous!" Henry put on an exaggerated expression of horror. "I shall find your familiar and put an end to your evil larks!"

"I have outwitted you. I have made my familiar a shapely Frenchwoman of nineteen. You'll never be able to do anything to my familiar but be compelled to make her like you." Mary smirked.

"That's all *you* know," Henry smiled. "I am immune to the charms of all other women; my heart belongs wholly to Fanny Price. She has utterly bewitched me."

"I am still not in charity with Fanny," Mary scowled. "She makes me wish to use Billingsgate language."

"Now, Mary," Henry coaxed, "you must not be cross with Fanny. She is doing the morally upright thing in refusing me. When she accepts me I will know it is because I have won a heart worth the effort."

Mary looked at her brother thoughtfully. "And if *I* could propose to a man, and he should refuse me, how would you feel about it?"

"I would beat him about the ears with my cane, call him out as a blackguard, and abuse him from pole to pole as the veriest ignoramus."

"Then you must allow me to be very angry with Fanny Price." Mary gave a small flounce as she said it, causing her brother to laugh.

"Oh, Mary! How glad I am that you are my sister!"

"That is a remarkable sign of good taste on your part," Mary said complacently, and preceded him into the haberdasher's shop.

॥

The next morning, quite as Mary had expected, Edmund Bertram paid a call on the parsonage. Only she and Mrs Grant were at home, so Edmund had only female faces to greet him in the drawing-room. He looked very conscious; he had obviously been informed of Henry's proposal to his cousin, but he was too well-bred to mention it. Mary, with more permissible rights to the topic, had no such hesitation.

"I am very angry with your cousin," Mary launched into the subject as soon as politeness would allow after his arrival. "Fanny has vexed me mightily by refusing my brother. I will and must abuse her dreadfully to you."

Mrs Grant laughed at her sister. "My word, Mary! You've broached the matter speedily!"

"Your affection for your brother could hardly allow you to feel less," Edmund smiled at Mary, confident that her playful tone indicated that she would attempt no real abuse about Fanny.

"Her refusal is inexplicable," Mary asserted. "Henry is one of the most sought after men in London. Oh! If you knew how many women – lovely and accomplished women – had set their caps for him you would be astounded. If he were a deer he would be a twelve point buck that everyone wished to bag."

Edmund laughed at this description of Mr Crawford, and Mrs Grant lovingly scolded her for comparing Henry to a game animal. However, it was an apt metaphor. Women positively stalked Henry in ballrooms, and laid out metaphorical salt-licks to entice him closer. No highland stag was as assiduously hunted by men as Henry Crawford was pursued by women.

"At least Henry has chosen well," Mary continued. "Fanny is all that I would choose for my brother. She is modest, sensible, kind, obliging, and amiable. Neither her morals nor her principles could ever be questioned and her sweetness of disposition is astounding. She even shares Henry's taste in her admiration for nature. No, my brother could not do better, but Fanny doesn't seem to realise that *she* could not do better. Henry is all that is pleasing in a gentleman, and has the means and desire to treat her as well as even *she* deserves. He is as pleasing in person as he is in address. He is not a Turk or a twiddle poop or fop or in any way objectionable. He has never been a Bond Street lounger; he has too much taste and intelligence to waste his life as a fribble. He is a man of information, education, and discernment. I cannot understand. Pray, tell me Mr Bertram; do you know why Fanny refuses my brother?"

Edmund's brow creased. "I have given the matter no little attention, and I think I have enough knowledge of my cousin's character to speculate upon her thoughts. Fanny is, of all human creatures, the one over whom habit has most power, and novelty least: and that the very circumstance of the novelty of Crawford's addresses was against him. Their being so new and so recent was all in their disfavour; she can tolerate nothing that she is not used to. Fanny must have time to adjust to the *idea* of Crawford's regard. Although he has been paying her his addresses, she did not see them as a sign of his growing affection and interest. That would be too unlike the humble modesty of my cousin. Thus, his declaration came upon her with a Scarborough warning, like lightning from a clear blue sky. She is very nervous and timid, and the ardour of a man like Crawford's, which is sanguine and direct, would have spooked her even if she *had* had a previous inkling of its existence. She is more likely to be agitated than animated by a declaration of love.

Mary frowned. "I know Fanny is sensitive and easily overwrought, but surely she isn't such a Tender Parnell as all *that*. Is she really so delicate that she can, as they say, break her finger in a posset?"

"I assure you that Fanny *is* as timorous as that," Edmund said. "She is so exceedingly bashful that she cannot bear too much attention, and even the *thought* of your brother's ardent love overwhelms her. A mastiff may only wish to play with a rabbit and mean it no harm, but the rabbit will still tremble from fear when the mastiff seeks it out."

"Poor Henry," Mary smiled. "First compared to a deer, and now to a dog. Mrs Grant, compare him to a pig and we'll have done."

"Henry is too nice to be a pig," Mrs Grant smiled in return. "If I were to compare him to any animal it would be the otter. He is as handsome and playful and quick as the best of those creatures."

"Yes, and he eats fish," Mary gave a quiet laugh, "so he is clearly an otter. As his sisters, we must be otters as well. It is a positive romp of otters within the parsonage. How Dr Grant bears it must be left to speculation."

"As long as I do not *badger* him, he is content," Mrs Grant looked pleased with herself.

"Egad!" Mary cried. "My sister is now saying puns! Henry has entirely corrupted her. Now I know why Fanny will not marry him; her family fears she will break out in the lowest form of wit from his contagion."

"She is safe enough, I think. Fanny has a plethora of admirable qualities, but lively witticisms are not her forte," Edmund assured Mary in good fun.

"Ah, then there must be some other reason Henry cannot entice her to join him in his holt. Does she dislike swimming, sir? Is that why she cannot give her hand to an otter?" Mary quipped.

"I confess that Fanny is the farthest thing from a mischievous, playful otter as I can conceive of," Edmund admitted. "However, I cannot think of the animal she does remind me of; I am not given to flights of fancy."

"If I can say, without seeming impertinent," Mrs Grant interjected, "what animal Miss Price reminds me of, it would be a doe. They are very shy, yet lovely and graceful."

"Henry is in luck then, since he's a stag. With such compatibility between them, I will urge him to persevere with his courtship in the hope of his being loved in time, and of having his addresses most kindly received at the end of about ten years' happy marriage," Mary declared, causing both Edmund and Mrs Grant to laugh.

"For myself, I am better satisfied now that I can understand the basis of Miss Price's fears and reluctance to accept Henry," Mrs Grant said, when her chuckles had abated. "She only needs a little time to adjust to the concept of becoming his wife."

Mary shook her head. "I am not quite as satisfied, ma'am. I do not see why a whole night's pondering of Henry's perfections should not induce Fanny to accept him, let alone three days. It has been above a week since I have seen Fanny, and although I miss her company I cannot say that it hasn't been for the best. I am very angry and will have no choice but to scold her dreadfully when next we are together. Be advised, Mr Bertram, that I might harangue your cousin into a faint, so you must stand ready with smelling salts."

Edmund nodded solemnly. "Yes, I can certainly see you coming down on poor Fanny with a terrible wrath. I fear for her greatly."

"Tell her that if she will prove herself to be in her senses by her different conduct regarding Henry, then we shall not need to rebuke her," Mrs Grant added. "It would be best for her if she did not have to face such termagant as Mary and myself."

The party had to change topic shortly thereafter, due to the entrance of Crawford and Dr Grant, and after a half hour's further visit, Edmund excused himself and returned to the Park.

ıı

Shortly after Edmund left, Mary dragooned her brother into a walk among the shrubberies. She wanted to tell him everything Edmund had revealed about Fanny's strange fear of novelty in private, so he could vent whatever concerns he felt without restraint or hesitation. It did not take long for Mary to retell everything Henry, to enlighten him as much as possible as to the futility of hoping for an *early* change in Fanny's inclinations. Fanny would need time, and not a short amount of it, to acclimate herself to his love and consider his proposals with the justice they deserved.

Henry walked in thoughtful silence beside Mary for several minutes, reflecting on this new and rather unwelcome information. Finally, he spoke.

"It is not just the novelty of my addresses that make her unwilling to engage herself to me, I'm afraid," He told his sister reluctantly. "She also thinks me unsteady—easily swayed by the whim of the moment—easily tempted—easily put aside. With such an opinion, no wonder that she refuses me. She does not trust that my love will endure beyond the life of a mayfly. That, too, will need time to rectify. She must see by my constancy that I am not the Smithfield bargain and sybarite she thinks me."

"You are no Smithfield bargain, and she would be lucky to marry you, but your insistence that you are not a sybarite stretches belief. Draw it mild, won't you?" Mary's mouth quirked with amusement at her brother's sudden reformation.

Henry bestowed a narrowed gaze on his sister. "Fine. I am *no longer* the sybarite she thinks me."

Mary patted his arm. "If you have changed, then we must give Fanny the benefit of the doubt and assume that *she* can change as well. She can overcome her timorous nature and concerns regarding your constancy if given enough time."

Henry sighed. "Yes, I know what I must do. My conduct shall speak for me—absence, distance, time shall speak for me.—*They* shall prove, that as far as she can be deserved by any body, I do deserve her. My constancy shall answer for me. This I can do. Yet I am disheartened at the long months such a process will take. I am ready to perform any task to win her hand, but I would prefer the tasks not be such *protracted* ones."

"Well other than dipping her in the River Shannon, which is said to be the instant cure for bashfulness, I do not see what else can be done; hard as it may be," Mary sympathised.

Henry smiled. "I shall take her to Ireland for our honeymoon, then. We'll see if the River Shannon can act upon such a severe affliction of shyness."

"I expect to see the water boil and hiss," Mary nodded sagely.

The siblings rambled on, with Henry making every effort to not talk incessantly about Fanny Price. Sometimes he would halt their progress so that he could point out birds squabbling with one another in the trees and bushes, and share some ornithology that Mary didn't care about in the least. She did nod dutifully and feign a decent interest, though. Henry's naturalism was something she had learned long ago to pretend to enjoy for his sake.

"Fanny loves flora and fauna and nature as much as you do," Mary commented. "You will be completely compatible in *that* area at least. I would beg your pardon for bringing up Fanny again, but I think you are not reluctant to discuss her further. Tell me if I am I wrong and I shall stopper it instantly."

"No, you are right — as usual," Henry gave his sister's hand an affectionate squeeze. "She is consuming much of my brainpower. I have been wondering what I should do next, in regards to the strange, standoffish courtship I must conduct."

"I think it would behove us to be away as soon as possible," Mary replied. "Absence is your friend in this case. It will give Fanny time to contemplate and adjust, and to tenderly reflect on your love and all that you have done for William Price. You continuing to love her when not actually in her presence will prove your steadfastness and assure her that there is no more idle flirtation in your character. I fear you did yourself a good deal of harm this summer, when you trifled with Maria Bertram; you must sweep that mess away and begin anew."

Henry grimaced. "You are right. My idle flirtation with Maria Bertram has made her cousin think much less of me. I should have refrained from any such teasing intrigue. But how was I to guess that I would fall in love with Fanny, or that she would hold such a grudge against me for her cousin's sake? I am used to women glorying in their triumphs over their own sex in the captivation of men. Such unearned, undeserved loyalty to her cousin I could not have foreseen."

"I must agree with you there," Mary concurred. "The careless, negligent, and cold way her cousins have treated her would have inspired any other woman to accept you just for the satisfaction of rubbing the conquest into their faces. Instead, Fanny feels for them so acutely she wishes to punish *you* for the whole of the misconduct. I think she is *wrong* to blame you for her cousin's inconstancy towards Mr Rushworth, but there is no denying that she holds Maria Bertram's folly against you. Fanny is a paragon; I have never met anyone with her purity of heart."

"Then you see why I must have her," Henry grinned. "I would have the only paragon as a wife in all of Great Britain. I could put her in the zoo at the Royal Exchange and charge people to look at her as they would a unicorn or dragon, should I ever need ready money."

Mary laughed. "More likely the lion and unicorn in an English zoo." She sang:

The lion and the unicorn
Were fighting for the crown
The lion beat the unicorn
All around the town.
Some gave them white bread,
And some gave them brown;
Some gave them plum cake
and drummed them out of town

"Has your ability to recall poetry fallen so low that you speak in nursery rhymes now?" Henry mocked her lovingly. "You have nothing better?"

Mary gave him a side eye. "There is seldom any poetry involving unicorns outside the ones that are written for children. I think there is a dragon in Beowulf, but I draw the line at learning ancient Anglo-Saxon poetry by rote."

"Well then, what of the lion? Does the king of beasts not get immortalised in verse?"

"Many times, but I can only remember that somewhere in one of Phillip Sydney's sonnets was a line how 'I thus with this young lion played'. I shall write Lord Byron directly and beg him to include lions in some of his works, and memorise *them*."

"An elegant solution," Henry said pedantically. "However, if he could see fit to put unicorns, dragons, and lions in a poem, that would serve our purpose better."

"True, true," Mary agreed solemnly.

"In all seriousness, how do you remember such a vast quantity of poetry that you can summon it from your mind at a moment's notice?"

Mary shrugged one shoulder. "I don't really understand it myself. All that I can tell you is that when it comes to written words – especially poetic words – my brain is as sticky as spilt honey on a table. Ask me what those birds you were talking about were, and the inside of my skull is as empty as a beggar's pocket."

"I shall have to put all my information regarding birds into verse, then, if I wish you to be properly instructed in avian matters," Henry teased.

Mary put her hand into the crook of her brother's elbow, and gave him a sideways embrace. They walked together without speaking, lost in their own thoughts, for at least two turns around the shrubberies before Henry reintroduced the inhabitants of Mansfield Park.

"It may be best for me leave the country, but what of you? Are you so eager to leave Bertram?"

Mary affected nonchalance. "London is not so far away. Let him come there to court me if he chooses." She was slightly peeved that Edmund had not yet taken an opportunity to ask for her hand. Now that she had determined to accept him, she would like the matter settled. His shilly-shallying was trying on her nerves.

Henry gave his sister a knowing look. "Expected him to ask you by now, did you?"

"Pish-tosh," she wrinkled her nose at her brother. "I expected no such thing. A woman *never* expects an offer until it is made."

Henry made a poor effort to hide his smile. "Ah, I stand corrected. Shall we leave for London the day after tomorrow then?"

"That sounds fine. I will write Mrs Fraser a line or two tomorrow, to let her I am finally on my way. She has been expecting me to come any day for the last fortnight I believe."

"Are you still of mixed feelings about the visit?"

Mary hesitated, unsure herself how she felt. "It is odd. I want to go to London very much, but I shall miss so many people *here*. What I most earnestly desire is to transport the inhabitants of Mansfield whom I esteem to London. When you and Fanny have a house in town, I shall be most delighted to come and stay with you."

"You are always welcome," Henry promised. "Even when you exchange your name for another, you are always welcome. I daresay your husband would be glad to come with you, and be spared the expense of a letting a place."

"So, you expect me to marry a man who cannot afford a decent town house, then?" Mary challenged.

"I *expect* nothing of the sort," Henry insisted dramatically. "I do, however, *suspect* that you might receive an offer you would accept from a man's whose income would be sufficient to keep a carriage, but not to have a large house in a fashionable part of Town. And, *supposing* the fellow is someone who would get along well with myself, and was *perhaps* a beloved relative of my wife, it would make infinite sense to give you a standing invitation to my future home. I'll make sure to get a home with a large nursery, so all the little cousins can romp about in it, and my daughters and my nieces can come out at a ball in their own home."

"Dearest Henry," Mary's bright eyes were full of love, "you truly are the best of brothers. Of all the gifts fate has given me, you are the one I treasure the most."

"No need to get soppy," He cleared his throat.

"I shall be as soppy as I wish," Mary raised her chin. "It is an infamous fraud against me as a woman, that I should be denied the right of sop."

"Fine then, sop all you like," Henry agreed, "but I draw the line at sophistry."

"One day," Mary pursed her lips in pretend disgust, "a day far, far, *far* in the future, I may forgive you for that pun."

Chapter Thirty-Five

MARY WAS DETERMINED that she should see Fanny at least once before leaving for London, and the next day she set out for Mansfield Park. Mary, with her open temper and unreserved nature, had no idea how much the idea of her visit was agitating Fanny Price. She was wholly unaware of the seething, putrid resentment Fanny felt toward her, of Fanny's secret attachment for Edmund, and how little Miss Price was really her friend. Mary was also completely unaware of how much the idea of a 'scolding' was frightening to Fanny, and that Fanny quite dreaded seeing her alone.

Fanny was in the breakfast-room, with her aunt, when Miss Crawford did come; and the first misery over, and Miss Crawford looking and speaking with much less particularity of expression than she had anticipated, Fanny began to hope there would be nothing worse to be endured than a half-hour of moderate agitation. But here she hoped too much, Miss Crawford was not the slave of opportunity. She was determined to see Fanny alone, and therefore said to her tolerably soon, in a low voice, "I must speak to you for a few minutes somewhere;" words that Fanny felt all over her, in all her pulses, and all her nerves. Denial was impossible. Her habits of ready submission, on the contrary, made her almost instantly rise and lead the way out of the room. Miss Crawford was not to be resisted.

They were no sooner in the hall than all restraint of countenance was over on Miss Crawford's side. She immediately shook her head at Fanny with arch, yet affectionate reproach, and taking her hand, seemed hardly able to help beginning directly. She said nothing, however, but, "Sad, sad girl! I do not know when I shall have done scolding you," and had discretion enough to reserve the rest till they might be secure of having four walls to themselves. Mary could see Fanny trembling and was moved to pity, even as she was exasperated by the silly girl's refusal of a man as well-bred and eligible as her brother.

Their entry into Fanny's small sitting area further softened Mary's feelings toward the cowering Miss Price by the strong effect on her mind which the finding herself in the east room again produced.

"Ha!" she cried, with instant animation, "am I here again? The east room. Once only was I in this room before!"—and after stopping to look about her, and seemingly to retrace all that had then passed, she added, "Once only before. Do you remember it? I came to rehearse. Your cousin came too; and we had a rehearsal. You were our audience and prompter. A delightful rehearsal. I shall never forget it. Here we were, just in this part of the room; here was your cousin, here was I, here were the chairs.—Oh! why will such things ever pass away?"

Mary wanted no answer. Her mind was entirely self-engrossed. She was in a reverie of sweet remembrances. The looks of consciousness that Edmund had given her when speaking of love! The warmth – no, the *heat* – in his eyes when she spoke to him of that tender emotion! It was everything elevating.

"The scene we were rehearsing was so very remarkable! The subject of it so very—very—what shall I say? He was to be describing and recommending matrimony to me. I think I see him now, trying to be as demure and composed as Anhalt ought, through the two long speeches. 'When two sympathetic hearts meet in the marriage state, matrimony may be called a happy life.' I suppose no time can ever wear out the impression I have of his looks and voice, as he said those words. It was curious, very curious, that we should have such a scene to play! If I had the power of recalling any one week of my existence, it should be that week, that acting week. Say what you would, Fanny, it should be *that*; for I never knew such exquisite happiness in any other."

Mary sighed with her reverie at Edmund's proofs of love. "His sturdy spirit to bend as it did! Oh! it was sweet beyond expression. But alas! very evening destroyed it all. That very evening brought your most unwelcome uncle. Poor Sir Thomas, who was glad to see you? Yet, Fanny, do not imagine I would now speak disrespectfully of Sir Thomas, though I certainly did hate him for many a week. No, I do him justice now. He is just what the head of such a family should be. Nay, in sober sadness, I believe I now love you all."

And having said so, with a degree of tenderness and consciousness which Fanny had never seen in her before, and now thought only too becoming, she turned away for a moment to recover herself. Mary had been closer to tears in her time at Mansfield than she had in the decade before it. How strange that love could make such a change in one's abilities to control one's emotions!

"I have had a little fit since I came into this room, as you may perceive," said she presently, with a playful smile, "but it is over now; so let us sit down and be comfortable; for as to scolding you, Fanny, which I came fully intending to do, I have not the heart for it when it comes to the point." And embracing her very affectionately,—"Good, gentle Fanny! when I think of this being the last time of seeing you; for I do not know how long—I feel it quite impossible to do anything but love you."

Fanny was affected. She had not foreseen anything of this, and her feelings could seldom withstand the melancholy influence of the word "last." She cried as if she had loved Miss Crawford more than she possibly could; and Miss Crawford, yet farther softened by the sight of such emotion, hung about her with fondness, and said, "I hate to leave you. I shall see no one half so amiable where I am going. Who says we shall not be sisters? I know we shall. I feel that we are born to be connected; and those tears convince me that you feel it too, dear Fanny."

Mary was wrong, of course. Fanny's tears were the product of empty sentimentality regarding separations. Fanny, in spite of her weeping, could not wait to see the back of the friend who loved her and wanted her to be Henry's wife despite of Fanny's poverty and low paternal connections. All of Mary's true, disinterested, and unworldly feelings of friendship toward Fanny were thrown away on a woman who could *truly* love no one who wasn't related to her. Everything that Mary took as proof of Fanny's affection for her was false coin, the hollow noise of a brass farthing falling to the floor.

Fanny roused herself, and replying only in part, said, "But you are only going from one set of friends to another. You are going to a very particular friend."

"Yes, very true. Mrs Fraser has been my intimate friend for years. But I have not the least inclination to go near her." Mary shook her head, bemused by her feelings of distance from one to whom she had once been as close as a sister. "I can think only of the friends I am leaving; my excellent sister, yourself, and the Bertrams in general. You have all so much more *heart* among you, than one finds in the world at large. You all give me a feeling of being able to trust and confide in you; which in common intercourse, one knows nothing of. I wish I had settled with Mrs Fraser not to go to her till after Easter, a much better time for the visit—but now I cannot put her off. And when I have done with her, I must go to her sister, Lady Stornoway, because *she* was rather my most particular friend of the two; but I have not cared much for *her* these three years."

After this speech the two girls sat many minutes silent, each thoughtful; Fanny meditating on the different sorts of friendship in the world, Mary on something of less philosophic tendency. Sincerity in friendships between the women of the ton was more remarkable in its appearance than otherwise. Her experience was not novel; it was the closeness of her friendships at Mansfield that were surprising to her. Even good friendship, however, paled to the warmth romantic love. Edmund filled Mary's thoughts.

"How perfectly I remember my resolving to look for you up stairs; and setting off to find my way to the east room, without having an idea whereabouts it was! How well I remember what I was thinking of as I came along; and my looking in and seeing you here, sitting at this table at work; and then your cousin's astonishment when he opened the door at seeing me here! To be sure, your uncle's returning that very evening! There never was anything quite like it."

Another short fit of abstraction followed. Then she remembered her purpose. Shaking off her preoccupation with Edmund, she thus attacked her companion.

"Why, Fanny, you are absolutely in a reverie! Thinking, I hope, of one who is always thinking of you. Oh! that I could transport you for a short time into our circle in town, that you might understand how your power over Henry is thought of there! Oh! the envyings and heart-burnings of dozens and dozens! the wonder, the incredulity that will be felt at hearing what you have done! For as to secrecy, Henry is quite the hero of an old romance, and glories in his chains. You should come to London, to know how to estimate your conquest."

Thinking of how the ton would react to the news of Henry's engagement amused her further. What wouldn't they say!

"If you were to see how he is courted, and how I am courted for his sake! Now I am well aware, that I shall not be half so welcome to Mrs. Fraser in consequence of his situation with you. When she comes to know the truth, she will very likely wish me in Northamptonshire again; for there is a daughter of Mr. Fraser by a first wife, whom she is wild to get married, and wants Henry to take. Oh! she has been trying for him to such a degree!

Mary looked at Fanny fondly. "Innocent and quiet as you sit here, you cannot have an idea of the *sensation* that you will be occasioning, of the curiosity there will be to see you, of the endless questions I shall have to answer! Poor Margaret Fraser will be at me for ever about your eyes and your teeth, and how you do your hair, and who makes your shoes. I wish Margaret were married, for my poor friend's sake, for I look upon the Frasers to be about as unhappy as most other married people. And yet it was a most desirable match for Janet at the time. We were all delighted. She could not do otherwise than accept him, for he was rich, and she had nothing; but he turns out ill-tempered and exigeant, and wants a young woman, a beautiful young woman of five-and-twenty, to be as steady as himself. And my friend does not manage him well; she does not seem to know how to make the best of it. There is a spirit of irritation, which, to say nothing worse, is certainly very ill-bred."

Sighing, Mary took Fanny's hand and confided, "In their house I shall call to mind the conjugal manners of Mansfield Parsonage with respect. Even Dr Grant does shew a thorough confidence in my sister, and a certain consideration for her judgement, which makes one feel there *is* attachment; but of that, I shall see nothing with the Frasers. I shall be at Mansfield for ever, Fanny. My own sister as a wife, Sir Thomas Bertram as a husband, are my standards of perfection."

Releasing Fanny's hand, Mary rose to pace the room. "Poor Janet has been sadly taken in; and yet there was nothing improper on her side; she did not run into the match inconsiderately, there was no want of foresight. She took three days to consider of his proposals; and during those three days asked the advice of every body connected with her whose opinion was worth having; and especially applied to my late dear aunt, whose knowledge of the world made her judgement very generally and deservedly looked up to by all the young people of her acquaintance; and she was decidedly in favour of Mr Fraser. This seems as if nothing were a security for matrimonial comfort!" Mary shook her head resignedly.

"I have not so much to say for my friend Flora," continued Mary, "who jilted a very nice young man in the Blues, for the sake of that horrid Lord Stornaway, who has about as much sense, Fanny, as Mr Rushworth, but much worse looking, and with a blackguard character. I *had* my doubts at the time about her being right, for he has not even the air of a gentleman, and now, I am sure, she was wrong." Mary frowned at the remembrance of her friend's ill-bred and reckless behaviour, when was struck by another thought.

"By the bye, Flora Ross was dying for Henry the first winter she came out. But were I to attempt to tell you of all the women whom I have known to be in love with him, I should never have done. It is you only, you, insensible Fanny, who can think of him with any thing like indifference. But are you so insensible as you profess yourself? No, no, I see you are not."

There was, indeed, so deep a blush over Fanny's face at that moment, as might warrant strong suspicion in a predisposed mind and Mary's mind was certainly predisposed.

"Excellent creature! I will not tease you," She smiled kindly at Fanny. "Every thing shall take its course. But dear Fanny, you must allow that you were not so absolutely unprepared to have the question asked as your cousin fancies. It is not possible, but that you must have had some thoughts on the subject, some surmises as to what might be. You must have seen that he was trying to please you, by every attention in his power. Was not he devoted to you at the ball? And then before the ball, the necklace! Oh! you received it just as it was meant. You were as conscious as heart could desire. I remember it perfectly."

"Do you mean then that your brother knew of the necklace beforehand? Oh! Miss Crawford, *that* was not fair."

Mary laughed at Fanny's innocent confusion. What a sweet girl she was! "Knew of it! It was his own doing entirely, his own thought. I am ashamed to say, that it had never entered my head; but I was delighted to act on his proposal, for both your sakes."

"I will not say," replied Fanny, "that I was not half afraid at the time, of its being so; for there was something in your look that frightened me—but not at first—I was as unsuspicious of it at first!— indeed, indeed I was. It is as true as that I sit here. And had I had an idea of it, nothing should have induced me to accept the necklace. As to your brother's behaviour, certainly I was sensible of a particularity, I had been sensible of it some little time, perhaps two or three weeks; but then I considered it as meaning nothing, I put it down as simply being his way, and was as far from supposing as from wishing him to have any serious thoughts of me. I had not, Miss Crawford, been an inattentive observer of what was passing between him and some part of this family in the summer and autumn. I was quiet, but I was not blind. I could not but see that Mr Crawford allowed himself in gallantries which did mean nothing."

"Ah! I cannot deny it." Mary pressed Fanny's hand in agreement. "He has now and then been a sad flirt, and cared very little for the havoc he might be making in young ladies' affections. I have often scolded him for it, but it is his only fault; and there is this to be said, that very few young ladies have any affections worth caring for. And then, Fanny, the glory of fixing one who has been shot at by so many; of having it in one's power to pay off the debts of one's sex! Oh, I am sure it is not in woman's nature to refuse such a triumph."

Fanny shook her head. "I cannot think well of a man who sports with any woman's feelings; and there may often be a great deal more suffered than a stander-by can judge of."

"I do not defend him," Mary declared. "I leave him entirely to your mercy; and when he has got you at Everingham, I do not care how much you lecture him. But this I will say, that his fault, the liking to make girls a little in love with him, is not half so dangerous to a wife's happiness, as a tendency to fall in love himself, which he has never been addicted to. And I do seriously and truly believe that he is attached to you in a way that he never was to any woman before; that he loves you with all his heart, and will love you as nearly for ever as possible. If any man ever loved a woman for ever, I think Henry will do as much for you."

Fanny could not avoid a faint smile, but had nothing to say.

"I cannot imagine Henry ever to have been happier," continued Mary, presently, "than when he had succeeded in getting your brother's commission."

She had made a sure push at Fanny's feelings here, as she well knew.

"Oh! yes. How very, very kind of him!"

"I know he must have exerted himself very much, for I know the parties he had to move. The Admiral hates trouble, and scorns asking favours; and there are so many young men's claims to be attended to in the same way, that a friendship and energy, not very determined, is easily put by. What a happy creature William must be! I wish we could see him." Mary was not speaking puffery; she did regard the hearty young sailor with pointed fondness for his open temper and active mind, so like her own.

Fanny sat thinking deeply of Mr Crawford's kindness to William till Mary, who had been first watching her complacently, and then musing on something else, suddenly called her attention, by saying, "I should like to sit talking with you here all day, but we must not forget the ladies below, and so good bye, my dear, my amiable, my excellent Fanny, for though we shall nominally part in the breakfast parlour, I must take leave of you here. And I do take leave, longing for a happy re-union, and trusting, that when we meet again, it will be under circumstances which may open our hearts to each other without any remnant or shadow of reserve."

A very, very kind embrace, and some agitation of manner, accompanied these words. At that moment Mary Crawford loved Fanny as much as any sister. To see Henry and Fanny united was her prime object, and if she could likewise unite with Edmund then she would have every earthly happiness.

"I shall see your cousin in town soon; he talks of being there tolerably soon; and Sir Thomas, I dare say, in the course of the spring; and your eldest cousin and the Rushworths and Julia I am sure of meeting again and again, and all but you. I have two favours to ask, Fanny; one is your correspondence. You must write to me. And the other, that you will often call on Mrs Grant and make her amends for my being gone."

Fanny promised faithfully to write, and when Mary left the East Room she felt nothing but regard and affection for Fanny Price, whom she hoped to have as a sister one day. There was no inkling on her side that Fanny would have rather *not* been her correspondent, and that Fanny had agreed to writer her more from a weakness in her own character than anything else. Fanny did not know how to civilly decline Mary's request, and was too pusillanimous to coldly rebuff it. Their entire so-called friendship was the result of Fanny's powerlessness to make her true feelings known, and Fanny's inability to maintain constancy of emotion when directly faced with kindness. In contrast, Mary thought of their friendship as the natural outpouring of Fanny's tenderness and Mary's own affection for her.

It was with sincere regret that Mary was leaving Fanny, whom she considered a confidant and well-wisher. Mary's loyalty to her intimates, which endured long after the heart-warming effects of true camaraderie was over, made her very careful in whom she bestowed the title of friend, but she had given that appellation unhesitatingly to Fanny Price. Who could not be moved to offer friendship to such a diffident, demure, and downtrodden girl, especially one with such a devoted heart?

In Fanny, Mary felt she had once again found the kind of deeply rooted affection she had felt toward Janet and Flora when they had befriended her at boarding school. They, as upperclassmen, had taken Mary under their wing and guidance, and in exchange Mary had become their steadfast friend. Time had changed them all so much that Mary no longer felt as close to them as she once had, but gratitude and remembrance of what she had once felt toward them kept Mary by their side regardless of the emotional distance in her heart. Mary had no such distance with Fanny. She had completely and candidly opened her heart to Miss Price, whose quiet attention Mary had misread as agreement and affection, rather than the silent condemnation it actually was.

||

In the evening there was another parting. Henry Crawford came and sat some time with the inhabitants of the Park; and Fanny's spirits not being previously in the strongest state, her heart was softened for a while towards him—because he really seemed to feel.—Quite unlike his usual self, he scarcely said any thing. He was evidently oppressed, and Fanny must grieve for him, though hoping she might never see him again till he were the husband of some other woman.

When it came to the moment of parting, he would take her hand, he would not be denied it; he said nothing, however, or nothing that she heard, and when he had left the room, she was better pleased that such a token of friendship had passed.

On the morrow the Crawfords were gone.

||

The trip *to* London was not the pleasant journey that the trip *from* London had been just six months before. There was no open barouche with pleasant, sunny weather; there was instead a closed coach and a cold, sullen drizzle. The bare trees and grey sky reflected the mood inside the vehicle. Mary and Henry were both sadly out of spirits, and miles would pass with no sound other than the rattle of the carriage wheels.

Henry sat mute, dwelling on the length of time it would take to prove his constancy to Fanny. He had expected to need to be active, to press his suit with all that charm and manner could accomplish. In lieu of such happy activity, he had to be patient, sombre, and calm. This was so alien to his temper that he felt it to be a sore trial, and further proof of his love for Fanny that he was willing to endure it.

Having never been denied something he really wanted ever before, he felt rather sorry for himself. Each lurch of the carriage on the rutted winter roads seemed to him to be yet another way he was being buffeted by cruel circumstance.

Mary huddled within her witzchoura, physically warm enough but holding a bleak chill within her. Why had Edmund not proposed? She had given him every encouragement. She had made every sacrifice and compromise. Still, he dithered. Had she misjudged him? Was his seeming love an *illusion* of depth, like the painted backdrop of the stage? It hurt her, and under her hurt came a bubbling anger at his dilly-dallying. He was being selfish, thoughtless, and uncaring by making her wait and doubt him. She began to wonder if she *would* accept him after all, considering his lack of ardour. What if she made the same mistake as her aunt, and married a fortune hunter who didn't love her in the slightest? How could Edmund actually love her, and still let her go to London without a positive engagement? It would serve him right if she met someone else. Someone richer and more congenial, with a *warm* attachment for her.

And so the carriage bumped along, bearing its discontented passengers toward the bright hubbub and social flurry of London.

Chapter Thirty-Six

THE CRAWFORD'S CARRIAGE arrived at Janet and Drummond Fraser's town house on Brunswick Square before five o'clock in the afternoon, but because the heavy cloud cover prevented the feeble light of the setting sun from getting through it was dark enough to have been evening already. Thankfully, Janet had the windows of the house lit up like a drunken bishop. Mr Fraser had been an early adopter of the London and Westminster Gas-Light and Coke Company's services, and all the principle rooms of the house were brightened by coal-gas lamps. There was, of course, no need for such extreme illumination in the bedrooms, but Mr Fraser had been far-sighted enough to put coal-gas lamps in the kitchen, his study, and the private family sitting room.

The sight of vivid yellow light spilling out from the windows of the front drawing-room cheered Mary, and her excited anticipation of London amusements returned. During the bustle of unloading the chests and luggage, Mary and Henry were ushered inside to be greeted with enthusiasm by the Frasers and Mr Fraser's adult daughter, Margaret. Mary watched Miss Fraser flirt with Henry, fluttering her eyelashes to such an extent that Mary wondered that there was not a breeze to ruffle her brother's hair, and tried not to find mirth in Margaret's disappointment later. Alas, Margaret was such a frivolous and spoilt young miss that it was hard to whip up much sympathy.

Henry was very cordially invited to dine with the Frasers that evening, but he made his excuses and claimed the Admiral was expecting him. After a quarter hour of civility, Henry bid his adieus, promised to call again as soon as possible, and returned to his carriage. Mary begged to be excused to wash and dress for dinner, which Janet had told her would be ready in an hour and a half. They were dining *en familia* tonight and had made no plans to go out, having assumed that their guest would be worn out from her day in the carriage. Mary, touched by the consideration, embraced Janet and even went so far as to shake hands with Mr Fraser, and then followed a maidservant upstairs to the bedroom that was to be hers for the duration of her stay. Mary discovered that although her sleeping apartment was not quite as congenial as the one she enjoyed at Mansfield Parsonage, it was nonetheless pleasing. Instead of a bedroom and dressing room attached, there was just the one chamber, but it was of a good size and had been fitted up with a screens and a table in such a way as to give Mary a perception of a space for privacy and a small sitting room. Mary's chief complaint was that Janet had hung the walls with Turkey red paper embossed with a gold-coloured pattern of Grecian meander and had used a matching red and gold chintz for the bed's draperies. It was immensely stylish, but too eye-searing for Mary's taste. Even the two screens had been papered with the same materials. Mary couldn't decide if she felt she would be sleeping in a very expensive brothel or a gilded abattoir.

Beatty, who was a treasure, had already secured hot water for the ewer and basin and had arranged one of the screens to reflect heat back toward the fireplace. This gave Mary a relatively warm place between the fire and the screen to strip off her travelling clothes, have a quick wash, and redress. Beatty always packed a smaller valise with the necessary things for evening half-dress, and had them at hand. Mary was glad to see fresh flannel drawers were included. After donning a long-sleeved cream-on-cream brocade gown with a brown droguet petticoat underneath and having Beatty style her hair into a braided chignon with bandeau, Mary descended the three flights of stairs to the drawing-room once more.

Mary had always been impressed with Janet's house. It was one of the first-rate new homes in this part of London. The Frasers had been wise enough to leave the entire first floor open to use as a ballroom or concert hall when needed, and had put the family rooms and master bedroom on the second floor, leaving the third and fourth floor for guest bedrooms and the nursery. The ground floor was, like in all other town houses, taken up mostly by a lavish public drawing-room and dining room, with the master's study and private family parlour toward the back. She wasn't certain all this domestic splendour was worth marrying a grumpy old stick-in-the-mud twice her age, as Janet had done, but it did have some definite pluses.

When Mary entered the drawing-room Janet saw her first, and cried out effusively, "Mary, darling! You look as elegant as ever. It is so good to have you back in Town, where I can talk with you and tell you everything without having to write prodigious letters."

"You are looking splendid yourself!" Mary enthused. "I am so happy to be back in London, I can hardly speak of it. I cannot thank you enough for inviting me. I beg of you to tell me every scrap of *on dit* or scandal I have missed during my rustication."

"This being London, nothing is so easily accomplished," Janet assured her. "But first, tell me *your* news. Is there anything of interest in *your* life? A certain Mr Bertram appeared in your letters too frequently for him to not be a beau. Has the handsome vicar successfully made love to you and won your hand?"

Janet's question was more in fun than in earnest. The idea of Mary settling for a country clergyman was laughable; Mary was pretty and rich enough to captivate a man with a title, if she saw one she liked well enough to set her cap for.

"I have no news of *myself*, but I do have a great deal to say of Henry," Mary baited. Although Janet was a dear friend, Mary truly trusted and confided in no one but her brother, her sister, … and Fanny Price.

"Your brother? What news do you have of him?" Margaret asked with rapidity.

Mary's smile became distinctly naughty. "Henry has fallen before Cupid's bow at last. He has proposed to Miss Price, a niece of Sir Thomas Bertram who lives with the family in their seat of Mansfield Park."

The look of stupefied amazement on the faces of those around her was a quite satisfying reaction to her news. Mary looked forward to dropping this same verbal thunderclap often in the next week or so.

Mr Fraser recovered the soonest. "I must wish him joy when next I see him! When do he and this Miss Price plan to be wed."

"Therein lies the rub," Mary leaned forward in a confidential manner. "Miss Price has refused to accept him."

If the news of Henry's proposal was a thunderclap, then the news of Miss Price's refusal was lightning; the entire company, even the stoic Mr Fraser, was shocked into exclamations.

"How can this be?" Janet ejaculated.

"Miss Price is a moralist on par with Miss Anabella Milbanke, and she holds Henry's flirtations and peccadilloes against him. Henry is, as you and everyone in London knows, an unceasing flirt, and before he realised what Miss Price would mean to him he had exposed himself as a gallant. Miss Price, not used to town manners, thinks my poor brother is a bit of a cad. He is now seeking to prove himself worthy of her hand, in the hopes she will relent and accept him."

"Henry finds himself in exalted company then," Mr Fraser said cryptically.

"Whatever do you mean, sir?" Mary wondered.

Janet answered for him, "My husband alludes to the fact that Lord Byron is reported to have proposed to Miss Milbanke sometime between Michaelmas and Christmas last, and was sent away with a flea in his ear."

Now it was Mary's turn to be staggered. "You are Josephus Rex."

"No," Janet assured her, "I am not Jo-King."

"Lord Byron proposed to *Miss Milbanke*? What else has happened? Has Napoleon renounced the world and become a Franciscan friar? Has Prinny become a Methodist?" Mary could barely wrap her head around it.

Of all the scandalous shenanigans Lord Byron had done since he had become a famous best-seller last spring, the most *shocking* thing was his proposal to Miss Anne Isabelle Milbanke, because no one had suspected such nonsense would ever occur. Lord Byron was well-known to be a seducer, rake, philanderer and libertine. Annabella Millbanke was well-known to be a priggish bluestocking with a penchant for mathematics. She was the only child of Sir Ralph Milbanke, a respectable country baronet, and had been such an intellectual prodigy that professor from Cambridge University was called in to be her tutor. She was also renowned the length and breadth of England for her strict religious beliefs and puritanical outlook on life. The idea of Lord Byron and Miss Milbanke united in holy matrimony was as bizarre as a discovery of pixies in one's chamberpot; it startled and fascinated, but could not be thought of as anything but distinctly absurd.

"Well, Janet," Mary said, "I haven't been more surprised by anything since we saw the leopard in Haymarket."

"*You* saw the leopard in Haymarket?" Margaret exclaimed, turning toward her father's wife. "I did not know this, Mother. Why did you never tell me?" Margaret was still under the care of her governess in 1810, and it was one of her chief regrets that she had not been in Haymarket the day the leopard made his appearance.

"I suppose because the topic never came up," Janet said. "It's not as if someone frequently asks me, 'oh, by the way — did you see the leopard in Haymarket?' or there is a conversational opportunity to casually mention that I saw the leopard in Haymarket."

"Why don't you tell her now, Mrs Fraser?" Her husband suggested politely.

"Oh! Alright then. Miss Crawford, her brother, and I were all in Mr Crawford's curricle and were heading south down Haymarket toward Pall Mall to view an exhibition at the Royal Academy. Mary was, of course, in the middle between myself and Mr Crawford. We tolerated the crush because Mr Crawford's curricle was so light and stylish it was a pleasure to ride in it – even if one was pressing one's best friend up against her brother and that said best friend was *ceaselessly* complaining that she was being squished."

"I did no such thing!" Mary interjected with a laugh.

Janet raised her eyebrows and gave Mary a look of profound disbelief. "Be that as it *may*, traffic was more congested in Haymarket than normal, and we were practically at a standstill, when suddenly we heard one of the … Drury Lane Vestals, shall we say … scream in terror. We all looked about, convinced the unfortunate woman was being murdered at the least. But no, she was screaming because a very large leopard was sauntering, devil-may-you-please, down the middle of the street. It was in front of us, and heading our way, so it gave Mary and myself a terrible fright. Mr Crawford, however, seemed unperturbed by the sight, except he was moved to utter a rather vehement, "By George!" The horses were of the same opinion as Mary and myself, and would have bolted if Mr Crawford had not held the reigns so expertly. It was a positive clutter and rumpus! The only amusing part of the event was what the young tiger sitting behind us said, which was indelicate but which I will repeat it for the sake of accuracy." Janet then declaimed, in a very passable imitation of a lower-class accent, "Oi! That's a bleedin' leopard that is!"

Mary and Margaret dissolved into laughter, quite as Janet had expected, and even Mr Fraser essayed a small smile. When the merriment had died down a bit, Margaret asked to be reminded where the leopard had come from.

Mary answered her. "Wombwell's menagerie in Piccadilly. According to the papers, Wombwell had loaded the beast into a caravan in order to transport it to a fair, I forget which one, but the horse bolted down Haymarket and overturned the cart, which broke into pieces. The animal saw its chance to escape, and made its bid for freedom. By the time we saw it, there had already been quite the ruckus. Its handler had tried to throw a rope around the leopard's neck, but it bit the man savagely, although by good luck not fatally, and continued its perambulations up Haymarket. The beast-masters of the menagerie later found the animal in a cellar nearby, where it had gone to earth to escape the hullabaloo, and secured it again. The whole event was, in the end, sound and fury signifying nothing."

"And lucky it was, that it was no worse," Mr Fraser added. "We had a tiger — the furry beast, not the small groom – escape a travelling menagerie in Essex in '02, and the brute nearly killed a child. It was a little boy of nine, just the same age as you were, Margaret, and I made sure you were kept indoors until the animal was recaptured."

"How on earth did the child survive an attack by a tiger?" Mary asked, horrified at the thought of the animal's strong jaws on the tender flesh of a small boy.

"The tiger met with something more savage and more deadly than itself – a farmer's wife." Mr Fraser harrumphed in jingoistic satisfaction at the thought of the strength of the English yeomanry. "The boy was, by the grace of God, in the yard helping his mother and the maids with the washing when the animal attacked. Seeing the beast leap upon her son, the good woman grabbed her battledore, one of those sturdy oak paddles used to beat linens clean in the country manner, and set about the tiger's head with it. The beast let go of the child, and might have attacked the mother had she not continued to assault it like a Maenad. Shakespeare may say there is no fury like a woman scorned, but with all due respect to the Bard, I would say an affrighted mother is more terrible by far. The maids, brave lasses both, joined the fray with a broom and the handle of a butter-churn, and the tiger decided he had had enough of mad Englishwomen and ran away into the trees. No other children were attacked, but several sheep were killed before it was caught by some vigilant gamekeepers."

"Oh, I am so glad to hear that the child lived," Mary said, with feeling. "Was he disabled for life, or did he lose any limbs?"

"Except for some fearsome scars which are hidden by his clothes now that he is a man, he has recovered completely. It *was* a very near thing, though. The apothecary who treated him, Haigh, said that the boy had hovered upon the edge of death, but had rallied just when almost all hope was gone. Haigh speculated the child had recovered because Death was afraid to meet the lad's mother and her battledore," Mr Fraser smiled. "She was the wife of one of the farmers who rented land from me, a fellow by the name of Whittcomb, and I rewarded his wife's bravery by refusing their rent for the farmland that year. I assumed they would need it for the boy's medical expenses."

"Perhaps we should send this Mrs Whittcomb to the front lines, to dispatch Napoleon," Mary recommended, tongue in cheek.

"Considering how the Peninsular War is going, I'm sure Lord Wellington would be glad of the help," Mr Fraser said wryly. Every major engagement in Spain last autumn had been a reversal of Anglo-Portuguese fortunes and a victory for the French. In October, Wellington had been forced to give up the siege of Burgos and had been defeated by the French at the Battle of Tordesillas, and ever since then Iberia had sat at a seething standstill waiting for better weather to fight in.

It was at this point that the Frasers' butler announced that dinner was ready. Mr Fraser civilly offered an arm to both his wife and Mary, and Miss Fraser trailed dutifully behind them. The dining table had, sensibly, been laid out only on one end, with Mr Fraser at the head of the table with Mary on his right, and his wife and daughter to his left. This would seem to be a self-evident layout, but Mary had often dined among only three people where the husband and wife maintained the more formal arrangement wherein they sat at the distant ends of the table. She suspected that Mr and Mrs Fraser sat further apart whenever they dined only with one another.

As long as the footmen remained in the room to serve the dishes, conversation must remain on neutral topics suitable to the servants' ears. Thus, the topic of Henry Crawford's would-be fiancée was left fallow, after a single attempt by Margaret Fraser to bring it up. Janet's hand on her arm and a pointed glance at the footmen reminded Margaret of the need for discretion in front of the servants, and the girl subsided. Fortunately, there was always a great deal to discuss regarding politics, entertainment, and scandals unconnected to one's close family and friends, so dinners were seldom dull.

Knowing Mary's fondness for Byron, Janet wasted no time giving her the further details about the latest the exploits of her favourite poet. Lord Byron had been continuing his known liaison with Lady Oxford, whom he was reported to call his Enchantress, even as he had wooed Miss Milbanke. In fact, the ardent and highly sexed wordsmith was currently visiting Eywood, the county house of the earl of Oxford in Herefordshire, where he was staying with both his mistress and her compliant husband. Lady Oxford, who was an old hand at juggling extramarital intrigues, didn't seem particularly

perturbed that her lover had asked Miss Milbanke to be his bride
while still enjoying his mistress's favours. It was doubtful, in Janet's
opinion, that Miss Milbanke was as sanguine about this arrangement.

Mary also quite enjoyed talking politics with the Frasers, even
though Mr Fraser was never one to appreciate a pithy turn of phrase.
Happily, she had the felicity of being able to air her opinions freely
without fear of offending, because her host was also a liberal Whig.
Knowing that her commiseration for the enslaved was shared, Mary
could once again discuss the evils of sugar plantations in the West
Indies without worry that she was astounding anyone at the table.
Mr Fraser had met Janet at an abolitionist salon that she and Mary
were attending one evening, and it was during their discussion of that
jointly held opinion that Mr Fraser had formed a false impression of
compatibility with Miss Janet Ross, and resolved to make the young
woman his future bride. Sadly, Janet and her husband were alike in
no other way except their political leanings. They had not one other
single taste in common, with Mr Fraser liking to stay *in* of an evening
as much as his wife liked to go *out*.

Mary could finally speak sympathetically of the Luddites, the
downtrodden factory workers who were being subjected to show
trials and persecution in York, and to obtain the most recent news of
the Luddites' tribulations. While she had been bidding her adieus at
Mansfield, three suspected Luddites had been hanged. They were all
young, well-educated men, who had been judicially murdered as an
example of what would happen to Luddite "ring-leaders"; i.e. men of
social standing who dared support the rights of the mill workers. As
a further indignity, their bodies were given over to the local hospital
to be dissected. This not only horrified their friends and family, but
also prevented any funeral services which may have served to rally
dissidents.

They discussed the rumours swirling around Princess Charlotte
at length. Court tittle-tattle had it that the princess was fed up to her
back teeth with being kept a virtual prisoner at Windsor and Warwick
House, and had petitioned for her own establishment. The princess's
governess, Lady De Clifford, had resigned, leaving the perfect opening
for the recognition of the teenager's adulthood, but instead of giving
the princess a little freedom and allowing her to come out, Prinny
had saddled the young woman with a new governess, the Duchess
of Leeds, and two lady companions, all of whom were de facto spies
for Prinny and his mother. The princess, it was said, was miserable

about this and about her father's refusal to let her see her Mama with any frequency or regularity. Public opinion was as sympathetic to the princess as it was apathetic toward the regent. Mary and the Frasers, in particular, had reasons to support the princess other than a natural revulsion for the way she was being treated; the princess was a vehement supporter of the Whigs.

Princess Charlotte wasn't the only royal to be spoken of. Ernest, the Duke of Cumberland, was embroiled in scandal once again, but at least this time he hadn't murdered his valet. The duke had interfered in the parliamentary elections in Weymouth, rigging the rotten borough to go to a Tory named Thomas Wallace. Rotten boroughs, which were largely Tory constituencies and thus vigorously defended by Tory administrations, were enough of a blight on English politics in Mary's opinion, but for a peer (let alone royalty!) to tamper with a Commons election was quite beyond the pale. But what was one to expect from a man reported to have sexually assaulted his own sister and gotten her with child? While Janet and Margaret were united in believing that the duke *had* fathered a bastard on Princess Sophia, Mary and Mr Fraser believed that there had been an attack but that no pregnancy had resulted. No one was in any way inclined to suggest the duke was innocent of such savagery.

Janet also encouraged Mary to become affiliated with the Hampden Club that she belonged to. The clubs were devoted to the topic of radical parliamentary reform and universal male suffrage and were open to everyone interested in political progress, and a subscription to the club cost only a penny a week. Janet assured Mary that is was well worth attending, if only for those times when a septuagenarian firebrand named Major John Cartwright spoke on the topic of pure democracy. Mary, who was as interested in parliamentary reform as she was prison reform and abolition, was very willing to join. Mr Fraser, who thought the Hampden Clubs too radical and apt to stir trouble, disagreed with his wife about the advisability of joining, and the Frasers bickered over the merits of such groups for nearly a quarter of an hour before Mary could engineer a change of topic.

On a cheerier note, Mary was reminded of some of the many opportunities for enjoyment she would have during her visit. Drury Lane was going to be putting on Coleridge's *Remorse* in a fortnight or so, which she was as eager to see as Janet and Margaret Fraser. She had not shopped at Bond Street or Pall Mall for six long months and was made happy by the thought of seeing all the latest goods the next morning. Countess Lieven had introduced a shockingly intimate dance called the waltz at Almack's, and Mary looked forward to seeing such risqué cavorting in two nights time, but she was duly warned that only married women had the courage to try it; for an unmarried young lady like Mary to dance the waltz would likely ruin her. The Frasers furthermore promised Mary that they would personally escort her as soon as possible to the Hindoostane Coffee House at 34 George Street, opened in 1810 by an Indian national named Sake Deen Mahomed, so she could partake of Indian food again. Mary, in spite of the fact she was eating an excellent cut of beef at the time, could feel her mouth water at the thought of a good curry.

All in all, Mary enjoyed herself more than she had expected on her first evening away from Mansfield. Mr Fraser had made a real effort to be courteous and charming to Mary, and although he and his wife were far from loving toward one another, he seemed less inclined to deliberately irritate Janet's spirits than he had six months before. Even Margaret had improved in deportment and sense. The freshness of the information she gathered had served to content her, and she was distracted enough by the present company and situation that she did not miss Edmund's society the way she had just a few weeks before, which is what she had feared.

Chapter Thirty-Seven

THE FOLLOWING MORNING reminded Mary of the distinct benefits of living in London. She rose late, unworried that she might be preventing anyone's activities or impinging on anyone's happiness by her slugabed behaviour. Breakfast included freshly fried salted herring, a favourite of Mary's that she hadn't eaten since she had gone to Mansfield, since Dr Grant detested the dish and would not suffer it at his table. Granted, the honey available for her roll was not as nectarous as that provided in Northamptonshire, but it was good enough.

Following her breakfast, she joined Janet in a round of morning visits to old friends, all of whom seemed very glad to see Mary again and all of whom were delighted to tell her the recent *on dit*. From Mrs Woodbead she discovered that Lady Rummage was supposed to be involved in a dalliance with Mr Jarsdel. From Lady Rummage she learned that Mrs Woodbead and Mrs Febland should not be invited to the same dinner or party due to the tension caused over Mr Febland's insult to Mrs Woodbead's cousin's son, Mr Bonneville, an insult which was rumoured to be inspired by Mr Febland and Mr Bonneville's competition for the same member of the demi-monde, a bit of muslin known as Dolly Davis, who had thrown them both over to become a mistress of a high ranking cabinet member. In turn, Mrs Febland told her that Mr Jarsdel had recently become engaged to an heiress who knew nothing of his misalliance with Lady Rummage. Mrs Febland also let it slip that Mr Woodbead was said to have made some bad investments, and might be teetering on the edge of financial ruin, which would no doubt scupper the hoped-for match between a certain baron and the eldest Miss Woodbead.

What was even better than hearing about the minor squabbles and sins of her social circle and the wider ton was the information Mary received regarding the peers and power-brokers of the government. She was told in the strictest confidence by at least a dozen people that the relationship between Lord Charles Bentinck, who had been a member of the Privy Council less than six months, and his wife Georgiana, the daughter of notorious courtesan Grace Dalrymple Elliot, was said to be very strained by Bentick's affair with Lady Abdy. This was seen to be a great scandal in the making, because Bentick's wife was reported to be the natural daughter of Prinny himself, or at the very least the by-blow of the Earl of Cholmondeley, and her displeasure might lead to a royal censure of Lord Bentick, even though the cabinet member *was* the third son of the Duke of Portland. There was also delighted speculation about the perversions of Lord Bentick, considering that Lady Abdy was, like his wife, the illegitimate daughter of an infamous lady of pleasure. Formerly Anne Wellesley, Lady Abdy was the result of the liaison between the French actress Hyacinth-Gabrielle Roland and the Marquess of Wellesley. Although the Marquess and Miss Rolland had eventually married, their marriage wasn't until *after* the birth of their five children. No woman's reputation could survive being seen to socialise with the current Lady Wellesley, and her daughter was now a very famous adulteress. What penchant did Lord Bentick have for ladies born to birds of paradise? Were certain proclivities toward vice transmitted by blood, making the daughters as libidinous as their famous mothers?

Mary also heard of myriad engagements, jilts, heartbreaks, expectations, births, legal separations, and even a divorce or two. The social fermentation of Town made the mishmash of Mansfield seem to be very small beer indeed.

Not that Mary was without information herself. Everywhere she went the news of Henry's amore for Miss Price, a woman wholly unknown in Town, created a sensation. The fact that his idol did not return his attachment created a tumult of disbelief. Mary was pelted with questions about Miss Price's connections, appearance, milliner, mantua-maker, hairstyle, and teeth. The shock that was expressed when Mary explained that Miss Price was merely pretty, of medium height with soft, light eyes, connected only to a baronet in Northampton, and was a shy, diffident moralist as well, brought Mary a great deal of secret amusement. Mary, with a glee she wasn't proud of, explained to the worldly and witty women of London how a quiet, timorous paragon of delicacy and rectitude had not only captured Henry's heart, but had inspired the rake to decide to entirely reform himself. It was news that eclipsed and subsumed all other gossip in its wake.

Mary and Janet's last call was at Lady Stornoway's, where they were given the refreshment of a cold luncheon and hot tea, and Mary disclosed Henry's defeat at the hands of Eros once more. She bit her lip to keep from laughing when Flora Stornoway made a face like she had sucked on a bitter pickle.

"So, your brother has fallen heels over head for a young miss from the country," Flora sniffed in an affected manner when she had recovered her countenance. "I cannot say that was something I expected to come from your sojourn to the hinterlands. Is that why Mr Crawford cut lose his little opera singer?"

"Actually, that occurred before Henry had developed his passion for Miss Price. He had simply not found another *chere-amie* before being conquered by love rendered him unfit to look upon any other woman but his adored." Mary took a sip of her tea, which was not as good as the mixture brewed by Mrs Grant but was nonetheless tasty.

"And how long will his infatuation with this agrarian exemplar of virtue last, do you think?" Flora could not quite hide the snide undertone of her question.

Mary hid her irritation. "Oh, as madly in love as Henry is, I would not be surprised if he never ceased his adulation of Fanny. His attachment makes *me* very happy, because I cannot envisage someone I would wish to embrace as a sister more than she. I have never heard a cross word from her, and she has the mildest, sweetest temper and disposition imaginable."

"How lovely!" Flora smiled, but it did not reach her eyes.

"Isn't it?" Janet interjected smoothly. "I had not thought Mr Crawford had a heart to lose, considering the many inducements he has had to matrimony."

"True, true," Mary's natural kindness reasserted itself and she sought to pacify Flora's obvious jealousy. "I had even wondered if Henry would never marry at all. It was never that he was too nice in his requirements; it was a loathing for the very idea of the married state that kept his more tender emotions at bay. He was nearly ruined by the Admiral. I believe his affection for Miss Price arises from his absolute conviction that she will be forever mollifying and genial. He need never even suspect anything but a copacetic existence with her, as he would have had he become captivated by a woman with more spirit."

"Is she spiritless then?" Flora pounced on the suggested criticism.

Sighing internally, Mary assuaged her friend's resentment towards Henry's intended by painting Fanny's benign temperament in a negative light. "She is, of course, not flawless. No one *can* be, whatever their lovers might *think*. She does frequently want spirits, and is very reserved. Her temper is not an open one. Her nature is not active. I would be insulted by Henry's choice of a woman the complete opposite of myself in almost every characteristic, if I did not believe that he loved her for the domestic tranquillity and peace her placid and submissive nature promises him. You are well aware that while we enjoyed many advantages in living with my aunt and uncle, the comfort of a contented home was not one of them."

"What a shame Mr Crawford could only see himself happy with an insipid woman." Flora commented with an ill-concealed mixture of spite and self-congratulation to salve her wounded pride.

Mary reminded herself that Henry had broken Flora's heart, and let it pass.

"Do you think your brother will settle entirely at Everingham when he weds?" Janet asked, trying to move the topic away from Miss Price's virtues or lack thereof.

"I think he will be more likely to settle upon it a seven years lease and deputation," Mary answered. "He is thinking of buying land and building a residence near Mansfield, considering that it will be my main place of abode in the foreseeable future, and he will spend the rest of his time in town."

If she were being completely honest, Mary would admit that she suspected Henry would take another mistress and set her up in Marylebone within a year of marriage. It was not that she thought Henry would be less in love with Fanny; it was that Henry would need company for the *earthier* side of love. Fanny's disposition was not one that would find much elation in the marriage bed, and Henry was not one to go long without the gratification of carnal relations. Henry, being a gentleman, would not make demands of Fanny when he could set up a willing — even eager — woman of pleasure for those needs. She trusted that her brother would keep Fanny completely in the dark about his amorous activities, and what Fanny did not know could not shock her or wound her.

She had rather expected her own future husband to take a mistress as well, resolving only to make complaints if the fellow should waste too much money or form an entanglement with a lady of quality that would embarrass her. Provided that her husband would be courteous and liberal in all other aspects of the marriage, she didn't think she would mind his inamoratas. Her opinion had changed when her infatuation with Edmund had begun. She could not see Edmund ever taking a mistress after marriage, when he eschewed one prior to it, and she could not imagine herself continuing uneffected if he did.

"I am glad to hear you and Henry would be settled near to one another," Janet said, "and that you think he will be much in Town. There is never a dull party or soiree when Mr Crawford is around. A season without him risks the terror of becoming stale."

"Yes, it would be a shame to lose Mr Crawford's pleasant company," Flora agreed, her voice no longer laced with acrimony. "One not need fear tedium with *him*! Did he spare you the bucolic boredom you feared, Mary?"

"Surprisingly, it was not wretchedly dismal even when he wasn't there. My sister, Mrs Grant, is a woman of taste and information, so I did not suffer from a complete lack of conversation. I had books and exercise enough to fill up the rest of my time," Mary ate another morsel of ham.

"Not to mention the company of the Bertrams of Mansfield," Flora hinted with returned good humour. "The eldest brother is a handsome man; I was surprised when your letters contained so much of the younger one."

"The elder brother is a very good sort of fellow, and I am sure will be a very interesting parti for some young lady some day, but he did not make my heart pitter-patter," Mary said lightly.

"But the younger brother did?" Janet quizzed.

"I am not sure I would go *that* far," Mary laughed. She was fond of Janet, but had no intention of making herself vulnerable to gossip and potential ridicule by opening up the secrets of her heart. "He was pleasant company though, and even more handsome in his face and build than his brother. He comes to London in a few weeks, and you will meet him for yourself."

Flora grinned. "And *why* does the younger Mr Bertram come to London, pray tell?"

"To see Astley's I am sure," Mary said, leaving the giggling of her friends unaddressed.

ıı

After their repast, Mary was renewed to the bliss of browsing in the glorious excesses of London's many wares. The three friends climbed into the Fraser town coach and made an excursion to Harding, Howell, & Co., the very modern department store in Pall Mall. No Viking had ever raided a village with as much intent to pillage as that which Mary harboured in her breast as she penetrated the doors of the bedecked shop.

"Ah, to re-enter the Garden of Eden," she sighed theatrically upon crossing the threshold of the store, much to the amusement of Janet and Flora.

Mary had loved Harding, Howell, & Co since the moment it had opened in '09. How glorious it was too have so many articles of female attire and adornment clustered together under one roof! The building was one hundred and fifty square feet of sartorial paradise. It had four departments, the first of which contained furs, and — for some reason Mary was unsure of — fans. The second department was filled with an affluence of haberdashery goods, and the third department was bursting with toiletries, jewellery, and decorative knick-knacks for the feminine rooms of one's abode. The department farthest from the door contained the most commonly bought woman's garb, such as dresses and head-wear, so that the customer had to run the gauntlet of ornamental temptation to get to the hats. Mary was so happy to be in the store again she could have kissed the sales clerks.

"What do you want to see first, then?" Flora asked her. "What has your poor heart yearned for in the rustication of Shropshire."

"I was in *Northamptonshire*," Mary corrected her, "as you well know. My poor heart yearns for *many* things. However, since the first department contains the furs, let us look for me a muff to better match my witzchoura."

"If you see nothing here that suits we can also go by Nicholay and Sneiders," Flora offered. "If you cannot find a fur there to match then the animal that wore it first has gone extinct."

"I thank you very sincerely for the civility," Mary replied, "but we had better wait until tomorrow. It's after three now and if I am not *very* much mistaken we'll be here more than an hour. Janet's dinner begins at 6:30 and we have to return you to your house and then get back to Brunswick Square in time to dress properly. One ever knows what the traffic shall do, so it wouldn't be wise to leave it too late when we go."

"You're right of course," Flora agreed. "I let the thought of Nicholay and Sneiders overwhelm my faculties."

"Do you remember how *long* we were in Nicholay and Sneiders when you were picking out your trousseau?" Mary smiled in fond remembrance. "Never have so many furs been laid out for the estimation of a more fastidious group of women!"

"Lord yes!" Janet cried. "Flora found what she liked for a tippit soon enough but we were all in *agonies* over the right fur for her pelerine."

Flora chuckled behind her hand. "Mother was in a positive frenzy to choose the most tasteful and fashionable thing allowed to mankind. *Miss Ross* could make do with a wool spencer and her mother's second-best scarf or perhaps a bit of fox trim, but the future *Lady Stornoway* must have only the best!"

"I wish our mother had been is desirous that *I* should have good furs upon my wedding, as well," Janet mouth compressed briefly with old bitterness, but then she smiled. "Mary, do you remember what your aunt said when those poor clerks had brought forth yet *another* ermine for mother's inspection?"

Mary did a credible imitation of her aunt advising, "Perhaps you should ask them if they have recently skinned some angels?" before joining in the laughter.

"But to give credit where it is due, the furs your mother chose for your mantle trimmings were exquisite, Flora," Mary continued. "You'll be able to have those furs re-purposed for years. Fur that beautiful will always be the first stare of fashion, notwithstanding any changes to the shape or length of covering. When I get married I hope to find some even half so nice."

"Maybe they'll have found a way to trap and skin angels by then," Janet suggested, "not that Mr Fraser is any more inclined to buy such things for me than mother. How long must one save up one's pin money to buy enough angel-skin to trim a mantle?

"If I cannot find angels to wear, I'll settle for marten," Mary said.

II

Mary not only found an amber-coloured marten's fur muff that would go very well with her witzchoura, she also found angels to wear in the form of an enamel hair comb decorated with frolicking putti. Afterwards, she and Janet made it back to the Fraser town house in good time, preventing any sort of discombobulating bustle or rush when preparing for dinner. Mary was so well ahead of herself that she had an extra three-quarters of an hour before she needed to descend to the drawing-room, time which she used to write Fanny a letter.

"Dearest Fanny,

I am safely arrived in London, and have been greeted with every warmth by the Frasers. The trip was not as arduous as I had feared it would be; the roads were in better condition that I could have hoped. Oh! I dream of a day when all main roads are well-maintained toll-roads, but alas! I fear that will always be just fantasy. I might as well dream that carriages will come equipped with wings. Although if they did come with wings no doubt there would be immediate riots by the hostlers and coachmen who feared their labour no longer useful. If it is true that every cloud has a silver lining, then it is equally true that every boon must have some ill in it.

I have been causing quite a disturbance in town today, revealing to all and sundry that Henry has been made love's whipping-boy and Miss Price is the cause. I had predicted correctly, by-the-by; there were an absurd amount of questions about your person. Never fear, though, I told them all that Henry was attached to you for the purity of your heart and the strength of your principles, rather than the blushes of your soft skin or the delicacy of your features.

Now that I write that, your visage, and indeed all of Mansfield, opens up before my mind's eye. If carriages had wings I would visit you tomorrow, so much do I miss the company there. I cannot help but wonder how you and your cousin are faring in the absence of so many young people that made up such a happy party just a month ago! I also find myself sometimes regretting the quiet of country life when, as is currently happening outside my window, two carters get into a row, roaring abuse at one another at the top of their voices. The never-ending clatter and rattle of carriages and horses going by will take some getting used to again on my part. I do not think I could have slept so well last night if I had not been knocked up with the fatigue of travel.

I hope that you have already made at least one visit to the parsonage, although if the roads have been too dirty for travel I understand completely and do not chastise you in the least. My sister will be lonesome in the mornings, I fear. The weather will not always allow her to venture forth for the comfort of the cottagers, and Dr Grant — albeit an excellent husband — has too much to attend to that keeps him from being always in company with his wife. Of course, even as I solicit you to visit my sister, I realise you must leave your aunt, which makes me feel very selfish in my demands. I shall soothe my conscience by assuming Mrs Norris will come to be with <u>her</u> sister while you go to <u>mine</u>.

I have been shopping this day with Mrs Fraser and Lady Stornoway, at Pall Mall, and although I enjoyed myself, I found myself wishing for your company. There is always such sense and thought behind what you say, and those sorts of exchanges seem foreign in among this set. I also miss the familial felicity I was surrounded with at Mansfield, both at the Park and in the parsonage. I think that if men knew how much their own happiness depended on the care of their wives, they would treat their wives with more kindness as a general rule. This is the secret to the domestic tranquility of the parsonage and the park. Both Sir Thomas and Dr Grant take care to be obliging and thoughtful husbands (Sir Thomas invariably, and Dr Grant usually), and thus they have wives who are content and at peace in their abode.

I wish Mr Fraser would learn this wisdom. He is all charm and civility to <u>me</u>, but quarrels with Janet over the smallest of trifles. How dreadful it must be to be married to a person one finds uncongenial! I will predict that <u>you</u>, my dearest Fanny, have no need to fear <u>that</u> fate.

Speaking of a certain gallant, Henry's farewell words to me yesterday were to remind me to write to you as soon as possible. No knight-errant can be thinking of his lady more than my brother! Do write to me soon, and have the mercy to include a line for Henry!

Your obliging servant,

Mary Crawford

Mary blotted the paper, and locked it in her writing desk for privacy. She trusted Beatty, but saw no point in putting temptations to snoop before the Fraser's housemaids. Far too many of them could read nowadays, thanks to Sunday schools. Mary mused for a moment that she herself had often contributed funds for the maintenance of those schools, the fruits of which now required her to lock away her correspondence. Such were the hazards of improving the populace, she supposed. She was sure men would complain if women's suffrage ever happened, and factory owners would complain if labourers were ever allowed to negotiate as a united front. Giving up an advantage was always difficult, even when it was the right thing to do, and she was not as immune from mourning its loss as she had presumed herself to be.

Oh well, she supposed it was better to acknowledge one's shortcomings and hypocrisies than to be ignorant of them. The fact that most people she knew were completely unaware of their own flaws and self-deceptions, that they could not see that what was bad behaviour for one group of people was just as bad if done by a group they belonged to or favoured, was something that was a continuous source of marvel for her. So few people noticed their own affectations, and of those few who did only a small handful seemed to care enough to try to *change*. Of course, she must admit that continuing a strange sort of speciousness of character was *easier* than finding the will to restructure one's mental scaffolding. Thinking on it further, she realised she was just as guilty of ignoring her internal duplicities in her own way, being too comforted by the fact that at least she was *aware* of many of her foibles, and therefore she wasn't sanctimonious or pharisaical in her attitude or mode of conduct.

Or was she? What was her own enjoyment and thrill at defamation and gossip but a form of insincerity, since in her heart of hearts she saw that the *true* sin of those embroiled in scandal was exposure? Usually, the culprits had done nothing worse or different than the same acts that many of the people casting such vehement opprobrium upon them had also done. Yet, she would listen to the calumny heaped upon the unfortunate targets with as much interest and amusement as if she were a saint hearing about the impropriety of lesser mortals. How was this truly different from Henry's concern for the plight of the poor as a general thing, while neglecting all he could do to help the poor on his own estate? She saw the misconduct and lack of self-understanding there, but could she see it in *herself*? Was she unknowingly as blind as everyone else to her *own* folly and nonsense?

Mary shook her head. These were heavy thoughts, and she was in the mood for light ones. Lively conversation would soon cure her of such introspection, and with Henry joining the party for dinner she was sure of that satisfaction. Her brother's plethora of *bon mots* and jokes and his ridiculous puns would breathe cool air into her heated head. The chatter-chitter of politics and the information about the doings of their acquaintance among the ton would thankfully leave no room in her brains for any sort of philosophical pondering.

Accordingly, Mary rose, checked her image in the peer-glass one last time, took up her shawl, and sallied forth to be entertained.

Chapter Thirty-Eight

HENRY WAS A nearly a daily visitor to the Fraser's home while his sister was under their roof, and he was therefore in the drawing-room two days later, when Mary received an answering letter from Fanny. Mary could not help but be diverted by his eagerness to hear the contents of the missive; he looked like a retriever that was remaining at heel in spite of its trembling yearning to be given leave to pursue its quarry. Politeness dictated, however, that he allow Mary to read her letter first, so that she could see if any material must be edited out of it when she read it aloud.

Janet, with the decorum and good breeding Mary always counted on from her, began to put aside her things on a flimsy pretext so she could leave the Crawfords to hear and discuss the letter in private. Yet before Janet could leave the room, Mary, who was a very fast reader and in possession of a short letter, begged her to stay, since there was nothing in the letter that could not be heard by anybody. Janet readily agreed because she had no small amount of curiosity about the Miss Price who had subdued the unconquerable Henry Crawford.

"I shall read you both the entirety of the letter, since there is not a single word in it that speaks of private matters, and being written by Fanny it contains nothing indelicate as well. I do not think the child knows *how* to be indelicate! Henry, this is a sad blow to you, for all wit is predicated on at least a *hint* of indelicacy, and your idol will never be as witty as your sister. How will you bear it?"

Henry bowed, "I would never dream of comparing women who are incomparable."

"Good answer!" Mary smiled. "Your fairy godmother was excessive when she blessed you with charm, dearest brother, and as your reward, you shall now hear all that your inamorata has written."

Clearing her throat, Mary began:

Dearest Miss Crawford, ("Note how she will not yet call me Mary? So proper! So unassuming! So ... silly!")

We are all very well here, and the weather continues to be dryer than normal for the season. ("She begins with the weather. Henry, you are wooing the most English of all Englishwomen.") *We were all made happy by the news of your safe arrival in London, and the warm reception given to your by your friends the Frasers. You need not doubt that many of your friends here regret your absence.*

I have been able to visit Mrs Grant twice since your leaving, and she and Dr Grant dined at the Park last night. She misses you, as must be expected, but she seems tolerably cheerful. ("Bless Fanny; that *does* relieve me.") *She had much to keep her busy, inasmuch as she has been sitting every day with Mrs Thurston since that good woman was brought to bed of one child that turned out to be* <u>two</u>. *Mrs Thurston and both babes, a boy and a girl, are in good health; Mrs Grant sits with her only because the newly-made mother has such comfort in Mrs Grant's presence, Mrs Thurston's own mother having passed away when Mrs Thurston was not quite eight years old. Mrs Grant's good disposition and love of babies is, of course, something you have great familiarly with, so you will be unsurprised that your sister spends her time in this fashion.* ("What a great pity it is that our sister has no children of her own, Henry. She must make do with loving us and we have both become very difficult to swaddle as of late.")

My aunt has recently received a letter from my cousin, Mrs Rushworth. Mr Rushworth has taken a house in Wimpole Street, and they should be in residence in town soon. ("Wimpole Street? There are some whoppers on Wimpole Street. I wonder which one they shall have.") *My cousin Julia will be with them, as she has a great desire to see some of the many amusements in London and my uncle sees no reason why she should not be given this time with her sister, in spite of the fact she is missed at home. Edmund has desired me to tell you that he remains at Mansfield so that my uncle and aunt will not be deprived of all their young people precipitously, but that he plans to visit*

his sister in London in the next fortnight or so, and hopes to
see both yourself and Mr Crawford.
     Your obedient and humble servant,

     Miss Price

Mary folded the letter. "See? Everything most proper. No hints,
no leading questions, not even a mention of *her* interest in hearing
how Henry does."

"I admit that is not the sort of letter I was expecting," Janet
frowned. "It reads more like a dutiful steward writing his employer. I
assume that the lady is not so indifferent in person?"

Henry leapt to Fanny's defence. "It is not her way to be effusive,
and until I have engaged her heart she would not be able to display
warmth without fear that she was giving me false hope. In person she
is much warmer, and has very sincere attachments."

"I believe," Mary tried not to smile, "that Mrs Fraser was
referring to Fanny's lack of warmth toward *me*."

Henry's cheeks actually became faintly tinged with red. "Oh!
Of course. I beg both your pardons."

"I can answer for her, Janet," Mary addressed her friend. "She
is, as Henry pointed out, not effusive. Nonetheless, she is a tender
thing in person. How she cried, and clung to my neck when I took
leave of her! I was greatly affected by her tears, I will own it. She is
exceedingly shy and reserved, but there is a great deal of genuine
feeling underneath; I can attest to it. If you could but see her with
her brother and her cousins! Her cousins, excepting Mr Edmund
Bertram, have done little to deserve such affection, but she gives it
regardless."

Janet did not look entirely convinced. "I suppose that most
people cannot make the force of their feelings known in letters.
Doubtlessly I have been spoilt by the lively and affectionate style of
your own, Mary."

"I would be the last person to insist Fanny's letters were superior
to my own," Mary joked, "because I always have the extra stomach to
consume more flattery."

Henry smiled, returned to his accustomed suavity, and told
Mrs Fraser that, "You must come to visit us when I get Fanny settled
as my bride. You'll find nothing lacking in the way of tenderness and
friendship, I promise you. Fanny is full of gratitude for any kindness

and cannot do enough to secure the comfort of others. The only reason she is able to refuse my suit is that she must be entirely certain within herself that she is marrying me for reasons of true affection. She does not yet understand that many women make a prudent marriage with the knowledge that gratitude and time will allow them to fully return their husband's affections. She thinks there is but one way to find love."

Janet smiled at Henry. "It is true that many people cannot understand the distinction between a prudent marriage and a disinterested one. And I must say that sometimes even a marriage undertaken more from the hopes of an establishment than affections can turn out to be an advantage. Flora was certainly not thinking of Lord Stornoway's sterling qualities when she jilted Captain Faulkes for him, but she has rather landed on her feet."

"I agree," Mary nodded. "Between us, Flora seemed very discontented the first day we were with her, and I assumed it was because of her unhappiness with Lord Stornoway, but seeing them together the night before last showed me I was wrong. Lord Stornoway improves upon further acquaintance."

"In truth, I believe it was the news of Henry's engagement that caused Flora to be out of countenance," Janet admitted.

"Why?" Henry didn't bother to remind Mrs Fraser that he had not yet been accepted by Fanny Price. He, as much as everyone else, expected Fanny's capitulation to be a foregone conclusion. "What can *my* choices mean to *her?*"

"My sister has always had an abundance of pride," Janet explained, "and the fact she tried all she could do to win your heart and yet failed achieve her goal still stings. While you were unattached, she could soothe herself that you were simply impervious to the more tender emotions, but your submission to a country miss has wounded her anew. What can this girl, who is by your own account a timid little thing, offer you that is superior to the hand of Miss Ross?"

"It is hardly becoming that *Lady Stornoway* still resents a supposed slight on *Miss Ross,*" Mary noted, "but I must agree with you. Flora has never really gotten over her infatuation with you Henry."

Henry made a face indicating his derisive disbelief. "What bosh. I can believe I have offended her pride, but I cannot believe I have injured her heart. First, she would have to *possess* such an organ. After the way she tossed Capitan Faulkes (who was as much in love with her as I have ever seen a man in love with anyone) aside for Lord

Stornoway I cannot believe she has a heart for any other reason than to pump her blood."

Mary mostly agreed with Henry's assessment, but she did not like to disparage her friend so openly and so bluntly, especially in front of Lady Stornoway's sister. She felt moved to defend Flora's decisions.

"Just because Captain Faulkes was in love with her does not mean she had ever promised him that *she* felt the same," Mary argued. "She may have accepted him, but it does not follow that she had pledged her undying love. We have no proof that she would have been happier with *him* than she is with Lord Stornoway. There are many marriages begun on professed true affection that are a picture of misery within a year. At least Flora is content with her choice *now*."

"I think all marriages, or perhaps I should say *most* marriages, require a period of adjustment before one can fairly estimate the happiness of the union," Janet opined. "There are many little rubs when a new family is created, and it is hard to go from being courted to being a wife. One expects more agreement and indulgences from one's husband than what is natural."

"That sounds very reasonable, and I shall try to remember that when I change my name in the future," Mary nodded. "Notwithstanding the general wisdom of what you say, I think it is easier to adjust to marriage if one half of the union is *particularly* sweet tempered or *particularly* civil. My sister has what I consider to be a very happy marriage, but still she needs the fortitude of an angel regarding my brother-in-law's occasional periods of being out of sorts. She never loses patience with him when he is grumpy and overly-demanding, the way *I* certainly would, and in exchange he usually treats her with more than common consideration. I have also witnessed Sir Thomas Bertram, of Mansfield Park, treat his indolent wife with unceasing courtesy, and their marriage seems very contented."

"Yes, but neither of those marriages is a *new* one. Perhaps there was as much adjustment in the beginning of those unions as in others, and you are merely seeing the fruits of those efforts," Janet pointed out.

Mary smiled. "Alas, it goes against me for I must confess you are right. For all I know Lady Bertram used to throw crockery at Sir Thomas in a passionate rage."

Henry chuckled at the thought of Lady Bertram bestirring herself to feel passionate about anything, or to throw a plate at her husband's head. "It's more likely that she would fall asleep at him on the sofa."

"Perhaps she used to fall asleep at him in a passionate rage?" Mary chirped.

"She probably asks Fanny to do it *for her* nowadays," Henry said wryly. "She has Fanny do everything that could be thought of as even remotely taxing."

"Miss Price is helpful to her aunt, then?" Janet inquired.

"Oh, beyond anything," Mary answered. "I fear that she'll require Fanny to chew her food for her next."

Janet grimaced. "Well, *that* is an appalling thought."

"My apologies," Mary giggled. "That sounded much worse when I spoke it aloud than when I formed the words in my head."

ıı

Later, when Henry had left, after making Mary promise to allow him to add a line or two to the next letter she sent to Fanny, which he hoped would be forthcoming as early as the next morning, Janet Fraser reintroduced the subject of Miss Price.

"May I speak frankly of her, Mary?"

"Of course you may!" Mary assured her. "I am not a lover, or a would-be husband."

"But you *are* a would-be sister," Janet said reasonably, "and I would not like this conversation to be held against me later."

"I give you my oath that I will hold you blameless," Mary said lightly, but meaning every word.

"If that is so then I will confess that Miss Price seems a very cold person. There was no warmth, not even in slightest iota of it, in her letter to you. There was more warmth in her words for your sister and the birth of twins to a cottager than for you. And for her to ignore Mr Crawford entirely! Not even her compliments! Can you … can your brother … be happy with such an unnatural coldness?"

"Well, it will save Henry a great deal of money on an ice-house. Fanny can chill the sherbets on her breast."

"Please be serious, Mary."

"I will, but it is very hard to explain Fanny to someone who hasn't met her. In person her manners are warm enough, except for her natural timorousness. She is creepmouse, that is true, but her shyness is not the shyness of *reserve*. That would indeed be disgusting! *Her* shyness is the effect of excessive modesty and delicacy. Where she feels the *right* to express love she does it with genuine feeling. Her devotion to her brother and her cousin Mr Edmund Bertram are all that is praiseworthy. No, Fanny has a very warm heart; it is the easy expression of it that she lacks."

Janet was not entirely satisfied. "Perhaps she does not express her warmth for anyone other than her brother and her cousin because she *feels* none."

"If that were so, then her friendship and affection for me would be a lie, but I can assure you that Fanny is no actress to disassemble so well, or someone able to falsify regard. She has never shown me anything but the greatest attachment when we have been together. You must wait and meet her before you can judge. To know Fanny in person will alleviate all your kindly-meant fears." Mary leant forward and squeezed Janet's hand for a moment. "I do know it is an expression of your concern as a friend that you distrust Fanny's feelings and I am far from harbouring any resentment toward you for it. In all truth it makes me honour you, and appreciate your friendship more."

"I am relieved," Janet smiled. "I cannot say I am wholly approving of Miss Price yet, but I will withhold my judgements until they can be given with more justice."

ıı

For the following fortnight Mary's days were filled with engagements, but Henry's constant reminders, plus her own desire to learn how Edmund fared at Mansfield, guaranteed her frequent correspondence with Fanny. In each letter there had been a few lines from Henry for Fanny, warm and determined like his speeches, but Fanny's replies never held any acknowledgement of Henry's words, or even an acknowledgement of Henry's *existence*. Mary's generous heart and open temper put this all down to Fanny's fears of leading Henry on a false trail, and Henry himself simply became ever more determined to gain Fanny's affections.

Between Fanny's letters and the missives regularly sent between herself and her loving sister at the parsonage, Mary had a fairly complete picture of how things were going in Mansfield. She knew that the Bertrams were unchanged, and was kept abreast of all the minutia of the village and what Mrs Rushworth and Julia had written to their mother of their doings. She had the happiness, for her friend's sake, of reading that Fanny's brother William had been granted a ten days leave and was expected at the Park by the second day of February.

As for Edmund, Mrs Grant dutifully reported that he spoke of her often, and his compliments were usually conveyed in letters from both her sister and her friend. Mary's letters returned those compliments, in spades, along with fulsome remembrances of the pleasures of Mansfield, but her feelings were more mixed that they had been. When she came to Town, she had been determined to accept Edmund; now, she was unsure again. She had such extreme enjoyment of the delights of London that it was hard to remember how easily she had withstood the sameness and quietness of Northamptonshire. She was bombarded night and day with witty conversation and the juiciest morsels of gossip, all of which she relished, and she knew Edmund neither bestowed witticisms or approved of her exposure to the indelicate realities of life among the ton. She would be giving up so much by accepting him; could he make her happy enough to compensate?

When Henry married Fanny, his life would still be at his own disposal. If he wished to spend half a year in London, his wife would dutifully follow or be left at home without comment. With Henry's income, renting or buying a town house was no obstacle either. If Mary was to wed Edmund, he could say whether or not she was ever in town again in her life. If Edmund agreed to take her to London they could, if they used her yearly income as well, afford to rent a small house in town for the season, but they would hard pressed to keep a coach. Even renting a carriage and horses while in London would possibly be too expensive. They could probably rely on staying as Henry and Fanny's guests, but Mary disliked feeling like a dependent relation. She dreaded the thought of Edmund pinching pennies, just to allow them to go to the simplest things, like Astley's or Vauxhall Gardens. A box at the opera, something she had always assumed that she would have as a married woman, would be far beyond their means.

There were many hopes and dreams that she must surrender in Edmund's favour. Would his company be congenial enough to make up for the lack of worldly pleasures? If she missed her fun more than she enjoyed being his wife, she feared she would become termagant from her unhappiness, and ruin Edmund's life more than her own. But was this thought, this desire to put Edmund's happiness before her own, not a sign of how fond she was of him? Didn't that indicate love? Could she be happy if she were *not* married to the man she loved?

Mary feared that she was a very shallow person, possibly as heartless as Flora, because she was *indeed* happy in London without Edmund. She did not pine for him, except for sometimes when she was alone in her room or as she was falling asleep. She would wish him to be *here* in London, but she almost never wished herself back in Mansfield to be with him. She missed her sister, but she would also transport the Grant's hither if she could. She tried to remind herself of the felicities of Northamptonshire, the fresh air and the tranquillity and the pretty views and the good natures of everyone but Mrs Norris, but remembrances of dirty lanes and the bouts of boredom would intrude. There were people she loved in Mansfield, but she believed she loved the hullabaloo and excitement of London nearly as much.

If she married Edmund then even her literary pleasures would be necessarily truncated by her new life the country. Mail-order deliverers and the village's little circulating library were all very well and good, but how could they compare to jubilation of browsing the shelves of Hatchard's? Or the utter bliss of exploring the offerings available in a bookshop as commodious as The Temple of the Muses? If she resided in Mansfield, then how long would it take her to get the freshest horrid novels or all six volumes of Maria Edgeworth's *Tales of Fashionable Life?* Not to mention she would have to forgo the *discussion* of those works with a varied audience. It would be the same handful of intimates always purporting the same ideas. No matter how *worthy* those intimates or ideas, she would long to hear other interpretations of various works, even if those interpretations were all nonsense. She could at least *laugh* at nonsense.

Laughter! Edmund was made up of almost wholly of excellent qualities, but a turn for humour was not among them. Heaven knew Mary loved serious conversation; she had spent many a happy hour of debate and erudition in intellectual salons. She and Henry cherished their time spend in new art exhibitions discussing the merits of the works, styles, and artists. She, if she could be forgiven her lack of modesty, knew she had a very agile mind and she liked to use it. But, and it was an important qualifier, she also liked to laugh and make merry. She delighted in japes and jests and word play of all kinds. Living with Edmund meant she would be forced to wait to be in the company of her siblings or other acquaintance before she could enjoy good raillery and repartee.

These were all very consequential considerations. The bonds of marriage were, for all but the wealthiest and most powerful citizens in the nation, inescapable. She reflected on what Mrs Wollstonecraft had wrote, that too many women "marry a man before they're twenty, whom they would have rejected some years after." Only a fool would wed without a great deal of contemplation, and Mary was no fool.

ǁ

On the third day of February, as she sat in the drawing-room reading the third volume of a new book by the author of *Sense and Sensibility*, enveloped in a warm shawl and next to a superior fire, the footman brought her a letter on a silver salver. Mary glanced at the direction, saw it was from Fanny, and put aside *Pride and Prejudice* in order to go get a letter opener off Janet's writing desk. Slicing through the seal, Mary read:

> *Dear Miss Crawford,*
>
> *I have the best news in the world to impart! When my brother William returns to Portsmouth on the 8th, I am to go with him (I will include my new direction in Portsmouth as a postscript) so that I may visit with my parents and all the siblings who are at home (my brother Sam will be leaving soon after my arrival, for he follows William's footsteps and joins His Majesty's Service) for a month or two, perhaps as much as three! Oh, what felicity! I can barely describe my happiness!*
>
> *Please, I beg you, make allowances for my scrawl and lack of composition. My agitation is extreme. I am ashamed to send such a letter, and I would have waited until I was more myself before I wrote, but my cousin Edmund bid me to write you and tell you the happy news forthwith. He also wishes me to tell you that this will delay his coming to London, inasmuch as he is unwilling to leave my aunt and uncle entirely without the solace of one of their children. I am the happiest of mortals!*
>
> *Your obedient and humble servant,*
>
> *Miss Price*

"Well, Janet can hardly claim there is a lack of warmth in *this* letter," Mary said in soliloquy. Mary Crawford, usually so perceptive, neglected to notice that none of the warmth was for *her*. Fanny's joy was, as always, for herself and her family alone.

Chapter Thirty-Nine

MARY SHOWED THE letter to Henry later that morning, when he stopped in to see if he could oblige her in any way whilst he was at his next destination, Fleet Street.

"Hmmm," Henry mused, after he had read it, "I suspect that this was not done entirely for Fanny's benefit."

Mary's brows rose. "Why ever not?"

"Many reasons," Henry paced, tapping his palm with the folded letter. "Firstly, this inconveniences Lady Bertram. In all the years that Fanny has lived at Mansfield Park no one has ever bothered to give her the means and ways to visit her nearest relations; why now, when she is dearer than ever to the comfort of Lady Bertram? Why this sudden interest in Fanny's happiness? There was none before, and — if I may say it without sounding a buffoonish coxcomb — until *I* began to pay attention to Fanny there was no effort to do anything specially designed for Fanny's amusement or felicity. It may be a mere freak of vanity, but I think this visit is more for *me* than for the woman I love."

Quick on the uptake, Mary responded, "You mean you think it is an inducement to make her accept you? I am at a loss to see how so much happiness on Fanny's part to see her family would push her into an engagement."

"You would if you had been to Portsmouth," Henry told her grimly. "The direction tells the tale. I have made inquiries, and I know Fanny's father is of not only of very low birth, he's poor; the man commands less than three hundred a year. The street he lives on is a shabby one, fully of small houses and smaller minds. I would not be surprised to find that it is to be an object lesson in her destiny should she continue to refuse me."

"My, but they are *very* concerned with Fanny's happiness in marriage if they are willing to bully her into it," Sarcasm dripped from Mary's tone.

"Yes, indeed. There is nothing that secures a woman's happiness like feeling she has no other choice. Fah! I want to *woo* Fanny, not have her driven into my arms like a covey of quail."

Mary bit her lower lip, deep in thought. "But what can be done about it?"

"That's the devil of it — pardon my French. There is nothing I *can* do. Can you imagine the *delicacy* of a letter asking Sir Thomas not to do this thing? 'Dear Sir Thomas, we both know Fanny's happiness is because she is too unworldly to see what you are up to. Please crush Fanny's excited hope by putting a stop to this at once. Your ect & ect, Henry Crawford.' Yes, a fine note that would be."

"Yes, I am sure Sir Thomas would delight in it," Mary went against years of deportment lessons and slumped toward the table, resting her chin on the heel of her hand. "I suppose you think you could go to Portsmouth to care for her yourself."

Henry spun around, his face brightening. "That's the very idea, Mary! By Jove, there are no flies on you. I can rent a decent house in Portsmouth and stay there, making sure she is safe and has every comfort."

"No," Mary contradicted him, "you *can't*. It would be an insult to the Bertrams, an insult to the Prices, and an insult to Fanny. What of yours, other than flowers, do you think she would accept? The best you can do is visiting her for a day or two, and even then you must wait until she has been there *at least* a month, or you shall look like the villain of a threepenny opera stalking his maidenly prey."

Henry collapsed into a chair, the picture of discontent. "I hate it when you speak good sense."

"I know."

"I have to go to Everingham next week. I could go to Portsmouth after."

"Only if your business takes you through it after the first week of March, brother of mine."

"Bugger."

"What?"

"Beggar; I said I feel like a beggar, having to ask to go see the object of my adoration."

"Yes, I am sure that was *exactly* what you said," Mary retorted with scepticism. "Why do you have to go to Everingham, by-the-by? This is a strange time of the year for you going into Norfolk."

Henry stretched out his legs and crossed his booted feet at the ankles. "I have legitimate business there, relative to the renewal of a lease. I believe the welfare of a large and industrious family is at stake. The business letters from my agent have been dissatisfying of late. I suspect the Maddison of some underhand dealing—of meaning to bias me against the deserving — for some reasons of his own. I am determined to go myself, and thoroughly investigate the merits of the case. Maddison is a clever fellow; I do not wish to displace him— provided he does not try to displace *me*, but I will not be made a cat's paw or treated as a moon-raker by my any man living."

Mary was all approbation. "This is delightful! I cannot begin to tell you how happy it makes me to see you take an interest for the poor and deserving on your estate. This is the influence of Fanny, isn't it? To be a paragon must be contagious, for she has infected you with the desire to be all that any man *should* be."

Her brother shrugged, and looked a little abashed. "It's true that I want to make her think well of me, and it is equally true that I wish to deserve her — insofar as that is possible, of course. I *should* have been more attentive to my tenants and my business. I am thoroughly ashamed of myself that I have not done more. I have been selfish in my concerns, and I repent of it. Ack!"

Henry cried out because Mary had abruptly embraced him, grasping him so hard that it nearly drove the air from his lungs. "What on earth?" he said, and patted her on the back.

Mary's eyes were shining like twin stars. "Oh, Henry! I am so very, *very* proud of you. I will bless Fanny all her life for this change she has inspired. You were a good man before, but now — *now* — you shall be the *best* of men."

"That's no excuse for mussing my cravat," Henry said with feigned petulance. "It took Anderson the better part of an hour to tie it."

Laughing, Mary hugged him again. "You are a goose, Henry, but I cannot imagine having a better brother. How *glad* I am that you are mine."

ıı

Mary supposed that Henry had found an abundance of things to occupy him in the north, since she didn't see hide nor hair of him again for more than three weeks. Happily for Mary, those days were as full of activity for her as they must have been for Henry, and it was not until the 16th that she found time to write to Fanny again.

Mary started the letter with the usual plea of increasing engagements was made in excuse for not having written to her earlier, and continued with "and now that I have begun my letter will not be worth your reading, for there will be no little offering of love at the end, no three or four lines passionées from the most devoted H. C. in the world, for Henry is in Norfolk; business called him to Everingham ten days ago, or perhaps he only pretended to call, for the sake of being travelling at the same time that you were. But there he is, and, by the by, his absence may sufficiently account for any remissness of his sister's in writing, for there has been no 'well, Mary, when do you write to Fanny?—is not it time for you to write to Fanny?' to spur me on. At last, after various attempts at meeting, I have seen your cousins, 'dear Julia and dearest Mrs Rushworth;' they found me at home yesterday, and we were glad to see each other again. We *seemed very* glad to see each other, and I do really think we were a little.—We had a vast deal to say.—Shall I tell you how Mrs Rushworth looked when your name was mentioned? I did not use to think her wanting in self possession, but she had not quite enough for the demands of yesterday. Upon the whole Julia was in the best looks of the two, at least after you were spoken of. There was no recovering the complexion from the moment that I spoke of 'Fanny,' and spoke of her as a sister should.—But Mrs Rushworth's day of good looks will come; we have cards for her first party on the 28th.—Then she will be in beauty, for she will open one of the best houses in Wimpole Street. I was in it two years ago, when it was Lady Lascelles's, and

Mary stopped and wondered if should scratch out that last bit. Pointing out that Maria Rushworth, who was almost sure to turn that dimwitted Mr Rushworth into a cuckold, was living in the house once occupied by a family connected to one of most notorious jades in the Ton (which took some doing on the lady's part) might be too shocking for poor Fanny. Almost the entirety of that area of Marylebone was a nest of slave-owners whose money came from the sugar plantations and trade of the West Indies, and there was a general notion of licentiousness about the place. Not that the rumours of lax morality would stop anyone from attending their dinners, balls, and parties, of course. Not unless they were caught. As Lady Worsley, the step-daughter of Edwin Lascelles, had surely been.

After some consideration, Mary decided to leave the sentence as it was. There was a strong chance that Fanny, sheltered and delicate as she was, had not been told about the accusation that Sir Richard Worsley, called Sir Richard Worse-than-sly in the scandal sheets and newspapers that permeated London, had acted as a pander and displayed his wife in her bath to her would-be lover, Captain George Bisset. Even if Fanny did know, it hardly signified; Sir Thomas Bertram had business dealings with the Lascelles – who were sugar factors – and must not be too shocked by the scandalous elopement between Lady Worsley and Captain Bisset since he continued to associate with the family. Besides, it was an old scandal, and the former Lady Worsley was living well in Farnham with a husband half her age who had taken her maiden name of Fleming. Lord and Lady Fleming were even received by several members of the Beau Monde, since Lady Fleming's brother-in-law was the virtuous and upright General Charles Stanhope, 3rd Earl of Harrington, who had forgiven his wife's sister and allowed her into his home. There were few sins that could not be forgiven by the glittering throng if one was rich and supported by well-connected family members.

Mary gathered her train of thought, reread her last sentence, and continued:

prefer it to almost any I know in London, and certainly she will then feel—to use a vulgar phrase—that she has got her pennyworth for her penny. Henry could not have afforded her such a house. I hope she will recollect it, and be satisfied, as well as she may, with moving the queen of a palace, though the king may appear best in the back ground, and as I have no desire to tease her, I shall never *force* your name upon her again. She will grow sober by degrees.— From all that I hear and guess, Baron Wildenheim's attentions to Julia continue, but I do not know that he has any serious encouragement. She ought to do better. A poor honourable is no catch, and I cannot imagine any liking in the case, for, take away his rants, and the poor Baron has nothing. What a difference a vowel makes!—if his rents were but equal to his rants!—Your cousin Edmund moves slowly; detained, perchance, by parish duties. There may be some old woman at Thornton Lacey to be converted. I am unwilling to fancy myself neglected for a *young* one. Adieu, my dear sweet Fanny, this is a long letter from London; write me a pretty one in reply to gladden Henry's eyes, when he comes back—and send me an account of all the dashing young captains whom you disdain for his sake."

Mary blotted the letter and sealed it, and sent it to Fanny with all the warmth and goodwill that Fanny did not reciprocate.

॥

Fanny's reply came three days later, and was, to Mary's disappointment, rather dull and made no mention of Mrs Rushworth's reaction to the news of Henry's love for Fanny. The chief substance of it was split between the humdrum activities of the everyday and a dispute between Mrs Price and a near neighbour, a woman by the bizarre name of Mrs Dickens. Apparently, Mrs Dickens had invited a few friends for dinner, ostensibly because she was jubilant her youngest son, a sickly baby named Charles, had just reach a full year in age despite his family's fears to the contrary. Mr and Mrs Price had *not* been invited to this dinner, and there was a preponderance of heartburning in the household because of it. Mary supposed Fanny must be enduring a life of extreme tedium is this was the only subject she could find to fill her letter. Poor girl!

Mary resolved to write poor Fanny soon, but then recollected that she might as well wait until after the 28th, so she could tell her all about the Rushworth's party.

॥

"I see someone has no worries about paying for coal-gas," Janet said to Mary as the Fraser's carriage waited its turn to disgorge its passengers onto the Rushworth's doorstep.

Illumination poured out of the windows on the ground and first floor of the most grandiose town house on Wimpole Street. Mary was unsure if the Lyceum Theatre was so well-lit. Thinking upon it, she was unsure that even Apollo in his chariot of fire had ever emitted such luminous rays as the ones beaming from the frontage of the Rushworth's abode.

"Mr Rushworth has twelve thousand a year; he could nearly light London" Mary replied. "I would envy *Mrs* Rushworth, but sadly I have *met* her husband."

Mr Fraser smiled sardonically. "So an advantageous marriage is not advantageous if the man be a dullard?" He cast a meaningful look at his wife. "Women marry for fortunes but are then unhappy because they wish they would have wed for love instead. At least Rushworth can rest easy knowing that he has enough cash on hand to keep his wife from turning into a virago."

Janet flushed at her husband's unsubtle innuendo. "That presupposes that Mr Rushworth isn't a miser determined to be mean in all his dealings, and gives *his* wife a decent amount of pin money."

Mary diverted a quarrel between the couple by interjecting, "My dear Mr Fraser, it would take a college of tutors and the wishes of a fairy godmother to help Mr Rushworth *rise* to level of dullard. The man has a three sheep's worth of wool between his ears, or I serve in Queen Dick's court. A woman may be *prosperously* married to Mr Rushworth, but never *advantageously* married to him."

Janet composed herself and smiled at her friend. "I've heard that the flames of his intellect couldn't make toast."

"Frankly," Mary said with acid humour, "the flames of his intellect couldn't melt butter, let alone toast the bread to spread it on."

II

As accustomed to wealth and elegance as Mary was, she was astonished by the opulence of the Rushworth residence. Everything, from the wallpaper to the paintings to the furnishings to the décor to the floors, *everything* was marked by expense and modernity. Even more amazing was that while this display reeked of money and pride, it somehow remained on the tasteful side of ostentatious. It did not veer into vulgar flamboyance or exhibitions. Its magnificence was not garish. It was glorious rather than vainglorious. She did not think that even the home of Sir Thomas Hope on Duchess Street was its superior.

Mary had the urge to begin applauding Maria Rushworth, and to cry out "Brava!" What Mrs Rushworth had accomplished, in terms of style and splendour, was unprecedented in Mary's experience. Usually one could satisfy any envy by the subtle mockery of too much showiness, but Mrs Rushworth's niceties of presentation pulled one's teeth before they could be bared.

Nonetheless, Mary would not have been herself is she hadn't murmured snidely to Janet, "When you go to the necessary room, do tell me if you think the bowl solid gold or merely gilded."

Even in the number of guests, Mrs Rushworth committed no error into pageantry. Dinners were considered best if one invited "at least the number of Graces and no more than the number of Muses." Maria had invited exactly eight other dinners to sit at the table, and with the inclusion of her sister Julia, the number hit the recommended maximum of nine. Another hostess would have been tempted to exclude Julia from the head-count since she was in residence there, but Maria made no such quibbles at the risk of social perfection.

There were many, many more people who were invited to the party afterwards, which was sure to be an absolute crush, but for now only the blessed few were going to dine in grandeur with their hosts, singled out for the honour of intimacy. Mary suspected the inclusion of herself and the Frasers in the august company was more to guarantee that a report of the evening's lustre would reach Henry than from any true partiality for herself from Mrs Rushworth.

Mrs Rushworth herself was in all respects as resplendent and fashionable as her house. Maria had wasted no time in embracing the darker colours worn by married ladies, and was wearing a Pomona green gown which set off her white skin and fair hair admirably. Brilliant cut diamonds encircled her throat, cascaded from her ears, and winked out from among her blond tresses. Mary could say, in all honesty, that there were few women in London — even among the actresses and courtesans — who could equal Maria in looks … and none who could surpass her.

Even Mr Rushworth looked very much the handsome gentleman, standing tall in a coat tailored by Weston himself, and provided he did not talk, he was an asset to his wife's cachet.

"My dear Mrs Rushworth," Mary chimed, "if you were not so handsome I would have eyes for nothing but your home!"

Maria thanked her graciously, and then introduced her to the three members of the dinner party not already known to her. They were two young gentlemen by the names of Captain Nuttal and Mr Farley, and Lord Greenwood, an elderly widower who had been a close friend of Mr Rushworth's father.

The remaining two members of the party were Mr and Mrs Aylmer of Twickenham, who had been friends of Mary and Henry for several years. John Aylmer had gone to Eton with Henry and Mrs Aylmer had been a confidant of Mary's when the lady still had the name of Miss Annamaria Simples.

Annamaria and Mary shook hands with warm cordiality, and fell easily into conversation.

"How are things in Richmond?" Mary asked her. "Not that it can ever be as lovely as it was before Lady Howe destroyed Pope's villa in '09."

"Lady Howe! It is still all I can do to be civil to her when we meet," Annamaria confessed. "Never have I disliked a fellow Whig more, or struggled more not to throttle one. To destroy the home of Alexander Pope because she found the stream of his admirers who came there to honour his memory to be a nuisance to *her*!"

Mary gave her friend a look of sympathetic agreement. "I comprehend you perfectly. Does it not strike you how strange it is that Pope's villa should be destroyed, when you look at his last verses in *Ode to Solitude*? "Thus unlamented let me die/ Steal from the world, and not a stone/ Tell where I lie." I know it is not the same; Pope's grave marker has not been destroyed. Yet is in not similar in *feeling*? Those who visited his former home did so in remembrance of him, and now there is not one stone left of it, thanks to the disgusting whims of Lady Howe."

"Never have I thought of it *that* way." Annamaria contemplated what Mary had said. "I believe you are right; it does have a strange echo of his *Ode to Solitude*."

"At least there are some consolations left in Richmond," Mary offered. "You can still visit Strawberry Hill at your leisure."

"That *is* a comfort worthy of the claim. Or I suppose I must say it is a comfort until the Earl of Walgrave comes to claim his inheritance. As long as Mrs Damer resides there it is as lively as it is interesting to look at," Annamaria smiled.

"I am sure it is very lively," Mary's eyes twinkled, "especially if Lady Derby comes for a visit."

Annamaria giggled behind her hand. "Now, now. We cannot know if Mrs Damer and Lady Derby are lovers, or were even when Lady Derby was still Miss Eliza Farren. Besides, the authoress Mary Berry still resides in Little Strawberry Hill House, and would not be happy to hear such speculation, considering the enduring nature of her *close friendship* with Mrs Damer."

Mary lowered her voice. "In all seriousness, now that you know Mrs Damer personally – do you think the rumours that she is a Sapphist are true? Or is it all down to Hester Thrale's spite and a general resentment that Mrs Damer's talent as a sculptor exceeds that of so many men?"

"Honestly, I don't know," Annamaria shrugged. "Mrs Damer certainly has some manly ways about her, but she's never acted inappropriately toward me or any other women in my presence. Where there is smoke, there may be fire, but everyone says that Hester Thrale turned into a bitter old cat after she married that Italian music master of hers thirty years ago and got cut from so much of good society. Mrs Damer indubitably moves in much better company than *Mrs Piozzi*. At this point, they are all elderly ladies, and I don't suppose it matters much."

"True," Mary conceded, "but scandals are so *tame* nowadays compared to the brouhaha about Mrs Damer in her youth."

"Be of good cheer," Annamaria grinned, "Prinny is likely to be caught out in bed with Lady Hertford, two chickens, and a bishop any day now."

Mary laughed more loudly than she had meant to, but fortunately she was saved from inquiries as to what had amused her by the arrival of the butler to announce that dinner was served.

‖

If Mary had been awestruck by the entranceway and drawing-room of Rushworth's house, it was nothing compared to the amazement she felt when she saw the dining table. Not only was the table huge, Mrs Rushworth had taken a leaf from the Regent's book and had commissioned a working fountain for the centre of it. Mary could not figure out how the hydraulic ram for it worked, and she assumed such clever workmanship must be correspondingly expensive. The fountain was flanked by two long silver troughs, roughly six inches high and nine inches in width, that extended to each end of the table. The troughs were decorated with aquatic flowers and there were actually little goldfish and gudgeons swimming around in them.

The enormous and fantastical gaslight chandelier above the table removed any need for candles, which was just as well since the water feature took up so much table space. The table had been decorated with small ceramic vases as snowy white as the Irish lace tablecloth they rested upon, all bursting with hothouse roses of multiple shades. Intricately cut crystal decanters containing white wines matched the goblets readied by each plate, and the dinnerware itself was painted and gilded Sèvres porcelain in the neoclassical style.

When the fish course came, Mr Aylmer declared, "It seems perverse to eat these piscine dishes in front of their finned fellows in the fountain; what if I am consuming a friend or relation?"

Animated conversation flowed as freely as the wine all through dinner, with everyone providing witticisms but Mr Rushworth. The most that could be said for the master of the house was that he did an admirable job of carving the pheasant.

Mary was not in the least surprised when the dessert course featured a multi-tiered and elaborately decorated cake that could have only come from Gunter's Tea Shop. The Duchess of Bedford had served Gunter's desserts instead of those made by her own pastry chefs at a ball two years before and now it was a mark of fashion for the dessert course to consist heavily of the shop's confections. She was also not unprepared to be offered pineapple in various guises. They were a delicious fruit to be sure, but they functioned more as a way of saying 'look! we can afford pineapples' than to delight the palate of the guests. The only thing the table was missing were sherbets, sorbets, and ices, which Mary supposed were too easily obtained in winter to be worth for Mrs Rushworth to bother providing.

ıı

After dinner, Mary found that the crush she had predicted had come to pass. There were so many of the beau monde crowding into the town house that, even as capacious as it was, there was scarcely room to move. The success of the party was stamped when no fewer than three young ladies fainted from the heat and stifling press of bodies. Mary would not have been startled to hear that children were conceived by women attempting to go through a doorway in differing directions than some member of the opposite sex.

It was nearly five o'clock in the morning, and the thin light of dawn was showing by the time Mary and the Frasers returned to Berkeley Square. As large and well-appointed as her friends' town house was, she could not help but think it appeared drab and insignificant compared to the magnificence of the home on Wimpole Street. Beatty helped her strip down to her shift, and Mary crawled half-asleep beneath her blankets. In spite of the roar of the sounds of the rest of London waking up, Mary drifted off almost instantly, and dreamed that she was watching Maria Bertram drown in river of rose petals.

Chapter Forty

MARY HAD MEANT to write Fanny to tell her all about the wild success of Maria's first party, but she was too stupid from tiredness the next day, and the day after that Edmund Bertram arrived in town and threw all her thoughts into confusion.

Janet kindly invited Edmund to tea as soon as his card appeared in her salver. Mary, who had thought she had been doing tolerably well of not thinking about him, found that her stomach was aflutter and her heart beat faster at the idea of seeing him after dinner. He was sure to be as handsome as ever, but would his formal country manners do as well in the city as they had in Mansfield? And his solemnity! Would it stifle conversation? Mary could not help but wonder if she *truly* loved Edmund, if doubts like these would occur. Surely a woman in love was blind to her lover's faults, and she did not feel blinkered by her preference for him, let alone deprived of her sight entirely.

When the butler announced Mr Edmund Bertram, Mary felt his arrival — if she was willing to permit herself the melodrama — in all her pulses and all her nerves. He came — he was in the room — she rose and walked to him and offered him her hand and welcomed him with words she could scarcely remember saying — introductions were made — they sat. Mary, who was truly affected by Edmund's presence, tried to bring herself back into equilibrium. She was grateful that Janet and Mr Fraser and Margaret were speaking to him while she struggled to make herself calm.

"How was your trip, sir?" Mr Fraser asked him civilly.

Edmund, who had perhaps grown even more handsome than Mary remembered him, replied with equal civility. "It went well, sir. The roads were better than I could have expected for this time of year."

"Did you travel with company?"

"I am afraid I was quite the solivagant."

"Then I hope your sojourn was peaceful, rather than tedious. I will own that while there are pleasures to be had in travelling with someone to converse with, there is tranquillity in solitude that is often the most restful and welcome."

Edmund made a slight bow in acknowledgement. "I found it comfortable, but I am luckily able to read in a moving carriage without becoming ill, and therefore was able to entertain myself with ease."

"That is indeed lucky, sir. I am not so fortunate."

There was a small pause in the conversation while Edmund accepted a cup of tea and thanked Mrs Fraser.

"Are you come to London for leisure or have you come on business matters, sir?" Mr Fraser likewise accepted his tea from his wife.

"It is both, sir. My father asks me to see to some business matters, but I will be free to enjoy the pleasures of London for the most part."

"Do you stay with friends or family members here?"

"I have the good fortune of claiming my hosts as both. My father's cousins are in town and they have welcomed me with great cordiality to reside with them for the three weeks I am to be here."

The harsh illumination of the gaslights could sometimes make otherwise attractive people look sickly, or strained, but they did nothing to lessen Edmund's physical appeal. His skin retained the robust pinkness of good health and the light made the blue of his eyes appear darker, stronger. Mary obliquely watched him sip his tea, fascinated by the way his hands, as large and masculine as they were, held the fragile china with such a gentle and easy grip. She had almost forgotten how beautiful his mouth was. Like his sister Maria's, his bottom lip was pillowy but his top lip was a sharply delineated Cupid's bow. His hair was too short to curl in full, but she could see from the way it flounced that if he grew it out another inch it would form itself into the same golden ringlets with which nature had blessed his sisters. With such a tender mouth and girlish locks, only the strong bones of his cheeks and the squareness of his chin kept him from looking effeminate. She remembered how it had felt when he kissed the backs of her knuckles in farewell the last time he had seen her at Mansfield Park; the softness of his mouth almost startling. How could what she felt toward him not be love?

Having handed round the tea, Mrs Fraser now spoke up. "We are recently acquainted with your sister, Mrs Rushworth. Do your cousins live in proximity to her?" Janet studiously avoided asking him why he wasn't staying on Wimpole Street with his nearer relations.

"They live just off Berkeley Square, ma'am."

"Then you are not far from my sister, Lady Stornoway."

Janet waited in vain for Edmund to make some comment about the felicity of having a sister nearby, or to ask for an introduction to the Stornoways. Instead, her guest merely sipped his tea. However, Edmund was too well-bred to let the silence drag out to the point of discomfort or obvious rudeness on his part, so he complimented his hostess on the brew.

Nonplussed, Janet tried to give him an opening to ask for an introduction once more. "It is most likely that you have seen my sister's town house, without knowing it. Hers is the largest one on the east side of the square, and has a vermillion door with some particularly fine iron scroll-work around it that catches the eye. Of course, it cannot compare to your sister's house on Wimpole Street!"

"We dined at the Rushworth's less than a week ago," there was a faintly nasty undertone to Mr Fraser's voice, "and my wife was all agog. She can never get enough of looking at such finery."

Mary wasn't surprised when Janet stiffened at the implication she was overly interested in material goods. Janet's elder sister Flora had been their mother's loll and Janet had been regarded as second best in all things, and the constant feeling of being lesser-than had left Janet's pride as thin and prickly as a nettle leaf. Her husband, rather than noting Janet's over-sensitivity to criticism and speaking gently to her, had developed a nasty habit of jabbing at her within weeks of their wedding. Mary suspected that he resented the fact Janet only married him for his fortune, but she thought his rancour unreasonable; why else would a lovely young woman marry an old, crabby man? Fraser should have known that from the beginning and made his peace with it, or not asked Janet to marry him at all. To ask Janet to marry him and yet punish her for the motivations of her acceptance was sheer ill-breeding as far as Mary was concerned.

Two red spots appeared high on Janet's cheeks, but she smiled and said in a voice like honey laced with arsenic, "One cannot help but admire such elegant taste, Mr Fraser. Do not fret, though. I shall not ask for the money to imitate Mrs Rushworth's style *here*, even if the house were as grand in size. I know how even giving me pin money causes you *suffering*."

A muscle in Drummond Fraser's cheek jumped at the accusation of parsimony. "I don't think there is enough pin money to be had to satisfy *you*, darling."

"Nonsense," Janet's expression and tone was fond, as though she were only jesting with her spouse, but her eyes were hard as flint. "My wants are modest enough. Haven't I have demonstrated that I can be easily satisfied with hardly more than a pittance?"

The Fraser's banter could have passed for playful in another couple, but Mary was fairly sure that Edmund could detect the venom hidden in the words as well as she could, and she was embarrassed for all of them.

"You cannot blame any woman for being agog at Mrs Rushworth's house, Mr Fraser," Mary breezily interjected, trying to lighten the darkness filling the room with some sunny speech. "I hear men admire a stylish curricle readily enough, but your sex all seem to find a woman's admiration of décor amusing. With our concerns being so domestic in nature, why shouldn't we notice domestic beauty? Doesn't it serve the men as well? Why, Mrs Fraser has already gotten sugared almonds from Mrs Rushworth's confectioner and you complimented them after dinner last night."

"You have a very good point, Miss Crawford," Mr Fraser, polite to every lady but his wife, agreed. "The almonds were excellent and it behoves me to encourage such niceties."

Edmund, as uncomfortable as Mary was with the Fraser's sub-textual spat but hiding it perfectly, asked his host if sugared almonds were a particular favourite and diverted the conversation to the topic of confectioneries. Edmund and Mr Fraser discovered that they both thought that although the best comfits and macaroons were available at Duvall's, Gunter's was the superior for ices and cakes, while Margaret Fraser declared that nothing pleased her so well as the silky marshmallow treats known as pâté de guimauve available at Parmetier's.

After a quarter hour in Edmund's presence, Mary felt that she could speak directly to him without any appearance of fawning upon him. She had seen many women, most of them young but some old enough to have known better, positively *gush* during conversation with Henry, and Mary had a horror of appearing at such a disadvantage in talking to a beau. Was there anything more ridiculous and gauche than a woman who revealed her preference?

"How is everyone at Mansfield, Mr Bertram? How does your mother get on with no Fanny to secure her entertainment and comfort?"

Edmund smiled at her. "They all do very well, I thank you. My mother does miss Fanny I believe, and speaks often of having her home again, but my aunt Norris spends a great deal of time at the Park so my mother is not left alone much. Before your sister went to bath, Mrs Grant was good enough to be a frequent visitor as well."

"My sister writes to me at least once a week — I am remiss at writing her back with punctuality but I am comforted to know that her sweet temper and cheerful disposition will always forgive me more readily than I deserve — and her tales from Mansfield made me really feel as though I were there. She wished your mother and Sir Thomas could be enticed to visit Bath, but did not ask because she thought it would be too unlikely for them to accept and feared it would seem impertinent of her to advise it."

"It is very unlikely that my mother would be willing to make such a trip; she prefers quiet evenings at home to anything and would probably not enjoy Bath the way your more sociable sister does. It was kind of your sister to think of it, and wise of her to see the futility of it."

Mary could not help but notice that Edmund did not insist that such an invitation or recommendation by Mrs Grant would *not* be considered impertinent. For a man who expected her to lower herself by marrying a country parson he was most high in the instep in regards to his parent's rank compared to that of Dr Grant. It vexed her, and brought other irksome memories into her mind, such as the fact that he had squandered an opportunity to be given her hand six weeks ago by failing to propose. *Then* she had been determined to accept him, but *now* she was beset once more by romantic velleities and worries. It put her out of charity with him, and made her want to tease him in spite of her attraction to him.

"It is true that my sister does enjoy being out much in company, but that is a blessing for Henry and I. We are both of us so fond of society that a sister who is always willing to make merry simply adds to our harmony as a family. The more I am in the world, the more grateful I am for such loving siblings. Both have offered me their home as my own as long as my name remains Crawford, and not everyone has the luxury of such closeness of thought and opinion as I have with my brother and sister."

"You are indeed lucky," Edmund's exquisite mouth compressed briefly at the corners as he was reminded that he shared very few characteristics with his brother or sisters, beyond the shallow and the physical, and that Mrs Rushworth had not invited him to stay with *her*.

The idea that Mary could have aimed that subtle barb at him in reprisal for his snobbery did not cross his mind. Mary had become his Ideal, and his Ideal woman could never be cross or retaliatory. Nonetheless, Mary was worried she had been a little *too* pointed, and offered Edmund the comfort of thinking about his cousin.

"I may be luckier still, if Henry can secure Fanny for my sister. *She* is not one to love society, but her goodness and sweetness of temper must make her welcome in any family of good sense."

Edmund's face grew more relaxed. "If I may confess it, Fanny is as dear to me as either of my sisters, and I am as eager as you are for your brother to win her hand. I can think of no one better for her than a man of Crawford's keen mind and easy-going outlook. Crawford will keep her blue devils at bay, and she will give him a gentle check on his high spirits."

"I have to say that I was unsure of what I found most surprising about Mr Crawford's submission to Cupid; his fall or his object's refusal," Janet's voice had lost its earlier animation. "I cannot think of a single unattached woman in all of London who would have not accepted him had he asked her. He has everything in his favour, both in fortune and in character."

Mary knew that her friend, who was still smarting from her husband's comments earlier, would be stiff and cold in her speech and manner for as long as she was trying to conceal her hurt feelings. What a pity that Edmund should see Janet this way at their first meeting! First impressions were so important.

"It says a great deal of the lady that Miss Price did not let Mr Crawford's property and wealth secure her hand." Fraser was less interested in complimenting Miss Price than he was in reminding his wife what the world thought of women who married for money.

Mary briefly considered picking up a nearby vase and smashing it over Mr Fraser's head for provoking Janet again.

"As if women were encouraged to make imprudent marriages to penniless men every day!" Mary laughed, her lively manner and candied tone obscuring the sting of her disagreement. "When someone seeks *your* daughter's hand in marriage, I am sure that *you* will be very persistent in establishing his ability to support her and her security in the articles. Yet if a woman dares to even consider then benefits of being rich rather than poor, then she is painted a mercenary! You must admit this is unfair, dear Mr Fraser."

"There is something in what you say," Fraser smiled at Mary, as charmed as everyone else by her sparkling eyes and ability to make refutations appear to be wit. "I will amend my statement to compliment Miss Price on not accepting Crawford *only* out of consideration for his wealth."

"There is another consideration," Edmund said before Mary could reply to Fraser. "It is a man's place and purview to consider such matters for his daughter. It shows a want of delicacy for a woman to be overly aware of such matters. I am sure my cousin gave no thought to Crawford's wealth one way or another. She cannot marry where she is not *sure* she loves; that is the crux of it. She is too aware of what misery such an evil would bring."

"And I think too well of Fanny's brains to believe fortune does *not* weigh in Henry's favour in her considerations," Mary rejoined, tilting her head beguilingly to imply a playfulness that was not actually there. "Did not her own mother marry imprudently? Can Fanny be unaware of the folly of marrying where want may follow? "

"As much as it pains me, I cannot agree with you. In my opinion, it is not a matter of brains," Edmund contradicted, frowning. "It is that Fanny's natural delicacy of mind cannot even consider the other benefits of the marriage if she does not love Crawford as she should. I know that my father had to point out the prudence of accepting your brother to her when he explained his approbation to the match."

Edmund now joined Mr Fraser on Mary's list of men she would like to hammer over the head with a heavy object for their delusional insistence that *good* women gave no thought to money.

"It is, of course, to Fanny's credit that she will not marry Henry if she is unsure she could secure his happiness and her own. However, whereas Henry's proposals are viewed as a compliment, I doubt even Fanny would be unoffended if some local farmer's lad had the temerity to ask for her hand — and his lack of substance would be the chief reason for the offence and his instant rejection. Moreover, I am *very* much mistaken if this fictional farm boy's expectation that Fanny should join him in comparative poverty would not offend Sir Thomas as well." Her expression was syrup and sparkles, but the acid in her meaning could have etched glass.

"Perhaps Miss Price is prudently waiting until she knows Mr Crawford longer," Janet added. "She might not be entirely sure that

Mr Crawford will *remain* the gentleman that he is while he is wooing her. A husband can be very different from a suitor," She looked at Mary, "Do you remember Miss Harbinshire?"

"Very well!" Mary answered with a sigh.

"Miss Harbinshire," Janet explained to the men and Margaret, "was a school-friend of Mary's and mine. She married a Mr Horatio Leguna in her first season. We were all delighted for her; he was the most charming man I have ever met — and that includes Mr Crawford! Everything was in his favour. He was rich and handsome and treated Miss Harbinshire as if she were a queen and he a mere knight in an Arthurian tale. Oh, how we all envied her such a lover! But she had not been enrolled in the lists of Hymen six weeks when she fled back to her father's home. Apparently, he was ... well, the least said the better! He refused to divorce her, though, and demanded Mr Harbinshire return her to him. The poor girl's parents were so afraid that they would be forced to relinquish their daughter to him that they up and immigrated to Canada to keep her safe from her husband. One never really knows a man until one marries him, and it is far too late to find out one has been taken in *then*," She pointedly did not look at her husband.

"Someone should write to them and tell them it is safe to return to England," Mr Fraser said. "Leguna was killed last night in a duel."

There were exclamations of surprise from his listeners.

Fraser spread his hands in a manner that indicated both his indifference and disdain, without having to be so crass as to shrug his shoulders before a guest, and addressed Edmund. "I heard of it this morning in my club, but thought it an unfit topic of conversation for ladies. If I had known that either Miss Crawford or my wife were familiar with Leguna, I would have mentioned it earlier."

"Can you tell what precipitated the duel, sir, without offending the ladies?" Edmund asked.

"The man was caught cheating at cards. It left him so friendless that he had to use his solicitor as a second."

Beating his wife so badly that she lost two teeth didn't ruin him, but cheating at cards did? How revoltingly typical, Mary thought to herself.

"If I knew the Harbinshires' direction, I would indeed write them," Janet averred. "I believe Mrs Glowder, who was Miss Anna Coster when we were at school, was a particular friend of Miss Harbinshire. Mrs Glowder is at home tomorrow, I believe. Mary, will you come with me to call upon her? We can make sure she has heard

the news about that odious Leguna, and I am sure she will write to
the Harbinshires if she has their direction."

"Of course," Mary assured her. "I always thought Mrs Glowder
to be a sweet girl; I should like to see her in any case."

"May I come too, Mother?" Margaret asked. "I am acquainted
with Mrs Glowder. My friend Miss Sleed is her cousin, and we were
introduced last summer when I stayed with the Sleeds for a few weeks
at their estate in Cornwall."

Janet hesitated. Although preferring to have only Mary as her
company, she felt she must to Margaret's request, as civility demanded.
Although she could not feel close to a 'daughter' only four years
younger than herself, Janet did *try* to be as well-bred and obliging as
possible to her husband's child.

"I had to consider for a moment if Mrs Glowder might have
other acquaintance at home to whom I would prefer that you — or
I, come to think of it — would not be introduced," Janet said to
Margaret, to explain away any sting the girl might have felt from her
stepmother's less-than-prompt response.

Janet turned to Edmund to clarify. "My friend Mrs Glowder,
although a very good sort of woman who was born with excellent
connections, married into a family of tradesmen. They are rich and
respectable, to be sure, but I do not think it would benefit Miss Fraser
to have one of the vulgar women of the Glower family's social circle
be able to claim her as an acquaintance."

Mary knew this was no more than the simple truth, and knew
how suddenly one could find oneself no longer received in the best
houses if it was believed you were becoming vulgar by association. In
Janet's situation, Mary would have done likewise for her stepdaughter.

Edmund believed he was of a differing opinion. Although
pained by his Aunt Price's disobliging and disadvantageous marriage,
he sneered inwardly at what he thought were Janet's pretensions at
gentility. Who were the Frasers, to be concerned with such things?
He was not a man who spent a lot of time in self-reflection, and did
not see his own snobbery as analogous to Janet Fraser's cares. For
Edmund, *his* pomposity was *justified* by his father's rank of baronet,
whereas the Fraser family was merely a generation or two removed
from the wool merchants that made their fortune. Ms Fraser, as far as
Edmund's opinion went, had lowered herself nearly as much as Mrs
Glowder had done.

Edmund's notions of Mary's friends would not shift during his upcoming three weeks in Town. He was not honest with himself regarding how much his own antipathy for Mrs Fraser and Lady Stornoway was based largely on his belief that they would discourage Mary from accepting his proposal because he was an obscure second son and a clergyman. He had been unconsciously seeking reasons to validate his dislike of Mary's two closest friends in London, and thus he found a basis for his disdain in nearly everything they did or any opinion they expressed. The irony of the fact that *he* was bitterly assuming the worst of Mary's friends because he feared that *they* were presupposing his unworthiness as a husband for Mary based on his career and birth order was totally lost on him.

Chapter Forty-One

"HENRY!" MARY LOOKED up from her book to see her brother enter the family parlour. It was hardly noon, a time when only the most intimate friends would visit, and with Janet at her mantua maker's and Fraser at his club, she hadn't expected anyone to disturb her time of leisure with her new novel. A disturbance from Henry, however, was always welcome. She stood to embrace him.

"Hello, sister mine!" Henry took both her hands in his and kissed her cheeks. "You look even more beautiful than ever."

"Don't be silly. No one looks beautiful in March. The weather simply *demands* a haggard appearance. The month of March is why Englishmen have no need of purgatory." Mary rang the bell for the servant before she resumed her seat. "Sit down and I'll order us a cup of tea to warm us. How was Norfolk?"

"Cold as a Tory's heart," Henry lamented in jest, "but not nearly so black. I am nonetheless glad I came. Maddison needed to be put back in his proper place. He needed a reminder that I will not be tricked on the south side of Everingham, any more than on the north, that I will be master of my own property, by Jove! He's been up to mischief again. He's trifling with a tenet's wife and is giving preference to some tenets in exchange for favours, which may be even called bribes. It's a muddle, Mary. He's a good steward in most ways — it is not as though he is embezzling or letting things go to rack and ruin – but he thinks he can impose upon me! I am sure he's trying to get a cousin of his own into a certain mill, which I design for somebody else. I've come back to Town for a few weeks as a kind of test. If Maddison does what he ought, he'll be well. If not, I shall give him his notice."

"I hope for your sake the fellow behaves himself," Mary gave her brother a look of sympathy. "Finding a good steward can be tremendously difficult. I went to dinner last Tuesday at the Febland's and met a lawyer by the name of Mr Knightly who told me the tribulations of finding a good steward for his father-in-law's estate in the *minutest* detail. He nearly bored me stiff, and he would *not* give over talking about it. I think the only person there fonder of the sound of his voice than himself was his wife."

"An admirable quality in a wife," Henry opined.

Mary laughed. "Well, you've your eye on the right gel for that! Fanny would much rather listen than talk."

"Fanny," Henry looked briefly fretful. "It has been an age since I have gotten to see her, but I've made up my mind; I go to Portsmouth tomorrow."

"I think she's been there long enough that Sir Thomas won't think it an impertinent judgement on his decision to send her," Mary agreed. "How long will you be there?"

"Only one night. Longer would make her uncomfortable, I believe."

"The poor thing has been there a month. I hope those terrible sea breezes have not ruined her skin."

"You and our aunt always made too much of the sea air, Mary," Henry showed some of his exasperation. "The sea air is *good* for one's health."

Mary narrowed her eyes at her brother. "Fine, then. Take poor Fanny to the seaside and turn her tender cheeks as rough as the heel of my foot and as red and blotchy as a persimmon. That will do *wonders* for her health."

"It's not like I am going to have her working the docks or on a fishing boat! A walk in a fine wind for exercise is plenty," Henry became thoughtful. "I wonder if sea-bathing would help her not get knocked up so easily?"

"Better find a good dipper if you take her to sea bathe. As frail as Fanny is, the waves will sweep her right out into the channel without a sturdy dipper to hold her."

"I'll settle for no other dipper but Mary Gunn herself," Henry promised.

"It's is *Martha* Gunn," Mary laughed. "I see I'll have no choice but to go with you, to secure Fanny's safety in the waters."

"Even better, I'll take Fanny on a tour of the southern Italian spas for our honeymoon, and you can come with us," Henry's eyes softened as he thought about it. "I will take you and Fanny to the Acque Albule Springs. They stink of sulphur but the heat seeps into your bones and gives you new life, I could swear it. I cannot wait until you both see Tivoli. It is beautiful beyond the telling, Mary.

The falls where the Aniene river begins — the ruins of Hadrian's villa and the Temple of Vesta — the Villa d'Este where Lucrezia Borgia's son lived — it all befuddles the mind with wonder. It is also close to Rome; you've always wanted to go to Rome, and we can certainly stay there for a fortnight or so. Then we can go to the Almalfi coast. Just thinking about it makes me think I can taste limoncello! We'll go to Positano. To sea-bathe there is to float in the heavens. The water is as blue and as clear as the sky, and as warm as true love's kiss. And the natural beauties of the landscape! Fanny will be in raptures."

"If I didn't want you to marry Fanny *before*, I do *now*," Mary teased, "if for no other reason than that I will finally get to see some of the Italian coast and Rome! You have no idea of how much I envied you your grand tour, Henry."

"I do have some idea of it, yes," Henry raised an eyebrow. "I heard about it with every breath you took for a year before it and the year after it."

"You exaggerate," Mary waved away his assertions. "I may have mentioned it once or twice."

"Once or twice an *hour*," Henry declared.

"Never fear, I shall be forever rendered mute with gratitude the instant I dip one toe into Mediterranean," Mary promised mockingly.

"You may be rendered mute if I held your head under it long enough, but never before that."

"With any luck, a handsome Roman would save me from my cruel brother."

"With any luck, I'd trip him and throw him into the sea before he could lay a hand on you. Those Latin men have blood much too hot to marry my sister."

"Says the man who has taken many an Italian opera girl under his protection."

"That's how I know Italians are hot blooded. Marry a nice German fellow, if you must wed abroad."

"A calm, sedate man of temperance ... like our German regent I suppose?"

"Touché!" Henry pressed a hand to his heart as if wounded by his sister outsmarting him. "It is plain that I can trust no one other than an Englishman to wed my gentle sister."

"I could marry a Spaniard. English royalty has mixed with Spanish blood. That should be good enough for me."

"Bah. Look what happened to Henry VIII when he married a Spanish lady."

"And look what happened to Anne Boleyn and Katherine Howard when *they* married an Englishman," Mary pointed out in return.

Henry grinned. "Don't give your husband a bull's feather to wear and you'll be fine."

"As if I should ever be such a fool as to risk my reputation and happiness for an intrigue," Mary snorted. "As long as I have more wit than peafowl my husband is assured a wife more loyal than Penelope."

"I used to think that women such as Penelope were myths invented by hopeful men, until I met Fanny."

"And what cause for worry did our mother give our father, or our aunt ever give the Admiral?" Mary was affronted.

Henry looked chagrined. "You are right, dearest. I cry peccavi. I paint with too broad a brush and see with too jaded an eye."

Mollified, Mary conceded, "There are many women in the Ton who have given you just cause to wonder. You cannot be held entirely to blame for your biased opinions of my sex."

"Never Fanny, though." Henry no effort to hide his romantic sigh. "I would not have believed such virtue could wear a human form. She is such as will make even the Admiral bow before her, like a Tarasque before Saint Martha."

"Who on earth," Mary looked quizzical, "is a Tarasque?"

"You've not heard that legend?" Accustomed to his sister's nearly encyclopaedic knowledge of myths and literature, Henry was somewhat taken aback by her ignorance of the beast St Martha tamed.

"I've no idea who that is. Are you going to tell me, or leave me in suspense?"

"This is a nice reversal; I tell you something *you* don't know!" Henry looked pleased, and earned himself a slanted look from his sister. "The Tarasque is a what, rather than a who. St Martha and the Tarasque is a tale from Provence. I had to translate it from French into Greek at Eton, and it caught my fancy. The Tarasque was supposedly a scaly water beast as big as an ox that lived in the marsh along the banks of the Rhone and ate travellers. It had a fearsome hodgepodge of animal characteristics; a turtle's shell and a lion's head and six legs like an insect and either a scorpion's sting or a snake as its tail – I have forgotten the exactitudes of its makeup. Naturally, the Tarasque's appearance and dining habits dismayed the people living in the area.

They sent knights against it but it would just eat the knights, possibly as a dessert course after all the travellers ..."

"The travellers might have been an apéritif before the knights, Henry. You can't just wildly speculate on that sort of thing," Mary interrupted him playfully.

"Regardless, the beast was a nuisance. Fortunately, St Martha happened to be in the region and lulled the monster with her prayers. She then led the tamed beast into the nearest city, where the poor thing was promptly slaughtered. The populace, grateful to St Martha for their deliverance and sorrowful after she scolded them for killing the monster, converted to Christianity forthwith and declared the name of the town to be Tarascon from that moment on, and it still stands to this day."

Mary cocked her head. "And how is this different from St George and the dragon, how?"

"On some very important points, dear sister. For example, the saint's name was Martha and the Tarasque wasn't technically a dragon."

"Ah. I see," Mary nodded sagely. "And how is it different from various fairy-tales about Beauty and the Beast?"

"In the fairy tales, the beast isn't slain by upset villagers."

"Crucial differences, I know," Mary agreed drolly. "Nonetheless, one cannot help but notice how similar the idea of a beauty — one either pure in heart or pure in soul or pure in face — can tame a beast. Or that if someone is but good enough, he or she can render a violent evil into a calm companion. The tales all seem to be offshoots of the story of Enkidu from the *Epic of Gilgamesh*, in my opinion."

"Imagine," Henry said with a straight face, "a world wherein not everyone attends lectures on the Epic of Gilgamesh with a gaggle of ladies intrigued by Middle Eastern antiquarianism, and explain Enkidu to me."

"Enkidu was a beast-like man who was tamed by a priestess named Shamkat. She was a Magdalene, but in service to the gods, and when she befriended Enkidu he became civilised and was transformed into a boon companion for the heroic king, Gilgamesh. Gilgamesh was kind of Sumerian Odysseus, or rather Odysseus is a Greek version of Gilgamesh, since the Mesopotamian epic pre-dates Greek civilisation by more than a thousand years."

"Since Fanny has tamed me with the goodness and purity of her heart and soul, does that make me analogous to pagan hero-kings?" Henry asked flippantly.

"As if your pride needed bolstering in that manner," Mary told him witheringly. "You are too well aware of your own superiorities as it is. I may think Fanny's rejection of you to be ridiculous on her part, but I cannot deny that it is a beneficial thing for you to find out that not *all* women would leap at the chance to lead you into the parson's trap."

"Does my pride make me more of a beast, then? Either way, Fanny has lulled me into the fold."

"I cannot deny it. Fanny has quite transformed you into the best possible aspect of yourself. I think you will do as much for her, Henry. You can lessen her shyness and timidity, and give her the comfortable life I believe she deserves."

"I will devote myself to her happiness," Henry was uncustomarily serious. "Her contentment will be my only object. She need never fear that the beast will re-emerge."

"Dear Henry! I know you will. I am aware, as no one else can be, of your kindness and devotion where you are sincerely attached."

The siblings were interrupted by the arrival of the tea things, accompanied by no less an august servant than the housekeeper. The housekeeper apologised for the tardiness of the tea's arrival while the footman set the tea tray upon the table; one of the scullery maids had been badly scalded when she slipped while carrying boiling water and it had set up a great deal of confusion below stairs. Mary and Henry expressed their sympathy for the scullion, and assured the housekeeper that they felt there had been no excessive delay in the tea's arrival.

"Do you ever find yourself missing Mrs Grant's tea?" Mary asked as she sipped the brew. The smell and taste of tea always brought her time at the parsonage with her sister strongly to her mind, and with it a small pang of longing for Mrs Grant's company. In the absence of both mother and motherly aunt, the attentions of her older sister had been a renewal of the feeling mothered, and Mary missed the warmth of being cosseted in such a way.

"I find myself missing many things about the parsonage and Mansfield that I would have never believed possible at this time last year," Henry said, "Mrs Grant's tea among them. Who would have thought a small village in Northampton could have such charms to an inveterate city dweller such as myself?"

Mary considered. "I think it is the *people* we miss, rather than the place. If I could have our friends from Northampton join us in London at the snap of my fingers, I would. I would be happiest to have all the benefits of Town wedded to all the blessings of Mansfield."

"You have a point," Henry nodded. "However, I have always been more for the countryside than you have been. Natural beauties and the picturesque do not thrill your heart the way they do mine. It is why I travel so frequently to the Bath or to Richmond; I want more variety in my landscape than what the city parks can offer."

"When I find a landscape as interesting to look upon as a painting exhibit or a play, I shall agree with you," Mary smiled. "But until I find a view that matches Kean on stage, I shall remain a Londoner through and through."

"Does this mean Bertram will be getting a broken heart?" Henry inquired. "You know he is as bound to Northampton as a country parson."

Mary made a creditable appearance of unconcern. "Mr Edmund Bertram has given me no indication that my choices in life should affect his heart in any way. He's come to London to visit friends — although he is not staying with the Rushworths. I cannot fault him for that. Can you imagine the mortification of having a brother like Mr Rushworth? I don't think Mrs Rushworth much wants him there either. She cannot act the coquette when her moralistic older brother attends her at every move. You should have seen her at her party, Henry! I have seldom seen a greater flirt. Be that as it may, Mr Bertram has visited me here at the Frasers, who have paid him every attention and courtesy, many times and he has never declared himself. I think that any belief he ever wished to pay me his addresses was the result of a shared brain fever between you and our elder sister."

"I doubt that, Mary," Henry was not fooled by her casual dismissal. "I have never seen a man more smitten that Bertram when he looks at you, excepting myself when I look at Fanny. I will wager that he quibbles because he fears rejection. He knows you have no yen to be a parson's wife in the hinterlands."

"If what you say is true, it is no credit to him," Mary sniffed derisively. "Faint heart never won fair maiden. He should, in the advice of Lady Macbeth, "screw his courage to the sticking point." Moreover, it is not his profession as much as his manner that is off-putting to me as of late. He is like a civil block of wood! I know he was never lively, but at least at Mansfield his manners were engaging.

Has he changed, or does he but suffer by comparison? Either way, it pleases me *not*."

"I would think it is just his natural reserve, dearest. It increases among strangers, and seems larger than it is when he is in company with those with easier manners. If you were more charmed by smooth and easy manners than serious and sincere ones, then you would have been more interested in Mr Tom Bertram than his sober younger brother."

"I don't remember him being quite so sober when we were at Mansfield," Mary protested. "Honestly, sometimes he sits around with such a sour, pious expression that he looks like a Methodist who's bitten a lemon. His morality seems to run amok in society. One cannot even give a slightly risqué anecdote or bit of gossip without making sure he cannot hear. I thought he would cluck his tongue like an old maiden aunt at Janet's tale of Lady Hertford!"

Henry frowned. "If he is so little concerned with your happiness that he cannot make himself agreeable to your friends, then he deserves to lose you, and is no loss. Just remain friendly with him, I beg you. He's dear to Fanny and I foresee him to be a frequent visitor when she becomes Mrs Crawford. I would not wish to see a coldness between those I most want to be guests in my home."

Mary was dissatisfied with his reply. "I don't think *coldness* would be the proper adjective. His behaviour vexes me too much for me to feel *cold*. But — supposing that Mr Bertram were interested in obtaining my hand, which I do not admit to — can my vexation be thought of as *indifference* to him? Is not this some sign of feelings on my part? If so, it is an injury to all my sex for me to admit it, even to a brother, but I cannot help but speculate upon the nature of … attachment." Mary was too aware of propriety to use the word "love" regarding a man to whom she was not engaged, even if it was only in front of Henry.

"I cannot help you there, I am afraid," Henry looked sympathetic. "My feelings for Fanny have no elements of vexation at all, but it might be very different for women. Perhaps Fanny feels vexed with *me*; and if so I can but hope it is a symptom of her interest."

"Why would Fanny be vexed with you?"

"For two reasons. First, because I ignored her when I was flirting with the Miss Crawfords, and secondly, because I command her taste and attention when she wishes she could dismiss me entirely."

"I cannot ascribe the first to Mr Bertram, but it *is* true he commands my taste and attention when I would rather he not," Mary bit her lip in thought. "I cannot understand *why* it is that he preys on my mind. He is nothing like the men I find most agreeable."

Henry's brow furrowed. "Bertram *is* a very handsome man. Many men have fallen in love with a pretty face only to discover they had married a very silly woman whom they wished they could never see again. Surely your sex is not immune to mistaking an appreciation of beauty for regard?"

"I should like to think women are immune from such folly, but I know very well that we are not. Nonetheless, I would like to continue to think *myself* immune from that foolishness, and I, therefore, reject your argument completely," Mary said with a comic air of fastidiousness.

"Then it must just be that you yearn to attach yourself to a staid clergyman," Henry chaffed his sister.

"Yes, I have often lain awake night in devout prayer that Almighty Providence send me a rusticated second son in the church to win my heart."

Henry laughed at Mary's expression, but her jocular statement jogged her memory and made her wonder about how much of her frustration with Edmund was the result of his taking orders. The other night at dinner, the main dish of the first course had been an 'alderman', a roast turkey ringed with linked sausages. When her host was carving the bird, he made a reference to the crispy rump of the fowl known as the parson's nose, starting a round of jests regarding men of the church. Would Edmund become another ecclesiastical panjandrum to be mocked for his gauche self-righteousness and ludicrous self-satisfaction? Would she become a joke by association, as a parson's wife?

Even if Edmund was never clownish (and she did not think a man of his gravitas *could* be clownish), there were other worries attached to his profession. She had already noticed that Edmund tended to think a little too well of himself; surely that would only increase if he were the focus of the attention and adoration of a congregation? If Dr Grant, who was far past his prime and plain as a cowherd's boot, was feted and cooed at by the women in his congregation, how much more would the young, handsome Edmund be fawned over? She did not fear that Edmund, upright and stalwart as he was, would stray from his vows, but did she want to be married to a man who was constantly reminded of his own charms? Wouldn't he, regardless of his good sense, become conceited?

Mary's soul shrank away from the thought of being married to a conceited man, one who was convinced that he was infallible and would not listen to anyone's advice. Many times she had seen her beloved aunt try to dissuade the Admirable from a course of action or plan, and never once had her aunt succeeded. The Admiral was impervious to her aunt's reasoned arguments, her pleading, or her gentle coaxing. Worse, the Admirable used his authority to bully his wife, to force her to change her plans to accommodate his demands at a whim, not from cruelty, but simply because he thought it was natural and just for him to have his way at all times.

Nor could she believe that Edmund would attend to her and remain courteous when wed on the basis that she would have brought a substantial dowry with her. The fact that her aunt had been an heiress, and her wealth had sustained them while the Admiral had made his fortune, had not helped Mrs Crawford one jot; the Admirable had always considered his wife's money and property as his own and his to do with as he saw fit. What reason did she have to think Edmund, hide-bound and traditionalist as he was, would think any differently?

Her thoughts all gave her dissatisfaction. She steered the conversation to other topics, confident that her brother would be too witty to fail to entertain and distract her, and she was not disappointed.

Chapter Forty-Two

THE HENRY THAT returned from Portsmouth was much more melancholy than the Henry who had gone. The morning after his journey back to London he came to the Fraser's to see Mary, taking her to a tea shop so they could talk unreservedly without neglecting Mary's hosts.

"My God, Mary," Henry was rigid with dismay, "you should see the hovel they've got her in."

"Surely it isn't a *hovel*," Mary protested. "Sir Thomas might be trying to strong-arm her into marrying you, but he wouldn't send her into absolute squalor."

"Supposing he knows what the conditions there really are," Henry reminded her. "He may have sent her into a much worse abode than he suspected. You may not *want* to call it a hovel because it pains you to think of Fanny in such a place, but if you had seen it with your own eyes you would have been as appalled as I was. I've seen better kept and cleaner cow byres."

"Do not exaggerate, please. I want to get an accurate account of the place. Now, with complete honesty and in a rational manner, if Windsor Palace is a ten on the scale of buildings and one of the slums of the Irish rookery is a one, where would you truly place the Price house?"

Henry took a deep breath, and thought. "In all fairness, I'd give it a four."

"That bad?" Mary was shocked.

"Possibly worse," Henry confirmed glumly. "It was one of a row of terraced houses on a narrow street not far from the harbour — the stink of fish and the estuary were inescapable — and each house looked as if only the neighbouring houses were keeping them all from falling down together. You've seen three drunkards lean on each other and stay upright? It looked very much like that. Honestly, I don't know how the end house doesn't collapse. The whole street is covered with dirt and filth; I had to step over a dead dog on my way to her door. The frontages of the houses were all as grimy as a chimney-sweep's face, and maybe one out of three had actually bothered to scrub their front stoop. You know a *true* slattern lives within when the steps are left grubby. I was hoping that Fanny's house was the best of the lot, but no such luck. I actually hesitated to knock. Even with the great love I bear for Fanny, I was loathe to enter such a sordid little dwelling."

"When I did finally knock, the most wretched servant I have ever seen in person answered the door. I thought one of the scullery maids had come upstairs and opened the door without permission, but no; that was the upstairs maid. She conducted me down a short hall that was as clean and brightly lit as any coal mine and into a cramped parlour not fit for a dog's use. Everything was scuzzy and spotted with grease and in ill-repair. To see Fanny sitting there, in that vile place! It took everything I had not to look as aghast as I felt."

"Dearest Henry," Mary cried compassionately. "How hard it must have been to see Fanny in such a setting, when you were powerless to remove her."

"It was like seeing a diamond in pig muck," Henry looked as though he could weep. "Then, to meet her mother! Mrs Price was as slatternly a woman as any I have ever laid eyes on, which seemed *worse* than it should be because she is so like Lady Bertram in feature. It was like seeing a thoroughbred tied to a knacker's cart. One cannot help but be revolted, even as one pities the circumstances."

"Was Fanny alone with her mother?"

"No, there were two sisters there with them, and they both bore a strong resemblance to Fanny, in face if nothing else. One, a girl named Susan, is a sturdy young lady of fifteen who was trying to emulate Fanny in manners, much to the child's credit. But the other! The youngest girl was a spoilt, disagreeable child named Betsey, who needed a good thrashing. To look upon the object of my affection in the midst of such coarse relations was a positive torture!"

"The Prices cannot all be so bad, dearest," Mary tried to comfort him. "Her brother was everything a young man *should* be, and Fanny herself is perfection. Perhaps her siblings will improve under Fanny's guidance and example?"

"There is something in that," Henry admitted. "Her sister Susan seems sensible and intelligent, with aspirations to gentility that I do not despair of. The brothers, whom I met the next day on the walk after church, were rough cubs, but that will do them no harm once they join His Majesty's Service and go to sea. But, Mary, if you could have met Fanny's father," Henry stopped, momentarily at a loss for words.

"Is it too clear that he is of low birth?" Mary asked, with sympathy.

"He is no different than any of the layabouts on half-pay that scrounge around the docks like wharf rats. He is dirty and gross and uncouth beyond even those of his breed. I smelled strong liquor on him in the middle of the day, and he was in every way an oaf. It was an embarrassment to be seen with him."

Mary reached her hand out to clasp her brother's. "Dearest, she has not accepted you. If you do not renew your addresses, you need never trouble yourself with the Prices again so long as you live." As fond as Mary was of Fanny, she would not encourage her brother to debase himself by marrying into poverty and disgrace.

"I admit I have been soul-searching, wondering if my love for Fanny is made of such stern stuff that it can survive her paternal connections. Would I be wiser to leave off, knowing that time will heal my wounds?" Henry stared down into his tea, as though there would be a solution to his dilemma in its creamed depths.

"I support you with my whole heart, regardless of what you choose," Mary assured him.

"Whether it is prudent or not, I love her too well to give her up," Henry sighed. "I never thought a time would come that it would pain me to say so, but there it is. I cannot make her father other than he is, but William Price fills me with hope that her brothers can all rise to respectability and modest wealth. If her sisters will but model themselves upon her, then there is hope for them as well. Her mother's connections are, as we both well know, unexceptionable. *There*, at least, I am on firm ground."

"Dear Henry," Mary sipped her tea, clearly struggling to think of how to say what she wished to say in the least offensive manner, "I must tell you the most troubling aspect of this is the light it casts on her refusal of you. It is one thing for a young woman in secure circumstances to choose to remain unmarried than to wed for reasons other than true affection, but it is quite another for a woman to choose privation and abasement rather than a gentleman's proposals. It seems as though she not only lacks fondness for you, but is resolved against you."

Henry was obviously unhappy, but he gave Mary's comments due consideration. "I do not think she knew quite what the alternative *was*. She was electing to remain at Mansfield Park rather than to wed without love, and only now can she understand what she could be reduced to if she remains unmarried. Perhaps Sir Thomas was right to send her to Portsmouth, as much as it pains me to see her there in that rancid place."

"But do you want her to marry you solely to escape a dreadful fate?" Mary asked. "Is that the foundation of a happy union?"

"I believe that if any woman could come to wholeheartedly devote herself to her husband, Fanny is that woman," Henry smiled wanly. "It would be against her principles to do anything other than love me, once she had sworn to do so at the altar."

"Is that enough?"

"Considering her purity of mind, her gentleness, and her sweet temper, I believe it will suffice," Henry was convincing himself as much as Mary. "Can you conceive of Fanny giving her hand where her heart was not?"

"No," Mary admitted, "but I want you to be loved and adored the way you *deserve*, Henry. I want her to, as Pope wrote, 'breathe what love inspires, warm from the soul, and faithful to its fires.' You are sacrificing all hope of an equal alliance for her; it is the least she could do."

"I think her to be worth every sacrifice," Henry said earnestly. "If you could have seen her gentle patience with her buffoon of a father and fool of a mother! She did everything she could to soften their vulgar manners and to present them in the best light, in spite of the humiliation she was *sure* to be feeling. She is all gentle attention and solicitude, once her heart is engaged. It would be a very good thing to be the object of her devotion."

"Then I will tell you that there is no other woman in the world whom I would rather be my sister," Mary smiled. "You need not have much to do with the Price clan, if that is your wish. At most, you can invite her brothers and sisters to visit, as their station and manner improves, and eschew Portsmouth and her progenitors like a plague house. Mansfield Park and all her relations within will be the family bonds that are strengthened."

"Provided that Fanny survives to return to the Park," Henry commented dourly.

"Whatever do you mean?"

"She has grown so thin and pale, Mary, that I fear she is starving. I put about inquires, and found out that she sends a brother to buy biscuits and buns daily, which I suspect is the only food she is eating due to the foul nature of the fare offered to her in that place. God knows I wouldn't have drunk tea in that house for a king's ransom. Her father invited me to eat with them, but I made an excuse of a prior engagement. I was hard pressed to keep my countenance and not appear to be gagging at the thought. How I wish that I could have taken Fanny away then, and given her a good meal as well! I felt like a brute for leaving her."

"Sir Thomas is the brute, because he is the one who has left her there all this time. He could fetch her away with a snap of his fingers."

"True," Henry looked brooding. "She said it will probably be at least another month, perhaps two, before Sir Thomas comes for her. I told her that if she would but write to you and say she is ready, that we would come for her together. I hope that is not overreaching myself, to commit you?"

"Of course I would join you!" Mary smiled. "I'll write Fanny as soon as I get home, to reaffirm your offer and assure her of my compliance. There is nothing here in London so important that I cannot do it during another visit, perhaps the next time staying with my brother and his lovely wife. I am having a gay time of it, but there is no comparison between the happiness of entertainment and the happiness of helping a brother."

Henry grinned, more relaxed now that he had shared his burden of concern for Fanny with his sister. "Yes, I am sure spending hours in a coach would be much more enjoyable than going to Astley's or dancing at Almack's."

"If you had to dance with some of the louts I have to dance with at Almack's, you'd been happier to be in the carriage, too," Mary said with some asperity. "I swear that the men of the ton grow dimmer and more clownish by the day. The want of elegance and wit is *deplorable*."

"Maybe they simply become tongue-tied and inept because they are dazzled by your beauty?" Henry suggested.

Mary gave a ladylike sound that was almost, but not quite, a snort. "Goose. You remain as ridiculous as ever. Now, you must tell me the good as well as the bad, so I can include that in my letter. What did you do at Portsmouth that was unexceptional and delightful?"

"

True to her word, and feeling rather guilty that she hadn't written Fanny more often, Mary composed a letter to her friend.

"I have to inform you, my dearest Fanny, that Henry has been down to Portsmouth to see you; that he had a delightful walk with you to the Dock-yard last Saturday, and one still more to be dwelt on the next day, on the ramparts; when the balmy air, the sparkling sea, and your sweet looks and conversation were altogether in the most delicious harmony, and afforded sensations which are to raise ecstasy even in retrospect. This, as well as I understand, is to be the substance of my information. He makes me write, but I do not know what else is to be communicated, except this said visit to Portsmouth, and these two said walks, and his introduction to your family, especially to a fair sister of yours, a fine girl of fifteen, who was of the party on the ramparts, taking her first lesson, I presume, in love. I have not time for writing much, but it would be out of place if I had, for this is to be a mere letter of business, penned for the purpose of conveying necessary information, which could not be delayed without risk of evil.

Mary paused. She was having unaccustomed trouble thinking of the lively things that would entertain Fanny. She had been taught not to weigh down a social letter with serious matters, for fear that it would bore the reader, or worse yet give the recipient ammunition against you in the future. Surely *that* was not a worry with dearest Fanny, but there was no point in pouring out all her conflicted feelings about Edmund on the girl. After all, he *was* Fanny's cousin; in all likelihood that Fanny — a lover of the bucolic and worshipper of her cousin — would not think there was any *good* reason for resisting his attentions, even if Mary explained herself fully. Sighing, she wrote:

My dear, dear Fanny, if I had you here, how I would talk to you!—You should listen to me till you were tired, and advise me till you were still tired more; but it is impossible to put a hundredth part of my great mind on paper, so I will abstain altogether, and leave you to guess what you like. I have no news for you. You have politics of course; and it would be too bad to plague you with the names of people and parties, that fill up my time. I ought to have sent you an account of your cousin's first party, but I was lazy, and now it is too long ago; suffice it, that every thing was just as it ought to be, in a style that any of her connections must have been gratified to witness, and that her own dress and manners did her the greatest credit. My friend Mrs. Fraser is mad for such a house, and it would not make *me* miserable. I go to Lady Stornaway after Easter. She seems in high spirits, and very happy. I fancy Lord S. is very good-humoured and pleasant in his own family, and I do not think him so very ill-looking as I did, at least, one sees many worse. He will not do by the side of your cousin Edmund.

She frowned, thinking of the Stornoways and her mixed feelings for Edmund. It mystified her to see Flora so content in her marriage. Flora, who was a jilt who still had feelings of resentment toward Henry, resentment that could only come from the fact she still loved him, was happier with a cad like Lord Stornoway than Janet was with the upright and respectable Mr Fraser. Mary suspected that Mr Fraser teased Janet for the same reasons Flora said snide things about Henry; a bitterness due to unrequited love. Flora and Stornoway, however, didn't care enough about each other to impair their mutual civility. Mary had learned that Stornoway had a mistress in Marylebone, and that had been the initial source of contention between himself and Flora, but once his wife had learned to not concern herself with his profligate nature they got along famously. But forbearance of a husband's infidelity was not *necessarily* a key to a happy marriage. Her good aunt didn't care a tuppence for the Admiral's peccadilloes and mistresses, but the Admiral was unkind to her anyway. What *was* the surety of a happy union, or at least one that was not miserable? How could she know she would be happy with Edmund, when there were so many variables to take into account?

Vexed with her train of thought, Mary dipped her pen in ink again and continued:

> Of the last-mentioned hero, what shall I say? If I avoided his name entirely, it would look suspicious. I will say, then, that we have seen him two or three times, and that my friends here are very much struck with his gentleman-like appearance. Mrs Fraser (no bad judge), declares she knows but three men in town who have so good a person, height, and air; and I must confess, when he dined here the other day, there were none to compare with him, and we were a party of sixteen. Luckily there is no distinction of dress now-a-days to tell tales, but—but—but.

> Yours, affectionately."

Mary had been on the point of folding the letter when she remembered she had not broached the real purpose of the missive. Shaking her head at her own distraction, she penned a postscript:

"I had almost forgot (it was Edmund's fault, he gets into my head more than does me good), one very material thing I had to say from Henry and myself, I mean about our taking you back into Northamptonshire. My dear little creature, do not stay at Portsmouth to lose your pretty looks. Those vile sea-breezes are the ruin of beauty and health. My poor aunt always felt affected, if within ten miles of the sea, which the Admiral of course never believed, but I know it was so. I am at your service and Henry's, at an hour's notice. I should like the scheme, and we would make a little circuit, and shew you Everingham in our way, and perhaps you would not mind passing through London, and seeing the inside of St George's, Hanover-Square. Only keep your cousin Edmund from me at such a time, I should not like to be tempted.

Again, Mary started to fold her letter when she remembered another thing Henry had particularly asked her to include:

What a long letter!—one word more. Henry, I find, has some idea of going into Norfolk again upon some business that you approve, but this cannot possibly be permitted before the middle of next week, that is, he cannot any how be spared till after the 14th, for we have a party that evening. The value of a man like Henry on such an occasion, is what you can have no conception of; so you must take it upon my word, to be inestimable.

Thinking of the party to come, Mary grinned wickedly to herself. Maria would be there, and have to see Henry for the first time since her marriage and hearing the news of his being in love with Fanny, the cousin who could not hold a candle to Maria in looks or wealth. Would Mrs Rushworth be able to compose herself, as Flora was always careful to do around Henry? Or would Maria expose herself to the world as scorned woman by behaving coldly to her former flirt? Mary thought Fanny would also like to know how events unfolded. Human nature always loved to see those who were supercilious brought down a peg or two, and how could Fanny be different? Even someone as gentle as Fanny Price *must* want to know that the cousin who had long neglected and dismissed her was about to be humbled.

He will see the Rushworths, which own I am not sorry for—having a little curiosity—and so I think has he, though he will not acknowledge it.

Having finally finished the letter, Mary folded it neatly and sealed it with wax before writing Fanny's directions in Portsmouth upon it. She rang for a footman, whom she sent to post the letter. Baring contingencies, Fanny would get the missive tomorrow. Mary thought of her friend's happiness at getting such a letter, and resolved to write Fanny more often. Sadly, like many of Mary's resolutions, her intentions would be better than her execution of them.

॥

The Fraser's party on the 14th went as well as Mary had hoped, in every particular. She had danced twice with Edmund, and his attentions toward her were so marked and so pleasing that more than one of her acquaintances had commented on her obvious conquest. Edmund also brought her cups of ratafia, and stood talking to her whenever she was not engaged in dancing. He was, in her estimation, the most handsome man in the room and she was not unaware of the envy of some of the other single women there. Whether they would have remained envious if they had known he was a clergyman was open to speculation, but for the present Mary was disinclined to think of it.

Mary also had the felicity of talking with Julia Bertram, who was a good conversationalist with a quick wit. Julia was so often overshadowed by Maria that it was easy to forget that Julia's looks and brain were superior to most women of the ton. Mr Yates, it was certain, was well aware of Julia's eminence, because he was as attentive to Edmund's sister as Edmund was to Mary. She observed them minutely, but Mary saw no sign that Julia returned Mr Yates regard. Nonetheless, Mary was sure that Julia was in love — with life in London. She had seldom heard anyone recount their time in Town with as much excitement and pleasure as did Julia.

Henry was, as ever, the life and soul of the party. Mary noted that both Julia and Edmund regarded Henry with the same friendliness that they had shown him at Mansfield. Henry flirted with Julia, which caused her to blush a little, but he spoke so determinedly of his adoration of Fanny Price that his gallantries could not be mistaken for *serious* flirtation. Edmund told Mary how happy it made him to see

Henry's love for Fanny remained fixed and unwavering, and Mary was able to assure him that her brother thought of no one else.

The one dark spot on the evening was the coldness and reserve with which Mrs Rushworth greeted her former favourite Mr Crawford. If it wouldn't have caused a small scandal, Mary suspected that Maria would have given Henry the cut direct. Henry, being always oblivious to the feelings his flirtations could create, was surprised and disconcerted by Maria's behaviour. Although Mary did experience some epicaricacy at Maria's exposing herself in such a manner, she was embarrassed for Edmund and Julia, who were obviously abashed by Maria's mode of conduct. This was, Mary knew, on top of the humiliation they both felt to have Mr Rushworth, whose dullness and stupidity was more evident in London than in the country, as a brother.

When Mary finally went to bed, closer to dawn than to midnight, she promised herself that she would write to Fanny as soon as she arose the next morning. In spite of Mary's sleepy resolve, it would be over a month before she wrote Fanny again.

Chapter Forty-Three

"I SAW THAT you visited for great while in the Rushworth's opera box last night," Mary said to her brother as they sat together in the Fraser's family parlour. They were, happily, alone, and could be frank. "Much longer than you visited with your sister in the Stornoway's box, I may add. Did Mrs Rushworth have such interesting news to impart then?"

"Actually, Mrs Rushworth did have news. She told me her brother is ailing," Henry said with a creased brow, remembering Maria's nonchalant attitude toward her sibling's health.

"Edmund is ill?" Mary's face blanched, and Henry was filled with remorse.

"No, no! Edmund is well. It is Tom Bertram who is poorly."

"Thank God!" Mary's pale cheeks bloomed colour once more as she experienced a rare blush. "That sounded horrid. I am not happy to hear Mr Bertram is sick."

"I understand," Henry smiled in commiseration. "I think it is more than humans can do, to think of the tribulations of those to whom we are less attached as important as tribulations afflicting those that we hold dear. My first thought was not for the one ailing, but for his parents and brother. This is perhaps unfair to Miss Bertram, who may feel it deeply, but I know that *Mrs Rushworth* seemed completely unconcerned."

"Julia has gone to stay with her cousins near Bedford Square, so she isn't enough alarmed to return to Mansfield at any rate," Mary informed him. "Perhaps his illness is not serious?"

"I believe, from what Mari – that is, from what Mrs Rushworth communicated to me, his illness is thought to be rather severe," Henry told her.

Mary arched a brow, silently letting her brother know she had noticed his near faux pas by using a married woman's Christian name. Such an intimacy would announce to the world that Henry was about to put horns on Rushworth … if he hadn't already. Henry pretended his sister was blessedly free of eyebrows and continued his report.

"Tom got full as a boiled owl and fell off his horse in Newmarket, and then contracted a fever during his recuperation from being thrown. Tom's fair-weather friends all absconded, and when his fever lingered, the physician attending him became concerned enough to contact Mansfield Park.""

"Then I marvel at his sisters staying in London," Mary's lips compressed in disapproval. "Illness is never pleasant, I admit, but I should never stay away from *you* where you in need of me."

Henry looked at her fondly. "I know. You have a very good heart."

"Not so good," Mary confessed shamefacedly, "In the small amount of time since you told me Tom Bertam was unwell, I have already thought how likely it is that Edmund has neither returned or written to me due to his brother's illness."

Henry shrugged. "Unpleasant truths will intrude into even the kindest mind, but that doesn't make them less true or the mind less kind."

"Upon reflection of the matter, I am sure it is not *too* serious," Mary opined. "Tom Bertram is one who would make sprained ankle into a broken leg. I am too severe on Maria and Julia for staying in London; they know their brother's character well enough to feel no alarm."

"Well, I shall be able to keep abreast of it," Henry assured her, "since Mrs Rushworth and I are both going to be staying with the Aylmer's in Twickenham over the Easter holidays. I will, of course, keep you informed."

"You are …" Mary suddenly broke into a smile, "I know what you are doing! I have not forgotten the date. You are pulling my leg, trying to make an April's fool of me."

"Not at all," Henry looked bewildered. "I am going to Twickenham. What's so odd about that?"

"What do you mean you are going to Twickenham?" Mary demanded incredulously. "With Maria Rushworth there also?"

"Yes," Henry said, in what was very close to a sulky manner.

"Have you gone mad? Why is coaxing Mrs Rushworth back into the fold of your admirers so important that you would spend Easter with her at Twickenham, and expose you both to what will be *at the least* impertinent remarks? Do you think the ton blind, or kind? Because I assure you they are *neither.*"

Henry looked aggrieved. "The Aylmers were kind enough to ask me to visit, and Mrs Rushworth had already accepted their invitation. You think too much of it Mary. I am only trying to get on Mrs Rushworth's good side for *Fanny's* sake. Fanny does not need to have contention between her husband and her cousin. It costs me nothing to smooth Maria's ruffled feathers."

"Maria, is it?" Mary scowled. "Calling a married woman by her first name is abhorrent, Henry. You might as well put a notice in the *London Times* that you are poking her."

"Dearest Mary," Henry smiled reassuringly, but Mary noticed he did not meet her eyes, "I am not — as you so elegantly put it — *poking* Mrs Rushworth. I am as much in love with Fanny as ever."

"I have no doubt you are in love with Fanny," Mary said with asperity. "What's that got to do with you frolicking under a married woman's petticoat? I am not an idiot; I know you can play with ease on pitches you do not love."

"Really," Henry frowned in what he hoped was a quelling manner, "this is not a topic for a man to discuss with a sister, let alone an unmarried sister."

Not quelled in the least, Mary continued. "I know what you are about, Henry. Maria Rushworth is a gilflurt and there are few things you like better than to let the air out of a gilflurt's balloon. But this is different! Maria will be your cousin when you marry Fanny, and if you think she will ever forgive you for dallying with her you are sadly mistaken. Once she knows you are done with her, her cold behaviour toward you at every family gathering will announce to the world that you cheapened her. I don't think even Edmund could blind himself to it. Leave Maria Rushworth be or you will come home by weeping cross, mark my words."

"Don't be nonsensical," Henry snapped, annoyed with Mary's insistence and the unwanted plausibility of her warning. "Do you think Maria wants her family to know she is a trollop? She has everything to lose by exposing herself."

It was closest thing to a fight Mary had ever had with her brother, and they were both made unhappy by it, but she felt she had no choice but to try and dissuade him from his dangerous course.

"I am sure Lord Byron thought the same of Lady Lamb," Mary pointed out with heat. "What if there is no one to save you when

Maria shows up at your door disguised as a page and demanding you elope with her?"

Henry tried to deflect his sister's scolding with humour, which had always been his best defence and had gotten him out of many scrapes in the past. "How would such a bushel bubby as Maria disguise herself as a page? She would never get the waistcoat closed."

Mary was not diverted. "You jest, but it isn't in the least amusing. If Fanny ever finds out you sullied her cousin's marriage bed you will lose her forever. Are you willing to risk that, just to tumble Mrs Rushworth?"

Henry's face was a thundercloud. "That will never happen, Mary, and I dislike you saying that it might."

"Well, I dislike you tumbling Maria all over Richmond," Mary shot back. "I thought you had more brains than this, Henry."

"You are just in the mood to slight love because Edmund left London without proposing, and *still* has not written you a declaration." Henry retorted. "If your *own* love life were going better, you would not be such a harpy about *mine*."

"Edmund Bertram has nothing to do with this," Mary's voice was cold enough to have frozen the fire. "This is about *your* idiocy, not *his*."

"Perhaps Edmund is clever and realised he didn't want to marry a harridan," Henry threw a punch below the belt.

Internally reeling at her brother's unfamiliar cruelty, Mary nonetheless kept her countenance and retaliated. "And perhaps Fanny Price realised she didn't want to marry an unprincipled, knavish puppy who couldn't refrain from tom-catting with her cousins."

Henry's nostril's flared, and he bowed his farewell with icy formality before almost stomping away from his sister.

ıı

Mary's emotions remained in turmoil for the next few weeks, even as she joked, danced, and played cards with her usual aplomb. She heard not one peep from her brother, although she *did* get to hear several insinuations that he and Maria Rushworth were involved in, at the *least*, a very flagrant indiscretion. There were other house guests at Twickenham, and as all of them could see a church by daylight and tell a hawk from a handsaw, letters with reports of Henry's dalliance with Mrs Rushworth had been sent back to London and the scandal rapidly permeated the ton.

She did what she could to staunch the flow, by laughing it all off as a flirtation, but inside she was sick with dread that the inhabitants of Mansfield Park or the Parsonage would find out. How the Bertrams, whom she sincerely cared for, would feel if Maria was revealed as a strumpet did not bear thinking about, and if they found out that Henry, whom they esteemed so highly, was the author of Maria's disgrace it would be ten thousand times worse. As for the Parsonage, Dr and Mrs Grant would be mortified and would flee Mansfield's environs rather than staying to be socially cut out by the most prominent family in the parish.

Mary thought herself sorely aggravated before, but when she went to stay with the Stornoways after Easter her situation became nearly unbearable. Henry's probable dalliance with Mrs Rushworth was a topic Flora wanted to return to again and again, as proof Henry was unprincipled and had never *really* loved Fanny Price. Lord Stornoway was no bar to his wife's near-obsession, finding the whole matter diverting and privately making plans to seduce the luscious Mrs Rushworth as soon as he could. To his mind, the woman had shown herself to be a wanton, and he foresaw no difficulties in getting her into bed at some house party or another. He was far from the only man in the ton to be making such plans, and not one of them felt the irony of their own infidelities in conjunction with the judgement they passed on Maria Rushworth.

Only Mary's ability to act a part kept the rumours about Henry and Maria from being put down as a certainty. As long as she stayed merry about the whole thing, pooh-poohing it as hyperbole, some doubt remained as to Henry Crawford's relationship with Mrs Rushworth. Mary may have cried from vexation and worry, but she did so at night, alone in her room, and no tell-tale traces of tears remained on her cheeks in the morning.

Things only began to improve for Mary when Henry returned to London, leaving Maria at the Aylmer's. Her brother came to see her on the 23rd, to tell her he had resumed residence at the Admiral's. Any rift between the siblings was healed when Henry poured out his heart to her, declaring that she had been in the right and that he should have listened to her. He was deeply concerned about the behaviours Mrs Rushworth was now showing; she claimed that she loved him and appeared to believe that a few torrid couplings meant they would be eloping together forthwith. He had, as he put it, ran from the Aylmer's with his tail between his legs like a frightened cur, and the prime object of his life was now to avoid Maria Rushworth and to prevent Fanny from ever finding out what had occurred.

"The more I know of Maria, the more repellent I find her," Henry confessed. "She is the most vain, self-centred, and selfish woman I have ever known. She wants me, but with the same greed that a brat wants a sweet in a confectioner's window and with as much willingness to throw a fit in the hopes of getting it. I am terrified that she will seek me out in London, or make her so-called love for me public knowledge. I have given my word to the Admiral that I will stay with him for a fortnight, but then I am decamping for Everingham, where I *should* have gone in the first place. There I hope I shall be safe, until Fanny returns to Mansfield and I can set myself up at the Parsonage to continue wooing her."

"Dearest Henry!" Mary loved her brother too much to revel in his pain, or to gloat over having been right. "I am sure you shall be safe there. This is all a tempest in a teacup and will blow over soon. There is no *proof* you and Mrs Rushworth were ever intimate in an untoward manner, and when you marry Fanny people will lose interest in the old gossip entirely. I am afraid my friend Maria has ruined her reputation in London forever, since even a whiff of scandal can drag a woman's character into the muck, but there is nothing I can do to help her. Perhaps if she doesn't make a habit of seducing other men, and people are reasonably sure that Rushworth's heirs are Rushworth's get, then she *may* recover her footing in time, but I cannot say for sure. I will, for your sake, and Fanny's, remain her friend, and do all I can to keep doors open for her."

Henry leaned forward with his elbows on his knees and his head in his hands, the picture of despair. "Oh, *why* didn't I listen to you in the first place?" Sun coming in from a southern window showed the russet hidden in his dark hair, and reminded Mary of the reddish-brown locks he had had as a boy. She felt deeply tender toward him, even though he was in a mess of his own making.

"There is no changing the past, dearest," Mary patted him gently on the back. "We can only go forward. It does you no good to flog yourself with what-ifs."

"You are the best sister a man could ever have," he told Mary warmly, straightening up and taking one of her hands between his own. "If I had not already known it, a few weeks in Maria's company would have shown it to me. When she received word that her brother's illness was worse she didn't turn a hair. *You* would never be so insensitive to my fate."

"Tom Bertram's illness is worse?" Mary asked, nonplussed. "How did I not hear of it?"

"I am surprised you haven't; it's all over Town. In his hurry to go home, Tom was moved from Newmarket a little too soon and his fever came back. Maria didn't give a fig, but Dr Grant wrote to me that for a full week they actually feared for Tom's life. He has amended some since then, yet he is far from well and remains invalided in his room. If his fever returns again, the physician told Dr Grant that he feared it would carry Tom off. That is, I am sorry to say, what I know of the matter."

Mary was distressed, thinking of the unhappiness that must be attending all those who remained at Mansfield. Then, to her chagrin, the idea of how Tom's death would benefit *her* came into her mind, and for a brief moment she wished him gone. She felt like a ghoul for acknowledging it, but she could not deny how much *better* her life would be if Edmund were master of Mansfield Park instead of his brother. Any hardships entailed in marrying Edmund would be removed. Edmund would no longer be the second son; he would be the heir. In time, she would become Lady Bertram.

Even as she was revolted with her own internal honesty, she salved her conscious by thinking of the great benefit *everyone* would reap if Edmund was Sir Edmund one day. Tom cared nothing for his home, his tenants, or the poor on his estate. In contrast, Edmund was excessively attentive and merciful. It would be wrong for her to want Tom's death, and she would — if it were possible — heal him rather than have the burden of second-hand murder on her conscience, but she could not lie to herself and say there were no advantages in his death.

"I'll write to Fanny," she told her brother. "*She* will know more."

ıı

Too eager to hear news of Tom's health and the details of Mansfield Park to be distracted from her task, Mary actually *did* write to Fanny the next morning:

> "Forgive me, my dear Fanny, as soon as you can,
> for my long silence, and behave as if you could forgive
> me directly. This is my modest request and expectation,

for you are so good, that I depend upon being treated better than I deserve—and I write now to beg an immediate answer. I want to know the state of things at Mansfield Park, and you, no doubt, are perfectly able to give it. One should be a brute not to feel for the distress they are in—and from what I hear, poor Mr Bertram has a bad chance of ultimate recovery. I thought little of his illness at first. I looked upon him as the sort of person to be made a fuss with, and to make a fuss himself in any trifling disorder, and was chiefly concerned for those who had to nurse him; but now it is confidently asserted that he is really in a decline, that the symptoms are most alarming, and that part of the family, at least, are aware of it. If it be so, I am sure you must be included in that part, that discerning part, and therefore entreat you to let me know how far I have been rightly informed. I need not say how rejoiced I shall be to hear there has been any mistake, but the report is so prevalent, that I confess I cannot help trembling. To have such a fine young man cut off in the flower of his days, is most melancholy. Poor Sir Thomas will feel it dreadfully. I really am quite agitated on the subject."

Mary stood up and paced her bedroom, half-pleased, half-disgusted with herself. She *was* sad to hear of Tom's illness, and she *did* pity the Bertrams, but that was not *all* she felt. A small part of her also wanted Edmund to inherit Mansfield Park, which meant that a small part of her was hoping Tom would die. She believed she had laid on her concern too thickly. If she left her sympathy undiluted by rationality it would make her a hypocrite of the lowest sort.

She sharpened her quill with a penknife, and resolved to lighten the tone of the letter:

"Fanny, Fanny, I see you smile, and look cunning, but upon my honour, I never bribed a physician in my life. Poor young man!—If he is to die, there will be *two* poor young men less in the world; and with a fearless face and bold voice would I say to any one, that wealth and consequence could fall into no hands more deserving of them. It was a foolish precipitation last Christmas, but the evil of a few days may be blotted out in part. Varnish and gilding hide many stains. It will be but the loss of the Esquire after his name. With real affection, Fanny, like mine, more might be overlooked. Write to me by return of post, judge of my anxiety, and do not trifle with it. Tell me the real truth, as you have it from the fountain head. And now, do not trouble yourself to be ashamed of either my feelings or your own. Believe me, they are not only natural, they are philanthropic and virtuous. I put it to your conscience, whether 'Sir Edmund' would not do more good with all the Bertram property, than any other possible 'Sir.' Had the Grants been at home, I would not have troubled you, but you are now the only one I can apply to for the truth, his sisters not being within my reach. Mrs R. has been spending the Easter with the Aylmers at Twickenham (as to be sure you know), and is not yet returned; and Julia is with the cousins, who live near Bedford Square; but I forget their name and street. Could I immediately apply to either, however, I should still prefer you, because it strikes me, that they have all along been so unwilling to have their own amusements cut up, as to shut their eyes to the truth. I suppose, Mrs R.'s Easter holidays will not last much longer; no doubt they are thorough holidays to her. The Aylmers are pleasant people; and her husband away, she can have nothing but enjoyment. I give her credit for promoting his going dutifully down to Bath, to fetch his mother; but how will she and the dowager agree in one house? Henry is not at hand, so I have nothing to say from him. Do not you think Edmund would have been in town again long ago, but for this illness?—Yours ever, Mary."

Mary looked up as she heard footsteps, and was surprised to see a rather ashen-looking Henry.

"Are you well?" She rose to go to him, concerned. "Whatever is the matter?"

"Mrs Rushworth sought me out," Henry took a deep breath. "Thank Heavens that I had just left the Admiral's and thus intercepted her on the street; otherwise I believe she would have come to the house itself. I cannot conceive of what a scandal that would cause. Has she taken leave of her senses?"

Mary was astonished. "She was actually coming, by herself, to see you at the Admiral's residence?" When Henry nodded, she made a distressed noise of sympathy and concern. "Did she say why she was doing something so asinine?"

Henry was so distressed he sat down on the sofa without Mary's leave. "I made as if I thought she were there totally by coincidence. Mrs Rushworth senior is returned from Bath today, and that is Maria's ostensible reason for leaving the Aylmer's and coming back to her own home, but I think it is more that she is pursuing *me*. I was able to avoid promising to call on her by the skin of my teeth," Henry shuddered at the idea of Maria clinging to him in her own drawing-room.

"Let me ring for tea," Mary told him, and proceeded to do so. By the time the brew arrived Henry had regained some of his savoir-faire.

"I am wracking my brain, trying to think of a way to get out of staying with our uncle the whole fortnight," Henry took a cup from Mary and sipped his tea, comforted by the taste and smell of the beverage as only an Englishman could be. "I want nothing so much as to leave immediately for Portsmouth and take Fanny to Mansfield Park, and if I could not have that, then to travel to Everingham. Surely Norfolk would be far enough away that Maria wouldn't pursue?"

"I am just now finishing a letter to Fanny," Mary said. "Let me plead with her to allow us to come for her."

"Dearest beloved Fanny," Henry murmured remorsefully. "What I would not give to be with her now. Every day I grow to love her more, and winning her hand becomes more important to me. If she will not be my wife, I will never know happiness again."

Mary knew that Henry's melodramatic yearning for Fanny was partly a manifestation of the novelty of having finally fallen in love, but it was nonetheless rooted in true affection. She pitied her brother, even though his problems were of his own creation. She returned to the table, and tried her best to elide Henry's sins and coax Fanny into leaving Portsmouth without Sir Thomas's permission:

> I had actually begun folding my letter, when Henry walked in; but he brings no intelligence to prevent my sending it. Mrs R. knows a decline is apprehended;

he saw her this morning, she returns to Wimpole-
Street to-day, the old lady is come. Now do not make
yourself uneasy with any queer fancies, because he has
been spending a few days at Richmond. He does it every
spring. Be assured, he cares for nobody but you. At this
very moment, he is wild to see you, and occupied only
in contriving the means for doing so, and for making
his pleasure conduce to yours. In proof, he repeats, and
more eagerly, what he said at Portsmouth, about our
conveying you home, and I join him in it with all my
soul. Dear Fanny, write directly, and tell us to come. It
will do us all good. He and I can go to the Parsonage,
you know, and be no trouble to our friends at Mansfield
Park. It would really be gratifying to see them all again,
and a little addition of society might be of infinite use
to them; and, as to yourself, you must feel yourself to
be so wanted there, that you cannot in conscience
(conscientious as you are,) keep away, when you have the
means of returning. I have not time or patience to give
half Henry's messages; be satisfied, that the spirit of each
and every one is unalterable affection."

"Let us hope," she told her brother, as she folded the letter and
added the direction, "that this will convince her."

Chapter Forty-Four

FOR THE REST of her life Mary would remember that second morning of May with absurd clarity.

The day had started out ordinarily enough. It was one of those mizzling and chilly spring mornings that reminded Englishmen why they loved to holiday abroad in sunnier climes. Mary had spent the hours between waking and breakfast lazily in her room, well wrapped in a shall and sitting near the fireplace reading Mary Russell Mitford's recently published *Narrative Poems on the Female Character*. In defiance of the overcast sky, she had donned a brilliant yellow walking dress before coming down for breakfast.

Both Lord and Lady Stornoway commented on the cheer she brought to the table when she sat down. As usual, breakfast was served at the table in the family's informal sitting room, and Lord Stornoway was reading his newspapers. It was one of the three days a week that *The London Chronicle* was published, and he was harrumphing over the predicted corn prices while Flora made soothing sounds of agreement.

The sound of a knock at the front door startled them all. Only a great exigency would bring a visitor at such an early hour. Mary thought the most likely candidate to be Henry, and she hoped he was only stopping by to bid farewell on his way to Everingham. It had been more than a week since Fanny had declined to allow them to rescue her, and there was nothing for Henry to do but leave London before Maria Rushworth's attentions attracted even more comment.

Instead, it was Janet Fraser who swept into the room. One look at her face showed them that she was in great distress.

"Janet!" Flora cried, both she and Mary spontaneously rising from the table to go to her. "What is wrong? Is it Mr Fraser? Margaret?"

Janet shook her head vigorously. "No, no. They are both in good health. I came so early because Mr Fraser just told me … how do I begin?" Her eyes filled with tears.

"Come darling, and sit down. A cup of tea will help calm you." Flora led her sister to the table, where a trembling Janet sat and accepted the drink Mary poured her.

"Now, what is it?" Flora coaxed, when they had all resumed a seat.

Janet took a deep, steadying breath. "It is regarding Henry Crawford."

Mary felt the room swoop around her as the blood drained from her head, and grabbed the table to keep from falling over. For a moment, she thought she would faint. She gulped air to steady herself, but seemed to be looking at Janet's pale face from the bottom of a well.

"He's alive," Janet hastened to assure her, seeing the fear written on Mary's countenance "and in good health as far as I know. I did not mean to alarm you in that manner, but to be honest my news is *nearly* as bad as the worst I could tell you."

Mary's cup clattered in the saucer as she picked it up and wrapped both hands around the warm china, hoping some of the heat would seep into her suddenly chilled fingers. She was so upset that she broke a lifetime of training and rested her elbows on the table without thought.

Janet's eyes were bleak as she looked at Mary. "Your brother has eloped with Maria Rushworth."

ii

The acrid stench of smelling salts brought Mary back into awareness of herself. Her left hip was throbbing, and she could only assume she had thumped it hard when she had toppled out of her chair and onto the floor. Her head was resting on Janet's lap, while a puddle of tea and shattered china spread out under the table in front of her. *I must have dropped the cup.* Then, in the nonsensical manner of shock, she thought: *Drat, that was a lovely breakfast set. I hope Flora can replace it.*

Dimly, she was aware of someone saying her name, and she struggled to sit up. She sat still for a minute, her head spinning, before she was ready to stand again. It was the first time she had ever fainted, and she found it a singularly unpleasant experience.

Lord Stornoway gave her his arm and led her to the divan, where she was encouraged by her hosts and Janet to recline and recover her nerves. Lord Stornoway, disregarding her protests, sent a footman for the physician.

"Please," Mary pleaded with Janet, grasping her friend's hand tightly. "Tell me what you know."

"This morning at breakfast, Mr Fraser told me he had heard a rumour at his club last night that Mrs Rushworth had left London under your brother's protection. I left immediately to come to you, so you wouldn't be caught unawares by callers asking impertinent questions."

"But that is all it is?" Mary clung to the idea like a barnacle. "It may be just baseless gossip? Nothing is sure?"

"Perhaps," Janet said, reluctant to lie, but unwilling to wound Mary further.

Looking over Janet's shoulder, Mary saw the gleam of pleased malice in Flora's expression. Mary realised that Flora was not her friend, and had probably never *really* been her friend. No friend would be relishing Henry's downfall with such hateful joy. Mary was bitterly aware that Flora would embellish the tale of how Mary had fainted at the breakfast table and repeat it all over London.

Flora's enjoyment had the effect of stiffening Mary's spine, and giving her courage.

Affecting lightness, she sat upright and smiled. "Janet dearest, you frightened me witless, but it is probably for naught. I am sure that if Henry *did* leave London with Mrs Rushworth, her sister Julia Bertram was with them. Their brother is very ill you know, and my brother is a close friend of the family. It would be entirely natural for him to escort them to Mansfield if they received word that Tom Bertram was failing."

"Why wouldn't Mr Rushworth accompany his wife and sister?" Flora asked, her eyes as predatory as a cat's as she watched Mary's face.

"Oh, many reasons." Mary made a languid motion with her hand, waving away any idea that Mr Rushworth was the one who *should* have escorted Maria and Julia. "If you had met Mr Rushworth's mother, you wouldn't even ask. I don't think she would allow her precious boy to leave her side for something as trivial as a wife's ailing brother."

"Then why did she go to Bath alone?" Flora asked slyly.

"Bath is entirely different," Mary asserted with false confidence. "*There* Mrs Rushworth was the centre of her friends and connections. She has fewer acquaintance in London; her son would be necessary to her here in a way he was not in Bath. She did the same thing when she resided at Sotherton. I assure you that she hardly let him out of her sight in the country."

"I am convinced that is what has happened," Janet agreed stoutly, glaring briefly at Flora. She was no less aware than Mary that Lady Stornoway was thrilled to see the Crawfords' social downfall. "I should have thought of that. I will be sure to ask Mr Fraser to tell everyone he knows that there is almost certainly an unexceptional explanation. I am sure," Janet met her brother-in-law's eye, "that Lord Stornoway will do the same."

"Of course," Stornoway promised, but his glance slid away to his wife.

⸿

Later, after the physician had come and pronounced her fit as a fiddle, Mary wrote a quick note to Fanny:

> "A most scandalous, ill-natured rumour has just reached me, and I write, dear Fanny, to warn you against giving the least credit to it, should it spread into the country. Depend upon it there is some mistake, and that a day or two will clear it up–at any rate, that Henry is blameless, and in spite of a moment's étourderie thinks of nobody but you. Say not a word of it–hear nothing, surmise nothing, whisper nothing, till I write again. I am sure it will be all hushed up, and nothing proved but Rushworth's folly. If they are gone, I would lay my life they are only gone to Mansfield Park, and Julia with them. But why would not you let us come for you? I wish you may not repent it.

> "Yours, &c."

Mary also sent a note to her uncle's house, asking if he knew where Henry had gone. That done, Mary spent the rest of the day gaily assuring the deluge of callers at the Stornoway residence that there was naught amiss, that time would reveal the baseless nature of the scandal, that Mr Rushworth was one in whom it was easy to stir unmerited alarm.

It wasn't until nearly midnight, when she retired to bed, that she was able to indulge in her tears. She feared with all her being that Henry had been well and truly trapped and was now doomed to social disgrace and a life with the haughty and spoilt Maria Rushworth. She could see so easily how it could have happened. If Maria had taken a page out of Lady Caroline Lamb's book and presented herself unescorted at the Admiral's town house, Henry would have been nearly powerless to refuse to elope with her. No man of his rank could think of disobliging a lady in such circumstances. Backed into a corner, he would have taken Maria away with him as she had demanded. With this gloomy thought haunting the corners of her mind, she drifted away into a troubled sleep that left her very little refreshed in the morning.

She had barely been awake ten minutes when Flora knocked on her door to tell Mary that her efforts to stem the tide of gossip the day before, heroic as they were, were all in vain. Every thing was now public beyond a hope. The servant of Mrs Rushworth, the mother, had exposure in her power, and, supported by her mistress, was not to be silenced. The two ladies, even in the short time they had been together, had disagreed; and the bitterness of the elder against her daughter-in-law might, perhaps, arise almost as much from the personal disrespect with which she had herself been treated, as from sensibility for her son. There was no chance that Mr Rushworth would not seek a divorce. Mary was going to have to undergo the agony of a brother testifying in crimcom court regarding adultery. It may even go so far that Mary herself would have to give testimony as well. Her social standing, as well as Henry's, would never be the same.

Only the gloating underneath Flora's false concern allowed Mary to hear it all with composure. She refused to give Lady Stornoway the satisfaction of hysterics.

Nevertheless, even Mary's resolve was not up to dealing with visitors, the theoretical well-wishers who would come to the Stornoway house to collect gossip in the guise of offering sympathy. She stayed in her room for the rest of the morning, with only Janet and Flora given admittance (it *was* Flora's home, and Mary didn't feel as though she had the right to forbid her entry), pleading a very real sick headache. Janet, proving herself to be a true friend in opposition of Flora, read to Mary throughout the day as a means of keeping her spirits from sinking too low.

Mary thought hearing that her brother's elopement with a married woman had been made public was to be the nadir of her day, but she was overly optimistic in that respect. Flora could not resist bringing the newspaper that trumpeted, "it was with infinite concern the newspaper had to announce to the world, a matrimonial *fracas* in the family of Mr R. of Wimpole Street; the beautiful Mrs R. whose name had not long been enrolled in the lists of hymen, and who had promised to become so brilliant a leader in the fashionable world, having quitted her husband's roof in company with the well known and captivating Mr C. the intimate friend and associate of Mr R. and it was not known, even to the editor of the newspaper, whither they were gone."

Seeing it in black and white was somehow worse that just knowing of it. Her brother's senselessness — the destruction of all his hopes and hers — sneered at her in print. Reading the notice again, Mary felt wretchedness such as she had never known. She had felt *grief*, profoundly, at the loss of her parents and her aunt, so she was not unfamiliar with suffering, but she had never felt the pangs of *humiliation* before. Never had she felt that she could not show her face. For a gregarious creature like Mary, with her lively manners and heart designed for friendship, this feeling that she could not see and be seen was grievous indeed.

Janet was her only consolation at this time. Her friends among the ton had shown themselves to be of the same cheap stuff as Flora; they wanted to enjoy a juicy scandal more than they wanted her happiness. Only Janet proved herself to be in possession of a loyal heart – or any heart at all, really. If Janet's motivations were not entirely altruistic – remaining loyal to Mary she could finally know that *she* was the preferred friend, and after a lifetime of feeling second-best she was able to consider herself secure in someone's affections — the reasons for her kindness did not mitigate the effect it had on Mary's comfort.

In spite of her day of voluntarily confinement, it was not in Mary's nature to remain bowed by the winds of misfortune. She was too active, too intelligent, to meekly accept the world's caprices. Henry had erred and she pitied him, and she mourned the loss of Fanny Price as a sister, but her agile mind was not idle. She pondered from every angle how she might best salvage the situation. Perhaps even she and Edmund — but there she shied away for her own thoughts. She could not, with any pretence of reason, imagine that

she and Edmund could still have a future together, but neither could
she yet admit to herself that they were separated forever by Henry and
Maria's foolishness.

By the time Janet was able to bring her word the next morning
that Edmund and his father were in London, Mary had formulated a
plan that she hoped would be the salvation of Henry, and incidentally
of Maria too. If Henry and Maria were saved, then perhaps — just
perhaps — she could once more think of Edmund as a potential
husband. If nothing else, Edmund was an ally. He was as involved
in this turmoil as she. He could be counted on for succour, and they
could find mutual support in each other. She was sure he needed the
consolation of a confederate as badly as she did.

Mary asked Flora to send Edmund a note asking him to come
to the house that day, so they could talk. She didn't like Flora knowing
that she had been the one to solicit Edmund, instead of Edmund
attempting to contact her, but it could not be helped.

At Janet's urging, the Stornoways had vacated the private
drawing-room, to allow Mary and Edmund privacy for their meeting.
Thus, only Edmund was in the room when Mary entered it.

"'I heard you were in town,' said she, 'I wanted to see you. Let
us talk over this sad business. What can equal the folly of our two
relations?

Edmund didn't reply, but his face showed such distress that
Mary was worried he believed her to be blaming his sister for Henry's
actions. If she told the absolute truth, she *did* blame Maria; to be sure
Henry did not want to elope. Nonetheless, she had no desire cause
Edmund more hurt than that which he was already suffering.

With a graver look and voice she then added—'I do not mean
to defend Henry at your sister's expense.'

Edmund closed his eyes and turned his head, seemingly too
moved for speech. She urged him to sit down, and joined him on the
sofa. She reached out a hand to lay on his forearm, but hesitated and
withdrew it to her own lap. She waited for him to say something, but
finally realising that he would not – could not — speak, Mary went on.

"Dearest Mr Bertram, I comprehend you, although you are
voiceless. I am also angered and disgusted by the imbecility of their
elopement. It is the most foolish, asinine thing I have ever known!
The folly of both is beyond comprehension. My brother's folly in
being drawn on by a woman whom he had never cared for, to do what
must lose him the woman he adored, is reprehensible enough, but

still less can I understand the actions of Mrs Rushworth. The idea of her sacrificing such a situation, plunging into such difficulties, under the idea of being really loved by a man who had long ago made his indifference clear — what could have possessed her to do so? It is but folly upon folly!"

Edmund, still silent from what she assumed was mortification, could not meet her eyes, and she feared she had wounded him further by dwelling on Maria's lunacy. She began then to speak of Henry's folly, particularly his great loss of any hope of Fanny Price, knowing that she and Edmund were united in their estimation of his cousin.

"What pains me the most about my brother's folly is the loss of Fanny. He has thrown away such a woman as he will never see again. She would have fixed him, she would have made him happy for ever." Here though, a flash of temper got the best of her. "Why, would not she have him? It is all her fault. Simple girl!—I shall never forgive her. Had she accepted him as she ought, they might now have been on the point of marriage, and Henry would have been too happy and too busy to want any other object. He would have taken no pains to be on terms with Mrs Rushworth again. It would have all ended in a regular standing flirtation, in yearly meetings at Sotherton and Everingham."

Mary took a deep breath and restrained herself. "The loss of Fanny as a sister pains me, but we must think of the future. We must think of how to help Henry and Mrs Rushworth survive this crisis. We must persuade Henry to marry her, and what with honour, and the certainty of having shut himself out for ever from Fanny, I do not despair of it. Fanny he must give up. I do not think that even *he* could now hope to succeed with one of her stamp, and therefore I hope we may find no insuperable difficulty. My influence, which is not small, shall all go that way; and, when once married, and properly supported by her own family, people of respectability as they are, she may recover her footing in society to a certain degree. In some circles, we know, she would never be admitted, but with good dinners, and large parties, there will always be those who will be glad of her acquaintance; and there is, undoubtedly, more liberality and candour on those points than formerly. What I advise is, that your father be quiet. Do not let him injure his own cause by interference. Persuade him to let things take their course. If by any officious exertions of his, she is induced to leave Henry's protection, there will be much less chance of his marrying her, than if she remain with him. I know how he is likely to be influenced. Let Sir Thomas trust to his honour and compassion, and it may all end well; but if he get his daughter away, it will be destroying the chief hold."

Finally, Edmund spoke. "Peace, I beg you! I had not supposed it possible, coming in such a state of mind into that house, as I had done, that any thing could occur to make me suffer more, but you have been inflicting deeper wounds in almost every sentence. Though I had, in the course of our acquaintance, been often sensible of some difference in our opinions, on points too, of some moment, it had not entered my imagination to conceive the difference could be such as you have now proved it. The manner in which you are treating the dreadful crime committed by your brother and my sister—(with whom lay the greater seduction I will not say)— the manner in which you speak of the crime itself, giving it every reproach but the right, considering its ill consequences only as they are to be braved or overborne by a defiance of decency and impudence in wrong; and, last of all, and above all, recommending to us a compliance, a compromise, an acquiescence in the continuance of the sin, on the chance of a marriage which, thinking as I now think of your brother, should rather be prevented than sought—all this together has most grievously convinced me that I had never understood you before, and that, as far as related to your mind, you have been the creature of my own imagination, not Miss Crawford, that I had been too apt to dwell on for many months past. It is, perhaps, best for me; I had less to regret in sacrificing a friendship—feelings—hopes which must, at any rate, have been torn from me now. And yet, that I must confess, that, could I restore you to what you had appeared to me before, I would infinitely prefer any increase of the pain of parting, for the sake of carrying with me the right of tenderness and esteem."

Mary was astonished, exceedingly astonished—more than astonished. She turned extremely red. She was profoundly abashed by Edmund's judgemental harangue. Never had she been lectured to in such a manner in her life! Was he right? Was she in error to look at Henry and Maria's indiscretion as folly? To wish to help them? Did it show a lack of character in herself? Completely taken aback, she sought refuge in lightness, much the way her brother always did.

With a sort of laugh, she answered, 'A pretty good lecture upon my word. Was it part of your last sermon? At this rate, you will soon reform every body at Mansfield and Thornton Lacey; and when I hear of you next, it may be as a celebrated preacher in some great society of Methodists, or as a missionary into foreign parts.'

464   MANSFIELD PARSONAGE

Edmund, with grave and cold formality, stood and bowed. He looked down his nose at her and said, ice forming on each word, "From my heart I wish you well, and earnestly hope that you might soon learn to think more justly, and not owe the most valuable knowledge we could any of us acquire—the knowledge of ourselves and of our duty, to the lessons of affliction. Gladly would I submit to all the increased pain of losing you, rather than have to think of you as I do now."

He bowed once more, turned on his heel, and made his exit.

Mary was briefly stupefied with shock. Then she leapt to her feet and darted to the door. It could not end thus! Not the affection that had been between them! She wrenched the door open and saw his retreating form already halfway up the hall.

'Mr Bertram,' said she. He looked back, his face like a mask of marble. 'Mr Bertram,' she said again with a smile— a saucy playful smile, inviting him back, showing him she was willing to forgive him his harsh words and repair the friendship between them.

Edmund, however, appeared unmoved. He did not answer her. He simply turned his back and walked out of her life, as though there was nothing there that could tempt him — or had ever tempted him – to be part of it.

Chapter Forty-Five

MARY STOOD WITH her mouth agape, stunned by the sound of the front door shutting behind Edmund. Everything had a curious lack of reality to it, as though she had seen it happen to someone else. How *could* it be real? One minute she was trying to salvage Maria Rushworth's happiness from the consequences of her own spoiled folly, even at the expense of Henry's peace of mind, as a sign of her friendship and affection for the Bertram family, and the next moment Edmund was looking at her as though she were filth, and admonishing her as though *she* were the one who had committed adultery in so public a manner, rather than his sister.

She would never, ever forget the pure loathing on Edmund's face. His every feature made it clear she disgusted him. The blue eyes that had looked upon her so warmly, so approvingly, were filled with revulsion. If she had been a dockside whore who had propositioned him, he could not have given her a sharper rebuke regarding her lapsed morality.

Once, when she was a girl, she fell out of a tree and had the wind knocked out of her. She felt that same agonising inability to draw breath now. It was as if Edmund had slapped her to the floor without having raised a hand.

She walked to the stairs with an eerie feeling of calm and began to ascend toward her sleeping quarters, putting each foot down carefully in front of her, as though she were expecting the floor to give way. She heard Flora call out to her from the drawing-room, a jumble of noise that she couldn't understand. Mary couldn't summon the strength to make herself turn her head or force words through her numb lips, and continued to climb the stairs without acknowledging her hostess's existence. An hour before Mary would have sworn that she was incapable of such rudeness, but now she barely registered her incivility. She cared for nothing but reaching the privacy of her bedroom.

Mary entered her room, locking the door carefully behind her. She then climbed into her bed fully dressed, pulled the up blankets around her ears, curled into a ball, and lay there shivering. She was cold. Had she developed an ague? Was Edmund's sermonising and repugnance enough to have brought on a fever? Her teeth chattered. A winter's fog had formed around her heart, and she was freezing to death from the inside out.

There had always been a kernel of doubt in Mary's rational, semi-agnostic mind on whether or not humans were really imbued with a soul, but she no longer wondered if she possessed such an unprovable item. She knew she had a soul because she could feel it bleeding. It was if Edmund had torn strips of raw meat from the core of her being, and she was exsanguinating from the unseen wounds.

When the tears started, she tried to remain silent but couldn't prevent thin whimpers from escaping. They seemed to press outward from her benumbed face without requiring her mouth. She had not cried with such desperate, aching loneliness since her mother had died. She felt utterly bereft, rudderless in a roiling sea. She had not known how important it was to her to believe Edmund loved her until all hope was taken from her. For his love to be replaced, supplanted by, abhorrence and detestation was pain upon pain. Her whimpers became sobs, and she could only hope that no one could hear her.

What had she done that had been so terrible? She had only wished to help Edmund's family survive the humiliation Maria had caused them. Would it have been better if she had rent her garments and poured ashes over her head in mourning? If she had raved like an evangelical about hellfire and the doom of the wayward pair? Were their sins so repulsively unique that her brother and Maria were beyond all hope? Was she a hardened monster to not see it as the end of the world? To want to mitigate the social repercussions of their elopement? After all, it was Maria, not Henry, who would be lost to all good society if there was no marriage. Her brother, rich and personable as he was, would be able to wed another. Maria, if Rushworth divorced her and Henry did not take her, would never have even the smallest hope of remarriage.

She cried alone until her eyes could make no more tears and her head was aching. As she lay in the bed, feeling as though she had been beaten by unseen rods, a small spark of anger at Edmund began to rise in Mary's breast. Who was *he* to look at her as if she were filth? A second son, a country parson without means to rise, the brother of a wastrel and a woman who would be deemed a slut by the entire ton. How did falling apart in the face of Maria and Henry's elopement make *him* morally superior? He did not want the stain of a remarriage to Henry to besmirch his family, but what good family would want any of the Bertram children now? Tom may have some success, being the eldest son and heir to Mansfield Park, but what could tempt anyone else to connect themselves with an infamous adulteress like Maria Bertram for less than a baronetcy? Who would want Julia, for fear she was no better than her sister? What did Edmund have to tempt a woman to accept his addresses and a parson's pittance, when his family was no longer unexceptional?

Slowly, the newly ignited anger began to burn, rising into a white-hot heat of searing rage when her pride, sorely bruised by Edmund's animosity, fed the flames by reminding her of her shame when he castigated her. That *she* should feel ashamed for Maria's folly and degradation! How dare Edmund Bertram judge *her*!

She threw back the covers and began to pace the room, the tears streaming down her face anew from vexation.

What an unbearable prig! What a self-righteous, conceited puppy! How dare he consider himself a moral adjudicator when it was *his* family that produced an adulteress, not *hers*! If he was the product of such a saintly home, then why wasn't an upbringing in the bosom of piety able to prevent his sister's wilful disobedience to her marriage vows?

His family did not wish Maria to marry Henry! That Henry not be considered *fit* to marry her! Ha! Maria was beneath contempt now, let alone beneath Henry. All the Bertrams were tainted by association. What the Crawfords would suffer for Henry's gaffe was nothing compared to the sneers that would be aimed at the Bertrams. If Edmund had enough brains to fill a teaspoon he would have fallen to his knees and kissed Mary's hem when she revealed that she was willing to encourage Henry to sully himself by marrying a vain, headstrong strumpet like Maria Rushworth!

How Edmund, whose family's money came from the sweat and agony of slaves, could think himself worthy to be an arbiter of morality beggared the mind. He could roll in the gelt that sugar had given the Bertrams without worry of the human cost, but found *her* willingness to "defy decency" appalling? She would rather her brother tup a thousand loose-legged wives than own a slave! Edmund found *her* impudent? At least *she* wasn't impudent enough to think she could judge how well others were following the commandments to love their neighbours as themselves while willing to *own* those neighbours and beat them for more profit!

What a hypocritical, pompous, puffing, bastard! He thought *his* moral compass was so unswerving, when he was as changeable as anyone else for his own comfort. Hadn't he capitulated and agreed to play Anhalt when it suited him? His staunch refusals could change in a jiffy if needs be. Oh, he had *said* that the change was to spare her the embarrassment of acting with Mr Maddox, but she had seen how he had enjoyed her declarations of devotion to Anhalt once he was in the role. She had felt him tremble when she rested her hand on his arm. He had relished his time acting with her or she would eat her best hat.

How she would like to have the last five minutes of that conversation again! What she wouldn't tell him! Not only would she skewer him for his own hypocrisy, she would point out that he was a complete failure as a swain and could hardly be called a gentleman. His attentions toward her at Mansfield had been so marked, and so persistent, that they had led to comments from more than one corner. Many people, of all rank, had hinted to Mrs Grant that all that stood in the way of her sister's marriage to Mr Edmund Bertram was her sister's willingness to bestow her hand. What sort of gentleman would behave in such a manner and not propose? He had potentially exposed a lady to ridicule! If Mary had let it be known that she was considering his suit, or if she had shown him the decided preference he had shown her, and yet he had not offered for her hand, then her reputation would have been materially harmed. Edmund's reputation would have been harmed less than her own by his unannounced jilting of her, but his character would have suffered in a way mortifying to him; he would have been seen as an ungentlemanlike cad without sufficient honour to raise expectations in a young lady but not meet them. It was *her* prudence and forethought, not his, that had saved them both from disgrace when he dithered over his proposal.

She would do more than put her indignation into words if she could. She would slap that expression of loathing and disdain off his self-righteous countenance! Mary allowed herself a very pleasing mental fantasy of Edward's face when she struck him. However, no sooner had she thought of reddening his cheek or splitting his lip with a blow, she was reminded of his handsome visage on other occasions. She wept afresh as the memories of him walking with her, talking to her, and looking at her as though she were an incomparable beauty, rose in her mind to cut up her peace like pike in a trout-stream. Mary spent the entire morning in her room, vacillating between bitter hatred and tender sentiment, weeping for either cause. When a maid came to tell Mary dinner was nearing, she sent the girl away. Her face was too swollen from crying for her to come down to dinner. When the maid returned to offer to bring Mary a tray, she told her to thank Lady Stornoway for her kind thoughts, but she was not hungry; she had a severe headache. It was Flora herself who came the third time, to ask if she need to send for a doctor or apothecary. Mary thanked her with a perfect counterfeit of sincerity, but knew from the avaricious way Flora looked at her tear-ravaged visage that her old school friend wanted to be able to tell others first-hand how distraught Mary had been after Edmund left.

"

Flora's unsuccessfully hidden gloating motivated Mary to pull herself together as little else would have. It also fixed, for the present, Mary's feelings of hurt outrage toward Edmund Bertram; if he had not wounded her, Flora would not be in a position to gloat over her tears. Mary also resolved that if Edmund did not consider her brother worthy of his sister, then *she* should not hesitate to express how unfit Maria was to be Henry's wife. Stiffening her spine, she rang for Beatty, and had her lady's maid bring cold water and cloths to place over her eyes to reduce the swelling. By the time dinner was over, the cold compresses and lightly applied makeup hid the tell-tale signs of Mary's distress well enough for Mary to venture down for after-dinner tea.

"Darling!" Flora was clearly shocked to see Mary enter the drawing-room. "I thought you ... your headache had quite incapacitated you."

"It *was* dreadful," Mary said cheerfully, "but it has abated for the most part."

"It was probably brought on by your sorrows," Flora oozed with sympathy, "considering all that has happened."

The dinner guests were all part of their habitual circle; Flora wouldn't have been so crass as to imply the topic of Henry's elopement in front of strangers. However, among the theoretical close friends as Mrs Woodbead and Lady Rummage, Flora felt well able to drag the subject out into the open.

Mary, her composure unshaken, agreed. "Yes, I am sure it was. Especially since Mr Edmund Bertram came today with the news that his brother has suffered something of a relapse from the shock, and his mother is nearly incapacitated. I was a frequent visitor at Mansfield Park, you know, and I was very much grieved for their distress." Mary lay false trails, determined to never allow either her reproach from Edmund — or her emotional turmoil as a result of it — to become public knowledge. "What is worse, my particular friend, Miss Price, whom Henry had asked to marry, is also in a very bad state. The poor girl regrets with all her heart her hesitation in accepting Henry. If she had not caviled then Henry would have been safe."

"Safe?" Mrs Woodbead asked eagerly.

"Oh yes," Mary smiled, inwardly burning with the remembrance of Edmund's disdain for a marriage between his harlot of a sister and dearest Henry. With a raging heart that could feel no mercy she threw Maria, whose brash selfishness she considered the author of the deplorable elopement, to the wolves. "Even Mrs Rushworth would have hesitated to strong-arm her cousin's betrothed into flying with her."

"So Mrs Rushworth forced Mr Crawford to elope with her?" Lady Rummage, with the security of a woman who knew the true crime of adultery was in its exposure, was all atwitter at the idea of the beautiful Maria Rushworth's idiocy. She had disliked Mrs Rushworth from the moment she saw how approvingly her own lover, Mr Jarsdel, had looked upon the blond Venus.

"What else?" Mary asked with every impression of candidness. "Henry was, perhaps, foolish in choosing such a near relation of Miss Price's to distract himself, but my brother has always had a weakness for woman of, shall we say, a certain *character*. He simply cannot resist being seduced, poor fellow. I tried to warn him that Mrs Rushworth would go to any length to have him, but he wouldn't believe me. He said it would be too *unnatural* in a woman to pursue a man. Alas, he was too generous-minded for his own good."

In truth, Mary was certain that Maria had bullied Henry into leaving town with her. It was beyond contestation that Henry had wanted nothing more to do with Maria the last time the siblings had spoken. When Mary had hoped to facilitate a marriage between Henry and Mrs Rushworth, she planned to try to paint the vile elopement in the most *romantic* light possible, presenting her brother and Maria as a sort of star-crossed pair of lovers, and emphasising the disgusted dismay any woman would have felt being married to a nitwit like Mr Rushworth. Now that Edmund had made his revulsion of the Crawfords known to her, she had no reason to try to help Mrs Rushworth recover her reputation, and Mary had no qualms about blackening Maria's reputation further in an effort to mitigate Henry's disgrace. As angry and hurt as she was by Edmund scolding and his scorn, Mary was also happy to cause the him further heartache by letting the entire Bertram family be tarred with the same brush that would smear Maria.

"Do you know where they have gone?" Flora queried, hoping for further gossip.

"Of course not," Mary sipped her tea. "If Henry had been given enough warning to tell me anything, he would have gone immediately into hiding."

"Isn't your brother an acquaintance of Mr Rushworth's?" Lady Rummage leaned forward confidently. "Is it true that Mr Crawford became close to Mr Rushworth in pursuit of his bride?"

"Quite to the contrary," Mary assured her. "He was introduced to Mr Rushworth when Mrs Rushworth still bore the name Miss Bertram. It was *Miss Bertram* that fostered the acquaintance, hoping Henry would become jealous and ask for her hand himself. Henry quite pitied Mr Rushworth his wife. He was sure the man would wear horns in a fortnight."

"Then perhaps he Honourable Mr Yates should be pitied as well," Mrs Woodbead smirked.

"Whatever do you mean?" Mary asked.

"Haven't you heard?" Mrs Woodbead looked astounded. "Miss Julia Bertram has eloped with Mr Yates. It is assumed they are heading for the Scottish boarder."

Mary boggled internally, but quickly rallied and did not give even so much as an extra blink to outwardly show her surprise. "No, I hadn't heard. Mr Bertram was understandably unwilling to mention the disgrace of his second sister. I can attest that Miss Julia Bertram was not very fond of Mr Yates before, but if he offered for her when the news of Maria's escapades reached her, I can see why she accepted. She probably feared it would be her last proposal, due to the potential worry among suitors that she was too much like her sister."

"And *is* she much like her sister?" Flora all but licked her lips.

"Not in the least," Mary announced. She was willing to add to Edmund Bertram's pain and shame, and did not care if his parents and elder brother were similarly distressed, but she had no desire to destroy his youngest sister's happiness with an outright falsehood about Julia's character. Even at her most enraged and vengeful, there were things Mary Crawford would never stoop to; she would expose, perhaps even show things to the least advantage, but she would not spin evil from thin air. Julia would suffer enough from the association with Maria's scandal, and from enduing a marriage to a blockhead like Mr Yates, without Mary's unreasonable enmity. "I wish Mr and Mrs Yates every joy."

"I think Mrs Rushworth must be *naturally* very bad," Mrs Woodbead pronounced, "and I wonder if the whole family doesn't have some sort of flaw in the blood. Isn't her brother, Mr Tom Bertram, a wastrel?"

Mary did not show even the smallest crack in her façade that the matter was of little account to her. "You may be right, my dear Mrs Woodbead, but I suspect that it has more to do with their *upbringing* than any *inherent* flaws within them. Their father is a slave-owner, and what can be expected of his children when he sets them such an example of callousness toward his fellow man? How can they truly know what is moral, and just, when they have been shown by example that they can benefit from slavery without the veriest twinge of conscience?"

Nothing, absolutely *nothing*, would hurt Edmund Bertram more than the idea that his ability to make moral distinctions was called into question, Mary thought to herself with the caustic satisfaction of someone who felt unjustly injured. Let him judge *me* as dissipated, but I'll make sure anyone over whom I have any influence is judging *him* as unprincipled in essence, if not in action.

Lady Rummage frowned in thought. "Wasn't Mr Edmund Bertram one of your beaus, my dear?"

"Does it seem likely that I would be encouraging the attentions of a country parson with hardly a penny to his name?" Mary grinned, as if the whole concept was inexpressibly amusing.

Lady Rummage laughed. "No, it does seem too odd now that I think on it."

"The Bertrams are, I will own, very pleasant people, all things considered," Mary said condescendingly. "Certainly they are all handsome, and appeared well-bred. I will also say, with absolute candour, that Sir Thomas was an absolute paragon as a husband. It is such a pity that there should be such lack of moral rectitude in their eldest daughter, and that Henry could not see his danger in Mrs Rushworth, but my brother *will* be gallant to the fair sex, regardless of situation or temper," She sighed, as though she were resigned to Henry's inability to detect and avoid any succubus that set her cap for him.

"Henry *is* a sad flirt," said Flora, not altogether kindly.

"Oh yes," Mary agreed. "I have warned him that his flirtations and attentions to every pretty woman were too much. Yet Henry, sensible in all else, thought that as long as he kept from paying sufficient attentions to arouse expectations *in general*, that the young ladies *themselves* would not form expectations of him either. What my dearest Henry did not calculate on was *vanity*. A truly vain woman, such as Mrs Rushworth, would not be able to conceive that his flirtations were not signs of love. I would lay my life that Henry did not have an inkling of Mrs Rushworth's intentions to quit her husband's home and go to him until it was all too late."

The men, leading with Mr Woodbead, began to rejoin the ladies in the drawing-room, necessitating Mary to repeat the gist of what she had already told her female acquaintance. Mary was confident that the men, who, despite their belief to the contrary, were every bit as gossipy and scandal-loving as the women of the Beau Monde, would disseminate the information throughout their gentleman's clubs. Nothing cemented an idea as fact quite like it becoming the general opinion, and if Mary could establish a general belief in Henry's reluctance to elope, then his reputation would escape almost unscathed.

II

Devoted to her brother and having no reason to spare the Bertrams, Mary carefully maintained the charade of her nonchalance and the insistence of Henry's victimisation for the entirety of the painful weeks that followed. She remained in the Stornoway home as long as had been originally planned, and attended balls, routes, parties and plays as if nothing were amiss. Her brazen refusal to admit that Henry was in any way culpable for his elopement had a reasonable degree of success in blackening Mrs Rushworth's name while exonerating Henry's. Happily for Mary, no one ever suspected that she, whose surface was appeared unruffled, was nursing the turmoil of a broken heart herself.

Although Mary did not waver in her resuscitation of Henry's character at the Bertrams' expense, her animosity toward Edmund was continually peppered with moments of remembered friendship that caused her more hurt than any amount of choler toward him. Had Mary not still loved Edmund, she would have hated him less. Indifference, not hatred, is the true opposite of love, and Mary's deep pain and deeper yearning for Edmund's affections melded together in a witch's brew of rage and recriminations against him.

Mary's self-awareness was also the enemy of her peace. She knew herself too well to think that she was wholly antagonistic toward Edmund. She knew rationally that he, and Sir Thomas, were her examples of the kind of husband she wanted to ensure her domestic happiness. Not even Dr Grant's affections for his wife could equal the unceasing consideration Sir Thomas gave to Lady Bertram, or Edmund's purity of heart. Thus, Mary was forced to admire Edmund even as she felt a profound umbrage regarding the way he had treated her. This mixture of ire and respect caused Mary more emotional suffering than a greater amount of simple hatred would have done.

Her anguish was increased by her knowledge of her siblings' misery. Letter's from Mrs Grant brought consolation, but the directions by which Mary returned the letters was a constant reminder of how the Grant's trip to Bath had been for some months purposely lengthened; after what had passed to wound and alienate the two families, the continuance of the Bertrams and Grants in such close neighbourhood would have been most distressing. Henry's folly with Maria Rushworth had in effect driven their sister and her husband from the home they loved, and although she was not the cause, Mary could not help but be sorry for it.

One of the few bright spots in Mary's life was that the Grant's exile in Bath ended very fortunately in the necessity, or at least the practicability of a permanent removal. Dr Grant, through an interest on which he had almost ceased to form hopes, succeeded to a stall in Westminster, which, as affording an occasion for leaving Mansfield, an excuse for residence in London, and an increase of income to answer the expenses of the change, was highly acceptable to those who went, and those who staid. Mrs Grant, with a temper to love and be loved, must have gone with some regret, from the scenes and people she had been used to; but the same happiness of disposition must in any place and any society, secure her a great deal to enjoy, and she had again a home to offer Mary.

Chapter Forty-Six

IN JULY, EXACTLY one year to the day, Mary found herself once more travelling to stay with the Grants. What a difference a year had made! Instead of the pleasure of her brother's barouche and her brother's company for a long trip into the country, Mary travelled in the Grant's carriage with her maid a mere two miles across London, from Berkeley Square to Westminster. This move was much more welcome than the last, as well. Mary had had enough of her own friends, enough of vanity, ambition, love, and disappointment in the course of the last half year, to be in need of the true kindness of her sister's heart, and the rational tranquillity of her ways. Mary hoped that her sister's home, while still accessible to the entertainments of Town, would nonetheless give her succour from the ton's voracious curiosity regarding Henry's scandal.

Secure in the Grant's abode, Mary had the inexpressible luxury of being allowed to grieve without pretence. With her sister and brother-in-law, she found a shared pain at Henry's actions, shared regrets, and shared consolations. Mary could now reflect over the opportunities for domestic happiness she and Henry had lost, or alternately to seethe over the way Edmund Bertram expressed himself in their final parting, and have someone she trusted enough to confide in about these feelings. Mrs Fraser had stood by her admirably, but Mary was reluctant to reveal the conflicted notions in her heart to Janet; the gallimaufry of emotions within her breast made her feel ridiculous, and Mary's pride revolted at the exposure. It was only with Mrs Grant that Mary could allow herself to be seen as foolish without feeling naked as well.

Mary was glad, however, that Janet's fixed kindness to her had been rewarded. Mrs Fraser's devotion to her friend restored Mr Fraser's opinion of his wife. Although she *had* married him for pecuniary reasons, he saw that was a woman of *genuine* feeling, and was not wholly mercenary. Janet's noble actions inspired Mr Fraser to try to woo his wife, hoping to win her heart *after* their marriage if not before.

His new gentleness and consideration for her brought him success earlier than he could have imagined. By the Yuletide, the Frasers' were refurbishing the nursery in preparation for a midsummer's occupant.

It was to the Grant's new abode that an abject Henry finally wrote to explain himself to the relations he had not ceased to value. Henry poured out his heart, and his self-reproach was harsher than anything his sisters would have said to him. Henry was well aware that had he done as he intended, and as he knew he ought, by going down to Everingham after his return from Portsmouth, he might have been deciding his own happy destiny. But he was pressed to stay for Mrs Fraser's party; his staying was made of flattering consequence, and he was to meet Mrs Rushworth there. Curiosity and vanity were both engaged, and the temptation of immediate pleasure was too strong for a mind unused to make any sacrifice to right; he resolved to defer his Norfolk journey, resolved that writing should answer the purpose of it, or that its purpose was unimportant—and staid. He saw Mrs Rushworth, was received by her with a coldness which ought to have been repulsive, and have established apparent indifference between them for ever; but he was mortified, he could not bear to be thrown off by the woman whose smiles had been so wholly at his command; he must exert himself to subdue so proud a display of resentment; it was anger on Fanny's account; he must get the better of it, and make Mrs Rushworth Maria Bertram again in her treatment of himself.

In this spirit he began the attack; and by animated perseverance had soon re-established the sort of familiar intercourse—of gallantry—of flirtation, which bounded his views, but in triumphing over the discretion, which, though beginning in anger, might have saved them both, he had put himself in the power of feelings on her side, more strong than he had supposed.—She loved him; there was no withdrawing attentions, avowedly dear to her. He was entangled by his own vanity, with as little excuse of love as possible, and without the smallest inconstancy of mind towards her cousin.—To keep Fanny and the Bertrams from a knowledge of what was passing became his first object. Secrecy could not have been more desirable for Mrs Rushworth's credit than he felt it for his own.—When he returned from Richmond, he would have been glad to see Mrs Rushworth no more.—All that followed was the result of her imprudence; and he went off with her at last, because he could not help it, regretting Fanny, even at the moment, but regretting her infinitely more, when all the bustle of the intrigue was over, and a very few months had taught him, by the force of contrast, to place a yet higher value on the sweetness of her temper, the purity of her mind, and the excellence of her principles.

Any desire his sisters or brother-in-law may have had to rail against him or castigate him was quashed by the obvious misery and guilt; he was tormenting himself well enough to need no help.

That his sisters and Dr Grant forgave him was Henry's only comfort during this time, since much to his dismay all that Maria's family could do to persuade her to leave him bore no fruit. She hoped to marry him, and they continued together till she was obliged to be convinced that such hope was vain, and till the disappointment and wretchedness arising from the conviction, rendered her temper so bad, and her feelings for him so like hatred, as to make them for a while each other's punishment, and then induce a voluntary separation. She had lived with him to be reproached as the ruin of all his happiness in Fanny, and carried away no better consolation in leaving him, than that she *had* divided them.

Freed from Maria, a penitent Henry returned to London for the 1814 season. The seeds Mary planted had grown strong and flowered, and Henry found himself regarded as victimised by, rather than culpable for, his own lunacy in involving himself with the former Mrs Rushworth. If anything, the scandal made him *more* popular, since he now had a Lord Byron-like aura of excessive Romanticism. His friends, and anyone whom Mary could influence, invited him to the dinners, routes, and card parties. He began to make public appearances at Vauxhall, Astley's, and Drury Lane. He even secured a voucher for Almack's, thanks to his long-standing friendship with William Molyneux, the 2nd Earl of Sefton, whose wife was a lady patroness.

That punishment, the public punishment of disgrace, should in a just measure attend <u>his</u> share of the offence is, we know, not one of the barriers which society gives to virtue. In this world the penalty is less equal than could be wished; but without presuming to look forward to a juster appointment hereafter, we may fairly consider a man of sense, like Henry Crawford, to be providing for himself no small portion of vexation and regret: vexation that must rise sometimes to self–reproach, and regret to wretchedness, in having so requited hospitality, so injured family peace, so forfeited his best, most estimable, and endeared acquaintance, and so lost the woman whom he had rationally as well as passionately loved.

Henry and Mary, although completely sanguine in public, both felt severe pangs of unhappiness when they heard of Edmund's marriage to Fanny. Henry, knowing himself to be entirely in the wrong, tried to derive comfort from the fact that Fanny would be as beloved and treasured by Edmund almost as much as Henry himself would have done. If *he* was miserable, at least Fanny was safe. Mary, who would always believe herself to have been injured by Edmund at the last, could not find surcease in contemplation of Edmund's and Fanny's wedded bliss. She did not think it right that Edmund should be happy while she still suffered from his treatment.

Mary tried to gratify her acrimony toward Edmund by thinking of the newlyweds dining at four o'clock then playing cribbage until bed, as though they were people who wore hobnailed boots. Unfortunately, her knowledge of how much he would enjoy such a simple and unsophisticated evening thwarted her. Edmund *would* be happy with such dull employment. All the fashionable world could mock him, but it could not in any way diminish his joy by sneering at his countrified ways. Edmund had been cruel to Mary, and had said things to her that had scarred her forever, but he was rewarded with marriage to Fanny. It vexed Mary heartily.

Just as unwelcome as the idea of Edmund's constant felicity with his wife was the idea that Mary herself might never recover her former happiness. What if she was left to play Patience, alone and unwanted, having never found anyone who made her as happy as Fanny surely made Edmund?

The only thing that brought her even a hint of satisfaction was that Edmund was now a fixed protector of his tender and gentle cousin. Mary remained the dupe of Fanny Price forever. Never did she ever suspect Fanny's friendship had been a façade, a whited sculpture that stank of a charnel house on the inside. Mary remained ignorant of the judgemental malevolence and self-righteousness of Miss Price, even after Miss Price became Mrs Edmund Bertram. Not once did it cross Mary's mind that to be Edmund's wife was what Fanny had hoped for, or that Fanny's hopes in that direction had made her regard Mary as her evil nemesis, even as she cried and hugged Mary's neck. Until the end of her life, Mary would regret losing Fanny's friendship, long after Henry would cease to regret never gaining Fanny's hand.

When Dr Grant had brought on apoplexy and death in 1815, by three great institutionary dinners in one week, the sisters continued to live together for more than two years after Mrs Grant's widowhood;

for Mary, though perfectly resolved against ever attaching herself to a younger brother again, was long in finding among the dashing representatives, or idle heir apparents, who were at the command of her beauty, and her 20,000*l.* any one who could satisfy the better taste she had acquired at Mansfield, whose character and manners could authorise a hope of the domestic happiness she had there learnt to estimate, or put Edmund Bertram sufficiently out of her head. Nonetheless, Mary did find love again and was made happier than she could have ever believed possible … but that is a tale for another day.

READING GROUP QUESTIONS

We hope that you enjoyed reading this book. Jane Austen's books are a great inspiration for writers and readers alike. Kyra Kramer has put together the following questions to help inspire you to enjoy the book more:

» Fanny Price is the heroine of Jane Austen's original novel, *Mansfield Park*. Mary Crawford is the central protagonist of *Mansfield Parsonage*. Which character did you find the most sympathetic? In short, which character did you like more?

» Do you feel the author of *Mansfield Parsonage* stayed true to the original Austen depictions of the central characters in *Mansfield Park*? If not, in what ways do you believe the author changed them?

» Do you consider Mary Crawford to have been a good friend to Fanny Price? Why or why not?

» Do you think Mary Crawford and Edmund Bertram had anything in common or was their attraction based solely on the physical appearance of their love interest?

» How did the author reconcile Mary's abolitionist principles with Mary's interest in the Bertram brothers as suitors? Do you think this was a reflection of human complexity or a character violation that lessened your enjoyment of the story?

» If Mary and Edmund had gotten married, do you think they would have been happy together?

Whom do you think would have needed to adjust the most in their role as a spouse to facilitate marital happiness?

» Was Fanny Price acting rashly or wisely when she rejected Henry Crawford? If she had accepted his proposal, do you think she would have found happiness? Do you think she could have effected any change in Henry's habits or behaviours?

» Do you believe that Mary Crawford's suggestion that her brother Henry be induced to marry Maria Rushworth was a rational kindness with the intent of helping the Bertrams or a callous attempt at damage control to protect herself by association? What do you think motivated Mary's plan?

» Taking Regency mores into consideration, do you think Edmund Bertram was justified in his revulsion for Mary's lack of "feminine delicacy" regarding Maria Rushworth's adultery? Or do think Edmund overreacted even by 19th century standards?

» Many movies have been made based on Jane Austen's works. If a movie was made about *Mansfield Parsonage*, which actor would you cast as each character?

Meet the Author

Kyra Kramer is a medical anthropologist, historian, and devoted bibliophile who lives just outside Cardiff, Wales with her handsome husband and three wonderful young daughters. She has a deep – nearly obsessive – love for Regency Period romances in general and Jane Austen's work in particular. Ms. Kramer has authored several history books and academic essays, but this is her first foray into fictional writing. You can visit her website at *kyrackramer.com* to learn more about her life and work.

Toni Mount

A
Sebastian Foxley
Medieval
Murder Mystery

The
Colour
of
Poison

ISBN: 978-84-944893-3-4

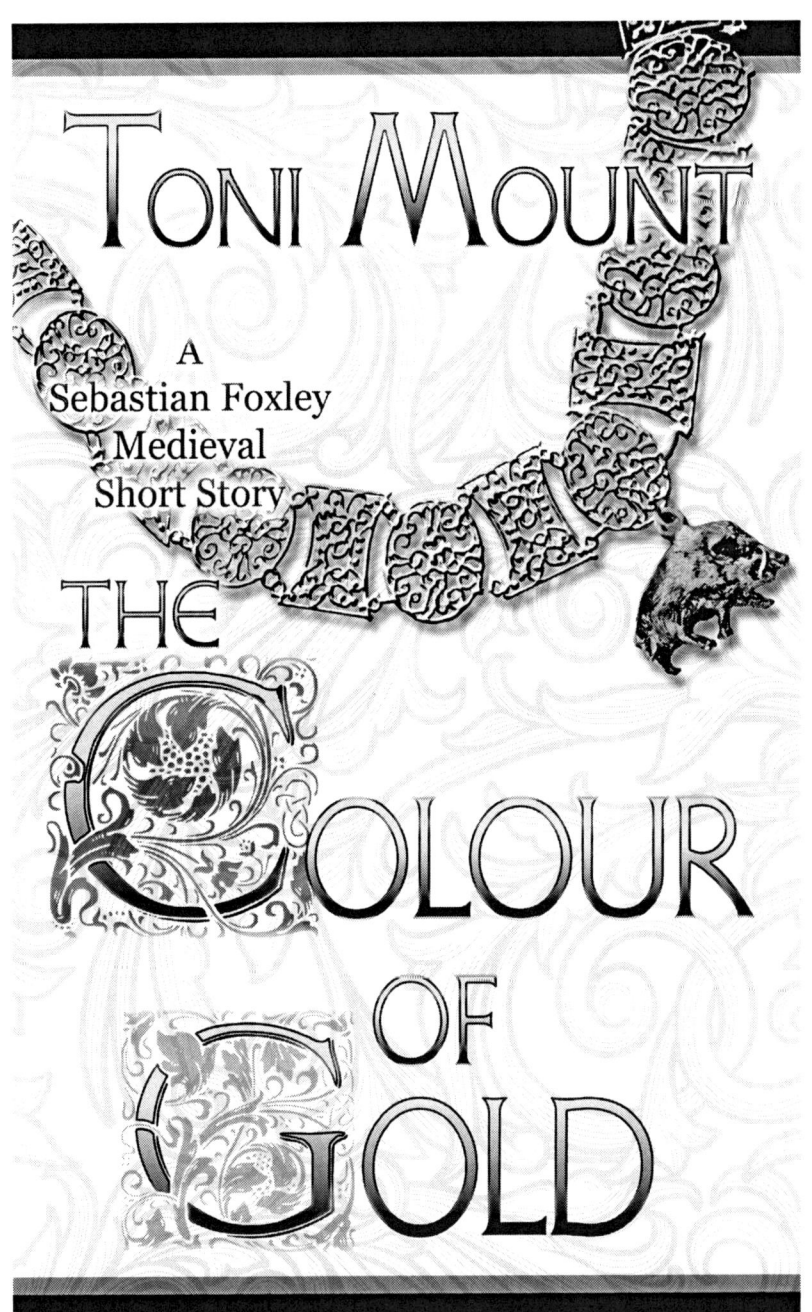

TONI MOUNT

A
Sebastian Foxley
Medieval
Short Story

THE

COLOUR

OF

GOLD

ISBN: 978-84-946498-0-6

TONI MOUNT

The Third
Sebastian Foxley
Medieval
Murder Mystery

THE COLOUR OF COLD BLOOD

ISBN: 978-84-946498-1-3

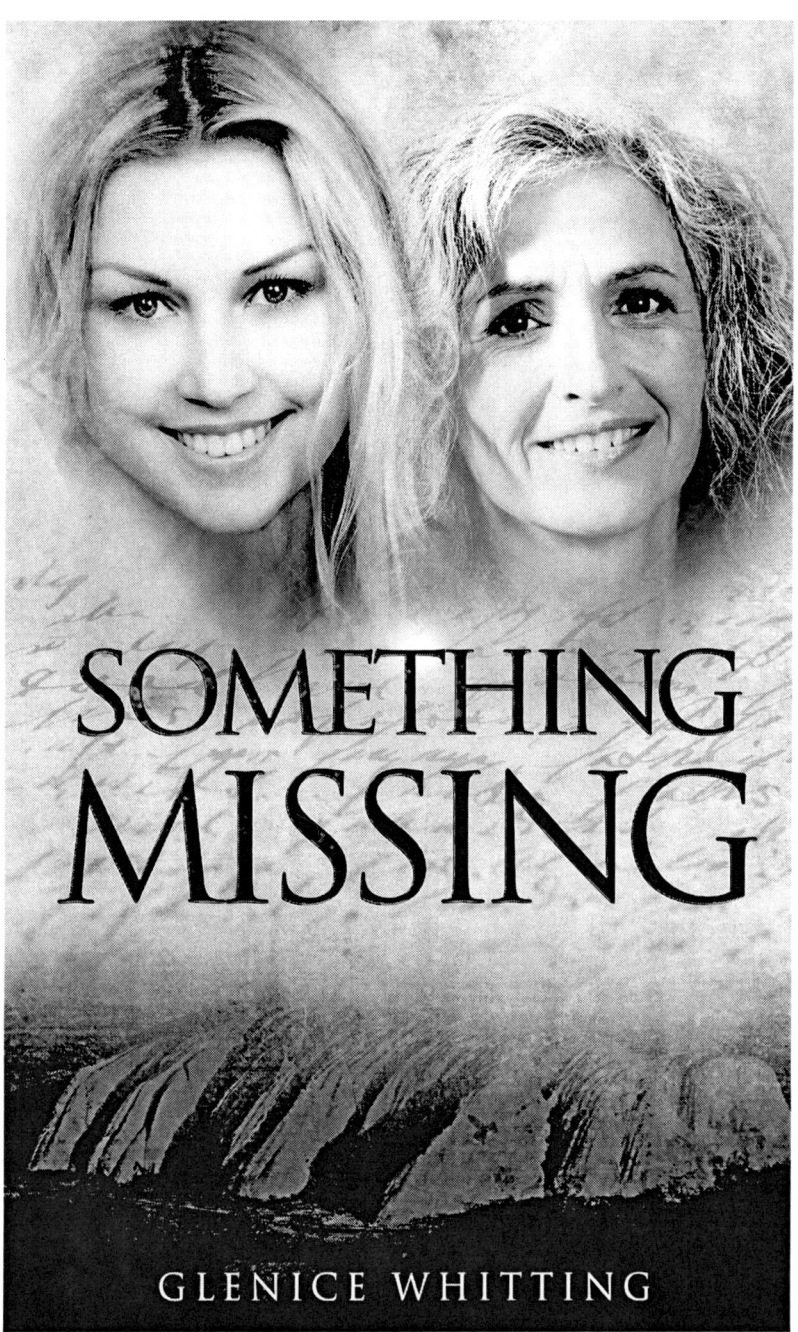

SOMETHING
MISSING

GLENICE WHITTING

ISBN: 978-84-945937-6-5

Remhurst
MANOR

Tamasine Loves

ISBN: 978-0-9942080-7-1

1549
Black arts
and rebellion
in Tudor
England

The Devil's Chalice

D.K. WILSON

Based on real
TUDOR CRIME
RECORDS

ISBN: 978-84-944893-8-9

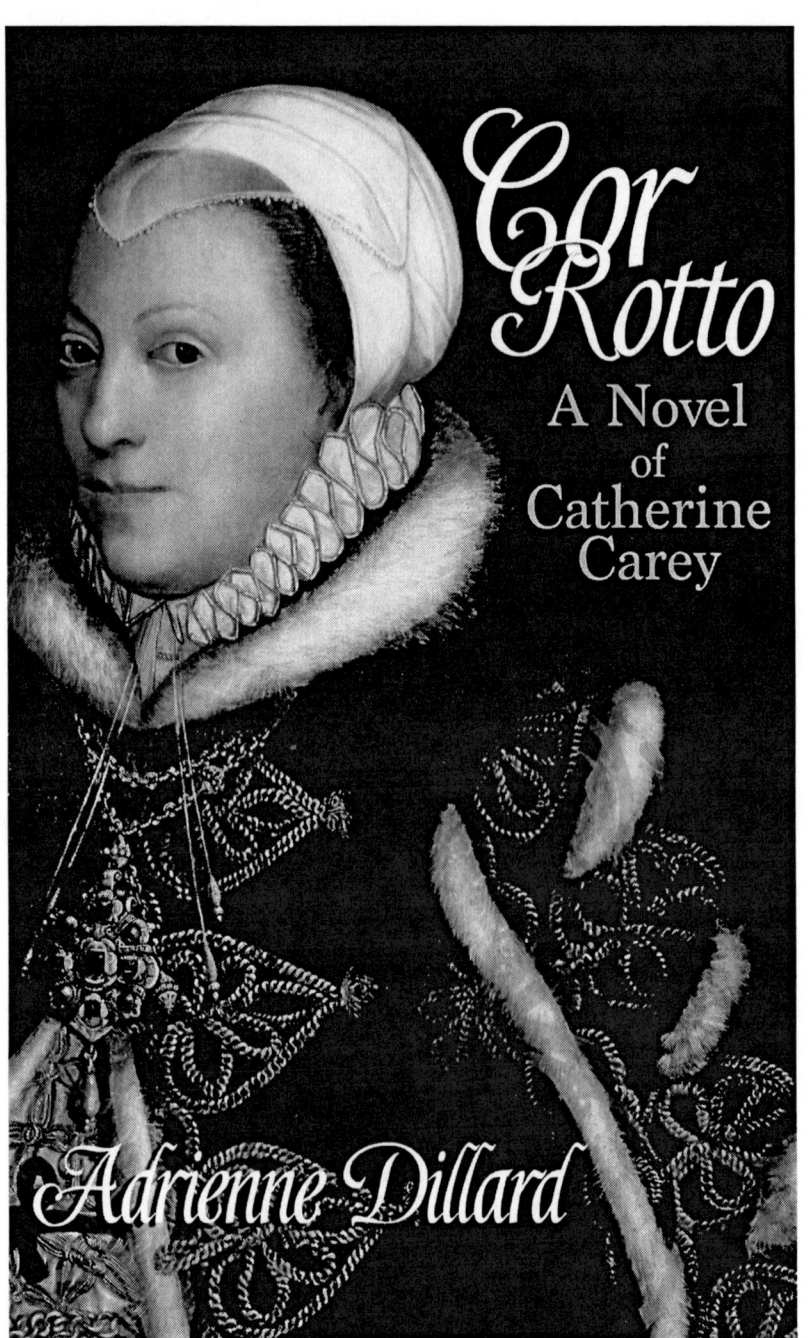

Cor Rotto

A Novel
of
Catherine
Carey

Adrienne Dillard

ISBN: 978-84-937464-7-6

THE RAVEN'S WIDOW

A Novel of
Jane Boleyn

ADRIENNE DILLARD

ISBN: 978-84-946498-3-7

AMAZING FICTION
from MadeGlobal Publishing

Falling Pomegranate Seeds - **Wendy J. Dunn**
Struck With the Dart of Love - **Sandra Vasoli**
Truth Endures - **Sandra Vasoli**
Phoenix Rising - **Hunter S. Jones**
Cor Rotto - **Adrienne Dillard**
The Raven's Widow - **Adrienne Dillard**
The Claimant - **Simon Anderson**
The Truth of the Line - **Melanie V. Taylor**
Remhurst Manor - **Tamasine Loves**
The Devil's Chalice - **Derek Wilson**
Something Missing - **Glenice Whitting**
The Colour of Poison - **Toni Mount**
The Colour of Gold - **Toni Mount**
The Colour of Cold Blood - **Toni Mount**

PLEASE LEAVE A REVIEW

If you enjoyed this book, *please* leave a review at the book seller
where you purchased it. There is no better way to thank the
author and it really does make a huge difference!
Thank you in advance.

Lightning Source UK Ltd.
Milton Keynes UK
UKOW08f0101120517

301042UK00001B/31/P